AUNTIE CLEM'S BAKERY

BOOKS # 4 - 6

P.D. WORKMAN

ISBN: 9781774680780 (KDP Paperback)

ISBN: 9781774680797 (Ingram Paperback)

ISBN: 9781774680803 (Ingram Hardcover)

ISBN: 9781989415023 (Kindle)

ISBN: 9781989415030 (ePub)

pdworkman

STIRRING UP MURDER

AUNTIE CLEM'S BAKERY #4

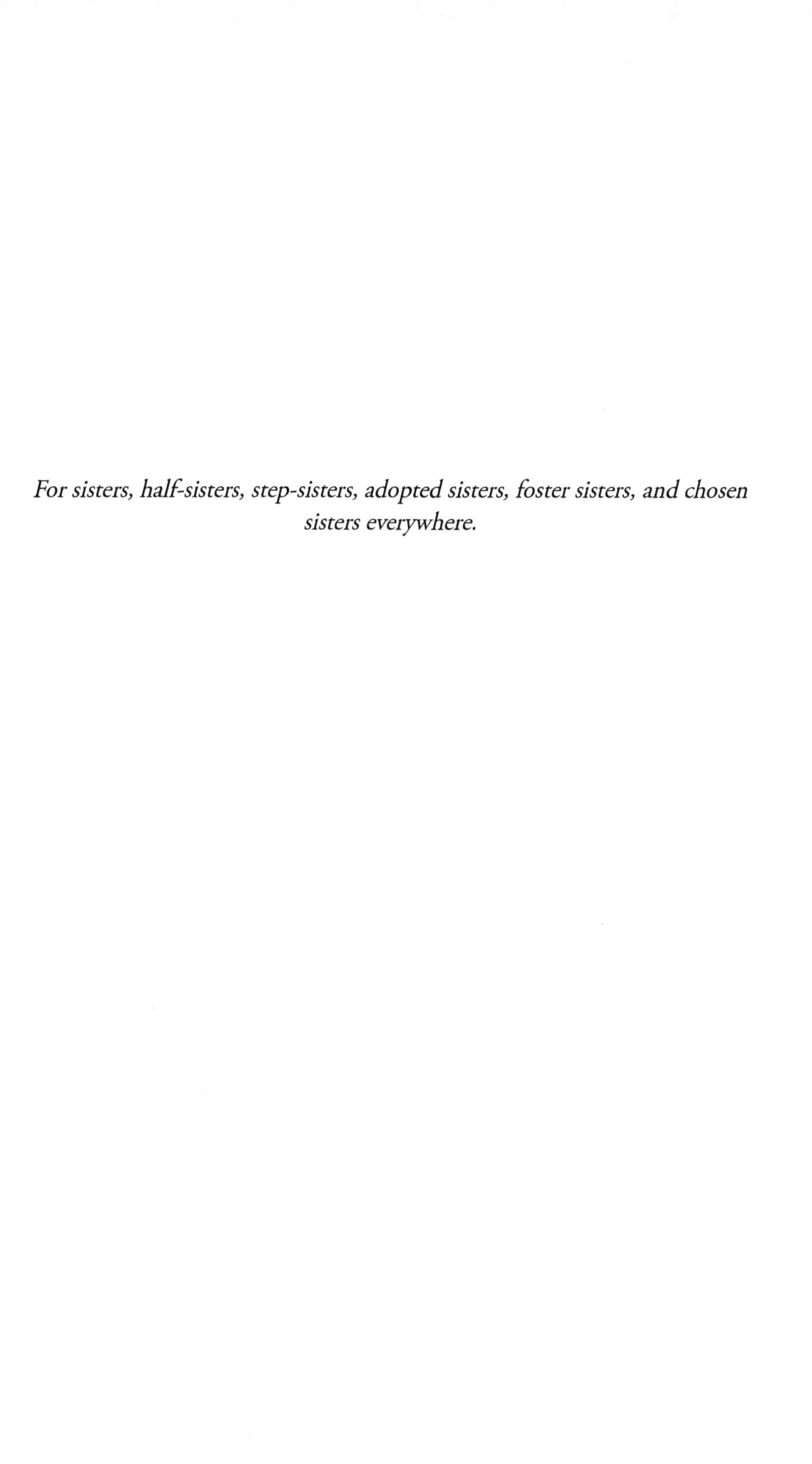

For sisters, half-sisters, step-sisters, adopted sisters, foster sisters, and chosen sisters everywhere.

CHAPTER 1

*E*rin managed to block Orange Blossom from getting out the door as she took out the garbage. She drew in a deep breath of fresh air and enjoyed the stillness of the early morning. There would be plenty of action at Auntie Clem's Bakery. It was good to cherish the quiet for a moment at the beginning of her day. Adele told her that she needed to take more time for herself and be at one with nature and the universe. It probably wouldn't hurt, but Erin's mind was always racing ahead, already working on the next thing.

She held her breath when she opened the garbage bin and threw her bag in. Even though she washed it out regularly, it still made her gag if she caught a whiff of it from a few feet away. Erin glanced up and down the street for any sign of activity and then went around to the back of the house.

There was a light on in Vic's loft over the garage, so Erin knew she was up and around and would be joining Erin before long to start their day at the bakery.

As soon as she was in the door, Orange Blossom was winding around her legs, *mrrowing* for food and attention. Erin bent down to pat him and then to pick him up and give his ears and chin a good scratch.

"Hey, Blossom. How was your night?"

The orange and white cat yowled and yipped chattily, telling her all about it. Even after having had him for a few months, it still made Erin laugh at how vocal he was. She'd never known any cat to be so noisy and interested in carrying on a conversation with his two-legged companions.

"I see. Well, that all sounds very interesting," Erin told him. She put him down on the floor and washed up, then went about getting his breakfast ready while her coffee brewed. Blossom stood up on hind legs and batted at her with soft paws while she opened a smelly can of cat food and scooped it into a dish for him. When she put it down on the floor, he immediately pushed his nose into the bowl and began to chow down, his loud purr rumbling through the kitchen.

The coffee finished brewing just as Vic tapped at the back door and entered. Erin wasn't sure how she managed to look fresh and polished so effortlessly first thing. Erin always felt so awkward and plain beside her young bakery assistant. Vic's height was the only aspect of her appearance that hinted at her transgender identity, and her height only increased her poised, willowy air.

"Morning," Vic drawled. "If it isn't just as crisp as a new dollar bill out there this morning. I do love this time of the year!"

Erin smiled at her Tennessee twang. "It really is lovely," she agreed. "If it could only stay like this all year instead of getting so blasted hot."

"We had such a mild summer, you don't know hot."

Erin shook her head. "Ugh. Don't tell me that."

Erin poured them each a cup of coffee.

"Now that the holidays are over, we need to be thinking about what else we can do to draw customers." Erin studied her coffee as if the answer might be there. "We don't want to go through a big slump because people aren't buying gingerbread men and pumpkin pies."

"We don't exactly have a big pool to draw customers from. Bald Eagle Falls isn't the biggest place."

"I know, but I think we still have untapped resources. Not everyone comes to Auntie Clem's. What are people buying in the city? What are they getting at the grocery store that they should be buying at the bakery? And why aren't they coming to the bakery for it?"

Vic sipped her coffee. Orange Blossom, having finished gobbling down his breakfast, sat back on his haunches and stared at them as he applied tongue to paw and washed his face.

"People who can eat gluten buy bread and baking at the grocery store because it is cheaper and convenient. Easier than making a separate trip to Auntie Clem's. And because of the stigma of gluten-free food being inferior."

Kicked into a higher gear by the caffeine, Erin's mind was already whirring, thinking about all the factors involved. "What if we sold bread to the grocery store? They could sell it off the shelves with their commercially produced stuff. People wouldn't have to make an extra trip. It would be right there."

Vic pursed her lips. "I'm not sure about that. If people don't come into the bakery, we can't up-sell. If they pick up a loaf of bread from the shelf at the grocer, how are we going to sell them cookies or cupcakes? Can we really stock the shelves at the grocery store too? That would be a lot of extra work."

"It would be. And we wouldn't be able to build a relationship or to up-sell… unless we sold cupcakes and cookies to the grocery store as well…"

Vic was shaking her head.

"Which would also be extra work," Erin admitted. "And if people didn't buy as much at the grocery store as we expected, Mr. Cooper would lose money. The margins are so thin, we couldn't afford to sell it to him much lower than we sell to bakery customers."

"I don't think you can be in both the bakery and the grocery store."

"No. You're right." Erin was quiet while she thought about other possibilities. Orange Blossom finished his bath and went over to Vic, rubbing up against her and yowling to be picked up.

"He's so demanding," Vic complained. But she put her coffee cup to the side to pick him up and cuddle him.

"That's because he's spoiled," Erin said.

"He is not!" Vic planted a kiss on the top of Blossom's head. "He was demanding even when you first got him. Before either of us had a chance to spoil him."

"That's true," Erin admitted. She eyed the clock on the kitchen wall. "I guess we'd better head out."

Vic gave Orange Blossom one more scratch and put him down. "Okay, Blossom, you'd better be good today. Marshmallow is here to keep you company, so no noise."

Orange Blossom stood looking at her for a minute, eyes intent and ears pointed forward. Then he turned and left the room. Erin got a carrot out of the fridge for Marshmallow and gave him his treat on her way out.

~

It wasn't long before Officer Terry Piper stopped by the bakery as he patrolled the neighborhood. Since it wasn't hot, his water bottle didn't need to be topped off yet, but Erin gave his partner, K9, a gluten-free doggie biscuit.

"How is everything today?" she asked Terry.

"Pretty quiet. Mrs. Sturm reported some vandalism last night, but I don't know if we'll be able to get anywhere on that. Kids, most likely."

"Vandalism? What happened?"

"Her car has been egged. No damage, just a mess."

Erin shook her head, thinking about the woman with the girlish blond pigtails and the people she had seen interact with Lottie. "You're probably right. Sounds like kids. Did she have any idea who it might have been?"

"Nothing too certain. Unfortunately, Lottie Sturm is... not well-liked among the younger generation."

Vic snorted. "Lottie isn't liked by a lot of people in any generation. If I had a nickel for every time she tried to stir up trouble..."

"I don't know if she tries to, or if she's just awkward," Erin said.

"She's not awkward," Vic said. "It's totally on purpose. She's a trouble-maker. That's the kind of person she is."

"We really don't know anything about what kind of person she is. Some people say the wrong things and hurt people's feelings without meaning to."

"And you think Lottie Sturm is one of those people?"

Erin considered. "No," she admitted finally. "You're probably right. She seems to get a certain amount of enjoyment out of it."

Vic nodded vigorously in agreement.

"Regardless of whether or not she brought it down on herself," Piper said, "I've taken her statement and opened a file, and if the culprits are found, they will be dealt with. Other than that, it was a quiet night, and it's shaping up to be a quiet day." His eyes met Erin's. "No bodies. No twenty-year-old mysteries. Just the normal Bald Eagle Falls stuff."

"Good. I don't think I'm up for any more bodies. I'll stick to baking. That's what I'm good at."

"Well, I can't disagree with that," Terry agreed. He was eyeing a fresh batch of chocolate chip cookies that Vic was starting to lay out in the display cabinet.

Vic and Erin exchanged a look. "Do you want one?" Vic asked, eyes twinkling.

"I don't know, I probably shouldn't…" Piper patted his belly like he might be putting on weight. But if he was, Erin certainly couldn't tell. His police uniform fit him as neatly as it ever had and didn't pull or bulge around the middle.

"Oh, come on." Vic put one into a paper sleeve for him. "With the amount of walking you do on a day of patrol? You'll walk this off easily. "

"I suppose." He took it when Vic handed it across the counter to him. "But even so, the sugar probably isn't good for me."

"It's gluten-free," Vic said with a wave of her hand. "That means it's good for you."

Erin opened her mouth to object that just because something was gluten-free, that didn't mean it was healthy. The cookies were full of refined sugar and flours, chocolate, and butter and were far from being a health food.

She saw the way that Piper was looking at her, expectant, waiting for the lecture, and closed her mouth. Was she that predictable?

"It's a dessert," she said instead. "As long as you don't go overboard, I don't think it will harm you."

"One little cookie never hurt anyone," Vic declared.

"Well…" Erin couldn't help objecting to this. Her muscles tensed up in spite of the fact that she was just talking to her friends. "If they're allergic or intolerant, then one cookie could cause damage, even an anaphylactic reaction—"

"Terry's not allergic, though."

"I know that. I mean that if he was…"

"I'm just going to eat this cookie," Terry said.

Erin looked at him. He took a bite of the warm cookie, leaving a smear of chocolate on his lip. The tension drained out of Erin and she laughed weakly.

"Okay. Good. And you two quit teasing me."

They both grinned like kids caught with their hands in the proverbial cookie jar. Erin shook her head.

The bells on the front door chimed, and Erin turned to greet the next customer.

CHAPTER 2

The fixer sat across the table from his boss. The man was physically unimposing, but if he could pay, that was the only thing that mattered.

"You found her?" the boss asked.

"Of course I found her. It wasn't hard. She's not in hiding."

"If you could find her, so can someone else."

He ran his fingers through his hair. "Sure. Anyone who is looking and has a little experience and the right tools could find her too."

"Even though you didn't know her name…"

"A name is nothing. Just one piece of the puzzle. If you have enough of the other pieces, you can figure out the solution."

The boss's eyes flicked around him, and he lowered his voice so it was almost a whisper. "Then I need for her to… disappear."

The fixer sat back in his chair considering the boss's words. "And by disappear, you mean…?"

It wasn't that he hadn't ventured over the line before. He worked outside the law at least as much as he worked within it. But if the boss was looking for a permanent solution, the fixer wasn't so sure. He would charge a much higher price, but he was also taking on a lot more risk. Was he willing to put his own tail on the line?

The boss scratched his head, twisting his face into a grimace. There was a long silence between them. He looked around to be sure no one was paying them any particular attention. Eventually, the boss wet his lips and cleared his throat. But he continued to speak in a whisper.

"I don't want her dead," he said. "That wouldn't be right. But if she disappeared, fell off the grid…"

"Why would she do that?"

"Maybe… she had to go into hiding."

The fixer thought about this, rolling it around in his mind and trying to formulate a plan. "Why would she go into hiding?"

"Why does anyone go into hiding? Maybe her boyfriend is abusive. Maybe she stole something. Maybe she was in danger. Be creative. Sometimes people leave just so they can start over again somewhere else."

"But how would I make any of those things happen? If you really do want to drive her into hiding, and you don't want her… dead… then making her decide to disappear… that's a lot more difficult than trying to warn her off or to blackmail her. I'm not sure how to work that."

"You've done well until now. I thought you were pretty competent."

The fixer was encouraged by these words. He did his best. He was willing to outwork everybody else to get the results his bosses needed. But he wasn't sure this current boss quite understood what he was getting into.

"You do know what family that boyfriend is part of, don't you?"

The boss narrowed his eyes. "Are you telling me you're afraid of some two-bit Tennessee family?"

"I didn't say I was afraid of them." But of course, any contact with organized crime made him nervous. He didn't like to be put in the line of fire of family business, big or little. "But it isn't like dealing with one person or one family. This is an organization. If we interfere with the girl or with her boyfriend, we're going to have targets on our backs and a lot of people looking for us."

"Are you saying I should be getting someone else for this job?"

The fixer chewed on his lip and ran his fingers through his hair again. "I have to think it through. We need to come up with a plan here. Something that makes sense."

"I don't need anything complicated. The fewer details I know, the better. Just make sure she goes into hiding where no one is going to find her."

"What's the payout for making her disappear permanently?"

The boss studied him carefully. "You understand that I don't want her dead. I'm not saying hide the body where it won't ever be found. I'm saying don't kill her."

"Killing her is not part of the deal. That's agreed."

"Not just that we haven't made it part of the deal. But it can't happen. I don't want her death on my conscience."

"Yes. Agreed. That's understood."

The boss looked down at the top of the table, scarred by many hands and nails. Using his body to shield anyone from seeing what he was doing, he traced invisible numbers with his index finger. The fixer watched the numbers and counted the digits. It wasn't a windfall. It wasn't the type of money he could retire on. But it would be enough to live in comfort for a while and not have to survive hand-to-mouth.

How far was he willing to go for that kind of money?

How much was he willing to put on the line?

It had been a while since Vic and Erin had gone out together to eat, just the two of them, so when Vic suggested a girls' night out, Erin accepted. She knew that Vic didn't have many other friends. Even though Vic was a fun, friendly, compassionate girl, she wasn't well-accepted in Bald Eagle Falls. The town was part of the Bible belt and, while the women there weren't any more perfect there than anywhere else, they were judgmental of the moral wrongs they saw or imagined. And Vic being a transgender girl meant that they would not have anything to do with her socially. It would have made for a lonely existence without Erin and Adele around or being able to go into the city for larger gatherings. And of course, she had Willie too, but he was out of town attending to some unnamed business. Erin wondered fleetingly what he was up to. But Willie was Willie, and he kept his business dealings pretty close to his chest.

They decided to go for Chinese, where they hadn't been for a while. Willie preferred the 'meat plus three' at the family restaurant, or maybe the hot chicken at the BBQ.

Erin watched Vic struggling with her chopsticks, a w-shaped wrinkle of concentration between her eyebrows. Vic looked up and saw Erin watching her, which made her drop the mouthful she had finally managed to wrangle.

"Shut up," she said sheepishly, "I can do a lot of things, but chopsticks are not my forte!"

"You're doing fine. You just need a little practice and you'll be an expert."

"At home, we always used forks when we went out for Chinese. It never even occurred to me to use chopsticks."

"You can use a fork here if you want to."

Vic always had before. But she shook her head. "No. I want to learn how to do this. Eating with chopsticks is different than eating it with a fork. I want the authentic experience."

"Okay. You're doing fine, so don't mind me."

Vic nodded and went back to work. Erin ate her meal slowly. She didn't want to be done when Vic was still trying to get her first few mouthfuls down.

"How's the research going?" Vic asked. "Did you mind being taken away from it tonight?"

"No, not really. I keep running into dead ends and I just get frustrated. Other people seem to manage to find long-lost family members, so why can't I?"

"You've just started. Sometimes those searches take years, you know. Decades, even."

"Don't tell me that!" Erin's heart sank. "That was pre-internet. Now, it should just be a matter of doing a few searches, and then... bingo, here's your new family!"

"Even when you know someone's name, it can be hard to find them on the internet. Not everybody even has email or social accounts. Some people who do still don't leave any tracks. And since you don't even know her name..."

Erin shook her head and wound noodles around her chopsticks. "How can I not even know my own sister's name? I mean... not even her birth name. How do you begin a search when you don't even have a birth name? Every time they talk about tracing adoptees on TV, they always say 'her birth name was...' Where do you start if you don't even have that?"

"I wish I could tell you. Usually there is a friend or family member who knows the history. Or hospital records. Or an attending nurse. Pretty hard when you don't have any of those things to start with.

"Everybody who knew anything is dead. The hospital only keeps five years' worth of records, and even if they did keep them longer than that, they've had black mold and a fire. Not just one or the other, but both!" Erin sighed in exasperation. "If I believed in God, I'd think he was trying to tell me not to look any further. Every time I think I found a way to track her down, it's blocked."

"God will make a way for you." Vic gave her a mischievous grin. "If there is a God."

"I can't just sit back and rely on some power of the universe to take over and direct my life." Erin used a pot sticker to wipe up juices on her plate. "If I did that, I never would have gotten anywhere in my life. I haven't gotten where I was by sitting still."

Vic gazed at her for a minute. "No... but you didn't get the bakery because you decided that was what you wanted to do and saved up and bought it."

"No," Erin admitted. "I just took the opportunity when it was presented to me. I thought this was my one chance to do what I always wanted to and make gluten-free baking for people with dietary restrictions."

"But you don't think an opportunity like that was more than just chance? Maybe fate? Or God? Or the universe?"

"It wasn't chance or God. It was Clementine. I guess she knew how much I liked it when she ran the tea shop. She didn't have any other living relatives. So she left it to me." Erin shrugged. There was nothing coincidental about that.

"I'm not convinced it wasn't by divine design. How do you explain the fact that you wanted to start a baking business and that's the opportunity that Clementine gave you?"

"I hadn't ever thought I'd be able to start a baking business. I just liked making gluten-free food for friends and clients who wanted it. I liked baking because I liked working with Clementine when I was a little girl. It's no coincidence or design. It's just history."

"Okay." Vic gave a wide shrug. "Whatever you say, Erin. It was all just you and Clementine and your history together. I just think it all fits together rather nicely. That doesn't always happen, you know. I liked hunting when I was little, but if my Uncle Archibald left me a hunting lodge, I wouldn't run it. I'd just liquidate it and get out of there."

"It's not the same."

"No. Because for *you* it was meant to be."

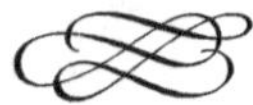

When Erin got home, she invited Vic to join her for the evening, but Vic sighed and shook her head.

"No, it's okay. You've got things to get done tonight, I'm sure, and we need to get to bed soon."

Having to start baking bread before dawn, they always tried to be early to bed and very early to rise. Erin sensed that Vic had other things on her mind.

"Are you sure? We can talk if you want. I don't have anything that has to be done tonight. Just taking care of the animals and making my lists for tomorrow."

"Goodness, if you don't have your lists made yet, I'd better leave you alone for sure. You'll need at least a couple of hours for that."

"I'm not that bad," Erin protested. "No more than an hour, I swear."

Vic laughed.

"Really, though, Vicky. If you want to talk, or just sit together a while…" Erin couldn't quite bring herself to use the local 'set a spell.'

"We just had dinner. I'm talked out. Thanks, though."

"Okay. Have a good night. I'll see you in the morning."

Vic nodded and headed for her loft apartment. Erin shut and locked the door. Maybe she'd read a bit before bed. Or have a long soak in the tub. Or look over Clementine's genealogy books for some tiny clue that would help her to find her sister.

But as she had told Vic, she still had to take care of the animals, feeding them and changing their litter. And she needed to write up her lists for the next day.

She had just finished changing Orange Blossom's and Marshmallow's litter and was again considering the idea of a nice hot bath when the door-bell rang.

Erin checked the peephole before opening the door. There had been too many threats to her life over the last year to be casual about opening the door. But she only needed a peek to see that it was Terry Piper. She opened the door and invited him and K9 in.

"Your light was still on, or I wouldn't have stopped," Terry said. "You aren't headed off to bed yet?"

"No, not yet. I can visit for a bit. I still have to write up some lists—and no comments from the peanut gallery."

He grinned. "You're not *that* bad."

"Saying it that way makes me feel worse than when Vic wisecracks about it. I can't help it if lists make me feel good. Call me weird, but it's my way of calming down and getting everything out of my head so I can sleep at night."

"If you can multi-task, we can visit at the same time as you are writing. Then you don't lose any time because I'm here. Or you'll lose less, anyway."

"Sounds good."

They both sat down. Neither of the animals had had much attention, with Erin being out to dinner and then working on other things, so they both wanted her attention. Marshmallow hopped over and started nibbling at her bare toes and Orange Blossom jumped up beside Erin onto the arm of the couch, keeping a close eye on K9. Erin laughed. She gave Orange Blossom an ear scratch and patted Marshmallow with her foot. It was going to be a few minutes before she would be able to get started on her list.

"Vic said you've been looking for your half-sister," Terry commented. "Any luck?"

"No. She was asking me about it tonight too. But I'm really not getting anywhere. I kept putting it off over the holiday season, because I always had so much going on and wanted to be able to really give it my attention, but I feel like I've lost momentum by not getting right onto it."

"It's been twenty years. It's not like a few more months makes that much difference."

"Logically, that makes sense, but that's not what it feels like."

"You're not getting anything from the hospital or government searches? I thought you could search adoption records now."

"If you're the adoptee, yes. But you have to have standing in the file, and that's only the adoptee and the birth parents. Biological siblings are just like the public. No access."

"Oh. Well, that's not too helpful."

"No. I thought getting my own DHS records was hard, but that's nothing compared to the roadblocks I'm running into here."

"What about court records?"

"What?"

"Court records are public, for the most part."

"Wouldn't that be just the same as the adoption registry information?"

"No. I don't think so. You should be able to do a search."

"How? Is it a name search? Because I don't know what her name was either before or after adoption."

"Normally, yes, but I think you can get paper copies of adoption orders for a certain window of time. If you had all of the adoption records for the year after she was born… would that do it?"

Erin nodded slowly. "I guess it's a start. It would at least reduce the pool from all of the residents of Tennessee to everyone who was adopted during that period."

"Only half of them."

"Why?"

"Because the other half are boys."

"Oh! Duh. Of course. Still, it's going to be a lot of names to sift through, isn't it?"

"It shouldn't be too bad. Just this county, girls, the year after your sister was born. It should be a fairly small set."

"That's a really good idea. I'll see what they'll let me do next time I go to the city."

"What about adoption reunion boards? It seems like they're all over the internet."

"It all seems a little daunting."

"I could help you with it, if you like. I don't think it would be too hard. And it can't hurt anything. Just putting your name on a forum with the information that you know. Place, hospital, birth date. A lot of people don't have any more information than that."

"Maybe you could use some of your police databases," Erin suggested.

"And what would I look for? Search DMV for all women with that date of birth? There's no guarantee that she still lives in Tennessee or has a driver's license. You didn't stay here. You moved to Maine, and all over the east coast. At least I had a name when I was checking your background. Even then, you weren't so easy to keep track of when you kept changing it."

Erin could feel herself blushing. She shrugged. He had asked her before about her past, but there were plenty of things from her past life that she just wasn't willing to have to tell him about. A person was entitled to a little privacy.

Orange Blossom had settled in beside Erin and was purring happily and Marshmallow was sprawled on top of her feet. Erin picked up the notepad that Vic had given to her for Christmas and opened it up to list everything she needed to remember for the next day. Terry bent down to scratch K9's ears, then leaned back in his seat, relaxing.

"I have an ulterior motive to helping you find your sister."

Erin didn't lift her eyes from the page. "Mm-hm?"

"You realize that if she is found, she's entitled to half of the Plaint estate?"

At this, Erin did look up. "What?"

"Her father was Adam Plaint."

"Well, yes. That's what it looks like, anyway. Obviously, no one has done a paternity test."

"Assuming her parents had a pretty good idea about when they had been with each other, your parents were both pretty sure she was not your father's."

"Right." Erin nodded, saddened by this. As excited as she was to find she had a sister, it would have been even more amazing if she had been Erin's full sister.

"Well, if Adam does prove to be her father, then half of Trenton's estate would go to her. He died intestate, so it goes first to his parents—who we now know are both dead—and then to his siblings. The sister, Sophie, is dead. That leaves Davis and your half-sister, who is also Trenton's half-sister."

"Davis can't inherit Trenton's estate anymore, can he? He's in prison."

"That doesn't stop him from inheriting, unless it can be proven that he had something to do with Trenton's death. And so far, all we have on that front is speculation."

CHAPTER 4

The fixer presented his thoughts to his boss and waited for his feedback.

"These all seem half-baked," the boss said finally, shaking his head. "What are the chances that any of these approaches are going to work? We can't leave it to chance."

"If you don't want her killed or kidnapped, then everything else is just chance. All I can do is give her a push in the right direction and see how she responds. I'm usually pretty good at reading people, figuring out how to influence them. But some people… Even when you think you've found the right trigger, they still don't respond." He shook his head, his mouth twisting into a bitter grimace. "*Some* people are extremely stubborn and can't be blackmailed or bullied."

"Kidnapping is no good," the boss said, shaking his head. "It could take months, even years, to get everything sorted out. We can't keep her under wraps for that long. It has to be voluntary. We need her to go into hiding and to stay there."

"So you don't have a problem with any of the plans I've outlined? I can't guarantee the success of any of them, but one of them… it only takes one of them to work."

"We've both dealt with this family before." His boss shook his head in disgust. "You know she might respond exactly the opposite way to what you expect. If she's anything like the *other one...*"

"I can't make any promises. There is only one permanent solution, and you said no to that."

"It needs to be soon," the boss said, ignoring the suggestion. "It won't be long before they manage to trace her."

He nodded and stood up. "Okay, then. I'll do my best to get her out of the way."

"Do it," the boss said. "Make sure it works."

CHAPTER 5

*E*rin measured orange zest into the muffin batter, the sharp oils tickling her nose.

"So you're still looking for her?" Vic asked.

Erin focused her attention on Vic, trying to pick up the thread of the conversation. But they hadn't been talking about anything. There was only one person that Vic could have been referring to, though, only one person Erin was looking for.

"Yes, Terry gave me some other suggestions of places to look or get searches. I kept running into dead ends."

"You think it will work? You'll be able to find her? Even though you don't know her name?"

"I don't know." Erin gave the batter a few stirs and looked at her recipe card. "I hope so. I'd really like to. Terry seems to think that it's possible. But after all of the issues I have had dealing with DHS and government agencies, I can't let myself get carried away. Who knows what problems I could run into."

Vic was quiet. She turned on the mixer for the cookie dough and didn't try to carry on the conversation over the loud motor. Erin looked over at her. Vic's usually sunny disposition seemed to have been dampened. She stared into the mixing bowl as if reading tea leaves, her expression dour. Had people been saying things to her again? Erin policed the customers who were prone to say rude or ecclesiastical things to Vic, trying to make sure that Auntie Clem's was a safe place where Vic didn't have to worry about being attacked for being transgender.

Or was there something else on her mind?

"Have you heard from Willie?" Erin asked.

Vic looked at Erin with a jerk, startled as if she hadn't even known Erin was in the room. "What? Oh… no, not really. He's sent me a few texts, but we haven't had any real conversations. He did say that he might not be able to call me much while he was out of town."

"But everything is okay?"

"Sure. Everything is fine."

"I just wondered. You seem like you're sad or worried about something."

"What do you think she's going to be like?"

"Who?"

"Your sister."

"Oh." Erin pressed her lips together, thinking about it. She'd had a lot of different foster siblings over the years, all different personalities. Some had been angry or cruel. Others had just drifted through like ghosts, barely registering in Erin's world. A precious few had been friends, or closer, like family. Like Carolyn. But Erin hadn't stayed in one home for long, never more than a year or so. She had learned to be like the ghosts, not investing anything in the relationships. Just drifting through the homes, trying to remain invisible. "I don't know, Vic. I've never had a biological sister. I don't have a clue what she'll be like. Will she be like my mother or Adam Plaint? Aunt Clementine? Me?" She shook her head. "I really don't know what to expect."

"Do you think you're going to be close? Keep in touch?"

"She's the only family I have, so I hope so…"

She saw Vic's lips form a protest, and then Vic turned off the mixer and the kitchen seemed unnaturally silent. Vic pulled off the mixing bowl and started to form teaspoons of dough into balls.

"I mean she's my only biological family," Erin said. "Of course I have other family. The homes I grew up in. My friends." She tried to give Vic a reassuring smile. "You and the animals. You're my family too. Just a different kind of family. The kind you choose."

"But you'll have more in common with a biological sister. I've read those studies. Twins separated at birth, and how alike each other they are when they are reunited. All the funny quirks that are actually family traits."

"But those are identical twins. This sister of mine… she's eight years younger. And we don't even have the same two parents. We only share one parent, so our shared genetic traits are more like… one quarter instead of one hundred percent like identical twins."

"I know with my family, though, siblings and cousins… when we get together at family reunions or funerals, there are family traits. Things that automatically connect you. Like magnets. They draw you together. You have more in common than strangers."

Erin felt a little thrill at Vic's words. She longed for that attraction. For people who were somehow the same inside as she was. Some person who wouldn't find her strange or an outsider, but who would connect with her like Erin never had with any friend or foster family.

"Those are people you grew up with," she reminded Vic. "The reason you're alike is that you were raised in the same social structure."

"Nurture, not nature? I don't know. I don't think so. Some of it. But there is something, like a pattern in a tapestry, a common thread. There's something more than just being raised in a similar way in a similar place."

Erin stirred sugared cranberries into the batter. She needed to focus on her work, or she was going to be behind before they even opened. "I'd like to think I'm going to find something like that with my sister. But I'm not counting on it. I don't think… I don't think shared genetics are going to make us the same in nature."

Vic rubbed the back of her arm across her forehead. "Blood is thicker than water."

"Think about Trenton and Davis," Erin said. "You've heard Melissa say how different they were. We saw it ourselves, even if we only saw Trenton briefly. Those two boys couldn't have been more unlike. Trenton was a bully. Good at everything. The Midas touch. And Davis was the opposite. A victim. Depressive. Unpopular. An addict. They didn't even look anything like each other. Not only that, they hated each other. Davis killed Trenton. Plotted it out and killed him, not just an accident or heat of the moment. What if my sister is like one of them?"

Vic tossed her head. "Well, maybe…"

"I hope she's someone who can be a friend," Erin said, "but I'm not counting on it."

The fixer knew going in that it was risky. They were talking about mob, even if it was only a small Tennessee clan. They might not have the reach of some Italian or Asian connection, but their bloodlines ran through most of the families in the county and it was impossible to know who was connected or could be leaned on.

He watched the young man for a few days. Robert Dyson was not at the top of the organization, but he was son, brother, and nephew to members who were. Bobby himself was a small-potatoes street soldier who still needed to make himself. A man couldn't just rely on his father's high position to get him a place in the Dyson clan. He was far below a hundred men who didn't even bear the Dyson name. But they'd worked to earn their positions, and so far, Bobby boy simply swaggered, expecting to be given everything.

The fixer watched for the right time and opportunity. Bobby had his coterie of admirers, people who hoped to ride his coattails in his ascent up the ladder, and the fixer needed to catch him alone to do his job.

Subtlety wasn't his strong suit, but he suspected it wasn't Bobby's either. Maybe the Dyson clan had become too inbred, knocking off a few IQ points with each new generation until it seemed that only the grandfather's generation had the smarts it took to run anything in the organization.

So Bobby found the fixer in the hall outside Bobby's apartment, banging on the door late at night. Bobby looked him up and down, the sneer becoming more deeply ingrained in his smooth face.

"Who are you? What are you doing here?"

The fixer turned slightly toward Bobby, allowing a little sway and sloppiness in his stance. "Where is she?" he slurred slightly, motioning to the closed, locked door. "I thought Charlotte was supposed to be here tonight."

Bobby Dyson looked confused. "She isn't here. She's out with the girls tonight."

"I know," the fixer agreed with a leer. "The girls." He snickered and snorted. "That's what she tells him."

"Tells who?"

"You know." He gave a broad wink. "Her old man. When she needs to get out and have a little fun. He doesn't exactly give her everything she needs to put a smile on her face."

Bobby was having obvious difficulty working through the clumsy innuendo. Too much to drink at the pool hall before making his way home, shaving even more IQ points from his already low score. He inserted his key into the apartment door lock, a process that took multiple attempts between his double vision and the shakiness of his hands.

At first, the fixer thought Bobby was just going to go into his apartment and shut the door, forgetting all about the conversation. But Bobby waited, motioning for him to enter. *Come into my parlor, said the spider to the fly.*

"You're friends with her?" he asked. He blinked, trying to focus.

"Friends…?" the fixer let the word hang. "Well, you could call us friends with benefits. But it's more about the benefits. She has plenty of friends."

Bobby's face flushed red. He was finally getting it, starting to put the pieces together. He would confront her the next time he saw her. Hit her. Threaten her with his mob connections. He owned the city. He had friends everywhere. There was nowhere safe for her to go.

And if she were smart, Charlotte would disappear. A girl like she was shouldn't need to be told to make herself scarce more than once.

He drifted toward the door, still open.

"What are you talking about?" Bobby demanded, still trying to make all the connections. "You don't know her. I've never even seen you before."

"If she's not here, I know where to find her," he said. "It's not like it's the first time I've been *one of the girls*."

Bobby threw a punch, but the young soldier was drunk, and his girlfriend's alleged paramour was only pretending to be, so Bobby couldn't land a blow.

"What's up with you, bro?" taunted the fixer. "It's not like a girl would look at you twice, if it wasn't for your money. That's all she wants. You should have known from the start she'd be fooling around on you."

Bobby came after him again, flailing like an untrained child.

The fixer easily avoided Bobby's flying fists and drifted out the door, leaving Bobby screaming incoherently behind him.

CHAPTER 7

I *think I know your long-lost sister.*

Erin looked at the words on her phone screen, not quite believing it. She'd placed messages on a number of adoption reunion boards, but she hadn't actually expected to get any hits.

And there was no guarantee that it was a hit. *I think,* not *I know.* It wasn't her sister writing back that she'd been looking for Erin. Would her sister even know about Erin's existence? Had she been told? Had her adoptive family been told?

It was probably nothing. How many adoptions had there been in the state? Just because the responder knew a woman who had been adopted around the appropriate time, that didn't mean she knew Erin's sister. It could be almost anyone.

Erin thought about whether to answer. What was the point in pursuing the poster? What were the odds it was legitimate? It could be some creep who wanted to meet her somewhere quiet. A predator.

Erin closed her email, checking her social networks instead. She only had a few quiet minutes for lunch, she didn't have time to be answering random emails. She picked up a grilled tomato sandwich.

"Are you okay?" Vic asked.

Erin wondered how she knew. Had Erin gone pale? Could Vic tell how hard Erin's heart was beating?

29

She hadn't expected to find anyone so quickly. She wasn't ready for it yet.

"Uh, yeah. I'm fine."

"You look like you just swallowed a live frog."

Erin laughed. "Just a weird message in my email. Whatever. Lots of creeps out there."

"Nasty pictures?" Vic suggested.

"Uh… no. It's nothing. No worries."

"If it's someone in town, you should let Terry know."

Erin shrugged. She made a quick conversation switch. "So Willie's back tonight?"

"No… he said he got held up. Going to be a few more days."

"Oh, I'm sorry. Are you okay with that?"

"Going to have to be." Vic gave a shrug. "He'll get back as soon as he can."

Bobby Dyson was in a state by the time his girlfriend got home from her evening out with the girls. As soon as she opened the door and walked into the apartment, the fixer heard Bobby snort and awaken, and then the screaming started.

"Where have you been? You think you can just treat me like this? Taking off and hooking up with some other man? Nobody does me like that!"

"What's your problem, Bobby? Are you drunk?"

"What's my problem? What do you think? You're running around all over town and you think I won't find out about it? Who do you think you're dealing with here? What exactly makes you think I'm just going to sit back and take it?"

"Bobby…" her voice was pitched low and soothing. "What's the matter? I told you I was going to be out with the girls tonight. I'm not cheating on you!"

He cursed her up and down, calling her every name in the book.

Meanwhile, the fixer was listening from outside the apartment door, leaning with his ear against the wall to try to catch every word.

"If you're going to treat me that way, I'm leaving." There was a snap in her voice. All of the soothing calm was gone.

Bobby swore even more at this. There was a crash from within the apartment. The fixer got closer, his whole body tense. Everything was going to plan, but if Bobby ended up killing her, that would screw everything up. He didn't fancy having to go to the boss to tell him that.

"Let me go, Bobby," the woman warned, her voice getting strident. "You take your hands off of me."

"You're not going anywhere. You hear me? You're never leaving here again!"

More sounds of struggle.

The fixer touched the doorknob. He was prepared to pick it, but he didn't think Charlotte had locked it. It turned smoothly and silently in his hand. Not that silence was needed this time. The screaming that was going on within would mask any small creaks and squeaks the fixer made.

He followed the noise of the struggle, the argument now going hot and heavy. Then he caught sight of them. If he'd imagined that Bobby was simply holding on to his girlfriend's wrist, he was wrong. He had both hands on her, and she wasn't just standing still and taking it. The two grappled, crashing into walls and furniture, kicking and clawing, neither one sparing the other because of tender feelings. But Bobby's superior strength was gradually overcoming the woman's desperate struggles. He managed to pin her against the wall. Then, holding her there with his body, he put one big hand around her throat, squeezing her windpipe and then the carotid. A few seconds without oxygenated blood to the brain, and she would be unconscious, unable to fight back against him any longer.

Her eyes glazed.

"Let her go, Bobby!" the fixer yelled.

Bobby was so startled by the unexpected voice that he released Charlotte, whirling around to face this new threat.

"Who are you?" he demanded, staring into the eyeholes of the fixer's black balaclava.

"I'm here to stop you from killing your girlfriend."

Bobby's brain was stuttering, trying to work through the possibilities and figure out what this strange man was doing in his apartment.

"Get out of my house! I'll call the cops."

"You'll call the cops with your girlfriend unconscious on the floor?"

Bobby's eyes went to the woman, who was not unconscious and was only now realizing it, coming back to herself.

"Who the—"

Maybe he was starting to put the clues together, figuring out that the man in the balaclava might be the drunk he'd been talking to the night before. But before he was able to finish the sentence, Charlotte's leg snapped out, and she kneed him, aiming straight for the groin. She wasn't fast enough and telegraphed the move, and Bobby was able to turn his body slightly so that she only kneed him in the leg, making him grunt with the impact instead of disabling him. Bobby grabbed her again, spinning in a circle to throw her down, but she clawed at him as he tried to put her down, pulling him off balance and making the two of them fall together, right through a glass coffee table.

The fixer winced as they both went down and glass flew everywhere. He took a few steps closer, fearing the injuries he would discover. The woman was struggling. He grasped her by the arms and pulled her to her feet. She didn't ask him who he was. Her eyes were wide with shock. Like Bobby, she'd probably spent half the night drinking, and she wasn't able to keep up with all that was happening. Bobby was still at first, then he reached behind him, and the fixer was sure he'd broken a vertebra or otherwise injured his back.

But Bobby brought his hand back out from behind his back holding a baby Glock. He pointed not at the masked intruder who had come into his apartment, but at his girlfriend.

If she were killed, the contract was off, the fixer's boss had made that clear. The fixer reacted as quickly as he could, pulling his own gun and aiming for center mass.

When he pulled the trigger, the effect was instant. Bobby lowered his gun, eyes glazing and mouth opening. He took a couple of spasmodic breaths, but it was obvious that the body's rhythm had been disrupted and, in a few seconds, all movement ceased.

Charlotte shouted at the fixer. She shoved him and ripped the gun out of his hand, her eyes wide with shock and horror.

"No! Bobby!"

She was on her knees over the man who had, just moments earlier, been trying to kill her. She laid the gun down on the floor as she held him, feeling for some sign of life.

"Lady, you'd better get out of here," the fixer told her. "If someone didn't call the cops when they heard you fighting, they surely will have now."

"You killed him!"

"I was never here. But everybody in the place heard the two of you fighting."

She didn't understand right away. "I didn't kill him! You did."

"They're going to come after you. They're going to be here within five minutes, so if you don't want to be cooling your pretty behind in prison for the next twenty years, I'd get up and get out."

"No."

He stared back at her and she didn't waver. For a minute, he thought she was going to hold firm. She really wasn't going to leave, but would wait by her boyfriend's body until the police came and arrested her.

Then she finally broke eye contact with him and looked around the apartment.

"Nobody heard," she disagreed. "Even if they did, nobody called the cops. They know better."

The fixer raised his brows, which was, of course, useless because the mask covered his expression. "They know better?"

"Everybody knows who Bobby is," she insisted. "No one is going to risk turning him in to the cops. We've fought before, and no one has ever called the police."

"Somebody will have heard the gunshot. It's pretty obvious how this argument ended."

"No," she told him again. She stood up and dusted crumbs of the tempered glass table off of her pants. Shocked sober, her brain was in high gear. "I do need to get out of here, just in case. But nobody is coming." She cocked her head for a moment. "No sirens."

The fixer stared at her. That was one cold broad. She had turned off horror and sorrow and was operating purely on logic. She looked around. He didn't realize what she was looking for at first, and then saw her purse where she had put it down on the counter when she came in the door. She picked it up and slung it over her shoulder.

The fixer tried to work out what she was going to do. If framing her for murder didn't keep her away, what would?

She gave the fixer one last long, appraising look, and then she was gone.

CHAPTER 8

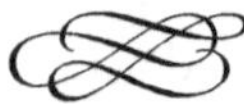

*E*ventually, Erin broke down and told Vic about the possible tip she had received on the adoption reunion board.

"I don't know what to do about it."

Vic rolled her eyes and shook her head. "What do you mean you don't know what to do about it? You know exactly what to do about it. Answer them and get more information. You're not going to know if it is her or not without doing some more investigating. So find out."

"I know… I should… but I'm not so sure I want to find out now. What if it isn't her? What if it is her? What if we hate each other? Davis and Trenton hated each other, and they grew up together. They should have had a good relationship."

"I think it's *because* they grew up together that they hated each other. Trenton was the golden boy and Davis never measured up. And Trenton was a bully. Not exactly conducive to a good relationship."

"What if we don't get along?"

Vic raised her hands in a shrug. "Does it matter? Do you get along with everyone as soon as you meet them? Some people you need to get to know. And some people are always going to rub you the wrong way."

Erin's stomach roiled and twisted. All her life she had wanted a family. Ever since she had lost her parents when she was eight. She'd suddenly been cut off from everything and everyone she knew, shoved into alien environments and left there to sink or swim. How many years had she dreamed that it was some mistake and one or both of her parents would find her and take her home and they could be a family again?

Even before that, growing up as an only child, she had dreamed of having a baby brother or sister to help take care of and play with. Now she was finally on the brink of getting what she wanted, an actual biologically related sibling, and her brain was shutting down.

"I think I'll go to bed. I don't feel very good."

"You can't just avoid it, Erin."

Of course she could.

Erin had lots of experience with avoidance.

Erin sat at the kitchen table with Vic, going through her notes and sketches.

"I was thinking about what we talked about. That we don't have the time or resources to be supplying bread and baking for the grocery store as well as Auntie Clem's."

Vic nodded. "Good. Because I think we'd need at least another three people to stock the grocery store. If they sold well. And if they didn't, then all of our work would be for nothing. Not really a good business plan."

"Yes. I think we need to keep it to what you, me, and Bella can do for now. I can't really afford to be paying for more staff."

"Yeah."

Erin paused, tapping her pen to her chin. She looked sideways at Vic. "Has Bella used the commode yet?"

Vic laughed. "She won't even look at the door to the stairs, let alone go downstairs and use the loo. Don't bother asking her to run downstairs to get you something, unless it's just because you want to see that panic-stricken look on her face."

"I've told her that there isn't anything scary down there. Everything has been cleaned up, and it isn't like it was a horrible bloody death in the first place. It was really a very clean murder, when you think about it."

"Yeah... but I don't think she cares how bloody it was. It's the ghosts."

"There are no ghosts."

"She's sure Angela Plaint is down there, if not the entire Plaint clan.

Doesn't matter that their bodies have been properly buried in consecrated ground. She's convinced that their spirits are stuck downstairs."

Erin shook her head. "I suppose I should be glad she even agreed to work for us. It's amazing she would even come into the bakery, if she's that terrified of restless spirits."

"You shouldn't mock what you don't understand," Vic warned.

She said it deadpan, and Erin studied her, trying to figure out if she was joking or serious. Even though Vic said she didn't believe in magic or ghosts or anything other than God and spirits either going to heaven or hell, her actions suggested she wasn't quite so sure. Erin decided to drop the subject altogether and go on.

"Where was I?" She scanned her notes. "Right. No more staff. Not yet. But I was thinking about the restaurants. How when Davis went to the family restaurant while I was there, he was so disgusted that they were using store-bought, mass-produced white rolls. He said that when he got The Bake Shoppe reopened, he would talk to them about a contract to supply them with good quality rolls and bread."

Vic nodded. "That would be nice. The store-bought stuff just doesn't measure up to handmade. But wouldn't that be just as much work as supplying the grocery store?"

"I don't think so. Not if we're careful. We can start just by supplying them with a gluten-free option. They can have frozen rolls and other bread products available for when someone orders them. Then we can look at offering them an upgrade on their meals. You can have turkey salad on brown bread, or you could pay a dollar fifty more and get it on an artisanal multigrain, handcrafted, roll."

"Work our way in."

"Right. People get exposed to it as an upgrade over regular bread instead of thinking of gluten-free as an inferior replacement. They maybe decide that was a really good bread and stop by Auntie Clem's to pick up a loaf when they've got company over. And we can scale it over time. There's more room for profit if it's a premium product. We can see how it is succeeding before we have to scale up our man hours."

"Does that mean—"

The doorbell rang. Erin looked at the clock and got up. As she walked into the living room, Orange Blossom was jumping up onto the couch to stick his head out through the curtains and have a look to see who had arrived. He meowed loudly a few times.

"Who is it, Blossom?" Erin asked him. "Is it our friend Terry?"

She looked out the peep hole and saw that it was. She opened the door to let Terry and K9 in. Orange Blossom promptly arched his back and frizzed out his fur, hissing at K9 as if he were a dangerous intruder, instead of a friend that visited them regularly several evenings a week. Erin laughed and shook her head.

"Don't pay him any attention. Come on in; have you had anything to eat?"

She knew that even if he'd had supper, he would still have bread and jam, so they automatically headed for the kitchen table. Vic swiped Erin's papers into a pile and put them on the sideboard.

"Look who's here. How's it going, Officer Piper?"

Terry grinned at her. "Everything is fine, Miss Victoria."

Erin shook her head at their mock formality and got out some leftover rolls from the bakery and a selection of Jam Lady condiments.

"I searched that name for you," Terry said, after a couple of bites of bread. He wiped crumbs from his mouth. "Did a little bit of background on her."

Erin felt like her heart would stop. She put her hand over her chest and forced herself to breathe. She knew that Terry was waiting for a proper answer from her, but she was unable to formulate one right away. She got K9 a biscuit from the cookie jar and handed it to him. K9 lay down with it between his paws to eat it. Orange Blossom was sitting in the doorway watching him with haughty disapproval.

Marshmallow lolloped past Orange Blossom and circled the kitchen. K9 looked up and gave a little woof of interest, which Marshmallow ignored. He acted as if he had no idea that dogs and rabbits were naturally predator and prey, acting instead as if K9 were just another piece of furniture. He approached Erin and snuffled at her pant leg.

"You want a treat too?" Erin asked him, laughing. She got a stick of celery out of the fridge for him, and soon Marshmallow was crunching away at it. Erin looked at Orange Blossom. "What about you, silly cat, are you going to ask for a treat?"

Orange Blossom hunched his shoulders, a quiver running down his back, and disdained Erin. She shrugged.

"Oh, well."

Terry and Vic were both looking at Erin. Terry took another bite of roll. "Did you hear what I said?"

"Who did she ask you to look up?" Vic asked, when Erin didn't answer right away. "That name she got from the reunion bulletin board?"

Terry nodded. "Charlotte Campbell," he pronounced. "Do you want to know?"

Erin sighed. She swallowed, hoping her stomach would stay still and not misbehave. "I suppose."

Terry pulled out his notepad and flipped back to find the right page. Erin doubted that he actually needed to look at it to tell her what he had found. It was not complicated.

"The birth date matches. That's really the only thing we have that shows it could be her. Everything else on the birth certificate changes with her adoption. We can't tell what her birth name or place were. You'd have to go back to the court documents to hopefully find out more details there."

"So it's a 'maybe,'" Erin observed. "It could be her. But it could be someone else who just happens to have the same birth date too. And there's bound to be a few of those in Tennessee."

"Right. It's a good starting place, but you'll have to find out more information to prove anything."

"Are you going to contact her?" Vic asked.

Erin knew she should sit down at the table to join Vic and Terry, but she was too anxious to sit still. She pretended instead that she was just standing up to watch the animals and get them their food.

"I don't know."

"You have to at least contact her to see if she's the right person. And if she is… you'll want some kind of relationship with her, won't you? You'll want to get together and compare notes," Vic persisted.

"I'm not sure."

Terry frowned. Both Vic and Erin caught the subtle tightening of his mouth and wrinkle between his brows.

"What is it?" Erin asked.

"I told you I did a little background. More than just pulling up her DMV to check her date of birth."

Erin took a couple steps closer to the table. Her voice was lower, like it was a secret and she didn't want anyone else to overhear, when it was just the three of them and the animals.

"What else?"

"She has a record. Just petty stuff."

"Anyone could have a record…"

"Anyone *could*," Terry agreed. The way he looked at Erin made her wonder again just how much he knew from her past. She had used different names in different places, across several states, and he had told her once that he'd had trouble following the thread, just as Alton had.

"But…?" It was Vic who prompted Terry to go on. Erin wasn't at all sure she wanted him to. She didn't want to know what kind of trouble Charlotte had been in. She didn't want to hear that the whole thing was just a scam. What would be the point in pretending to be someone's long-lost half-sister? It wasn't like Erin was rolling in dough. Well—maybe she was rolling in dough, but not in cash. Terry's sharp eyes caught Erin's brief smile, and he cocked his head slightly, trying to analyze it. Erin didn't fill him in on her erratic train of thought.

"Charlotte Campbell has some involvement with an organized crime family here in Tennessee."

Erin suppressed a curse. She took a couple of slow, even breaths. "You have organized crime here? I thought most of the crime in these parts was just vandals and moonshiners. Nothing serious."

"Don't get me wrong, it's no mafia. But there are a number of families that have been involved in some pretty nasty stuff for a number of generations… as far back as the civil war, some of them."

"Which one is this Charlotte part of?" Vic demanded.

"Dysons."

Vic, her complexion naturally fair, went a shade whiter. "The Dyson Clan? How did she get involved with *them?*"

"I don't know. There's only so much information I can get from official sources."

"You don't want to get involved with this," Vic told Erin firmly. "She's probably not really your sister, but even if she is… stay away from her. You don't want to get tangled up somehow with the Dyson clan."

Erin felt the first stirrings of curiosity, but also something else. One of her foster mothers had observed once, 'if you want Erin to do something, the surest way to get her to do it is to tell her not to.' Rebellion rose up in her at Vic's words. Charlotte was Erin's sister. If Charlotte were in trouble, maybe Erin could help her out. How bad could some backwoods Tennessee family really be?

"They're not really organized crime," she asserted, even though she knew nothing more about them than what Terry had just said. They were just an old Tennessee family with a bad reputation.

"Maybe not like *The Godfather*," Vic said, "but they're still some nasty people with deep connections all over these parts."

"You didn't say there was anything serious in her background," Erin said to Terry. "Right? Just minor stuff."

"Yes… but being involved with these people… there may be a lot more going on than has made it to her official record."

"But you don't know that. And you don't know how she's involved with these guys. She might have been adopted by someone in this Dyson family, right? She can't help that and it doesn't mean she's a bad person."

"No one is saying she's a bad person," Terry said, holding up one hand to stop her. "What we're saying…" He looked at Vic to make sure they were on the same page. "…is just that you don't want to get involved with this family."

"So you think I shouldn't contact her? That I shouldn't meet her, just because of the family she is in?"

Terry looked again at Vic, squirming. It was unusual for him to be at a loss for words. "I don't know, Erin. I wouldn't want you to get mixed up in anything."

"Just by talking to her and finding out if she's really my sister?"

"It sounds perfectly safe, I know. But I've seen innocent encounters turn into something else. I'd hate to see you get hurt."

"These are bad guys, Erin," Vic chimed in. "I grew up around them. Knowing who they were and what things they were involved in. Maybe it's not the mafia, but they're the closest you're going to get to it in these parts."

"You're the one who's been telling me I should get in touch with my sister. That I should do whatever I could to find her and not just forget about it. You were the one talking to me about how she was going to be like me, she was going to have more in common with me than any random friend. So if she's like me, she's not going to be involved in anything dishonest, right?"

"I don't think you can go that far. I don't think you can be sure. Not if she's been raised by these guys."

Erin shook her head in frustration. She looked at Terry. "You must know something. Was she raised by them? Or does she have some other connection with them?"

"All I can tell by what I was able to pull up was that these convictions on her record are gang-related. She is associated with the Dyson clan. Whether that means that she was in the wrong place at the wrong time, or that she's actually a member of the family, I can't tell."

Erin threw herself into her work at the bakery. If there was one thing she was good at, it was avoidance. She didn't know yet what to do with the information that her sister might be in some organized crime family, so she ignored the issue and pretended not to care. Vic didn't say anything to her about it, but Erin knew from Vic's glances when she thought Erin wasn't looking that Vic still wanted to talk to Erin more about it, to persuade her that the best course of action was just to leave Charlotte Campbell alone.

Erin looked up at the jingle of bells on the front door, and saw Mrs. Foster, Peter's mother. She had Traci, the baby, with her, but it was afternoon and the other children were still at school. Traci started begging for a cookie, and Erin got one out from the display case and handed it to her so that she and Mrs. Foster would be able to talk.

"She's getting to be such a big girl!"

"She sure is," Mrs. Foster said. "She's growing like a weed. It's a good thing we have lots of hand-me-downs, or I'd have trouble keeping her in clothes!"

Erin packaged up the bread and other baked goods that Mrs. Foster selected. "Do you find that your kids are a lot alike?" she asked. "Do they share a lot of traits and interests?"

"Lands, no. They all come with their own unique personalities. Peter was never like this little one. He's the firstborn, and firstborns are always a little bit of a perfectionist, you know. He had a lot of health issues, but when he was feeling well, he was always quiet and eager to please. He's such a mature little man now. The little girls, they're more like each other than like Peter. Karen and Jody are so close in age, they're almost like twins. Take their cues from each other. They're both girly girls, all into fashion and Barbies. This one," Mrs. Foster adjusted Traci on her hip, "I think she's going to be a little tomboy. She's far more interested in trucks and climbing and creepy-crawlies than in dolls or dresses."

She picked out some muffins and Erin went over to the till to ring up the purchases. Vic was in the kitchen, taking some fresh rolls out of the oven.

"Why do you ask?" Mrs. Foster asked. "Just idle curiosity?"

"Oh… I don't know. I just wonder what it would be like to have a sister, I guess. What it would be like to find out that I have one now. If we didn't grow up together, if we weren't playmates like your little girls, then how much alike would we be?"

"You never can tell." Mrs. Foster shook her head unhelpfully. "Some siblings are so different, you'd never believe they were even related to each other. Others… they're so much alike in looks and in the way they act, you know without even being told that they're from the same family."

Vic returned to the front of the store. She smiled and greeted Mrs. Foster and Traci. Erin made change for the purchase, but her brain was rabbiting off in a new direction. What about looks? Would her long-lost sister be dark-haired like she was? Or would she be a blond or even a redhead? Erin's mother had brown hair, and so did Adam Plaint, so Erin assumed their child would have as well. Would she have the same delicate facial features as Erin and her mother? Or the coarser, more chiseled look that Adam and his sons had? Terry must have seen mugshots of Charlotte if he'd looked at her police record, but he hadn't said a word about whether the woman looked similar to Erin or not. Wouldn't Terry have said something if they looked remarkably like each other?

"Erin?"

Erin brought her attention back to Mrs. Foster. "Oh. Sorry. What?"

"I just wanted to thank you again for all of the Christmas treats. Peter was just in heaven to have a whole platter of different kinds of cookies and sweets to choose from this year instead of one bag of store-bought gluten-free cookies. It was so nice for him to be just like anyone else."

"You're welcome. I'm glad I could make it special for him. I remember my sister… my foster sister that was celiac. She always felt so left out. She would sneak foods that she knew were bad for her because she wanted so much to be a part of the social experience. She wanted to be just like everyone else instead of being left out and forced to eat unappetizing substitutes, if anyone even thought of her."

Mrs. Foster shook her head. "I can't imagine. I'm so sorry she had to go through that. I've tried to do everything I could to make things normal and happy for Peter. Staying up late at night after putting a fussy baby to bed, just to make him a half-decent loaf of bread."

Erin nodded. Her foster parents hadn't worked that hard to make Carolyn feel normal. Maybe a biological parent, one like Mrs. Foster, would have been able to reach her.

"I'm always happy to do something for Peter."

The bells tinkled again and, looking up, Erin saw Clara Jones enter. Erin looked at Vic in disbelief. Clara had only been in the bakery once or twice before, and then only to cause trouble.

Vic shrugged. She greeted Clara pleasantly, but her expression was guarded. Neither one of them had any expectation that Clara was there to buy a dozen cookies for the police department, where she worked as a part-time administrator for Terry, the sheriff, and Tom Banks.

"What can we do for you today?" Vic asked. "I'm afraid Terry isn't here, if you were looking for him to sign something…"

"I'm not looking for Officer Piper," Clara said. She waited for Mrs. Foster to pick up her bag and depart. She leaned in toward Erin. "You should not be using police resources for your own personal investigations," she warned. "Terry may look the other way, but I think if the sheriff knew, that would be a different story. And if someone further up the line figured out what was going on…"

"Who is further up the line than the sheriff?"

"The mayor, for one. You really want the mayor investigating Officer Piper for misuse of department funds? How do you think that would end?"

Erin swallowed. She hadn't really thought about the possibility that Terry could get in trouble for running background on Charlotte Campbell for her. He was the one who had offered. Terry was always conscientious about his time, and Erin was sure he would have conducted the background search on his own time, not the department's. As far as using department resources… she had assumed that they had a monthly subscription to the databases, not that they were charged per transaction.

"You'd have to bring that up with Terry," she said icily. "He knows all of the ins and outs of the system and the politics, I don't. I don't see why you'd come here to harass me about it."

"I couldn't believe it when I saw those printouts," Clara said, eyes glittering. Her smile made Erin think of a shark. "I couldn't think of what trouble the Dyson clan would be up to in our town."

"I'm sure I wouldn't know anything about it."

"He told you about them, didn't he? You being from Maine, I could understand you not knowing what you were getting into with this family, though I would think that someone like Victor, growing up in these parts…"

"Don't call me that," Vic growled. Her tone was hard and Erin could see that Clara was surprised, having miscalculated how far she could push Vic before the girl would snap. Erin knew that Vic hadn't even gone by Victor before transitioning, so it was doubly insulting. Not like she was just an acquaintance who had forgotten what Vic's preferred name was, but making it obvious that she was intentionally misgendering her.

"Well, I'm sure sorry," Clara said dramatically, clearly not one bit sorry for what she had done. "I can't keep straight what it is you want to be called…"

Vic's mouth was in a tight, forced smile. "Since you're not actually a customer here—"

"Oh, I'll buy something." Clara looked over the goodies in the glass-fronted display case. "How about some gingersnaps? I don't think you can do anything to ruin gingersnaps…"

Erin was relieved when the bells rang again, needing someone else there to help dissipate the tension. Clara turned her head to see who was coming in as well, but she didn't get the eager audience she was hoping for. Instead, it was Willie Andrews, who Clara knew would not hesitate to jump to Vic's side and champion her case. Clara's mouth pursed into a sour knot while she waited for Vic to count the cookies out into a paper bag. Seeing who was there, the corners of Vic's mouth curled up slightly, and she counted out the cookies even more slowly and deliberately.

"Hi, Vicky," Willie's voice was warm and pleasant, happy to see her after he'd been away on whatever business had taken him from Bald Eagle Falls. He only had eyes for her.

Vic passed the bag of cookies down to Erin, who rang them up for

Clara, taking her time just as Vic had. Clara paid for them, then practically snatched the paper bag and made a dash for the door.

"If you know what's good for you, you'll stay away from the Dyson Clan," she warned. "You're not from around here, so maybe nobody has bothered to tell you." She looked at Vic when she said *nobody*. "You better stay out of the way of the Dysons. Or you're going to end up in a heap of trouble. The trouble you could get in from the sheriff for wasting department resources isn't even close to what's going to happen if you get involved with that bunch."

The bells jangled wildly when she shoved the door open, sending them dancing. Then the door swished shut behind her.

Willie looked at Vic, then at Erin, his brows raised. His soot-stained skin made the whites of his eyes stand out even more, so he seemed almost comically surprised.

"Uh… what was that about?"

"It's a long story," Erin sighed.

Vic looked at her. "Can I tell him about it? Do you mind?"

Erin threw her hands up in a shrug. "No, I suppose not. Looks like it's on its way around town now anyway. By tomorrow, everybody will be in the know."

"It's Erin's new sister," Vic said. "She got a lead on the identity, but the girl is involved with the Dyson clan. Terry did a background on her. We've been trying to explain to her that she should just stay away from them, give up on pursuing this woman any further. But you know Erin. Once she gets an idea into her head…"

"I'm not stubborn," Erin protested. "I'm a perfectly reasonable person!"

Willie and Vic exchanged a look that said otherwise.

Erin rolled her eyes and shook her head. "I'm not stubborn. You can compare me to a pit bull all you like, but that doesn't make it accurate!"

Neither one of them said anything. Erin didn't have anyone to argue against if they wouldn't push back, so she let out her breath and tried to just let it go.

"Nice to see you're back in town, Willie. Need your water refilled?"

"No, it's good. I just wanted to see Vicky and make sure we were on for tonight."

"I'm free if you are," Vic agreed.

"Good. I'll come by tonight when you're off."

Vic nodded, a brilliant smile advertising how happy she was to have him home again. Willie turned his gaze back to Erin, his mouth twisting into a grimace.

"And the Dysons, Erin? You really don't want to get involved with them. When I was—I know some of them… you really don't want to be mixed up in anything to do with that family."

Erin arched an eyebrow. "Really. I'm sort of surprised to hear that coming from you."

Willie was taken aback. He blinked at her. "Why? What do you mean?"

"I mean, usually, that's what people are telling me about you. He has a past. He's been involved in things. He has some bad connections. And I never listened to any of them."

"Well… it's all true. I do my best to be an upright citizen, but if you were to start digging into my skeletons… well, you might be surprised."

"But I don't care about your skeletons. And I don't care about Charlotte's. All I care about is finding her and getting to know her. If she is involved with some of these bad characters, or wants to get involved with one, that's her business. It's got nothing to do with me." Erin hesitated to say anything else, then forged on. "Everybody is entitled to some privacy about their past. You don't know everything about me, and I don't know everything about you, and that's okay. We should be able to evaluate each other without all of that baggage."

Willie gave a nod. "Normally, I would go along with that. But we're talking about a brutal gang here. Really, you don't want to underestimate them."

Erin considered his words. She was beginning to wonder if she could be wrong. It wasn't like it was just one of them telling her to stay away from the Dysons. Everybody acted like they were bad news.

"I'm not joining this clan," she pointed out. "I'm not getting involved in anything shady. I'm just talking about meeting someone who happens to have a connection to them. Do you really think they're going to kidnap me and induct me into their dark practices?"

Vic snickered. "They're not witches, Erin. Just… criminals."

"Exactly. I'm not going to be committing any crimes. I just want to meet my sister."

CHAPTER 9

*E*rin did think things through seriously. She considered all of the warnings from her friends. Willie's warnings in particular, weren't to be ignored, she'd learned in the past. She wondered what dealings he'd had with the Dysons in the past. Had he done jobs for them? Fought them for some kind of territorial right? Maybe just known some of the clan kids his age when he was going to school?

In the end, Erin had to follow her heart. She couldn't go another twenty years without meeting her sister. Now that she knew Charlotte's name, she couldn't just erase her. She needed to meet her. She needed to know what her sister was like and what it was like to actually have a family relationship.

She had a phone number, but she couldn't imagine just springing the news to someone over the phone that they were siblings. Erin had no idea what Charlotte's past was, whether she'd had any other siblings or had grown up as an only child. Whether she had lost either of her parents. Whether she'd had good relationships or bad ones. It wasn't something Erin could just spring on her over the phone.

She left Vic and Bella to watch the store one Friday afternoon, and headed to Moose River to find her sister.

Would Erin recognize Charlotte? She should have asked Terry if he had a picture of her. But she didn't want any preconceived notion of what Charlotte looked like. She wanted somehow to recognize her mother or Adam

Plaint in Charlotte's features. If Charlotte didn't look like either of them, could she really be the right person? There must have been other Charlottes out there. Plenty of people with the same birth date who could have been the missing sibling.

The information from the adoption board contact gave Erin a home address, but no work address. She had no idea what kind of work Charlotte did or what time of day she worked. She aimed for six o'clock, figuring that would give her time to get home if she had a nine-to-five job, but before she would have to leave for a night shift. Erin could be completely wrong. Charlotte could go out for dinner or drinks at six o'clock. But it was the best Erin could do.

The address was an apartment building, but Erin was able to get in without having to buzz someone from the lobby. She went to number 309 and took a few deep breaths before knocking on the door. Too quietly. She knocked again, rapping her knuckles sharply, then worried that it had been too hard and Charlotte would think it was the police. The police always knocked like they were going to break the door down if the homeowner didn't answer right away. Erin had been roused from a deep sleep by that knock more than once.

She waited, chewing on the inside of her lip, practicing in her head exactly what she was going to say if Charlotte came to the door. To begin with, there didn't seem to be anyone home. Erin knocked again, criticizing herself silently for even being there. She didn't know for sure that Charlotte was her sister. She didn't know what to say to her. She didn't know what she would do if they didn't have anything in common. If there was a long, awkward silence and she didn't know how to fill it.

There were footsteps within, and then the door was opened. Not even a pause to check the peephole or call through the door to see who it was. Maybe Charlotte was expecting someone.

Erin could instantly see familiar features in her sister's face. How many times had she wished that she looked like one of her foster sisters or a foster mother? That she was the one who belonged instead of the ugly duckling. She scrutinized her face in the mirror and saw only the vaguest resemblance to her mother's features, and nothing of her father's. There was no extended family to review for inherited traits she might have that had skipped her parents' generation. No long-lost cousins to say she looked just like this aunt or that great-grandmother. The pictures in

Clementine's genealogy were black and white, too fuzzy to make out details.

"Yes…?" Charlotte asked, giving her head an impatient shake.

Erin tried to pick her jaw up from the floor and come out with something coherent. It took a bit of stammering to get her greeting out.

"Charlotte? You must be Charlotte Campbell."

Charlotte gave a scowl. "Who are you?"

"I'm… my name is Erin. Price. I'm… well, I've been looking for you. Could we… sit down and talk for a few minutes?"

"I don't have the time right now, I'm getting ready to go out."

Probably that was just an excuse. Get rid of the crazy lady at the door and continue with whatever she had been doing before Erin arrived. Charlotte was in blue jeans and a black t-shirt that was too small for her. Erin could see the edge of a tattoo under the neckline of the shirt. She had scratches on her arms. Maybe she had a cat. She seemed far too young to be Erin's sister. Almost as young as Vic. But Erin had known that. She knew that Charlotte was eight years younger than she was. Barely an adult.

"I'm sorry… maybe tomorrow? Could we have coffee?"

"Coffee?" Charlotte shook her head irritably. "I'm sorry, who are you?"

"You don't know me, but you're…" Erin still couldn't bring herself to say it right out. She considered telling Charlotte the information she had, the date and hospital where she was born, so tiny, to a mother who had been brain dead for months. But surely no one had ever given her those details, so Erin didn't either, holding back.

"Yeah, I'm what…?"

"Are you adopted?"

Charlotte's eyes narrowed. She looked at Erin with new understanding, looking at her face, and then up and down her, making the same comparisons as Erin was. Petite build and pleasant, small facial features. Dark brown hair. The same eye shape.

"Maybe you'd better come in."

Charlotte opened the door wider and Erin entered. The apartment was small and sparse, but neatly furnished. Charlotte picked up a pair of socks and a few other things from the floor, giving an embarrassed laugh. "I'm really not that bad a slob, let me just pick these up…"

But it was obvious she wasn't a slob. For the most part, everything was put away in its proper places. It was a pleasant place, if a little bare. The type of place Erin would have lived if she weren't in Clementine's old house. The type of place she had lived many times.

"It's fine," Erin assured her. "It's not messy, it's just comfortable."

"Lived in," Charlotte agreed.

Erin sat down on a couch. She swallowed and tried again to find the natural way to start the conversation. "I'm not sure what to say," she admitted. "I guess… you might be my sister. I don't know. Maybe."

"Your sister." Charlotte shook her head. "But I don't have any family. Any biological family, I mean. Both my parents died in a car accident."

That part was true, at least.

"I know they did. But I was eight at the time. I survived the car accident. They put me into foster care."

"Foster care. Wouldn't they put you up for adoption, like they did me?"

"I was free for adoption… but people don't really want eight-year-olds. Infants, but not older kids."

"Eight isn't that old."

"No… I know other kids who got adopted. But mostly… if you're older than five… you're hard to place."

Charlotte's eyes searched Erin's face. "How do I know you're telling the truth? How do I know this isn't just some scam?"

"Well… I guess you don't. Not really. But I know… if you're my sister, your biological parents would have been listed as Kathryn and Luke Price."

Charlotte quirked her head slightly. A movement that was vaguely reminiscent of Erin's mother. "Listed as…?"

"I believe that your father was actually Adam Plaint. Not Luke Price. Making us only half-siblings."

"Adam Plaint. Who is that? Is *he* still alive?"

"No. He was… it's a long story. He was killed about the same time."

"So it's just you and me."

"On our mother's side, yes. If Adam Plaint was your father, then you have a half-brother as well. Older. His name is Davis."

Charlotte sat back, thinking about this. "All of this comes as a bit of a shock. I was always told I was an only child."

A sharp pain sliced through Erin's chest. Why had they told her that? What was the harm in sharing that she had a sister? They wouldn't have known about Adam Plaint being her father and having other children, but they knew about Erin. Erin was there at the hospital. In the car. They put her into a foster family. DFS knew very well that baby Charlotte had a sister. Did they think it would be more attractive to her adoptive parents if she were an only child? Maybe they didn't want to put pressure on them to adopt the two of them as a sibling group? Or had Charlotte's adoptive parents known about her sister and not wanted to tell Charlotte about Erin? Had they wanted a child who was unconnected and would never go looking for her biological family?

"You're not alone," she told Charlotte.

"Of course I'm not alone," Charlotte snapped. "I've got my parents, friends, a boyfriend—" She cut herself off abruptly and shook her head. "This is too much."

She went into the little kitchen and in a minute was pouring herself a tumbler of amber liquid. "You want a drink? I can't do this without a drink."

Erin's whole body was tense, her stomach a lead weight. She shook her head. "No… I don't drink."

"Of course little miss goody two-shoes doesn't drink," Charlotte muttered.

Erin looked down at herself. Had she done something to make Charlotte think she was condescending or judgmental? Was it the way she was dressed? Something she had said? Erin had been through plenty of scrapes herself and, while she might not be tattooed or a drinker, she wasn't like one of the Bald Eagles church ladies, outwardly self-righteous and telling everyone else how to behave.

"I'm not… I just don't drink," she said lamely. "After our parents… the car crash… and I lived in foster homes where… I saw what it did to other people. I just… never wanted to take the chance."

She thought of Davis and his long-time addictions. Did it run in the family? Was Charlotte already, at this tender age, an addict herself? She had certainly been quick to go for the alcohol.

"I don't need your preaching. You don't know what my life has been like. Maybe you're fine to go through life without a little help, but I could use a little something to take the edge off now and then."

Erin opened her mouth to object, but Charlotte didn't give her a chance to talk.

"I'm not an alcoholic. I just have a drink now and then and I don't see anything wrong with drinking socially. It's what I do with my friends. So you can take your judgmental attitude and—"

"I just said I don't drink." Erin gave Charlotte a steely glare. One of the looks she'd been practicing for dealing with the Bald Eagle Falls ladies when they started preaching or harassing Vic. Both Adele and Vic had been helping her, encouraging her to be assertive and not worry so much about pleasing others or meeting with their approval.

And it worked. Charlotte stopped ranting and looked at her, cheeks flushing red. She took a steadying drink from the tumbler, looking embarrassed by her behavior.

"I'm under a lot of stress," she explained. "You're right. You didn't do anything to deserve me acting like that."

"I know this must be weird for you," Erin said. "Just showing up like this and telling you we're sisters. Especially when you didn't even know you had any siblings. I'm sorry... but I didn't want to do it over the phone or email. I thought that face-to-face would be better... and I wanted to see you. To see if there was... a connection."

Charlotte sipped her drink, still holding herself aloof. "And is there?"

"You really look like our mother."

Charlotte considered this, shaking her head. "I've never been told I look like anyone. I mean, people will say I look like my adoptive mom, but she's always very quick to tell them that we're not biologically related. Like she doesn't want them to mistake me for a blood relative. I've never... your face seems really familiar. It's weird."

Erin nodded. Seeing her own features and her mother's features in Charlotte's face was disconcerting. It had been years since she had looked anyone in the face who had resembled her so closely. It had been more than twenty years since she had looked a blood relative in the face.

"I know. It's weird for me too."

They were both silent for a few minutes. "So, you live around here?" Charlotte asked. "You don't sound like you're from these parts."

"I do now, but I wasn't raised here. I had a foster family who moved north, out of state, and they were given permission to take me with them. I didn't have any relatives here I needed to stay available to. So I didn't grow up in Tennessee, even though I was born here and lived here until the accident."

"So, was it just the one foster family?"

"Oh, no. There were a lot of foster families."

"Oh." Charlotte nodded. "Sorry."

"Don't be. It was fine. I got to know lots of different people… different places…" She didn't focus on the bad stuff. Never being able to keep any personal possessions. Never knowing if the family she went to was going to be nice or abusive. Knowing she was a throwaway no one ever really wanted. Charlotte didn't need to hear any of that. Not yet.

"Must be nice," Charlotte said. "You don't know how many times I wished I could get out of Moose River. How I wanted to be anywhere but here."

It seemed like an odd complaint coming from a twenty-one year old. What was stopping her from pulling up stakes and moving somewhere else? She obviously wasn't still living with her parents. She had a place of her own. She could have moved anywhere else she liked. Erin had disappeared and left her old life behind enough times to know that it wasn't that hard. Unless, of course, being part of the Dyson clan, Charlotte wasn't allowed to make her own choice in the matter.

There was a knock on the door, so sudden and loud that Erin nearly leapt out of her seat and Charlotte spilled some of her drink. Charlotte swore and shook her head.

"What is it now?"

She went over to the door, and this time she did look out the peephole before opening the door. She stood there with her hand on the doorknob, hesitating.

"Who is it?" Erin whispered.

There was another loud knock, followed by "Police, open up!"

Erin stood there with her mouth open, all of Terry's, Vic's, and Willie's warnings flooding her brain. Don't get mixed up with her. Don't go meet her. It was too dangerous to chance getting mixed up with Dyson clan business.

"What are you going to do?"

Charlotte threw a look over her shoulder, clearly irritated.

At the third knock on the door, so loud it sounded like they were already using a battering ram, Charlotte opened the door.

"You trying to get me in trouble with the landlord?" she demanded. "What's with all the noise?"

One of the uniformed cops grasped Charlotte by the arm. "Charlotte Campbell, you're under arrest for the murder of Bobby Dyson."

Erin's heart dropped to her stomach. The murder of Bobby Dyson?

"Murder?" Charlotte repeated, her voice going higher. "Of Bobby? What happened to Bobby? Why would I kill him?"

"Young Bobby isn't exactly known for his discretion. Maybe you decided you didn't like him fooling around on you and making it known far and wide."

The cop pulled Charlotte's hands behind her back to handcuff her, then checked each of her pockets and did a cursory pat down.

"Any weapons?"

"No. I'm sitting in my house visiting, why would I be wearing a gun?"

"Or maybe you don't have it because you left it at the scene."

"Left it at the scene? You think I shot Bobby? I loved Bobby, I'd never do that!"

"Yeah. I'm sure," he sneered.

"I'd never hurt Bobby! Do you have any idea what they would do to me?"

The cop chuckled. "Well, I don't imagine they'll be too happy about it, will they?"

It wasn't until then that the little knot of policemen seemed to realize there was someone else in the apartment.

"And who are you?" the cop in charge demanded, putting his hand on his holster.

Erin tried to swallow a lump in her throat.

"I'm—I'm Erin Price. I'm Charlotte's sister."

He blinked at her, frown lines appearing in his forehead and his mouth turning down. "Her sister? Charley Campbell doesn't have a sister."

Exactly how well-known to the police was Charlotte?

"We were separated when our parents died." Erin swallowed and licked her dry lips. "She was adopted. I wasn't."

The cop approached her, leaving the other officers to supervise Charley, securely handcuffed. He studied Erin's face, and nodded slightly, perhaps seeing enough similarities in their features to accept the explanation.

"Jack Ward," he introduced himself. "How long have you been with Charley today?"

Erin looked over at Charlotte. "Not very long," she said. "Just a few minutes."

"Where were you last night?"

"Uh—not here."

"That's not an answer."

Erin wasn't keen on telling the policemen any more about herself than she had to. She didn't need everyone knowing who she was and where she was from. And more than that, she wasn't sure she was ready to tell Charley where she was from. She didn't need the Dyson clan following her home.

She jerked her chin a fraction of an inch in Charley's direction. "I wasn't around here," she repeated.

Jack Ward apparently got her meaning. He scratched his jaw, looking from Erin to Charley and back again.

"You got yourself in a heap of trouble now, Charley."

"I didn't do anything."

"We've got enough to arrest you and search your apartment."

"You need a warrant!" Charley's face was bright red.

Jack Ward unfolded a paper and flapped it in her direction. "I have a warrant."

Charley fumed silently. Ward grinned at her. He walked closer to her. "I've told you before, Charley. You hang with these guys and you're going to get burned, sooner or later."

Ward had Charley escorted from the apartment. He motioned to Erin.

"If I could also get you to come to the station, Miss Price."

Erin's stomach was clenched in a giant knot. "I didn't do anything. I'm not under arrest."

"As you heard, Charley just killed her lover, and there is going to be maelstrom like you've never seen before when the rest of the Dysons find out. Every aspect of this investigation is going to be tracked and scrutinized. If you think I'm just going to let a potential witness walk off without being questioned..." He shook his head. "It's just not going to happen. So you can come voluntarily, or you will be compelled. It's up to you."

"I'm not a witness. I didn't even get to town until this afternoon."

"You can put that in writing, and when we verify it, you'll be on your way."

"This just all seems so..."

"It's a murder investigation, ma'am. If you've never been caught up in one before, then everything is going to seem a little strange. But that's just the way it works."

Erin kept her mouth closed and did not inform him that she had been involved in a murder investigation before. More than once.

The murder investigations that she had been involved in, though, had not been shootings. They had appeared to be accidents. The investigations had been stressful, but she hadn't been in imminent danger of being thrown in jail, even when she was a suspect.

She followed Ward out of the apartment. There were more officers in the hall outside, and once Ward had escorted Erin out, they streamed in.

"My car is just parked down on the street—" Erin attempted to split away from Ward to go get her own vehicle, but he put his hand on her arm and held her back.

"We'll take you in. Once you're released, someone will drive you back over to get your car."

"But that's ridiculous, I can just drive it over…"

"No."

Erin again opened her mouth to remind him that she wasn't under arrest and could therefore do what she wanted to, but she closed it and breathed deeply instead. He was doing his job. He had a mobster who had been shot. Erin imagined that such a murder could result in retaliation against anyone who was suspected of having been involved, as well as having political ramifications, as Ward had suggested. He wasn't concerned with her convenience. He had a murder to solve while sitting on a powder keg.

Ward let go of her arm and let her walk beside him unrestrained.

"So you've known Charley since she was a baby?" Ward asked. "I never heard any whisper that she had a sister before."

"No. I never met her before. I didn't even know she existed until just a few months ago. Then I had to track her down… This was the first time I made contact with her. We've never met before, not even on the phone or email."

His brows shot up. "Well, this is quite the introduction, then. I guess you didn't know that she was involved with an organized crime family."

"I… kind of did."

"Kind of?"

"I had a friend check her out… you know, to see if her birthdate was right and make sure she wasn't just some online scammer… He said that she was involved with this family somehow, but we didn't know how. I thought... maybe her adoptive parents were part of it... something that wasn't really her fault. I thought maybe she just had some peripheral involvement."

"Her parents are good, hardworking folks who are heartbroken to have a daughter get involved with these guys. Charley is a wild child who's been nothing but trouble for them since she was a teenager."

A wild child? Erin frowned, thinking of Charley's apartment. It had been fairly neat and clean, not some rat-infested drug den. Charley wasn't passed out with a bunch of other junkies, spent after a night of riotous living.

"So her involvement with these guys..." Erin was reluctant to call them a gang or syndicate, or whatever they considered themselves. "That's because she's the girlfriend of one of them?"

Ward gave a bark of laughter. "You're not listening to me, honey. She isn't in the Dyson clan because she's Bobby Dyson's girlfriend. She's his girlfriend because she's in the clan." He paused for a moment, and amended his statement. "She *was* his girlfriend. Now that's all changed."

He opened the door of a dark sedan for Erin and she slid into it. He shut her door and walked around to the other side. When he got in, he didn't speak to her, but started the car with a scowl on his face, lost deep in thought.

Erin watched out the window at the unfamiliar city streets whipping by. She'd only left Vic to take care of the bakery for one afternoon. What if she weren't back there by morning? How was she going to explain it to Vic? And worse—to Terry? Ward had said that all she needed to do was to sign a written statement, and then she could go home. Erin could only hope that it would really be that easy.

CHAPTER 10

*E*rin finished writing up her witness statement, which was really no more than couple of lines saying that she hadn't ever met Charley before six o'clock and had no knowledge of what had happened before then, and then she waited for Ward to return to the room and tell her she could go home. She was tired, in need of dinner, and trying to figure out if she should drive back to Bald Eagle Falls or stay overnight and let Vic know that she wasn't going to make it back in time to open up in the morning. Vic could either keep Auntie Clem's Bakery closed for the day, or she and Bella could work out some arrangement that suited them.

But Erin really didn't want to leave Vic in the lurch, so once Jack Ward told her she could go, she would probably grab a burger at a drive-through and hit the highway. She might not get much sleep, but she could at least be there to lend a hand. With an extra cup of coffee in the morning, she should be able to function, at least.

There was a polite knock on the door and Ward entered, reading a sheaf of papers in his hand. Erin shifted in her seat to get up and he motioned her to stay put. He sat down across from her without looking at her, and continued to flip through the printouts, absorbing whatever important information had been gathered. Erin's statement wasn't long, so she wasn't sure why he was still keeping her. It wouldn't have taken more than thirty seconds for him to read it and send her on her way.

Finally, Ward put the papers down on the table in front of him. He cocked his head to the side, looking at her.

Erin shifted uncomfortably. "What?"

"You don't exactly have a squeaky-clean record yourself, do you?"

Erin licked her lips. "I've never been convicted of anything. Unless you count parking tickets. And I've paid all of those."

He stared at her for a minute, letting the silence lengthen. "What makes you think this is a good time to joke?"

"I'm not. I'm telling you—I don't have a record. I don't have any criminal convictions."

"Maybe not. But you've certainly been investigated a number of times, on a number of different charges. Under a number of different names or identities."

"I haven't done anything wrong. It's not illegal to use an alias."

"You haven't done anything wrong?"

Erin shook her head. "None of those charges have gone anywhere. I haven't done anything."

"These accusations just keep popping up," he said sarcastically, "all by themselves."

"Misunderstandings. Or circumstances. There was never any real evidence against me for anything."

He looked down at his printouts. Erin swallowed and tried to keep her face open and unemotional. Yes, she'd been investigated in the past, but she'd always been proven to be innocent, or there hadn't been enough to proceed. He couldn't hold those charges against her.

"You've been investigated for murder," Ward pointed out.

"It's not like that. A woman died in my bakery from anaphylaxis. But it wasn't from anything I did. It wasn't even an accident, it was somebody else. And she went to prison for it. I was completely cleared."

He frowned, still reading through the pages. "If I'm reading this right… not once, but twice."

"It wasn't me either time. Just because someone uses my baking as a vehicle for poison, that doesn't mean I'm guilty of anything. If someone pushes someone else in front of your car and you run over him, are you guilty of murder?"

Ward gave a little smile. "I guess that would depend on the circumstances."

Erin's face warmed. "I didn't have anything to do with either one of those deaths. I didn't set them up, or hire someone, or do anything. I had no motive. They ate baked goods that I made. That's all. I had nothing to do with it."

"Your record goes back further than that. You weren't exactly pure as the driven snow before you moved to Tennessee were you?"

"I didn't have an easy life up north. I ran into trouble a few times. But I was never convicted of anything. You can call up any of those cops who had anything to do with me, and they'll tell you. I never did anything."

"Seems like maybe this rebellious streak runs in the family."

"I was never rebellious," Erin insisted. But even as she said it, she knew it wasn't true. No, she had never gotten into drugs or crime or other things she shouldn't have as a teenager and young adult. She'd known from an early age that she was going to have to be able to support herself once she aged out of the system, and had planned accordingly. But she had defied her foster parents. Many foster parents. She had never been able to believe what she was told and trust in adults who had more experience than she did.

Instead, she'd had to figure it out herself. She had to test the limits. She disobeyed. She did the opposite to what she was told. Sometimes the adults in her life were right, but sometimes they were wrong, and she never had figured out a way to tell which was which without testing it out herself.

"You weren't rebellious," Ward repeated.

"I was responsible. You feel free to talk to any social worker or cop who ever worked with me. I worked. I educated myself. I supported myself. I was no 'wild child' like you say Charley was."

"But it sound like maybe you lined your own pockets when the opportunity presented itself. Felt free to accept gifts that you didn't deserve. Took advantage of those who were vulnerable."

Erin clenched her teeth. "No. I didn't. I worked hard as a caregiver. I never talked anyone into giving me anything. Sometimes... people would give me gifts. Was I supposed to turn them down? I worked hard."

"I'm sure you did."

"If someone gave you a gift, you wouldn't accept it?"

"It's called accepting a bribe. No, I wouldn't."

"But it's not accepting a bribe if you're not a police officer. It's just someone showing gratitude. And why would you turn it down? Especially if you were struggling to make ends meet. I don't think it's fair to expect that."

"I doubt if you were on the skids."

Erin shook her head slowly. "You have no idea what it was like for me."

"I know that now you're a business owner. You've got your own shop. Sounds to me like you managed to make out pretty well."

"I have all that because my aunt died. I've got no one else left in the world, and she didn't have anyone else to leave it to."

"Except Charley."

Erin was taken aback. "Except Charley," she admitted. "But Clementine didn't know about Charley. I didn't know about Charley. No one knew about her."

"Why wouldn't your aunt know about her?"

Erin realized that Ward was missing big pieces of the puzzle. She sat back, letting her breath out.

"I really need to get back to my bakery tomorrow. Do you think we could arrange to discuss this some other time? Or over the phone? Or I can email you answers to your questions? I can't just leave my partner to take care of everything."

"This is a murder investigation, Miss Price. The first few hours of case are vital. We need to get all the information we can as quickly as we can. Maybe your information won't have any bearing on the case, but we can't know that until we hear it. Leave it to us to figure out what is important and what is not."

"I don't see how this has anything to do with the murder. What does my Aunt Clementine leaving me the bakery have to do with Charley allegedly killing her boyfriend?"

"I don't know. I won't be able to make connections until I have all of the details. Maybe you have motive to set Charley up. Maybe she was threatening to take your inheritance. Maybe the two of you aren't quite as buddy-buddy as you would like me to think."

"We're not buddy-buddy. We just met each other today."

"I don't know that. I don't have any proof of that. I'd like to hear about why you inherited this property and she didn't."

Erin closed her eyes and covered them with her palms for a few minutes, trying to rest her head and stay clear.

"Okay. I'll try to explain it as concisely as I can. Clementine never knew Charley. None of us did. Charley was born after the accident that killed our mother. Our mother was kept on life support in order to carry Charley to term. I don't think Clementine found out about what had happened to our parents until years later. I don't know for sure, because the journal is still missing. But she didn't take either of us in. She might not have ever even known about Charley being born; it took me a long time to get any information out of DFS, and that was years later. Clementine knew that I was still alive… or was last she had heard… so she left everything to me."

"Did Charley challenge the will?"

"I just met Charley today!"

"So you say."

"You don't have any evidence that we ever met before this. I've got a business to run. I barely ever leave Bald Eagle Falls for anything other than supply runs."

Ward looked at Erin for a long time. Erin didn't crack. There wasn't anything else for her to say. She didn't have anything to confess to.

"Do you think your sister killed Bobby Dyson?" Ward asked.

"How would I know? I don't know anything about her or about him. I didn't get to town until after he was killed. I'm not Charley's alibi. She never said anything to me about him. I never heard his name until you arrested her."

"You'd heard of the Dyson clan, though."

"I told you that. I had a friend run background…"

"If you had him run background, why didn't you listen to him when he told you to stay out of it?"

Because Erin always had to test it out for herself. She should have listened to Terry, but she figured he was just being an overprotective boyfriend. She should have listened to Vic, who had grown up hearing about the Dyson clan and had warned Erin not to get involved with them. But Erin figured she was a little bit jealous of Erin meeting her long-lost sister and didn't want to take the chance of losing her place as Erin's close friend and confidante.

And Willie… how many times had Terry told her that Willie might not be quite as trustworthy as Erin thought him? She'd heard, not just from Terry, but from others as well, that Willie was suspected of being involved in shady practices. That he would do anything for a buck. That he didn't care who he worked for, as long as he got his money. Maybe she should have listened to Willie. Maybe he knew more about the Dysons than the others did. Not just rumor and innuendo, but actual first-hand experience.

Erin rubbed her forehead. "I guess I just really wanted to meet my sister. I didn't see how that could be a problem. It wasn't like I was getting involved in anything with this Dyson gang. I just wanted to meet my sister."

"Next time, maybe you should listen."

Erin sighed and nodded. "Yeah. Maybe next time I will."

Before Erin left, she was allowed to see Charley. She hadn't expected Ward to allow it, but he'd looked at his watch and considered the request, and eventually nodded.

"Sure, why not?"

"Really?"

"You're going to have to wait just a few more minutes. I need to make sure we're not interrupting the flow of an interrogation. Obviously, we can't just break in in the middle of something important."

"Aren't you the one questioning her?"

"No, I have someone else talking to her right now. We take turns. Have to stay fresh. Questioning a suspect can be exhausting and can take a long time."

Erin suspected that Charley did not get to take breaks. They would keep questioning her, trying to wear her down and tire her out and break her down until she confessed to what they wanted her to. Erin watched TV. She knew how it worked.

She looked at her watch again, worried that it was going to be hours before she got a chance to see Charley and was able to start on her way home. But it was only twenty minutes before Ward was escorting her to the interview room where Charley was being kept. The police officer interrogating her was pulled out and Erin was allowed to enter. The door closed, sealing them in. Erin felt like they were in an echo chamber. Every sound was too loud. They were bound to be recorded and observed.

"What are you doing here?" Charley demanded.

"I asked if I could see you before I headed for home."

"That was nice of you. Why?"

"I just wanted to make sure you were okay, and to make sure you could get ahold of me if you needed to. I don't know… maybe you don't care. But if you did want to keep in touch…"

"It would be nice to have a pen pal while I'm in prison?"

Erin gulped. The conversation was certainly not going the way she had expected. "No… I didn't mean that… I'm hoping this is all just a mistake, and they're going to let you go, and then we'll have a chance to get to know each other."

Charley shook her head. Her eyes were angry. Probably not even at Erin; she was wound up after having to talk to the police for hours on end. Looking more closely, Erin could see lines of fatigue around her eyes, and puffiness that suggested she had concealed bags under her eyes with makeup earlier in the day. If she'd already been sleep-deprived before the arrest, Erin could only imagine how exhausted she must be with several hours of questioning on top of that.

"You seem like a nice person," Charley said. "But I don't know you from Adam. You could just be someone the department planted to get my confidence. If you are legit, then I'm sorry. You just got me at a really bad time. Maybe some other time—some other lifetime—we could get to know each other. But for me now… it's just not going to work."

Erin nodded. "Okay. Just for the record, I'm sorry this is happening to you, and I'm not a police plant. If you change your mind…" Erin slid a slip of paper across the table to Charley. "That's my cell number. You can call me if you want to. Otherwise… I guess we just go our separate directions now."

Charley looked down at the paper. It was a while before she nodded and picked it up.

"Okay, sis. Maybe I'll call you sometime."

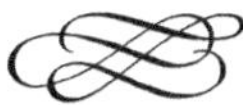

*V*ic was writing up price labels for the display case. She looked over at Erin and caught her yawning again. Vic raised an eyebrow.

"You sure you're going to be able to manage today?"

Erin had gotten back to Bald Eagle Falls in time to start the early-morning baking at Auntie Clem's, but she hadn't actually had more than an hour or two of restless sleep before that. She hadn't even bothered to put on her pajamas, but had just fallen into bed. She had at least managed to get her shoes off. Orange Blossom had prowled around, walking overtop her on the bed and sniffing at the abundance of unusual smells that clung to Erin, snuffling and sneezing at her.

"I know, I know," Erin had told him. "I'll shower in the morning and these clothes go straight into the washing machine. Though her nose wasn't as sensitive as the cat's, she could detect a number of the smells from the police station. Her own sweat, smoke from Jack Ward, who had obviously sneaked out for a cigarette at some point before talking to her, leftover fast food dumped into garbage cans, the bodies and bodily fluids of various detainees Erin had been forced to sit with while she was waiting to make her statement. Even if there hadn't been anyone else there, the furniture itself seemed to have absorbed their odors. Erin had gagged more than once at the foul smells.

Vic had fed the animals in her absence, so they didn't need to be taken care of, but both Orange Blossom and Marshmallow had seemed to understand that something was going on with Erin and had given her extra attention.

"I'm fine," Erin told Vic, rubbing her eyes. "I'll have another coffee and that will keep me going."

"You've had enough coffee to float the Titanic. What you really need is sleep."

"I don't think I'd be able to get it now even if I tried. Don't worry about me. It's just a day like any other."

Vic carefully filled loaf pans with dough. "So, are you going to tell me how things went? I guess you guys must have gotten on pretty well, to stay out there talking so late."

"Well… no, not exactly. I'm not sure if I'll ever hear from her again."

Vic turned her head to look at Erin, puzzled. "What? But you were out there…"

"I wasn't so late because we were visiting." Erin sighed. She wanted to talk it over with someone, but she also didn't want to have to divulge what had happened. She wasn't exactly going to be able to keep it from Vic. She knew Vic would keep whatever she said in confidence. "I was there late because I was talking to the police."

"What?" Vic dropped the spatula she was using to scrape out the bowl.

"I… uh… Charley was arrested, so they were questioning me as a witness."

"Who's Charley?"

"Charlotte. My sister. Apparently, that's what she goes by."

"She was arrested? Your sister was arrested?"

"Err… yeah."

"What for?"

Erin swallowed. She pretended to be concentrating on the muffin recipe she was assembling, even though she could have done it in her sleep.

"Murder."

"Murder? Who?"

"Her boyfriend, one of the Dysons." Though Vic hadn't asked, Erin knew what question would be coming next. "Shot."

Vic's mouth worked for a few seconds before she managed to get anything out. "Land sakes! She shot her boyfriend?"

"That's what the police think. I don't know. I barely met her. I… hope she didn't."

"Goodness, I hope not. I can't believe it, Erin. That's just crazy! I'm flabbergasted! I don't know what to say!"

Erin nodded. "That about covers it."

"What did the police want from you? They didn't think you had something to do with it?"

"I didn't," Erin asserted, "and they'll know that if they verify my alibi. I was here with you yesterday morning."

Vic nodded, her eyes wide. "Do you think *she* did it?"

"I don't know. They didn't exactly discuss any of the details with me. I didn't talk to Charley about it, before or after she was arrested. I'm afraid I wouldn't want to know the answer."

"Wow."

"You're nice not to say 'I told you so,'" Erin told Vic. "You all told me not to get involved with her after you found out she was involved with the Dyson clan."

"Well… yes. We didn't want you to get involved in anything nasty. But I don't think any of us imagined that there would be a murder the day you met her. We were thinking more about you being exposed to some disreputable characters. Not… being caught in the middle of a murder investigation."

Erin looked at the clock. It was just about time to turn the sign to 'open.' She looked sideways at Vic and caught her looking back.

"I know," she said. "But it's not like it's the first murder investigation I've gotten caught in the middle of."

Erin was dreading having to tell Terry about her first visit with her half-sister. She didn't know how she was going to explain how she had ended up at the police station giving a statement about her movements over the previous twenty-four hours. But as it turned out, she didn't have to bring it up with him.

Terry came into the bakery for a water bottle refill and a visit during the slow part of the afternoon. He took a seat at one of the small cafe tables by the front window. Erin took a deep breath and looked at Vic, not sure about how to proceed. Vic just gave her an encouraging 'get on with it' gesture. Not helpful. Erin prepared a pitcher of water and got a doggie biscuit out of the cookie jar on the counter.

She approached him, forcing a smile. "Hi, Terry. How is everything?"

"Everything is quiet here."

"Good! I know quiet is better in the police business."

"Things are not so quiet in Moose River; but I gather you already know that."

Erin's heart sank. She sat down on the chair across from him. She gave the biscuit to K9. "Uh… yeah. Interesting story."

"Jack Ward says hi."

"He seemed like a very competent policeman. I'm sure he'll have it all sorted out before long."

"He called the PD to ask about you. Imagine my surprise."

Erin swallowed. She wished she had brought a glass over for herself. "I didn't know he was going to call you."

"Would it have made a difference?"

Erin searched his face. He wasn't happy, that was clear. His jaw was clenched. His voice was flat and cold.

"I was going to tell you about it later on. Tonight. There wasn't any point in calling you last night, it was almost time to get up by the time I got back here. I didn't have the energy to do anything but fall into bed. But if I'd known he was going to call you, then yes… I would have called you while we were making preparations this morning. I didn't think anyone in Bald Eagle Falls was going to know anything about it if I didn't bring it up."

"I *warned* you."

"But I didn't do anything, Terry. I was just there. Not even when the murder happened, I wasn't there until hours later. At Charley's house, I mean. Not at the crime scene. I was just there to meet my sister."

"Who I told you was involved in organized crime."

"Would you have let that stop *you* from meeting a long-lost relative?"

Terry frowned. He took his time unscrewing the top of his water bottle and topping it up from the provided pitcher. A wave of relief washed over Erin. At least he hadn't just snapped back an answer without seriously considering it. She waited, giving him time.

"I don't have a long-lost relative," Terry said finally. "I can't imagine what it would be like to have a sibling I had never met before. But I know that if one of my brothers was in trouble... I would go see him even if I knew he was involved in something shady."

Erin breathed out a sigh of relief. "I didn't go there thinking that she was actually involved in anything like a murder. I honestly couldn't see how going to see her could be dangerous to me."

Terry opened his mouth to interject, but Erin held up her hand and went on.

"I just wanted to meet her. I wanted to talk to someone I was blood-related to. I haven't been able to do that since I was eight years old. I haven't had anyone. I never planned to get involved in anything she was involved in. I never thought anyone would be suspicious of me just for talking to her. Maybe that's naive, but what were the odds she was going to be arrested for murder the day I met her?"

Terry cracked a smile. "With you...?" he took a sip of his water. "I wouldn't even want to speculate."

Erin tried to look aloof, though her face was burning. "I've never done anything to actually get myself mixed up in a murder investigation. Except maybe for maybe Adam Plaint's, and I wasn't involved, I was just helping the police department with the information I had uncovered. You suspected me in Angela's death, but even you have to admit I didn't do anything wrong. It wasn't like I was holding drugs for someone and got accused of dealing. I didn't do anything, I was just in the wrong place at the wrong time. Or *she* was."

Terry was nodding. "I know. I know. But this time you did have warning. Because I warned you."

"You didn't warn me that she might be involved in a murder."

"Well... no. How could I, unless I was clairvoyant?"

"Exactly. No one could have expected it to happen. None of us could have predicted *that*."

"Okay. Agreed."

Erin looked out the front window, but all was quiet on the street outside. Nothing for Terry to investigate. No approaching customers for the bakery.

"What did Jack Ward have to say to you?"

"He didn't know that you and I were... together. He thought he was just calling me to get the background of an ordinary citizen. To check in and see whether you were a troublemaker, or just someone that landed in the middle of things."

"And you told him…"

"The latter. You've never been a troublemaker, Erin… but trouble certainly has a way of finding you."

Erin shrugged helplessly. "I know. I don't know how. Maybe since the car crash… I'm cursed. Maybe it altered my magnetic field."

He raised an eyebrow. "That sounds suspiciously like some new age witchcraft. Did you get that from Adele?"

"No. I've never heard her talk about magnetic fields. She'd say my spirit or some such nonsense. But she knows I don't believe in that kind of thing."

Terry took a long drink of his water. He bent down to scratch K9's ears, which Erin recognized as a sign he was getting ready to leave.

"What exactly do you and Adele talk about when you get together?" Terry asked.

"I don't know. Just like anybody else. Things going on in our lives, around town, books, politics…"

"She's interested in politics?"

"Not particularly. Neither am I. It's just something we talk about in passing. What's going on in the world."

Terry nodded. "I'd better be getting back out on patrol." He stood up. "I assume you're going to be staying away from Charlotte in the future?"

Erin stood up as well. She bit her lip, considering. A shadow passed over Terry's face.

"You *are* going to stay away from her, right Erin?"

"She's my sister. You said if it was one of your brothers who was in trouble, you would still go see them."

He looked troubled. "I know, but I'm a cop. I'm trained to deal with things like that. I could offer advice and try to help out. What could you do to help Charlotte? You'd just be exposing yourself for no reason."

"No, not for no reason. Because she's my sister."

A couple of days passed uneventfully. Erin caught up on her sleep and followed her usual routines, glad to get back to normal, but still wondered about her new sister and what was going on with her. Charley hadn't called her, so Erin tried to just put her sister out of her mind, but that wasn't as easy as it sounded.

Then one morning when her phone rang and Erin glanced down at the screen to see who it was, she saw the words Moose River Jail scrolling across. Her heart leapt—there was no one else it could be, it had to be Charley— but she felt anxious and queasy at the same time. The morning sales were still pretty brisk, and Erin looked at Vic, gauging whether she should answer the call or not.

"Go ahead," Vic said, jerking her head toward the kitchen in the back. "I can take care of things here."

"I'll just be a minute," Erin promised. She hit the answer button and ducked through the door. "Hello?"

"Yeah, is this Erin? Erin Price?"

"Charley? Are you okay?"

"Yeah, yeah, I'm just fine."

"I didn't think you were going to call. How is everything going? I guess you're still…"

"I'm still here," Charley confirmed the obvious. "My lawyer is working on getting me out, but they don't move quickly around here. They like to leave you here and give you a taste of what it's going to be like if you have to be incarcerated long term. Throw a scare into you. Pigs. It's just taking a little longer than I expected."

"Uh-huh…" Erin had no idea what to say to this. She supposed she should commiserate. Express sympathy. Tell her sister that she knew Charley wasn't supposed to be there. And that she would get out soon. But Charley knew that world better than Erin did, and Erin was sure she probably had a pretty good idea of what her chances and the timeline were without any false encouragement from Erin.

"You said if I needed anything, I could call," Charley said tentatively

Erin was pretty sure that wasn't what she had said. But it was an olive branch. Charley was reaching out to her and Erin wasn't about to slap her down.

"Is there something you needed?"

Maybe Erin could take her some muffins or other baking. Was that kind of thing allowed in jail? Did people really try to smuggle things in to prisoners inside a cake, like in the comics? Surely with the advent of x-rays and metal detectors, that kind of thing was antiquated.

"Yeah. It's just… I wouldn't ask, but I really couldn't think of anyone else I could trust. I don't have a lot of close friends. I mean, there are girls I hang with but…"

"Trust with what?"

"I don't have anyone to feed Iggy."

"Iggy?" Erin pictured a little black puppy or kitten. Charley had already been away for a few days, but maybe she had an automatic feeder for it that would last that long. Charley had thought that she would be back to take care of him, but it was going to be too long.

"Iggy is… my lizard. Don't gross out. He's not slimy or poisonous. But… he's going to need to be fed. No one but Bobby had a key to my apartment. Obviously, the cops aren't going to step in and take care of him. I'm lucky they didn't just turn him in to the Humane Society."

A lizard? Of course Iggy was a lizard. It figured that her prickly little sister wouldn't have a fluffy puppy or kitten. Or rabbit. Instead… a lizard. A cold-blooded reptile. Just like the guys she worked with.

"Uh… I don't know much about lizards."

"Everything is set up. Just make sure that his environmentals are all okay, give him some crickets… he doesn't need to be taken out for a walk or anything."

"Good, because I'm afraid I'd lose him. Uh… how big *is* this lizard, anyway. Is he… I mean, he's not too big if all he eats is crickets, right?"

"It's not a gila monster," Charley laughed. She sounded natural and friendly for the first time. Just a girl talking about her lizard. "He's a chameleon."

"Named Iggy? I thought he'd be an iguana."

"Yeah… it's sort of a joke."

"I don't know how big chameleons are. They're the ones that change color, right?"

"Yes. He's not big and he's not going to bite you. Is that okay? Do you think you could…?"

Erin thought about it. Of course she wanted to rush over and do something for Charley. It was the first opportunity she'd had to bond over something. But it was a couple of hours driving each way. She hadn't told Charley she lived in Bald Eagle Falls, and Charley had just naturally assumed Erin was in town.

"Yeah… I can do that. But I won't be able to get there until late. How do I get the key? You don't have a neighbor that can let me in?"

"No. You'll have to come to the jail to pick it up. Sorry about that. And go to the pet store for crickets because I don't have any at home. The landlord freaks out over me keeping *la cucaracha* in the apartment." Erin could practically hear Charley's eye roll. "So you can do it?" Her voice took on a plaintive quality. "I know it's a pain…"

She had no idea how far out of the way it was for Erin. But Erin wasn't about to tell her and make her sister feel guilty for asking. She'd wanted a connection, and now she had it. She would be the lizard sitter. If Iggy only needed to be fed every few days, then Erin would probably only have to do it once or twice before Charley got released or got out on bail. When Charley learned how far Erin had gone to take care of the lizard, she would be super grateful, and it would be the beginning of a warm, sisterly relationship for them.

"I'll do it," Erin agreed. "I'll get over as soon as I can. How late can I get to the jail to pick up the key? And what are the pet store hours?"

Charley let out a sigh of relief. She gave Erin the details, and Erin bent over the desk in her tiny office scribbling them down.

"Thank you so much for doing this," Charley said. "It's a big relief. I've been so worried…"

"Of course. I'm happy to help."

"Looks like my time is up. I gotta get off the phone. Do you have everything you need? You don't need to know any more?"

"How many crickets do I need to get? And do I just drop them into his cage?"

"Reptarium. Yes. You don't need a lot, just the smallest container. Just open the tank and dump them in. Make sure the dripper is working and his heat and humidity are okay—"

There was a growling voice in the background, and Erin knew they were kicking Charley off the phone.

"That's all," Charley's voice was fading as she was getting farther away from the handset. "It's not hard. Thank you, Erin!"

The phone connection was cut. Erin stood there for a moment with her phone still to her ear, as if Charley might come back and continue the conversation.

What had she gotten herself into? She knew absolutely nothing about caring for a chameleon. Charley might say it was nothing, but if Erin did something wrong and the lizard was sick or dead by the time Charley got out of jail, that would not be a good relationship builder.

Eventually, Erin lowered her phone and slid it into her pocket. She looked at the time, and started calculating in her head what time she was going to need to leave if she were going to get to the jail and the pet store before they closed, so she could take care of Iggy properly. Then she'd need to immediately turn around and return home in time to get the sleep she needed to be functional at the bakery the next day. She didn't have the reserves she needed to stay up late more than once in a blue moon.

"Is everything okay?" Vic asked, as Erin walked back out to the store front, her thoughts miles away.

"Yeah. Fine. Just… thinking."

"Who was that on the phone?"

Erin looked at the customers who were listening in. None of them knew anything about Erin's sister or what she had gotten herself into.

"That was Charley."

Vic's eyes widened. "Charley? What did *Charley* want?" Vic carefully avoided the use of a pronoun so that no one could catch on that Charley was a girl rather than a boy.

"Uh… Charley has a… friend… who needs a babysitter. Just tonight. After that, Charley should be home."

Vic followed this easily. "This friend is… all the way *out there?*"

"Yes. So…" Erin looked at the time again. "I think I'm going to have to leave early today, so I can pick up a meal and the key, and still get home in good time tonight."

"Yeah. For sure. You just go when you have to. I can take care of things here for one afternoon."

"Do you want me to call Bella and see if she can come in?"

"No. Don't worry about it. We already have her coming in on the weekend, and that's more important. It's not like it's all day, and everything is already made. It's just the after-school crowd and clean-up."

"Are you sure?"

"Of course. You have to take care of Charley's friend. It's important."

"Okay."

Mary Lou looked at Erin and Vic, a little frown on her face. "Charlie who? What's this all about?"

"It's nothing," Erin assured her. "I just have a little errand I need to run. Nothing to worry about."

"Then why are you being so mysterious?"

Erin did feel a little like they were drawing attention to themselves by being so cloak-and-dagger. Would people really care if they found out that Erin had a half-sister who needed her help?

And that that sister was in a criminal gang?

And currently in jail?

Erin decided that there was no way she was going to let that gossip loose in Bald Eagle Falls. She would keep it a secret for as long as she could.

*E*rin was relieved that everything was in order at the jail. They seemed to be expecting her, and she had only to show her identification to get the key to Charley's apartment. She had been worried that they would interrogate her and make her sign some kind of statement about why she wanted it. Maybe the police would even insist that she had to have an escort to go back to the apartment, so they could be sure she wasn't tampering with evidence. But the police had already had their chance to search Charley's apartment to their hearts' content, and if they hadn't found the evidence they were looking for, that was their own problem. The jail didn't appear to have any problem with Erin picking up the key, so she didn't argue with success, and just smiled and thanked them politely.

Charley had told her which pet food store to go to. Not all pet stores would have crickets. She followed the noise of their chirps to the back of the store, where there were various sizes of container and varieties of bugs in tanks. It felt a little like take-out for insects.

The girl who helped Erin out didn't look like she was old enough to be out of high school. She was completely relaxed and matter-of-fact about all of the creepy crawlies.

"I'm helping out a friend who's out of town," Erin told her. "I haven't ever taken care of a lizard before, so I'm a little nervous."

"It will be totally fine," the girl assured her. "What kind of lizard is it?"

"Chameleon."

"Oh, I love chameleons! You will too. Did she tell you what to get?"

"Just crickets. The smallest size container."

"Sure. These babies are gut-loaded and calcium-dusted, so they're all ready to go."

Erin had to look away as the girl dipped a little bowl into the tank full of hoppers and then snapped the lid into place.

"All safe and sound," the girl promised. "It's nice and tight and isn't going to pop open in your car. When you have the chameleon's tank open, just dump them in. Did she tell you what else to do?"

She ran through the procedures with Erin, and Erin was much more reassured than she had been after the hurried talk with Charley at the jail.

Erin wrote down all of the details for later reference.

"Can I call you if I run into any trouble?" she joked.

"Of course! Here." The girl picked up a business card and wrote her name and number on the back of it. "I'm Olivia. If you have any questions when you get there or something happens or seems wrong, just call me up and I'll be happy to help. Any time, day or night."

"Really? You're a lifesaver, Olivia. I'm Erin. Hopefully, I won't need you, but if something happens… I'm really glad I have someone to call."

"You could call your friend," Olivia suggested. "The one who owns the chameleon."

"No, she's… not available most of the time. She can call me now and then to check in, but I can't really call her or ask her any questions."

"She must be in the mountains," Olivia decided. It wasn't really a question, so Erin wasn't actually lying by not telling her yes or no.

Erin was soon on her way back to Charley's apartment. There were no police cars outside like there had been when Charley was arrested. Erin had kind of expected there to still be one cop hanging around to keep an eye on the place, but if there was, he was well-disguised, because Erin couldn't pick out anyone she thought was a cop or who was paying more attention to her than they should.

The apartment door looked just as it had. No crime scene tape or notice telling her to stay out. Erin fit the key into the lock and slowly let herself in. She waited once the door was open, listening. She strained her ears for any sign that someone else was in the apartment. There was not a movement, not a breath that she could hear. The apartment smelled as if it had been shut up for several days, the air still and undisturbed. Erin hadn't noticed the smell of the lizard's cage the last time she had been there but, either because she was expecting it or because it hadn't been cleaned for a few days, she could easily detect it.

Erin followed her nose to the small study that had been converted into Iggy's room, with a screened reptarium full of green growing plants and environmental monitoring equipment. She followed the instructions that Charley and Olivia had given her, staring through the screen to find the green lizard before opening the door and dumping the container of bugs into a corner. She closed the door again.

Iggy was still. Erin waited for him to go after the bugs. He blinked lazily and one of his eyes seemed to follow her, independent of the other. *Ugh. Gross.* It was a minute before there was a subtle shift in his position and she thought he was aware of the crickets.

"Yeah, see? Hungry?"

She was used to her cat and her rabbit. She understood their body language and behaviors, the ways that they talked and responded to her. The chameleon was like an alien. She didn't know whether they responded to voices, or whether they responded more to smell or movement. Did Iggy know that she wasn't his usual caregiver? Did he know Charley and respond to her?

It happened so fast that Erin completely missed it the first time. The chameleon's sticky tongue shot out, and a cricket was gone. Erin blinked.

"Whoa. That was fast. You're like a frog."

He blinked his eyes one at a time. Slowly, as if mocking her. The next time his tongue shot out, she was expecting it. And another cricket was gone. She waited for him to eat more, but he didn't, he just stayed there clinging to the branch, rolling his eyes around in different directions. The only other movement in the cage came from the crickets, wandering around aimlessly, apparently unaware of the predator that lurked above them.

Erin looked at the thermometer and hygrometer to make sure they were within the limits that Olivia had recommended. The dripper and heater were doing their jobs.

"Your mom will be back in a day or two," Erin promised Iggy. "Just as soon as she can get out."

He didn't respond to her voice.

In spite of how interesting the reptarium environment and the lizard were, her eyes started to wander around the study, taking in other things.

She didn't mean to snoop. That wasn't why she was there. She was just there to take care of Iggy, but she thought maybe she should have a look around to make sure everything else was in order as well. She was there and she was the only one with a key, so she was the only one who could make sure that everything was as it should be while Charley was away.

There was a writing desk on one side of the room, the chair between the desk and the wall so that when Charley sat down to use it, she would be facing the chameleon's environment and be able to watch him. Erin thought about the way that Orange Blossom would come up to her little attic hideaway while she was at her writing desk or reading nook, wanting to know why she was being so quiet and why she didn't want to play. It seemed a little sad to have only a lizard, who couldn't do that, but who just crawled along branches flicking out his tongue at insects. But maybe it was different for Charley. Maybe she felt a connection with him even though he did look like something from another planet. Maybe she was allergic to animal dander, or had grown up with parents who were allergic, so she hadn't been able to have a warm-blooded pet that would be more responsive to her.

Erin looked at the neat, tidy desk. What did Charley write there? Letters? A journal? It had a warm feeling and Erin couldn't imagine Charley conducting gang activities from there, writing orders for other clan members or keeping a double set of books. What was Charley's role in the clan? Did she have a specific function? Was it a well-organized group, or did the members just have casual roles? Erin could picture herself sitting there writing out recipes or making her lists for the next day. It was well-lit and tidy, with all of the writing materials and supplies she would need close at hand.

No laptop. Did that mean the police had taken Charley's computer or that she didn't keep one? Or maybe it was in another room. She might watch DVDs or a subscription service before bed and have a laptop in her bedroom.

Erin made sure that she had properly latched the lizard enclosure and left the study. After a few seconds of hesitation, she went to the fridge. She wasn't snooping. She was there to help her sister out. Charley hadn't said anything about Erin taking care of anything else, but she had been worried about her pet and the conversation had been cut short by impatient jail staff. She hadn't had a chance to ask Erin to do anything else while she was at the apartment. But Erin was there, and she might as well check on other things that she could be reasonably expected to do.

She opened the fridge, expecting to find nothing but old takeout containers and half-empty bottles of condiments. But it wasn't empty and there wasn't a takeout container in sight. Not even a frozen dinner or deli package. Everything seemed to be home cooked.

Erin took out a small carton of milk and, after checking the expiry date, poured it down the sink drain. She poked through the produce and the cooked dishes in covered glass bowls, adding a few things to the green compost bin under the sink. She noticed that the garbage can was empty, and that gave her pause. Charley hadn't had a chance to empty the garbage when she had been arrested. Had she emptied it before then, earlier in the day? There was no garbage pick-up schedule on the fridge that would give an indication of whether it would have been normal for Charley to have taken out the garbage that day.

It occurred to Erin that she hadn't eaten supper or made any plans to. She'd been focused on Iggy's needs and hadn't even thought of her own. Should she go out to a fast-food joint before heading home, or would Charley mind if she helped herself to some of the food in the fridge before it started to go bad?

In a few minutes, Erin had a small plate of food warming in the microwave and pulled out her phone to check for any new voicemails, texts, or social media messages.

Charley was a surprisingly good cook. She'd missed her calling in choosing to be a mobster. She should have gone into the food services industry. Erin thought back to helping in Clementine's tea room. Maybe it ran in the family. Maybe it was one of those inexplicable family traits. An interest in food services. A talent for food preparation. Erin had always found it comforting to make food and had enjoyed making other people happy or more at ease by making them food. It wasn't just Carolyn's death that had prompted her interest in cooking for others. It had spurred an interest in gluten-free and cooking for other special diets, but years before that, she had spent happy hours as a child helping Clementine in the tea room. She could remember playing with child-sized dishes when she was little, pretending to serve her mother and being frustrated that she wasn't allowed to be involved in the cooking of real meals. She knew she could do better than her mother, who seemed to struggle with even the basic heating of prepared meals.

She washed up and put away the dishes she had used. The kitchen was well-stocked and everything seemed to be in its logical place. Erin picked up the small compost bin and poked around in the corridors of the building until she found a room with a trash chute and a larger green bin smelling of rot that she emptied the small bin into.

Erin looked at her watch. She had saved some time by eating at Charley's instead of having to find a restaurant or fast-food place. She could spend a few more minutes making sure that everything had been properly taken care of in the apartment before heading home, and she'd still have time to work on her lists for the next day before bed. She found that thought comforting.

There was a little more mess in Charley's bedroom than in the rest of the apartment. Evening clothes draped over the back of a chair instead of hung up. Makeup strewn over the top of a dressing table with a mirror. The bed had been made, but Charley had certainly not been drilled in making hospital corners or a military-tight bunk.

Erin sat on the edge of the bed and looked around.

Was Charley really a wild child? A mobster? Nothing in her rooms seemed to indicate anything other than a normal, everyday existence. She could have easily been an office or retail worker, restaurant cook or hostess. But a career criminal? Her apartment was nothing like what Erin would have expected from a mobster or a mobster's girlfriend. But then, what did she actually know about what a mobster's room would look like? If she was to go from TV, it could range from a rat-infested flop house to a sumptuous mansion a king would envy. What exactly did a Tennessee organized crime clan look like?

There was little to indicate that Charley had had a boyfriend. There was a picture of her with a young man on the bedside table, but there wasn't a lot of jewelry, wilting flowers, or other romantic keepsakes that Erin could see. A quick glance through her closet and drawers did not turn up any men's overnight gear. Not even a toothbrush or change of underwear. How serious could they be if he wasn't even sleeping over occasionally?

Erin's face flushed warmly even though there was no one there to see her embarrassment. Who was she to be making judgments over how serious Charley's relationship with Bobby was? It wasn't like Terry was spending nights at her house either. There was plenty of room for another person in the family-sized house, especially now that Vic had her own place over the garage. But she and Terry had kept their lives separate and had not taken that step. They were moving slowly, content, for the most part, to spend time together as friends and not to do anything that would have caused tongues to wag among the Bald Eagle Falls gossips.

CHAPTER 13

*E*rin texted Vic that she was on her way home. When she arrived, she parked her car in the new garage. As she walked across the yard, Vic stuck her head out the door at the top of the stairs that climbed the outside of the garage to her loft apartment.

"Hey, Erin. Everything go okay?"

"Yes, Iggy was fine and has enough bugs for the next few days."

"And he didn't gross you out?" Vic grinned. She was far less squeamish than Erin, having grown up farming, hunting, and fishing. Critters didn't bother her.

"No, he's pretty weird looking, but at least he wasn't slimy."

"Did he change color for you?"

"No. Just green while I was there."

Vic nodded. "Okay. Well, have a good night." She started to pull her head back.

"You got company?" Erin asked. Vic usually came over for a few minutes before bed if she was by herself. But if Willie was over, she didn't.

Vic gave her a grin. "Yes, Miss Nosy Parker. Willie's here."

"Hi, Erin." Willie's voice drifted out from behind Vic.

Erin smiled and gave a little wave. "Hi and good night to both of you. I'm going to have a bath and head to bed."

"And make lists," Vic added.

"And make lists," Erin admitted.

Vic withdrew and Erin went into Clementine's house through the back door.

She had bathed and was in her pink flannel jammies when she heard voices coming from outside. Not Vic and Willie out for a moonlight stroll, but shouts and jeers.

Erin hurried to the kitchen, nearly tripping over Orange Blossom, and peered out the window. She caught sight of a few dark shapes flitting across the yard, and then they were out of view of the kitchen window. Erin opened the back door. Willie was coming down the stairs of the garage apartment at a run.

"Willie? What happened? What's wrong?"

"Stay inside, Erin. Call Terry."

"But what—"

"Stay inside."

Erin closed the door and locked it. She couldn't see what he was doing through the little arched window high in the door, and when she went back to the kitchen window, it was just in time to see him step out of view. Erin swallowed and concentrated on doing what Willie had said. She dragged her phone out and hit the speed dial for Officer Terry Piper.

"Piper. Oh, hi, Erin."

"Terry, something is wrong. I don't know what's going on. There were people in the back yard. And then Willie came out, and he said to call you."

"There was someone in your back yard?"

"More than one. I saw at least three."

"Stay inside."

"Willie already told me to. I locked the door. What's going on?"

"I don't know yet. Did he lock the apartment door?"

"No, I think he went after them. He was outside…"

"Of course he did," Terry grumbled. "Okay, stay put, I'll be there in a shake."

He must have put a call out to the rest of the police department, because Tom Banks pulled up in front of the house at almost the same time as Terry pulled in behind the garage. Both got out and took a look around the yard. Erin saw Willie join them. When they walked toward the back door, Erin opened it and stepped out to meet them.

"What is it? What happened?"

"It's nothing," Terry said, "just a little vandalism." He gestured toward the garage and walked with Erin toward it.

"Heard car doors slam," Willie growled. "Didn't even see the car before they were gone."

Even with the security lights turned on, Erin couldn't see the mess of the raw eggs until she got up close to it.

"If you've got a pressure washer, we should clean it off before it dries. Even just a garden hose…" Terry suggested.

Erin felt distant and removed from the situation as she went into the garage and got the little pressure washer she had picked up at a Black Friday sale after Thanksgiving. Terry took it from her and set it up outside the garage. His eyes flicked over her.

"You're going to catch a chill. Go put on a coat."

Erin looked at her pink pajamas. She had slipped sandals on her bare feet. "I'm fine."

K9 snuffled around and made an irritated huff when he sat down, disappointed at the lack of excitement. Tom was taking pictures of the vandalism. When he finished, he nodded at Terry. Terry aimed a stream of water at the mess and washed it off. Vic stood at the top of the stairs until he was done, then joined them.

"Who was it?" Erin asked Willie. "Why would anyone do something like this?"

Everyone was silent, looking at each other but not answering. Willie cleared his throat.

"They were shouting slurs," he said. He indicated Vic with his eyes, and Erin understood without his saying anything more that it was prejudice about Vic's gender identity. "I didn't see them clearly enough to identify who it was. Young people. Probably out drinking. Bored. Looking for trouble."

Erin shook her head. She looked at Terry. "Do you know who would do something like this?"

"Sure, I know a number of people who would do something like this. But I don't have any evidence of who it was. You don't have any security cameras, do you?"

"No."

Maybe Erin should have anticipated it. Vic hadn't exactly been welcomed with open arms by everyone in Bald Eagle Falls. Erin had already had rocks thrown through the window and an attempt to burn her house to the ground. It shouldn't have taken so long for her to figure out that she might benefit from a few security cameras.

"It's okay," Vic said. Her face was pale. "It doesn't matter who it was. It was bound to happen sooner or later. If we react to it, it will just get worse."

Erin scowled. She hated for Vic to think that it was acceptable. People might not choose to like or be friendly with Vic, and that was their right. No one was universally liked. But it wasn't okay for them to yell slurs and vandalize her home.

"I'll get cameras this weekend," she promised. "The guys can help install them, right?" She looked at Terry and Willie for confirmation.

"I can install cameras," Vic said with an offhanded shrug. "I just don't think… well, it's not like they tried to hurt me. If we overreact, they'll just think I'm a good target."

"Installing cameras isn't overreacting," Erin said firmly. "I'm worried about security. If these guys come back again, I want to be ready."

"If you want to upgrade your security, you can do a few other things," Tom said. "Put the security lights on a motion sensor. Put alarms on your doors and windows and keep it armed at night or when you're not home. You two ladies both live alone…"

Even though they were on the property and always in and out of the house, they did live separately. If someone broke into Vic's loft apartment in the middle of the night, or into the main house, the other would never know it.

Erin nodded. "Yeah. You're right. I should probably get something over at Adele's in the cottage as well. She's even more remote than we are."

"She's not going to like that," Vic said.

"No, probably not. But I wouldn't want anything happening to her, either. People might not realize that she's… you know what… but she's still isolated, and kids might not like the fact that she's taken over their old hangout and keeping an eye on things out there."

Vic sighed. She rubbed her bare arms. "I just hate that we have to change anything because of people like this."

"I know," Erin agreed. She thought about Charley living alone as well. With her enemies, why hadn't there been security measures at her apartment? Erin hadn't even needed to be buzzed in at the lobby door, and there was only a single lock on the apartment door. Was Charley so sure of her position in the Dyson clan that she had no fear of anyone breaking in when she was away or when she was home alone?

"You can file your reports in the morning," Terry said. "You ladies need to be up early, so you'd better get off to bed."

Erin yawned, but at the same time, felt wide awake. Her brain was going to take a long time to settle down. "I don't know if I can. Are you on call tonight?"

Terry shook his head. "I'm off. Tom's on. But you can still call me if something happens. You never use the dispatch line anyway." He smiled, showing that this was not something that bothered him. Just a statement of fact.

"Okay." Erin hesitated, then gave him a brief hug. The various badges and equipment on his uniform poked uncomfortably into her, but she ignored it. "Thanks for coming. I'll see you tomorrow."

He gave her an extra squeeze and let go. K9 whined, looking at Terry.

"We'll do one patrol around the house and yard and then we have to go," Terry told him. "If there's anything to find, you'd better find it."

He gave K9 a hand signal and let him lead the way. K9 smelled the remains of the smashed eggs on the ground and started to cast around for a scent trail. Erin knew that the perpetrators had escaped in their vehicle, so K9's search was unlikely to turn up anything of interest. Terry knew that too, but K9 wanted to do his job, and it was always possible that one of the young people had dropped something in the dark. A set of keys or a wallet with identification would be nice. Erin watched them for a few minutes, then waved at Terry.

"Night, Vicky. You be okay? Do you want to come sleep in the guest room tonight?"

Vic looked at Willie. "I think… are you going to stay?"

Willie nodded. "I don't like to leave you alone after this. I'll hang out tonight and make sure nothing else happens."

"Good." Erin nodded. "Thanks."

"What about you? Are you going to be okay alone?"

"Sure. It was Vic they were targeting, not me. They probably didn't give me a second thought."

"All right. See you in the morning."

"Bright and early," Erin agreed.

It might take her a while to get to sleep, but she was still going to have to be up in the morning.

~

The boss was not pleased with the way things had gone down.

"What were you thinking? The idea was to get her out of town and into hiding, not arrested for murder! How did this happen?"

The fixer raised his hands in a placating gesture. He looked around at the other tables, making sure that no one was listening in.

"Things didn't go to plan. Obviously. But I handled it the best I could, and the result is, she's out of the way. That's what you wanted, isn't it?"

"That's what I wanted? No, it's not what I wanted. I wanted her to quietly disappear. How do you think she's going to disappear when she's in the system? Got guards over her day and night? If they're able to get her name, they'll trace her here. Just like that. She's got a great big neon sign over her now. And if they find her, then I lose out. Understand?"

The fixer considered this, examining the situation from several angles.

"You've worked on these things before," the boss growled. "You've got experience. So why are you behaving like such an amateur?"

"Give me some time to sort it out. You want her to get out."

"Of course I want her to get out. Having her behind bars doesn't help anything."

"Maybe if she gets out, she'll run."

"She should," the boss agreed. "They've got enough on her, she's got to know that they've got enough to convict her and keep her behind bars for twenty years."

"Less than that for manslaughter," the fixer disagreed. "They won't convict on intentional murder. Anyone looking at that apartment or hearing about the fighting will know it was in the heat of the moment."

"Manslaughter, then."

"If she lives long enough to be convicted. Because the clan can't be too happy about her killing Bobby. Getting her out puts her back in their sights too."

"I don't want her killed. I just want her gone."

The fixer cleared his throat. "I can't be her guardian angel. If you want her out of jail, there could be consequences. I can't stand up against the whole clan. I'll do my best to get her to run, but she might try to tough it out."

"She has to run."

"If she has any sense, she will."

"I don't care about sense. She *has to run.*" The boss spaced the final words out and bit each one off, making it a sentence all by itself. Has. To. Run.

The gears in his head were turning, and the fixer nodded, focusing on the whole machine. It was one of the strangest jobs he'd ever had. But that didn't mean he couldn't do it. One way or another, the girl would have to disappear.

"I'll get her out," he agreed, "and then I'll get her to run."

Erin looked at the phone and saw it was another call from the jail. It was, at least, a quieter hour at the bakery, so she didn't feel as bad about leaving Vic to handle the counter and ducking into the back to take the call. Melissa was there, and Erin didn't need all of the church ladies in town knowing she had a half-sister in jail. She knew it shouldn't matter. She should be able to just be who she was and not worry about if the ladies were judging her for her sister's sins. But the fact was, a lot hinged on Erin's reputation. There had been threats before that the ladies would stop coming to the store because of perceived faults, and Erin knew that the success of the bakery was tenuous. If it were blackballed because not only was she an atheist employing a misled youth, but she also had family in jail, she would have to pull up stakes in Bald Eagle Falls and find something else to do. And she didn't want to. She really wanted to make the bakery work.

"Hello?"

"Erin, it's Charley."

"Hi. I did get to see Iggy and gave him the crickets and checked everything out. He seems to be perfectly happy and healthy."

"Great, thanks. I really appreciate it." But Charley's words were cold and clipped, like she was just saying it out of duty and not because she really felt anything. Erin instantly felt disdained.

"Was there something else, then?"

"They've scheduled a bail hearing for tomorrow. That no-good lawyer must have finally done something right. I was starting to think he was taking his orders from the Dysons. So I might be getting out."

"That's great! I'm really glad to hear it."

But what did she need Erin for?

"I just wondered… I might need someone to pick me up. I thought I could buy you supper. You know, for helping me out with Iggy and everything. And… I've been thinking about the things you said about my biological family… I thought maybe you could tell me a little more about them. I haven't… I haven't ever had a biological connection with anyone before…"

Erin listened to the beating of her own heart. Charley was saying the right things, but Erin didn't feel any warmth from her. She had the feeling that Charley was only saying what she thought Erin wanted her to say. What did Charley really want?

"So… tomorrow? I won't be able to get there until later in the day. I have my work."

"You can't get off?"

"It's my own business, Charley, and I don't have someone who can step in and take care of things on short notice like that. We're on a shoestring as it is, and if I'm not there, I have to pay someone else to be there. I don't even know if our usual girl will be available."

There was silence from Charley.

"You can't expect me to just drop everything to be there," Erin said. "You could probably get a cab or a bus or another way home. Maybe you should do that instead."

"No. No, it's okay. I don't mean to be ungrateful. You've been really nice and you don't even know me."

"Okay. So late tomorrow afternoon is okay?"

Erin really wouldn't mind if Charley decided she could get a cab after all. It was a little silly of Erin to keep making the trip back and forth when it was a couple of hours each direction. She needed to tell Charley the truth about how far away she lived so she could be more reasonable.

"Yeah, okay. Late tomorrow afternoon."

"All right. Will you call me after you get bail, when you know for sure you're getting out? It would be silly for me to come pick you up if you didn't even get bail."

"I'll let you know," Charley agreed.

Erin went back to work and to explain to Vic why she would, once again, need to cover the last few afternoon hours while Erin ran back to Moose River.

Terry insisted on taking Erin out for supper, and she should have guessed by how hard he pressed her even when she said she had other things to do, that he had a reason other than just the pleasure of her company.

She didn't want to tell him that she had to get ready to go out of town again to see Charley and help her out of a scrape. He would find out anyway, but she would rather he didn't.

The way he looked at Erin when they sat down at the table told her that he already knew far more than she wanted him to. She ignored the feeling and they studied the menus they already knew off by heart and ordered meat plus three, and they both pretended they were just there to have a pleasant evening meal. Terry waited until they received their dinners to start in on the conversation he had planned.

"I hear you're going back to Moose River."

"I guess you've been talking to Vic."

"Why is it I have to hear it from her instead of from you? Why weren't you the one to tell me?"

"I suppose because I knew you wouldn't approve. Vic wasn't supposed to run to you and tell you."

"That's not exactly how it happened. Why did you think I wouldn't approve?"

"Well, you don't, do you?" Erin challenged.

He looked back at her steadily and didn't disagree, nor did he reword his question. He just waited.

"You already told me you didn't think I should have anything to do with Charley. But I'm a grown-up. I can decide for myself who I'm going to see or not see, or what to do or not do. Charley needs me, so I'm going to go give her a hand."

"Charley needs you?"

"Yes. She asked for my help. So I'm going to help her. It doesn't have anything to do with the Dysons or this murder or anything else shady. I'm not getting into anything dangerous. I'm just going to help out a friend. Family member."

Terry leaned forward, ignoring his steaming food. "Erin. This is not good. I know your instinct is to believe that she didn't have anything to do with killing Bobby Dyson, but the evidence against her is overwhelming."

"Then why are they letting her out on bail?"

"They haven't yet. If they do give her bail, it's going to be high. How is she going to pay for it? I hope you're not mortgaging the house or the bakery to help her out."

"No!" Erin was horrified at the thought. Give up her security on the chance that Charley hadn't killed Bobby Dyson and wouldn't run the first chance she was given? The second thought that she had was how glad she was that Charley hadn't asked her to. She wasn't sure what she would have done. "No, she didn't even ask. She must figure she can make bail on her own."

"Or that someone else will put up the money. Maybe even the Dysons."

"Why would they put it up?"

"Because while she's in jail, they can't do anything about her. Once she gets out, they can put a bounty on her."

"They can't do that while she's inside?"

"Well…" Terry considered. "Not as easily. Not without being traceable. Anyone who kills her on the inside is likely to get caught. If they want to get away with it, their best bet is to get her on the outside."

"But why would she take it? Wouldn't she know she was walking right into a trap?"

"I don't know. Maybe she thinks she's smart enough to get away with it."

"She must have money of her own. The apartment she lives in isn't any flophouse. And if she works for the Dysons like Jack Ward claims, then she must make pretty good money. I always thought organized crime paid pretty well."

Terry nodded slowly and took a couple of bites of his meal. "You're right. She might be using her own money."

"All I know is, I'm not putting it up. She said she was going to get out on bail, not that she needed me to pay for it." Erin pushed peas around her plate. Her stomach was hurting and she didn't feel like she could keep anything down. "What kind of evidence is there? They wouldn't be releasing her if it was overwhelming, would they? If there was that much, wouldn't they just keep her without bail?"

"I imagine she's pulled some strings. It's pretty bad, Erin. She was heard fighting with Bobby. Her fingerprints are on the murder weapon."

"He was shot? Ward said the gun was left at the scene."

"That's right."

"If she's supposed to be some kind of organized crime figure, why would she leave the gun at the scene? Wouldn't she know better?"

"People do things when they're in a panic that they wouldn't do if they were thinking. Criminals make mistakes, or we'd never catch them."

"I guess." Erin ran her finger down the side of her glass, making a track through the condensation. "So you think she did it?"

"I don't think there's any question she did it. The only question will be what she's convicted of."

"But what if she *didn't?*"

"She did, Erin."

"You thought I killed Angela Plaint. But I didn't."

"I thought…" Terry trailed off and decided that whatever argument or clarification he was going to make wasn't going to get him anywhere in the conversation. "It's not the same at all."

"You could be wrong."

"Everybody could be wrong… but it's unlikely."

Erin was quiet, thinking about it. Terry was watching her between bites.

"Tell me you'll just stay out of it, Erin."

Erin shook her head.

"Erin!"

"I know. I'm stubborn. I should listen to you because you just have my best interests in mind." How many times had she heard those words from foster parents?

Terry nodded.

"But you said if it was your brother, you'd help him."

"You're going to keep holding that over my head, aren't you?"

"I don't know why you think I'd behave any differently."

"I have training. I have connections. I'm in law enforcement, so if I get involved in an investigation, it's a little different."

Erin shrugged. "I may not have any training, but I have some experience. And I care what happens to her."

"I don't like you going there by yourself and putting yourself in the middle of this thing."

"I need to. I'm sorry, but I'm going to pick her up tomorrow and do what I can to help her out. You can't talk me out of it."

Terry's mouth tightened. He stared down at his plate and continued to eat in silence. Erin picked at her food, but didn't really have any appetite for anything.

CHAPTER 15

*L*ate the next afternoon, Charley climbed into Erin's car and sat back with a sigh. "I appreciate you picking me up, Erin. I really… don't have anyone else to call."

Erin resisted asking her about her adoptive parents or any friends that must have lived in the area. Or what about other members of the Dyson clan? Surely some of them must have been on Charley's side. Even if Bobby Dyson's parents blamed her for his death, there had to be others who didn't.

"Did you want to go straight to your apartment? Or did you need to run any errands first?"

"The least I can do is to take you out to dinner," Charley said. "Where do you like?"

"Uh… I don't really know what's around."

"Wherever you want to go," Charley urged. "It doesn't matter. We can head back to… what neighborhood do you live in?"

Erin licked her lips. Charley fiddled with the shoulder strap of her seatbelt.

"Where do you live?" she repeated.

"Bald Eagle Falls."

Charley stopped playing with the seatbelt and looked at Erin. "Where?"

"Bald Eagle Falls."

"Is that one of the new developments on the west side?"

"No. It's a town. In the mountains."

"You don't live in Moose River?"

"No."

"How far away is Bald Eagle Falls?"

"A couple hours."

"Why didn't you tell me?"

Erin gave an embarrassed shrug. "I wanted to help you out. So I... made the time."

"That's crazy! I wouldn't have called you. I thought you said you were here in town. I guess I just assumed. I've always lived here, I thought you had too."

"I wasn't raised here—"

"I remember that," Charley interrupted. "You said you'd been raised away from here, but then you came back. Here."

"Here... to Tennessee. You weren't born in Moose River. I just meant I came back to Tennessee."

"Well, this is a mess. I guess you can stay overnight on the couch, if you like. You can head back in the morning. If you need to work. If you can take a day or two off, you're welcome to stay. You don't have to do all that driving in one day."

"I need to be at work early. It's better if I get back tonight and get a few hours of sleep in my own bed."

Charley looked at her for a minute, then shrugged. "You can do whatever you want. But you have to eat. You like sushi?"

"Uh... no. Not big on sushi. Family Style? Chinese? Pizza?"

"Pizza," Charley decided. "And for that, we can just go home and order in. You'll want some time to relax, at least."

"Sure. Sounds good."

"But I'll need to stop at the pet store on the way, can we do that? Iggy can celebrate with some worms."

"Worms?"

Crickets had been bad enough. Vic and Charley might be able to stomach wrigglers, but Erin didn't want to see Iggy eat worms any more than she wanted to eat sushi. She was queasy just thinking about it.

"As long as I don't have to do it," Erin said.

Charley laughed. "I gather you're not a reptile person."

"I didn't mind Iggy, but the bugs..." Erin gave a shudder that made

Charley snicker. "I have a cat and a rabbit," Erin said, trying to make a connection with Charley. "I never had any pets as a kid, but I've acquired two since moving to Bald Eagle Falls."

"And it doesn't gross you out to feed your cat meat or fish? It's no different."

"Uh… it's a little different. I don't feed him anything that moves."

"I bet he'd like it better if you did."

"He probably would, but I'm not going to try."

"It's the natural order of things," Charley pointed out. "Predators and prey. Survival of the fittest."

Erin glanced over at her, wondering if she had a similar view of the place for violence in human society. Since human society had always been violent, did that mean it was okay? Might makes right, so use of force and deadly weapons was perfectly natural and acceptable? Charley was looking out the passenger window and didn't catch Erin's look. Erin stared at the road in front of her.

Charley directed Erin to the pet store once more, and Erin elected to sit in the car while Charley went in to get Iggy's celebratory treat. She came out with the little takeout container in a paper bag.

"All done up tight," she promised. "No worms are going to escape in your car."

"Good thing."

She knew the way from the pet store to Charley's apartment fairly well and Charley only had to redirect her a couple of times. Charley called her favorite pizza place on the way, and they arrived there just ahead of the delivery man.

Inside the apartment, Charley put the pizza and the bag from the pet store down on the kitchen island while she kicked off her shoes and sorted through her mail.

"Make yourself comfortable," she advised. "You must be tired after working all day and then driving out here. You need to get some rest in before going back to Eagle whatever."

"Bald Eagle Falls."

"The backside of the mountain," Charley scoffed. "I don't know why you'd want to live somewhere so isolated."

"It isn't like I live by myself. It's a little town, but I have friends."

Charley sighed. "More than I can say."

Erin looked again at the pizza and the pet food bag on the counter. Her stomach felt like it was filled with worms. She wasn't sure she was going to be able to eat any of the pizza with the worms in such close proximity.

"You want to see them?" Charley offered, following Erin's gaze.

"Ugh, no!"

"Oh…" Charley picked the bag up. "I see. Did you know there are places you can order crickets or mealworms on your pizza?"

Erin felt dangerously queasy. "Uh, no. I don't think I'm going to be going for that. Your pizza place doesn't, right?"

Charley snorted. "No. Too bad, I could order for myself and Iggy at the same time! We could share a pizza…"

She laughed at Erin's expression and gave the bag a little shake. "I'm going to go see the little bug-eater and give him his treat. Come and watch if you want."

"I'll just wait out here."

Charley nodded and went into the study. Erin looked around the apartment. If it was a false front, a mask for what kind of person Charley really was, it was a good one. It certainly didn't look like the apartment of a wild, rebellious child. Nor did it look like anything she envisioned a mobster living in. It was perfectly normal and not too showy. There was no sign that she normally kept weapons, drugs, or large amounts of money there.

"Okay, let's eat," Charley invited.

Erin was startled out of her serious thoughts. She was about to say that she didn't know if she could eat, but when Charley opened the pizza box and the apartment filled with the fragrant smells of garlicky tomato sauce, pepperoni, and mozzarella, her stomach gave a loud growl and she realized she was more than a little hungry.

"That smells amazing! No wonder you like this place."

Charley nodded. She got out plates, and she and Erin each grabbed a couple of slices. They sat down at the table. Erin took a bite of the pizza and contemplated the pillowy, crispy crust. "Do they offer a gluten-free option?" she asked.

"I never asked. Why, you aren't allergic, are you?"

"No, I just—"

"Are you on one of those diets? Paleo or grain free? Caveman stuff?"

"If I was, I wouldn't be eating this. No, my bakery is gluten-free and caters to special diets. I'm always on the lookout for other opportunities."

"You're going to start selling pizza?"

"I already sell some pizza crusts. And pizza pretzels. But I should check with the local pizza joint and see whether they stock a gluten-free crust for special orders, or if I could supply them with frozen crusts so they could offer them."

"Oh. Cool. Good idea. So you can eat normal food, but you bake gluten-free just as a marketing plan? For commercial opportunities?"

"No, I just want to... make sure that people who do need to follow special diets can get everything they need right in town."

Charley looked up from her pizza and gazed at Erin. "Why?"

"I had a sister... a foster sister, I mean... She was celiac, and she did a lot of damage to her system because she refused to eat gluten-free. She couldn't stand to be different than everybody else and to have to provide her own food. It was more important for her to look normal than to stay well. I want the kids in Bald Eagle Falls to be able to eat where everyone else eats and to be able to order food that looks the same as everyone else's. And the adults too."

"Well, that's nice... but I don't know how you could keep a place like that afloat. In a little town? I don't even know how a normal bakery could stay in business."

"It's been okay, especially since... the previous bakery had to close. So we only have the one. People who want regular bread can get it at the grocery, but if they want fresh bakery bread and baking..... Auntie Clem's is the only place to go. And it's good food."

"Auntie Clem's? Is that the name of your bakery?"

"Yes." Erin took a bite of her pizza. "After my—our—Aunt Clementine. She used to run a tea shop there. She left it to me when she died. I didn't want to reopen the tea shop, but I thought I would take a run at seeing if a gluten-free bakery could make it."

"Huh." Charley chewed a mouthful of pizza thoughtfully. "I never would have thought of doing something like that."

Erin shrugged and looked down at her plate.

"Go ahead and ask," Charley said. "I can tell you're dying to."

"What?"

Charley just leveled a look at her and waited.

"Okay... did you do it?"

"No."

Erin was a little surprised at the denial. She'd expected excuses and explanations, not a flat-out no.

"You didn't have a fight with Bobby Dyson and end up shooting him?"

"I had a fight with him, sure. Bobby and me were always fighting. He was a passionate guy. But I didn't kill him."

Erin looked Charley in the eye. The woman's gaze didn't waver. But Erin did realize that under Charley's makeup there was something more than bags under her eyes. She hadn't managed to completely cover up a black eye. Erin remembered Terry's comment about the state of Bobby Dyson's room. It had, she guessed, been more than just a heated argument.

"Did he hit you?"

Charley touched the bruise briefly, as if checking to see if it were still there. "He was a passionate guy," she repeated.

"Was it self-defense?"

"I told you, I didn't kill him. I have an alibi, so they're not convicting me of anything."

"You have an alibi?" It was the first Erin had heard mention of this.

"Yeah. I was out with girlfriends. They'll confirm it. Like I say, nobody is railroading me for Bobby's murder. It wasn't me."

"Then how...? People heard you there. The gun had your fingerprints on it."

Charley raised her eyebrows. "How do you know that?"

"I... talked to Jack Ward."

"Why would he tell you my fingerprints were on the weapon? They're not going to reveal details like that to the public."

Erin wasn't sure what to say. Charley had already demonstrated some suspicion toward Erin, accusing her of being a police plant. How was she going to react if Erin told her that her boyfriend was a policeman and that he'd been in contact with Jack Ward?

"You're a terrible liar," Charley said, "so how about the truth?"

"I didn't say anything; how do you know if I'm a bad liar?"

"Because everything you think is written on your face. Haven't you ever played poker?"

Erin shifted uncomfortably. "I think I used to be a better liar. Or maybe it's just because it's you. I don't want to lie to you."

"Then don't." Charley's voice was stern. She looked Erin straight in the eye. "Obviously, you're not a cop, or you wouldn't be having any trouble telling me a believable story. So why would Ward be telling you any details of the case? Unless the two of you…" she held up two crossed fingers. "Maybe you had some extracurricular time away from the police station?"

"No. No, not Ward."

"Ah. Who, then?"

Erin dropped her eyes to her pizza, uncomfortable with the scrutiny. "I know the police in Bald Eagle Falls."

"And they thought they'd share the details with you."

"They didn't want me to come and help you."

"Because I'm a murderer. Already convicted in their minds."

Erin shrugged.

Charley shook her head. "Well, get this through your head. I have an alibi. Whoever Bobby was arguing with, it wasn't me. And if my fingerprints are on any gun there, it was a frame. Maybe there really was a gun with my fingerprints there. Or maybe the police just made it up. My gun is still here and I never touched any of Bobby's."

Erin was relieved. She glanced around the room. "You keep a gun here? Is that safe?"

"Yes, it's safe. That's how I keep myself safe."

"The police didn't confiscate it?"

"It's in a safe." Charley went suddenly still. For a moment, she sat there frozen, then she jumped to her feet and ran out of the room. She popped into her study, and was back a few seconds later, swearing like a sailor. "They stole my safe. Just grabbed the whole thing and took it with them! They can't just take my property!"

"If they thought it had something to do with the murder…"

"Something like what? They already had the weapon, why would they take mine, unless they wanted to screw with the evidence? They're going to swap my gun with the one at the scene, and say that it was mine all along. That's why Ward said it had my prints on it. Because they planted my gun!" She swore loudly.

"They wouldn't do that," Erin protested.

"Oh, they would do anything they could to get me permanently behind bars. Or in the ground. If they tell Bobby's family that I'm the one who killed him…"

Erin kept her mouth closed to prevent herself from defending the police a second time. She wasn't the one who was in Charley's position. Charley obviously knew the situation with the Moose River police much better than Erin did. Just because the police Erin knew wouldn't have ever dared contaminate evidence, that didn't mean that all police would be just as diligent and honest. Terry had leaped into action on a previous case in order to keep Alton Summers from being killed, even though he was a miserable specimen of a human being and continued to harass Erin. Summers had initially been hired by Clementine's estate to track Erin down, but after he spent his money from that job, he'd been back, trying to blackmail her into giving him more. Even so, Terry had been willing to protect him as a citizen, and Erin knew he would never do like Charley suggested and encourage the Dysons to take her out of the picture.

Charley started to pace back and forth, her movements tight and controlled.

"They wouldn't dare do anything without Dwight's blessing," she said, obviously talking to herself more than to Erin. "So it's him I've got to talk to. If I can. How am I going to get a call through to him?"

"You won't get anywhere without asking," Erin said.

Charley stopped and looked at Erin, looking baffled to find anyone in the same room as she was.

"Just ask. That's your suggestion? Just call them up and say I want to talk to Dwight Dyson."

"If he's the only one who can help you. What good is it going to do to talk to anyone else? Or to beat around the bush and try to get to him another way. If he thinks you might be Bobby's killer, won't he want to talk to you? To get your story?"

Charley laughed. "You know nothing about how it works in the family. This isn't about justice. It's about vengeance. And you get that wherever you can. If it looks like someone is unfaithful to the family, you get rid of them. It doesn't matter whether they really are or not. If people think that they are, that's more than enough reason to get rid of them."

"Call," Erin urged again. "What's the worst that can happen?"

"They know I'm here and come here and kill me. And you too, for good measure."

"Won't they already know you're here?"

Charley resumed her pacing. "Of course they'll know. They'll know I was getting bail. Either they pulled strings for me to get it, or they had someone keeping tabs and would know. They just watch for me to get back here. If they wanted to, they could already have come up here and killed me."

She stopped and looked at Erin.

"Does that mean they don't want to? If they wanted to, they could have done it by now?"

Erin shrugged and didn't point out that they might simply have wanted her to get nice and worked up first. Maybe they wanted her to fully realize what kind of trouble she was in before taking care of her. It wouldn't be quite as satisfying to just take her out at the first opportunity, without seeing that understanding on her face.

Charley picked up her phone from where she'd left it on the table beside her plate. Then she put it down. Then she picked it up again. She stared down at it in her hand. Finally, she started moving her thumb over the virtual keys. She put the phone up to her ear, and breathed out a long, heavy breath.

"This is stupid," she said quietly. "This has seriously got to be the stupidest thing I've ever done in my life."

After waiting for several rings, she apparently got an answer.

"It's Charley Campbell. I need to speak with him."

A pause while she listened.

"I need to talk to him. And he's going to want to talk to me. You know what happened, don't you? You think he's going to be happy if he hears that I tried to get ahold of him, and you wouldn't put it through? He's going to start by cutting off your fingers and feeding them to you. Is that how you want to die?"

Apparently it was not, because after waiting in silence for the next few minutes, Erin could tell by Charley's face that it was ringing again. She seemed to withdraw into herself. She looked lost and bleak. Erin wished she could give Charley a hug and make it all better. But Charley had gotten herself into something that a hug wasn't going to fix.

What about the police? Did they really want the Dyson clan to just murder Bobby's killer, eliminating the need for the state to do anything in regard to prosecuting her? It was much cleaner and cheaper if the Dysons would just kill each other. Or had they also stationed guards to watch for Charley, and to watch for anyone else who was watching for Charley, to try to protect her?

"Dwight." Charley's voice was hoarse, almost a whisper. "Yeah... it's

Charley." She swallowed. "I didn't kill him. I swear it. You know I loved Bobby. I'd never do anything to hurt him. I'd never kill him. The cops are setting me up. I just got home, and they've taken my gun safe. That means they've got my gun, and they're going to swap it for the one that was found at the apartment and make sure everything points to me. But I didn't do it. I wouldn't do anything to hurt him."

She stopped speaking. Erin couldn't hear what was being said on the other end of the conversation. She pictured Dwight Dyson, a godfather with a Tennessee accent, sitting behind a big black walnut desk and giving Charley his theory of the crime.

"I don't know what happened," Charley said. "I don't know who it was. Some guy—I don't know. I wasn't even there."

Erin watched Charley, frowning, trying to follow everything that was being said when she could only hear half the conversation. It was like dinner theater, except that she knew gangsters could come through the door to end it at any time, and she and Charley had no way to protect themselves. She wasn't at home, there was no Terry Piper to save the day. Though they might actually have 9-1-1 service, and Erin could covertly call the police while Charley was on her call…

"Maybe it was a hit and it was meant to look like it was me. A frame. I was out with the girls…"

Erin slid her own phone out of her pocket. If she called 9-1-1, could they trace it to her location? Would they find her if she didn't say anything? How about if she texted? Could she text 9-1-1? Erin glanced at the apartment door. It was still shut. No intruders. No Tennessee mafia showing up to kill them. Had Dwight Dyson called them off when he took Charley's call, or did he want to hear it go down while he was still on the phone with her?

"You've got to believe me," Charley begged.

Her shoulders dipped down and her eyes closed. Erin thought for a moment she was going to faint, but then Charley lowered her phone and looked down at its blank screen.

"What did he say?" Erin squeaked.

"I'm supposed to go talk to him. He's sending someone over to take me there."

Then there was a knock on the door.

CHAPTER 16

*E*rin and Charley both stared at each other, wide-eyed with alarm.

"It's them," Charley hissed.

"How did they get here so fast?"

"They didn't. They were already here. Just like I said."

She reluctantly went to the door, unlocked it, and turned the handle to face her visitors. Erin couldn't see the man clearly. The angle she was at to the door obscured most of her view. It took a minute for her to realize what was wrong with him. He wore a ski mask to obscure his face. Erin's stomach tightened, even more anxious than before. Wouldn't the Dyson clan soldiers be guys that Charley already knew? Why would he cover his face? And was it odd that there was only one of them? She had been expecting two, at least. The eye holes turned in Erin's direction for a minute, then the man took Charley by the arm and pulled her firmly through the door. Erin covered her mouth and tried to keep from screaming or calling out after her. But the masked man didn't take Charley away. The door did not shut again, and Erin could still see their figures in the hall. The masked man stood close to Charley, and his words were too quiet for Erin to make anything out. Charley's body language exuded confidence that Erin certainly didn't have. She suspected that Charley didn't either; it was just a bluff.

It was only a minute or two before Charley slipped back in through the door, alone again. She looked at Erin, her forehead wrinkled and sweat gathering at her hairline.

"What happened?" Erin asked.

"He told me to get out. He said the clan was coming after me and that I should run. Disappear. Never show my face here again."

Erin nodded slowly. She wasn't sure why that was so surprising. "Who is he, then? Not someone from the clan?"

"No. He's not."

"Do you know him?"

"He was—no. I don't. I have no idea who he is."

"Not a policeman?"

"A policeman wouldn't tell me to disappear. I'm on bail. If I disappear, they don't get to prosecute me. If they don't want the Dysons to kill me, then they want to prosecute me."

Erin's head was whirling. "Then who is it? Another gang? Do the Dysons have a rival? Or is it someone from your family that wants to protect you?"

"No, I said I don't know him. It isn't someone from my family."

"Should we go? Before the guys Dwight sent get here?"

Charley bit her lip, considering, then shook her head. "I'll look guilty to the Dysons. And I can't disappear that fast, I need to make arrangements— get money and ID. Make a plan. I can't just run out of here and be gone."

They both looked at the still-open apartment door.

"You should go," Charley told Erin. "You shouldn't be here when they arrive. I don't want you getting mixed up in this."

"I don't want to leave you like this…"

"Go on." Charley made shooing motions. "I shouldn't have brought you here in the first place. I wasn't thinking. Thanks for helping out with Iggy, but I think I'd better not call you again. It wasn't a good idea. We've lived this long without knowing about each other. I don't think we should talk to each other again."

Erin walked toward the door, anxious and uncertain. She looked back at Charley but, like someone trying to chase away a puppy, Charley again made motions for her to scram. As Erin walked down the hall, the elevator dinged and the doors slid open.

There were the men from the clan. Almost twins in appearance, tall and spare, with blond sun-kissed hair and freckled faces. They weren't in mafioso suits, but they weren't in shabby t-shirts either. They had on polo shirts and slacks with sharply-pressed creases. They moved with purpose down the hall toward Charley's apartment.

They obviously knew Charley by sight, because they didn't spare Erin a second glance. She walked right by them without either one registering her presence. Erin got on the elevator and, as the doors closed, watched them enter Charley's apartment.

~

Erin was in a daze as she rode the elevator down to the main floor and headed over to her car. She was completely unaware of anything going on around her. It was dark, and she should have been far more worried than she was about being alone in a strange parking lot in the city.

Someone hit her hard from behind, slamming her into the body of her car. Erin tried to fight her way free from the man's grip, but there was no use.

"Be still and I won't hurt you," he whispered in her ear.

Erin was sure that was what all muggers and rapists told their victims. *Be still. Be quiet. I'm not going to hurt you.*

"Let me go, or I'm going to scream."

"I know who you are, Erin Price, and you need to stay out of this."

Erin was paralyzed hearing her name come out of his lips. How would anyone know who she was? She wasn't from Moose River. No one in Moose River knew her. Only Charley and the police. And Charley had said it wasn't the police who had warned her to run. Likewise, Erin didn't think the police would be whispering warnings to her in the parking lot.

"Who are you?"

"Did you hear me?" His arm was against the back of her neck, pushing her harder against the car. "I know who you are. Stay out of it. It has nothing to do with you. Go back home, and never come back here or make contact with Charlotte Campbell again."

Erin couldn't raise her voice to answer him. She was so shocked by the sudden attack that she couldn't think of what to say to him. She couldn't argue with him, couldn't figure out who he was. She couldn't put her brain into gear to figure out the best course of action. She just stayed there, frozen, pressed up against her car.

"I know where you live. I know who your friends are. You wouldn't want anything to happen to anyone you love, would you?"

Erin swallowed. "Leave me alone."

He gave her another shove. "Why do you have to be so stubborn? You just don't understand how this works, do you? You may fancy yourself an amateur detective, but you don't know anything. Stay away from Charlotte and just let things take their natural course. Quit poking around and stirring up trouble. Go home and make cookies."

CHAPTER 17

$\mathcal{E}$rin sat in her car and shook.

She told herself it was just the adrenaline. It would make anyone shaky. She'd been unexpectedly attacked and threatened, and it was only natural for her to react emotionally and physically.

She checked again to be sure the car doors were locked. Could she drive all the way back to Bald Eagle Falls without having an accident? Or should she call Terry or someone else for help? The trouble was, it would take anyone from Bald Eagle Falls two hours to get there, just to have to turn around and drive another two hours home. She couldn't sit there in the parking lot for two hours waiting. Even if Terry used his lights and siren, it was still going to take a significant amount of time for him to get there. Assuming he could get someone to cover for him if it was his turn to be on call.

Erin turned the key and tightened her grip on the steering wheel, trying to ground herself. She could drive home. There was nothing to it. The trip down the highway would be soothing. It was just what she needed to relax. She backed out of her parking space and focused on the journey.

The fixer watched Erin drive away, fuming to himself. Charlotte Campbell was supposed to run as soon as she got out on bail, and instead she had ended up meeting with Erin Price. One of the very people that the boss didn't want her near.

He continued to surveil the building, hoping to see Charlotte leaving with a hastily-packed bag. Her car was in its reserved space. Did she not realize the danger she was in if she stayed around? The Dysons would be out for blood. They weren't going to listen to any fanciful stories about the appearance of a mysterious stranger. They would simply put her in the ground for Bobby Dyson's death.

Instead of being rewarded with the sight of her emerging with her luggage and making straight for her parked car, the fixer saw Charlotte exit the building between two of the Dyson boys. There were no visible weapons trained on her, but she had undoubtedly been threatened and they would have whatever arsenal was needed to ensure her compliance.

The fixer was a little surprised that they would remove her from the apartment rather than just leaving her body there in a pool of blood. But they surely had a plan and were acting under orders. Charlotte Campbell looked as cool and collected as if she were headed out for a Sunday stroll in the park. Like a lamb to the slaughter.

CHAPTER 18

$\mathcal{E}$rin was calm when she got home. The shakes had disappeared. But she didn't want to be alone and it was going to be hours before she was ready to sleep, which meant another caffeine-charged day at the bakery.

Willie's car wasn't parked anywhere that Erin could see, so she figured he must be off on a job. Willie always had something going on. Even over the Christmas holidays, it had been hard to get him to commit to a time when they could all get together. Erin picked up Marshmallow and cuddled with him on the couch. Orange Blossom yowled and complained and, after telling her all of his troubles, jumped up on the couch next to her and butted her with the top of his head, demanding that she give him just as much attention as she was giving Marshmallow. Erin rubbed and scratched both of them until they eventually settled comfortably against her, Blossom purring and Marshmallow flicking his ear every few minutes.

"You wouldn't believe the critter my sister has," Erin told them. "Green and scaly, eyes that go two separate directions, and a tongue that's twice as long as he is! What a thing."

With both pets quiet and content, Erin texted Vic and then Terry to see if they wanted to come visit.

Vic only had to cover the back yard, so she was the first to get there. She didn't bother knocking; Erin considered it Vic's home just as much as her own.

"You're back! How did everything go?"

Orange Blossom abandoned his place beside Erin. He jumped to the floor and stretched his back, then flopped over and offered his belly to Vic for a scratch.

"Watch out for his pointy ends!" Erin warned. Though, of course, Vic knew this as well as she did. Orange Blossom would tolerate a tummy scratch for all of about five seconds, and then would attempt to grab Vic's hand with his front paws while kicking with his back. An unwary victim would end up being raked with claws from all four 'pointy ends.' Vic gave Orange Blossom's belly one quick scrub, then picked him up to cuddle, and sat down on one of the easy chairs.

"So, Charley is out on bail? Everything is okay?"

"She's out, but everything is… pretty uncertain. I'm really worried about what's going to happen to her."

Vic frowned. "Why? What happened?"

Erin looked at her phone to read Terry's text response, then slid it away. "May as well wait for Terry, then I don't have to explain twice."

"Okay, sure."

They played with the animals.

"Did you eat?" Vic asked.

"Yeah… pizza." Erin tried to remember how much of it she had eaten. Had she even finished one slice? It had been good pizza, but once their conversation had turned to matters of Charley's safety, Erin wasn't sure she had eaten anything more. She shook her head. Either way, she wasn't hungry. She didn't need anything else before hitting the sack. "Where's Willie? Not around today?"

"No. He had an *important* job. Not sure what, but he didn't know when he would be back."

"Out of town, then?"

"I guess so."

Erin stroked Marshmallow's long, velvety ears. "He doesn't tell you what he does?"

"Sometimes. It just depends on what kind of job it is, I guess. There are plenty of times he'll tell me who he's working for and what he's doing for them. But other times it's confidential… I just don't ask. He tells me what he wants to offer."

Erin supposed it was no different from Terry with his police work.

Sometimes, he had no qualms telling Erin about what he was up to. Other times, he had to protect the privacy of the citizens he served.

There was a soft knock on the front door, and Vic got up to answer it, depositing Orange Blossom on the couch beside Erin so she wouldn't get clawed up when Blossom spotted K9 and decided to make his disapproval known.

Terry entered and settled on the couch with Erin, giving her a hug and then touching her cheek with the back of his fingers. It was one of those rare occasions when he was wearing a t-shirt instead of his uniform. Obviously, not on call.

"You're pale. Too many late nights?" he asked.

"I guess, yeah."

"I figured you'd be heading to bed. You're going to get sick if you keep staying out late."

"I can't get to sleep yet. Terry… do you know any more details about Bobby Dyson's murder? Or could you get more?"

He settled back, the cleft in his chin more pronounced than usual. "I thought you were going to leave it alone."

"I'm not," Erin said, surprising herself with the vehemence in her own voice. "The more people tell me to stay away from it, the more sure I am that there's something going on. It wasn't Charley. She's being set up."

Vic and Terry both shook their heads automatically. But they didn't know anything. They just didn't want her looking into it.

"I know you're worried that I'm going to get mixed up somehow with this Dyson family. I get that. They're… scary. They're dangerous. But I'm not doing something that's against their interests, I want to find out who really killed Bobby."

"What makes you think it isn't Charley?" Terry asked. "She was heard there. Her fingerprints are on the weapon. You can't get much more certain that that."

"But what if it's a setup? What if the female voice the neighbors heard wasn't Charley? What if the gun was a plant? What if the police are setting her up?"

"Contrary to what you see on TV, that's not something that's usually done," Terry said. "Sure, half the people who get arrested are going to tell you they were set up or that drugs or weapons found in a search were planted by the police, but that doesn't make it true. Most police officers would never consider tampering with evidence."

"But that doesn't mean it never happens. And with cases that do involve criminals who keep getting away with breaking the law over and over again, don't the police get more and more frustrated? It would get more and more tempting to do something about it to get the person put behind bars."

Terry shrugged. "Again… TV. Do you think I would do that?"

"Get tempted? I don't know. You're human, so I assume you could be tempted just like anyone else."

"I just do my job. It isn't my job to ensure convictions. Just to make sure that there is enough evidence to perform an arrest. If they get off, that's not on me. That part isn't my job."

"I just want to know what else you know about Charley's case. You talked to Jack Ward, right? So tell me what you found out. Were there any other fingerprints on the gun?"

Terry hesitated. He looked at Erin and at Vic, then down at K9. "Yes, there were unidentified prints on the gun. Most of them too obscured to get a good match. The ones that were clear had not been identified. But it takes longer to get a hit when you don't have a short list of suspects to compare it against. It isn't like you can just pop it into the scanner and have an identity ten minutes later. Not usually."

"Was the gun registered to Charley?"

"No. Still registered to a previous owner. It changed hands a number of times, and the final owner never registered the change of ownership."

"So it wasn't Charley's."

"They can't prove it was Charley's. That doesn't mean it was not."

"She said her gun was still in the gun safe in her apartment. But the safe wasn't there, so the police must have confiscated it in their search."

"Which would be within their rights. They would need to catalog any firearms and to account for any that might have been registered to her."

"Did they take her safe? Was her gun still inside?"

Terry gazed at her. "I'd have to ask Jack Ward. That's not the kind of thing he would just offer up to me in casual conversation. And by now, he's probably heard about the connection between the two of us, so he's not going to want to divulge details to me that he knows are going to get back to you."

"She says they're going to swap her gun for the one that was found at the scene. As proof that it was her."

"They can't do that when the other gun has already been logged and its serial number noted."

"Then don't you think it at least points to the fact that it wasn't Charley? If it was her, why would her gun still be at home? Whose gun did she use?"

"There's nothing to stop her from owning more than one gun. If I was going to kill my boyfriend, I would choose the unregistered gun over the one registered in my name."

"But they don't think it was premeditated, do they? She didn't go there to kill him."

"We don't know that. If he was cheating on her—and from what I understand, there's no question of that fact—that might be exactly why she went there."

"What if it wasn't her he was arguing with? If he was cheating on her with other women, couldn't it have been one of the other women who confronted and killed him?"

"Witnesses say it was Charley. I'm sure the Moose River police department will be getting whatever surveillance video is available inside and outside the building."

"If they just heard her, it could have been someone else. They might have just assumed it was her. They probably didn't hear Bobby calling her by name…"

"Erin… you're so determined to prove that it wasn't Charley. But what if it was?"

"I just… can't believe that." Erin closed her eyes, trying to separate her emotions from the facts of the case. "My parents… they're gone. Maybe their deaths were accidental, but if they'd made better choices… maybe they'd still be around. I just found Charley. I don't want to lose her. And I don't want to think that she's a murderer. I want… a sister."

She let out a long, shaky breath. "Before I left her place… a couple of the guys from the Dyson gang came to get her. And someone… threatened me to stay off of the case. Someone who knew my name."

"What do you mean, someone?"

"He came up behind me, so I didn't see him. It was a man. Bigger than me. Strong. But I never saw him."

"He knew you?"

"He called me by name. He knew I was from Bald Eagle Falls. He knew I was a baker."

Terry scratched the back of his neck, frowning. "Those are all basic background, but it's still disturbing. He would have to know who you were to look you up. And you aren't known in Moose River. Or at least, you weren't. You were questioned when Charley was arrested, so your name is on the police records. They could have a leak."

"Did you recognize his voice?" Vic asked.

Erin tried to replay it in her head, and immediately shook her head. "No. He was whispering. So I couldn't recognize it."

"Words he said? Phrases? Diction?" Terry interrogated.

"No... not that I can think of. It was all so fast. It's not like it was a long conversation. He just told me to stay away from Charley. To stop causing trouble."

"I'd tell you that myself if I thought it would do any good," Terry said in a teasing tone. Erin knew that he was partially serious. He had told her and would probably continue to tell her the same thing, but Erin had already proven that she wasn't going to listen to his warnings. It was a source of frustration for Terry, but Erin couldn't make herself abandon her sister just because her friends were worried she was going to get in some kind of trouble.

"I don't know who it was," Erin said. "But it did kind of freak me out. I guess you're right about the police knowing who I was, and maybe someone leaking the information... I was afraid it was someone I knew here in Bald Eagle Falls."

They were silent, thinking about it. They'd all had run-ins with various members of the community who were not as welcoming or pleasant as they ought to be. But no one was going to start throwing accusations around.

"You're sure it was a man?" Vic asked.

Erin looked at Vic, disconcerted. The crisp line that she used to see between male and female had blurred since she had met Vic. Her experience with Vic and the few things that Vic had shared about her growing-up years and her gender identity made Erin reluctant to classify anyone's gender without knowing how they self-identified.

"Uh... no. I'm assuming it was the same person who warned Charley to get out of town before the Dysons showed up, and I thought that he was a man. But I only caught a glimpse and he was wearing a mask."

Terry's expression was almost comical. Erin realized she was telling the whole story out of sequence and he was getting more frustrated and angry with each revelation.

"Oh… uh, yeah… Somebody came to Charley's apartment… and…"

"And warned her to get out of town," Terry finished. "A man with a mask, apparently."

Erin nodded.

"What kind of mask?"

"Like a ski mask. I could just see the eye holes."

"And possibly that it was a man."

"I thought so, yes."

"Height? Build?"

"It was just a glimpse, across the room, through a doorway…"

"You saw him near a doorway? Did his head reach the top?"

"No. Just… average height, I guess. A strong build… you know, not blocky or paunchy, but… not slender."

"All pretty average. That's not very helpful in identifying him."

"I know. I wish I could tell you more…"

"Any tattoos? Anything else that would help identify him? Something you'd recognize if you saw again?"

"No."

Terry pondered the clues they had. "So he warned Charley to take off before the Dysons showed up. And he told you to leave town, to go home and forget about her."

"So it doesn't sound like he was aligned with the police or the Dysons, does it?" Erin said. "That's what I can't figure out."

Erin pulled out her phone and looked at the screen. She told herself she was only checking the time, but she was checking to see whether Charley had called too. Charley had said she wasn't going to involve Erin any more, because she didn't want to put her in harm's way. But Erin was hoping she would have changed her mind. Surely she would want to tell someone about what happened when she went to see Dwight Dyson, wouldn't she? If she were still alive to tell the tale.

"What is it?" Vic asked.

"I was just hoping… Charley would have called me. I wish I knew if she was okay."

"Are you afraid that this masked man might have done something to her?"

"No, the Dysons. She was going to talk to one of them… I don't know if he's the head of the family, or Bobby Dyson's father, or both. But she said the only way she was going to be able to convince them that she hadn't killed Bobby was to talk to him face-to-face."

"That's a pretty dangerous proposition," Terry commented.

"I know. She was pretty scared about it. But she figured if she didn't talk to him, they were going to kill her anyway. So I guess… she really didn't have much choice one way or the other." Erin rubbed her forehead. It was pulsing with fatigue. "I just don't know what to do. It's not like I can call the police to tell them what happened. She doesn't want the police involved. And I can't call the Dyson family to see what's happened. Charley said not to contact her again. But how can I go through life not even knowing if she's alive or not?" A few tears escaped Erin's eyes and dripped down her face.

Terry rubbed her back. Orange Blossom squirmed away from Vic and jumped back up onto the couch, where he climbed over Terry and Marshmallow to reach Erin and bump her face with the top of his head. Erin scratched his ears, sniffling.

"This has been really hard on you," Terry observed. "I never expected it to turn into something like this."

"You guys all said to stay away from her when you found out about the Dysons. I guess I should have. I would have been better off not knowing what was going on."

Neither of them argued with the statement, but they both looked sympathetic.

"Should I call her?" Erin asked. "Do you think it would be okay?"

"If she told you not to… maybe you shouldn't," Vic said tentatively.

"How about Jack Ward?" Erin appealed to Terry. "Do you think we could call him tomorrow and see if he knows anything? Maybe he'll give you a little more information about the murder… and he could check in on Charley, see if she's okay?"

"I suppose we could check," Terry conceded. "But don't expect to be able to get anything out of Ward. Chances are, he's going to keep his cards pretty close to his chest."

"Okay." Erin rubbed her eyes. "I just hope she's okay."

There was a tap at the door, and the three of them looked at each other, startled. Terry put his hand on his holster, which he was wearing even with his casual clothes.

"It's not Willie," Vic whispered, "he would have let me know if his plans changed."

It was too late for casual visitors. Terry got up and moved to the door. He checked the peephole and his stance relaxed. He opened the door and ushered their visitor in with a half-smile.

"Adele!" Vic, unencumbered by animals, jumped up to greet her.

Erin made a little gesture indicating that she would get up, but Adele motioned her back. "No need. I just saw your light on and popped in to make sure everything was okay. You're not usually up this late."

"I just got back from Moose River," Erin explained. She looked at her phone, and realized that quite a bit of time had elapsed since she had made it home. It was getting very late. "Oh… a while ago."

"You're okay?" The tall, spare woman peered at Erin, looking like she didn't quite believe it. "You look a little piqued."

"Things are… not so great. I'm tired and I'm worried and hyped up. My heart is still pumping like a train engine, I don't know how I'm going to get to sleep tonight."

"Let me make you some tea," Adele said, heading into the kitchen without an invitation. "Do you have any herbs?"

Orange Blossom jumped down, figuring that anyone in the kitchen was fair game for him to beg for an extra treat. Erin moved to get up to help Adele, but Terry sat back down beside her, taking her hand to keep her seated. "Stay and relax. I'm sure she can find her way around. You two both need to relax and get some sleep before work."

Vic shrugged. "I'll just take an Ambien and be out like a light."

"I'd be too dopey if I did that. I'd be hung over." Erin knew her limits. She had a few herbal sleeping remedies, but anything pharmacy grade would still affect her in the morning.

She could hear Adele putting the kettle on the stove and opening various cupboards to see where everything was.

"Should somebody be keeping an eye on her in there?" Vic whispered anxiously. "What if she… makes a potion?"

"A sleeping potion?" Erin suggested, trying to keep a smile from her face.

"No… I don't know, something else…"

"You're the one who said that witches don't actually perform magic," Erin pointed out.

"I know that… but she could still make something that… affected you the wrong way. She could poison you."

"With a policeman right here?"

"She could poison him too."

Terry shook his head. It was clear from his expression that he was also trying to keep from smiling at Vic's concerns. "I won't drink anything, Vic. You and Erin can have it. I don't need to be up as early as you do. I still have plenty of time to get to bed."

"I'm not drinking it!" Vic insisted.

"Why not?" Adele was standing in the doorway. "Do you really think I would try to poison or magick you, Victoria?"

Vic turned a brilliant red at having been overheard. "No! No, I know you wouldn't do anything, I just mean… I just was worried that… I don't know, you're not exactly *licensed*."

"Does someone need to be licensed to serve tea now? I wasn't aware of this new requirement."

"You can serve the tea," Erin laughed. "But it looks like you and I will be the only ones who are having any."

"I'll have it ready in a minute. Just waiting for the kettle to boil."

"Thanks, Adele. That's really nice of you."

"Just want to do right by my boss. She's a pretty nice person, you know."

Adele disappeared back into the kitchen. Vic covered her face and then dropped her hands back down to look at Erin. "I'm so embarrassed!"

"I don't know why you're so worried about Adele. She's never done anything to hurt any of us."

"It's the way I was raised. I guess I still have a few prejudices I didn't realize I had," Vic admitted.

In a few minutes, Adele brought a tea cup to Erin and sat down with one of her own.

"Try to let your troubles go," she advised. "Release them… tomorrow morning when you are refreshed, things will not seem as bad."

Erin nodded. "Yes… things are always worst at night when you're tired."

"Let it all go tonight. Tomorrow is another day."

Erin smelled the tea before sipping it. There were many tins, bags, and boxes of teas of all kinds in Clementine's cupboards. Clementine had been forced by her poor health to close the tea shop, but that had apparently not stopped her from enjoying a wide variety of teas herself. When Erin closed her eyes and breathed in the aroma, she could see her younger self helping Clementine in the tea shop when her mother left her there for Clementine to keep an eye on. Erin loved to identify each of the teas by smell, and was right ninety-nine percent of the time.

"Is it okay?" Adele asked softly.

"Chamomile and lemon balm," Erin guessed. "Good Night Tea." She opened her eyes again.

Adele smiled broadly. "Yes, that's right. You know your teas."

"The nose knows." Erin tapped the side of her nose and took another breath of the steam before bringing the teacup up to her mouth to have a sip.

*E*rin and Vic had a bit of a rough morning getting up and getting prepared to open. Erin was still tired and found that it made her clumsy as well as a little bit irritable. Part of her irritability also had to do with her concern about Charley, and the fact that she still didn't even know whether Charley was alive or dead.

Vic seemed better-rested than Erin, though she too seemed a little thick-headed, having to write some of her labels twice and to pull out the calculator for math she could normally do in her head. Together, they managed to bungle their way through the pre-opening routine and eventually the morning rush as well. They normally took their lunch early, and Terry stopped by to see if he could take Erin away for a few minutes. She promised Vic she would be back soon, and went with Terry to the police department in the Town Hall. Terry closed the door to his office and turned on the speaker phone to call Jack Ward.

It didn't take him long to get past the receptionist, and then they heard Ward's gruff voice over the speaker.

"Jack, it's Terry Piper in Bald Eagle Falls. I've got Erin Price with me."

Ward grunted. "You got something for me?"

"Actually, we were hoping for a little information from you."

"It's still an active investigation," Ward said, his words clipped and impatient. "I don't have anything to share with you."

"Erin might have a few things that you are unaware of," Terry said. "But she would like a little information in return."

"It's not a two-way street. We can't release anything to a civilian."

"Which is why I'm the one calling you," Terry said. "I figured you might be able to tell me…"

"Not when it's going straight to the ears of the public," Ward countered, not giving an inch.

"Do you know where Charlotte Campbell is this morning?"

There was silence for a moment while Ward considered the question. Erin could hear papers being moved around.

"Why do you ask?" Ward asked cautiously.

"Charlotte was visited by a couple of the Dyson boys yesterday. Erin was concerned that something might happen to her."

"Then why did Miss Price not call emergency or call my number yesterday?"

"I didn't know what to do," Erin protested. "She called them and was okay with them coming over… so I didn't think it was an emergency. I didn't know what to do."

"You should have called me anyway. I'll have someone follow up with her, but it's a little late now. If she was in any danger, it's way too late to do anything about it now."

Erin's stomach was tight, cramped up with the fear that Ward was right and it was too late to do anything for Charley.

"There was apparently another man who came by Charley's last night as well," Terry informed Ward. Erin put her hand out to stop him, not sure she wanted anyone else to know about the masked man, but Terry ignored her and continued on. "He told Charley to get out of town, and Erin to go home and stay out of the way."

"Not bad advice for Miss Price," Ward grumbled. "Who is this guy?"

"Erin doesn't know. He was wearing a ski mask. But he knew her name and where she was from."

"It's a small community. Wouldn't take much to find out who she was. Are you okay, Miss Price?" His voice was still gruff, but noticeably softer. "Did he hurt you?"

"No, I'm okay," Erin found herself choking up at his more sympathetic approach. "He grabbed me and pushed me up against the car, but he didn't really hurt me. Just scared me."

"You should have called me. You'll need to file an official report."

Erin shook her head. "An official report of what? Like I said, he didn't hurt me, and I don't know who he is."

"It's still an assault. Did he threaten you? That's a second charge."

Erin tried to remember all of the man's words to her. "No… I don't think he said anything that would be considered a threat. He said he knew who my friends were. Told me to go home and stay away from the investigation."

"Like I said, that's good advice."

Tears escaped the corners of Erin's eyes. She wiped at them, trying not to let Terry see she was crying or to sob or sniffle so that Ward would be able to hear. Terry reached over and rubbed her shoulder, which didn't help stanch the flow of tears.

"Jack, how sure are your witnesses that it was Charley they heard fighting with Bobby Dyson?"

"It was Charley. She was well-known to the neighbors."

"It couldn't have been another woman? Bobby Dyson might have been seeing others."

"Of course he was seeing others. But they didn't come to his apartment. Charlotte was his official girlfriend and the others were kept out of sight."

"That doesn't mean one of them couldn't have shown up."

"We're sure it was Charley," Ward said flatly.

"She said she had an alibi," Erin protested. "She said once you checked her alibi, you'd know it wasn't her."

Ward's derisive snort carried over the phone line. "Her ironclad alibi? Yeah, that's not going to hold any water."

"You think it's fabricated?" Terry guessed.

"She and her girlfriends were out enjoying chimichangas and margaritas. We have independent verification until about one in the morning. After that, everything falls apart. The party broke up and went their separate directions. Charley has a couple of the ladies saying that they went out together for a nightcap at that point, and then she went back to her own apartment to hit the sack."

"So she does have an alibi," Erin asserted.

"Until one. After that, no one saw Charley with the others. No surveillance cameras. No waiters or bartenders. Just her girlfriends. She's asked them to cover for her."

Erin recalled how Charley had said she had no other friends. But apparently, she'd had friends that night. Maybe they figured they'd done enough for Charley and she couldn't tap them for anything else.

"Charley Campbell killed Bobby Dyson," Ward growled. "She did it and we know it. The judge was stupid to grant her bail, but sometimes judges can be bought. The Dysons aren't exactly short on cash."

"You think the clan paid her bond?" Terry asked.

"I don't know whether they paid it, or whether she paid it out of her own ill-gotten gains. Either way, you can bet it was originally Dyson money. And either way, she was stupid to bond out. She would have been a lot safer in isolation at the jail than on the outside."

Terry cleared his throat. "Is there any way you can follow up and find out if she is okay today?"

"I already said I would. You should have called last night."

"Yes," Erin agreed in a small voice. "I guess I should have."

When Terry hung up the phone, he looked at Erin. "Are you okay?"

"I guess… it's been harder on me than I thought. I know Charley and I have lived completely different lives, and I've only had a few days to get to know her a little… but I let myself get attached to her. She's my sister."

"It's been quite a whirlwind. You haven't really had time to sort out how you feel."

"Yeah."

"I'll take you back to the bakery. You probably have low blood sugar too, and that doesn't help anything."

"Do you think… Ward will be able to find her? Do you think she's okay? He's right, I should have called someone last night. But she didn't want me to, and these Dyson guys only showed up because she had called them. It wasn't… exactly an emergency."

"You could have called me. Especially when this guy approached you and tried to scare you off."

"I thought about it. But I just wanted to come home. If I'd called you, I would have had to wait there for hours. I wanted to get out of there as fast as I could."

He nodded. "Understandable."

Terry delivered Erin back to the bakery, with strict instructions to Vic that Erin was to sit down and have something to eat, no matter how close it was to the lunchtime rush. Vic took the direction seriously, going immediately into mother-hen mode and not even letting Erin prepare her own lunch.

Terry looked satisfied with Vic's compliance, but he didn't leave to recommence his own duties immediately.

"Is Willie around today?" he asked casually.

"He should be," Vic confirmed. "But he hasn't stopped by or contacted me yet, so he might have been held up."

"He was out of town yesterday?"

Vic nodded as she prepared a sandwich for Erin. "Yeah. Some emergency call."

"You don't know what it was about?"

"He doesn't give me details." Vic looked at Terry, her gaze stern. "And that doesn't mean he's up to anything he shouldn't be. It just means he's a private person and he likes to keep his business to himself."

Terry opened his mouth to answer, but Vic beat him to the punch.

"He's got mining claims that could be really valuable, and if word got around town about what he was taking out of which mines…"

"So you think he was at one of his mines yesterday?"

Vic made a face and put the sandwich in front of Erin. "No, I don't think he was at a mine. He's got a lot of other work he does too for other people. One of them called him and needed him."

"Did you see him take the call?"

Erin was starting to get the feeling that there was something more going on than Terry just asking how Willie was doing and when he'd be back in town. Vic's expression was suspicious.

"Did I see him take the call? Why? He got a call. He needed to go out of town to deal with a problem. You think it's something else? You think he's cheating on me?"

"No. Not at all. I was just curious. I just wondered if he seemed concerned. Or if it was just something routine. Willie's a bit of a loner and I like to keep an eye on him. After he disappeared last year, with that knock on the head…"

Erin saw the words hit Vic like a blow. All of the anxiety she had suffered when Willie had dropped out of sight and then when they found evidence that he had been injured flashed across her face in a microsecond. She put her hand on the counter to steady herself.

"It's nothing like that. If he's away for too long and doesn't text me, I'll get in touch to make sure he's okay. I was there when he got the call. It was just a job. Nothing for either of us to be worried about."

"He didn't seem like he was concerned about it?"

"No. Not at all."

"It seemed like it was just a routine call, not anything that was too difficult or worrisome?"

"Right."

"But he said it was an emergency call?"

"I don't know whether he said emergency. It might have been urgent or important."

"So not routine, but not something that upset him."

Vic scowled and shook her head. "I have no idea why you're interrogating me over this. Do you think something happened to him?"

Terry weighed his words. Erin munched on her sandwich, knowing she had to eat before they opened up again, which would have to be soon. But she hardly tasted what she was eating and couldn't have said what was actually in the sandwich later. She just forced it down, focused on Terry's strange behavior.

"It's not so much that I'm worried about something having happened to Willie," he said slowly. "It's just that I know he has family connections in Moose River, and with all that's going on there at the moment..."

"Wait." Vic faced Terry straight on, her expression thunderous. "Wait just one dang minute here. Family connections in Moose River? What's going on? You think he's one of the Dysons?"

K9's ears were up and he stared at Vic as if waiting to be given the word to take her down. He'd been trained to identify threats, and he obviously didn't like Vic's angry tone.

"I don't *think* he's one of the Dysons." Terry licked his lips and kept his gaze focused on Vic. "I know."

Erin gasped out loud. *Willie?* What could he possibly have to do with the Dyson clan? He'd always been kind and courteous to Erin and Vic. She knew that Terry was overly suspicious of Willie's activities, but she'd always just figured that was jealousy.

"He's not!" Vic insisted.

"His mother was a Dyson. You think I'm making this up? You wonder why Willie is such a pariah around Bald Eagle Falls? You think it's just because he works odd jobs? People have good reason for being so suspicious of him. You've heard him admit to being involved in shady dealings growing up. I'm not just making this up, Victoria. He should have told you where he came from a long time ago."

Vic shook her head. "I don't care. I didn't care where he came from before, and I don't care now. I don't judge anyone because of the family they came from. He can't help who he was born to or how he was raised. All he can control is the life he lives now. And you know he's a good man!"

Terry reached for K9, scratching his ears and the scruff of his neck, motioning for him to sit. K9 relaxed his alert posture, letting his tongue loll out in a doggie grin.

"I've said before, Willie has certain skills that I would trust my life to in the right situation. But he also has a past and a present that he keeps well-hidden. He's not open about everything he's involved in, is he? He doesn't tell you where he's going or who he's working for or what type of job he's going out on. He keeps that all under wraps."

Vic swallowed as she tried to come up with an argument, but she just shook her head. "I know what kind of man he is."

Terry stood there silently, letting Vic think about it. Giving her some time to let it all sink in. He took a step toward the door, having gleaned everything he could from her. He still had other work to do. He looked back at Vic.

"And is he the kind of man who would tell Erin to get out of a dangerous situation and to come home?"

CHAPTER 20

*E*rin and Vic looked at each other for a long moment after Terry was gone. Erin guessed they had similar expressions. Mouths open, eyes wide, skin pale. They were both shocked at the suggestion.

It was Vic who broke the silence. "Could it have been him, Erin?"

Erin tried to replay the one glimpse she'd had of the man through the doorway. She tried to remember the feel of his hands and the timbre of his voice. But it had all been too quick. He'd been well-disguised and he hadn't given himself away.

"I don't know. I can't rule him out. I didn't get a good look. I just… don't know."

"I can't believe this."

"That Terry would accuse him?"

"That Willie didn't tell me. Why wouldn't he tell me his mother was a Dyson? Why didn't he tell you, when we were talking about Charley being in the clan?"

"I don't know. Maybe it was just like he said, that he wanted privacy. He didn't want to be judged by his upbringing or who his family was. He wanted to be his own person and live his own life, the way he wanted to."

"He could have! I wouldn't have judged him! Heaven knows, my family ain't no gathering of saints."

Erin put her plate into the sink. It was time to open up again for the lunch rush. The conversation would have to wait until a more appropriate time.

"I'm sure he would have told you in time. He was just waiting until he was comfortable with it. He was just waiting for the right time to let you know."

Vic's face looked pinched and pale as she followed Erin to the front of the bakery. Erin turned the sign to *Open* and unlocked the door.

Mary Lou brought over a fresh batch of Jam Lady jams to add to their stock. The jams sure helped to sell bread, and vice versa. Erin and Vic knew the Jam Lady's secret—that it was actually Mary Lou's husband who made them while Mary Lou acted as the distributor and kept the maker a secret— and neither had ever breathed a word that would even hint at the truth.

"I figured you were about due for a new shipment," she told Erin, holding up the flat of jars. "How's your inventory?"

"You're right, as usual," Erin assured her. "Thanks."

Mary Lou gave Vic a frozen smile and smoothed her form-fitting blazer over her hips. "And have you heard anything from your family, my dear?"

Vic stared at her. "Have I heard anything from my family? No. Why would I?"

"I just thought that with all of the trouble going on, they might have stopped by to see you or gotten in touch with you by phone or email…"

"All of what trouble?"

Mary Lou looked from Vic to Erin and back again. "Well, I… you are from Moose River too, aren't you?"

Erin looked at Vic, stunned. Was everybody in on the inside track of politics and society in Moose River except for her? Vic had said nothing about being from Moose River.

"I'm from *outside* Moose River," Vic corrected icily. "My folks have never lived in town."

Mary Lou gave a little laugh and shook her head at this.

"Well, outside Moose River, then. It's all the same. I just thought that with a murder happening, and the threat of violence between the clans…" she trailed off, letting Erin and Vic complete the thought.

"What's she talking about?" Erin asked Vic. "Am I that dense? I don't understand."

Vic stared down at the baking in the display case. "I'll tell you later. For now…" she raised her voice so that the rest of the customers could hear her clearly. "Thanks for the jams, Mary Lou. Did you want anything from the case?"

Mary Lou took her time looking over the baked goods on display. "Everything always looks so good here." She smoothed her jacket again. "Of course, I can't eat any of it, or it would go straight to my hips. But the boys would like something, I'm sure. Oh… why don't we go with chocolate chip? Always so good with a glass of cold milk."

"Certainly," Vic agreed.

Mary Lou was looking around the store to greet the other patrons with a smile. While she always made Erin feel welcome and included with her friendly manner, she had never quite extended the same courtesy to Vic. She didn't give her the same smile, the same thanks, the same effort at being pleasant. Erin realized that Vic was giving Mary Lou a baker's dozen, and made a motion to stop her and remind her that Mary Lou always requested an even dozen so that the desserts would split evenly between her husband and two sons. Vic smiled and raised a brow at Erin and with an expression of mischief, slid thirteen cookies into the bag for Mary Lou.

Erin stifled a giggle. She was tired and stressed and if she started laughing, she wouldn't be able to stop.

"Is there anything else?" she asked Mary Lou, calling her attention back to the transaction.

"Oh, no. That's all I need today."

They settled up the bill, and Mary Lou went on her way with the thirteen cookies. Erin shook her head at Vic. "You're incorrigible."

"Mary Lou was being very kind to inquire about my family," Vic said. "Of course I would want to do something nice for her."

Erin shrugged, baffled by whatever had passed between Mary Lou and Vic. There would be a story coming later, and Erin wanted to hear it.

~

"Has Erin Price been take care of?" the boss demanded. "I wanted her kept out of this situation. Now she's walking all over it like chickens scratching in a yard. For an outsider, she has certainly managed to muck things around."

"She's taken care of," the fixer assured him. "She's been warned off, and both Terry Piper and Jack Ward are doing their best to pull her back. She's not going to cause any more trouble."

"I wish I could believe that. The woman is relentless. She's determined not to leave things alone until I'm completely ruined."

"It's just coincidence. She's not going to be a problem anymore."

"Better not be. And what about Charlotte? Where is she?"

"Well…" the fixer grimaced at that. The one question he couldn't answer. "I did get to her ahead of the Dyson gang, but not by much. Told her to get out of there and not come back. But she didn't have time to get packed and get out before they got there."

"And now…? Where is she now?"

"I'm sure we'll turn her up before too long. She's too important to just leave hanging. There will be too many people looking for her."

"That's not an answer. Dyson got her? And did what? Is she still there or back home?"

"She's not home. The cops are looking for her. I haven't found anything out yet. I'm doing my best to monitor what's going on, but people don't exactly trust me."

"You're not particularly trustworthy."

The fixer snorted. "I'm a lot more trustworthy than you!"

The boss didn't disagree.

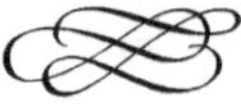

So explain to me what Mary Ann was going on about today," Erin told Vic as they cleaned up, preparing to leave.

"Oh, Erin… you don't want to hear all about my family's dirty laundry."

"Their dirty laundry? What kind of dirty laundry? And how would Mary Lou know about it?"

"Because it's been going on for generations. And when something has been going on for that long, word spreads, and people know."

"What's been going on for generations? I'm at a definite disadvantage as a newcomer in these parts."

"Except you're not, you're part of the community too. You just… don't know what you don't know. If your parents had raised you here, you'd know all about it too."

"But they didn't. So you're going to have to fill me in."

Vic sighed. "Well… you know Victoria Webster isn't my birth name."

"Of course. I know that."

"There's a reason I didn't just change my given name. Victor was my middle name, and I always liked Victoria. But I also changed my last name, from Jackson to Webster."

"Right. So you wouldn't be as easy to track when you ran away."

Vic nodded. "But not just because my family objected to me being transgender."

Erin slowly washed the dishes, scrubbing them under the warm, soapy water.

"What is it about the Jackson family, then? It's an old name in these parts. Pretty common."

"Yeah. There's lots of us around, and everyone is related to everyone else on the mountain."

She waited. Vic could dance around the issue all day for as long as Erin continued asking her questions. She wasn't going to get to the crux of it until she decided it was safe to do so.

"The Dysons and the Jacksons have been rivals for a long time," Vic said finally. "They've been fighting each other for generations."

"Like a feud?"

Vic shrugged. "Like a feud. Or like two mafia families fighting for territory. It's like with Romeo and Juliet, you don't get to choose which family you're a part of. You're just born into it, and there you are. You have to live with it."

"Is that why you were so surprised to hear that Willie was a Dyson?"

"That's just one more curve ball. I don't know what to say, Erin. Your sister… she's one of the Dysons. She's my mortal enemy. Stupid, I know, but that's the way it's been for years. You can't just change that kind of thing on a whim. You can't just say 'Oh, she seems nice, so we'll accept her as one of us'."

"So do you hate her?"

"Me?" Vic laughed. "No, not me. How could I? She's your sister. I can't hate anyone who's part of your family. But my family…? Yes. They can hate her. They're not going to give her a chance, they're just going to hate her."

"Even though she killed Bobby Dyson? Or they think she did?"

"That's just the way it is with a rivalry like this. Even if she killed Bobby Dyson, Charley is still a Dyson herself, so we hate her. *They* hate her."

"That's crazy." Erin shook her head, putting the pans on the drying rack and grabbing a few more to scrub off. "I couldn't hate anyone without even meeting them. What about your religion? Doesn't Christianity say you're supposed to love everyone?"

"Everyone but the Dysons," Vic agreed. "They wrote that part into the Bible themselves."

"You can do that?"

"No. You can't do that. I'm joking."

"So… all this time… I thought you grew up on a farm shooting varmints and climbing trees. Are you telling me you hunted the Dyson family? That you learned to shoot so you could fight this feud?"

Vic looked troubled. She set out the clean and dry cooling racks for the next day.

"No, it wasn't like that. I *did* grow up on a farm. I haven't ever shot a person, only squirrels and coons and such. But I always knew we were part of the Jackson clan and that we were enemies with the Dyson clan. If we ever ran into Dysons at school or in town… there was tension. Nobody killed anybody, not while I was around, but we didn't have anything to do with each other. And the politics… I always knew my uncle was a big boss in the clan. I never really understood what that meant. Just that we showed him respect. People didn't go around talking about whatever the clans are involved in… protection scams or drugs or black market weapons… but even when I was little, I knew that… a lot of what the grown-ups said had double meanings. One thing to little ears or outsiders, and something different to the adults who were in the know."

Erin couldn't fathom being part of a big family organization like that. Most of the families she had been a part of had been very small and insular. Sometimes there were aunts and uncles and grandparents, but she was a foster child, so she wasn't treated like a real family member. There had been many times when she'd been shipped off to a respite family so that her foster family could entertain the extended family. The real kids stayed home and the foster kids were sent away.

"So… have they called you like Mary Lou said?"

Vic didn't answer right away. "I'm still estranged," she said finally. "Most of them don't want anything to do with me."

"Most of them," Erin repeated. "What about Jeremy? Has he called?"

"A couple of times. Since we got back in touch at Christmas, you know."

"I know," Erin agreed. She remembered the joy Vic had greeted her brother with. The exuberance of her reunion with him after being away from each other for months, shunned by a family who wouldn't accept her gender identity. What kind of sense did it make to be involved in whatever organized crime they were involved with, and yet to shun a person for being a girl? "Has he been in contact with you in the last week or so? Since I met Charley?"

"Well, yes."

"And…?"

"I wouldn't ever do anything to put you or your sister in danger, Erin. I swear it. When Jeremy started nosing around, asking questions that were none of his business, I told him so. I told him to just take a hike if he was going to interfere with my friend's family. You're family to me, Erin. You took me in when my family of birth wouldn't have anything to do with me. So you're my first priority. I chose you to be my family."

Erin felt a little twinge of guilt at Vic's words. She felt guilty for going against what Vic had told her and seeking Charley out anyway. Vic, Willie, and Terry had all told her to stay away from Charley and the Dysons. They all had different reasons, different kinds of experience with the Dysons, but they had all seen trouble brewing and warned her to stay away. And Erin hadn't. She had chosen her sister, someone she didn't even know, over friends who had stuck with her through thick and thin and three murder investigations.

Erin wiped her hands on a dishtowel and gave Vic a hug.

"I'm glad you're my family too. I know I haven't always been the best friend…"

"What are you talking about? You have been the best friend. Every minute!"

"Not when I went to see Charley…"

Vic brushed that away with a gesture. "I'm not enemies with Charley. I'm not enemies with anyone. My family can choose to ignore the Bible if they want. But I'm not going to live like that. I'm not going to live my life under the thumb of some criminal organization. I can't help where I was born. But I can help where and how I live now that I'm an adult."

They looked around the kitchen to make sure everything was ready for the next day, then turned toward the door together.

"You never knew Willie was a Dyson?" Erin asked.

Vic laughed. "No. I suppose I should have guessed. Aunt Angela said he was no good. That should have been my first clue. But I never asked him anything about his family, and have only gleaned a few bits and pieces about his past. Nothing clear. I never got why he was shunned in Bald Eagle Falls. I just figured… it was because of the way he looked, and that he didn't have a regular job."

"Do you think he knows you were a Jackson?"

Vic considered this. "Yeah… I'm pretty sure he does. I never hid my birth name from him. I'm sure I must have mentioned it at some time."

"What a rascal," Erin said. "He really should have told you. It's not fair that he knew who you were, and that you were supposed to be enemies, and that you didn't. He should have said something."

"I was okay with him knowing I was a Jackson… but that doesn't mean he had to be comfortable with me knowing his roots. I knew he had secrets. And I'm pretty sure that's not the only one."

"You're a lot more forgiving than I would be."

"What about your boyfriend?"

Erin frowned. "What do you mean?"

"He did tell you he was a cop, right?"

Erin laughed. "Yeah, it might have come up in conversation at some point."

"And did you tell him everything about your past?"

There were a few seconds of silence. Erin swallowed. "The salient points."

"So the two of you are okay with not being on exactly the same page too."

"Uh… yeah, I guess," Erin agreed.

"Terry is willing to wait for you to tell him about yourself. Or to be kept in the dark indefinitely."

"It's not like I have this deep, dark past," Erin said. "He knows the basics. So do you."

"Uh-huh. But you're not ready to expose everything, are you?"

"No."

"I'm not going to insist that you tell me everything about your past. And I'm not going to insist that Willie tell me everything about his. We'll figure it out. We've got years to get to know each other."

Years. It was such a foreign concept to Erin. She didn't stay in the same place, associating with the same people for years. She stayed around for a few weeks, a few months, and then she would be off on a new adventure.

She would leave everything behind, shed it like the skin of a snake, and start over again as a new person. The idea of staying in the same place and getting to know the same people over a period of years was a daunting concept.

"It's okay," Vic repeated. "We've got plenty of time."

It had been such a tiring week that Erin was asleep the instant her head hit the pillow. Orange Blossom could make all the noise he wanted to, because she wasn't waking up again for anything.

So when she awoke to Vic shaking her, she knew she must have overslept. The alarm had probably gone off, and she had just slept right through it. She sat up abruptly, her heart thumping wildly.

"What time is it?"

"I'm sorry, Erin. We've got to go."

Erin looked at the clock and frowned. She hadn't overslept. It wasn't even time for the alarm to go off yet. She'd only been asleep for a couple of hours. She put her hand over her pumping heart and took a long breath.

"Vicky, are you sleepwalking? It's not time to get up."

"We have to go," Vic repeated. "You took so long to wake up, I thought I was going to have to carry you. Get up. I'll explain on the way."

She tugged on Erin's arm, and Erin slid her feet off the bed and got unsteadily to her feet. "What's going on? It's not time to get up."

"Get your shoes on." Vic grabbed Erin's bulky purse and chivvied her toward the bedroom door. "We have to go out. Come on."

"Is it Adele? Is something wrong?"

"It's not Adele. I promise, I'll explain. Just keep moving."

Erin rubbed her eyes with both hands as she stumbled down the hall. At the back door, she put her shoes on over bare feet, trying to process what was going on. Vic pulled her out the door and stopped to lock it and arm the new alarm system.

"The car," she instructed. "Let's go."

Erin led the way to the garage, blinking in the moonlight. She had no idea what Vic was up to. Where in the world were they going in the middle of the night. And how were they going to be awake enough in the morning to run the bakery?

Vic motioned to the passenger side. "You ride shotgun. You're not awake enough to drive yet. Did you take something to sleep?"

"No. I was just really tired. Can't we just sleep tonight and do whatever this is another day?"

"No. Get in."

Erin was already opening the door on the passenger side of her car. She hadn't ever ridden in the passenger seat before. She always drove. She settled in and Vic handed her her purse and made sure she had done up her seatbelt. They were on their way in less than a minute.

Erin yawned widely. "Now can you tell me what is going on? I don't understand where we're going in the middle of the night. Is something wrong?"

Vic nodded grimly. "Willie called me. Told me to get out of there and get you out right away."

"Why?"

"He didn't have time to tell me and I didn't ask. If he's a Dyson, Erin, and he says we're in danger, I trust he knows what he's talking about. I'm not going to wait around to find out the details."

"Where did he say to go?"

"I don't know yet. Just get out of the house and get out of town. I'll call him now and see if he can tell us what's going on."

Vic pulled out her phone and was fiddling with it while racing down the dark highway. Erin took it away from her and found the speed dial for Willie. She put it on the Bluetooth radio. They both held their breaths while they waited for him to answer. One ring... two... three... it went on and on, and Erin was waiting for it to disconnect or go to voicemail. Then there was a click.

"Vicky?"

"We're fine," Vic assured Willie. "We're on the highway. Can you tell us what's going on? Where do you want us to go?"

"Erin is with you?"

"I'm here," Erin acknowledged.

"Good." Willie's voice was relieved. "I was afraid I wasn't going to be able to get to you in time."

"What's going on?" Vic demanded. "Is it the Dysons?"

There was a pause while Willie thought through what it was he wanted to say. "Vic, I never told you, but…"

"I know. Terry told us. Your mother was a Dyson."

"Well, thank you Officer Piper… okay, well… Erin probably shouldn't be driving. Can you pull over for a few minutes?"

"She's not driving, I am."

"Oh. Do you even know how to drive?"

"Oh, please. I've been driving tractors and back roads since I was seven. I'm a good driver!"

"Do you have a license?"

"Willie, will you get on with it?"

"The two of you are in danger. Well, Erin anyway. The Dysons don't like her poking around Bobby's case, and—"

"And even though she went home when you told her to, they decided that wasn't enough."

For a few seconds, Erin thought they had lost the connection. There was dead air, with no response back from Willie. She looked down at the phone screen to make sure the call was still active.

"Willie?"

"What do you mean, when I told her to?" Willie demanded.

"You were the masked man, weren't you? It was Terry who figured it out—"

"What masked man?"

Vic looked over at Erin, who was finally fully awake and alert.

"The man who told Charley to run," Erin said, "and who told me to go home and stay out of it."

"That wasn't me. Back up. What happened?"

"When I went to Moose River to pick up Charley. She made bail, but she needed a ride and I still had her apartment keys. When we were at her apartment, a man in a ski mask came to the door, and he told her she should get out of Moose River and disappear. But she had already called the Dysons to try to explain to them, and they had men on the way. I left, but in the parking lot, he came up behind me. He told me to stay out of it and go home."

"It wasn't me." Willie reiterated. "What made you think it was?"

"It was Terry—"

"What made Terry think it was me?"

"The man knew me by name. He knew I lived in Bald Eagle Falls and was a baker. So Terry thought either the police department had a leak, or it was someone…"

"Someone who knew you personally. Like me."

Erin nodded mutely, even though he couldn't see her.

"You were called away right when Charley was released. I just thought…"

Willie was quiet for some time.

"Willie… I don't even know where you want me to go," Vic reminded him.

Willie gave a short laugh. "I don't either, so don't feel left out."

Erin had to smile at his dry sense of humor. She ran her fingers through her hair to tame it into some semblance of order. There weren't exactly a lot of places she could go, dressed in her pajamas, bed head and no makeup, with only the shoes on her feet and whatever was in her purse. And what about the animals? Someone would need to feed them. And open the bakery. It couldn't run without Erin and Vic opening up and getting every-thing ready.

"Do you know if Charley is okay? Or did they…?"

Willie made a humming noise, considering. "I'm not on the inside, so I can't tell you anything with certainty, but from what I can gather from the whispers I've heard, they've got her under wraps, but still alive. Her turning herself in to Dwight was either desperation to prove herself innocent, or an audacious bluff, but they don't know which yet." He paused a few seconds. "They're leaning toward a bluff, which wouldn't be good for Charley's health."

"We have to help her."

"There's nothing any of us can do, Erin."

"What about the police? If you know where they're holding her…"

"I told you, I'm not a trusted insider. They're not going to give me information like that. It's only luck that I know what I do."

"Do you really think they were coming for Erin tonight?" Vic asked. There was a quiver in her voice, the adrenaline of their escape affecting her.

"They were," Willie said flatly.

Erin shivered.

Vic reached over to rub Erin's knee comfortingly. "Can we meet you somewhere?" she asked Willie.

"Yes… Let's pick a random hotel in a random town along the way. Hillard Bluff?"

"Hillard Bluff," Vic agreed. "Is there a Best Western off the highway?"

"Yes. I'll probably get there before you, so I'll get a room. I don't want to be waiting around in the lobby." He cleared his throat. "I don't exactly blend in."

"Just dress like a construction worker," Vic advised. "No one will even notice you."

*E*rin was self-conscious walking into a hotel in her pajamas, but there was nothing else for her to do. They couldn't stop somewhere to buy clothes and change in the middle of the night.

Vic caught Erin eyeing her clothes, and gave an apologetic smile. "I know. I got changed and then I hustled you out the door. But by the time I got you to wake up… I was really panicking about getting out of there fast enough. I didn't know for sure what was up, but I wasn't about to piddle around when Willie said to get out now." She swept her hands through her ponytail. "I really didn't take time to do more than pull on pants and a shirt."

Erin shrugged. Nothing could be done about it at that point. The important thing was that they were both safe for the moment. She wasn't sure whether she could say the same about Charley. Willie said she was still alive, but Erin wondered what kind of shape she was in and what she might have been going through.

The desk clerk made no sign that she noticed their attire or disheveled condition and merely directed them up to their room. Vic texted Willie from the elevator, and when they reached the hotel room, Willie opened the door and let them in. He stayed at the door and looked up and down the hall. He stepped back and let the door shut, and still stayed at the peephole looking out into the hallway. Eventually, he relaxed and joined Vic and Erin in the bedroom. He sat down on one of the beds and Vic joined him, cuddling up against him. Erin sat down on the other bed. Despite how fast her heart was still beating, she really wanted to lie down and go back to sleep. She rubbed her eyes and stifled a yawn.

"Doesn't look like you were followed," Willie said in a low voice. "Not up here to the room, anyway. There could still be someone watching the hotel and waiting for you to leave again."

"I didn't see anyone following us," Vic said. "They wouldn't know where we were going, so they would have had to follow us all the way from the house. There were lots of times on the highway when I couldn't even see any other headlights."

"I hoped that if I acted fast enough, I could get you out of there before anyone showed up."

Erin and Vic nodded.

Erin looked Willie over. She was used to his usual grubby appearance, his skin stained dark by the mining and processing work he did and his clothes frequently worn. He had done as she had suggested and dressed like a blue-collar worker, so he looked less like a homeless person and more like he was just in the middle of a dirty job.

Willie tapped the bill of his hat. "Sewers and sanitation," he pointed out. "No one wants to look too close at someone who just climbed out of a sewer."

Erin chuckled. "No, you're probably right there. How did you get your hands on that in the middle of the night?"

"Don't ask me any questions, and I won't have to lie to you."

"So what are we going to do now?" Vic asked. "We're safe, but what do we do next?"

"Best would be to get some sleep, if you think you can. We can try to sort things out in the morning."

Erin kicked off her shoes and lay down on the bed, looking at them. "What about the bakery? We have work."

"Tomorrow is Sunday," Vic said. "So, thank goodness, it's not a regular work day. If you want, we can just stay closed. If not, you could call Bella and see if she can manage it herself. It's just the ladies' tea. They all know where everything is and can help her get set up. There are enough cookies and treats in the freezer that she can put a couple of platters out and no one will be the wiser."

"Those are for an emergency," Erin protested.

Vic raised an eyebrow. "Uh… yeah," she agreed.

Erin's face warmed. Running for their lives didn't constitute an emergency? Exactly what was she saving them for? "Okay. I guess we can call Bella. She hasn't had to handle it on her own before, but she's been there enough times… and it's not like serving the rush crowd on other days."

Vic nodded in agreement. She followed Erin's example and pulled off her shoes. She lay down, and Willie stretched out behind her, spoon style. Erin didn't close her eyes. She was tired and hyped up at the same time. Vic looked back at her across the gap between the two beds, not closing her eyes either.

"Tell me about when you were a kid," Vic told Willie. "Since I know where you come from now, you don't have to worry about giving yourself away."

"You already knew where I was from," Willie said, his voice gravelly. "Bald Eagle Falls, just like I said. None of that has changed."

"What was it like growing up as a Dyson?"

"I don't imagine it was so different from growing up as a Jackson. My parents left Moose River before I was born. Wanted to get away from the clan. Be their own people and not have to worry about the politics or about having the cops on their case all the time."

"What did the family think about that?"

"No big deal, I don't think. Not everyone stays involved in family matters. Not everyone is made for it."

"Your dad was a trucker; what did your mom do?"

Willie grunted. "Dad was a trucker when he was employed, which was not very often. Mom did what she could from home. Sewing. Laundry. Going out and cleaning houses when we could be left alone for a while. When we got old enough, we picked up after-school jobs to try to contribute to the household."

"How bad was it?" Vic asked. "Were you really poor?"

"Grindingly poor. We didn't have many clothes, always got made fun of for that. Why people think it's okay to make fun of those who have less, I'll never understand. Like poverty was a crime or a choice. Believe me, we didn't choose to live that way."

Vic shifted, reaching behind her to pat his cheek. "In a way, your parents did. If they'd chosen to live with the clan, you wouldn't have been poor. You would have had everything you needed."

"At a cost."

Erin closed her eyes, thinking about the hollowness in Willie's voice. Just what had he suffered in his life, first living without enough food or clothing and being bullied by Trenton Plaint or boys like him? Then leaving Bald Eagle Falls to strike out on his own.

"What did you do when you got out of school? You left Bald Eagle Falls?"

"Yes. I figured my parents had made the wrong choice. That they didn't know what they were talking about. So I went to the Dysons."

Vic caught her breath sharply. "You went back?"

"Technically, I didn't go *back* because I'd never been there before. But yeah, I went back to what my parents had abandoned, thinking that they were just naive and out of touch and I knew better than they did."

Erin closed her eyes. She wanted to block out the pictures and to see them at the same time. She didn't want to look at Willie, but to give him his privacy. Even though he was her friend, it seemed like a more intimate moment, one that he should have shared with Vic alone.

"How could you do that?" Vic asked. "You knew they were... criminals. Bad guys. That's not the kind of person you are."

"I was a teenager," Willie said. "Teenagers know everything. I wanted the money. I wanted the power and the respect. I didn't want to be looked down on anymore." Erin cracked her eyelids briefly to see him shaking his head. "I didn't want to be hungry anymore."

Vic turned over to face him. She put her arms around him and buried her face in his chest. She rubbed his back comfortingly. "I'm so sorry..."

"I learned pretty quick that there were worse things than being poor. And that being part of the clan didn't get me the respect I wanted. I was the lowest man on the totem pole. I knew nothing about the family or the way things worked. There were twelve-year-olds with more skill and experience than I had. People outside the family didn't respect me. Fear, yes. Plenty of people who would look away or kowtow to me. But real respect for me and my skills... no."

"How long before you decided to go back home to Bald Eagle Falls?"

"I had committed to... something like an apprenticeship or internship.

I had to do my time so they could see what kind of an asset I was and how they could use me."

"For how long?"

"Five years. And after that, I was allowed to decide what I wanted to do. It wasn't easy, but I left it all behind. I decided my parents had been right in the first place. Better to be poor and be your own man. Better not to be a slave to the organization or to have to give up your standards and beliefs for theirs. I didn't come back to Bald Eagle Falls. Not right away."

Vic murmured a sympathetic sound. She continued to rub Willie's back and to hold him close. "What did you do, while you were apprenticing? Was it hard? Was it…?"

"I can't talk about it. I can't tell you what things I did or what I was involved with. You know the kind of people who run the family. You know what kind of organization they are and what they're involved in. An apprentice doesn't get to avoid anything. He has to learn the organization from the ground up."

Erin thought about some of the skills Willie had shown in the time she had known him and how Terry was so wary of him, never fully trusting him. He'd run away, a teen starving for attention as much as for food. He'd returned a man, with years of knowledge and experience in things he should never have had to witness or participate in. Erin was glad that he and Vic had connected. Vic was still way too young for him, but maybe he needed her inexperience and non-worldliness to balance his own cynicism and weariness. It shouldn't have worked between them, but it did.

*E*rin had apparently fallen asleep sometime during the night or the early hours of the morning. She couldn't remember all that they had discussed during the night or when she had fallen asleep, but by morning they were all snoring away, exhausted by the emotion and the events of the night.

Erin was the first to awaken, and decided to take advantage of the fact to have a shower. The hot water felt good and the white noise of the droplets was soothing. She really needed it.

And whatever the reason for it, she was going to have a day off. A full day off, away from the bakery and thinking about how to keep it solvent.

But before long, her mind went to Charley and she lost her zen state, returning to full worry mode. They had to find Charley. They have to figure out how to help her. There had to be a way.

By the time she got out of the bathroom, all dried off and dressed again in her pajamas, Erin could feel the frown lines creasing her forehead. They couldn't afford to just let the hours drift by without doing anything. Vic shifted in her sleep, and Erin shook her arm.

"Vic. Vic, we should get up and figure out what we're going to do."

"Five more minutes." She sounded like a child trying to avoid getting up for school.

"No more minutes. You're getting out of bed right now, young lady."

Vic squinted in the bright light of the hotel room. "Are you channeling my mother?"

"That's right. Up and at 'em. Time's a-wasting. The early bird gets the worm."

"You are evil," Vic groaned. She stretched and sat up, rubbing both eyes with her fists. "What time is it?"

"Later than we ever get up for the bakery, so you shouldn't have any trouble getting up. You got to sleep in."

"I barely got any time," Vic objected. "I just barely got to sleep."

"We need to figure out what to do."

"Okay." Vic elbowed Willie none-too-gently. "Hey. Willie. Time for action."

"Five more minutes."

He'd obviously heard Erin getting Vic up. Vic laughed and attacked him, tickling and kissing him while he played possum, pretending he was still asleep. Eventually, Willie put an end to it, pulling Vic into a bear hug and kissing her firmly until she stopped struggling. He released her, and Vic got to her feet, face red, giggling at Erin. She disappeared into the bathroom.

Willie yawned and stretched. He cracked his fingers and his neck joints and ran his fingers through his close-cropped hair.

"I know you said you don't know where they have Charley," Erin said. "But can you find out? Can we figure out some way to help her? We can't just leave it up to the clan to decide that she was responsible for Bobby's death and execute her for it."

Willie ran his hand briskly over his head, back and forth, like he was trying to warm up his brain.

"Let me think about it. I need caffeine."

"I would offer to go down and get you some from the breakfast buffet, but I need some clothes."

Willie looked at Erin's pajamas as if seeing them for the first time. "Oh. Yeah, I guess we'd better get you something more appropriate. Did Vicky bring anything?"

"We didn't have time to pack," Vic said, coming out of the bathroom. "I barely stopped to throw on clothes myself. All we brought is what we've got on."

Erin lifted up her purse. "And this."

Vic looked at it. "Somehow, I doubt you've got a change of clothes in there."

"Uh… no." Erin dug around in it. "I do have breath mints."

They both looked at her.

"No toothbrush," Erin explained. "So…"

Vic laughed. "At least if we have to face down the Dysons, we'll have fresh breath."

"We are not facing down the Dysons," Willie said.

"I hope not," Vic agreed. "But how are we going to help Charley? I think we're going to have to talk to someone."

"Coffee first."

"And clothes," Erin added. She pointed at the in-room coffee maker. "We can start some coffee brewing here. But someone is going to have to pick up some real clothes for me before I leave this room."

Vic and Willie looked at each other. Vic looked down at herself, getting pink. "And I didn't do anything more than pull on the closest things I could find. I don't even have on a bra."

Willie shifted uncomfortably. "You want me to go out and buy Erin an outfit and you a bra?"

"No, I won't make you go bra shopping."

Vic was getting pink and Erin suspected that Willie would be too if she'd been able to see his natural skin color.

"You and me will go together. We'll check the gift shop first. See if they had some souvenir t-shirts. And hopefully some pants. Then we can all go together to get the sundries Erin and I need."

Willie nodded. "Okay."

"We can't spend too much time shopping," Erin worried. "Popping down to the gift shop is fine, but going to the department store or mall for other things… I don't want to waste any more time than we have to. They could decide that Charley is guilty at any time. And then she could be gone before we have a chance to do anything."

"We won't waste time," Vic promised. "And Willie will be working the phone while we're getting what we need. Right?"

Willie raised an eyebrow. "Maybe if I can figure out who to call to get some help with this… situation."

"Charley called someone named Dwight. What about him?"

Willie shook his head. "I don't have an in with Dwight. He's way higher than anyone I have any connection with. Maybe someone on his staff would know something…"

Erin moved over to the coffee maker. "Okay, caffeine coming up. Get ready for it, because once you get this, you're not going to want to stop until everything is sorted out."

"That must be some magical coffee."

~

With coffee on board, Willie was functioning a little better, and was able to start putting together some plans.

"Dwight is Bobby's dad. He's also sort of the boss of the Dysons in Moose River."

"Like the Godfather?" Erin suggested.

"Well, more like one of his capos," Willie said. "But close enough. All you need to know is that he's important, high up in the organization, and he's dangerous. You can't mess around with this guy. Understood? There's no trying to trick him or lie to him. He won't take it."

"But Charley—"

"Charley went for broke. I don't know whether she was telling the truth or playing the biggest bluff ever. But we can't do that. We can't bluff our way into anything, but especially not into Dwight Dyson's inner circle."

"How are we going to—"

"Dwight has another son. Not a bigwig like Bobby was. Not wild and flamboyant like Bobby. Quiet and studious."

Erin and Vic nodded, listening intently, trying to memorize every word as if their lives depended on it. Because they probably did.

"Nelson, I can probably get in to see. I've helped him out with his computers. Other projects. Dwight wouldn't know me from Adam, but Nelson does."

"Nelson," Erin repeated. "That sounds good. And would he be able to help with Charley? Telling us where she was or even getting her out?"

"One step at a time. He's still living at home with Dwight, so there's a chance he would have heard something about what has been going on. For sure, he'll know that Bobby is dead, even if he's had his head in the sand about everything else. We'll start with that. Find out if he knows about Charley." Willie sighed. "I want to be able to play this like a chess game, staying four moves ahead of them. But I can barely even see what's on the board. It's frustrating."

"So how do we get in to see Nelson?" Vic asked.

"I'll call him… I'm going to need to offer him something of value. He's not going to let us just march in there and do whatever we want to."

"What's he into?"

Willie shook his head. "Computers, sound systems, drama. He's mostly a loner, but he gets together with some friends for gaming or putting on little plays."

"Kind of a geek, huh?"

Willie shrugged. "I'm not going to judge. If he's managed to keep himself separate from the family business, then good for him. Whatever it takes. If he had to lock himself in his room for the first twenty years in order to avoid it, then good for him."

"How about a double-date?" Vic suggested. "If he's kind of awkward, then maybe if you just told him the four of us wanted to go out to dinner together…"

"No one said he was awkward. Being a geek is not the same thing. He doesn't have a steady girlfriend as far as I know, but that doesn't mean he doesn't know any girls. The drama clubs include a lot of women."

"Say we have a play we want to get produced and we want him in it?"

"I told you, we can't bluff our way into this. We have to have something of value to offer him."

"A way to avenge his brother," Erin said. "To impress his father and do something for Bobby."

Willie pursed his lips and raised both eyebrows as he considered this. "Not bad. And what do we actually offer him when we get there? We can't exactly say that we know what happened or that we can offer him anyone in place of Charley."

"No… we tell him we can get the truth from Charley."

"How are we going to do that?"

"She wanted the chance to tell Dwight her story. I don't know if he heard her out. We could get Nelson to listen to it, and then he'd be able to offer something to his dad. An alternate version of what happened. Even if Charley doesn't know who did it, if she could tell what she knew…"

"You're putting an awful lot of faith into the idea that Charley didn't do it. Are you really that sure?" Willie challenged.

"I can't understand why she would go to Dwight if she did. Why would she do that? Wouldn't she just run? Isn't that what you would do if you had this family after you?"

"What I would do and what some girl I've never met would do aren't necessarily the same thing. This kind of business attracts and rewards big egos. And people who have big egos think they can talk their way out of anything. What do you really know about Charley?"

Erin sighed. She scratched at a spot on her pajamas. "I wish I could get a chance to know her better. I really don't think she did it, Willie. She just wants to live her life. Why would she throw everything away like that?"

Willie didn't answer immediately. He took a sip of his coffee. "I think *you* just want to live your own life. You're putting your own motives on her. She wasn't raised in the family. She didn't just fall into it naturally. She had to join up. And this wasn't something that was planned. If she killed Bobby Dyson, it was in the middle of a big blow-up. If she was smart, she'd be arguing self-defense."

"But if she really didn't do it…"

"Then she should definitely be arguing self-defense and trying to get a deal."

Erin frowned. "No, if she didn't do it—"

"If she doesn't want to spend the next few years in court, and to be able to get off without prison time, she should be working a deal."

Erin felt a lot better once she had on real clothes, even though they were new and a little stiff and didn't quite fit her the way that her own clothes did. She might look a little juvenile in her touristy gift store t-shirt and pants, but they were better than walking around town in her pajamas.

When she and Vic got out of the department store with their unmentionables also dealt with, Willie was waiting in his car talking on the phone. Erin and Vic got in quietly and listened to Willie's half of the conversation, trying to analyze how he was doing with getting them inside the Dysons. Erin's stomach was tight with nervous anticipation.

"You know I usually don't get involved in this kind of thing," Willie said. "I keep my nose out of other people's business. But this is different. I actually know Charley's sister. If anyone can get the truth out of her, it's Erin."

There was a long pause while he listened to the voice on the other end, Nelson Dyson, Erin assumed.

"Would he still have her there if he'd gotten everything he wanted out of her?" Willie countered. "He obviously doesn't have everything he needs. And the longer he's got her, the hotter things get. The cops are looking for her. Other people are looking for her. It's only a matter of time until they come by there with a warrant, and then what?"

More waiting.

"Of course Dwight is careful. He wouldn't be where he is today if he wasn't. But this is your chance, Nelson. Your one chance to do right for Bobby and show your father that you're not second-best."

Erin and Vic looked at each other, gauging each other's reaction to Willie's conversation. Erin had a strange sense of being in an alien world. She'd always seen Willie as a blue-collar worker. He did his mining, he did odd jobs that involved physical labor, like moving boxes, painting buildings, and putting flyers on cars. She knew that he had advanced skills in caving and first aid, but those were hobbies, not a professional skill-set. Listening to him smoothly negotiating with Nelson Dyson was a freaky, out-of-body experience. She'd never even imagined him in that role before.

Willie started to nod. "Yeah. Yep. I know. I can't guarantee results, but this is about as close as I can get. Give me this chance. If it doesn't pan out, then nothing is lost, right? You're no further behind than you were to start with. It's not your job to get the story out of Charley, so if you can't, no skin off your back. If you do, though… Well, Dwight isn't going to ignore it, is he?"

Wrapping up noises from the phone, which Willie acknowledged, and then hung up. He looked at Erin and Vic.

"Okay. We're in. I just hope we're not jumping into a hornets' nest." He swallowed, lips tightening. "I want to keep you girls safe."

*E*rin had been expecting a big house. The foster families she had grown up with had always lived in little places, relying on foster parenting checks to help pay the bills. She had worked in some bigger houses, cleaning or caregiving, and that was what she had pictured in her mind. A mob boss would obviously live in a big house. But she had never seen anything like the mansion that Willie drove up to.

There was a big gate with a guard booth. Willie handed over his wallet. "Here to see Nelson."

The guard took his time going over Willie's ID and checking it against his list, then handed it back and pressed the button to open the motorized gates. "You have a nice day, sir."

Erin thought she detected a sneer in his voice, but she couldn't think of anything that warranted his contempt, so she brushed the feeling aside. They drove down the long driveway, and then the house came into sight. It was at least as large as the hotel they had slept in. Erin stared, her mouth gaping open.

"That's… a house?" she asked weakly.

Willie nodded. The muscles in his jaw and neck were tight, belying his calm exterior.

Erin shook her head in amazement. A dozen regular houses could have fit into the same footprint.

"How many people actually live here?"

"Good question. Dwight and his second or third wife and her kids. Nelson. I think there are a couple of grown daughters. Household staff. Security. Gardeners and groundskeepers. Whatever soldiers or guests he has at any time. All in… somewhere over fifty, I would think."

At least it wasn't just Dwight and Nelson, but it still seemed like an incredible waste of space and resources.

"It's huge," Vic observed.

Erin was glad to hear it from someone else. Willie hadn't grown up in a house like that, but he'd been there before, so he had known what to expect. Vic had grown up as part of the Jackson clan, but she hadn't lived in a mansion like that. She'd lived on a farm. Erin didn't know anything about it, but she pictured a quaint little traditional farmhouse when she thought about Vic growing up there as a child.

"It's insane. I can't imagine anyone living in a place like that."

Willie shrugged. "People live in all kinds of places. It blew me away when I first saw it too. But when it comes right down to it, it's just like animals living in different cages at the zoo. You can have a little barred cage, or a huge fenced environment they can roam around in. But either way, it's still a cage."

Was that what it was? Erin didn't consider her home a cage, and she didn't think Willie saw his that way either. But the people who lived in that huge mansion—he saw them as caged animals. That was how he had felt when he had lived there, or whatever place they'd put him in while he'd been an apprentice to the clan. He'd felt trapped and penned in—Willie, who could crawl through the narrowest caves and tunnels without feeling a flicker of claustrophobia.

They drove up to the house and Willie pulled into a small parking lot around the side, screened from sight by a row of trees. He led the way to a side door. A servants' entrance, not the front door.

He knocked a couple of times and opened the door, leading Vic and Erin in.

It was a small anteroom, where a receptionist sat at an antique desk with an appointment book and there were a number of doors leading in different directions. The receptionist looked at Willie. She raised one eyebrow.

"Mr. Andrews. I wasn't expecting to see you today."

"I have an appointment with Mr. Nelson."

"Yes, I saw that. I meant before that… no one had told me that your services would be required."

"Something came up. I arranged it with Mr. Nelson this morning. There shouldn't be any problems."

"No, no problem." She picked up the wired phone handset on the desk and pressed a button. "Mr. William Andrews," she announced. She waited for a reply. "I'll send him up."

Her gaze slid to Erin and Vic as she hung up.

"I didn't realize you were bringing anyone with you."

"Miss Victoria Webster and Miss Erin Price."

The receptionist wrote their names down. She was obviously waiting for more information, but it was not forthcoming. "And they are here as your… assistants?"

"Yes."

The woman studied Vic for a long time, frown lines between her penciled eyebrows. Then she smoothed her face and nodded. "Take the back stair," she gestured to one of the doors leading out of the room. "You know the way."

Willie jerked his head at Vic and Erin and led the way through the door and into the warren of back halls and passages. Erin tried not to gape at the wealth on display as they moved through the halls. Paintings on the walls, antique furniture topped with priceless vases, lamps, and other ornaments. She wasn't as well-versed as a collector would be, but she knew quality when she saw it.

"This is amazing," she breathed, not daring to raise her voice above a whisper.

"If you think the back rooms are something you should see the ones intended for public viewing," Willie murmured back.

Erin didn't touch anything. She was intensely aware of the video cameras that undoubtedly recorded every move. In the locations she couldn't see any cameras, she assumed they were only better hidden. Miniaturized and placed in a crack, a button, or behind a mirror. They wouldn't leave an inch of the place unmonitored. And Erin had thought she'd be able to just walk in and get Charley out of there? She could just unlock whatever door Charley was imprisoned behind and spirit her away? Even though she'd been told repeatedly how dangerous the Dysons were, she still thought she could just walk in and walk out.

Vic gave Erin a look that eloquently expressed she was thinking the same thing.

Then they were there. Willie led them through a door into an office. The carpet on the floor was thick, big tomes lined the bookshelves along the walls, and a man sat behind the walnut desk. He didn't look up immediately when they arrived, but continued to read whatever report he was paging through on his desk. Willie stood quietly waiting, and Erin and Vic followed his example.

The man eventually put the report down and looked up at them.

He was blond, with a long face, impeccably dressed and groomed. When he looked them over, he didn't seem haughty or self-important. Curious and tentative. Not sure how to proceed. He looked at each of Erin and Vic in turn, then back at Willie, the one of them that he knew, eyebrows up in a query.

"Willie. I see you brought the whole gang."

It calmed Erin to hear him call Willie by his nickname, just like he was a friend. No Mr. Andrews for him. Just a couple of guys who had worked with each other.

"This is Victoria Webster. And Erin Price."

Nelson looked at them and nodded. His eyes went back to Vic.

"Victoria Webster?" he repeated.

Vic nodded. "Vic," she advised.

He pressed his lips together, frowning, then caught himself and looked at Erin. But she apparently didn't set off anything on his radar. He looked back at Vic.

"Willie said Charley is your sister."

Vic looked over at Erin, and Erin raised her hand tentatively. "Mine."

"Yours. Erin Price…" he seemed to be consulting his mental files. "I don't think I know your family."

"No. We weren't… involved with your family in any way. Not that I know of. My parents died years ago, around the time Charley was born. I haven't been around until just recently." She was about to offer up that she had a bakery in Bald Eagle Falls, then thought better of it. Did she really want him knowing all of her business? She was sure he could ask a few questions and find out, but there wasn't any point in just handing it to him. She bit her lip and waited for him to ask anything further.

"I never knew Charley had a sister," Nelson said.

"We didn't grow up together."

"I see." He nodded. "Even siblings that grow up together can sometimes be estranged. You and Charley aren't close, then?"

Erin could feel the chance to find out where Charley was and to make sure she was okay slipping away from her. If the man decided she wasn't close enough to Charley to make any difference to them, he might just send Erin on her way.

"We met just recently, but we've hit it off. I think I can help you, Mr. Dyson. I think I can convince her to tell what happened between her and Bobby."

"Nelson, please. There are too many Mr. Dysons around here for me to keep track of when anyone is talking to me."

"Oh. Okay. Mr. Nelson."

"Just Nelson. I could call you Erin, if that would help."

Erin nodded slightly. "This is all a little bit new to me. I don't know what I'm supposed to say."

"I'm not my father. I don't expect any kind of formality."

"Okay. I'll try."

"Why don't you have a seat. Would you like drinks? Anything I can do to make you comfortable?"

"Oh, no," Erin said. "We just ate." She looked down at her clothes, not feeling much more comfortable than she would have if she'd still had on her pajamas. "I mean… nothing for me. I don't know…?" She looked at the others for their input. Vic and Willie both shook their heads.

Nelson pressed a button on his desk. "Bring Charley in."

Just like that. Erin had been expecting to have to do some heavy negotiating, but apparently that was not required. Willie had already smoothed the way for them, and Nelson, not standing on ceremony, was ready for action.

Erin swallowed and looked at the floor, not wanting to have to meet Nelson's eyes.

There were a few minutes of silence, and then a door clicked open, and Charley was escorted in.

Her eyes were down. They were dark and deep-set, like she'd lost weight in the couple of days since Erin had seen her last. Erin couldn't decide whether they were bruised or if it was just the lighting. Charley walked in under her own power, free of any restraints, but they might as well have been holding a gun to her. She walked into the middle of the room and waited there for further instructions.

"Sit down."

Charley looked around and selected a seat. She raised her eyes for a moment to look at Nelson, glanced at the rest of them, and looked back down again.

Erin waited for Nelson to say something to Charley, but he didn't. He looked at Erin and made a motion toward Charley. *There she is. All yours.*

Erin licked her lips and wished she had at least asked for a glass of water. She had no idea what she was supposed to say. She had been the one to suggest to Willie that she might be able to get Charley to talk, but she couldn't find anything to say. She swallowed.

"Uh… hi, Charley."

Charley raised her eyes to look at Erin for a moment, as if she hadn't been expecting any sound to come out of Erin's mouth.

"Hi."

"I was really worried about you. When those guys showed up to talk to you, I was really afraid of what was going to happen."

"Bright girl."

Erin was amazed that Charley could still use sarcasm as a weapon in the situation they were in. Erin was there to help Charley, but Charley was acting like they were talking privately.

"I was hoping I could help you to get out of here."

"I don't see how. You don't know the way things work around here."

"I thought that if we could prove that you were innocent, that you didn't have anything to do with Bobby's murder…"

Charley let out a short, sharp bark of laughter. "How are *we* going to do that?"

"If you'll just tell the truth about what happened that night. I know you didn't kill Bobby. If you just explain what happened…?"

"How can I do that? I wasn't even there."

"Ward is pulling surveillance video from inside and around the apartment. If you weren't in the apartment, he'll be able to verify that."

But inside, Erin knew he wasn't going to be able to verify that Charley wasn't there. The police had already reviewed her alibi and decided it had been fabricated. Why would she need to fabricate an alibi unless she was really there?

"Erin… you shouldn't be here."

"I know. But… I was in danger too. People came looking for me last night." Erin looked at Nelson. "Dysons."

"Why would they want you?" Charley scowled "you don't have anything to do with this. There was no need to bring her into this," she told Nelson. "Erin doesn't know anything. I didn't even meet her until after Bobby was dead. You know she doesn't have anything to do with her death. You shouldn't have brought her here."

"I didn't bring her here," Nelson said mildly. "She brought herself."

"She shouldn't be here. The Dysons have no reason to interfere with her."

Nelson looked at Charley, his nostrils flaring. "You seem to be under the mistaken impression that I have something to do with Erin being here. I don't. She and her friends were the ones who called me. I don't know what might have happened last night…" He looked over at Willie.

"I don't know if it was something Dwight ordered, or just a couple of soldiers deciding they needed to take care of any threats. Whatever it was… I caught wind before they got there and got Erin and Vic out. Whether there is still any kind of planned action against them, I have no idea."

"We can sort that out later," Nelson made an uncaring motion. "They can't be any safer than they are here."

"Charley, what happened?" Erin begged. "Can't you tell me? If you didn't kill Bobby, then tell them what did happen, so that they'll let you go."

"What makes you think anyone is going to let me go if I tell the truth?" Charley demanded. "I've been trying to tell them for two days that I didn't kill Bobby. I threw myself on their mercy. What else can I do?"

"Charley. Just tell us what happened. The truth."

"I was out with the girls," Charley maintained. "I have no way of knowing what happened to Bobby."

"You were out having margaritas," Erin agreed. Ward had confirmed that.

Charley looked surprised. "How… who told you that?"

"And then what happened? After last call, when everybody went home, where did you go?"

"A few of us went out for a nightcap. Just because the restaurant closes, that doesn't mean you can't go to someone's apartment and have a few more. We were having a good time. We weren't ready to hang it up for the night."

"You didn't go to the apartment of one of the other girls. You went home to Bobby."

"You don't know anything," Charley asserted. "You don't know what you're talking about."

Nelson just rubbed his chin and watched the two of them.

"You went to Bobby's apartment," Erin repeated.

"You weren't there. You don't know anything." Charley coughed. It was a deep, croupy cough that sent a chill through Erin. What had they done to Charley? Had they tortured her? Waterboarded her? Left her in a cold, dark dungeon under the big house?

The coughing didn't stop. Nelson pressed the button on his desk, but didn't give any directions this time. A woman poked her head in the door, looked at Charley for a minute, red and gasping for oxygen between the deep, wrenching coughs, and then withdrew. She was back a couple of minutes later with a tea tray. She placed it beside Charley and picked up the cup, pressing it into Charley's hand.

"Here. Drink this down. It will help, just take a few sips…"

She helped Charley to hold the cup and to take a drink. After Charley managed to get a few swallows down, her coughing gradually eased. Erin sniffed at the air. Honey and lemon. But something else, too. Something medicinal underneath it.

Charley leaned back in her seat. She closed her eyes, resting.

"She's sick," Erin said. "You need to let her go. She should be at the hospital."

"Charley's fine," Nelson said, with great unconcern. "She's tough."

"I don't know what you've been doing to her, but she's not that tough. You want her to die from pneumonia?"

Nelson raised his brows at her and didn't say anything. Erin rubbed at the goosebumps on her arms. Nelson couldn't care less whether Charley died of pneumonia. She had, as far as he was concerned, killed Bobby. Maybe pneumonia would kill her, and maybe the Dysons would, Nelson didn't really care which.

"I'm fine," Charley whispered.

Erin looked at Vic and saw the same concern in her eyes as Erin felt. At least someone else in the room cared.

"Charley. You need to tell them," Erin encouraged yet again. How many times did she have to say it before Nelson decided that Erin didn't have any sway over her sister after all and sent her on her way? Or sent her down to whatever dungeon they had been keeping Charley in?

Charley rubbed her chest. She took another drink of the honey and lemon tea. The woman who had brought it in nodded respectfully at Nelson and left again. The door closed silently behind her.

"It won't make any difference," Charley said. "They're not going to believe me."

"They don't believe you because you're lying."

"You don't know that. You don't know anything."

"Remember how you told me I wasn't a very good liar?"

Charley nodded.

"You aren't either."

Charley opened her mouth to object. Then she closed it again, scowling.

"Did you go back to see Bobby?" Erin asked. "You're the one who was yelling and fighting with him?"

Charley didn't respond for a long time. Then she finally nodded. "But I didn't kill him," she reiterated.

"Someone did."

Charley nodded. "Someone did," she agreed. "Someone set me up."

"Who?"

"Someone who wanted me to run."

Erin thought immediately of the masked man. He had told Charley to run. Erin had thought he was trying to protect Charley for some reason, but what if that weren't true? Maybe he didn't want to help her. Maybe he was trying to push her. To frame her.

"The man with the mask?" she asked.

Charley's eyes riveted on Erin. Her mouth twitched. The moniker had an obvious effect on her.

"Who is the man with the mask?" Nelson asked.

Willie looked back and forth at Erin and Charley.

"The masked man is someone who came to the apartment right before you guys picked up Charley. He talked to Charley then, and he grabbed Erin in the parking lot and threatened her and told her to stay out of things that weren't any of her concern."

"Good advice."

"The point is… there is someone else involved here. Someone whose identity we don't know."

"Or you're bluffing."

"Do you know who he is?" Erin asked Charley. "He knew who I was and where I was from. Did you tell him? Did the police leak it? Or is he from…" Erin glanced aside at Nelson, "…where I'm from?"

Charley shook her head. "How would I know? I have no idea who the guy is. I've only seen him twice and he was wearing that stupid mask both times."

"You couldn't recognize him? His eyes? His voice? His build?"

"No. No idea."

"Is he one of the Dysons? Is he with the family?"

"I don't know," Charley insisted more vehemently, raising her voice above a whisper. She coughed a couple of times and had more of the tea.

"Tell me what happened when you went back to Bobby's," Nelson said.

Charley glared at Erin, like it was her fault that Charley had gone back there and gotten herself into such deep trouble. Erin hadn't even met Charley until after that, so she didn't know how it could be her fault.

"I just went home," Charley said. "Back to Bobby's apartment to hook up. Everything was fine when I saw him earlier that day. He knew I was going out with the girls. He didn't care. We didn't have to spend every minute together."

"And maybe he had someone else he wanted to see," Nelson suggested.

Charley looked at him. Her mouth formed a thin, straight line. "Maybe he did," she agreed. "She wouldn't be the first."

"But she'd be the last. You saw to that."

"It wasn't me. That's not what happened. I got back and he was flipping out. Accusing me of all kinds of stuff. Saying that I was out with a man, showing him up and making a laughingstock of him. But I wasn't. I was just out with the girls, just like I said I'd been."

"He came after you."

Charley swallowed hard. She took another drink of her tea. For a few minutes, she didn't answer.

"Yeah," she said finally. "He did. He was raving like a lunatic. I've never seen him so mad. He was all over me, grabbing me, throwing me around. He put his hands around my neck. We crashed through the coffee table. He was freaking out. He was seriously acting like he was going to kill me with his own hands."

Nelson nodded. His nostrils flared. He kept his thoughts and feelings hidden. Erin didn't know whether he was upset over his brother's death, or the fact that he had been murdered, or if he was upset about the way his brother had treated Charley. Maybe he'd sometimes been on the receiving end of his brother's temper himself. But he maintained the mask of indifference. He would be a good poker player.

Charley set her teacup back on the tray. She covered her sunken eyes with both hands.

"He was my boyfriend," she said brokenly. "I never gave him reason to be jealous of me. I don't know if he was drunk or high, why he thought I was doing anything. I just went out with the girls."

"You had to protect yourself," Erin said. "It was self-defense."

Charley looked at Erin, her red-rimmed eyes wide. "No! It wasn't self-defense," she insisted.

"If he came after you—"

"He was going to kill me. He had his hands around my neck."

"So it was—"

"No, I didn't kill him! It was *him*. The man in the mask."

CHAPTER 26

The atmosphere in the room was electric.

Charley shook her head. "I was there and saw him do it, but I can't tell you who he was or why he did it."

"Wait—the masked man? *He* killed Bobby?" Erin's head whirled. The masked man wasn't protecting Charley. He was setting her up. He was the one who had killed Bobby, framing Charley for it. But he was the one who had told her to run. Both actions were so contradictory, she couldn't make them fit. Setting her up and then trying to save her. Were there two masked men? Two opposite sides? One from the Dysons and one from the Jacksons or somewhere else?

"Yeah." Charley shook her head bitterly. "I told you no one was going to believe me. Sure, Charley, it was a masked man. *I* wouldn't believe me."

"But if that's what happened… There must be something on the security cameras. He couldn't have gotten in and out of there without being recorded. Could he?"

There were surveillance cameras everywhere. Inside, outside, city cameras and private cameras. No one could escape them all.

"The police haven't turned up anyone wearing a mask on the surveillance cameras," Nelson said.

"How do you know?" Erin questioned.

He just looked at her.

Of course they had someone on the inside. Of course they had someone who was feeding them everything Ward turned up in his investigation. They had to know all of the details of who had killed Bobby. The Dysons couldn't have known anything about Erin unless it came from the police.

Just the same as the masked man had known who Erin was. Was he a cop? Had the police been the ones to set Charley up, hoping to either put her in jail or for her to run? Either way, she was out of the picture so they no longer had to worry about her committing crimes on their turf.

But why would they have set up Charley? Surely there were bigger fish to fry. They could have set up someone higher up the food chain. Not Nelson or Bobby, maybe, but someone who had more influence and was doing more damage than Charley.

They had gotten rid of Bobby too, though. Gotten rid of him and put Charley in the hot seat for it. Maybe Bobby was the primary target, and Charley was only a secondary consideration.

"I saw the masked man," Erin told Nelson. "He does exist. I saw him."

"You saw *a* masked man. Maybe. If you're telling the truth. But Charley could have set you up. She could have arranged for someone to act the part so you would corroborate her story."

"Charley wouldn't do that."

Charley chuckled. "The hell I wouldn't. That would be brilliant."

Erin looked at Charley in exasperation. How was she supposed to help her little sister if she was going to say things like that?

Nelson cracked a smile at Charley's retort. "Of course she would. Look, nothing about this story makes any sense. Like Charley said, we have no reason to believe her. Bobby gets blown away. Everyone heard them fighting. Charley's fingerprints were on the gun. So she's the one who killed him."

He leaned back in his chair and rubbed his head, concentrating deeply. Everyone waited on pins and needles to hear his decision. He obviously had no reason to believe Charley. Was he making up his mind whether to have Charley executed without any further regard to her protestations of innocence? What good would any further investigation do? If things had happened the way Charley said they had, then there was no way to prove it had been the unknown stranger rather than Charley.

And if he got rid of Charley, then there was no reason to leave Erin, Willie, and Vic alive. Why leave witnesses who could go to the police?

"Willie," Nelson finally spoke, "that firewall you set up for me, is it any good?"

Erin shook her head. Firewall? Why was he talking to Willie about computers? The situation was dire. His brother had been killed and, as far as he was concerned, the killer was sitting right there in front of him. Had he already decided that their lives weren't worth anything, and was more concerned with the minutiae of his life than what happened to them?

Willie shifted in his seat. "It's the best money can buy. You're looking at the level of security that the FBI or NASA has. It's very secure."

"The FBI and NASA have been hacked. You develop an encryption that's supposed to take billions of years to break, and a twelve-year-old does it with his Xbox. Anything is hackable."

"Then I'm not going to tell you it's not," Willie said. "Every system has flaws. There is no perfectly secure system."

"You've never steered me wrong in the past."

"But I'm not going to tell you it's perfect when it's not."

"And you," Nelson turns to Erin, "do you believe her?"

Erin floundered, not sure what to say. "Yes," she said finally. "I saw the masked man myself. I never believed Charley killed Bobby."

"Why do you care?"

"She's my sister."

"You never met her before."

Erin swallowed. "She's still my sister."

"Why would you get mixed up in something like this? Why don't you just go home and bake cookies?"

Erin stared at him. Was *he* the masked man? But his build wasn't right. His voice didn't have the right qualities. Terry had said that it wouldn't be hard to learn these basics about Erin. Of course Nelson had done his homework.

"I don't believe she did it. I don't want to lose her after I just found her."

Nelson turned to look at Vic. "James Jackson."

The color drained from Vic's face, turning her chalk white. "That's not my name anymore."

"Why would you bring a Jackson into my house?" Nelson demanded. He didn't look at Willie's face.

Willie reached out and took Vic by the hand. He held it protectively. "I brought Vic here to protect her."

They had walked into Nelson's office thinking they knew more than he did. They walked in there figuring they had their secrets intact. But he knew all along who each of them was and what each of them was. Of course. Had they thought he was some kind of patsy? The geeky son. The second in line. He wasn't the playboy, bold and brash and sure of his inheritance. He was a long-legged spider, sitting in the middle of his web, inviting them all in.

Had *he* sent the masked man? Had he been the one to kill Bobby and set Charley up to take the fall? If he had been the masked man, then surely Charley would have recognized him, but that didn't mean he couldn't send someone to act the part, just as he had accused Charley of doing. Had it all been a ploy for him to get in line to inherit the role of capo in his family?

Nelson watched Erin, his eyes quick and cunning. "No," he told her, "I have no interest in becoming the boss of this family or any other. I'd rather play with my toys. Willie knows that."

Erin took a quick glance at Willie, hoping for some reassurance. But Willie didn't look reassuring. He held Vic's hand in his, eyes darting around the room looking for an avenue of escape.

"But that doesn't mean I'm stupid. I've always been a much better boss than Bobby, even though he was the heir, the one groomed to take over the running of the family. I wouldn't have survived this long if I had just been sitting around, ignorant of the jealousies and politics of this organization. You think there are people who wouldn't take my position if they could? You think they want some nerdy upstart giving them orders and being promoted to a position he doesn't want or deserve?"

Nelson's voice hung in the air. No one dared say anything to him. Erin feared that, just like on TV, this was the monologue leading up to their deaths. The explanation as to why they had to die.

"Willie brought you here. Willie can tell you that I'm not just some kid who's acting too big for his britches. He knows I've been building my own network. My own organization within the family. Loyal to me. Firewalled from the rest of the system, just like my computers. I may look dull, but I've been planning this for years."

It was him. He was the one who had arranged to have Bobby killed, setting Charley up to take the fall. He hadn't been sitting on the sidelines in ignorance. He'd set the whole plan into motion.

Nelson shook his head. "No. I don't know who the masked man is. He comes bumbling into the middle of everything, winding Bobby up and then killing him when things get out of hand. I have no idea who the guy is or where he came from. With the mask on, there's no way to get facial recognition. He avoided the cameras like a pro; he'd obviously scouted the area ahead of time. So I've got nothing to go on. Nothing but what the two of you can tell me about what you saw."

"You knew all along?" Charley demanded, her voice hoarse. "For two days, I've been interrogated by your father and his thugs, and you knew all along that I wasn't the one who killed Bobby?"

Nelson lifted an eyebrow. "I'm sorry, but when you joined up with the Dysons, were you under the impression that everyone was going to play fair and have consideration for your feelings? Or did you think you were joining a criminal enterprise? When you chose Bobby over me or someone else in the organization, was it because you thought he was a kind and sensitive soul who would take care of you?" He snorted. "You knew exactly what you were getting into, Charley Campbell. Don't blame me for getting burned when you chose to play with fire."

"You got it all on video?" Erin asked, parsing what he had just told them. "You saw what happened and you have physical evidence that it wasn't Charley?"

"If you really want to clear your sister," Nelson paused to give Charley a look of distaste, "even after seeing what kind of a person she is, then you need to cooperate with me. Otherwise... no, there is no evidence. You'll have to rely on the evidence the cops have got, and the only person it implicates is Charley."

"Cooperate with you?" Erin exchanged glances with Willie, Charley, and Vic, trying to gauge their reactions. "What do you expect me to do? I don't have connections with any of these people. I don't have any skills that would benefit you, unless you're in need of a batch of chocolate chip cookies."

Nelson's mouth twisted into a smirk. "Don't sell yourself short. I think you've demonstrated considerable skills."

"Nelson, Erin isn't one of your employees. She doesn't want to be associated with the Dysons or any other family," Willie said.

"Unlike James," Nelson said, looking hard at Vic.

"Victoria," she corrected evenly.

"Changing your name doesn't change who and what you were born as,"

Nelson said. "If I'm right, this all goes back to the Jacksons, and here is little James Jackson sitting in my office."

"I didn't have anything to do with it. If you've looked into my background, you know I don't have anything to do with my immediate family, let alone the extended Jackson clan."

Nelson leaned his head back against the headrest of his chair and gazed at her.

"I think you could find out."

"Find out what?"

"Who the masked man is, or who sent or hired him."

"What makes you think it was one of the Jacksons?" Willie asked.

"It wasn't internal. It wasn't the cops. The next logical suspect is the Jacksons."

Vic leaned forward in her chair. "So you want me to go to my family and casually find out if they happen to know who killed Bobby."

Nelson shrugged. "I don't care how you do it."

Vic looked at Erin. Erin knew how much Vic hated the thought of running to her family or having to deal with them and their prejudice.

Erin shook her head. "You don't have to, Vicky. We'll find another way to sort it out. Charley didn't do it and there is video out there that proves it. The masked man is out there. People know things. We can figure it out."

"How? Mr. Dyson obviously isn't giving up the video. If the masked man is smart enough to wear a mask and avoid the cameras, he is smart enough to avoid our bungling attempts to find out who he is. We're bakers, not detectives."

"We know people with skills," Erin said stubbornly. She was thinking of Terry and Willie specifically, but she wasn't going to name names in front of Nelson, who was obviously too smart for his own good. Terry was a trained investigator, and Willie had set up that firewall and would know its weaknesses. Maybe there was a backdoor or administrative password in case Nelson forgot his. And if Nelson had captured video of the masked man killing Bobby, then there was a chance that someone else had seen it or had access to it. "Let Charley go with us," she told Nelson, "and we'll see what we can find out."

"Why would I let Charley go?"

"Why would you keep her here in the first place? You knew she wasn't the killer. Why would you let her take the punishment for something she didn't do?"

"She hasn't been punished for the murder." Nelson's eyes glittered. "There's only one punishment for killing a member of the family. She's just been incentivized to tell us what she knew. And apparently, to motivate you to act. Why would I take away that motivation?"

"We're still going to be motivated if she comes with us. I get that you've got people out there who can take us at a moment's notice. I get that you have eyes and ears all over the place, including in the police department. I'll be motivated because I don't want to come back here, and I don't want any of my friends coming back here."

Nelson raised one eyebrow. He went back to the report on his desk, ignoring them. Erin assumed he was thinking it through, clearing his mind by focusing on something else for a few minutes. She often distracted herself in order to relax and look at a problem again with fresh eyes.

After a few moments of silence, Nelson looked up at them. "Nobody is keeping you here," he pointed out. "I have other things to work on."

Erin looked at Willie. He was the one who knew Nelson and understood the dynamics of the clan, something Erin couldn't even come close to doing. Willie got to his feet. He motioned the three women to come with him. Erin felt panic rising as they left the room and wound their way back through the halls again. She felt like they were walking in slow motion, and that any minute, they would all be the target of one of Nelson's minions. They would shoot her in the head, or drag her back to the cell Charley had been imprisoned in. But he wasn't just going to let them walk out of there.

None of them said a word as they traipsed back to the car. They piled in and fastened their seatbelts with shaking hands. Vic sat shotgun beside Willie. Erin looked anxiously at Willie, trying to assess his stress level. He was the one who knew Nelson and the family. He was the one who knew how scared they should be. But his face was a mask and Erin didn't know what he was thinking or feeling. He shifted gears and pulled out into the driveway. They backtracked the curves and came up to the gate again. It swung open in front of them, and Willie drove through.

Erin let out a huge sigh of relief. She wasn't the only one.

"Oh, lordy," Vic exclaimed, fanning herself with her hand. "I was scared as a jack-rabbit that's heard the howl of a wolf. I about wet my pants!"

"I never would have guessed it," Erin said admiringly. "I couldn't tell."

"You don't need to lie to me. I was sweating buckets. Must smell to high heaven." Vic slumped back in her seat, trying to relax. She wiped her forehead.

"If you two are done," Charley said, "we should talk about what we're going to do."

"If one of the options is to run away and never come back..." Vic suggested.

"You think we could ever run far enough that they wouldn't find us?" Charley shot back.

"We've all run away before," Erin said, looking at each of them. "I don't think it solved all of our problems, though, did it? If we ran… there'd be no more Auntie Clem's, Vic. That life would be over. We'd go somewhere else, use new names, and start all over again. New friends, new jobs, new city…"

"I know," Vic admitted. "I'm just scared, and it's so tempting."

"I've done it before. More than once. And it never solves all the problems."

"Right now, we've only got one problem," Charley said. "And that's keeping alive. If we're going to keep alive, we have to figure this out. Who this guy was that killed Bobby."

"Should we go to the police?" Erin suggested. "Jack Ward? Terry? One of them could help us."

"No, Erin," Willie growled. "The police are not going to help us get out of this. You go to the cops, and the clan is going to come gunning for us. And I don't mean that in a figurative way."

"Then what? Do you know how to get into his system to get the video?"

"It's a possibility," Willie said. "But I think our first step should be to show compliance, not to hack his system."

Erin looked at Charley, then at Vic. Vic's arms were folded over her stomach and she was looking down. Despite her earlier jocularity, Vic looked ready to cry.

"Tell me you don't mean going to my family," she begged.

"I know that's the last thing you want to do," Willie said gently. "No more than I would go back to mine, if I could. But we need information. We need to get some clue of whether the Jacksons are involved in this. And I don't know how else to get it. I can't exactly go walking into one of their watering holes."

Vic held her hands over her face, giving a sob. Erin wished that Vic were sitting in the back so Erin could give her a hug. She had to settle instead for reaching up and giving Vic's shoulder a squeeze.

"I'm sorry, Vicky. I'm so sorry."

"It's not your fault." Vic's voice was muffled by her hands. "I'll be fine."

"What can I do? I want to help you."

Vic shook her head. "I don't know what to do. I swore I'd never go back there. They all thought it was a big joke, that I'd be back in a day or two, tail between my legs, having learned my lesson. I swore it wouldn't happen. I'd never go back there."

"You didn't. You came and worked with me and made a life for yourself. You made adult choices and took responsibility for yourself. This isn't crawling back to them, Vic. If we go back…" Erin scowled at Willie for saying that it was the next logical step. He had to know how that would affect Vic. "It's a fact-finding mission. Not because you made a wrong choice and regret what you did."

"But I can't go back there as myself. If I go back as Vic, no one is going to trust me or tell me anything. They'll just laugh and tease and keep things from me like I'm an outsider."

Erin didn't know what to say. She knew how important it was for Vic to be true to herself and her identity. If she couldn't go back as herself, she couldn't go back. Expecting her to was just too cruel.

"Willie… we need to come up with another plan," Erin said. "There has to be another way."

Willie shook his head. "Okay. We'll see what else we can come up with. We need a place to land for a few minutes to recoup." Willie looked in the rear-view mirror toward Charley. "You have a suggestion?"

"Let's just go back to my place. It's not like they're going to come back for me again. Nelson let me go. He knows the truth. If Dwight decides to overrule him… well, it doesn't really matter where we go, they'll find us one way or another."

"Your place it is," Willie agreed. He took a right turn at the next intersection, and Erin realized as they went back to Charley's apartment that Charley wasn't giving Willie any directions. He knew exactly where he was going. Erin glanced at Vic to see if she noticed, but Vic's thoughts were far from the occupants of the car and their destination.

"What about the man in the mask, though?" Erin asked. "What if he comes back to your apartment? He knows where you live."

"If he comes back, he'd better come guns a-blazing, because I'm not putting up with any more mystery nonsense. If he shows his face—or his mask—I'm blowing the dude away."

Erin wasn't sure that made her feel any better. Willie glanced at her and didn't say anything.

Once parked, everyone followed Charley up to her apartment. Charley and Willie entered cautiously, checked out the extent of the small apartment, and returned to the door to let Erin and Vic know it was safe to enter.

Erin looked around the front room and kitchen of the now-familiar apartment and gave a sigh. The day was slipping away. They needed to make a plan. The next day was Monday, and Erin would need to be up bright and early to run the bakery. It seemed like a long time since she had been at Auntie Clem's, and it felt farther away than ever before.

Charley had her head in the fridge. Erin suspected she probably hadn't eaten well, if anything, in the previous two days. At least the rest of them had started the day with coffee and a continental breakfast. But when Charley straightened and backed up, she didn't have leftover casserole or takeout in her hand, but one of the flat bowls Erin recognized as coming from the pet store.

Of course. Iggy hadn't eaten in two days, and Charley was more concerned about looking after the lizard than herself. Charley put the dish on the counter. She caught Erin's eyes on her.

"Have to let them warm up a bit," she commented. "They get too slow when they're cold. They'll be more active once they warm."

"What—?" Vic started to ask, and then cut herself off. She saw Erin's expression and realized what they were talking about. She gave Erin a little smile. "You're so squeamish. We need to take you fishing sometime."

Erin gagged at the thought of having to bait hooks. She couldn't imagine touching the worms or other bait that would be required, let alone impaling them on sharp hooks.

"No, thank you! I'll get my fish at the grocery store."

Though the truth was, Erin wasn't much of a fish person. The nauseating smell was enough to put Erin off her feed for the rest of the day.

"They're not that bad," Charley said, nodding to the bowl. "They don't stink and they're not slimy…"

"I don't want to hear about it," Erin insisted. "You go ahead and feed Iggy, but leave me out of it. I don't want to see or hear or smell what you're giving him."

"They need to warm up for a few minutes. Then I will. Sorry."

She turned back to the fridge. "Man, am I hungry! You know, there were roaches in the room they kept me in, and I just kept thinking how Iggy would love them. And with getting hungrier and hungrier, I was thinking… people can eat bugs. They're a delicacy in some countries. Lots of protein, a real lean meat."

"No way," Erin said. "Doesn't matter how hungry I got, I would never eat a bug. Not on purpose."

"What about cricket flour?" Vic suggested. "I've seen it online. It's gluten free."

"I don't care. I'm still not putting it in my baking. That's disgusting."

"You know there are bug eggs and larvae in the flour you use, don't you?" Charley asked. "That's why you have to put it in the freezer if you don't want it to go bad."

"No," Erin protested, covering her ears. "You guys cut it out. No more talking about bugs."

Willie was sitting on the couch, thumbing through his phone. The insect conversation was going right over his head. Erin knew that she and the others were giddy with their nervousness and anxiety over what was going on, but she sobered at Willie's grim expression, and Vic and Charley quickly became serious as well. Charley pulled a plastic box out of the fridge, along with a bottle of juice.

"Anyone else wants anything, just help yourself," she invited. And don't worry, there's no more bugs in there. You can open anything up without fear."

She sat down with her scavenged lunch.

"So. What are we going to do?"

"Maybe you could make some phone calls," Willie suggested. "Is there anyone you can call on who might have an idea of what's going on?"

Charley pursed her lips and shook her head. "No... not really. If it's something to do with the Jacksons, I can't think of anyone I could touch."

"There are always people who have a foot in both camps."

"I've stayed as far away from those types as possible. I've got no intention of being accused of being a turncoat." She paused for a moment. "I thought staying away from those kinds of people would keep me safe, but obviously not. What about you? You're the big disappointment. The one who did his five years and then decided it wasn't for you." Charley popped the top of the can and had a swig. "Usually after five years, you're either dead or in too deep to pull out," she informed Erin and Vic. "People just don't do their tour and then bow out."

"Usually," Willie amended.

"Usually."

"I've got a couple of people to tap," Willie said, his eyes still on his phone screen. "But it's a long shot. I'm not confident they'll know anything or want to talk to me."

～

In another hour, Willie had exhausted his contacts. Pale but determined, Vic looked to Charley for help.

"If I'm going to go visit my family, I'm going to need to dress down," she said. "I'm going to need some clothes that look a little less…" She looked down at herself, trailing off.

"Less feminine?" Charley suggested.

Erin winced. Vic loved her clothes. She loved dressing up and looking good. While Erin was happiest in a pair of jeans and a t-shirt, Vic had a flair for making herself look pretty.

"Yeah," Vic agreed. "That."

"I have to admit, I've been wondering since Nelson called you James. I never met a transvestite in real life."

"Transgender," Erin corrected her quickly. "And it's really no one's business—"

"It's okay, Erin," Vic said. "I can deal with it. Yes, it's transgender, and I just need to know if you've got… tennis shoes and a hoodie… something that will make me a little less… different. More like I dressed before I left home."

"Sure," Charley agreed. "Come with me. We'll find you something."

Vic followed Charley into her bedroom. Erin looked at Willie, not sure what she should do. Follow them and try to run interference and make Vic feel as comfortable as possible? Or stay out of the way and not make such a big deal of it?

"Nothing we can do," Willie said. "Just be supportive. She knows you love her for who she is. She can take strength in that."

"And you too," Erin agreed.

"I'm not so sure. This is not something I should be pushing her into. I just don't know what else to do. I've done my best to stay on the good side of these guys in spite of not staying inside the organization. I never foresaw it causing Vic any pain."

"It's not your fault. I'm the one who made contact with Charley. If I hadn't done that, we wouldn't be here. We wouldn't be in this situation."

"You had no way of knowing."

"Neither did you."

They both sat there, lost in their own morose thoughts, waiting for Vic and Charley to return.

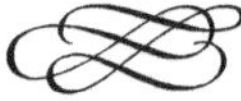

Erin barely recognized Vic when she came into the living room after changing and washing off her makeup. She wore a shapeless, faded hoodie with the logo of a Tennessee college on it, sneakers, and had her hair pulled back and hidden under the hood of the sweatshirt. Her face looked rougher and more angular without the softening lines of her makeup. Erin could still see the familiar face and expression of her friend, but she could also see the face of the boy she had first seen in the "missing" advertisement of the Bald Eagles weekly newspaper months before. She was still Vic, but she was much closer to James than she had ever been in the months Erin had known her.

Erin bit her lip and looked away, not meeting Vic's eye. Vic didn't need anyone telling her that she looked fine or that she was still the person she had always been. She hadn't changed as a way of exploring another side of herself, but because she had a job to do.

"Okay," Vic said. "Let's go."

Willie stood up. "Where to?"

"I'll have to put in an appearance at the farm. I never associated with the wider clan, so I'll have to start with where I'm known."

Willie nodded. After Charley fed the room-temperature bugs to Iggy, they all headed back down to the car.

"It's just a costume," Charley told Vic, trying to cheer her up. "Just like for Halloween or a play. It doesn't change the person you are. It's just clothes."

Vic nodded.

"It's going to be all right," Charley encouraged.

"Charley…" Willie said. "Just shut up, please? You're not helping."

"I'm just trying to—"

"Just drop it. You don't know what you're talking about."

Charley opened her mouth to argue. She stopped, looking at them, then shook her head.

"Okay. I admit I don't know thing one about being transvestite. Transgender. I'm just trying to be positive."

No one said anything to her.

"Got it," Charley sighed. "Shutting up."

They didn't say anything as they got into the car. When Willie and Vic were once again settled in the front, Vic gave Willie directions in a soft, husky voice. It took almost an hour to get to the farm.

In spite of Erin's concern for her, she was interested in seeing where Vic had come from. Here she had grown up climbing trees, shooting squirrels and other varmints, and doing whatever chores were expected of her. She wrestled with her brothers, went to church on Sunday, and went to school, all as James, another one of the boys.

A man walked out of the whitewashed farmhouse when they stopped. He walked with a cane, leaning heavily on it but giving the impression of great strength rather than frailty. She could only imagine how imposing he had been before the accident that had left him with what Vic had simply called 'a bum leg.'

"Can I help you folks?" he asked gruffly, confident they had just taken a wrong turn off the highway.

"Pa," Vic said.

He looked at her. He stared. His brows furrowed deeply. "James Victor Jackson," he rumbled. "As I recall, you said you were never setting foot on this property again."

"I know, Pa," Vic said. "And I wouldn't. I just… there's been some things going on, and I needed to see you and Mom again. I needed to make sure… everything is going okay with you."

"Your ma and I are still above ground. Every day is a blessing of the Lord."

"It's just… could I come in and talk for a bit? And my friends?"

Mr. Jackson looked at the four of them with a calculating look. Was he trying to divine their relationships? Deciding whether they were two couples? If Erin had been in front with Willie and Vic in back with Charley, it would have been a more likely scenario. His eyes lingered on Willie and he took a long, slow blink. Erin was used to Willie getting second looks due to his darkly-stained skin and the state of his clothes, but this didn't look like one of those looks. Erin was expecting him to say he knew Willie.

"Maybe you know each other," she said, "from Trenton Plaint's funeral?"

Mr. Jackson blinked. "Mebbe."

Vic didn't offer up that Willie was her boyfriend. Not when she was there looking for information. Not when she needed to be an insider for just a little while. For as long as it took to get the information they needed, and then they would be gone.

"Can we maybe come in?" Vic prompted again.

He gave a shrug and stepped back, using his cane deliberately to avoid losing his footing. "Your ma would hogtie me and beat the livin' tar out of me if she knew you'd been here and I turned you away. So you may as well come in. But you know what we think of this nonsense. You're not coming back here unless you give up these ideas about being something you're not. It's unnatural and it's a sin."

"Yes, Pa."

They all got out of the car. Not looking at each other, embarrassed to be caught between the opposite ideologies. They followed Mr. Jackson into the house, in through a door that led to the kitchen. It was overly warm. The stove was on, the air humid and redolent with the smells of fresh baking, roast, and potatoes. Mr. Jackson took a deep breath of the savory air as he stepped in.

"Like walkin' into paradise, Mother."

The heavy woman at the stove turned around, smile wide, to answer him. But her smile and words dropped away when she saw the three visitors entering her domain.

"Oh, my stars, it's James!" She put down her spoon and strode over to Vic, enfolding her in a big hug.

"You're home! You came home! I prayed every day you were gone. Thank the Lord for his goodness."

Vic pulled back from the hug. "I'm not home, Mom. Just for a visit. I wanted to make sure y'all were okay. Catch up on everything that's been going on." She glanced over at Willie for reassurance. It was putting a lot on her to expect her to be able to walk into her family home and somehow to extract a clue as to what had been going on in Moose River. Even if Bobby's death had been orchestrated by the Jacksons, there was no guarantee that her family knew anything about it, or that they would have any reason to tell her.

Mrs. Jackson held Vic at arm's length, looking over her critically. "I swear, I don't know what's wrong with you, child. I raised you right. We raised all of you to be strong, hard-working, faithful men. And you…" She shook her head.

Vic swallowed. She indicated the other visitors. "Mom and Dad, this is my friend and boss, Erin, and her sister Charlotte, and William, a friend of ours."

"Well, it's might nice to meet y'all. I'm grateful to you for being good friends to my boy."

They all tried to smile and nod and be pleasant, but Erin was fighting back her fury at them for treating Vic the way they did. Not accepting her identity, telling her it was a sin, refusing to call her by her chosen name. Vic had run away from home as soon as she could to escape their condemnation and recriminations. Erin couldn't understand how people who claimed to love everyone could treat her like a pariah for being true to herself.

"Should we go to the sitting room?" Mrs. Jackson suggested. "I can leave the stove for a bit now. We'll be more comfortable."

Everyone agreed and followed her into the next room. The sitting room was dim, almost too dark, due to the closed blinds and curtains shutting out the Tennessee sun. It was much cooler than the kitchen. Mr. and Mrs. Jackson took their favorite seats and Vic motioned to her friends to pick what places they wanted. She sat on the couch with Willie, but she didn't cuddle up to him like she would have if they were at Erin's house. Instead, she sat several inches away from him, her back stiff, hands in her lap.

"Erin is my boss at the bakery," Vic said. "She gave me a job and I rent an apartment over her garage. It's my own little place, and it's really nice. We drive to work together."

"Sounds like a good arrangement," Mr. Jackson said. "That's where you were working when we came out for the funeral?"

"Yes, sir."

"People told us about the bakery when we were there," Mrs. Jackson recalled. "Said it made those weird, trendy foods…"

"It's a gluten-free bakery," Erin explained. "And we cater to other special diets as well."

"Well, I suppose there are them that need it," Mr. Jackson said doubtfully. "Though it seems to me that it's more of a fad these days. When I was a young buck, there weren't any of these places around. Everybody ate bread and potatoes and meat. Now, you have gluten-free, and allergies, and those crazy vegans. Seems like everybody's got some kind of special needs all of the sudden."

"They've been around for hundreds and thousands of years," Erin said. "It's hard to say whether they are more prevalent now, or if we just understand more about them so that so many people aren't dying from celiac disease and allergic reactions. Even a hundred years ago, if someone had a severe reaction, they would just die."

Mr. Jackson gave a ponderous shrug. "God takes who he takes," he pronounced. "We can't always divine the reason."

Erin tried to work out what to say in response to that. The fatalistic attitude was one of the things that she never understood about religious people. As if man had no choice in his own life path, and there was no point in trying to stay healthy and extend his life. Because no matter what he did, one day, God would just reach down from the sky and point his finger and the man would die.

Mrs. Jackson whispered something to her husband and darted a glance at Erin, her face pink.

"An atheist?" Mr. Jackson repeated, as if the comment had been shared with the entire room. "I suppose that explains everything."

Erin blinked. She looked at Vic, trying to get a read on the situation, but Vic's face was blank and her attention was somewhere far away. Physically, she was sitting in the room, but it was obvious to Erin that she was in pain. It was all Vic could do to sit there and talk with her parents as if they were on perfectly good terms. All for Erin's sister. A half-sister who Erin had to admit she didn't even really like. And she wasn't sure Charley liked her either. It had been handy for her to have Erin around, but Erin wasn't at all sure Charley would have had anything to do with her if she hadn't needed someone to help her.

"Excuse me? Explains what?" Erin asked.

"Why you would hire someone like James, in spite of… his confusion. No Christian would ever have a—a person like that in their workplace."

"Then it's a good thing she came to me," Erin said, her jaw sore with how hard she was clenching it. "She's a good baker. You should be proud of how hard she works. I couldn't run the place without her."

Mr. Jackson glared at Erin.

Had she just thrown away any chance they had of finding out who Bobby's killer was? If she alienated Vic's father, how would they find out if something was going on with the Jacksons? But Erin couldn't bear to hear them maligning and misgendering Vic and not stand up for her.

"James was always good in the kitchen," Mrs. Jackson admitted. "Out of all of my boys, he was the only one who was ever interested in learning how to cook and bake."

She received Mr. Jackson's next glare and quavered under his gaze.

"I'm here now," Vic said, her voice cracking a little in desperation. "I, uh, heard some rumors about stuff going on down in Moose River and I was worried that there might be problems here…"

"What stuff?" Mr. Jackson demanded, pulling his eyes away from his wife.

"About Bobby Dyson getting shot," Vic said. "It's been all over the news. I was worried about relations between the families. Stuff like that always causes tensions."

Mr. Jackson nodded, frowning deeply. "You heard about that all the way to Bald Eagle Falls? Nasty business. Who would do a thing like that?"

Mrs. Jackson shook her head. "It could start a whole war," she agreed. "Things have been pretty quiet between the families lately. The usual upsets, but nothing major. And then Bobby Dyson." She closed her eyes and continued to shake her head slowly. "He was a horrible boy, but I would never suggest anyone killing him. It's a bad, bad idea."

Erin took a quick glance at Charley to see how she took the comment about Bobby being 'a horrible boy,' but Charley didn't seem to be offended by it. He had, after all, tried to kill Charley. If he was regularly violent with her and cheated on her as she'd said, Charley had probably had much worse thoughts about him than that he was a horrible boy.

"Do you know who did it?" Vic asked, eager to get the news and get out of there.

"I heard it was his girlfriend," Mrs. Jackson offered in a low voice.

"It wasn't," Vic said. "There was someone else there. It was all caught on video."

"Then you know who did it?"

"No, because the video didn't show his face. The police can't identify him. They need more evidence. Better proof."

"How do you know all that?" Mr. Jackson asked suspiciously.

"I… I know the police in Bald Eagle Falls. Erin is really good friends with one of the officers. So we see him and talk with him a lot. He knew I was from around here, so he thought I would be interested."

"And they have video of Bobby Dyson getting killed?"

Vic tried to avoid getting tangled up in the details. "It's so frustrating," she said, leaning forward confidentially, "because if they can't prove who it is, then they're going to think it was done by the Jackson clan. And I don't know if it was."

Mr. Jackson looked at his wife and shook his head. "I haven't heard anything like that. Do you think it was the family?"

"It *is* the Dysons," she said.

"I don't know." Mr. Jackson shook his head at Vic. "I don't think so. We would have heard something through the organization. Once news spread about Bobby getting killed, there would have been rumblings."

"And nothing…?" Vic asked. That wasn't good news. Not when they needed to prove Charley's innocence if they were all to stay safe. If it wasn't one of the Jacksons, then it was back to the drawing board, and Nelson was not going to like that. He was going to think they were just putting him off.

"No," Vic's father said. "Nothing at all. If it was someone in the family, they kept it quiet. Couldn't have been official business."

"Oh." Vic was trying to look reassured at this news. "I'm glad. I was worried that it was… someone in the family. Someone that we knew."

Mrs. Jackson's eyes flashed, picking up something from Vic's words and body language that Erin hadn't. "Your own brothers, James? For shame. I can't believe you would even think such a thing."

"No… I didn't really think so, but you worry about your own family. And the boys are always so… so brash and boastful. They'd love to be able to say that they had done something like that."

"Certainly not," Mrs. Jackson said primly. But Erin caught an uneasy look exchanged between Mrs. Jackson and her husband. Not this time, maybe. But sometime soon.

"Good," Vic repeated. "I guess that's all I wanted to know. I was just worried."

"You should know better. Don't speculate. Don't judge your brothers. They're good boys."

"I know they are. Is anyone around today? I kind of thought I'd be able to say hi. To Jeremy, at least."

"They're all out working. But they'll be back for supper. Which I'd better check on…" Mrs. Jackson leaned forward, hands on knees, until she managed to raise herself up. She shuffled toward the kitchen. "We wouldn't want it getting ruined because we're having so much fun visiting."

Erin's stomach growled at the thought of food, but no one invited them to stay. Vic's eyes followed her mother out of the room, and Erin wondered if Vic wanted to talk to her alone. Mr. Jackson quickly took advantage of his wife's departure.

"Why don't you come home for good, James? We never turned you out. You could come back, if you weren't so stubborn. You can see that you've made a mistake. We accept that. Everybody makes mistakes."

Vic chewed on her lip, looking down. "It wasn't a mistake," she said softly. "And if you're waiting for me to admit that it was, you're going to end up waiting a long time. I could never move back here because you and Mom would never accept me the way I am. Besides, I'm an adult now. I have my own life, and I like it. I'm comfortable in my own apartment, with new friends…" Her eyes went to Willie, but she didn't out him as her boyfriend. "I love my job. I like helping people and nourishing them. Making sure that they can get really good food that isn't going to make them sick."

"I wouldn't think that such a place would make much of a profit," Mr. Jackson said, rubbing the space between his eyebrows like he was getting a headache. "It doesn't seem to me that there would be that many people who would want to eat there. Maybe in the big city, where there is more demand for… unusual foods… but in a little town like Bald Eagle Falls? You would be much better off working at a conventional bakery. Like your Aunt Angela had."

"Erin's bakery has been doing really well. It's the only bakery in town, so we get plenty of people who are just looking for good freshly-baked goods, whether it is gluten-free or not. And we're always looking for ways to expand and place our products in more locations. Like the local restaurants, bake sales, county fair, everywhere you could think of."

"Who got Angela's bakery?" Mr. Jackson asked. "Are they going to reopen it?"

"He'd like to," Erin said, "but he's run into some legal trouble."

"Who is that?" Mr. Jackson asked.

"Davis Plaint."

"Davis?" He scowled. "How would it go to Davis? I thought Angela left everything to Trenton. Did Davis challenge the will in court? Or did she change it?"

Erin shook her head. "It's a little complicated. Angela left it to Trenton. But he died intestate—without making a will—and when that happens, then the state's intestacy laws go into effect. His estate goes first to his parents, if either of them is surviving. So that means it would go to Adam Plaint, who at that point was only missing. He hadn't been declared dead. The estate had to try to find him, so they hired Alton Summers for that. He's good at that, he's the one who tracked down Trenton and Davis." Erin looked over at Vic, worried she was monopolizing the conversation. But Vic was again staring off the other direction, apparently happy to have someone else keeping her father engaged. "I don't know how much of this you already know…"

Mr. Jackson was leaning forward, interested. "Go on," he encouraged.

"Then we found out that Adam Plaint was dead. He had been for years, long before Angela died. So her estate could never flow into his."

"Where does his estate go? If Trenton's assets go to him, then…"

"But Trenton's estate couldn't flow into his either. Same reason. Adam died years before Trenton did."

"So Trenton's estate, the bakery, goes to Davis?"

"Right." Erin nodded. "Since Trenton died intestate, and neither of his parents were living, it then goes to his siblings. Their sister also died a number of years ago. It was just Trenton and Davis. So the bakery that Angela left to Trenton actually ends up going to Davis… except he's in prison right now, so he can't actually start it up again. My guess is that he'll have to liquidate it instead…"

Vic's head suddenly went up and she looked at Erin. Erin tried to read the surprised expression on her face. Charley's head turned slowly toward Erin at the same time.

Erin's jaw dropped. "Except… it wasn't just Trenton and Davis."

Mr. Jackson snorted. "Of course it was. You're not telling me that Sophie is still alive and just faked her own death."

"No. Not Sophie. Adam Plaint fathered one more child just before he died."

"Angela never had any more children. He disappeared from the picture. Are you telling me he picked up with some other woman?"

"Yes!" Erin didn't mean to sound so delighted about something that had had such a lasting negative effect on her life. All eyes in the room were on her. Willie had caught up with what the others had realized and was looking not at Erin, but at Charley in wide-eyed shock. "He had an affair with my mother. And she became pregnant with Charley!" She quickly amended, as they had decided it was best not to use Charley's nickname with the Jacksons and give away who she actually was. "With Charlotte, I mean." Erin pointed to Charley. "My sister is also Trenton's sister. Since she and Davis both survived Trenton, they both receive equal shares in the estate. Half of the bakery!"

For a moment, the room just sat in stunned silence. Charley looked at Erin like she was crazy.

"What are you talking about?"

"I told you that you were my half-sister. My mother's child. With Adam Plaint. That means you're Trenton Plaint's sister too, and you and Davis both inherit a half share of the bakery."

"What bakery? Your bakery?"

"No, Angela Plaint's bakery. The Bake Shoppe. In Bald Eagle Falls."

"And you think I own half of it now?" She shook her head in confusion. "No one has contacted me about that."

Erin looked at Charley, blinking as the possibilities each clicked into place.

"Erin," Willie said, "maybe Bobby wasn't the target. Maybe that was just misdirection. Maybe this was all about Charlotte."

"*Charlotte,*" Erin repeated. "The masked man. He didn't say… your nickname. He said Charlotte."

"Why does that matter?"

"Because it means he didn't know you. He didn't know you personally, and he didn't know you through… your boss. He only knew your name."

"Okay. So he didn't know me. That's kind of a relief. I'd rather it wasn't someone I know. But again… what does it matter?"

"No one told you that you were an heir to Trenton's estate?"

"I think I'd remember that."

"Somebody should have come." Erin looked at Vic and Willie for their input. "Alton Summers was hired by Clementine's estate to find me. He was hired by Angela's estate to find Trenton and Davis and then to look into Adam's disappearance. It's what he does. So why didn't they hire him to find Charlotte?"

"Maybe they did… maybe Davis himself did," Willie said.

"I'm telling you, no one called me," Charley reiterated.

Willie's eyes were bright against his dark face. "Think about it. Davis doesn't want to split the estate fifty-fifty. He wants to run The Bake Shoppe. And if he can't open The Bake Shoppe, then he wants to get the money for it. All the money for it, not half. So he hires Alton to find Charlotte, but not to inform her of her rights in the estate. To get her out of the picture."

Charley swore under her breath. All eyes in the room were on her. "Nelson said that the masked man 'wound Bobby up' and then killed him when things got out of hand. *Why* would he intentionally wind Bobby up?"

"So Bobby would break up with you," Erin deduced.

"A messy breakup with Bobby Dyson would mean you would have to leave," Willie said. "There's no way you could stay here and continue to work with the Dysons if there was bad blood between you and Bobby."

"Wait a minute," Mr. Jackson was starting to clue in to what they were talking about. He pointed to Charley. "This is Bobby's girlfriend?" He turned to Vic. "You brought one of the Dyson clan into my house?"

"We had to find out who killed Bobby—" Vic started to explain.

"You're working for the Dysons? My own son?"

"I'm—no—they just… they kidnapped Charley, and she's Erin's sister, so we were trying to help her out…"

Mr. Jackson was struggling to his feet, using the cane to push himself up. "I thought when you left here that there couldn't be anything worse than my son deciding he was gay or a girl or whatever the crap you came up with. I thought I could never be more disappointed and embarrassed by your behavior." He made it to his feet and glared at Vic, his eyes blazing. "Was I ever wrong. Not only do you think you can switch sexes, you think you can switch families and start working for the Dysons as well!

You are a traitor to this family. You've gone against everything we believe in."

Vic got up. The rest of them did as well, not sure how to react to Mr. Jackson's anger. Vic stood before her father, hands up, watching him warily.

"We'll go," she said. "I'm sorry. I'm going."

"You'll go, will you?" He advanced on her. "You've stopped using the family name, and that's a good thing. You are no longer a Jackson. You will never come by here again. We shoot trespassers in these parts, keep that in mind. I don't ever want to see you or hear from you again. Your mother, either. No contact *ever again*."

Vic's voice was choked. "Okay. I won't."

He took another step and swung the cane. Erin wasn't close enough to do anything about it, but she reacted instinctively, throwing her hands up as if she could block the cane. "No!"

The first blow landed on the back of Vic's upper thigh, with a resounding thwack. There was no second blow. Willie grabbed the cane and wrenched it out of Mr. Jackson's hand. He got in Mr. Jackson's face, the cane held threateningly in his hand.

"You will *never* lay your hands on her again!"

"If he comes back here, I'll do what I need to. How about you keep him away?" Mr. Jackson stared at Willie, eye-to-eye, not backing down. "Now that I know you all came from the Dysons, I know who you are. William, he called you. Willie Andrews. Outcast from your own family. A filthy, lazy, degenerate. You and James…?" He flicked a glance at Vic. "You're disgusting. I should have you charged with corrupting a minor."

"Vic is not a minor."

"He was when he left here." Mr. Jackson took in Willie's look of surprise. "Oh, he may have told you he was eighteen, but he wasn't. He just turned eighteen this Christmas."

Erin looked over at Vic. She had wondered more than once whether Vic was telling the truth about her age. There were times when she seemed so young. A few months really didn't make a difference one way or another, but it did confirm Erin's suspicions that the runaway hadn't quite been able to wait until her eighteenth birthday to strike out on her own.

Vic was rubbing the back of her leg where her father had struck her, clearly aching from the blow. Willie gave Mr. Jackson one more warning look, then stepped back from him, took Vic around the shoulders, and escorted her out of the room. Erin and Charley followed them out, staying as far from Mr. Jackson as possible.

Mrs. Jackson was in the kitchen wringing her hands. "Oh, no," she wept. "Oh, no, James. Please. Talk to your father. Make up. Don't leave like this, with everybody on bad terms. You can come home. He'll cool down again and he'll regret what he said. Please don't leave."

Vic shook her head. She didn't hug her mother again before leaving. She just walked on by, protected by Willie's embrace. Before leaving the kitchen, Willie threw Mr. Jackson's cane down on the floor with a clatter.

Erin was relieved when they got out to the car, but it wasn't over. A pickup truck was bouncing down the road approaching the house.

Erin watched it with alarm. With four of them facing Mr. Jackson, she had felt threatened, but not too afraid. Having more men from the Jackson clan closing in, she felt just as scared as she had been in the Dyson mansion. It was a different setting, but again facing the possibility of armed clan soldiers with overwhelming force, she felt almost sick with fear.

Vic stopped in her tracks. Willie stopped and encouraged her to get into the car. They could get in the car and drive away. They could probably outrun the truck if they had to. They could call the police.

There was probably no 9-1-1 service and they'd have to wait until they got back into Moose River. Now that they knew—or strongly suspected—who had hired the masked man, they had something to take to the police. They could explain all that had happened and the police would drop the charges against Charley.

They would all be safe, because the Dysons would know that it wasn't the Jackson clan who had ordered his son killed. It had just been Davis, and he and Alton had screwed it up. Alton had planned to make Bobby mad enough to throw Charley out and make her run, but he hadn't expected Bobby to be so furious that he would try to kill Charley. After that, he'd done everything he could to get her to run.

The pickup pulled to a stop a few feet away from Willie's car, skidding in the gravel and sending clouds of dust into the air. The doors opened and the men jumped out of the truck, fanning out to look the strangers over.

"It's James!" one young man crowed. He pushed toward her, his blond hair streaming out behind him, and Erin recognized him as Jeremy. "Vic. How's it going, little sister?" He gave her a hard hug, and looked around at the rest of them, eyes sparkling. "Erin, Willie." He shook his head at Charley. "I don't know you, but welcome!"

"We're leaving," Vic said quietly. "Pa…"

"Aw, come on. Pa's bark is worse than his bite, pay him no mind."

Vic shook her head, rubbing the back of her leg. "His bite's pretty bad today too. I can't stay, Jer, and I won't be back."

He stared at her. The other young men were not as enthusiastic as Jeremy. They greeted Vic with awkward handshakes and slaps on the back, unsure what to call her or how to talk to her, too embarrassed to hug her.

"Y'all know where to find me," Vic said. "You want to visit, just come by Auntie Clem's Bakery in Bald Eagle Falls. It's not that far away. And Jeremy knows where the house is." She sniffled, her eyes glistening with tears. "I can't come back here and I can't call, so if you want to keep in touch, y'all have to reach out to me. Otherwise… I'll assume you don't want anything to do with me either."

They made noises of protest. Jeremy gave her another hug. "Vic. I don't know what happened, but don't just leave like this. Mom misses you so bad. She cries all the time. You have to come back and visit. Don't worry about what Pa says…"

"He said he'll shoot any trespassers, Jer. He'll shoot me. You think I'm going to take the chance that he might just be full of hot air? He near 'nough broke my leg with that durn cane of his! I'm not coming back. You know where to find me."

"Okay," Jeremy finally conceded. "I'd never forgive myself if something happened to you. You take care of yourself." He looked over at Willie. "You take care of my sister."

There were murmurs from the other boys. Embarrassed laughs over Jeremy calling Vic his sister. But Jeremy showed no embarrassment. He stood and watched as they all got into Willie's car, then waved as Willie pulled out.

Once they were out of sight of the boys and the white farmhouse, Vic put her hands over her face and sobbed.

Charley made no attempt to comfort Vic and tell her that everything was going to be fine this time. She didn't tell her that there was no reason to be so upset over some silly clothes. They were all quiet as Willie drove back to Moose River. Willie turned on the radio and managed to find a weak signal, and they listened to scratchy-sounding country on the way back, each of them lost in their own thoughts.

When they reached the city limits, Vic had stopped crying, had wiped her face with the voluminous hoodie, and was breathing more naturally.

"Why would Davis just try to scare Charley off?" Erin asked Willie. "After killing Trenton and Bernie, why would he balk at Charley?"

"Maybe he didn't," Willie said, glancing back at Erin. "Maybe that was Alton, if Alton is the masked man. Maybe he drew the line at murder. He's never had a problem with verbal threats and blackmail. Maybe just scaring Charley off was his idea."

Vic cleared her throat. "Or maybe it's because Davis has already lost one sister." She wiped her eyes.

"Sophie?"

Vic nodded. "He doesn't have any family left other than Charley. Maybe he couldn't bring himself to do it. She is his baby sister, just like she's yours."

They called Terry rather than Jack Ward. Terry knew them and he would trust their deductions before a cop who barely knew anything about them. He got Tom to take the remainder of his shift and drove into Moose River to meet them at Charley's apartment.

They had talked about finding somewhere neutral where the Dysons wouldn't know to find them. But Vic desperately needed to put on her own clothes again and none of them had the mental energy to go shopping for replacements. So they went back to Charley's apartment. Willie scouted it out before they went in, looking for anyone who might be keeping surveillance.

"At least if they come, we'll have something to tell them this time," Charley said, not too worried about it.

"But anything we tell Nelson, he's likely to take action on," Erin pointed out. "We don't want to get anyone killed when all we have is speculation."

Charley shrugged. "Doesn't sound like these guys are exactly upstanding citizens. If they get themselves into the middle of an organized crime murder, they can expect to be targeted."

"Like you? You managed to get yourself into the middle of it, but you didn't do anything. Nelson or his father can act as judge, jury, and executioner, but that doesn't mean justice is served. Killing you would have been a mistake, and the same might be true of Davis or Alton Summers. We don't know the extent of their crimes and we don't want to get them killed."

Charley shrugged. "I'm not trying to get anyone killed, but if the Dysons show up... I don't feel like being the sacrificial lamb."

Vic had disappeared immediately into Charley's bedroom. It was a while before she came out, herself once again. The makeup was flawlessly applied, all signs of distress eliminated, other than her red-rimmed eyes and the slight puffiness under them.

Erin gave her a hug. "Are you okay?"

Vic nodded and forced a smile. "I'm just as fine as a home-cooked meal. How long will we have to wait for Terry?"

"He's going to get Tom to finish out his shift, so we don't have to wait that long. Just a couple of hours for him to drive here."

"Or however long it takes," Vic agreed. "I have a feeling he might just use his lights and siren and shave off a bit of time."

"Maybe. At least we don't have to wait until tonight."

"You really *do* look good," Charley said, looking Vic over. "I never would guess that you were…" she trailed off, suddenly awkward over how to finish the sentence.

"Vic always looks good," Erin said firmly. "I guess we just sit down and relax and wait now. Maybe order in something to eat? I'll cover the bill this time."

"You want pizza again? We didn't exactly finish it last time."

"Sure." Erin nodded. She looked at Vic. "You'll love it. It's the most amazing pizza ever. Willie…?"

Willie was distracted, looking out the window. Daydreaming or watching for bad guys? Willie looked around at his name.

"Sorry, what?"

"Pizza?"

"Sure. Sounds good."

Erin sat down with a sigh. Vic lowered herself carefully to the couch, wincing as she settled on it.

"Are you okay?" Erin asked. "Do you want… some ice or something for your… leg?"

Vic shifted uncomfortably. "Feels like I got hit by a car. That old man really has an arm."

"It must really hurt."

"I've been whipped worse, but not many times. If you guys weren't there and he got me down…" Vic rubbed the injured area, trying to sit in a way that didn't put pressure on it. "What makes him think he can still hit me like that? I'm an adult, I'm not a child anymore!"

Erin's anger rose again at the thought of Mr. Jackson hitting a defenseless child with his cane. How could any person treat a child like that and consider themselves a good person? Erin couldn't even call him a Christian in her mind, knowing that the myths of Jesus had him preaching kindness toward children. Mr. Jackson couldn't profess to follow such a man and then whip his own child like an animal. Erin would never even have treated an animal that way.

She swallowed and tried not to let her anger show.

"He's got no right to hurt you. You could charge him with assault." She knew Vic never would.

"I know… but I don't want any trouble. Things are bad enough already. You saw that. They can disown me, but I don't want to end up in a feud with them. Despite what they might say… I haven't joined the enemy. I'm just helping out Charley."

Charley had been talking on her phone, Erin presumed with the pizza restaurant. She hung up and looked over at Vic at the mention of her name.

"What?"

"Just saying that I wasn't going against my family by helping you out…"

Charley nodded slowly. "Hey, I didn't follow everything you were saying at your house, but…"

Vic raised her eyebrows. "Yeah…?"

"You're a Jackson."

"Right. Born one, anyway, I've changed my name."

"And your aunt is related to the guy who killed Bobby."

"Related to the guy who hired him, anyway," Erin clarified. "Davis. He's Angela's son."

"My half-brother."

Vic and Erin nodded together.

"So it *was* the Jacksons who were responsible for Bobby's death."

Vic hesitated. "Well… I suppose technically. But he was just doing it for himself, not because the family ordered it."

"And I'm a Jackson? Was my father a Jackson, or just his wife?"

Vic shrugged. "They're all clan. So I guess you are too."

Willie chuckled. Charley turned and looked at him.

"A Jackson working for the Dysons?" Willie said. "I think you're going to be out a job, if you weren't already."

Charley rubbed her head. "This is crazy."

Erin felt like she hadn't seen Terry in days. The handsome policeman in uniform was a welcome sight, and she felt much better with him there.

"Terry, thanks so much for coming!" She threw her arms around him. "You don't know how glad I am to see you!"

Terry cuddled her close and kissed the top of her hair.

"I'm glad to see you too." He scanned the room, evaluating each of his tired friends. "So… what have you gotten yourselves into now?"

"We didn't exactly have any choice," Vic defended them. "It wasn't like we asked to be mixed up in a murder.

"You never do…"

He sat down with them and snagged a slice of room-temperature pizza from the coffee table.

"Why don't you start at the beginning, and tell me how you ended up here again?" Terry looked at Erin. "I thought we had agreed that you should just stay out of this."

"I didn't think there was anything else I could do. I never said I would stay out of it."

He rolled his eyes and took a bite of pizza, gesturing for her to begin her explanation. Erin looked at the others, not sure where to start. "I told you about the Dysons taking Charley…"

"Well, we knew she had gone with them. By choice." He cocked an eyebrow at Charley. "Right? You wanted to go talk to Dwight Dyson."

Charley shrugged. "Yeah… I figured it was the only way not to get killed. But things didn't exactly go as well as I'd hoped."

"They kidnapped her," Erin said.

"Kidnapped?" Terry repeated. "Were you held against your will?"

Charley nodded. "Well, yeah. I didn't exactly choose to stay there in a creepy basement room full of bugs and rats."

"Have you reported this to the police?"

"No."

"If you want to have them arrested, you need to report it."

"That's not what I want. I'm out now. Nelson let me go after he talked to Erin."

"So what do you need my help for?"

"We think we figured out who killed Bobby," Erin said.

"How did you do that?"

Erin didn't explain the how, which was too long and convoluted, and she didn't want to highlight Vic's dysfunctional family. "We think that Charley was the target, not Bobby. The idea was to force her to leave town. Killing Bobby was an unexpected development."

"You think."

"We're pretty sure."

"What makes you think that?"

Erin expanded on what they had learned from Nelson, from Charley's recollection, and their analysis of Trenton Plaint's estate succession. Terry sat, rubbing his jaw, thinking about it.

"Nelson has surveillance video of what happened."

"Yes… but I don't think he's going to give it to anyone," Erin admitted. "Even if we can prove who it is in the video, I think he's keeping his cards close to the vest. He's not going to share it with the police."

"So how do you expect to prove this? Davis has already avoided charges a number of times. He's pretty savvy where the law is concerned. He's not going to confess."

"Then we go after Alton, get him to admit who hired him and the whole conspiracy."

"Because Alton has always been so open and honest before," Terry said wryly. "So easy to get along with."

"Well… no… but he knows which side his bread is buttered on. If he sees he could end up going to prison for Bobby's shooting, he's going to turn on Davis and make a deal, don't you think? He's always been in it for his own gain."

"We need some leverage. We need to start somewhere. We can't just go in and say that we know he killed Bobby, but we have no evidence that it was him or that he was working with Davis."

Charley shuffled forward in her seat. "We need a sting," she said. "Catch the two of them together. Maybe they'll say something incriminating."

"That might be an idea. But we'll have to get Jack Ward or someone else local on our side. Again, going to them without any evidence…"

"Davis is still in prison, isn't he?" Erin asked.

"Yes."

"Then if Alton has been meeting with him, he'll be on the visitor records."

Terry nodded. "Maybe right after Bobby's death. The timing of the visits might be informative."

"And if they've been seeing each other, there might be video or audio recordings of their visits…"

"If you're lucky. But I don't think any of the prisons around here are very high-tech."

CHAPTER 30

It took some convincing, but eventually, Jack Ward agreed to at least consult with the prison on Davis's visitor list and any surveillance they might have available. When he got back to Terry, his tone was cautiously optimistic. "You were right about the two of them meeting, anyway," he admitted. "Unfortunately, Plaint is only in medium security, and their visits have not been subject to audio or visual surveillance."

"So where can you go from there? Is there anything I can lend a hand with?"

"You've been helpful, but there's not a lot anyone can do until Plaint and Summers meet again. If they do. We just have to wait and see."

As luck would have it, it wasn't long before Alton returned to the prison to report to Davis on developments.

Davis had apparently already heard some whisperings of trouble through the prison grapevine. He leaned in close to Alton, his voice low, difficult to hear over the background of all of the other conversations in the medium-security visitor's room. But they had a microphone under the table that picked up most of the conversation.

"What's going on?" Davis demanded, leaning close to Alton. "First I hear she'd been killed by the Dysons and then I hear she's fine and still hanging around Moose River!"

Alton ran a hand through his thin, stringy hair. "She's not dead," he said. "I'm not sure where that rumor came from, other than that she dropped out of sight for a few days. I think she was taken by Dwight Dyson." He looked back and forth, watching for anyone that was paying more attention to him than they should be. "Things are getting pretty hot, boss. I think we should pull out. Cut our losses."

"That's not good enough," Davis objected. "You said you could get her out of town. That's what we agreed to. We can't pull out. She needs to disappear."

"There's only one way I know of to make sure she disappears and never comes back. We've tried everything else. She's just as stubborn as her sister. I couldn't get anywhere with that one, either."

Davis's face was getting red. "You said you could do it. We've wasted all of this time. This whole thing has blown up into a huge mess. You need to fix it."

Summers sat back in his seat, folding his arms. "All right," he agreed. "I'll fix it."

Davis stared at him. "What are you going to do?"

"I'm going to make her disappear."

"How?"

"You don't want to ask me that."

"You remember what I said before. You promised."

Summers shrugged. "If you want me to act for you, you need to give me the freedom to do what I need to. If you're having second thoughts, I can pull out. If you want me to go ahead, then don't put restrictions on me."

"Fine." Davis's mouth formed a thin, straight line. "You do what you said you would."

"We've got police guards on Charley Campbell," Jack Ward assured Terry. "They're not visible, but they're close by and monitoring all of the approaches with video surveillance. As soon as Alton Summers makes his move, we'll be ready for him."

Erin, listening to the call on speakerphone, shook her head. "Why can't you just arrest him? As soon as you tell him you know what he's been doing, he'll confess. He'll make a deal so he doesn't have to go to prison too."

"Not likely," Ward disagreed. "If he's the one who shot Bobby, he's got blood on his hands and he won't confess to that, because it's a sure trip to prison."

"But he'll plead," Erin argued.

"Maybe he would plead if we had some evidence, but we don't. We just have a theory and a cryptic conversation at the prison. He didn't admit to killing anyone and didn't say exactly what it was that he was going to do, other than make Charley disappear permanently."

"Which means he's planning to kill her."

"That's your interpretation," Ward said. "He can argue that he meant he was going to talk to her. Persuade her, bribe her, whatever."

"But you know that wasn't what he meant."

"What I think he meant is beside the point. That doesn't hold up in court. Juries need proof, not speculation. Don't worry, Miss Price, we are guarding your sister. Nothing is going to happen to her. When Summers proves his intent, then we'll be able to arrest him. And when we have proof of wrongdoing on his part, then we have something to bargain with to put Davis away permanently."

Terry put his hand over Erin's, giving her a reassuring smile. Erin did her best to smile back.

"Okay. Just please take care of my baby sister."

CHAPTER 31

The fixer moved stealthily, his feet barely making a sound as he approached the door. His heart was pounding hard and fast in anticipation, feeling the euphoric adrenaline rush that was getting harder and harder for him to achieve.

She thought she could defy him, that she could ignore his warnings and just go ahead and do whatever she wanted to. She thought she was smarter than he was. She thought she could outwit him, when she didn't have a clue what was going on.

Now she was a sitting duck, oblivious to his presence. He took a careful look around to make sure that nobody was watching and no wireless cameras had been installed since he'd been there last. Stupid of her to think that a burglar alarm triggered by an opened door or window was going to stop him from doing what he was there to do.

He disabled the front door sensor and jimmied the lock to let himself in. The place was quiet. After all of her excitement over the last few days, she was asleep early, thinking herself beyond the reach of the clans. But he knew better. Charlotte needed to be shown that no one was out of reach. He could always find a way to fulfill a contract.

The carpet inside the door was thick enough to muffle any noise from his movements. There was nothing to wake her up. He went down the hall to the room that he'd previously noted as being her bedroom, his arm down at his side, finger inside the trigger guard, savoring the moment.

Just as he stepped forward, there was a horrible screeching noise. Something thumped against him in the darkness, the howling filling his ears.

He was distracted from his target for only a moment, but when he brought his weapon up and pointed it at the bed, the covers were thrown back and it was empty.

Alton swore. It was only one misstep, but it was a big one. He couldn't complete his mission without a target.

"Erin," he said softly into the darkness. "Where are you, Erin?"

CHAPTER 32

$\mathcal{E}$rin lay on the floor on the other side of the bed, panicked and disoriented. She could hear Alton moving into the room, his feet whispering over the carpet, his voice pitched in a low, soothing tone as he hunted her down.

Orange Blossom let out another furious scream, yowling and screeching like a cougar at the intruder. Alton stumbled and swore, obviously tripped up by the angry puffball.

Why hadn't the burglar alarm gone off? What was the point in having it if it didn't give her any warning of a break-in and didn't let the neighbors, Vic, or Terry know that something was wrong?

Her phone was on the bedside table on the other side of the bed. In order for Erin to get it, she would have to expose herself. But it wasn't going to take that long for Alton to make it across the room, around the bed, and to find her where she cowered. By then, it would be too late for Erin to go anywhere or try anything.

She tried to squirm under the bed. It was a pretty tight fit. She was skinny, but that didn't make her skull any smaller. She was glad the mattress on the antique frame was raised more than three inches, but she still wasn't sure she could crawl underneath without getting stuck. All Alton had to do was fire through the mattress or lift it up off of the bed so that he could get a clear shot at her.

It was dusty. Erin spent a lot of time at the bakery and not so much time vacuuming the house. With two furry pets, the dust balls reproduced at an alarming rate.

Alton was still advancing, speaking to her in that creepy, soothing voice. He knew she was in the room and he had only to get her in his sights. Orange Blossom was still dancing around him like a Tasmanian devil, hissing and yowling and occasionally clawing or biting Alton when he could. Alton tripped, scraped his shin on the iron bed frame, and swore.

"Why are you giving me such problems, Erin? It's time to stop playing around."

Erin squirmed the rest of the way under the bed, and took a couple of deep breaths, even though the dust tickled her nose and filling her lungs made it an even tighter fit. At first, she had only been trying to hide from Alton, but once she had the mattress over top of her, she had another thought. If she could get to the other side of the bed without exposing herself, then maybe she could get ahold of her phone and place a call to Terry. If only someone else knew she was in trouble, she had a chance of surviving.

Erin inched forward under the bed. She kept running into boxes and other items that had been stored under it, and was beginning to wonder if there was any clear route to the other side. She tried to gently move things out of her way without making any sound to give away where she was and what she was doing. Luckily, Orange Blossom kept making a racket and giving Alton trouble.

Erin felt a sudden shifting of air on her hand. It was out from under the bed. She felt for the phone's charge cord, and used it to drag the phone over to her, catching it when it fell. Just a few seconds, and she would be through to Terry. She couldn't tell him what was happening without alerting Alton, but she was sure he would go to her house if she didn't say anything. He would know that a call that late wasn't just a pocket dial. Erin tried to hide the brightly-lit screen from Alton as she turned on the display.

All of a sudden, the burglar alarm started shrilling. Erin jumped and hit her head on the iron frame of the bed, making her see stars and nearly black out.

Alton swore and turned toward the bedroom doorway. They could both hear footsteps in the kitchen.

"I'm sorry! I was half asleep and I forgot about the stupid alarm," Vic called out. "Is everything okay, Erin?"

The footsteps left the hard tile of the kitchen and Erin knew Vic was in the hall walking toward the bedroom.

"Stay back, Vic! He's got a gun!"

Alton swore irritably at Erin. He turned around to face the door, his gun raised to the level, waiting for Vic to appear in the doorway.

Erin had called Terry's number and laid her phone face-down on the floor so that the light would be covered and Alton couldn't use it as a beacon to shoot her. As Alton moved toward the door, Erin retreated farther back, putting space between them and sheltering behind the bed.

There wasn't a sound from Vic. Erin strained her ears. Did Vic understand? Was she still there or had she retreated? Erin held her breath, which was rasping in her own ears, and listened harder. She could still hear nothing but Alton moving and cursing under his breath at Orange Blossom, the cat still yowling and trying to drive the stranger from his territory.

There was a tinny voice coming from Erin's phone, muffled because the speaker was against the rug. Terry trying to figure out what was wrong.

Erin heard a creak from the hallway floor. She recognized it. She knew where every creaky floorboard in the house was, and she now knew where Vic was, just outside Erin's bedroom door.

Without thinking it through, Erin grabbed her phone and threw it across the room. Alton whirled toward it and fired. At almost the same instant, Vic moved into the doorway and leveled her gun, taking careful aim at Alton before firing. At her shot, Alton turned slowly back to look at Vic. The hand gripping his gun started to lower slowly, like a plant drooping without water.

Vic remained motionless in the doorway, gun still up, waiting for Alton to make a move. Erin wanted to shout at her to get out of the way and to take cover. She shouldn't just stand there where Alton could shoot her. He'd already fired his gun once, he wouldn't hesitate to do it again.

But Alton's hand lowered all the way to his side. Then he dropped his gun. Erin thought she should probably grab it before he could bend over and pick it up again, but she was paralyzed.

Sirens sounded outside. More than one. Terry had dispatched the sheriff and Tom as well. They were all closing in on the house.

Alton just stood there. Vic stood at the ready in the doorway, not moving, even though Alton had dropped his gun.

~

The cars stopped outside the house. She could hear running footsteps up the front walkway. Terry's voice sounded from the front door.

"Erin? Are you okay?"

Erin tried to answer, but her voice was so small it didn't register. She still didn't want Alton to hear her, even though he seemed to be folding into himself, slowly getting closer to the floor.

"I'm in the hall," Vic called to Terry. "Erin is in the bedroom. I think the gunman is Alton Summers."

Terry's voice got closer. Erin could hear K9 panting, and imagined he was eagerly pulling on his collar, wanting to get closer to the action.

"Where is he?" Terry asked. "Are you safe?"

"He's here. I shot him. He dropped the gun, but he hasn't been secured."

Terry's form appeared behind Vic. He stood there for a moment, allowing his eyes to adjust to the dark and assessing the situation.

"Alton Summers, you're under arrest. Put your hands above your head."

Alton didn't move his arms. His knees continued to buckle, and it wouldn't be long before he reached the tipping point and either toppled over or collapsed. Erin tried to tell Terry that Alton was injured, but still couldn't raise her voice enough for him to hear.

"Move aside, Vic. Holster your gun, but I'm going to need to take it from you later."

Vic lowered her weapon. She drew aside to allow Terry to get into the bedroom. Terry entered as Alton hit the floor. He put a hand on Alton's back to keep him down.

"Can you turn on the light?" he asked Vic. "I can't see a thing. Where's Erin, is she okay?"

"I don't know."

The light came on, blinding at first, making Erin's eyes water. Terry saw Alton's gun and pushed it farther away. He turned Alton onto his back and they all saw the blood-soaked shirt. Terry pressed one hand over it, and clicked his radio with his other.

"Gunshot victim, need EMS. Center mass, heavy bleeding."

Terry's eyes caught on Erin, peeking out from under the bed. "Erin. Are you okay? Are you hurt?"

Erin swallowed. "I'm okay," she whispered. This time he was close enough and it was quiet enough for him to hear.

"Good. Are you sure? Come out of there and let Vic check you out. Sometimes you can get hurt and not even know it."

It seemed like a long time before Erin's limbs obeyed and she was able to crawl out. Vic moved around the perimeter of the room, giving Terry lots of space, and helped Erin to her feet. They both looked Erin over, looking for any injuries. Vic found a crease across Erin's forehead, bloody but not deep.

"Is that from his shot?" Vic asked, sitting Erin down on the bed and pulling several tissues from the box on the bedside table to wad up and hold over the cut.

"No. I hit it on the bed when the alarm went."

Tom and the sheriff had cleared the rest of the house and hovered around the door, not entering because the room was already too crowded with the four of them.

"Everything is clear, Terry," the sheriff advised. "Do you want me to take over there?"

Terry looked down at the bloody mess under his hand. "I'd better keep pressure on. I don't know if it's doing any good, but if we can keep him alive to prosecute, I'd sure like to see him rotting in jail."

"What happened?"

"Orange Blossom woke me up," Erin explained, trying to speak up loudly enough that they could all hear her. "I guess he didn't like Alton coming in. I don't know how he got in. The alarm didn't go until Vic came. He had a gun. He was trying to kill me."

Terry nodded, his expression grim and set.

"Why did he come after me?" Erin demanded. "He was supposed to be going after Charley! Charley was the one being guarded!"

"Maybe he knew that. Or maybe you were the final threat that was supposed to scare Charley into doing what she was told and disappearing for good. I don't know."

Erin blinked at Vic, still pressing the tissue to Erin's forehead. "How did you know?"

Vic shook her head. "I heard Blossom. He never makes noise like that when you're around. I just knew something was wrong."

Orange Blossom jumped up on the bed beside Erin and turned around. He puffed out his fur and hissed at K9, who was panting and watching all the excitement with interest.

*E*rin met up with Charley at her apartment. It had been a long, strange week. Strange because it had been so normal. No mysteries, no worries, no sleepless nights. Just working the usual bakery routine. So Sunday afternoon, after the ladies' tea, she headed over to Charley's.

Everything in Charley's apartment had been packed up and was in boxes, other than Iggy's reptarium.

"Where are you going?" Erin asked.

As they had expected, once word got out about Charley's familial connection with Davis, and how Davis had been implicated in Bobby's death, Charley was no longer welcomed by the Dysons.

"It's not really fair," Charley complained. "It isn't like anything has been proven in court. And I didn't choose to be related to the Jacksons. It isn't like I was even raised by them."

"I know," Erin agreed. "So… where…?"

"If I'm heir to Angela Plaint's estate, then I thought maybe… there might be a place in Bald Eagle Falls I could live."

"Half-heir."

Charley gave her a narrow look. "If Davis killed Trenton for the inheritance, then he can't profit by it, right? And that would make all of it mine."

"But we can't prove that Davis had anything to do with Trenton's death.

Trenton had an allergic reaction to the cupcakes that Joelle bought. It looks like an accident."

"Yeah, that's what you said. And that might be good enough for you, but it's not good enough for me. Not when it's the difference between half of the Plaint estate or all of it. So I'm going to prove it, one way or another."

Erin shifted uneasily.

Everything they had just been through had been because Davis didn't want to split the inheritance with Charley. Now Charley was turning the tables.

Erin wasn't sure she was going to like the results any better.

BREWING DEATH

AUNTIE CLEM'S BAKERY #5

For true friends.

*E*rin was surprised to hear the back door opening. Vic, her partner at the bakery, entered the kitchen. The tall, blond girl surveyed the mess the kitchen was in, cookbooks and boxes of herbs and tea strewing the counters and tables and shook her head in mock dismay.

"I leave you alone for the day and come home to the house looking like it was hit by a tornado!" she drawled.

Erin looked at the clock on the wall. "It can't be that late already!"

"I suppose this means you didn't make supper."

Not that they usually had anything fancy for supper. Even on the rare days when one of them took the afternoon or the day off while Bella covered a shift at Auntie Clem's Bakery, there was usually so much else to do that the evening meal was a frozen dinner or something at one of Bald Eagle Falls's fine eating establishments. Erin shook her head ruefully.

"I don't think I even had lunch."

Vic walked toward the fridge. In the living room, Erin heard a thump as Orange Blossom jumped off of the couch, and by the time Vic had her hand on the handle of the fridge door, he was into the room, meowing chattily at one of his favorite people. Vic looked over at his food dish.

"It doesn't look like you forgot to feed Blossom, though."

"How could I? He'd never let me forget that!"

Vic opened the fridge. Orange Blossom wound around her legs, vocalizing loudly. "Oh, is there something in here you would like?" Vic teased him, looking over the shelves.

He would have been happy to stick his head in the opening and climb right up into the fridge, but Vic blocked him with her leg. She found the roast chicken from a couple of nights before and pulled the container out of the fridge. He followed her as she cleared a little space on the counter to set it down.

"Sorry," Erin apologized, looking around at the mess, "I've been cleaning."

"I think you've got it backward. Cleaning is when you put things away."

Vic cut a little slice of the chicken and put it in Orange Blossom's dish, and he attacked it with vigor. Erin's nostrils flared at the smell of the chicken, and her stomach rumbled loudly, reminding her that she had neglected it since breakfast. Used to bakers' hours, breakfast had been a long time before.

"I wanted to clear some space in the cupboards," Erin explained. "These things are taking up so much room, there's nowhere for me to put my own recipe books."

Vic nibbled at a piece of chicken. "You're getting rid of all of these?"

"No, not all of them. They're sorted into groups…" Erin knew that it looked like chaos, but there really was a method to all of the books strewn around. "I'm keeping most of the handwritten ones," she indicated the hardcover notebooks full of recipes; the same kind of notebooks that her Aunt Clementine had written her journals in, "and a few other classic ones that look really interesting. I thought Adele might be interested in some of the ones on herbs and remedies, and maybe take some of the teas."

Vic nodded. While Erin had spent some time helping Clementine back when she was a little girl and the bakery was a tea room, she hadn't made a dent in the wide variety of teas and herbs that had stocked Clementine's cupboard. Adele, who lived in the cottage at the other end of Clementine's wooded property and acted as Erin's groundskeeper, would put them to better use.

"And the rest of them?" Vic inquired.

"You can take what you want. What's left over after that… I'm not sure what I'm going to do with. I don't know whether there is anyone in town who would be interested in them."

"Maybe you could put some of them on display at the bakery and see if anyone had any interest in them. Or we could hold an auction and get you a new car!"

"There's nothing wrong with my Challenger," Erin protested.

"Nothing that a complete overhaul of the engine, transmission, and exhaust system wouldn't cure," Vic agreed with a wry smile.

"Do you want to make some sandwiches?" Erin's stomach was protesting at the smell and sight of the chicken Vic was nibbling away at. "I'll clear some space…"

"All of these recipe books, and you just want to make sandwiches? Shouldn't we be making chicken á la king, or chicken fettuccine alfredo, or something more sophisticated than sandwiches?"

"I can't wait for anything fancy. Just slap some mayo and mustard on some bread and we can have a quick supper."

"Do you want them on buttermilk biscuits?" Vic suggested. "We had a few left over."

"That sounds great." Erin started to gather the books into piles, so they would take up less room, arranging them by the type of recipes they contained. "I can't believe how fast the time flew by today. I thought I could have this done in an hour, but it's stretched out to take all day."

"Did you get anything else on your list done?" Vic rummaged through the fridge to pull out the condiments and a salad. Orange Blossom had finished his chicken and was sniffing around the edges of his bowl like he might have missed some. He wandered over to Vic, making inquiries to see whether she would give him anything else. "That's enough, Blossom, or you're going to get fat!"

The cat sat back on his haunches, looking offended. He licked his paw and started to wash his face.

"I did some laundry and some other general cleaning up and tidying. Took three bags out to the garbage bin, so I must have gotten something done today." Erin stopped and surveyed the kitchen, hands on her hips. "It won't take that long to put these away, into boxes or back in the cupboard. At least I'll have gained some cupboard space." She had her own recipe books that she needed a place for, mostly printed on letter-size paper and inserted in clear plastic sleeves in binders. Running a gluten-free bakery that tried to cater to a variety of dietary restrictions, she was always on the prowl for new recipes and techniques, and she couldn't store all of them in the kitchen and tiny office at the bakery.

She and Vic worked together for a few minutes, Vic getting supper prepared and Erin sorting the books into boxes and putting a few back into the cupboard.

"You didn't find any journals mixed in with those?" Vic inquired, nodding to the hardcover notebooks.

"No. I was kind of hoping that that missing journal might be in there. But I'm afraid it must be lost or stolen for good."

"You think Uncle Davis has it?"

"I don't know. I don't see how he could have gotten his hands on it, but we didn't have an alarm system yet around the time of the funeral. So, who knows? Maybe."

"Officer Piper has already searched his house. It wasn't there."

"I don't think Terry could have missed it," Erin agreed.

Vic helped get the table cleared and put out the sandwiches and salad.

"Why don't you wash off the dust and take a break?"

Erin agreed. She was used to being on her feet all day at the bakery, but for some reason, her day of cleaning and sorting out the kitchen had left her feeling more tired and sore than usual. She was happy to get off her feet to enjoy a light supper with Vic.

Erin's usual routine of sitting with Vic in the living room and making lists before bed to organize the next day's activities was comforting to her. She liked to get everything down on paper and have some idea of what the shape of the day would be. Of course, she never got everything on her lists done, but she was pretty productive.

Orange Blossom was curled up on Vic's lap while she read a book, and the brown and white rabbit, Marshmallow, was lying on Erin's feet.

The next day was Sunday, which meant the ladies' tea at the bakery, an old tradition Erin had resurrected from when it was a tea room. Tea, cookies, and gossip. Even though Erin wasn't part of the church community at Bald Eagle Falls, she had come to enjoy the quiet Sunday ritual and the chance to visit with her friends in a more relaxed environment.

"You could take a few of Clementine's teas to the ladies' tea," Vic suggested. "There might be a few adventurous souls willing to try something new."

"I might do that." Erin added it to her list of things to take with her to the bakery in the morning.

"Just make sure they're labeled. None of those bags of unlabeled herbs."

"I can tell what most of them are, even if they don't have labels. I can identify any of the teas Clementine used to serve in the tea room."

"But some of those… I don't know. They just look *dubious* to me."

"I'll give them to Adele. She can use them or compost them if she doesn't know what to do with them. Her herbal knowledge is pretty good."

"As long as no one expects me to drink anything unidentified."

Erin laughed. "We're not going to poison you, Vicky! Has Adele ever given you anything that's hurt you?"

"So far, I've been able to avoid drinking anything she has made."

Erin was almost expecting her to make the sign of the cross to ward off any evil. Adele was a practicing witch, and despite Vic's acknowledgment that Wicca was just a pagan religion and Adele was not going to work any magic on them, she avoided eating or drinking anything Adele made. Erin had never suffered any ill effects from Adele's herbal teas, but Vic just couldn't bring herself to take the chance.

"I think Charley is going to come by for the ladies' tea tomorrow," Erin said, changing the subject.

"Really? I thought she said she wasn't comfortable around 'all those church ladies.'"

Erin smiled and nodded. "I know. But I think I've persuaded her just to give them a chance. If she wants to make friends in Bald Eagle Falls, she's going to have to socialize somehow."

"And if she's going to open up The Bake Shoppe, she's going to need to know her clientele," Vic agreed.

Erin's stomach clenched into a knot. She took a few deep breaths, waiting for it to subside. She knew she should be happy that her newfound half-sister was willing to consider opening up a legitimate business, putting her criminal activities with the Dyson clan behind her. It was just that Erin wasn't sure how it would impact her business at Auntie Clem's Bakery. She'd said from the start that she believed the town could sustain two bakeries but, deep down, she wasn't one hundred percent sure it was true.

"She won't be opening up The Bake Shoppe for a while. She's still fighting over whether she can open it up on her own while Davis is in prison, when they are each only fifty-percent owners once Trenton's probate goes through."

"She'll be able to open it. It's more valuable as an operating bakery than sitting there closed up. Uncle Davis really can't win that argument."

"I suppose."

Thinking about Charley and Davis made Erin uneasy. She was happy to have her sister in Bald Eagle Falls so that she could get to know her. But Charley had some pretty rough edges and wasn't the kind of person that Erin would have associated with normally. And Charley was determined to prove Davis's involvement in Trenton's death and get his half of the inheritance.

Erin added a couple more items to her list, and wiggled her toes, making Marshmallow shift and look up at her. "I think I'm going to head to bed."

Vic lifted Orange Blossom from her lap to cuddle him and kiss the top of his head. "Yeah, me too," she agreed. "Even though we can sleep in on a Sunday, my body just doesn't get the message."

Erin nodded. "See you tomorrow, then. Where's Willie these days? Working out of town again?"

Vic stood up and put Orange Blossom down. "I don't know. We decided to take a break for a while."

Erin stared at her, mouth open. "You decided to take a break? From each other? What happened?"

But even as she said it, Erin knew. Things had not been the same since they had returned to Bald Eagle Falls after rescuing Charley and solving the murder she'd been wrongly accused of.

Vic sighed. Her mouth twisted into a grimace that she tried to hide. "I told him who I was. I didn't keep that from him. But he didn't tell me who he was. He knew our families were enemies, and he didn't tell me."

Willie had initially had a hard time with Vic being a transgender woman, but had eventually been able to get past it. But he hadn't told her that he was a Dyson, the clan that had been feuding against Vic's family, the Jacksons, for generations.

"You told me once that you knew Willie had secrets, but you were willing to wait until he was ready to share them with you."

"Yeah." Vic considered. "I guess that's one that I would have liked to have known up front. Other stuff from his past I could wait for, but he should have told me that. At least given me the chance to decide if I wanted to get involved with someone who'd fought against my family."

It wasn't just that Willie had been born a Dyson. Vic probably could have handled that. But he had been a soldier for them for five years, and that wasn't so easy for her take.

"I'm sorry," Erin said softly, shaking her head. "You should have told me. I just thought he was off working. I didn't know the two of you were having trouble."

"I wasn't ready to talk about it. I'm still not ready. But you're a friend. You should at least know."

"Okay." Erin looked down at her lists instead of staring at Vic and trying to analyze her. "I won't ask about it. You just let me know when you're ready."

"Okay. Thanks."

Vic bent down to give Orange Blossom one last scratch. Marshmallow got up and hopped over to her for a share of the attention, and Vic scratched the base of his long ear.

"All right, babies, time for bed. You guys be quiet for Erin and let her sleep."

Orange Blossom followed Vic into the kitchen, yowling at her about how hungry he was, but she wasn't fooled. She went out the back door and across the yard to her apartment over the garage. Erin heard her pause on her way out to arm the burglar alarm. Erin wasn't sure she felt any more secure with the alarm set, since the last intruder had managed to disable it on entering. But it was just a precaution. There was no one after Erin. Not anymore, thanks to Orange Blossom and Vic's marksmanship skills. It was a good thing she'd had so much practice shooting gophers and other critters when she was younger.

Erin had expected that Charley would jam out at the last minute and not show up for the ladies' tea when church let out. She wasn't an atheist, like Erin. She'd been raised Christian, but had obviously left those beliefs behind when she had left home to work with the Dyson clan, whose views were distinctly opposed to any of the teachings Erin knew of the Christian faith. Even if they went to funerals and to Easter and Christmas services, they really didn't follow the teachings of Christ as Erin knew them.

But Charley showed up. She wasn't in a dress like most of the church ladies would be, but she wasn't in blue jeans either. She'd taken the time to find something appropriate, to put her hair, dark like Erin's, back in a knot behind her neck, and to keep to a natural look with her makeup, just accenting her brown eyes and small mouth.

"I made it," Charley declared. "I actually got myself out of bed early and got myself all dolled up for your friends."

Erin couldn't help looking at the clock on the wall. Early?

"Considering I'm usually going to bed when you're getting up, that's early for me," Charley asserted.

"Yes, it is," Erin agreed. "You're here just in time, the others should be arriving soon."

Mary Lou was the first to arrive. As usual, her short gray hair was perfectly coiffed and her neatly tailored skirt suit looked like it had been made just for her. She smiled and nodded at Charley. "I'm so glad you could make it, Miss Campbell."

"Oh, no! Just call me Charley. No one calls me Miss Campbell."

"Have a seat, Mary Lou," Erin invited, gesturing toward the tables, all ready for the group of women. "How were your services today?"

"Very nice," Mary Lou said. She chose her usual chair and sat down. She closed her eyes for an instant, looking tired. "Yes, it was a beautiful spring service. I always enjoy a talk that centers around renewal and new life."

"Good." Erin waited for Mary Lou to pick out her usual English Breakfast, and then poured the water from the waiting teapot for her.

Mary Lou nodded her thanks and stared off, distant.

"What kind of tea do you like?" Erin asked Charley.

"Oh, I don't know. I'm pretty easy. Just tea. Black, green, I don't really care."

Erin considered, mentally cataloging the kinds of tea in the baskets at the middles of the tables. "How about... Earl Grey?" she suggested, pulling one of the yellow packets out.

Charley shrugged. "Sure, sounds good." She sat down, not right next to Mary Lou, but not off on her own, either. Erin put the teabag in Charley's cup and poured the water for her.

Other women started coming in the door. Melissa, with her mass of brown curls, eyes sparkling as she gossiped with Clara Jones, who she some-times worked with at the police department's administrative office. Clara was wearing a green dress, which Erin wasn't sure looked good with Clara's brassy curls and oversize jewelry. Clara seemed to enjoy drawing attention to herself, positive or negative.

Lottie was there, along with several others of the usual crowd. They all got quieter at the sight of Charley. Though Erin was sure they knew who Charley was, she introduced her anyway, trying to make everyone feel comfortable. Vic brought out the platters of cookies and confections, and everyone chattered at once, admiring the treats and discussing which were their favorites. Erin circulated, pouring water and making sure everyone had everything they needed. Eventually, everyone had been served, and there was nothing much more for Erin to do than just enjoy her guests and listen to them talk.

"I understand you are trying to open up The Bake Shoppe again," Melissa said to Charley. "How is that coming along?"

"Slower than a herd of turtles," Charley answered, shaking her head. "I mean… I know small towns do things slow, but how long can it take to decide the place is worth more open than closed?"

Sympathetic nods from around the table. They all knew about small-town bureaucracy and how hard it was to get people to make a decision.

"I managed to get ahold of Joelle Biggs," Charley went on. "Asked her if she'd come meet with me to go over everything."

The room fell utterly silent.

Charley looked around, her eyes wide. She looked over at Erin and raised her brows. "Uh… what?"

"Why would you ask her to come back to Bald Eagle Falls?" Erin asked, her voice coming out much more calm than she really felt.

"She holds Davis's power of attorney, so if I can get her to agree with me, she can just sign a consent on his behalf, and then the trustees don't have a leg to stand on. We're the only two beneficiaries of the bakery, and if we both say we want to go ahead and open it up again, why would they object? As soon as it's gone through probate, we're the ones who are going to be making all the decisions on it."

"Why would Joelle agree to come back here?" Lottie demanded. "She's the one who killed Trenton Plaint! How could she dare show her face here again?"

"We couldn't prove that it was done intentionally," Vic pointed out. "I guess she knows there's nothing we can do about it."

Erin saw Charley's eyes flash. She certainly intended to do something about it, and Erin worried that it wasn't just having a little chat with her. Yes, she wanted the bakery open, but that wasn't all she wanted.

But instead of protesting, Charley just gave a lazy shrug and raised her teacup to her lips. "I don't see how it's anyone's business but my own."

The other ladies huffed and rolled their eyes but didn't come up with a reason that Charley should have to justify herself to them. It was true, as much as they liked to know all of what was going on and to give endless advice on the right way to do things, they didn't have any control over what Charley and Joelle did and weren't in a position to be making any demands. Of course, that hadn't stopped them when Erin had moved into Bald Eagle Falls to open a second bakery. She had been the outsider then, and everyone had made it clear that she should be reopening the tea room rather than a bakery. Especially a gluten-free bakery, of all things.

"We'll just have to see how it all unfolds," Erin said, hoping to soothe the nettled tempers. She looked over in Vic's direction. Vic was the one who was best at defusing things. She always seemed to know the right thing to say.

"Can't knit a sweater before the sheep is shorn," Vic agreed, making everyone laugh.

In a few minutes, the conversation moved on to other things, and Erin gave a sigh of relief. She would have to keep an eye on Charley. Maybe inviting her to the ladies' tea hadn't been the best idea.

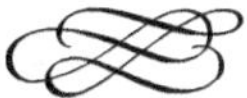

Surprisingly, it was Mary Lou who was the first to stand up and make motions toward leaving. She was usually one of the last ones to go, sticking around to help gather up the dishes and brush away the crumbs to help Erin and Vic out.

She caught Erin's eyes on her. "I'm sorry. Duty calls. Roger hasn't been feeling well this week. I don't want to leave him to himself for too long."

"Oh, I'm sorry," Erin sympathized. "Is there anything he'd like? I could send you home with some cookies…?"

"No, that's fine, thank you. Don't want to do business on the Sabbath. What he really needs is for me to be home."

"I meant I would give them to you, not that you had to pay," Erin tried to correct the misunderstanding.

"I'm certainly not taking anything without paying for it. You're running a business here, and you're going to need every sale you can get." Mary gave a significant look in Charley's direction. Her meaning was clear. Erin was going to be in trouble when The Bake Shoppe reopened.

"We'll manage," Erin assured her. She didn't feel quite as certain as she let on. The bakery's first year had not been an easy one, and she wasn't yet mentally prepared to face the competition of another bakery in town. There would still be people who had to come to Auntie Clem's for the gluten-free baking, but not enough of them to support the business. How many others would stay loyal to Auntie Clem's if they didn't need gluten-free or other allergen-free goods? Would they all just go back to The Bake Shoppe when it opened?

Mary Lou put her thin, well-manicured hand on Erin's arm as she walked by. "That's right, dear," she agreed. "I'm sure it will be fine."

~

Erin didn't expect Joelle to show up in town right away. In spite of what Charley had said, Erin figured Joelle would play it cool, saying that she would come but in no hurry to do so. What murder suspect in her right mind would just waltz back into town as if she didn't have a care in the world?

But the week wasn't out before Erin saw Joelle, with her chic yoga pants and long, spidery limbs, walk right by the bakery. Erin turned to Vic to point Joelle out, but Vic had already seen, and had turned toward Erin, eyes wide, mouth open to make a comment about it.

Erin grinned. "Miss Joelle Biggs is back in town," she acknowledged.

"Still can't believe Charley was able to talk her into coming."

The bakery was pretty quiet, with only the elderly Potters standing there looking at the display case and waffling over the choices. Vic slipped out from behind the counter and walked to the front window to watch Joelle's progress down the street.

"Where is she going?" Erin asked.

"They must be meeting at The Bake Shoppe."

"Should somebody go over there…?"

Vic's eyebrows went up. "And do what, exactly?"

"I don't know. Make sure they don't kill each other."

"And pray tell, how would we do that?"

Erin leaned on the counter, trying to come up with an answer. The last time she had been into The Bake Shoppe was when Trenton had died, poisoned by the muffins Joelle had purchased at Auntie Clem's Bakery. Just thinking about it made her muscles tense up and her breathing grow shallower. She and Terry Piper had spent hours keeping up CPR until an ambulance from the city could get there. Erin rubbed her biceps. What an ordeal that had been. And a hopeless one, as it turned out. Trenton had never revived.

"I don't know. But I don't think they should be left alone together."

"We've got no reason to go into their place of business. We can't stop them from having a meeting."

Erin fought the urge to bite her nails. She tried to distract herself, turning to the Potters with a pasted-on smile. "See anything you like today?"

"We were thinking of the chocolate muffins," Mrs. Potter started out, her quavery voice slow and deliberate.

"Good choice," Erin approved. She reached for the muffins. "How many would you like?"

"But then we were looking at the blueberry ones," Mr. Potter put in.

Erin wasn't fooled a second time. She waited for the next installment in the story.

"We did have muffins last week," Mrs. Potter noted.

"Yes. So, something a little different this week? Maybe cookies or some fresh rosemary bread? I know you like that..."

"Mrs. Potter likes the rosemary," Mr. Potter disagreed. "I like the poppyseed."

"I have poppyseed bagels today," Erin said desperately, pointing to them.

"Mmm..." Both of the Potters gazed into the display case, considering the poppyseed bagels and everything else in turn.

Erin raised her eyes to Vic, who was turning away from the front window with a mirthful smile. She walked back to her place behind the counter. "You can't rush the future," she advised placidly.

Erin settled back to wait. It wasn't like there was a line up behind the Potters. Things would be quiet until school let out. Assuming Charley and Joelle didn't kill each other.

The doorbell rang after supper, and Erin had a pretty good idea who it was going to be. She hadn't set the burglar alarm yet, and she took a careful look through the peephole before opening the door to him.

Officer Terry Piper and his faithful partner, K9, stood on the steps waiting. Erin smiled at her favorite police officer. "Come on in," she invited.

They made themselves at home, Terry sitting down in his preferred chair, and K9 lying down at his feet with a snort and a sigh.

"What can I get you?" Erin offered. "Coffee? Cinnamon rolls?"

"Oh, both of those sound great," Terry approved. "I don't know when the last time I had a cinnamon roll was."

"And you're on duty tonight, so coffee is okay?"

He nodded his agreement. K9 watched Erin intently while she went into the kitchen to warm up a roll. Orange Blossom jumped down from the couch, hissed at K9, and then stalked after Erin on stiff legs.

Erin tossed him a couple of kitty treats while she warmed up the cinnamon roll, and he skittered across the kitchen after them like a kitten, making her laugh. Erin put a doggie biscuit in her pocket to free up her hands for the coffee and roll, and took them into the living room.

"I should probably have come into the kitchen to eat this," Terry commented, taking the plate from her. "I don't want to make a mess in your parlor."

"If you drop crumbs, the animals will vacuum them up."

K9 put his head back down between his paws with a grumble. Erin pulled the biscuit out of her pocket.

"Did you think I forgot about you?"

K9 sat up eagerly and took the treat from her, then lay down with it to eat.

"They're just like kids," Terry said. "Feed them once, and you can expect to have to do the same thing every single time you see them. It's a good thing we spend plenty of time walking, or we'd both be fat."

"You don't need to worry about your weight," Erin dismissed, glancing at Terry's heavy work belt, buckled at exactly the same hole as always.

"Where's Vic tonight? Did she and Willie make up?"

"Did you know they were on the outs? I didn't realize it until Saturday."

He nodded, grunting something through the cinnamon roll.

"She went to see Adele," Erin said, in answer to his question. "We haven't seen much of her lately and I have something to give her."

"How is that working out? You don't regret letting her live in the cottage and being your groundskeeper?"

"No. She's great. She doesn't get in the way and make demands. She makes improvements and keeps rowdy teenagers to a minimum. It's worked out just great."

"Good. I wasn't sure, when you took her on, that it was the right thing to do. None of us really knew anything about her."

Erin gave a little shrug. "We all have to start somewhere. I felt good about her, and I know what it's like to be new in town and need a little bit of help. She doesn't ask much. She just... needed a friend, I guess."

"Sometimes people can mislead you... I'd hate to see someone take advantage of you. You can't trust everyone."

"I don't."

He studied her for a moment, then nodded and went back to eating his cinnamon roll. He licked his fingers. "Oh, those are so rich. Great job, Erin."

Erin's face warmed at his words of praise. She took the empty plate from him, trying to mask her embarrassment.

There were voices in the back yard, and then Vic and Adele came in through the back door and into the kitchen.

"Hello," Vic called out, giving Erin and Terry a wave.

Adele hesitated for a moment. "You have company."

"Come in, come in. Terry's not company, and neither are you. You're family. The more the merrier."

Adele considered, then inclined her head. She walked through the kitchen into the living room. "I'm sorry I haven't been around much the last week. Nothing is wrong, I've just had... a lot to do."

"That's fine. We just wanted to make sure that you were okay. You're kind of isolated, and if something happened to you... well," Erin shrugged uncomfortably, "I'd want to know about it sooner rather than later."

The stately woman said nothing.

"Anyway," Erin realized she was still holding Terry's empty plate in her hand and walked into the kitchen to put it in the sink. "I have some things that you might like. You don't need to take anything you don't want, but..."

Erin gestured to the boxes she had filled for Adele. Adele opened one of the lids and looked at the jumble of teas and herbs.

"Sorry, it's not organized..."

"No, this is fine," Adele said, poking through the contents. "I'd be happy to take it back to the cottage and have a look through it. Thank you." She opened the other box and picked up the recipe books on top. "These look intriguing."

"I don't know if any of it is worth anything to you, or if you already know all of this…" While Erin had kept a few baking books for herself, she really didn't have any use for the old herbal remedy books Clementine had collected.

"These are lovely. There's always more wisdom to be gathered."

"Good."

Adele opened the hardcover notebook that had Clementine's own recipes in it. "Oh, are you sure? This looks special."

"They're Clementine's tea recipes and other herbal remedies. I've kept some of her other recipes, but I don't have room for everything. If you don't want it…"

"No, I'm honored. I just wanted to make sure you really wanted me to have that one. You can ask for it back if you change your mind…"

"No, really, it's for you. I don't have the time to spend on herbal remedies as well as everything else already on my plate." Erin giggled at her own pun. "Go ahead, use it as you like. I hope you can get something out of it."

"Thank you. I'll put it to good use."

Erin nodded and headed back to the living room. Orange Blossom sat in the doorway of the kitchen, staring intently at Adele, but not going in and demanding a treat like he normally would.

"Why is he looking at you like that?"

"Maybe he would like to talk to me."

Vic laughed. "Orange Blossom talks to everyone. It's when he shuts up that it's surprising."

Adele extended her fingers and called softly to the cat. "Puss, puss?"

Orange Blossom looked at Erin, then back at Adele, and entered the kitchen, approaching her cautiously. Erin glanced over at Vic and saw that her eyes were big as she watched the cat and the woman who called herself a witch.

"Did you want to tell me something?" Adele asked the cat.

Orange Blossom sniffed Adele's fingers, then bent his head and smelled her shoes, raising his head again with his mouth partly open.

"You must have stepped in something good," Vic chuckled.

"Maybe catnip," Erin suggested. "Does catnip grow around here?"

"Certainly," Adele said. She gave Orange Blossom's ears a scratch. "He probably smells Skye."

"Skye?" Erin echoed.

"The crow."

"Oh," Erin had seen the crow that was not Adele's pet a few times. She got the feeling that he wasn't often very far away, but he didn't go into Adele's house, and he only landed to perch on her shoulder or hand briefly, and then after communing with her would fly away again. "I guess I never knew his name. You never really talk about him."

"There's not much to say," Adele said with a shrug. She straightened. "He's a crow."

"You said he's not your pet; is he—"

"He's her familiar," Vic interrupted. "A spirit helper. Isn't he?"

Adele looked at Vic, her brows drawn down. "Skye is a crow. He likes the peanuts I give him. I wouldn't speculate on things I knew nothing about if I was you, Victoria."

Vic flushed. "I just thought… well, witches have animals to help them, no matter what you call them, don't you?"

"You like having animals around, don't you?" Adele said. "Orange Blossom and Marshmallow? You grew up on a farm with other animals, probably dogs and livestock, at least."

"Sure. I like animals."

"So do I. I like to be close to nature and I like to be close to non-human animals. When you've been around an animal for a while, you get to learn its body language and habits. You develop a friendship."

Vic nodded. "Yeah."

"Skye doesn't belong to me. But I miss him when he's not around."

Vic didn't pursue it any further.

"Come in for a visit," Erin invited, motioning to the living room. They all joined Terry in the living room. Erin sat down next to Terry. "I guess you know Joelle is back in town."

"Yes, I saw her."

"Joelle?" Adele repeated.

"Joelle Biggs," Erin explained, and proceeded to tell Adele the details of Trenton Plaint's death.

"But what is she doing back in town?" Adele asked. "Does she have friends around here? Other than Davis?"

"No, no one that I know of. Charley wanted her to come back. But I don't know why she came. I certainly wouldn't if it was me!"

Adele stared at the dark window. Erin suspected she had other things she would rather be doing. She had come back with Vic to be accommodating and to let them know she was fine, but she had said she had a lot of things to do. They were probably keeping her away from something else. While Erin and Vic had to retire to bed early, Adele would be up past midnight doing whatever it was she did in the woods.

Erin covered a faked yawn. "Well... I'm going to need to hit the sack. Stay and visit if you like..."

Terry looked at his watch. K9 looked up quickly, reading the signal that they were going to leave. "I'd better get back to it," Terry commented. He gave Erin a quick hug and brushed her cheek with a kiss. "See you tomorrow."

Erin nodded. "Keep an eye on Joelle while she's in town..."

"I'll keep my eyes open," he promised.

"I suppose I should get to bed too," Vic said grudgingly.

Adele looked relieved. She rose to her feet in one fluid movement. "Good to see you, Erin. I need to pop over and see Mary Lou. Thank you for the goodies. I'll have a lot of fun going through them."

In a few minutes, everyone was gone, and Erin was left by herself to think about the events of the day.

CHAPTER 3

"Isn't it nice to have everything back to normal?" Vic asked, as they closed up the bakery to take their early lunch.

Erin flipped the sign to *Closed* and they got out sandwich makings and freshly-baked bread for their repast.

"I suppose so," Erin said slowly.

Vic looked over at her, eyebrows raised. "Don't tell me you prefer mortal peril," she teased.

"No! Certainly not that. I just can't help feeling like… something is bound to happen. I'm just waiting for the other shoe to drop. Ever since I came to Bald Eagle Falls, things have been happening. There have been quiet intervals in between, when everything *seems normal*, but that's when the scary music starts to play, before the characters realize that something bad is going to happen."

Vic laughed. "There are only so many shoes," she quipped. "I think they've all dropped by now." She slathered mayonnaise on her sandwich. "I don't hear any music."

"The characters never do."

"I really don't think you need to worry, Erin. Everything has been settled. Davis is in jail, Charley is out, and there are no more mysteries to be solved."

"Well…"

Vic gave her a stern look. "There are no more mysteries."

"Okay. If you say so."

Erin still had questions, both about her family's past and about things that had happened in Bald Eagle Falls since she had moved there. But those were just questions, not mysteries. A person never had all of their questions answered. Life just didn't work out that way.

But several weeks had passed without anything eventful happening. Charley was settling into the Bald Eagle Falls routine, resigned to the fact that things were not going to move as quickly as she wanted them to. She had been unable to convince Joelle that it was in Davis's best interests to open the bakery immediately, and was still doing whatever she could to convince the lawyers in charge of the estate to hasten things along at faster than a turtle's pace. Joelle had, Erin knew, been up to the prison to see Davis a few times. But that hadn't resulted in any threats on Erin's life, and Joelle hadn't even bothered to poke her head into Auntie Clem's in the time she had been in town. Joelle and Charley both had to find temporary living arrangements, as the estate would not choose one of them over the other to live in the Plaint house, so it sat cold and empty while the two ladies lived out of suitcases in rented cottages.

Erin layered thin slices of tomato into her sandwich. Vic was right. For the time being, everything was quiet. Everything was back to normal. There was no scary music playing.

~

Peter Foster came to the bakery after school with his mother and little sisters. He was one of Erin's favorite customers, and it always made her day when he stopped in.

He and his sisters pressed their faces up against the glass, considering the various treats. Unlike at The Bake Shoppe before it closed, Peter could choose any of the cookies or treats that appealed to him and know that they would be safe for him to eat. The little boy who had rarely been able to have any baking other than some dry, store-bought gluten-free cookies, thought Auntie Clem's Bakery was heaven.

"Marshmallow cookies," Peter breathed, fogging up the glass.

"Is that what you would like today?" Erin asked.

Peter nodded emphatically. "Yes, please!"

"Me too!" the girls chorused.

Usually, Peter suggested to them that they each get a different variety of cookie so that they could each have a bite of three different sorts of cookies, but this time, Peter didn't say anything about them all having the same kind of cookies. Each of them drooled over the chocolate-covered marshmallow and cookie confection and took them almost reverently from Erin.

"Cook-kie!" toddler Traci insisted, slapping Mrs. Foster's arm excitedly.

"Maybe something not so messy for this one," Mrs. Foster said with a laugh. "She'll have chocolate everywhere."

"Oatmeal?" Erin suggested.

"That would be great."

Erin gave Traci her cookie. Traci looked at the other children and seemed uncertain whether to take it, but was eventually tempted into it. She jammed the oatmeal cookie straight into her mouth, humming a pleased *mmmmm* sound as she slobbered over it.

The children taken care of, Mrs. Foster looked over the baking to pick out what she would need for meals during the week.

"How is it going?" she asked, sounding a little tired. "Everything good with you ladies?"

Erin nodded. "Yes, everything is good with me."

She glanced over at Vic for her response, wondering what Vic would say. Vic smiled and brushed the question off. "Every day above ground…"

"…is a good day," Mrs. Foster finished. She seemed satisfied with the response and didn't pursue it any further.

Erin wondered how Vic really was. Erin knew that Vic and Willie had talked a couple of times, and even met for dinner one evening, but things didn't seem to be progressing. Erin hadn't seen Willie at Vic's apartment at all and he didn't stop by to visit at Erin's house. Vic occasionally borrowed the car to go into the city but, as far as Erin knew, she hadn't gone to Willie's house. While she had never thought them a particularly good match, with Willie so much older than Vic, she was sorry that things didn't seem to have worked out between them.

But it wasn't any of Erin's business. Vic didn't talk to her about it, and Erin just let it go, wishing she knew more.

"Did you hear about Joelle?" Mrs. Foster asked.

The question was aimed at Vic, but Erin snapped to attention. "Joelle?"

"That girl—woman—who was mixed up with the Plaint boys. You know, the one who came back…"

"Yes," Erin nodded impatiently. "I know who you mean. What happened?"

"Poor girl had a nasty fall, out doing her power-walking thing. I *hear* she broke her leg."

"I don't think it was broken," Vic provided. "I think she just messed it up pretty good. Road rash and a sprained knee."

Erin winced. "How did she do that out walking?"

"She goes pretty fast," Mrs. Foster provided. "I don't know if you've seen her out striding around, but I know joggers who wouldn't be able to keep up with her. I guess she tripped over something. I don't know."

"I heard she fell into the creek," Vic said, frowning. "Standing too close to the edge, and just tumbled in."

"That was last week. This was just yesterday."

Erin blinked and shook her head. "Two falls in a week? That seems strange."

"I guess she's accident prone," Vic said. "Doesn't sound like there was anyone else involved. City girl, maybe she's just not used to the challenges of hiking in the woods."

Mrs. Foster laughed. "Well, it can be dangerous, I suppose. I would have thought that with all of her workout clothes and talk about yoga and wellness and what-not that she was a little bit better-coordinated than that."

"Well…" Erin tried to think of a way to tactfully voice her opinion. "I think that Joelle… isn't always what she would like people to think she is. I think she is more about outward appearances than actually being fit and healthy."

Vic nodded her agreement. "She likes to look well-to-do, but that's just an act. Same with being vegan. I guess it's not a stretch that she's not really athletic either."

"I wonder what she's really like," Erin mused. "Under all of that outward stuff, what is she really like inside?"

Vic handed Erin Mrs. Foster's purchases to ring up on the till. "My guess would be that she's either really mean and nasty, or just a scared little girl. The trouble is, I don't know which one."

CHAPTER 4

ic looked at the amount of soup that was left over from supper and shook her head. "I guess we're having chicken soup again tomorrow," she said. "Were you expecting Terry to come by for dinner, or something?"

Erin shook her head. She hadn't said anything to Vic, because she didn't want to be held to anything if she ended up chickening out in the end. "No. I just thought… it would be neighborly to take some soup over to Joelle. I don't know how well she's getting around on her injured leg. If it's as bad as people are saying, she's probably on bed rest for a while, and I don't know of anyone she has on her side. I don't think she's made any friends around here."

"If Joelle Biggs has been trying to make friends, she's going about it the wrong way," Vic declared.

They both laughed.

"I just felt like I should do something for her," Erin said. "But I'm kind of nervous about going over there by myself. Do you want to come along?"

"You think I want to go visit with Joelle? Not my first choice about how to spend the evening."

"I know. Me either. But it doesn't have to take long. We can just stay for a few minutes, and then get on our way. We wouldn't lose the whole evening."

Vic wrinkled her nose. "I suppose if you really need me to go."

"Wasn't there something in that Bible of yours about feeding the hungry or the sick?" Erin needled. It was dirty pool, she knew, but she really didn't want to have to face Joelle alone, and Vic was being unexpectedly obstinate about going to visit her.

Vic's eyes flashed. "For someone who is an atheist, you're always surprising me with your knowledge of what Christians believe."

Joelle's rented house was not far from Erin's as the crow flew, but the crow flew through the woods, and Erin had to drive around them. It was similar in age and style to Clementine's house. It probably belonged to one of the older residents who had moved to a larger house or a care home in the city.

Erin and Vic stood on the doorstep and waited after Erin rang the bell.

"If she's laid up in bed, how is she going to answer the door?" Vic asked after a few minutes of waiting.

Erin considered. She had been giving Joelle extra time, picturing her having to hobble to the door on crutches, but if Joelle were confined to her bed rather than just limping around, standing on the doorstep wasn't going to do much good.

"Uh… good question. I guess we should have called first."

"You could call now."

Erin felt her pocket for her phone. "I don't have her number."

Vic shook her head. She gave a sharp rap on the door, calling out Joelle's name, and they listened for a response from within. Erin couldn't hear anything. They waited for a little longer. Vic tried the handle, but found it locked.

"City folk," she muttered. "If she was from around here, she would have just left it unlocked."

"I guess this isn't going to work," Erin admitted. "I should have come up with a better plan."

Vic looked around. She stepped off of the concrete stairs and picked up a large rock, looking underneath.

"What are you doing?"

"Looking for her key."

"She's not going to put a key under a rock in the front garden."

"Maybe, maybe not." Vic put down the rock and picked up another large, decorative rock. There was a ceramic toad nestled down among the flowers, and she picked it up. "Bingo."

"I can't believe she would leave it there! That's just not safe."

"Maybe she didn't. Maybe the landlord did. Either way, we've got a key."

Vic climbed the stairs back to Erin's side and fit the key into the lock.

"Maybe we shouldn't," Erin warned.

"We're not exactly breaking in. We're checking in on a neighbor and bringing her lifesaving chicken soup."

"Well, maybe not lifesaving."

"Of course it is. If she didn't have any food, what would happen to her?"

"She would die."

"Therefore, chicken soup is lifesaving. We don't know if there is anyone else looking in on her. We could be the only ones."

Erin was still hesitant, but Vic didn't wait for her to agree. She just turned the handle and pushed the door open.

"Hello? Joelle? Are you home?" Vic stepped right in. Erin followed behind her uncertainly, a nervous cramp in her guts. It wasn't right to just walk right into Joelle's house. "It's Vic and Erin," Vic continued. "We brought you something to eat."

There was no sign of Joelle in the living room or kitchen. The house was still and quiet.

"Maybe she went out," Erin suggested.

"I thought she was hurt so bad," Vic countered.

"Maybe she went into the city. To stay with someone else, or to go to the hospital."

"Come on."

Vic led the way down the hallway to the bedrooms. The house had a similar floor layout to Clementine's. Probably most of Bald Eagle Falls houses had a similar floor plan. Most of them had been built around the same time.

"Joelle? Are you home?"

There was a soft response from the back of the house. Erin clutched at Vic's arm, listening. "Did you hear that?"

Vic looked at Erin and rolled her eyes. Of course she had heard. And it wasn't unexpected. Vic led the way to the bedroom in the far corner of the house. It was dark within, and Vic pushed the door open the rest of the way with one finger. They both looked in. The room was darkened by blinds that had been pulled shut, and there was a form lying in the bed under the blankets.

"Hey, Joelle, are you awake?" Vic asked.

Silly, since Joelle had just called back to them. Erin and Vic approached the bed. Erin wasn't sure what to do with the container of soup in her hands.

The room was warm and close. Erin's nostrils flared at the smell of sweat and dust and the tang of a sharp, bitter herb.

Joelle made another incoherent sound, and she turned over, pulling the blankets back from her face to see them.

"Hi," Erin greeted. "We… uh… brought you some soup." She gave the container a little lift to show it to Joelle. "We didn't know if you'd be able to fix anything for yourself. We heard you got hurt."

Joelle groaned. She pushed herself up, struggling to get into a sitting position. Vic helped her to get situated and turned on a bedside lamp.

Joelle shied away from the light and held her hand over her eyes to block it.

She didn't look well. Her face was pale, almost gray in the light of the lamp. Sweat stood out on her face. When she looked at them, Erin wasn't sure whether Joelle was really taking in what she saw and understanding it, or whether she was not even seeing Vic and Erin.

"We brought you food," Vic repeated loudly, like she was talking to someone hard of hearing.

"Not hungry," Joelle said. "Can't eat."

"When did you last have something? You need to eat something to sustain yourself."

"No. No, don't want any. Thank you."

Vic looked around the room. There were no empty dishes or trays to indicate that Joelle had eaten anything. There was a large mug on the bedside table. Erin bent over it. Tea. Loose leaves. She sniffed at it and found that it was the source of the bitter green smell that filled the room. She was unsure of the scent. It wasn't a tea that she was familiar with, and she thought she knew most of them.

"We'll warm some up for you," Vic told Joelle, still half shouting at her.

"I want to make sure you get a few spoonfuls inside of you, at least. You need to keep your strength up."

Joelle shook her head weakly. Her thinness made her face and body look frail in the dim light of the room. Erin had taken care of people who were failing, and she wasn't getting a good feeling about Joelle. Maybe she was in a lot of pain from her injury, and that was what was making her look so drawn and pale. Maybe the painkillers that had been prescribed to her were making her a bit dopey and suppressing her appetite. But Joelle did not look like the proud, vibrant young woman she had been.

Erin handed the soup container to Vic. "Would you warm it up?"

Vic opened her mouth to argue, obviously having expected Erin to do this part of the job. But she closed her mouth again and nodded. "Sure." She took the soup container and left the room.

Erin looked around the room again slowly. "How are you doing today, Joelle?" she asked, finding herself talking loudly as Vic had done. She opened the drawer in the bedside table to check for painkillers and didn't find anything. "Are you in a lot of pain? I heard you busted up your leg pretty good."

"It's fine," Joelle said, her voice a low moan that was at odds with her words. "Got some stuff…"

Some stuff. That bolstered Erin's thought that it might be painkillers that were affecting Joelle. Maybe she was hypersensitive or was having some kind of reaction. Maybe she had misunderstood the dosing or had taken too many by accident. Erin checked the other surfaces of the room, the dresser, and the other bedside table. No prescriptions.

There was an ensuite bathroom, something unusual in houses of that age, and Erin went into it, still talking to Joelle to distract her from the fact that Erin was snooping around her room.

There was a pill bottle with a red lid on the vanity counter, and Erin snatched it up. Bingo!

But turning it in her hand, she saw that it was just acetaminophen. Regular dose, not even extra strength. She unscrewed the red lid. The top seal had been punched through. Weighing it in her hand and looking down at the pills within, Erin was disappointed. The bottle had probably just been opened. It looked full. Joelle obviously hadn't overdosed on them. Erin continued her search, looking for any other signs of prescriptions or illicit drugs, checking the medicine cabinet behind the mirror, the shelves and drawers, and anywhere else she could think of that Joelle might conceivably have put her pills. She wouldn't have hidden them too carefully or too far away, because she needed to be able to get back at them with her bum leg, pain, and whatever other symptoms she was experiencing.

Erin was coming out of the bathroom as Vic was returning with a hot bowl of soup and a spoon. Vic raised her eyebrows questioningly. Erin shook her head.

"Here you go, Joelle," Vic announced. "Here's that chicken soup you wanted. Let's see if you can get some of it down."

Joelle's eyelids fluttered. She tried to focus on Vic, but seemed too drowsy to keep her eyes open all the way.

Vic perched on the edge of the bed and half-filled the soup spoon, then held it in front of Joelle's mouth. "Here you go. Open up."

Joelle obediently opened her mouth. Vic tipped the spoonful of soup into it. Most of it just dribbled down Joelle's chin.

"Let's try that again," Vic said with a bit of a laugh.

She again tried to get a spoonful of soup into Joelle. Joelle gagged and coughed.

"Maybe we should have gone vegan," Vic said. "What do vegans eat when they're sick?"

"I have no idea. Tofu?"

"This isn't working," Vic said more seriously. "What do you think we should do? We probably shouldn't leave her alone."

"No. I think she should be in hospital. She doesn't even have anyone watching over her here."

"Should we drive her? There might not be an ambulance available."

As if Erin didn't already know that. Bald Eagle Falls only had limited emergency resources, and if the dedicated ambulance was in use, they would have to get one from the city or make use of another option. "No… I think she'll be okay until they can get here. We'll just hang around to make sure she's okay and nothing happens to her before they get here. She'll probably just sleep."

She looked over at Joelle, whose eyes were already closed again.

CHAPTER 5

$\mathcal{E}$rin talked to the emergency dispatcher for Bald Eagle Falls, who broke the news that their ambulance was in use, but promised to scout around for another and get someone over to take care of Joelle.

"Do you need a doctor over there, honey?"

Erin smiled at the twang in her voice. "No, she's sleeping comfortably, so I think she'll be fine until the paramedics can get here. She's not in any pain or distress or throwing up."

"How about breathing? Good breaths?"

Erin leaned close to Joelle and watched her breathe. Joelle's chest rose and fell in a regular rhythm, long and slow in sleep.

"Yes. Her breathing seems just fine. Clear and regular."

"Okay. You be sure to call me back if anything changes. We'll have a doctor over there pronto if she takes a turn for the worse."

"Thanks. Any idea how long the ambulance will be?"

"It will depend on what is in use right now. I'll call around to see who I can get, but it might be a couple of hours."

Erin nodded. She'd expected as much. "Okay. Thanks for your help."

Erin stayed in the room with Joelle, wanting to keep an eye on her just to make sure she didn't run into any problems. Vic was restless and spent most of the time watching TV in one of the other rooms, only re-entering the bedroom occasionally to check on Joelle and make sure that Erin didn't need anything else from her.

Erin sat in a chair in the corner, listening to Joelle breathe and move around restlessly. Erin picked up a worn paperback copy of A Pocketful of Rye and started to read.

Joelle tossed and turned, getting increasingly agitated. Erin put down the book and went over to Joelle's side. She shook Joelle's arm gently to wake her up, figuring she was having nightmares. Joelle opened her eyes and stared at Erin, not seeming to take her in at first. Then she looked around the room and flapped her arm toward the bedside table.

"Drink."

Erin picked up the cup of room temperature tea. "Let me go get you some water. I don't know how long this has been sitting here."

"No! Give me the tea."

Erin hesitated. "It's not going to taste very good. It's not hot."

"It's for my leg," Joelle insisted. "Heal faster."

She reached insistently for the mug, and Erin eventually relinquished it. She expected Joelle to taste it and then decide it was too nasty to drink, but Joelle seemed oblivious to the bitter smell, taking a few swallows.

"What's in it?" Erin asked, thinking maybe she should let the paramedics know, just in case it was anything that might have an effect on her treatment at the hospital.

"Boneknit." Joelle's voice was weak, but her words were clear. "From Adele."

"Adele brought the tea?" Erin looked down at it in surprise. It wasn't like she would be able to somehow identify Adele's hand in the making of the tea, or that knowing who had made it would reveal what was in it.

She was surprised that Adele had gone to Joelle's house with tea for her injury. Adele knew who Joelle was, of course, and might have heard about her injury through the grapevine, as Erin had, but Adele spent most of her time in solitary pursuits and didn't hear the rumors like Erin did. But maybe it was usual for Adele to drop in with healing teas for the residents of Bald Eagle Falls. Just because she hadn't told Erin anything about it, that didn't mean anything. Adele was a private person and didn't share many of her inner thoughts.

Erin took the cup back from Joelle when she was done, and Joelle put her head down, closing her eyes again. Erin waited until she was sure Joelle was back asleep before leaving the room.

"How's it going?" Vic asked, looking up from the TV. "Everything okay?"

"Yes. She wanted some more of that tea." Erin wrinkled her nose. "I don't know how she could drink something that tasted like that, especially cold."

"Like what? Did you taste it?"

"No, but I can smell it, and that's bad enough."

Vic shook her head. "What did it smell like?"

"I don't know. She said it was boneknit, and that's comfrey, but that's not what it smelled like. It has comfrey in it, but something else that doesn't smell very nice. Bitter. Pungent. I don't know."

"I guess that answers what a vegan drinks when she's sick or hurt. She probably can't even taste it. Not everyone's nose is as sensitive as yours."

"No. I guess not. But I wouldn't be able to drink the stuff, that's for sure."

"See if there's some in the kitchen, and we can make some fresh for her. At least then it won't be cold. You can put some honey in it if it makes you feel better."

Erin went into the kitchen to see if any of the leaves had been left out.

"Did she go back to sleep?" Vic asked.

"Yes. She was only awake for a minute or two. Just long enough to have a few sips of tea, then she was off to slumberland again."

Erin was going through the cupboards and drawers in the kitchen when the doorbell rang. Erin listened to Vic answer it and deduced that it was the paramedics.

"This way," Vic invited, and led them down the hall to the bedroom. "Joelle. Joelle, honey, wake up. The ambulance is here, they're going to take you to the hospital to keep an eye on you. Joelle?" Vic's voice rose "Joelle?"

Erin paused in her search. Vic's voice was concerned, anxious. The paramedics spoke, taking over the scene and asking Vic to leave the room. Erin met Vic in the living room.

"What is it? Is everything okay?"

Vic's eyes were wide and panicked. "I couldn't wake her up, Erin. I think… she didn't respond at all. I don't know if she was even breathing."

CHAPTER 6

$\mathcal{S}$tunned, Erin steadied herself, putting her hand on the wall.

"What?" She looked down the hall toward the room. "I was just in there. She was fine!"

"I don't know. Maybe I'm wrong. I hope I'm just wrong!"

"Come in here," Erin led Vic over to the couch and sat her down. "Just relax and take deep breaths. I'm sure she's fine. There's nothing to panic about."

"What if she's dead?" Vic wailed, "I don't understand what happened. She just hurt her leg!"

"I don't know. We'll figure it out, okay? I'm sure it will all be okay."

Erin sat holding Vic's hand and rubbing her shoulder, trying to keep her calm, until one of the paramedics returned to the living room to talk to them.

"I need to know what happened," the man said. He had a stocky build, dark hair, and acne scars. Erin didn't recognize him from Bald Eagle Falls and assumed that he must have come from the city. Wherever the dispatcher had managed to find a free ambulance.

"What do you mean?" Erin asked. She shook her head. "We came here to check in on Joelle and bring her some chicken soup. She didn't seem like she was in very good shape, and we didn't want to leave her to take care of herself, so we called for an ambulance. That's all. I looked around for any pills, in case she had taken too many painkillers, but all I found was the Tylenol in the bathroom, and it looked full."

"What made you think she had overdosed on painkillers?"

"She hurt her leg, that's why she was in bed. So I thought maybe it had been bothering her and she had accidentally taken too many pills. She seemed really dopey and distant. She didn't want anything to eat, even though I don't think she'd had anything recently. Why? What's wrong? Is she worse? Vic said…" Erin looked at Vic and trailed off.

"She was non-responsive," the paramedic said. "We weren't able to detect any pulse or breathing. How long was she like that before we came?"

"She wasn't. I was just in there. She asked for more tea, so I gave her a sip. I came out here to make some more and then you arrived. I was in there and she was talking to me and awake not five minutes ago."

The paramedic looked from Erin to Vic and back again. He nodded, apparently seeing nothing that disturbed him. "Okay, then. We'll call for a doctor and your PD. I'm sure there's no reason to be concerned, but… it's an unattended death, and you did make an emergency call…"

Erin nodded numbly. "Okay… yeah. Of course. Whatever your procedure is. Do you want Vicky and me to stay here, or should we go home and stay out of the way?"

"I'd like you to stay put for now. We'll let the authorities make that call."

He went back down the hall to the bedroom. Vic raised her eyebrows at Erin.

"You see? I told you. I knew something was wrong."

"But she was just awake. She was just talking to me. What could have happened?"

"I don't know."

They waited for something to happen. But of course, nothing happened quickly in Bald Eagle Falls. The minutes seemed to drag into hours before the doctor showed up to examine Joelle's body and declare her dead. The doctor put the same questions to Erin and Vic as the paramedics had, shaking his head in confusion.

"I can't say what happened," he told them. "Maybe an embolism or a stroke. Even a heart attack. No way to tell until an autopsy is done."

"She's too young for something like that, isn't she? Women in their early thirties don't just drop dead."

"She had a leg injury. Probably there was a clot. It traveled to her lungs and she was gone very quickly."

Erin breathed out. "I suppose. I never thought of anything like that happening. Is there something I could have done? Some symptom I should have seen? Should I have elevated her legs?"

"There was probably no way you could have known. She might have had pain and tenderness in her leg, but considering that was where she had hurt herself... there would have been nothing to make you think it was anything other than just being sore after a fall."

Erin felt a little reassured by that. "Okay... thanks. This was really a shock!"

"I'm sure it was. I'll just wait for the police," the doctor looked at his watch, "and then we should all be able to get home. You two are the bakers, right? So you want to head to bed pretty early."

"I don't think there's much hope for that tonight," Vic sighed. "Normally, we'd be getting ready for bed now."

"It shouldn't take long for the police officer to arrive. He should be here any—"

There was a quick knock on the door, and Officer Terry Piper entered, K9 at his side. He looked at Erin and Vic, his jaw dropping. "What are you doing here?"

"Uh... we..." Erin was having trouble finding the words to explain their presence. "We were here for the soup."

"What?"

"Joelle, we heard that she was laid up, so we brought her soup."

"Joelle? What does she have to do with this?"

Erin swallowed. "She's the one who died."

Terry shook his head, his eyebrows drawing down in a scowl. "I wasn't told who it was that had died. Joelle Biggs? She seemed like a fit, healthy person. She was always going on about her yoga and healthy eating and training regime..."

He made it sound like he'd talked to her on a regular basis. Erin was puzzled, but pushed the thought aside, trying to bring Terry up to speed.

"I know. She always acted like she was really in good shape. I don't know if she was or not, but she had an accident and hurt her leg badly. We didn't know if she was going to be able to be up and around, so we stopped by with some soup..."

"Why?" Terry asked suspiciously.

"To be neighborly," Vic snapped. "That's the Christian way to behave, isn't it?" She glanced at Erin and got a little pink. "I mean… we were just trying to help out."

"Okay. And you discovered her body?"

Erin pushed her hair back over her ear. "No. She was alive when we got here. But she seemed like she wasn't in very good shape, so we called for an ambulance to take her to the hospital. So they could look after her."

Terry nodded encouragingly.

"She had some tea… I came out to the kitchen to talk to Vic… the paramedics came here, and when they went into her bedroom… they said she was dead."

Terry pulled out his notepad and started to scratch out some notes to himself. "So you were out of the room."

"Yes. The doctor said maybe it was a blood clot. From the injury in her leg. And she just… died when I left the room. Coincidentally." Erin looked over at the doctor for confirmation, and he nodded.

Terry looked at the doctor. "Stay here," he told Erin and Vic. "I'm going to go over the scene with the doctor and the paramedics, and then I might have more questions for you."

Erin nodded. She and Vic sat in silence while they waited for Terry to conduct his investigation and then return. The time crawled by. Erin pulled out her phone to peek at the time.

"Does it seem to you like he's taking a long time?"

Vic shrugged. "I guess. I'm sure he's just being careful…"

Erin rubbed her temples tiredly. "We were just being neighborly," she mumbled.

"No good deed goes unpunished," Vic quipped.

They exchanged weak laughs over this and were again quiet. Eventually, Terry and K9 returned from the bedroom, talking seriously with the doctor. Rather than leaving, the doctor sat down to join the further discussion.

"Can you go through everything that happened from the time you got to the house?" Terry suggested. "Did Joelle get up to let you in? Did someone else let you in?"

"Uh… no, we let ourselves in," Vic said. "She wasn't well enough to get up."

"So she had left the door unlocked for you?"

"No. The door was locked. The key was under the toad." Vic motioned in the direction of the front garden.

"Under the toad. She told you that's where to find it?"

"No, I just looked around. She didn't exactly know that we were coming. So I had to improvise."

"She didn't know you were coming, and you just searched out the spare key and let yourselves in."

"Well… yes," Vic agreed. "We knew she was hurt and probably couldn't get to the door to let us in. So we just did the logical thing."

"And broke in."

"We didn't break anything. We used a key to unlock the door. If she didn't want anyone to use the key, she shouldn't have left it in the front yard."

"Hidden out of sight under a toad."

"Anyone could have found it."

Terry made notes. "And what was it that concerned you about her condition when you went into her bedroom?"

"She seemed very weak," Erin explained. "She seemed… foggy. She couldn't sit up by herself. She didn't want anything to eat."

"Maybe she'd already had supper."

"She wouldn't even swallow the soup. I thought maybe she'd overdosed on painkillers and that was why she was so out of it. But I couldn't find any sign that she'd had anything but Tylenol."

"And tea," Vic contributed.

"Yes…" Erin agreed, unsure how to put her doubts about the tea into words.

"You made her tea and she drank it?" Terry asked.

"No. She had tea beside her bed. Cold. Room temperature. She said she wanted more of the tea, so I gave it to her. She didn't want anything else. I said I'd get her water and that the tea was cold, but she drank it anyway."

"So she was able to swallow."

"Yes. She swallowed the tea."

Terry nodded.

"She went back to sleep, and I came out to the kitchen to make some more tea. I was looking around to see if she had more leaves…"

At his questioning look, she tried to explain further.

"It wasn't *tea* tea. It was an herbal remedy. She said it was boneknit. Comfrey."

The doctor was nodding. "A lot of natural remedies are used in these parts. Comfrey is generally regarded as safe, if it is used in small amounts and for a limited period of time."

"What happens if a person takes too much?" Piper asked.

"Liver damage, if I remember right. Possibly carcinogenic. But those are long-term consequences. I've never heard of it causing a sudden death like this." He gave a smile. "I think you can disregard it as a causative factor in this case."

"But it wasn't just boneknit," Erin said.

Both men looked at her. "Oh…?" Terry prompted.

"There was something else in it. I know what comfrey smells like. Very fresh and aromatic… like sliced cucumbers. The tea had comfrey in it, but there was another smell, a stronger one. I'm not sure what it was. I know most of the common tea ingredients, but not all of the medicinal herbs."

"Can you describe it?"

"Not very well. It was bitter. Sharp. It was… unpleasant. I couldn't have drunk it."

The doctor gave a shrug. "There are many different plants used in folk remedies. Most of them are harmless. Some can be poisonous, or beneficial herbs have poisonous lookalikes, but reactions are usually mild, they don't end up being treated in hospital… or dead. I doubt if it was the tea."

"How long after drinking the tea did Joelle die?" Terry asked.

"A couple of minutes, maybe," Erin said uncomfortably. "It couldn't have been more than five minutes from the time she drank the tea until the paramedics got here and couldn't get a response from her."

"I think I'd better take this tea into evidence," Terry said. "Did you find any more leaves in the kitchen?"

"No. Just what was already made in the bedroom. I couldn't find any more loose leaves. They would probably be out on the counter if she had a supply of them. But there weren't any."

"We'll get it tested. Maybe there was something harmful it in. Between that and the autopsy… hopefully we'll be able to get some answers about what she died of." He made a face, and Erin wondered what was bothering him. "You guys really shouldn't have been here. I understand that your intentions were good, but you just landed yourself in the middle of another unexplained death. You want to stop doing that…"

"It isn't like I was planning to!" Erin protested. "We were just trying to do something nice. We didn't poison her."

"I imagine that's the conclusion people are going to jump to. This is the third time you're the suspect in a possible poisoning. People will stop coming to the bakery, afraid that you might poison them."

"They know I didn't poison Angela or Trenton," Erin shot back. "And there's no other bakery for them to go to. Not in town."

Her eyes locked with Terry's, and Erin knew in an instant that was exactly the wrong thing to say. There was no other bakery and there would be no other bakery, now that Joelle could not team up with Charley to open The Bake Shoppe. The potential opening of a competing bakery was, once again, on the back burner.

"I didn't poison Joelle to eliminate the competition," Erin said tiredly.

"No," Terry said. His voice was just as weary as hers. It didn't carry quite the conviction that she would have expected from him on her behalf.

Erin knew that it would take time for Joelle's death to be investigated. It took time to analyze unknown substances, and it took time for an autopsy to be performed and have anything useful for the police to investigate. In the meantime, Terry would be making inquiries with anyone who might have had motive or opportunity to kill Joelle. Unfortunately, if Joelle had agreed with Charley to sign on Davis's behalf and open up The Bake Shoppe, it would put Auntie Clem's Bakery's business in jeopardy, and nothing Erin could say would remove that mark against her.

She didn't get much sleep, but she was at the bakery the next day early in the morning as usual, trying to focus on her job rather than on Joelle's death. It wasn't just the fact that she would be a suspect that bothered her. Maybe even the prime suspect, since she had been on the scene when Joelle died. She couldn't erase Joelle's face from her mind. The pallid, frail look she had exhibited before her death. Should Erin have known that she was near death? She and Vic had recognized that something was wrong. Joelle shouldn't have been that ill just from a leg injury. The doctor had said that if it were a blood clot, there was probably no way Erin could have recognized it and nothing she could have done differently. Would Joelle have looked that way if she had a blood clot? If it were in her leg, would her face and her thought processes have been affected?

"Erin."

Erin blinked and looked over at Vic. "Hm? Sorry, I wasn't listening."

"You don't think it was the tea, do you?"

Vic's thoughts were apparently running parallel to Erin's.

"I really don't know. I don't think so. The doctor said most herbal teas are harmless. And she didn't have very much. Just a few sips…"

"But we don't know how much she might have had before we got there. She might have had several cups already, hoping to heal her leg faster."

"With medicine, more isn't always better."

"I know that. But would Joelle? People think that a natural herb can't do any damage, because it's natural, but… well, hemlock is natural too, right?"

"Hemlock?" Erin repeated, her voice jumping higher, "You don't think someone put hemlock in her tea, do you?"

Vic shook her head emphatically. "No, no. I didn't mean that at all. I'm just saying, it could have been something that was harmful to her. Even if it was a healing herb, it could still have affected her the wrong way."

Erin shook her head. "I don't think it was the tea. The doctor thought maybe it was a blood clot."

Erin hadn't told anyone that Joelle said it was Adele who had given her the tea. Adele wouldn't have done anything to hurt Joelle. Adele was a good person. She was a friend. Despite all that had happened since Erin had moved to Bald Eagle Falls, she still believed in the basic goodness of people. Despite all of the people and problems that lurked in her past, she still thought that most people, people like Adele, were good.

They continued to work in silence.

CHAPTER 7

True to her usual schedule, Charley didn't show her face until the afternoon, probably having slept away the morning.

"Can you take a break?" she asked Erin, motioning to the tables and chairs at the front of the shop.

There were no other customers and Erin expected it to stay quiet until the after-school crowd arrived. She nodded.

"You want a coffee? Danish?"

"Coffee," Charley agreed. "It's too early for anything too sweet, though. How about… a muffin?"

"Most of them are still pretty sweet. Maybe… lemon cranberry?"

"Sounds good!" Charley agreed.

In her first weeks living in Bald Eagle Falls, she had approached Erin's gluten-free goodies with some trepidation, sure they were going to be awful, or at least substandard. But she had gotten over her uncertainty of the food and was open to trying whatever was on offer.

Erin got them each a coffee and a muffin for Charley, and she went to the front of the store.

"Just let me know if you need a break for anything," she told Vic.

Vic nodded, unsmiling. Erin knew that Vic didn't particularly like Charley. Partly because of who Charley was—a Dyson and a rather abrasive personality—and partly, Erin suspected, because she was jealous of the time Erin spent with Charley and the fact that they had a familial relationship Erin and Vic did not. It wasn't like Erin was spending a lot of time with Charley and only a little with Vic, but that didn't seem to matter.

"So…?" Erin prompted, wondering what Charley wanted to talk about.

"So…? Someone practically dies in your arms, and you have to ask what I want to talk about?"

News traveled fast in Bald Eagle Falls, especially juicy gossip. Erin wasn't sure who had talked to Charley. She didn't have a lot of friends in town, but there were plenty of people who were happy to spread bad news.

"She didn't die in my arms," Erin countered. "I wasn't even in the room."

Charley broke off a bite of muffin. "Spill it," she said, "I want to know all the details."

"I probably shouldn't be talking to you about it. Officer Piper will want to talk to you…"

"Why would he want to talk to me? I wasn't there. I didn't have anything to do with it."

"But you'll be a suspect. Because of the bakery…"

"Why? I didn't want her dead. Who knows who Davis will appoint as his attorney now. I wanted Joelle alive, so she could sign whatever directions were needed to get the bakery opened up again."

"But she wasn't cooperating, so maybe…."

"Still no reason for me to kill her. I can't convince her if she's dead."

Erin considered it, but she couldn't think of any reason Charley would have killed Joelle. Not if she was telling the truth.

"Well…"

"Come on. Tell me what happened. All of it."

Erin surrendered and gave Charley a brief account of what had happened at Joelle's house.

"Bizarre," Charley said, shaking her head. "I never would have thought… she seemed really healthy. I know sometimes athletes have heart attacks just out of the blue… do you think that's what happened?"

"It's as good a guess as any. Until the autopsy has been done, we have no way of knowing what it actually was. Maybe she had a virus or an infection. I don't know."

She didn't suggest to Charley that it might have been a blood clot or that it might have had something to do with the mysterious ingredients of the tea. She wasn't comfortable talking to Charley about it like she was with Vic. Charley was still an outsider.

For a while, Charley was silent, sipping her coffee, her brow furrowed. Erin waited for her to spill what she was thinking.

"You know how you hear stories?" Charley asked finally. "Somebody who had several near-death experiences in a short period of time, and then things caught up to them, and they actually did die?"

Erin shook her head. "I don't know... I guess I've heard of a couple stories like that, but it isn't that common."

"No... but how would you explain it? Was that person fated to die? The person was supposed to die, and even if they escaped the first few incidents, it was bound to catch up to them..."

"I don't believe in fate." Erin shifted uncomfortably. She took a sip of her black coffee, knowing that she probably shouldn't have anything too late in the afternoon. She wouldn't be able to sleep at night, and she needed to be able to sleep.

"But you must see how some things are meant to happen," Charley pressed. "Things that just fall into place? Coincidences? Unexpected events..."

"No. Sorry. I just don't see it that way. There is randomness and there are patterns... but God or fate? I've never seen anything to convince me of that."

"Okay... well, then maybe you can explain this. Joelle kept having accidents and now she's dead. Do you think that's just coincidence?"

"Not exactly. She died because of one of those accidents. It's not a coincidence, it's related."

"But you don't know why she died."

"Not yet. But I think it was related to her getting hurt."

"What about the other accidents?"

"Maybe she hurt herself the first time, and that caused the others. She hit her head or pulled a muscle. Something that made her more clumsy."

"I talked to her, though. She said they weren't related. And if she had a head injury or was limping, I would have noticed."

"It might have just been more subtle than that." Erin shrugged.

Charley's face was tight, a mask. She shook her head.

"What other accidents did she have?" Erin asked.

Charley drew her chair in closer to Erin. Erin got the feeling that this was the question she had been waiting for. She was bursting at the seams to share what she knew, only she didn't have anyone to share it with.

"The first time, it was a black eye. She said that she had walked into a tree branch. We kind of laughed about it. She said she had never done anything like that before, and we laughed at what a crazy accident it was. She's a city girl, so I teased her about how she'd never learned how to be safe around trees, you know?"

Erin nodded.

"Then there was the accident at the river."

"Someone said she was standing too close to the edge and the bank crumbled."

"That could happen to anyone, right? But… I mean, she was a city girl, she would still be figuring out how close to go and be safe. Not like someone who's grown up climbing trees and jumping into rivers and all of the stupid things we did as kids."

Erin hadn't grown up in Bald Eagle Falls either. Like Joelle, she was a product of the city, not really at ease in the bush. Her childhood had not consisted of climbing trees and jumping into rivers.

Charley shrugged, as if acknowledging this.

"And that was the only other accident? Until she fell and hurt her leg?" Erin asked.

Three accidents. Only one of them had resulted in any serious injury. If they had happened months apart, no one would have thought anything of any of them. But because they had happened in a short time, they formed a pattern in Joelle's and Charley's minds. A false pattern, probably.

"She couldn't explain how she had hurt herself in the woods that day," Charley said, her voice low as if she were telling a ghost story. "She said that something had grabbed her foot and made her fall."

"Grabbed her foot? What grabbed her foot?"

"She couldn't say. When she fell, she was knocked out initially. When she woke up, she was in shock. She was bleeding badly, so she was faint and queasy. She tried to figure out how she had fallen, but she wasn't in any shape to sort it out. She told me about what had happened. Told me where it was, and I went back there to take a look around, and I couldn't see anything that she might have tripped over."

"Where was this?"

Charley chewed her lip. "In the bush, where she'd been out hiking. She had to flag down a passing vehicle to give her a ride because she was too hurt to walk back."

"How do you know you got the right place? And how do you know there wasn't anything she might have tripped over? I mean… I can trip over a crack in the sidewalk. All it would take is a stick or a pebble that she stepped on the wrong way. You can't tell that by going back and looking at the ground."

"I know it was the right place because her blood was still there. And there wasn't anything that could have tripped her up. Not like she said. Not something that could have *grabbed* her."

"That could mean anything. Her foot caught under an exposed root. It doesn't mean that there was a person lying in wait who reached out and grabbed her."

"There were no exposed roots," Charley said triumphantly. "There wasn't anything sticking up from the ground that she could have caught her toe under."

"Not that you could see. That doesn't mean that there wasn't something she had just caught the wrong way. A rock that caught her toe in a hollow, that she ended up kicking away when she tripped over it. With all of the experience you have in the backwoods, you've *never* tripped?"

"Sure. A hundred times. But I've never hurt myself that bad, and I could usually figure out what had tripped me."

"Usually. So not always."

Charley considered. "Okay, not always. Sometimes, it could just have been uneven ground, something that looked perfectly smooth to the casual eye. But I never thought I'd been grabbed." She considered and reworded. "Usually," she admitted again.

"When you catch your toe under something or run into weeds or branches that are ankle-high, sometimes it feels like you were grabbed," Erin said.

"I suppose."

Erin shrugged.

"So your answer is that it was all just coincidence. It wasn't just because it was her time to die."

"It wasn't really coincidence. She was doing activities she wasn't used to in a place she wasn't accustomed to doing them. She wasn't used to walking around in the woods or standing on riverbanks. So she made mistakes, and those got her hurt."

"She wasn't supposed to die?"

"Supposed to?" Erin shrugged. "Like I said, I don't believe in fate or God. There isn't any *supposed to* or *not supposed to*. She just did."

"I don't know how that is supposed to make more sense than fate," Charley said. "Death just being a random happening... that doesn't make me feel any better. Our lives are more than just *random*."

Her speech just served to convince Erin further that religion was mostly just people attempting to make themselves feel better about what they perceived as the unfairness of the short human life.

"Did Joelle talk to you about anyone else in Bald Eagle Falls?" Erin asked, wondering whether Joelle had mentioned Adele to anyone else. "Anyone that she had talked to or who was helping her out...?"

"No. I don't think she really had much to do with anyone around here." Charley's eyes narrowed. "Do you mean *you?* Were you helping her?"

"No. I just wondered whether she had made any other friends. Just you?"

Charley shrugged. "We weren't really friends, but I don't know that she had any friends here. I was the one who had the most to do with her, because of the bakery and her being Davis's power of attorney. But we weren't close."

"You went to see where she had fallen down," Erin pointed out.

"I was just curious. It was a strange accident."

"So you were visiting her at her house after the accident?"

"Yeah. She couldn't get out and around."

"Did she seem... okay? I mean, her spirits, pallor, energy level?"

"Sure. Seemed normal. In pain, of course, but nothing seemed wrong to me."

"What day was that?"

"Right after it had happened. I told her to let me know if she needed anything—I figured the more I helped her, the more she would be willing to work with me—but she never called to ask for anything. So I figured everything was just fine. I certainly never expected *this*." Charley rolled her eyes. "You've kind of messed things up for me."

"I didn't—"

"But then…" Charley's eyes were calculating, "We never were on the same side, were we? You never wanted me to come here and open up The Bake Shoppe."

"I never said that."

"You didn't have to. It's true, isn't it? You never did like the idea."

"I… was nervous about it," Erin admitted. "I didn't want to end up getting squeezed out by another bakery. But I was willing to ride it out and see how it went. I never would have… eliminated the competition."

"Easy enough to say. But I don't know. This bakery means everything to you, doesn't it?"

Erin swallowed and looked around at her surroundings. The bakery was important to her. It represented her independence, her one chance to run her own business and be her own boss, instead of constantly being subservient to someone else. It was the unexpected legacy Clementine had left for her. In the short time she had been there, she had made it her own. It wasn't just important to her, either. It also supported Vic and made it possible for her to be independent from the family that had disowned her for trying to be true to herself. Clementine's legacy also meant that she had a place to live where she didn't have to pay someone else rent every month, and also provided places for Vic and Adele to have their own homes. If the plug were pulled, and the bakery were no longer there to support them, what would happen to Erin, Vic, and Adele? Erin would have to find another job, working for someone else once more, and the odds that she'd be able to find something to support herself in Bald Eagle Falls were slim. The odds that all three of them would be able to find jobs, plus Bella, who worked part time to make sure they all got breaks, were almost nonexistent. No more bakery would mean changes to all of their lives.

"It means a lot," she agreed. "Not everything, because I still have my friends, and my family," she met Charley's eyes. "But I don't know what I would do without the bakery."

"I don't think you poisoned Joelle," Charley said, sitting back. "But her dying like this… it's pretty weird. Don't you think?"

"It's unexplained. I'm sure once the autopsy has been done… it will all make sense."

"A person doesn't die from falling down and banging up her knee."

"No… I mean, it could get infected, or get a clot… so it's possible… but I don't know if that's what happened. I just know… she wasn't in good shape when we got there. Something was wrong with her."

"I guess time will tell," Charley said, folding her arms across her chest. "We'll just have to wait and see."

CHAPTER 8

Terry hadn't been to the house or to the bakery for several days. Erin excused his absence; he obviously had a lot more on his plate, with an unexpected death on the books. He had a lot to investigate. It couldn't be easy to conduct an investigation while still performing all of his usual duties.

She was relieved when she heard the tap on her door. At least he hadn't totally cut himself off from her.

"Terry!" She opened the door wide to invite him in. "Come in! How are you?"

He didn't go to his favorite spot in the living room, so Erin assumed he was hoping for the kitchen. "Are you hungry? You know I've always got bread and jam."

"I could manage a little something…"

Which probably meant that he had skipped dinner altogether. Erin let him get settled at the table, going through the day-old bread she had brought home with her to pick out his favorite rolls. A few seconds in the microwave, and they would be as warm and moist as if she had just finished baking them.

"I'm getting low on some of the Jam Lady jams," she commented, as she pulled several out of the fridge. The statement seemed a little ridiculous when she set half a dozen different flavors in front of him on the table but, nonetheless, it was true. They consumed more than their fair share of the Jam Lady jams and, unlike the rest of the town, Erin knew that the Jam Lady wasn't even a lady, but was Roger, Mary Lou's husband. Disabled after a failed suicide attempt, it had taken him some time to find something he could do to help bring more income into the home, and that turned out to be creating handmade artisanal jams. As he did not consider it a 'manly' job, the actual source of the Jam Lady jams was kept a strict secret.

"Looks wonderful," Terry assured Erin, breaking open one of the rolls to slather it will butter and jam.

Erin got out a biscuit for K9 and tossed a couple of treats to Orange Blossom to quiet him down and to make sure he didn't steal K9's doggie biscuit. Blossom was getting altogether too bold recently, unconcerned that K9 was big enough to put a stop to any thievery if he decided to disobey his master. But K9 was well-trained and, though he grumbled, he didn't chase Orange Blossom when the cat teased him or stole his food.

Erin made small talk with Terry while he worked his way through a couple of rolls, waiting for an indication from him as to the reason he had stopped by. Was it just for a visit, or did he have news?

She caught a glimpse of Vic making her way across the back yard and, in a minute, Vic was at the back door, peeking around the door.

"Knock, knock? Am I interrupting anything?"

"No, come on in. You want a snack?"

"Better not." Vic patted her stomach. "I won't be able to keep my figure if I keep adding extra meals."

Erin sat down at the table and helped herself to a corner of Terry's roll. Like Vic, she didn't want a whole one, but she did want a taste. She savored the bite. Terry offered the rest to her, but she shook her head.

"No. This is good. Just want a taste of that blackberry jam. It's so good!"

"They all are. Choosing between the flavors is the hardest part." The handsome officer polished off the rest of his treat in a couple of bites. "We can sit in the living room, if you like."

They all agreed to go where it was more comfortable and took up their seats in the living room.

"Any news about Joelle?" Vic asked what Erin had been dying to know but didn't have the nerve to ask.

Terry let out a long sigh. He didn't look happy. Did that mean they didn't know anything?

"I wish I could say I had better news. But yes… we have made a little progress on the case."

"Better news…?" Erin echoed.

"The autopsy isn't done, but we were able to have the tea analyzed for its components."

"And it wasn't just comfrey, was it?" Erin asked.

"No."

"What else?"

"Foxglove."

Vic cocked her head. She was obviously more familiar with her herbs than Erin was. Erin was trying to think of any tea that had foxglove as an ingredient, and couldn't.

"You've heard of it?" Erin asked Vic.

"Uh, yeah…" Vic looked at Terry. "It has those tall clusters of flowers in the summer. They're really pretty."

"Pretty, but deadly," Terry said quietly. "They source a drug called digitalis from foxglove. A heart medication."

"So it's good for the heart?" Erin suggested hopefully, even though he had said it was deadly.

"In tiny, measured doses, it can be very effective. But you wouldn't put foxglove into a tea. The plant itself is quite toxic."

"It was supposed to be comfrey tea," Erin said. "Do you think someone could mix up comfrey and foxglove? Are they similar?"

"It's been known to happen. When they are not in bloom, comfrey and foxglove can look very similar. People have been known to confuse them."

"That must be what happened, then. Joelle knew it was supposed to be comfrey. Something to help her to heal faster. When she drank it, she didn't act like it tasted bad. I guess… she couldn't tell by the taste."

"You could smell it, though," Terry pointed out.

"Yeah, but you know Erin's nose," Vic said. "Just because she can smell something, that doesn't mean a normal person would have been able to. It didn't smell bad to me."

Erin closed her eyes and shook her head. "So it was an accident. That must be why she was acting so strangely when we got there. She'd already had some of the tea. And then when she had some more… I guess that was enough to finish her off? How much foxglove would she need to have to kill her?"

"I've got some experts compiling information for me, but from my nonprofessional internet searches… it looks like one or two leaves could kill within a few days. It's not a fast poison like cyanide or water hemlock."

His eyes were quick, focused sharply on Erin, watching her for her reaction. Erin looked away from him, frustrated that she would still be on his list, in spite of their personal relationship. "It wasn't me, Officer Piper."

"I don't think it was," he returned. "But I can't let my personal feelings get in the way of the investigation. I shouldn't even be here talking to you, I should get you down to the police department for an official statement. But like I say… I don't think it was you."

"Then why are you looking at me like that?"

"I'm still on the job. I'm still investigating an unexpected death. If it was an accident, then it was an accident. But if it wasn't, I can't let myself be swayed by a pretty face."

Erin rolled her eyes. "You can't sweet talk me and investigate me at the same time."

"Actually, I thought I was doing a pretty good job of it."

"Not bad," Vic agreed obligingly.

Erin wasn't willing to give Terry a break, though. If they were close friends, then he couldn't suspect her. He couldn't be investigating her. In the past, with Angela's murder especially, it was different. They weren't involved yet then. But now that they were friends, getting ever closer, he couldn't just step back and pretend to be objective.

"Erin, please…" Terry tried to take her hand. And while his warm grip felt comforting, Erin shook it off.

"No, Terry. You can tell me all you like that you don't think I did it. If you're still investigating me, then that's sort of beside the point, isn't it?"

He withdrew his hand. "I suppose I should hand the investigation over to someone else. The sheriff or Tom or some outside investigator… I could get someone from the county, or the FBI…"

"The FBI? For an accidental poisoning?"

"If that's what it was."

"What else would it be?" Vic demanded. "You think it was intentional? You think that Erin or whoever made that tea was trying to kill Joelle? I agree that no one around here liked her, but why would anyone try to kill her?"

"She might have hurt your business, Miss Victoria. Or Charley might have gotten sick and tired of trying to convince her to help open up The Bake Shoppe."

"My business? You know very well it's Erin's business, I'm not the one who—" Vic looked over at Erin, and blanched. "I mean… I'm sorry, Erin, but it's true. I'd lose my job if Auntie Clem's went under, but it isn't *my* business."

"I know that. And so does Terry. And so will whoever he passes the investigation over to."

Terry knew that she was telling him to go ahead. She wanted him to give the case to someone else, but she could see in his eyes that he was reluctant to do so. He didn't want to let it go and give it to someone else. Erin had no idea what kind of investigative experience the sheriff or Tom had. Terry had always taken point on everything in the previous investigations. If he couldn't trust the sheriff or Tom to be able to run down the culprit—if it was murder rather than an accident—then he'd have to get an outside investigator and take the matter completely out of the hands of the Bald Eagle Falls police department. Terry looked pained as he considered the alternatives.

"Okay," he agreed. "I'll give it to someone else."

He waited for her to protest, but Erin didn't. She didn't want him looking at her and considering whether she could be a killer, either accidental or intentional. He had done enough digging into her past previously. She didn't want her boyfriend—if that was what he was—being privy to the mistakes she had made in the past or the circumstances that she had found herself in that were beyond her control.

Vic raised her eyebrows. "Are you really going to make him give the case to someone else? What if he does and that person thinks you poisoned Joelle? Intentionally?"

Erin's stomach tightened. "I didn't do it."

"I didn't say you did. But some people… they're not going to look past the first suspect. And being innocent doesn't mean you're not going to get convicted and thrown in the pokey. Erin, you have to sit up and pay attention. Terry isn't going to accuse you of murder. But someone else might."

"No, Erin's right," Terry said. "I shouldn't be investigating it when she is a suspect. It's a conflict of interest."

"Then make her not a suspect."

"I can't do that, Vic. The circumstances are what they are. I don't want to end up censured or disgraced because I listened to my heart instead of the evidence."

Which again made Erin sound like she was guilty. The evidence would exonerate her, not convict her.

"Who are you going to give it to?" she asked.

"I have to think about it. Probably the sheriff."

Erin nodded. "Well, he knows where to find me."

CHAPTER 9

$\mathcal{E}$rin's heart was heavy as she made her way through the thick woods to go visit Adele. She didn't want to have to be the one to break the news to Adele, but she didn't want Adele to be surprised by the police investigation either.

She was sure that the investigation would prove that it was just an accident. Adele had accidentally included foxglove in the comfrey tea. She had been trying to help out. It was unfortunate, but not intentional. After Terry had gone, Vic had repeated to Erin that comfrey and foxglove looked similar enough to be confused with each other if they were not in bloom and the person gathering them was not experienced or careful enough. Erin hadn't told Vic that it was Adele who had prepared Joelle's tea.

It took a while to get to the cottage, and Erin hadn't called ahead, so there was no guarantee she would be home. Erin knocked on the door, quietly at first, and then louder. There was no answer. Apparently, Adele was out.

With a sigh, Erin turned away from the door. She saw Adele approaching from the other side of the clearing.

"Oh—Adele."

Adele's eyebrows went up. "Erin. I wasn't expecting you."

"I know. I should have called…"

"No, of course not. You're welcome to come by here any time. It is your property."

"That doesn't mean I can just come in whenever I feel like it. Anyway… could we talk?"

Adele nodded. "Of course," she agreed. She paused before approaching the door, looking around. Erin heard a caw, and Skye swooped in and landed on Adele's shoulder. Adele put two fingers out and stroked the bird.

"Hello, Skye," Erin greeted him softly.

The crow cocked his head at her curiously but didn't immediately fly away.

"Could I touch him?" Erin asked.

"You'll have to ask him."

Erin took a couple of steps closer and reached her hand out tentatively toward Skye. He cawed and flapped away, disappearing into the trees. Erin shrugged.

"I guess we have to get to know each other better first."

Adele nodded and let herself into the cabin. Erin watched as she took off her cloak, and then took a variety of greenery out of her satchel, which she arranged in piles on the counter.

"You've been out gathering herbs?" Erin asked.

"Yes."

"Comfrey?"

Adele turned to look at Erin. "No comfrey today."

She went back to laying out the various plants, and then sat down at the table. Erin sat across from her, feeling awkward without a cup of tea or something to occupy her hands.

"Did you hear about Joelle?" she asked finally.

Adele's brow furrowed. "I heard that she passed," she said after consideration. "But no one seemed to know what had happened. I knew that she had hurt herself, but I didn't know she was sick. It seemed very sudden."

"It was… and they still haven't confirmed the cause of death. Not officially, anyway."

Adele's gaze darted to Erin's face. "Not officially."

"They haven't completed the autopsy yet. Things like that take time."

"But you're here to talk to me about it, so you must suspect something."

Erin's instinct was to deny that was what she had gone to Adele's to talk to her about it. She could say that she had just gone there for a visit, and that the conversation had just led naturally to Joelle. But Adele wasn't an idiot. She knew something was going on.

"I… I saw Joelle just before she died. She said that you had made her the tea. Comfrey tea."

She wanted Adele to deny it. Joelle had been hallucinating or had some reason to make trouble for her. Adele hadn't even been over there. Why would she be? She didn't even know Joelle.

"I made her comfrey tea," Adele agreed.

Erin sighed. She looked around the little cabin.

"Why does that upset you?" Adele inquired. She was so calm.

Too calm.

"Because there wasn't just comfrey in that tea. They tested it. It also had foxglove in it."

"Foxglove." For the first time, Adele looked anxious. "There couldn't have been foxglove in it."

"There was. I could smell something. I knew it wasn't just comfrey."

"You smelled it? What were you doing there?"

"I stopped by with some soup. She wouldn't take it. All she wanted was the tea. She drank some… and then she died."

"Foxglove doesn't kill that fast."

"It wasn't the first time she'd drunk the tea. What day did you give it to her?"

Adele didn't answer.

"Could you have picked foxglove instead of comfrey?" Erin prompted. "Vic said they look similar. If they're not in bloom. One could be mistaken for the other."

"I would not mistake foxglove for comfrey." Adele's gaze was unfocused. She wasn't looking at Erin. Was she thinking back to when she had collected the comfrey? Picturing it in her mind and trying to determine if she could possibly have been wrong? "But you said the autopsy hadn't been done yet. They haven't determined cause of death."

"No. It could have been something else. But if her tea did contain foxglove… well…" Erin shook her head. "Digitalis is poisonous. What are the odds that something else killed her?"

"You were there when she died? Tell me what happened. Describe it to me."

Erin described the scene with as much detail as she could. When she was done, Adele didn't ask any questions, but sat there thinking about it.

"I don't want it to be the foxglove in the tea," Erin said. "But if she'd been drinking it for a couple of days… well then, it makes sense, doesn't it?"

"Deaths don't always make sense," Adele said. "I couldn't say whether Joelle died of digitalis poisoning. No one could say, not yet."

"No."

They sat in awkward silence for some time.

"Did you know Joelle?" Erin asked. "How did you end up taking her the comfrey tea?"

She didn't think Adele was going to answer her. But Adele was a person who didn't mind silences, and she took her time to consider things before answering. Erin found it unnerving, but she was getting more used to Adele's rhythms, so she waited.

"Sometimes women in town ask me to provide them with remedies," Adele said slowly, weighing her words. "They know that I am familiar with herbs and have decided I am good at more than just wreaths of dried herbs for use in their kitchens."

Erin was surprised. She raised her eyebrows at this revelation. "Does that mean they know that you are…"

"Wiccan?" Adele considered the question. "I think we're following the old army policy of don't ask, don't tell. They probably suspect, but they're willing to believe I'm just a wise old woman experienced with herbs. As long as they don't actually ask me if I'm a witch, they're not under any moral obligation to shun my teas and tonics. Remedies are okay; potions are not."

Erin nodded. She had always trusted Adele's ministrations before but, for the first time, she questioned her own blind faith in the woman's knowledge and abilities. What did she really know about Adele? Could Erin really be sure Adele could tell the difference between comfrey and foxglove? How much could she really be trusted?

"So Joelle sent for you? Asked you to bring her something to help her heal faster?

"I heard she was hurt, so I offered my services."

"Did you give comfrey to anyone else?"

Adele measured her words. "Not lately."

"I just thought… you wouldn't want to harm anyone…"

"I did not harm Joelle. I don't know what happened to her, but she was not poisoned by my comfrey."

No, not by her comfrey. But by her foxglove?

Adele rose to her feet, which Erin took as a signal that it was time for her to leave. She got up as well and turned toward the door.

"Okay. I just wanted to let you know what had happened, so you wouldn't be blindsided if the police came around. I didn't tell them that Joelle said the tea was from you, but I suspect they'll figure it out. Especially if you've been preparing remedies for other women."

Adele nodded. "It's not a secret. I imagine they'll be by here sooner or later. Will it be your friend, Terry?"

"No." Erin hesitated, not sure how much to tell Adele. Her tendency to be reserved and not jump in with any personal information made Erin more reticent to share with her. "They consider me a suspect, so it's not really right for Terry to lead the investigation."

"A suspect? You make it sound like they think it was murder."

"Since they haven't determined cause or manner of death yet… that has to be a possibility." Erin choked up, thinking of Joelle lying in her bed, weak and gray. "I was just there to help her. But it seems like I can't get close to someone in this town without them dying. *I'd* suspect me."

Adele paused in walking Erin to the door. "But you've told me about those other cases. You might have been close by, but you were exonerated. The police know it was nothing to do with you. You were just being used."

"It doesn't make me feel any better. I still feel like it's my fault. Stuff like this wasn't happening before I came to Bald Eagle Falls. I must have some kind of… karma."

Adele gave her a smile. "But you don't believe in karma."

"No. But I don't know of any other way to explain it. Why else would these things start happening when I got here?"

"How would you explain it to Vic, if she said it was some kind of divine destiny?"

Erin sniffled and thought about it. "I'd tell her that it was just random or coincidental. That she was just associating disparate events with each other…"

"The other possibility is that your arrival here threw something out of balance. Before you arrived, it was in stasis, but you… jarred something loose. Not in some kind of karmic or mystical way. You just changed the dynamics of the people here. Threw something new into the mix."

"Because I opened the bakery? That meant that the town didn't need Angela's bakery anymore, so Gema decided to fight back instead of being pushed around?"

Adele shrugged. "I don't know. But I have seen that things in this town are very unsettled. They are in a state of change instead of stasis."

"It makes me wish I hadn't come. If I'd just stayed away, sold the house and shop instead of coming and setting up here… everything would have just stayed the same."

"Maybe it's good that things changed. Still waters grow stagnant. A new source of water clears things away, freshens them up. Rather than being something harmful, maybe you are helping to heal this community."

Erin sighed and shook her head. "I don't know. I don't like feeling responsible for all of this stuff."

"Then stop."

How could Erin stop feeling responsible for all of the mishaps and death that had happened since she had arrived in town?

"Well… thanks for letting me vent. I hope you don't run into any trouble because of all of this."

"Don't worry about me. And don't worry about the investigation. It will all work out."

"I don't know how to not worry," Erin said with a bleak laugh.

Adele opened the door for her. "I could help you with that."

Erin didn't know whether Adele was suggesting an herbal remedy, or some sort of Wiccan ritual or prayer. Either way, she didn't stick around long enough to find out.

*E*rin knew Sheriff Wilmot, but she'd never really had anything to do with him directly. She knew him through Terry. Even though he was Terry's boss, she'd always gotten the impression that he didn't have the skills or experience that Terry did. He was always in the background, covering when there was too much for Terry to do, but never taking point. It was odd to have him taking over the investigation into Joelle's death.

She was summoned to the police department, a small business office in the civic building. Erin had attended interviews with Terry there, back when he was still mostly a stranger to her. Later, as they grew closer and she was no longer a suspect in any active cases, she had become more familiar with the offices, coming and going as she visited with Terry or stopped by to drop off a plate of cookies.

Terry's door was shut when Erin arrived to meet with the sheriff. Not by accident or coincidence, she was sure. Neither one of them wanted the awkwardness of trying to deal with their relationship while Erin was there as a suspect. With his door shut, Erin couldn't tell whether he was in or out, and that was probably for the best.

"The sheriff will be with you shortly," Clara Jones advised, her face as grim as if Erin were a known serial killer. "He's a busy man."

"I'm sure he is," Erin agreed. "But he did ask me to come over. If now isn't a good time, I could set up a more convenient time for both of us."

"I said he won't be long. Just have a seat, and he'll be with you shortly."

Erin conceded, sitting down in one of the tubular metal chairs in the waiting area. It was longer than a few minutes, but then, Erin had expected it to be. She stood up when the sheriff appeared in front of her.

"Miss Price," Sheriff Wilmot greeted. "Thank you for making the time to come in to talk with me. I know you are a busy woman and I appreciate you making the time."

"I want to help in any way I can," Erin said, "but I don't know what I can do for you. I've already given Terry—Officer Piper—my statement. I don't think I have anything else to contribute."

"No, no, understood. That's fine. I'd just like you to run through it one more time, just like you told Officer Piper. You pick up a lot more nuance talking to a person face-to-face than you do just reading a typed-up statement. I'm sure you understand."

"Yes, of course. That makes sense."

"Good." He ushered her into his office, crowded with old file cabinets and blanketed with a layer of paper that looked like it had been there for as long as he had held the job.

Erin sat down on an uncomfortable couch with scratchy material and upholstery buttons that bit into her flesh. Not furniture designed to make her comfortable while she told her story. The sheriff sat down at his desk and looked at Erin, his eyelids at half-mast.

"Go ahead, any time you'd like to start."

"You don't want to ask anything particular? You just want me to…"

"Just tell me about what happened."

Erin wasn't sure where to start. When they got into the house? When they decided to go? When they first saw Joelle? She decided to bypass the sticky part about how they got into the house, and went with what had happened from the moment they entered Joelle's bedroom. She kept going until the arrival of the paramedics and stopped there.

The sheriff nodded slowly and thoughtfully. Erin waited for the questions. Sheriff Wilmot did not disappoint.

"How did you know Joelle Biggs?"

"I didn't really know her well. We weren't friends. I met her when she was in town before, with Davis, for Trenton's funeral. Saw her at the bakery once, and then a couple more times around town after that. She didn't stop in at the bakery this time. I guess she just got whatever she needed at the grocery store."

"She didn't call on you?"

"No."

"Then why did you decide to pay her a visit?"

"I heard about her hurting her leg. I just thought it would be neighborly to take her some soup. We didn't know whether she could get around and look after herself."

"Why didn't you just leave that to her friends?"

"I… don't really know if she had any friends in these parts. She was from out of town, and she wasn't the type who made friends quickly. She was a little… abrasive."

"But you decided that in spite of that abrasiveness that you would look in on her."

Erin shrugged. "Yes."

"That was a very Christian thing to do."

Erin raised her eyebrows. "I'm not a Christian."

The sheriff shifted uncomfortably. "I didn't mean you're a Christian, just that it was the kind of thing that… a Christian would do. That we're taught to do. Love your enemies. Turn the other cheek. Don't judge."

"She wasn't my enemy. We weren't friends, but that doesn't mean she was an enemy."

Sheriff Wilmot tented his fingers, gazing over them at her. "You wouldn't have called her an enemy?"

"No."

"It was my understanding that you accused her and Davis of trying to burn your house down. You believe she was complicit in Trenton Plaint's death."

"Uh… well, yes…"

"Why would you take soup to a person who had tried to burn your house down? Out of neighborly concern? She wasn't exactly next door, now, was she? You had to go halfway around town to get to her house. Why not just assume that other people would look in on her? Let someone who wasn't her enemy look after her?"

"I said she wasn't my enemy."

"But you were hers. She'd tried to burn your house down. You don't do that to a friend." He raised a finger, silencing any response from Erin. "And don't try to tell me that just because you weren't her friend, that doesn't mean you were her enemy. I think it is quite clear that Joelle considered you her enemy. If I'm to believe what you claim."

Erin couldn't think of any response.

"And if she didn't try to burn down your house, then she had good reason to hate you because you accused her of it."

"I just… I wasn't really thinking about that. I was just thinking that someone should look in on her and make sure she was okay. I made a bigger batch of soup than I needed. It wasn't any extra bother, other than actually running over there to give it to her. I thought it would take half an hour, and then I'd be home again."

His expression suggested that he found the whole thing a little hard to swallow.

"I've been a caregiver before," Erin said. "I know that people need help when they are hurt or sick, even if they're disagreeable or hard to get along with. I just didn't consider what had happened in the past or the fact that she wasn't my friend. I was only thinking about the fact that she might need someone to help her out."

"I see." The sheriff made a few notes on a piece of paper in front of him. "Moving on, then. You said that you made her soup. You didn't say anything about making her tea."

"No, I didn't make her the tea. She already had that on her bedside table. I didn't even know what it was."

"You didn't know what it was, but you gave it to her to drink?"

"Yes… wouldn't you? Someone has a mug on their table and asks you to pass it to them, wouldn't you do it? You wouldn't investigate what was in it first, you'd just hand it over."

"You didn't think to make her fresh tea? This stuff had been sitting on her table stewing and getting cold and maybe even fermenting for who-knows-how-long. I wouldn't drink tea that had been sitting out for half the day. Or longer."

"I told her it was cold and that I'd make her some more, but she just wanted me to give it to her. So I did. I couldn't have drunk it either."

"And how did she seem after you gave her the tea?"

"No different. I put it back where I got it. She closed her eyes and went back to sleep. She seemed to be fine, so I left her and went out to the kitchen. I wanted to see if there was any more tea, so I could make her some fresh stuff. But there weren't any leaves. Not that I could find. She must have used the last of it."

"Or you did and didn't want to leave any trace of it behind."

"I didn't make the tea," Erin said firmly. "It was already there when I got there."

"It was already there."

"Yes. If I made it to poison Joelle, why would I have left it out like that? Why would I point it out to Terry? If I was trying to poison her, I would have dumped what was left down the loo after she died. I would have washed out the cup and not left any trace of it."

"People make mistakes. People do stupid things, and they think they won't get caught. I've dealt with a lot of stupid criminals before, Miss Price, it wouldn't be anything new for me."

"I didn't bring the tea. I didn't put anything in her tea. I didn't poison Joelle. Period. I just happened to be there, trying to be a good neighbor, when she passed away. If I could go back and change that, I would. But I can't."

"No. You certainly can't. Miss Biggs is beyond help now."

Erin looked down at her hands. "I know. I feel really bad about that. I wish I could have done something for her. I wish someone had figured out that there was foxglove in the tea a day or two before, when maybe the doctors could have saved her. But that's not what happened."

Sheriff Wilmot scowled. "How do you know there was foxglove in the tea?"

"I…" Erin mentally apologized to Terry. She was going to get him in trouble for talking to her. But she couldn't lie, and she couldn't leave the sheriff thinking that the reason she knew there was foxglove in the tea was because she had put it there herself. "Office Piper told me. Before he handed the case over to you. We both thought it was better if he wasn't the one investigating it. Because…" Erin trailed off.

"Because you are a suspect if it was intentional poisoning."

"Yes. But I didn't poison her. Not intentionally, and not accidentally. I just went over there to give her a hand."

"Because that's the kind of person you are."

"Yes!" Erin insisted. "You ask anyone who knows me. I like to help people. Especially looking after their dietary needs. Maybe you could have figured that out by the fact that I run a bakery for people with dietary restrictions. It's kind of what I do!"

She hadn't meant to reply so sharply, but the sheriff had hit a sensitive spot. He grinned at her suddenly. He'd been intentionally egging her on, trying to get an emotional reaction from her. Maybe he thought that she'd say something to implicate herself.

"I had heard a rumor to that effect," he chuckled.

"See if I ever bring *you* cookies."

"I'll just steal Terry's."

The frigid atmosphere warmed quickly. Erin shook her head, embarrassed by how she had let him get to her. After so many years of being teased and bullied by foster siblings, she should have had a thicker skin. Joelle's death had left her anxious and on edge. She was saddened, even though Joelle was someone she hadn't liked. Maybe *because* Joelle was someone she hadn't liked and would never come to like. There was no chance that the two of them would ever be reconciled and become friendly toward each other.

"Sheriff... you know I didn't kill Joelle. I would never do something like that. I'm a sucker for anyone and anything sick or suffering. I just wanted to help her while she was under the weather. Maybe I thought that if I did something nice for her, we could be... not friends, but maybe just... tolerant of each other. I didn't want anyone fighting me. I just wanted to be on good terms."

"That wasn't likely to happen, if she opened up a bakery that competed with yours."

"The other person trying to open that bakery is my sister. You think I'm going to kill her too?"

"I hope not. How *do* you feel about Charley Campbell trying to reopen The Bake Shoppe?"

"I'm nervous about it. But I'll stick it out. I'm hoping that I'll be able to survive the competition. If Charley can get Davis to agree to open it, or manages to take it away from him... I'm not going to fight her. I want her to succeed too. I'm hoping that we can carve up the Bald Eagle Falls business so that we can both survive."

Sheriff Wilmot nodded. "Do you think she's going to be able to?"

"I haven't talked to her the last couple of days, but I don't think things are looking too good right now. Davis tried to get her out of the way so that he could have the full estate to himself, and now she's trying to do the same thing to him. Legally, but still… they're not going to work together, so Charley is either going to have to convince the trustees that it's in the best interest of the estate to open the bakery, even with Davis objecting, or she needs to prove that he had a hand in Trenton's death, so that he can't inherit from Trenton's estate."

The sheriff raised his brows. "Is that what's going on? I admit I was confused as to why Joelle would be back in town. But if Charley was trying to get proof that Davis was involved in Trenton's death, then getting close to Joelle would be the best way to do that."

Erin nodded. "I couldn't have done it. I couldn't pretend to be interested in Joelle while secretly trying to find a way to convict them both of murder. But Charley's… different."

"She's been associating with people who would do that and a lot worse."

"Yeah. In her world, it makes sense. I just couldn't be that mercenary."

"Well, at least you're trying to stick it out."

Erin frowned. It sounded as if he knew about her past. As if he knew that in the past, when things got bad, Erin had moved on rather than tough it out. And probably he did. Terry had run background on her when she had first been implicated in Angela's death. He didn't know everything, but he knew a lot. And that file was probably fully accessible by Sheriff Wilmot and anyone else who did work for the department.

"I really want to make this work," Erin told him. "Bald Eagle Falls is the first place I could really call home in a long time. I don't want to have to leave."

"Well, let's keep working on that. No one thought that you could make a gluten-free bakery work in Bald Eagle Falls to start with. You've proven them all wrong. You just hang in there and keep at it. See what happens."

Erin nodded. Sheriff Wilmot closed the file folder in front of him, signaling the end of the interview. He stood up. Erin followed his lead and pushed herself up off of the lumpy couch with its uncomfortable buttons. She rubbed her backside.

"Sorry," the sheriff apologized. "I keep promising I'm going to replace that old monster. One of these days…"

"Oh, it's fine…"

"No, it's a dinosaur and there's no good reason for keeping it around. Well, I want to thank you for coming in, Miss Price. And thank you for trying to help a stranger out, even if things didn't work out the way you had expected."

"Maybe next time, I'll just mind my own business."

"No, I don't think so." He smiled at her. "And it would be a shame if you did."

CHAPTER 11

$\mathcal{E}$xiting the sheriff's office, Erin ran into Melissa Lee in the administrative office, sorting and filing a sheaf of papers in the rows of files. She smiled at Erin.

"Hey! How's it going? He wasn't too hard on you, was he?" Melissa shot a look at Sheriff Wilmot's closed door. "He really isn't too bad. He puts on a gruff front, but inside, he's really just a pussycat."

Erin nodded and stopped to chat with Melissa. "He was okay. He got me a bit wound up to start with… but he doesn't seem like such a bad guy. He's just doing his job."

Melissa nodded. "It's such a shame that Terry couldn't stay on the case. We all know you didn't have anything to do with it, but I guess he couldn't let himself be accused of having a bias toward you, with the two of you being so close, and all." Melissa's confidential tone was like that of a high school girl wanting to get all of the details of her friend's hot date. Erin's cheeks warmed, and she rolled her eyes.

"There's nothing between us," she declared. "I mean… we're friends, and we've gone on a few dates, but…"

"You two have been *the* item ever since Angela's investigation," Melissa argued. "You may not be all over each other, but…" She searched for the right words. "You definitely have stars in your eyes."

Erin laughed, blushing more. "I hope you're right. But right now… things are going to have to be on hold until this gets sorted out."

Melissa shook her head. "No, they don't. Terry isn't investigating the case anymore, so you two can be as involved as you want. That was the whole reason for giving the case to the sheriff."

"I know." Erin didn't want to have to explain her feelings to Melissa. They were too elusive for her to even label. The fact that Terry had considered her a suspect—probably the prime suspect—in Joelle's death, despite their involvement, left a bitter taste in her mouth. He shouldn't have ever even considered it. He knew what kind of person she was, and he should have known immediately that she didn't have anything to do with Joelle's death. But his professionalism had won out over his feelings for Erin. "But I think… we're going to wait until things are resolved with this case."

Melissa put her hand on Erin's arm. "You can't let things get in the way of your relationship with Terry. The two of you have to be stronger than that."

Erin thought back to what she knew about Melissa and her relationships. The number of men she had been involved with in the time since Erin had arrived in Bald Eagle Falls was easy to tally up. Zero. She had not been dating or even attracted to any man in the time that Erin had known her. Of course, Melissa could be going to the city and living a wild and crazy lifestyle there without anyone in Bald Eagle Falls knowing about it, but somehow Erin doubted it. Melissa was involved with community events and with her part time job at the police department, which seemed to provide enough income for her to live on. She was always up on the latest gossip, but Erin never heard anything juicy about her, except for the fact that she and Davis had been involved back in high school. Whatever had happened back then seemed to have soured Melissa permanently on the idea of a relationship.

"How are things with you and Davis?" Erin asked, not so much because she thought there was still a relationship there to be explored, but to distract Melissa from her interest in Erin's love life. "Do you go out there to visit him?"

Melissa withdrew her hand from Erin's arm like she had been burned. "Who told you that?" she demanded. "If I've been out to the prison, it's not because I have any feelings for Davis Plaint. And if I did, why would I pursue someone like that? He tried to kill you and he did kill poor Bertie

Braceling. He might say that was accidental, just an impulse that he acted on without having a chance to think, but that doesn't matter. Poor Bertie was a pillar of this community. Davis even admits that Bertie never did anything to hurt him. He helped Davis years ago, when he didn't have anyone else to turn to."

It certainly sounded like Melissa *was* seeing Davis Plaint. How else would she have known Davis's excuses for having run down Bertie Braceling in cold blood?

"Has he ever said anything about me?"

"Has he ever said *what* about you?" Melissa returned. "Why would he talk about you?"

"Well, if he talked about Bertie, he might just as easily have talked about me. We were together that day. And then there was Alton…"

"Davis didn't have anything to do with what Alton did. He never told Alton to go after you."

That sounded suspiciously like a 'yes' to Erin. She didn't say anything, not sure how to continue the conversation. Melissa leaned in closer to Erin. "Davis is trying to get himself turned around. That's not easy to do when you're in prison. He's lived a hard life and he's never really had the opportunity to change. He's getting counseling now. He really does want to be a better person."

"He hasn't had the opportunity to change before?" Erin challenged. "It isn't like anyone has been stopping him. He's a grown man. He could have decided to turn himself around long before he ended up in prison."

"You don't understand what it's like for an addict. He wasn't in prison, but he was the prisoner of his own body. You don't know what that's like."

Erin shrugged. "Okay, I'm not a drug addict, so I don't understand what he's gone through. But there are a lot of people who are, and who turn themselves around before they end up in prison or having done the things that he has. You said once that you'd never go back to him, after all he put you through when you were younger. I guess you changed your mind on that."

"I haven't 'gone back to him.'" Melissa disagreed. "We are not a couple. I'm not dating him. Just because I visit him, that doesn't mean there's anything between us. I wouldn't get into the middle of all of that drama again."

Erin raised her brows in disbelief. It certainly sounded to her like

Melissa was putting herself right back into the middle of Davis's drama again.

"Well, I'm glad you're not letting yourself be pulled in by him again."

Melissa's usual broad smile was gone. "I'm not," she asserted. "I'd never get involved with him again after all the stuff that happened when we were kids. I wouldn't let that happen."

"Good. I wouldn't want you getting hurt."

"He can't hurt me. He's in prison. There's nothing he can do to me while he's in there."

"That's good," Erin agreed again.

Melissa was getting more and more agitated, acting as if Erin were arguing with her rather than agreeing. "It's different than when we were kids. I didn't understand back then what a monster addiction was, how totally it could change a person. It wasn't his fault that he behaved how he did. And it wasn't his fault, the way that his mother and brother treated him. And his father, cheating on Angela and putting the family in jeopardy…"

"He couldn't help any of that," Erin agreed. "But he still had choices. I don't know exactly what happened between the two of you, but he could still choose how he treated you."

Melissa walked with Erin out of the police department's offices, away from the sharp ears of Clara Jones and anyone else who might overhear them there. "With the way his family acted, Davis really didn't have a chance. You don't know what it was like, the way he was bullied."

"He's not a teenager anymore. He's a grown man. He's got you feeling sorry for him, but he's the one who got himself in prison. Nobody bullied him into killing Trenton or Bertie or trying to kill me."

Melissa bristled. "He didn't kill Trenton. That was an accident. And that was Joelle, not Davis."

"Are you sure of that?" Erin held Melissa's gaze. "Are you really sure he had nothing to do with it? He didn't tell Joelle about Trenton's allergy? He wasn't involved in the plan to feed him something that would kill him?"

Erin thought about Joelle's death and couldn't suppress a sudden shiver. Had Davis planned a way to get rid of Joelle from inside prison? She was the one person who could testify if he had planned his own brother's murder. And it wouldn't be the first time that Davis had tried to orchestrate such a plan from behind prison walls. With Charley digging around and trying to get Joelle to admit to Davis's involvement in the plan to kill Trenton, did Davis decide that it was time to get rid of Joelle? With her dead, there was no one else who could testify as to Davis's role in the murder.

"What is it?" Melissa asked, studying Erin.

"I… nothing. I was just thinking about… something. Maybe I should tell the sheriff…"

"You don't need to tell him anything else," Melissa insisted. "You've already told him all that you know. So just leave it in his hands now. He's a competent investigator."

Had Melissa been able to read Erin's thoughts that clearly in her expression? She couldn't know what Erin had or hadn't told the sheriff, or what direction the sheriff would take the investigation. She might be thinking the exact opposite to what she was saying. Leave Sheriff Wilmot to flounder around with the information he already had, and he'd never figure out what had happened. Davis would be safe, because the sheriff would never figure out his part in Joelle's death. Could it be?

"You're right," Erin told Melissa. "I'm sure he'll sort it out all on his own."

Charley had told Erin on more than one occasion that she had a terrible poker face and could not lie without telegraphing it. Erin hoped that was just because Charley was her sister and had an intuitive grasp of Erin's mental processes. Hopefully, she wasn't quite as transparent to Melissa, or the woman would have no doubt that Erin didn't intend to stay away from Sheriff Wilmot. He needed to know of the possibility that Davis might have been involved in Joelle's death.

How Davis could have had a hand in it wasn't immediately apparent, but he had a stronger motive than anyone in Bald Eagle Falls, including Erin. He could have influenced Melissa or someone else to take action against Joelle. If Vic and Erin could find the key and let themselves into Joelle's house, then what was to stop anyone else from doing the same and spiking her tea with foxglove? Erin didn't want to think Melissa capable of such a thing, but maybe there were others Davis could talk into acting on his behalf.

CHAPTER 12

rin was glad to be back at the bakery, doing what she did best, surrounded by her loyal customers, with Vic at her side. That was where she belonged. She didn't really feel calm and at home except when she lost herself in her work at the bakery or was at home making lists or reading through Clementine's genealogy books.

"Everything went okay with the sheriff?" Vic asked, watching Erin mix up another batch of cookie dough.

"Yes, it was just fine. I was pretty nervous at first, and he was doing the best he could to get me worked up, but you know… he's not a bad guy. And I think he'll do a good job of the investigation."

"As good as Terry?"

Erin shrugged. "Maybe. Maybe he's the one who trained Terry."

"I never actually thought of that," Vic admitted. "He's always sort of in the background."

"I know. But he's smart. He'll do okay. I'm glad we've got him instead of the FBI. Take how nervous I was of Sheriff Wilmot and multiply it by about a hundred."

Vic nodded.

"You're supposed to see him this afternoon?" Erin recalled.

"Yeah. And talking about nervous… I'm about as nervous as a long-tailed cat in a roomful of rocking chairs."

"Just tell him what happened. Neither of us had anything to do with Joelle's death. We just happened to be there when she died. The sheriff doesn't have any reason to be suspicious of us."

"Except that we let ourselves into her house and were there when she died. We could have given her something, in her tea or a pill or injection. Or just a pillow over her face. Joelle could have ruined our business if she agreed to open The Bake Shoppe. That's a good enough motive for some people."

"He doesn't think you poisoned Joelle. No matter what he says, just stay calm and answer his questions truthfully."

"Is that what you did?" Vic's smile suggested that she knew Erin hadn't been the perfect interviewee herself.

"No. I lost it. But at least he knew I meant what I said…"

Vic chuckled. "Well, he didn't arrest you, so I guess that's a good sign."

Erin agreed. The bells on the front door jingled and Erin looked through the kitchen door into the front to see who was there. Mary Lou Cox walked in; she looked through the doorway and smiled as Erin wiped her hands on her apron.

"Good morning, Mary Lou," Erin greeted. "What can I get for you today?"

Mary Lou brushed a hand over her forehead in a gesture of fatigue. Her eyes looked tired and swollen. "Some bread for supper. Crusty rolls or a French loaf?"

Erin indicated the French bread and Mary Lou nodded.

"Yes," she said briskly. "That's fine. And something for dessert. Maybe peanut butter bars?"

"I don't do nuts," Erin reminded her as she selected a loaf of French bread for her. "Sorry. How about some fudge?"

Mary Lou swore. Erin's mouth nearly dropped open in her surprise. Mary Lou had never cursed around her before. She had never lost her temper or her composure. Was it possible that Joelle's death had had an effect on her? They hadn't been friends. As far as Erin knew, Joelle didn't have any friends. But sometimes, things were not as they seemed.

"I'm sorry," Erin said again. "What else could I get you? The marshmallow cookies have been really popular since we started making them…"

"Oh, don't mind me," Mary Lou said, shaking her head. "I'm just not myself today." She rubbed her hand over her eyes. "Sometimes I just don't know how I'm going to make it through the day."

"Can I help?" Erin asked, concerned. "What's wrong?"

"Nothing, my dear. You can't do a thing. You just keep baking up a storm. At least that's one thing I don't have to do."

Erin stood there awkwardly, waiting for Mary Lou to pick out what she wanted for dessert. Mary Lou blinked a few times, sighed, and looked at the goodies in the display case.

"Honestly. I can't even decide."

"How about an assortment of cookies," Erin suggested. "I'll just put a few different varieties together for you."

"Yes," Mary Lou agreed. She ran one hand through her short gray hair, mussing it up. Erin had never seen Mary Lou with a single hair out of place, even on the most hectic days. Looking her over, Erin realized that her impeccably tailored suit was showing wrinkles, and there was a smudge of green on one elbow.

Rather than asking again what was wrong, Erin decided to mind her own business, and got together the cookies Mary Lou had requested.

"Only twelve," Mary Lou reminded her tiredly. "Not thirteen."

"I know," Erin agreed. "I'll give you three each of four varieties. That way it's totally even. Each of your boys can have one of each kind."

"I'm not even sure it matters anymore," Mary Lou confessed. "Why do I try so hard?"

Erin was at a loss as to what to say. Mary Lou was always careful to treat her two sons and her husband with an even hand, making sure that one didn't get more than another. Erin knew from her own experience in many different foster homes that the fairness routine always broke down sooner or later. The parent couldn't help favoring one child over another, or their needs were so disparate that it was impossible to treat them equally, or their tastes were different, so you couldn't give them all the same thing. Mary Lou's children were teens; maybe they had started to reject Mary Lou's efforts to treat them equally and assert their own wants and needs.

Erin finished packaging the cookies and went to the till to ring up the purchase. Vic had remained in the kitchen to get the cookies divided up and put into the oven.

"Are you sure there isn't anything I could do to help?" Erin asked as Mary Lou carefully counted out exact change. "I hate seeing you like this."

Mary Lou smoothed at the wrinkles in her suit. "Like what? I'm just fine, dear. Just didn't get a good sleep last night. You know how a poor night's sleep can just make everything more difficult the next day. So clumsy and scattered and everything just falls apart when you touch it!"

Not to mention emotional and overwrought.

"Hopefully, you'll get a better sleep tonight," Erin encouraged. "You'll be extra tired, and sleep like a baby."

"Not likely," Mary Lou sighed.

"Maybe you could take a sleep aid, if you're having trouble? Melatonin or valerian or Xanax…?"

Mary Lou just shook her head as if Erin couldn't possibly understand. And she didn't. If Mary Lou wasn't going to tell her exactly what was going on, Erin didn't have very much chance of giving good advice.

"Well, I hope you're feeling better soon." Erin handed Mary Lou her purchases. "Take care."

"Thank you, Erin, you too." Mary Lou raised her voice. "And you, Vic. Have a good day!"

Vic moved into the line of sight of the doorway and gave a little wave. "Thanks, Mary Lou! Have a good one!"

Erin waited for a moment to see if anyone else was coming in before heading back into the kitchen to help Vic finish up.

"I've never seen Mary Lou so rattled," she said. She related how their friend had behaved. "Do you think it has something to do with Joelle's death? Or something else?"

"If she said she was short on sleep, then I believe she's short on sleep. You know what a bear I am when I don't get my beauty rest."

Erin laughed. "You're just as sweet when you're tired as any other time. And I've never seen Mary Lou like that before. I'm worried something is really wrong."

"Don't borrow trouble. She'll get over it, I'm sure."

"I hope so. If she's not sleeping, I have to wonder why. Joelle? Her husband? Trouble with one of the boys? Or is she sick?" Erin worried over this last idea. "What if she's really sick?"

"You're just worried because of what happened to Joelle. You're overreacting. Mary Lou will get a better sleep tonight, and she'll be just fine in the morning."

Erin gazed back toward the door, but of course Mary Lou was out of sight.

"I sure hope so."

CHAPTER 13

With Willie and Vic on a break and Terry avoiding Erin due to the police investigation into Joelle's death, Erin and Vic were spending more time together in the evenings, as they had before Vic's apartment over the garage had been built. It was a comfortable routine and, while Erin worried that Vic wasn't getting out and getting the socialization that she needed, she was happy to just stay home and relax when she could.

The evenings were pleasant, and Erin had taken Orange Blossom and Marshmallow out to the backyard for a run in the grass. Vic sat on a deck chair watching, laughing at Orange Blossom as he stalked bugs or imaginary critters through the grass, and at Marshmallow when he would creep up behind Orange Blossom and then give him a friendly nudge, making Orange Blossom take off like a rocket and leap around the back yard as if the devil had ahold of him. Erin kept close, trying to block Orange Blossom if he got any ideas of leaving the yard and going off on an adventure of his own. Though he didn't seem to have any desire to return to his solitary life as a stray, Erin was careful, not wanting him to get any ideas.

"You sound like you're having fun."

Erin looked across the yard to see Adele approaching from the gate that opened into the woods.

"Letting the animals out to play," Erin explained, though Adele could see that for herself.

Adele watched them for a few minutes, making no attempt at conversation. Erin heard a crow caw nearby.

"Is that Skye?"

"Yes."

"Is he afraid to come too close to us? Or to the animals?"

"No, he's just not sure what we're all doing. It's quite the motley crowd."

"I guess. Would he come if you called him?"

"He might."

"The animals wouldn't bother him, right? I know Marshmallow wouldn't. But he's too big for Orange Blossom to hurt, isn't he?"

"If he was sick or injured, the cat could do him harm. But while he's well, he's too smart to let a house cat sneak up on him."

"Call him. See if he'll come."

Adele looked in the direction of the woods. "Skye," she said softly, and touched her shoulder.

Erin didn't think Adele had called loudly enough or made the gesture big enough to get the attention of the crow, but in seconds, there was another caw, a swoosh of wings, and the black bird landed on Adele's shoulder. Adele raised her hand and stroked him.

"Wow," Vic said, "you've got him really well-trained. I knew crows were smart, but I didn't know you could train them like that."

"He's not trained," Adele corrected. "We're just familiar with each other. He's not a circus show. Just… a friend."

Vic nodded, and didn't make the mistake of referring to Skye as Adele's pet or her familiar again. If Adele wanted to use the word friend, she could use it. It didn't matter to Erin or Vic. "Okay. Well, does your friend do anything else?"

Adele shrugged and looked at the crow on her shoulder with her bright eyes. Skye looked back at her, making a soft, raspy noise like he was trying to purr. Adele whispered to Skye, but Erin couldn't make out what she was saying. She couldn't even swear that it was English. Skye cawed again and left Adele's shoulder.

At first, Erin was disappointed, thinking that Skye was headed back into the woods to sit in the trees and converse with the other crows and do whatever else crows did in their free time. But rather than flying away, Skye flew down to the grass and landed a few feet away from Orange Blossom.

Orange Blossom went rigid, as if electrified. He stared at the black bird in shock. His nose twitched eagerly in the air as he picked up the bird's scent. His mouth opened slightly, and he made a chattering sound at the bird.

"What's he doing?" Erin demanded. "Is he trying to talk to Skye?"

"No," Vic laughed, "that's just a sound that cats make when they see a bird or something else that interests them. I don't know why."

"Is it a threat or a warning?"

Vic and Adele both shook their heads. "It's just a noise cats make. Birds, squirrels, laser pointers… when they see something they want to hunt or chase, especially up in the air, they chatter."

"That's weird. Doesn't it scare their prey away?"

"Maybe sometimes," Adele said, "but it doesn't seem to matter."

"And Skye is being careful? He's not going to let Orange Blossom catch him, right?" Erin watched the bird nervously. Skye acted as if he didn't even know the cat was there. As if he had just landed there to peck at seeds or bugs in the grass and had no idea there were any other animals around.

"He's watching. With their eyes on the side like that, birds can see all around their heads. Skye knows the cat is there."

Reassured, Erin watched eagerly to see what would happen.

Orange Blossom began to stalk Skye, pressing his body to the ground to make himself as low as possible, and slinking closer and closer. He stopped a couple of feet away from the bird, his butt twitching as if it were a separate creature.

Then Orange Blossom exploded into the air, straight for Skye. Erin let out a little yelp, startled and still not convinced that Skye would be fast enough to avoid the fuzzy predator. But Skye flapped a few feet away, almost as if it was simply a coincidence that he had decided to move at the same time as the cat had pounced. He still didn't look at the cat.

Orange Blossom stood frozen for a moment as if he couldn't believe that his prey had gotten away from him. Then he sat back on his haunches and started to wash.

"He's embarrassed," Vic said with a laugh. "That's his way of saying, 'I meant to do that. I just had an itch, that's all.'"

Erin giggled. Orange Blossom stopped washing to glare at her. Erin and Vic both laughed loudly at his offended expression. Even Adele was smiling.

Orange Blossom marched a few steps farther away from them, and then started washing again. He stayed completely focused on his hygiene routine, and Erin almost believed he'd completely forgotten about the bird and how much he'd wanted to catch Skye.

Skye eyed Blossom, tilting his head up and down, and took a few steps closer to him. Erin watched in eager anticipation. Orange Blossom stopped washing, staring at the bird again. Behind him, Marshmallow decided he was being left out of the fun, and hopped closer to Orange Blossom, eventually giving him a playful nudge. Instead of jumping around like a dervish, Orange Blossom stayed still. He swatted Marshmallow on top of the head, which Marshmallow didn't like. Orange Blossom's message was clear. He was hunting something more important and didn't have time to play with Marshmallow.

Marshmallow nibbled at the grass, watching Orange Blossom with his sideways glance.

Orange Blossom watched Skye intently as the bird continued to act ask if there were nothing to be worried about. Erin shook her head. "Look at how he's playing with Blossom! I didn't know birds were so smart."

Orange Blossom's chest went down, and his hind end rose up, and he twitched his butt back and forth getting ready to pounce again.

But this time, Skye turned the tables, erupting into the air, flying straight at Orange Blossom. The cat flipped right over trying to avoid him, and all three women laughed at the spectacle. Orange Blossom looked at them, then stalked off and sat with his back to them, pouting.

"Oh!" Erin could barely catch her breath. "I've never see anything so funny. What a clever bird!"

"He is that," Adele agreed. She patted her shoulder again as an invitation to the crow. Skye instead flew at Marshmallow, seeing if he could be intimidated as easily as the cat. Marshmallow kept nibbling at the grass, ignoring him. Skye cawed and flew back to Adele's shoulder.

"I got some peanuts," Erin said. "You said that's what he likes, so I bought some to feed to him the next time I went to your house. Can I give him some?"

"You can try."

Erin could have predicted that was what Adele would say. But in spite of the fact that Adele wouldn't say yes or no and insisted that the bird was not her pet, Erin suspected she would have been offended if Erin had just offered food to Skye without checking with Adele first.

"They're just in the pantry. Stay here for a minute."

She was afraid that by the time she got the peanuts and returned, she would find Skye gone again, but he was still there, rubbing his beak against Adele's coat collar.

"Skye," Erin said softly, holding a couple of peanuts out toward the crow. "I got some peanuts. Do you want some peanuts? Are those good?"

Skye watched her sideways, much like Marshmallow did, but with a bit more head bobbing and animation. Erin stopped a couple of feet away, not wanting to scare him away or to get too close. Skye made that quiet noise in his throat again, which Erin took as encouragement. She pinched a peanut between her thumb and finger and held it right up to him. Skye took it politely from her grasp.

Erin was breathless. "He did it! He took it from me! He didn't fly away this time."

"Would you?" Adele asked. "If I brought you dinner, would you take off?"

"Well, no. But I thought he would be scared and just fly away again."

Erin watched Skye crack the peanut shell open and eat the nuts from inside it, dropping the shells to the ground. Orange Blossom put his ears back, listening to the bird eat, but refused to turn around to look at him again.

Erin fed Skye a couple more peanuts and watched him eat them. Then Skye took one from her hand and flew away into the woods.

"Oh." Erin looked around to see if something had scared the bird away. "What happened?"

"He's going to go hide it for later. He's full," Adele advised.

"Oh, okay." Erin smiled. "Well, that was fun. I'm glad you brought him by while the animals were out. It was so funny to watch him and Orange Blossom together."

Adele nodded. "It was," she agreed.

"Come set a spell," Vic invited, motioning to the deck chairs. "We're just enjoying the lovely evening."

"I believe I will," Adele agreed. She sat in one of the chairs and leaned back, closing her eyes. Erin stayed on her feet to keep track of Orange Blossom and make sure he didn't take off looking for the departed bird.

"You heard about Joelle?" Vic asked Adele. It was the hottest topic in Bald Eagle Falls, and Erin had not told Vic about her trip to see Adele and inform her of the investigation.

"Yes, I did," Adele agreed. She put her fingers up to her temples as if she were fighting a headache. "I suspect it will only be a matter of time before your sheriff comes by to question me… maybe to arrest me."

Vic's eyes opened wide in shock. "To arrest you?" she repeated. "He wouldn't do that. He's very good. He doesn't jump to conclusions. He's not going to judge you just because you're… not Christian."

"No," Adele agreed. "But he may judge me because I'm the one who prepared the tea."

Erin wouldn't have thought that Vic's eyes could get any bigger, and she would have been wrong. Vic's eyes were nearly popping out of her head.

"You made the tea?"

Adele turned her head to look at Erin. "You didn't tell her?"

"No."

"You knew Adele made the tea?" Vic demanded. "Why didn't you tell me?"

"I didn't tell anyone," Erin said. "I didn't want to get her in any trouble."

"You could have told me. I wouldn't have told anyone."

"I know. But I didn't think it was my place to spread it around."

Vic was flabbergasted. She shook her head. "Did you hear it had foxglove in it?" she asked Adele. "You must have made a mistake when you were gathering comfrey. They look very similar…"

"I did not make a mistake," Adele said calmly.

"How could you know that? It would be an easy mistake to make. And all it would take is a couple of leaves."

Adele gazed at Erin, sighing. "I didn't gather the comfrey myself," she said. "It was in with the herbs you gave me from Clementine."

CHAPTER 14

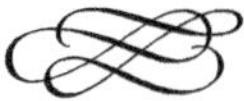

All of the oxygen went out of the air around Erin, and she could suddenly not breathe. Nor could she talk. She just stared into Adele's deep, dark eyes for an eternity, unable to believe it could be true.

Erin swayed on her feet, opening her mouth but still unable to find the words. Vic and Adele had both gotten to their feet without Erin being aware of it, and they took her, one on either side, and escorted her over to one of the empty deck chairs, murmuring to her and lowering her into the seat.

"It's okay," Vic said. "Just take a few deep breaths. It was a shock, but it's going to be okay."

Erin tried to push air in and out.

"Do you want a drink of water?" Vic suggested. "Tea?" She bit her lip, aware that tea was maybe not the best thing to offer on the heels of Adele's revelation.

Erin shook her head.

Adele sat in the chair across from Erin and waited. She didn't say anything else. She just waited.

It was some time before Erin was breathing normally again and thought that she could talk, even though her heart was hammering so hard in her chest that it hurt. Maybe some digitalis was just what she needed to slow it down.

"The comfrey in Joelle's tea was from the herbs of Aunt Clementine's that I gave you?" Erin asked.

It wasn't like she thought she had misunderstood. She just didn't want it to be true.

"Yes."

"And… it was labeled comfrey?"

"It was labeled boneknit," Adele said. "One of the folk names for comfrey."

"And boneknit… it wasn't used as the name for more than one herb?" Erin asked. "There are some names that are used for more than one herb, because they have similar properties…"

"No," Adele said. "Boneknit is only used for comfrey. Not for foxglove. Foxglove is never used for healing bones."

"Is it… used for anything?"

"Edema. A heart tonic. But you have to be very careful."

Erin was at a loss. She didn't know what to say. Her voice was echoing in her head and she felt removed from herself.

"So you think that Clementine collected foxglove, thinking it was comfrey, and labeled it wrong?"

"I'm not sure," Adele said slowly. "I didn't see anything that would suggest to me that it wasn't comfrey. It had the smell and look of comfrey. No damp or mustiness. It was all similar in color and texture of the leaves. I wouldn't have guessed, looking at it, that it was more than just comfrey."

Erin rubbed her forehead. "I can't believe it. I never would have given you Clementine's herbs if I had thought there was anything wrong with them. Clementine was careful. I never would have expected her to pick the wrong thing like that."

Adele nodded. "I've gone over it and over it in my mind. But there was nothing to indicate that it was contaminated. All of her herbs were carefully bottled and labeled. She seemed like a very competent herbalist."

"I thought she was."

"Anybody can make a mistake," Vic comforted. "Even someone who has handled herbs for years. Or maybe someone else collected it for her and she didn't realize they had made a mistake."

Erin frowned, thinking about Clementine's last days on the earth.

"Someone else could have brought it to her," Vic insisted, misinterpreting Erin's expression.

"Yes. You're right. She wasn't able to get around the last little while. She had to close up the shop and just stayed at home. Even just trying to get around here, she took a fall and broke her hip. So then she was confined to bed. She could have asked someone else to collect boneknit for her, to help her hip heal faster."

Vic's eyes widened. "And if someone collected foxglove instead of comfrey, they might have poisoned Clementine too."

"She hadn't been well. It's not unusual for people who are old and frail not to recover from a broken bone. Their bodies can't take the abuse. No one would think her death was suspicious. It wasn't like with Joelle, where a woman who had been vibrant and healthy a few days earlier passed away suddenly. She was already faltering."

"We don't know that Clementine ever took foxglove," Adele said firmly, "and there's no way to find out. You're only making yourself miserable thinking about it."

Erin shook her head slowly. "I can't believe it. What if she was poisoned?"

"If she was, it was by mistake," Vic said. "No one intentionally hurt her. She didn't have any enemies."

Erin didn't know of anyone who held a grudge against Clementine. But that didn't mean Vic was right. They couldn't know for sure. None of them had been living in Bald Eagle Falls when it happened. They didn't know anything that might have been going on below the surface, things that no one had known about or that no one had shared with Erin.

"At least this helps your case," Erin told Adele. "You weren't the one who collected the herbs. You just went by what the bottle said. They can test it. And you don't have any previous connection with Joelle, so you don't have any reason to intentionally poison her."

Adele's eyes cut to the side. A tell.

"What?" Erin asked, running through what she had just said in her mind. "You didn't know Joelle, right?"

Adele didn't answer.

Erin had assumed, since neither Adele nor Joelle were from Bald Eagle Falls, that they didn't know each other. Adele had definitely given Erin the impression that she didn't know Joelle, asking about what she was doing there and what had happened with Trenton and Davis when Joelle had been there previously. But Erin couldn't remember Adele actually saying she didn't know Joelle.

"You know Joelle?" Vic demanded, her eyes wide. "Well, don't that beat all. How do you know her?"

Adele folded her hands in her lap. "I don't know if I'm ready to discuss that."

"It isn't any of our business," Erin admitted. But that didn't stop her from being curious. Adele knew Joelle. The fact that she didn't want to talk about it probably meant they weren't best friends. Adele was back to being in hot water. She had been the one to make the tea, and she had some kind of grievance or past with Joelle. She could tell the sheriff that she hadn't been the one to pick the comfrey or foxglove for the tea, but she couldn't prove a negative.

"If the sheriff doesn't call on you, you'd better go see him anyway," Erin suggested. "It will look better if you're up front about everything."

Adele nodded. "I'll have to tell him that the herbs came from Clementine…"

"Yes. Go ahead. Tell him everything."

Vic and Adele both looked at Erin.

"What? What is it?"

"You're already a suspect," Vic said. "Now we're going to tell the sheriff that you had access to herbs from Clementine's collection."

"But I gave them to Adele. That's what she's going to tell him."

"You might have kept back foxglove. Or mixed it with the comfrey."

"I didn't. And how would I know to do that? I'm a city girl, I don't know what medicinal purposes the different herbs have. I can pick out ginger or comfrey by smell, but I can't tell you their properties."

"But the books you gave me from your aunt could," Adele said. "Both comfrey and foxglove are in the handwritten book. Maybe in others too, I haven't looked through them all. It would have been easy for you to figure out."

"Well, I didn't," Erin said flatly. "There's no point in trying to hide the details from the sheriff, he's going to ferret them out sooner or later anyway. If I try to cover it up, it just makes me look more suspicious."

"Sheriff Wilmot knows you didn't kill Joelle," Vic asserted.

"Whether he thinks I did or not, he's still got a job to do. Hopefully, Joelle died of natural causes and all of this is just academic."

Adele had left, and Erin had rounded up the animals to take them back inside. Orange Blossom was looking wild-eyed and was reluctant to go back into the house, but a few shakes of his treats can eventually convinced him, and he slunk into the house, looking at her reproachfully when she shut the door behind him.

"Sorry, you can't stay outside all night," Erin told him. She firmly believed that pets, even cats, should be kept indoors and didn't want to risk any mishaps with cars or cougars or other hazards. Besides which, she was pretty sure that he'd end up yowling outside the door to be let back in at the most inconvenient time, and with his volume, he would be waking the neighbors.

Vic said her goodbyes to the pets and headed back to her apartment. Erin watched her across the yard and then set the burglar alarm. She was going through her usual nightly rituals when there was a knock on the front door. Firm. A knock she recognized. For a moment, she just stood there, uncertain what to do. Then she went to the front door, disarmed the alarm, and let Terry in.

"I know it's late for you," he said. "I promise I won't keep you long."

He stood there awkwardly, K9 at his side, waiting for her approval. Erin motioned to the armchair.

"Help yourself."

He did. Orange Blossom had finished his treat and approached warily. He sat in the kitchen doorway and started to wash, staring at K9 the entire time. K9 settled at Terry's feet.

"Erin… I passed the case to Sheriff Wilmot so that you and I would still be able to see each other without there being any accusations of bias or conflict of interest."

Erin nodded. "Yes, I know."

"But somehow, it meant that we stopped seeing anything of each other. I don't know why. But it's not what I wanted. I thought we could just go on like we were before."

"Maybe that was naive. For both of us."

"I don't like things like they are. Is there any way we can get back on track? Anything I could do for you? Can I just… come see you again like I was before? Or we could go out for dinner?"

"Are you sure that wouldn't reflect badly on your reputation? Even if you have passed the investigation off to the sheriff, people will still think you're in a position of conflict."

"I…" He gazed off, considering the matter. "I'm okay with that if you are."

Erin sat down on the couch. She patted the cushion beside her for Orange Blossom to jump up, but the cat stayed stubbornly in the doorway, looking daggers at K9.

"I miss you," she admitted. "But I think it's also good that I'm spending more time with Vic, because she doesn't have Willie anymore… or not for now, anyway. If it's the three of us, she might feel like a third wheel and not be comfortable."

"But we can still see each other."

"I don't see why not. I'm not the one who changed my routine."

He smiled. Erin was happy to see the familiar dimple appear in his cheek. Nothing like a strong man in uniform with a cute little dimple. Erin suppressed a giggle, trying to remain serious.

"I need to get to bed. Do you want to get supper together tomorrow? Can you manage that on your shift?"

"Sure. You know I could get called away, but I won't leave you in the lurch if I can help it. I'll pop in at the bakery around closing and we'll decide where we're going."

"Okay."

They both stood up. K9 got to his feet and shook himself. Terry leaned over slightly to give Erin the whisper of a kiss, and then he was heading out the door.

"Sweet dreams, then, Erin."

Erin held the door, watching him go, before she shut it and secured it.

"Sweet dreams," she echoed.

CHAPTER 15

The day was a blur. Erin kept busy, so the day flew by quickly, and she wasn't left with a lot of time to worry about Terry or their upcoming date. Everything seemed fine between them. They would reconnect, and everything would go back to normal.

She was more worried about Adele meeting with Sheriff Wilmot. Would he treat her okay? Would he believe what she had to say? How would her confession that she had known Joelle before coming to Bald Eagle Falls impact the investigation? The last thing Erin wanted to hear was that he was arresting Adele and as far as he was concerned, it was all over. He wouldn't just jump to conclusions, would he? Just because Adele had been the one to prepare the tea, that didn't mean that she had poisoned Joelle, either intentionally or accidentally.

Knowing Joelle didn't mean she had poisoned her. The two might have been close friends. Why else would she have gone to Joelle's house with the tea? They were friends. Adele wanted to help out and had taken her the tea to help her to heal faster. She didn't know the comfrey was mixed with foxglove.

"Erin," Vic called. And then, "She's in outer space today."

Erin came back down to earth and saw Terry watching her. She flushed. "Sorry," she said. "I was just thinking about something. Easy to do when you're lost in a repetitive task." She motioned to the dishes she had been washing. "You're ready to go?"

"I can help clean up."

"You don't need to help," Erin protested. But he did, and pretty soon Erin was ready for dinner. "I'll see you later tonight?" Erin asked Vic. "There are frozen dinners in the freezer if you want, and—"

"I know where everything is. Have a nice time."

"Okay. Sorry—"

"Go with Officer Piper. I'll take your car home. I'll see you tonight."

Erin let Vic go, and she and Terry decided on the Chinese food place for their supper.

By the time they worked their way through hot and sour soup and dumplings, Erin felt like they had broken through the awkwardness and everything was back to normal. Yes, there was an investigation ongoing, but Terry wasn't directly involved in it, and the sheriff hadn't yet turned his attention back to Erin. She didn't know how things had gone with Adele's interview, but at least the sheriff hadn't immediately dropped what he was doing to arrest Erin. Every time thoughts of Joelle's death reasserted themselves, Erin pushed them away. She was going to enjoy her date with Terry, no matter what else was happening.

That is, until Terry's phone rang and, looking down at the screen, Erin saw it was Sheriff Wilmot. Terry hesitated, but Erin nodded.

"Go ahead. He is your boss."

Terry made a face as he picked it up, apologetic. "Piper."

The sheriff apparently went straight into whatever instructions or report he had for Terry, since Terry just sat there listening to the phone, occasionally nodding, but not answering or interrupting. Frown lines appeared between his brows. Eventually, he gave a more emphatic nod, and spoke.

"Yes, sir. I'll think on it and see what I can come up with. Uh… I'm with Erin Price, do you mind…?"

Erin could just hear the sheriff's tinny voice assert, "we're going to need as much help as we can get," before hanging up.

Terry put his phone down on the table slowly and deliberately. Erin waited, trying not to show her curiosity. The silence drew out, and Erin finally cracked. "Well? What was that all about?"

Terry startled, as if he had forgotten she was even there. He focused his gaze on her.

"There wasn't enough digitalis in the tea to poison Joelle. The concentration was quite low, so unless she'd had several cups of it, it's not likely what killed her."

Erin blinked, taking this in. "It wasn't the tea."

"Apparently not."

"So it doesn't matter who made the tea or where the comfrey came from."

He gave a little frown. "No. It doesn't matter."

Erin gave a sigh of relief. That took the heat off of her and Adele. Sheriff Wilmot might still consider Erin a suspect, because she had a motive, and who knew whether Adele had a motive for harming Joelle? There was no way for any of them to know what had happened in their past if Adele wasn't talking about it. But at least the murder weapon had not been provided by one of them.

Terry was still watching her. Erin thought about what he had said so far. "So what was the cause of death? It wasn't just a blood clot?"

"What makes you think it wasn't a blood clot?"

"Because you have to think about it and the sheriff said he could use all the help he could get. That doesn't sound like a random occurrence. It doesn't sound like an accident or natural causes."

"You're too smart for your own good," Terry said, the dimple making an appearance.

Erin smiled back.

"So here's the thing. She *did* have toxic levels of digitalis."

"But you said she couldn't have gotten enough from the tea."

"She couldn't have. There was only a token amount in the tea. Like someone wanted to mislead us into thinking that was the source of the poison."

"Then how was she poisoned? Was it a pill or injection? In something she ate? You can't accidentally get digitalis by walking past foxglove in the woods."

"You know how Joelle had hurt herself. How she'd tripped and hurt her leg."

"Right."

"Well, she'd applied a poultice to the wound on her leg to make it heal faster."

Erin waited for Terry to go on, and then realized that was the entire story. He didn't have anything else to add.

Erin finally connected it up. "There was foxglove in the poultice?"

"It was almost entirely foxglove."

"And she absorbed it through her skin?"

"Apparently, applying foxglove to broken skin speeds the absorption process significantly."

"Poor Joelle! Did she make the poultice herself? Maybe she's the one who contaminated the tea, because she'd handled the poultice. Maybe it was all just an accident."

"It's possible. The sheriff will need to explore the possibilities further. But right now… we don't know. The people who knew Joelle—and no one has claimed to know her very well—have said that it seemed unlikely she would know anything about poultices herself. It's something of a dying art. Generally, it's only the grandmas or great-grandmas that know anything about applications like that."

"Maybe she just looked it up on the internet and ended up picking foxglove instead of comfrey. She might have just made it herself."

"It's possible. But the sheriff has a hunch somebody was helping her. Or pretending to help her."

"But why? You really think someone wanted to kill her? She was annoying, but I don't know if there's anyone who had a serious grudge against her."

"Say, someone whose house she'd tried to burn down?" he teased.

"I don't have any experiences in poultices or anything of the sort. Do you need specialized equipment? Or is it just a matter of grinding up the leaves and making a mash?"

"I don't know how Joelle's poultice was applied, or what the usual method for making a boneknit poultice is. I think most poultices are boiled. Some might be fermented. Stills are used for medicinal purposes, but I think that would be more for tonics than anything you put on your skin."

"You sound like an expert." It was Erin's turn to tease.

Terry rolled his eyes and shook his head. "I had a grandmother who still had the knowledge," he said. "I used to find her work fascinating. But I imagine she took all of the secrets with her. My mother never made anything but supper."

"That's too bad. Funny how scientists are looking more carefully at folk remedies these days. Looking for things medicine might have missed. Remedies that they previously would just have dismissed as being backward or superstition. There are scientists who try to seek out tribes and cultures that haven't had much contact with modern man, who might still have traditional knowledge that pharmaceutical companies could use…"

"A lot of it was superstition," Terry admitted. "Or the placebo effect. Or just forcing the person to stay in one place and be calm and to let the body's natural powers of healing take over. But I imagine we've lost a lot by letting these remedies be forgotten."

Erin thought of the books that she had passed on to Adele. Maybe she shouldn't have been so quick to give them all away. Maybe she should have studied them and preserved them for future generations. It hadn't really occurred to her that they could be important.

"So if Joelle didn't know anything about natural healing," Erin said, "and for now we'll just have to assume that she didn't, who in Bald Eagle Falls would know all of that old-timey stuff? We have to assume it wasn't somebody's great-grandma, unless she was offended by Joelle's yoga clothes."

Terry chuckled. "I really don't know. It's going to take some research. I think we can assume that Adele does. She seems to be into all of that kind of thing. As far as anyone else goes, the police department is going to have to do the footwork to find out."

CHAPTER 16

$\mathscr{A}$t first, Erin had been relieved to hear that the tea hadn't been what had killed Joelle. But by the time she got home in the evening, her brain was working overtime to try to fill in the gaps in her knowledge, and she wasn't feeling more relaxed, but instead more agitated and anxious.

It couldn't be Adele. She knew Adele would never do anything to hurt anyone. She was gentle and attuned to nature, and that just wouldn't fit the picture. Erin slept restlessly, her brain continuing to offer up more images of suspects and possibilities, before again forcing her into consciousness to consider what she had seen.

"Just let me sleep," Erin moaned, trying to quiet her brain.

Orange Blossom was sleeping on the bed. He raised his head to look at Erin, but when she gave no indication that she was talking to him, he put his head back down, and cuddled up against her.

"You're a good boy," Erin whispered to him. "At least you're not keeping me awake tonight.

He rolled onto his back, looking up at her with one eye. Erin snuggled down and tried to go back to sleep.

Morning came as it always did. Erin forced herself to get up and get ready, pasting a smile on her face and hoping it would help her to cheer up and not be grumpy at the bakery.

Vic was rubbing her eyes when they got to the bakery. She kept her eyes covered as Erin turned on the lights inside, then slowly removed her hands and squinted at Erin.

"You look like something the dog drug in," she said, and yawned herself. "What's up?"

Erin was happy to have someone she could talk to about her theories. Though in the light of day, most of them withered up and died, making no sense once she was fully awake. She told Vic all about the poultice.

"So it wasn't the tea? That's a relief. I was really worried that Sheriff Wilmot was going to lock you up and throw away the key!"

"I'm glad he didn't! I wondered what was going to happen after Adele finished giving him her story, but I guess I didn't need to worry."

"Who woulda thought you could be poisoned through your skin like that." Vic shook her head.

"I guess if your body can be healed by a poultice, it could be poisoned by one too."

"Yeah… but I never really thought any of that stuff worked. I thought it was kind of like garlic keeping away vampires. Just because it's an accepted folk remedy… that doesn't mean it will actually do anything for you. I thought it was more the power of suggestion."

Erin nodded, understanding. She had always lumped folk remedies and witchcraft together with voodoo and religion and haunted houses. Just things that people liked to talk about and have fun with; not that really had any efficacy.

"You don't know anyone around town who would know anything about poultices and such, do you? I know you're not from Bald Eagle falls, but you did used to come here to help Angela out, and you're more outgoing than I am. People talk to you."

Vic looked for a moment like she would object to this, then shrugged. They went about getting loaves of bread into the oven and starting work on the rest of the baking they needed before opening.

"I don't know a lot of people who believe in that anymore. Like you said, it's not likely to be someone's great grandma, and there really isn't anyone really young who would know anything about it."

Erin was looking out the front window of the bakery when she saw Mary Lou hurrying by outside. Mary Lou was usually working at the General Store by then, so Erin was surprised to see her out on the street. Even at that distance and walking by at a quick clip, Mary Lou looked worried. And Mary Lou never looked worried. She always just smiled and calmly took everything in her stride.

"Did you see Mary Lou the other day?" Erin asked Vic, when there were no customers there to overhear her. "Did you notice how... poorly she's looking?"

Vic considered this. "She has always been one who doesn't show when things are getting her down. She pushes everything down and continues on as if nothing is happening. It's too bad... some people won't accept any help, even when they need it."

"You're right," Erin agreed. She rearranged cookies in the display case, moving them around to cover any gaps that had appeared and mentally preparing a list of what they would need to make in the afternoon. "When I think about all that she's been through, and how she always keeps a smile on her face and acts like everything in her life is just fine... So you think that's all it is? That she's stressed out and won't ask anyone for help?"

"What else would it be?" Vic asked, amusement in her voice. "Unless you think she's ill..."

"Well, I thought she might be. And then I got to thinking about Joelle, and how she got so run down and pale before she died..."

"Nobody is poisoning Mary Lou," Vic said flatly. "Don't even go there. She can take care of herself. She's not going to let anyone give her anything dangerous."

Erin got a cloth and wiped fingerprints from the customer side of the glass display case. "Sure. I know. It's just with her looking so tired and all..."

"I'm sure she's fine. Maybe she's got a flu bug, or maybe those boys are keeping her up late. You know how kids are, expecting their parents to pick them up from parties..."

"Kids," Erin repeated, smirking. Vic was barely eighteen herself. "I guess. Adele said she was going over to Mary Lou's the other day. I thought... she must be making a remedy for her..."

Vic cut her eyes sideways to look at Erin as she returned to the till. "You think?"

"I don't know. I don't mean I think Adele is poisoning her… I guess I'm just a little more wary about these remedies than I was before…"

Vic leaned closer, her voice dropping lower. "I don't believe in magic," she said, a refrain she had repeated more than once since Adele's arrival in Bald Eagle Falls. "But that doesn't mean that I don't think someone could mix up a potion that was harmful… or they could influence someone in a negative way… you know what I mean?"

Vic had always been wary of Adele's teas and other offerings. Erin had thought it funny before. But it wasn't funny after Joelle had died due to an herbal remedy gone wrong.

"Maybe one of us should drop in on Mary Lou later on," Vic suggested. "See if she's feeling okay. Make sure she's not taking something…"

Erin nodded. "Even if it isn't something poison, she could still be allergic to it, right? She could be having a bad reaction, and not even realize that's what is going on."

"So which one of us should go?"

Mary Lou had always been a bit stand offish where Vic was concerned. As pleasant as she tried to be, she just couldn't seem to accept a transgender woman into her circle of friends. She tried to treat Vic like anyone else, but her disapproval was still obvious.

"I guess I will," Erin said. "After the lunch rush, I'll pop over… say that I need something…"

"The Jam Lady Strawberry Jam is going pretty fast," Vic suggested. "That new crop of berries seems like it's got better flavor than any other batch I can remember."

"Okay. I'll go over and pick up some strawberry jam or put in an order if she doesn't have any in stock. And I'll ask her whether… she's feeling well… if she's using any remedies from Adele… She wouldn't have any way of knowing that the tea Joelle drank was from Adele, or she might think twice before taking any…"

"Be careful what you say. I wouldn't want Adele putting the evil eye on us."

~

Unfortunately, the visit to the General Store to see Mary Lou couldn't have gone much worse. Mary Lou obviously knew from the start that Erin was there for more than just ordering more strawberry jam. She could have picked up the phone to do that, or just waited until the next time Mary Lou stopped by the bakery to pick something up for dinner or dessert.

"I don't have time for any nonsense, Erin," she said irritably. "If you want something, just come out with it, okay? I'm worked to the bone, and don't have the patience for any more."

"I was just wondering… wanted to make sure that you were okay. You seem like you're tired or sick…"

"I told you before, I'm just fine. You should know better than to tell someone how bad they look." Even though she denied it, Mary Lou's hands fluttered quickly over her clothes, smoothing and straightening them, and over her hair to check that everything was in place.

"I didn't mean that. You look great. You always do. You just seemed tired…"

"Like any woman who is working and trying to run a household." Mary Lou's dismissal was obvious. She went about her work at the General Store, ignoring Erin and waiting for her to leave.

"And you're not drinking any teas that Adele prepared, are you?"

"I beg your pardon?"

"Adele made the tea that Joelle was drinking, and it had foxglove in it. I know that's not what poisoned Joelle, and Adele said that the herbs came from my Aunt Clementine's herbs, not ones that she had collected by herself, so that wasn't her fault, but…"

"I'm not sure Adele would appreciate you talking about her behind her back, especially accusing her of poisoning Joelle."

"I know. I'm not. I just wanted to check with you and make sure that you're not… allergic or anything…"

She wouldn't be the first one in Bald Eagle Falls to fall suddenly ill due to an allergy. It wasn't unheard of. But Mary Lou knew very well that Erin wasn't talking about an allergy.

"What I do or don't take is really none of your business," Mary Lou said bluntly. "I'll thank you to stay out of my personal life."

"Okay." Erin's throat was tight and hot, and her face was burning. "I'm sorry."

She walked back out of the General Store, humiliated. Somewhere nearby, a crow cawed.

Erin's next idea was to ask the bakery customers if there was anyone in town who was an expert in herbal preparations and remedies. Just a few casual, well-placed questions, and she would be able to start building a list of who in town could have helped Joelle by preparing a poultice for her leg.

But people looked at her oddly and few of them had any names to offer. Erin wasn't sure if they were suspicious of her motives, or if it was just that there really wasn't anyone around who did that kind of thing anymore. Maybe they couldn't think of anyone because there weren't any folk medicine practitioners around anymore.

Erin thought the Potters would be a good bet. They were an older couple, and they always took so much time to pick out what they wanted to purchase, it would give Erin plenty of time to drop a few hints and see if she could get anything out of them.

"I was wondering," Erin said to the Potters, "do you know anyone who has experience with natural healing? Herbal remedies?"

Mrs. Potter looked up from the display case, leaning on her cane. She had a tremor, making her head bob a little as she examined the baker.

"Why do you want to know about that?"

"I'm just curious. You know my Aunt Clementine was really into teas, what with the tea room here and all... I wonder whether she ever partnered with someone to give her advice on medicinal teas… you know, for people who had particular ailments…"

Mrs. Potter wasn't buying it. She looked at her husband, not for help remembering, but a warning.

"No, I don't think so, dear. Clementine didn't sell medicinal teas. Just plain old drinking teas."

"But she had all kinds of medicinal herbs at home, and books about what they were used for. She obviously had an interest in it."

"Then I guess that's your answer. She had books about it."

"There isn't anyone around here who practices herbal medicines? Natural healing?"

"I hear that new woman in your woods is a practitioner. Other than her, we haven't had anyone around here lately." Mrs. Potter brought her other hand up to her cane, leaning with both hands clasped over top. "No one was interested in it for a long time. Young people thought they knew better. Doctors told you to stay away from herbs. Prescription pills were better. Anyone who believed in that natural stuff was backward. Stupid."

"I don't think that," Erin assured her. "I think there can be a lot of good to be gained from the natural world."

"But you don't even believe in God."

Erin was startled by the turn in conversation. "What does that have to do with…?"

"Old timers believe that God put those things on earth for man to use. When Adam was kicked out of the Garden of Eden, God created medicinal plants for his use. That's why they're here. But then the witches came along and perverted them for their own uses, and doctors came along and told everyone they were useless, that we were only imagining that they worked, and everybody turned away from God."

Erin looked for something to say. She glanced sideways at Vic, looking for help. Vic was nodding, but didn't jump in with anything that would help Erin in her effort to find out who in the community possessed the knowledge of a natural healer.

"I don't believe in God," Erin admitted, "but I do think herbs and things found in the natural world can be helpful to us. A lot of the pharmaceuticals are actually based on plants that were used in folk medicines. So of course the plants themselves worked as well. The pharmaceutical industry just refined the process."

"Perverted it," Mrs. Potter asserted. "They try to distill all of the good-ness out of a plant, and they eliminate the balance. All herbs are created with good and bad qualities, with lots of different substances that can be used for different remedies. You can't just take one chemical out of the herb and expect it to work the same way."

"Oh." Erin nodded. "I'm sure you're right." Another glance at Vic, who was looking amused by the conversation, but didn't say anything. "That's why I'd like to know if there is anyone around who still knows the old remedies."

"Maybe you could look in your aunt's old books. I'm sure you could find what you needed there," Mrs. Potter said, her tone closing the subject. She shuffled a little closer to the display case and proceeded to place her order much more quickly than she ever had before. She and her husband both gave Erin frowns of disapproval before leaving.

Vic started giggling after they had left the shop. "I never would have thought you could get the Potters riled up," she told Erin. "Did you see how fast they ordered today?"

"Where was my help?" Erin demanded. "You couldn't think of anything to say?"

"No, I think you said it all," Vic giggled. "I guess atheists just don't ask about herbal remedies."

Erin still held out hope that she would be able to find something out on Sunday, when the church ladies would be by for their after-service tea. Their tongues were always a little bit looser for tea time, and with them all together, she hoped to foster conversation among them that would give her more information. What else would they be talking about than Joelle's death and anything surrounding it?

But things did not start out well. Mary Lou Cox was absent, which had never happened before. She was the backbone of the group. Melissa Lee was there, but she was wary of Erin, avoiding talking to her. She was usually a chatterbox, so it felt strange for her to be so terse with Erin.

It occurred to Erin that she never had followed up with Sheriff Wilmot on the possibility that Davis could somehow have been involved in Joelle's poisoning. Was that still possible with Joelle being poisoned by the poultice instead of the tea? While she could see him instructing Melissa to slip some foxglove into Joelle's tea, it would have been harder for Melissa to poison Joelle with a poultice. Did she or Davis have the knowledge of how to prepare a poultice? Would Melissa have been able to convince Joelle that spreading mashed-up leaves over her injury was the best way to heal it? Erin couldn't recall ever seeing them together. Melissa was not a friend or known associate of Joelle's. Then again, who was?

"Where is Mary Lou?" Erin asked Melissa.

"She wasn't at church." It was Lottie Sturm who answered instead when Melissa just turned her head away and pretended she hadn't heard the inquiry. "Mary Lou never misses church; she must be sick."

"I've been worried about her," Erin said. "She hasn't been looking very well lately. I was afraid she was coming down with something."

"She must have. She wouldn't miss church services for any other reason."

"Maybe I'll go over there after the tea. I'm worried about her."

There were significant looks exchanged around the tables. Erin tried to interpret them.

"What is it? You think I shouldn't?"

"Mary Lou doesn't cotton to uninvited guests," Lottie said, when no one else offered anything. "Roger doesn't do well with visitors. If you're going to go over there… it's best you at least call first. But she'll probably tell you not to come."

"Oh." It hadn't occurred to Erin that there would be any problem with just dropping in for a visit. Bald Eagle Falls was normally very casual about visitors. People often showed up on her doorstep without any advance warning, much as they had done with Joelle. It was commonly accepted that neighborly people just dropped in on each other. "I didn't know that. You don't think she'll want me there? Even if I'm bringing bread or soup?"

"You'd best call first."

Terry sometimes stopped in while the ladies' tea was going on, not to join them, but just to touch base with the community and make sure everything was running smoothly. And maybe to snitch a cookie or treat while he was there. And to make arrangements to see Erin later, if she wasn't going to be running to the city to do some shopping.

Erin smiled and nodded at him as he came in the door. She put her teapot down and got K9 a biscuit. Terry could help himself to something from one of the trays.

"Everything quiet?" she asked.

"Quiet as a Sunday afternoon."

Erin looked at the clock on the wall. "It's still morning."

"Well, then, I guess it's as quiet as a Sunday morning. Everything going well here?" He looked from her to Vic, chatting with a couple of the customers. "I thought you'd have Bella in today."

"She has a school exam to prep for; her mother said she wasn't allowed to leave the house."

Terry grinned and nodded. "Aren't you glad you're not a teenager anymore?"

"Am I ever." Erin shook her head. "I didn't have the happiest childhood; I was more than ready by the time I turned eighteen to just take off and start my own life, without parents or teachers telling me what to do."

"But didn't your family—" Terry caught himself. "Right. Foster family. But you didn't have any relationship with them? Any desire to keep in touch?"

"No. There were families that I had liked over the years… but I was never able to keep in touch with them. Social services discouraged that kind of thing. Once you were gone, you could just forget everything that had happened there. Move on and make a fresh start."

"That must have been depressing."

Terry's phone buzzed. He gave Erin an apologetic look and answered it. "Piper."

He listened to the report from the dispatcher. "Okay. Tell her I'll be right over." He hung up the call and looked at Erin. "Mary Lou Cox," he said.

Erin steadied herself on one of the chairs. "Is she okay? I've really been worried about her lately."

"She's okay. It's Roger."

"What happened? He didn't…?"

"He's disappeared. She's been out looking for him but hasn't been able to find him. I'll go over there to talk to her, but I may be back asking for volunteers to help look for him."

Erin covered her mouth. "What do you think happened? You don't think he's done something to harm himself, do you?" He had, after all, attempted suicide once before.

"Don't know anything yet, Erin. I'll need to talk to Mary Lou and find out how he's been and if she has any idea where he might have gone." Terry looked across the room, reaching out to Vic with his expression. She put down the tray she'd been passing around, and joined Terry and Erin.

"Roger Cox is missing," Terry told her, his voice low. "See if you can get ahold of Willie for me and have him meet me here. As soon as I've had a chance to go through things with Mary Lou, I'll be back, and between the two of us, we can coordinate a search."

Erin opened her mouth to argue that Vic and Willie were no longer together, but Vic nodded briskly. "I'll get him."

"Thanks. Back in a few minutes."

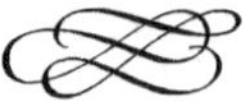

*E*rin had expected Terry to return with Mary Lou with him to be part of the search for her husband, but Terry returned alone. He was focused and serious, not smiling and casual like he had been earlier. The church ladies had quieted at the news that Roger was missing and, when Terry walked back in, they fell completely silent. Terry looked around at their expectant faces.

"I want everybody to go home," he told them. At their noises of protest, he raised his hand to silence them. "I want you to check your yards and outbuildings. Have your neighbors check theirs, and everybody keep passing the word along. Call the emergency dispatch number to report every property that has been checked. We'll start marking a map. If you want to be involved in a more extensive search, meet in the parking lot at First Baptist *after* you've checked your own property. We'll coordinate manpower from there."

He lowered his hand and waited for their responses. The ladies murmured to each other, gathering up their purses and Bibles and heading out. The bakery emptied quickly. Terry looked around.

"Did you manage to get Willie?" he asked Vic.

"He's on his way." Vic looked over at the clock on the wall. "He should be here within five minutes."

"What did you find out from Mary Lou?" Erin asked. "Is there anything you can share?"

"Roger has been having increasingly frequent bouts of agitation and confusion. They've tried to arrange it so that there is always someone at the house to keep track of him, but there are only three of them, and the boys have school, so sometimes it's just not possible. Even when they are home, sometimes he manages to sneak out without anyone noticing. He goes for walks to calm himself down, and usually he comes home on his own, but sometimes he gets confused and loses his way."

"Why didn't she tell us what was going on? Get some help? It sounds like they could use a home care worker, at the very least."

Having worked in the industry, Erin knew that family members were often reluctant to admit there was a real problem and to get the assistance they needed. Mary Lou had weathered her past troubles on her own, and maybe thought she could continue to keep track of Roger on her own too, but she was going to have to face up to the problem before Roger got hurt. Hopefully, she would have the opportunity. They would find Roger and return him home safely, and Mary Lou would get the help they needed.

"Not the time to be asking those questions," Terry advised. "She's already beating herself up. She's beside herself with worry. They've checked all of the places they know he normally goes, but there's no sign of him. Probably, he's just wandered to another part of town, but if he's off in the wilderness..." Terry shook his head grimly. People who wandered into the bush didn't often come back.

The bells on the door jangled and Willie came in. He was dressed for work, a filthy ball cap on, loose fitting clothes, and laced-up boots. His face was, as usual, stained dark by his mining and processing activities. He looked around at each of them briefly. He didn't avoid looking at Vic. Erin wondered briefly if he'd lost a little weight lately. He seemed like he had diminished since she had talked to him last. She'd seen him around town, doing the odd jobs that sometimes occupied his time, but he had remained at a distance and she hadn't had a chance to talk to him.

Willie nodded at Vic, then his eyes went back to Terry. "What have we got, Piper?"

Terry pulled out one of the wrought iron chairs previously occupied by the church ladies and sat down. Willie did the same. Terry started to outline the details he knew. As he talked, Willie pulled out a worn map of the area and spread it across the table. He studied it intently while Terry spoke.

"Where are his usual haunts? The places they've checked already."

Terry pointed out each location, explaining what it was and why Roger would go there, if they knew. Willie pulled a sheet of stickers out of his pocket and placed a colored dot over each of the locations.

Willie looked around the shop, as if just realizing that it should have been full, but instead was empty. Terry explained about sending the ladies home and telling them to check their yards and spread the word.

Willie nodded. "Okay, good," he agreed. "They may contaminate potential scenes, but the faster we can cover the town, the better. If he isn't found, the police will need to do an official door-to-door search, but that will take a lot longer. We might need to get Search and Rescue and the feds involved, if it goes that far."

Terry told Willie about having set up the church as the central hub for the search, and Willie got to his feet.

"Let's get over there, then. It won't be long before people start showing up, and there will be complaints if we aren't ready for them. No one wants to stand around waiting when Roger could be sick or hurt."

"We'll come too," Vic announced.

Terry frowned. "I was hoping I could get you working on the back end," he said. "We're going to have a lot of people to coordinate and take care of. We're going to need sandwiches, urns of coffee and tea. People aren't going to want to stop. They're not going to want to go home to make supper and then get back into it. They'll want to just grab something when they check in and continue working."

"Sure," Erin nodded. "I'll start a list of what we'll need…"

Vic bit her lip. She obviously would have preferred to have been a part of the actual search, but she accepted the job they had been assigned. "Go ahead then. We'll be up there with what you need as soon as we can."

oor Mary Lou," Vic said, as they unpacked the plastic-wrap covered platters of sandwiches and urns of coffee for the volunteers. "Can you believe that after everything she's had to go through, now she gets this thrown at her as well? The poor woman!"

Erin nodded. "After losing everything and then almost losing her husband… then just when it seemed like she was getting back on her feet with the you-know-what…" The rest of the town didn't know that Roger was the creator of the Jam Lady Jams, so Erin had to be careful what she said around other people. "Just when it seemed like things were going better, this happens."

They continued to load up the tables so that as the volunteers returned from their search areas, they could grab something to eat before heading back out.

"Why would God let that happen?" Vic said.

Erin looked at her. "I'm the last person you want to ask that. God didn't have anything to do with it. Roger has brain damage from trying to kill himself. That's all there is to it. They thought they could manage without bringing in more help, but they were wrong."

"I know you don't believe in God. But don't you think there has to be a limit? That at some point, things have to get easier?"

"No. People have to go through horrific things. We tend to have it pretty good in North America. Other countries, they would consider Mary Lou blessed to still have a husband and two nearly-grown sons. It's a matter of perspective."

"I suppose. It just doesn't seem fair, though. I think she's been through enough."

"Then maybe you should mention that to God next time you pray," Erin advised.

Vic scowled. "Are you making fun of my beliefs? You know, just because you don't understand how God works or about how to use natural remedies or you don't think magic could be real, that doesn't give you the right to make fun of other people who do."

Erin's jaw dropped, and she wasn't able to work out an answer immediately. Vic turned away from her abruptly and busied herself with getting another coffee urn out of the little car.

"Vic, I didn't mean it that way," Erin insisted, following her. "I wasn't mocking you, I meant it sincerely. You pray about things that bother you, so I just thought…"

She could see Vic take a few deep breaths before she turned back around. When she did, her face was calm, but flushed. "I'm sorry. I overreacted. I'm all emotional for no good reason and I just snapped."

Erin touched her arm tentatively. "You've been through a lot lately. This business with Joelle dying when we were right there in the house, and people suspecting that we were involved somehow. That maybe we poisoned her, when neither of us would ever harm a fly. And breaking up with Willie. Now you're worried about Mary Lou and Roger, just like I am. There's a lot of stress right now. Even Mary Lou snapped at me the other day. If she can lose her composure, anyone can."

"Well, now we can see why. The poor woman's been dealing with this all by herself."

"And Adele," Erin reminded her. "Adele was over there the other day."

Vic frowned. "I wonder why…"

"Maybe something to help her to sleep. She was looking so fatigued the other day I almost wondered if someone was poisoning her."

Vic shook her head but didn't put her doubts into words. They continued to work side-by-side, not saying anything for a while.

"You can't really say that I would never hurt a fly," Vic said.

Erin looked at her, confused.

"You said that they shouldn't have suspected us of having anything to do with Joelle's death, because neither of us would hurt a fly."

"Yes…?"

"But you can't say that. Because I have."

"Hurt a fly?"

"Hurt someone."

Erin just looked at her blankly before it finally dawned on her. "Alton Summers?" she asked finally. At Vic's nod, Erin shook her head vigorously. "Hurting Alton Summers doesn't count. The man was trying to kill me!"

"I know… but I didn't even hesitate. I didn't even stop to think if it was the right thing to do or if it was the only way to handle the situation. I just grabbed my gun and shot him the first chance I got."

"And a good thing you did, or I might be the one lying in hospital instead of him. Or worse, in the morgue, because I don't think he would have hesitated to shoot me at point blank range."

"So Alton doesn't count."

"Of course he doesn't."

Vic straightened the stacks of cups near the coffee urns. "I can't get shooting him out of my head. If it wasn't for my Xanax, I wouldn't get a wink of sleep. I've only ever needed it occasionally before, but now I can't sleep at all without them."

"It's no wonder you're emotional! I didn't even think about how hard that must be on you. I just… was so relieved that you were there to save me, that I never considered that you might have a hard time dealing with it. I'm so sorry!"

Vic swiped at her eye with her wrist and kept working away. Erin knew she should insist that they sit down and have a good talk over everything, but there was work to be done, and she and Vic had always talked best while they were working together. She gave Vic a quick sideways hug.

"I'm fine," Vic promised. "I guess I've just been holding a lot in."

"You need Willie. I wish you two would make up."

"It isn't that we're fighting. We just… have different viewpoints. Maybe we're not as compatible as I thought we were. I thought initially that our differences were just superficial, but now…" She trailed off and let out a deep sigh. "Maybe you were right about him being too much older than me. He's from another generation. He's set in his ways. He has… a longer history than I do. The wrong choices he made as a teenager and young man are way in his past, he's had years to get over them. But for me, I'm right in the middle of that stage of life, thinking that I know all of the answers; and if I do, then why couldn't he have made the right choices when he was my age?"

"It's not his age that bothers you. I don't think it's even the stupid stuff that he did, getting involved with the Dysons that bothers you."

Vic snorted. "You don't know."

"Okay, I don't know."

But in a minute, Vic was chuckling and wiping at her eyes. "What makes you so smart, Erin? That's not what upset me the most. I could deal with all that stuff."

"I only know because you told me. You're mad at him because you told him your secrets and revealed who you were, and he didn't reciprocate. He knew you were a Jackson and that he should tell you he was a Dyson, even if it meant you would break up with him. It isn't like he's just keeping his business secrets to himself. He was being dishonest because he knew being honest could mean that it was over between you."

Vic sniffled and nodded.

Volunteers began arriving in the church parking lot to check in with the police department coordinators to get their routes checked off. Terry and Willie had organized everything, but then left it in the capable hands of Clara Jones and Melissa while they left to help with the search. K9 might be able to track Roger, and Willie was an accomplished outdoorsman and might be able to find Roger's trail if he ran across it. Everyone was hoping that Roger hadn't gone wandering in the deep woods. A few hours of walking, and they might never get him back.

After checking in, the volunteers dug into the sandwiches, sloshed hot cups of coffee down their throats at a speed that made Erin wonder how they were not scalding themselves, and then headed out again. They had started early, so there were a lot of daylight hours, and Erin was hoping that Roger would be found before nightfall. How would Mary Lou get through the night if they hadn't found him yet?

"Has Mary Lou come by?" asked one of the men who had stopped to eat, wiping his mouth off with the back of his sleeve.

"No. She's staying at the house in case Roger goes back there. I don't imagine she could deal with everyone else right now, either."

"No, maybe not," the man grunted.

"She'll be happy when we find him," Vic said firmly.

Erin nodded. "Yes, she will. Any time now."

"We're praying for her," the volunteer said. He put down his empty coffee cup and walked away.

"Do you remember when we were searching for you?" Vic asked Erin, when the latest batch of volunteers walked away again, ready to continue their searches.

Erin remembered the excruciating hours in the pitch-black tunnel, injured, her body trying to shut down while she tried to keep it going. She had kept going, worried Vic was down there with her, also hurt, needing Erin's help. She remembered the relief at finally seeing Terry's and Willie's headlamps, knowing that she was found and that she wasn't going to die down there in the dark, her body left entombed there for an eternity.

"Oh yeah," she agreed. "I remember."

"We knew you were down there, but the tunnels can go on for miles, and they twist all over the place. I didn't know if they'd be able to find you in time, or if you were already dead."

"It wasn't so great for me either."

Vic giggled. "I guess not."

"There aren't any caves close by here, are there? You don't think Roger's gone anywhere like that?"

"No. There aren't any mines within walking distance, not that I know of. And no one has reported their vehicle missing. He has to be in town, or not far from it."

If he'd walked out of town, he could have hitchhiked. He could disappear into some other part of the country. Start a new life where he didn't have a reputation. He could have a new family. Or he could decide it was better to live alone and not drag anyone else down with him. What if he hadn't just wandered off, agitated or confused, but had planned it out? What if he had decided that the kindest thing he could do for Mary Lou and the boys was to get out of their lives? He'd tried once before. Maybe this was his second attempt to remove himself from their lives. Instead of killing himself, just walking away from them forever.

Erin kept her thoughts to herself. No one wanted to hear her speculation.

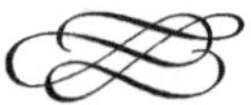

It was almost the end of the day. People were talking about what they were going to do when night fell. Would the search be called off until morning, and then they would regroup? Would some of them search through the night, using flashlights or night vision goggles, calling Roger's name and hoping for a response?

Then Erin detected a change in the body language of the volunteers near the check-in table. She nudged Vic.

"Is something happening?"

Vic followed Erin's gaze to the group of townspeople. Her eyes were quick. "Yeah… it looks like something is going on."

"They're not calling it off, are they? It's not dark yet, we still have time."

"No. I don't think it's being called off." Vic clasped her hands together and closed her eyes. "Come on," she urged. "Come on…"

Erin didn't know if it was a prayer or a wish, but she echoed the sentiment in her own mind. Mary Lou deserved a break. After working so hard to take care of her husband and keep her family together, she deserved to get good news, not a death notification or a missing persons case that remained open indefinitely.

Terry's truck sped up the road to the church. He had a police light stuck to the top, a rotating red cherry. He skidded into the parking lot, spraying gravel. He drove past the cluster of volunteers, up to the refreshment tables that Vic and Erin still manned, exhausted after a day on their feet on the unforgiving asphalt. Terry jumped out his door, and then went around to the passenger door, and helped out a man who was wrapped in a gray woolen blanket.

A cheer went up from the volunteers.

"It's Roger?" Erin asked. "They found him?"

But Vic didn't know Roger by sight any more than Erin did. He was always at home, out of sight, and had never been by the bakery or any social events in Erin's time in Bald Eagle Falls.

Erin's mind was buzzing with questions, not the least of which was why Terry had brought Roger to the church instead of home to his family.

Terry led Roger over to the table, Roger resisting and trying to pull back from Terry's grip the whole way. Terry positioned Roger in front of a platter of drying sandwiches and grabbed a water bottle from the chest of ice, mostly melted. He cracked the bottle open and handed it to Roger.

Another truck was speeding toward the church, and this one Erin recognized as Willie's. It raced up to the church to stop beside Terry's, and Willie jumped out. K9 was in the back of Terry's car and barked a greeting at Willie. From his tone, Erin figured he was probably annoyed at being relegated to the back when he was used to riding with Terry in the cab, and at not being released as soon as Terry stopped and got out.

Willie ignored K9 and went over to Roger and Terry. He took Roger's wrist, fingers expertly placed to check Roger's pulse. He spoke to him in a low voice and started a field test to determine Roger's condition.

Roger seemed somewhat dazed by all of the unusual activity to start out with, but his confusion quickly grew into anger and irritation.

"What's going on here?" he demanded. "Who are all of these people?"

The crowd was growing rapidly, word obviously spreading that Roger was safe and had been brought to the church. An ambulance rolled up, and the paramedics talked to Willie, but then climbed back into the ambulance and sat there waiting, not disturbing Roger.

A stream of cars was headed up the road toward the parking lot, their lights coming on as dusk drew closer. Erin saw Mary Lou's car, and breathed a sigh of relief. She had been afraid everyone in town was going to see Roger before he had a chance to be reunited with his family. Mary Lou pulled up close to her husband and got slowly out of the car. The two boys were with her and followed. Erin couldn't understand why Mary Lou and Roger weren't running into each other's arms.

Terry tried to turn Roger to focus him on Mary Lou and her cautious approach, but Roger didn't seem to even see her.

"What is everyone doing here?" he demanded. "Why can't I go home?"

"You can go home," Mary Lou promised, getting closer to him. "It's fine, Roger, they just wanted to make sure you were okay before they brought you home. You can come with me now, I'll take you home."

"Why? I don't understand what's going on."

Roger's voice was aggrieved. Erin tried to analyze him. She'd dealt with Alzheimer and dementia patients, but there was something different about Roger. He didn't act vague and uncertain. He acted ready for a fight. Was he sundowning? Some patients changed their behaviors dramatically in the evening and seemed like different people from who they were during the day.

He was a tall man with wispy brown hair and a thin build. Taller than Mary Lou. His face was red, but she didn't know whether that was his normal complexion, sunburn from being out in the sun all day, or his anger at not knowing what was going on. He looked around impatiently.

"Where was he?" Mary Lou asked Terry, ignoring her husband's complaint.

Terry looked around. "Can we get some space here?" he asked the crowd. "Move back to the check-in table, please. We need a little more room."

The excited volunteers were not happy to be told not to crowd so close, and getting them to move back and give the Coxes some space was not easy, but eventually, they cleared a perimeter.

"He was in a wooded area close to the river," Terry told Mary Lou finally. "Like you said, just out on a nature walk to clear his head."

"Was he lost?"

Terry shook his head. "Hard to say. I don't think he was aware of how long he'd been away. Or that you would be worried about him."

Mary Lou sighed and nodded. "We've tried to explain it to him, but that part of his brain just doesn't seem to be working. He has no idea why we get so upset."

"These sandwiches are dry," Roger complained. "I have a casserole ready to put in the oven at home. Let's just go home."

"Come on," Mary Lou agreed. She looked at Terry, as if expecting him to object. "It will be okay," she assured him. "He'll be tired tonight after being out for so long. He'll sleep soundly."

"He seems to be fine physically," Terry said, with a nod toward Willie. "But at this point I think it is fair to be considering whether he should be left without supervision."

"He won't be," Mary Lou promised. "Someone will be with him. I don't know what's been going on lately, he's been a lot more agitated than usual. I promise we'll keep a close eye on him."

Terry nodded. Erin wasn't sure whether there was anything he could do about it even if he wanted to. What would he do? Call social services and report them? That would cause all sorts of problems that he probably didn't want to be responsible for. "Let us know if you need anything," Terry told Mary Lou. "Look around you. There are a lot of people who care about you and are willing to help you out. You don't need to push everyone away."

"You're right." Mary Lou wiped at the corner of her eye. "I can't believe how many people came out to help look for him. This really is a great community."

"It is. And you and Roger and the boys have a lot of friends here. Don't shut them out and insist on doing it by yourself."

"Okay." Her voice was hoarse. She nodded and sighed, giving her husband a sad sort of smile. "Come on, Roger. Let's go home."

Roger put down the half sandwich he'd taken a few bites of and walked alongside Mary Lou. She put her arm around his waist, and he reflexively put his arm around her shoulders. They looked like any ordinary couple, just out for an evening stroll, sharing a few minutes together. They went to Mary Lou's car, and it took a minute for Mary Lou to redirect Roger to the passenger seat, as he apparently thought he should be able to drive. Erin didn't know how disabled his accident had made him. She knew that he tended toward depression and that the brain damage he had sustained left him unable to go back to the work he had previously been doing, but she didn't know what functions had been affected and which had not.

Roger got into the car and, once he was settled, Mary Lou went around to the driver's side and got in. Erin watched her pull on her seatbelt. Then Mary Lou just sat there for a minute. Erin was too far away to see if she was crying, praying, or just breathing. Or maybe all three. The boys were in the back seat and reached up and patted their father on the shoulder and the back, welcoming him back. As far as Erin could tell, he didn't reach back to them, but he might have been talking to them. Mary Lou turned her car around and headed for home. The volunteers waved and called out after them, and then the Coxes were gone.

"So that was Roger," Erin said.

Terry looked at her. "You haven't met him before?"

"No. How would I? He's always at home, and I gather they don't take visitors."

"Well… they do still go out to church as a family. Mary Lou goes to the ladies' tea afterward and the boys take Roger home. But you don't go to church, so how would you know that?" His gaze drifted to Vic. "Either of you."

Erin frowned at this comment. "From what I understand, you don't go to church either, Officer Piper."

He grinned. His face was tired, but the smile brought out his dimple and made Erin's heart skip a beat. "It wasn't meant as a criticism, Erin. Just an observation. You're right, I don't get there very often either. My work prevents it."

Erin shook her head. "You told me before that work was just a convenient excuse. You wouldn't be going regularly anyway, would you?"

"No. Not regularly," he admitted. "I get there once in a blue moon. Which is how I know that Roger still goes with his family."

"It's good he gets out for something. I imagine it would be pretty stifling for him to be shut up in the house all day."

"That isn't why he wandered off."

"I know… but it might still help to take him out places more often." At Terry's skeptical look, she defended herself, "I have had some experience as a caregiver, you know. You ran background on me, so I'm sure you know that. I've taken care of a lot of elderly people who needed a companion. Roger's not elderly, but it seems like he has some of the same problems as some of my patients did."

Terry shrugged. "You could be right. But I'd be careful about how you approach that topic with Mary Lou."

"I doubt I'll say anything about it. She hasn't exactly been open to suggestion lately."

"She's probably been worried about him."

Erin nodded. She started gathering up the leftover drying sandwiches. "I don't imagine anyone is going to be interested in these now. If anyone is hungry, they'll be heading over to a restaurant or home to cook something."

"I'll take one of those." Terry helped himself to a couple of half-sandwiches. "I'm still on duty for a while yet."

"You've been on since this morning. Can't one of the others take over?"

"Everybody's been working hard. I have a double shift today, but it will be fine. I'll be off in a couple more hours."

"Do you want me to bring you something else?" Erin said, looking down at the sandwiches doubtfully. "These have been sitting out for a while, they're not really that nice."

"They'll do fine for now."

CHAPTER 21

Erin didn't take a direct route home, but the scenic route around her woods. Across the bridge, close to the cottage that Joelle had rented, and as close as the road got to the old summer house that was Adele's home. Erin looked through the trees but didn't see any lights. Of course, that didn't mean anything. The house was set back a good way from the road, with a screen of trees in between, and Adele could have it lit with a low lantern or a few candles, and no one would be able to tell until they were right up to it.

"She didn't come out for the search," Vic observed, noting the direction of Erin's eyes. "Do you think anyone even told her what was going on?"

"I doubt it. She chooses to be more isolated back here, so she doesn't really have any neighbors. Someone could have phoned her and told her. Or Terry or Willie might have stopped in during the search. I don't know if she would come out and help with something like this."

Vic agreed. Adele wasn't exactly antisocial, but she was different from her neighbors and chose to spend most of her time alone. She didn't follow the same rules as the rest of Bald Eagle Falls. Erin thought about Mary Lou. At least she would be able to sleep soundly for once.

"Maybe Adele could give you something to help you sleep," Erin suggested to Vic, remembering how she had confessed to not being able to sleep since shooting Alton Summers.

Vic looked at her. "I already have something to help me sleep. And no matter what you say, I'm not going to go to a witch for a sleeping potion." She shook her head. "I have visions of Snow White or Sleeping Beauty."

Erin laughed at the image. Adele was certainly no wicked old witch. Erin would trust her. Or Erin always had trusted her. With all of the talk about poisoning and poultices, Erin wasn't sure who she trusted anymore. Adele had never given her any reason to be suspicious. She'd never given Erin anything that had harmed her or given her adverse symptoms.

But she thought of Joelle's pale, pinched face and Mary Lou's tired, swollen eyes. There was someone in the community who either didn't know enough about herbs and poisons, or who knew too much.

Erin was just feeding Orange Blossom a few treats before bed when she heard a truck coming down the lane. Looking out the kitchen window, she saw a familiar truck pulling in behind the garage. It was a truck that she had seen earlier that day.

She didn't mean to be snoopy, but she was standing there watching as Willie let himself into the yard and headed up the stairs to Vic's apartment. Willie looked at the house, and Erin realized that he could probably see her standing there with the light of the living room shining behind her. He raised his hand to wave.

Embarrassed, Erin waved back, and turned quickly away from the window to head back into the living room. She wasn't going to stand there to watch what happened between Willie and Vic. Would Vic refuse any approach from him? Or would Willie apologize for the secrets he had kept from her and persuade her to take him back? Erin wouldn't know, because Erin was going to bed, and Vic could tell her—or choose not to tell her—in the morning.

Orange Blossom followed Erin, *mrrowing* inquiringly. Erin turned and waited for him to catch up to her.

"No more treats," she told him. "It's bedtime. I may not have gotten my day of rest today, but tomorrow is a new week anyway, so I'd better get a good night's sleep tonight."

She looked in on Marshmallow, then brushed her teeth and climbed into bed.

~

"That Joelle wasn't a very nice person. I'm not saying I'm happy that anyone is dead, but I'm glad that she's not around anymore."

Erin's ears pricked. She looked up to see who was talking. It was a busy time of day, and she couldn't stop to gossip with anyone, but she couldn't help overhearing the words.

It was Melissa talking to Charley. Erin was surprised to see Charley up and around in the morning; usually, she acted like any time before noon was too early to be expecting people to be awake. But there she was, not only up, but dressed professionally instead of in blue jeans and a t-shirt. She saw Erin's surprised look.

"I *do* clean up pretty good."

"No, it's not that… I mean, partly that, but I didn't even expect to see you up yet."

"It wouldn't be my first choice," Charley agreed. "But I have an appointment with the estate lawyers, and with Sheriff Wilmot *again*. I don't know why he can't get it through his head that I didn't want Joelle dead." Charley cast a glance at Melissa. "I could have gotten her to help convince Davis to agree to open The Bake Shoppe again. Without her, I've got no in. I can't even get onto his visitor list at the prison."

Erin looked at Melissa, who didn't offer that she was on Davis's visitor list. Erin kept quiet about it.

"I'm sure the sheriff is just trying to cover all of the bases," Erin said. "I doubt if he has a lot of experience in investigating a death like this."

"Still, it shouldn't be that hard to understand that I wouldn't kill someone who I benefited more from alive. Besides the fact that I don't have any expertise in poisons or any of the herbs he's talking about. He could be speaking Greek, that's how much sense it makes to me. I was never interested in cooking or gardening or medicine. So why would I know anything about poultices?"

Charley gazed into the display case, holding up the line of customers behind her as she chattered on, ignoring them.

"I don't even know what a poultice is. I mean, I get it, you put this goop on someone's injury to help it to heal, but… how you make it or what you put in it, how you get it to stay on them, how long you keep it there… I don't know any of that kind of stuff. Basic stuff you'd have to know if you were going to poison someone with one. And I never knew you could poison someone through their skin. On TV, it's always a pill or an injection or something mixed into their drink. I don't have any experience with that kind of thing."

"Haven't you ever had poison ivy?" Melissa challenged.

"Yes, but that doesn't actually poison you. You just get itchy, you don't die. I didn't know that you could put something on someone's skin that would kill them."

Melissa rolled her eyes. "Of course you can. They can give you nicotine or other medications in a patch. That's just like a poultice… except not so messy…"

Charley picked out a muffin, and Erin rang it up for her and collected her money. She didn't look directly at Melissa. "Do you know a lot about poultices?"

"My grandma was sort of a healer," Melissa said. "I mean, she mostly did prayers or the laying on of hands, but she did use herbal treatments as well. Back then, everyone knew how to make a mustard plaster or other kinds of applications. It was just passed along in families."

"So your grandma passed it on to you?"

"No, not really. She was too old to still be practicing when I was a kid. I mean, she seemed like she was really old. I suppose she was only seventy and not a hundred, but I had in my mind that she was about a hundred. Too old to be doing anything."

"Did she talk about it? Try to teach you any of the old lore?"

Melissa had Vic package up some fudge for her. She didn't look directly at Erin as she paid for it.

"I told you, she was too old. She might have talked about it sometimes, but I never listened. All of that stuff was out of date. We were using modern medicine. Science. Not grass and bark and stuff that should just be thrown in the compost heap."

Erin nodded. Melissa's tone didn't give Erin any indication that Melissa was trying to deceive her. But Erin had caught her lying before and never had figured out any of Melissa's 'tells.' Some people could fool even themselves into thinking they were telling the truth, and maybe Melissa was one of those people. Someone who just redefined history to be what they felt like it should be. Melissa liked to be the center of attention, and never seemed as happy as when she was in the spotlight.

"It's too bad all of that knowledge went to waste," Erin said. "I imagine she knew a lot that could really be helpful today."

"I don't know. Was any of that stuff actually effective?" Melissa shrugged. "People don't really believe in these old-school remedies like they used to. They're almost always just snake oil."

Charley appeared to be waiting for Melissa to finish so they could walk together. Were Charley and Melissa friends now? Did Charley know that Melissa was another 'in' with Davis? Other people must know about Melissa's past relationship with Davis, and about her going to the prison to visit him in recent days. Some of them would have been around when Melissa and Davis were going to school. They would have seen it with their own eyes. A few well-placed questions, and Charley would know everything she needed to.

Melissa clutched her bag of fudge and followed Charley out of the shop. Erin could hear her already starting to complain again about how the sheriff just didn't understand that Charley had wanted Joelle to help her out and it was extremely inconvenient for her to have died.

They were all together again, and the mood in Erin's little house was almost festive as the four friends gathered around for an evening snack and to catch up with each other. Vic had agreed to start seeing Willie again, and he was beaming. Hearing that Willie was going to be over, Terry had agreed that he would pop by as well, and the four of them could have a little party.

It wasn't really a party. There were no balloons or streamers or wine. It was a different kind of a celebration. There might not be any decorations or cake, but there were rolls made fewer than twenty-four hours before, and Jam Lady jams, and they were just as sweet as cake and everyone could choose their favorites.

As Erin got the jars out of the fridge to put onto the counter, there was a tap at the back door. She turned to see Adele.

"Are you busy?" Adele asked, her eyes following the noise of chatter out to the living room. "You've got people over."

"Just the usual crowd. The more the merrier."

"Except I'm sort of a third wheel," Adele said. "A fifth wheel." She laughed.

"No, really, you're just as welcome here as anyone else. It's a few days since I saw you. Is everything okay?"

"Oh, just fine. I know things have been a little disrupted in town, but in my little cottage… everything is nice and quiet. The way I like it." Adele looked around. "Drinks? Shall I make some tea?"

"Sure. Sounds good. Nothing that is going to keep me up, though."

Adele shook her head. "No. Something soothing to help you sleep."

"Vic's been having trouble sleeping since—she's been having trouble sleeping lately, but I guess she wouldn't let you give her anything for it. You know how she is about your 'potions.'"

Adele chuckled. She moved around the room, getting the kettle out and checking the cupboards to see what varieties of commercial teas, herbs, and other ingredients Erin had kept for herself.

"Erin, come watch this!"

Erin turned at Vic's call from the living room. She was laughing hard, giddy. Erin guessed that just the relief of having Willie back in her life was enough to make her act a little silly. She went out to the living room to see what Vic wanted to show her.

"Willie brought this laser pointer," Vic said, pressing the button to turn it on, so that a bright red dot suddenly appeared on the floor. Orange Blossom eyed it hungrily, his body crouched and tense. Vic wiggled it around enticingly, making the dot run around the floor. Every time it disappeared from Orange Blossom's sight, the cat ran forward to spot it again. Several times, he tried to pounce on it, going wild when it just jumped on top of his paws when he expected to catch it underneath them. He yipped in protest and jumped from place to place, panting with the exertion of trying to catch the shiny red dot.

"That's hilarious," Erin agreed. It was funny, but she wasn't nearly as giggly as Vic was over the cat's antics. "Now let me finish getting everything ready out here, or the rolls are going to be cold or dry before we even start.

"Go ahead," Vic agreed. "Sorry, I just thought you would want to see. He's so funny!"

"He is," Erin said. "Silly cat."

She went back out to the kitchen and continued to get things ready. She warmed the rolls gently and opened the jars of jam, including the new batch of wild strawberries that everyone was raving about. The jar top didn't pop like they usually did, and she looked at it carefully to make sure it was okay. It might not have formed a proper seal, but it was fresh enough that even if it hadn't sealed during canning, it wouldn't be spoiled yet.

She checked the surface of the jam anyway to make sure there was no discoloration and saw that someone had already used the jam. It was no wonder the seal hadn't popped. *Somebody* had already opened it and taken some of the jam. Probably Vic had grabbed a midnight snack without Erin even realizing she'd been around. Although Vic had her own kitchenette, she and Erin usually ate together, and there wasn't much worth mentioning in Vic's fridge. She knew the burglar alarm code and knew she was welcome to use what she wanted to from Erin's kitchen any time.

"What was she doing to the cat?" Adele asked.

Erin startled and looked at her. "I almost forgot you were there, you're so quiet. Just teasing him with a laser pointer. Making him chase the light."

Adele nodded. "We used to use flashlights, but laser pointers work much better."

"It is pretty funny." Erin glanced toward the living room as Vic burst out in another fit of laughter. "But I don't know if it's *that* funny!"

The kettle was singing, so Adele took it off of the burner. "Does anyone else want tea?" she called toward the living room.

The laughter quieted, but there were no takers. Adele shrugged at Erin. "Their loss."

Erin finished putting everything on the table. "Okay, bread's on. Come on in!"

The kitchen was full of friends and the smell of bread and jam and spiced orange tea.

"Mmm," Vic held Erin's cup up to her nose. "That smells really good!"

"Did you want some?" Adele asked.

"No... thanks." Vic put the cup down and focused on the bread and jam. Everyone picked out their favorites and started to eat.

Erin helped herself to generous amounts of the new-batch strawberry jam before anyone else could. Vic had already helped herself to some and Erin wanted to make sure she got her fair share.

She had a couple of bites of bread and jam, then took a sip of the tantalizing-smelling spiced orange tea. Cinnamon and cloves and maybe just a hint of ginger? Sweetened with a little honey. Erin nodded approvingly at Adele. "That's really good."

Everyone was quiet for a few minutes while they ate the rolls. Erin took a second bite of her roll, savoring the sweet jam. But there was something that wasn't quite right. A slightly off taste that shouldn't have been there. Erin sniffed at the jam, trying to identify it. Maybe it had started to go off because it hadn't been sealed properly? Or maybe there was an ingredient in the jam that she wasn't expecting, like an artificial sweetener. Erin picked up the jar of strawberry jam to see if it was labeled sugar-free, but it wasn't.

"Is something wrong?" Vic asked, mouth full. She giggled and covered her mouth.

Erin took another sip of her tea, rinsing her palate, and took another bite of the jam smeared on the warm roll. The main taste was strawberry. But there was something else underneath it. Something like tomatoes? It wasn't unpleasant, it just seemed out of place.

"Erin?" Terry was looking at her, frown lines forming between his brows.

"What did you say?" Erin's mouth was dry. She took another sip of tea. She was glad it had ginger in it, because she was starting to feel a little nauseated. She wiped sweat from her forehead and took a couple of deep breaths to settle her stomach.

"You're not looking so good," Willie observed. He left his seat and walked around the table to take her hand, feeling her wrist for her pulse. "Talk to me, Erin. How are you feeling?"

"Fine... just... little icky..." Erin held on to the edge of the table because the room seemed to be shifting and tossing like a boat.

"Maybe she should lie down," Vic suggested.

"No... I don't think so. Erin, can you get to the car?"

"Don't think I can drive," Erin murmured.

"No, I don't want you to drive. I just want to get you into the car. Come on." He helped Erin to her feet. She wasn't quite sure why he was being so insistent.

"Just a little dizzy."

His strong arm was around her, hurrying her along much faster than she wanted to move. He was practically sweeping her off her feet. It was Vic he was supposed to sweep off of her feet. Erin tried to laugh and tell him that, but the words got stuck and she couldn't get them out.

"Terry," Willie said urgently, as the policeman followed him to the living room. Willie's body turned slightly as he looked back into the kitchen at Vic and Adele. "Crime scene. Don't let anyone touch any more of the food or drink in there. Get samples of everything. Right away."

"You don't think...?"

"I do. She was just fine until she started eating. Whatever it is, it's working fast, and I need to get her to help before it's too late."

"Wait—"

"No. I'll be in touch. Seconds count."

Willie hustled Erin out of the house and into Terry's truck. He threw her into the seat like a rag doll and hurried around to the other side of the truck to get in and drive. After turning the key in the ignition, his hands flew over the controls as if he knew exactly what he was doing, and Erin heard the siren start. She closed her eyes, but even with them shut, she could see bright pulses of light. She tried to tell Willie to turn them off, but he ignored her.

"Just stay with me, Erin. Who is going to bake us treats if you are gone? Tell me you're not going to leave me at the mercy of your sister!"

Erin tried to answer him. The words didn't come out as anything resembling speech. Erin couldn't figure out why nothing was working. She'd had strawberry tea and orange jam. Or orange tea and strawberry jam. Nothing that she was allergic to. She should be able to just get up and walk away.

But she was still in the truck, and even if she tried, she couldn't open the door and walk away. She felt like she was floating, suspended in the air.

Once they were out of town, she could hear the truck engine straining as they raced down the highway. She knew Willie must have the gas pedal pushed to the floor. She didn't want to know how fast they were actually going.

But chances were, he was not going to get pulled over for speeding! Not unless Terry decided to prosecute him for stealing the police vehicle. Erin's thoughts were growing jumbled. Had Terry given Willie the keys? If not, then how was Willie driving the truck? Maybe Erin was confused, and they were in Willie's truck. Maybe the siren was following them rather than coming from their ride.

"How do you always get yourself into the middle of these situations, Erin?" Willie demanded. "Why is it everyone is always trying to burn down your house, run you down, hit you over the head, or poison you? Did you ever stop to think about that?"

It wasn't her fault. It was Bald Eagle Falls. Erin had never had her life threatened before that. Not seriously. She'd dealt with people who wanted to hurt her in other ways or been in other dangerous situations, but it was different from what she had gone through since she had moved out to the middle of nowhere determined to start her own bakery. And that had all started with Angela's death. If it weren't for Angela, everything would have been fine.

Erin tried to push herself up in her seat. Her body was unaccountably uncooperative. It was difficult just to move, forget trying to shift her own weight.

"How are you feeling? Okay, Erin?"

Erin managed a little moan.

"Try to talk to me. Try to focus on what I'm saying."

She wished he'd put music on the radio instead of expecting her to carry on a conversation.

Willie started to sing. Erin was annoyed. If there was one thing that was worse than trying to talk when she was sick, it was having to listen to improvised karaoke from someone who didn't have the talent for it. When she moaned again, Willie just sang louder.

She didn't know how long it took to get to the city. It seemed like an eternity. Willie didn't need to ask for directions or turn on the GPS in the truck, he navigated directly to the hospital without any help. Erin was looking forward to being able to lie down and relax. It was late, and she should be going to bed if she were going to get to the bakery in the morning.

Willie opened the door beside Erin, and she nearly fell out. Willie didn't try to make Erin walk, but simply scooped her up in his arms and walked briskly into the hospital.

"I need help!" he shouted. "Poisoning victim. She needs treatment right away!"

There were doctors or nurses and hospital staff. Erin was soon on a gurney and hooked up to several monitors. She closed her eyes and tried to shut out all of the noise.

CHAPTER 23

$\mathcal{E}$rin dreamt for a long time. She didn't drift in and out of sleep like she did when she was sick or anxious. But she wasn't exactly in a normal state of sleep, either. There were lots of dreams, the kind where she didn't know whether she was dreaming or not until she woke up, but then she found out she wasn't awake, but was really stuck in another dream after all. There were people coming and going, talking to her and touching her, and the various monitors the hospital had put on her got in her way and kept her from getting comfortable. She just wanted them off. Her stomach hurt. Her body hurt. Her head didn't feel right.

Erin opened her eyes. "Why doesn't someone shut that light off?" she demanded.

Terry moved into her line of vision. "Erin?"

"I'm trying to sleep; can't they turn off the lights?"

He smiled. "I'll ask them."

Erin closed her eyes again. She lay there for a while, waiting to wake up again, or maybe to fall asleep.

"Willie has your truck," she told Terry.

"I got it back. Thanks."

"He's a really bad singer."

Terry laughed. "Is he? I've never heard him sing."

Erin waited. Sleep still didn't come.

"Can I go home? Is Vic feeding the animals?"

"I'm sure she is. You can go home when the doctors decide you're well enough. What do you remember about what happened?"

"Nothing. I was sick. Willie brought me here, but he should have just left me home to sleep. Then I could get enough sleep and still get up in time for the bakery."

"He did the right thing to bring you here. You would have died if he hadn't acted as quickly as he did."

Erin opened her eyes again and turned her head to look at Terry. "I wouldn't have died!"

"You were poisoned. Something very fast-acting. Not digitalis this time."

"I wasn't poisoned."

"You were. Can you tell me who would have had access to the tea and the jam?"

"Access?"

"Who could have contaminated them?"

"No one. They were just in my kitchen. No one touched them."

"Adele."

"Adele didn't poison me."

Terry raised his brows. "You're a little more... oppositional than usual. Did you know that?"

"No, I'm not."

He smiled. "I think you're still a little confused. Adele was in the kitchen alone, with access to the tea and the jam, wasn't she? Just for a few minutes?"

"No. I was in there with her."

"But you came out to the living room when Vic called you. To watch the cat chasing the laser pointer."

Erin remembered that. "She thought it was so funny. But Adele came out too. She said they used to get their cat to chase flashlights."

Terry shook his head slowly. "No, Adele didn't come into the living room with you. She was still in the kitchen."

"I don't think so," Erin said firmly.

"Tell me about the jar of jam. Do you remember which kind of jam you were eating?"

"Jam Lady jam. That's what we always get now."

"I know that. But what flavor, do you remember?"

"Strawberry. The new batch."

"The new batch?"

"Not last year's strawberries. This year's new wild strawberries. There was a really good crop."

"Oh, I see. So you must have bought it recently."

"Yes. Just…" Erin tried to narrow down the day she had bought the new jar. "A few days ago. I don't remember. What day is today?"

Terry ignored the question. "You bought the jam a few days ago. Did you just open it yesterday? Or had you had some of it before?"

"It was new."

"Unopened?"

"I hadn't had any of it." Erin frowned, concentrating.

Terry waited. "Is there something else, Erin?" he prompted.

"I hadn't opened it. But it wasn't sealed."

"You're sure?"

"Someone else opened it. Vic."

"Vic had opened it already?"

"She must have. Had a midnight snack."

"It's possible. I'll ask her. Could it have been someone else who had opened it?"

"No. It was Vic."

"You hadn't had anyone else in the house lately? And it was sealed when you got it?"

"Vic already had some." Erin blinked at Terry, the bright light still bothering her eyes. "See, it wasn't poisoned. Because Vic already had some, and she didn't get sick. It must have just been the flu."

"You were poisoned."

"With what?" Erin challenged.

"They're still testing to figure it out."

"But I didn't die, so I wasn't poisoned."

"You would have died if Willie hadn't gotten you straight here. They were able to give you something to stop you from absorbing any more of the poison and started cleaning your blood and giving you fluids and medications to keep you from succumbing to it."

Erin put her hand over her eyes. She couldn't remember any of that. She could remember little of what had happened since Willie had driven her to the hospital.

"He drove like a maniac. I was afraid he was going to go off the road."

"Good thing he didn't. If he totaled my truck and kept you from getting medical attention, I would have…" Terry cut himself off and shook his head. *Would have killed him,* Erin finished in her head. But there had been enough violent deaths in Bald Eagle Falls. Terry didn't want to say it aloud, even as a joke.

"Nobody killed Willie," she told Terry.

"No. Willie's fine. Everyone is fine, including you. Though you're a little loopy right now."

"Joelle isn't fine."

"No." Terry nodded soberly. "Not Joelle."

"Did they give it to her in the jam?"

"No. In her tea and the poultice on her leg."

"Oh. Right." Erin closed her eyes and waited for sleep.

"*Who* put it in the tea?" Erin asked, trying to remember the details.

"We don't know yet. That's what we're trying to figure out."

"The Jam Lady. I like the Jam Lady jam."

"We all do," Terry agreed. His chair creaked as he sat back, stretching his back. He probably had a stiff neck after sitting there all night. Erin didn't know how late it was, or if it was the next day, or even the day after that. "Is strawberry your favorite?"

"I like them all. The new-batch strawberry jam is so good. But I think there was something in that one. Something wrong."

"In the jam, not the tea?" Terry asked.

"Yes."

"What did it taste like? Was it bitter? Did you recognize it?"

"Don't ask so many questions." Erin rubbed her eyes with her fists. "That's too many!"

"Sorry. Your brain is still trying to catch on to what's going on. What did the jam taste like?"

Erin imagined she could still feel it on her tongue. The cloying sweetness. The soft, yeasty roll. The smell of the spiced orange tea in her nostrils. Maybe if the smell of the tea hadn't been so strong, she would have been able to smell what was in the jam before she had tasted it and poisoned herself.

"It tasted… kind of… tomato," she told Terry. She shook her head, trying to isolate it further. She'd barely been able to taste it under the sweet strawberry jam.

"Tomato?" Terry repeated. He leaned toward her, putting his hand on Erin's arm. "Tell me about it before you fall back asleep," he said. "It wasn't bitter? It tasted like tomato?"

Erin shrugged. "Sort of. That's the closest thing I can think of."

"Okay. Why don't you go back to sleep? I'll pass that on and see if it's something that will help narrow down what you were poisoned with."

*A*s luck would have it, that clue was exactly what the doctors and investigators needed to figure out what had been put in the jam.

"As soon as I told the doctor, his face kind of lit up," Terry told Erin. "He said that there was a deadly poison in the same family as tomatoes, and that the fruit of that plant was said to taste a little sweet and savory, like a tomato. In fact, people used to be afraid to eat tomatoes, because they thought they would be poisonous like—"

"Deadly nightshade," Erin filled in.

Terry grinned, a dimple appearing in his cheek. "Deadly nightshade," he agreed. "Belladonna. One of the most toxic plants in these parts. Though luckily, the fruit does not carry as much poison as the root."

Erin struggled to sit up, and Terry used an electronic control to raise the head of her bed until she was upright. Erin was feeling a little more like herself, her brain not running rampant down rabbit trails like it had been. She felt grounded for the first time since Willie had put her into his truck. Like she was actually held by gravity to the bed instead of floating or being in danger of floating away. Erin grasped the rails of the bed just to be sure, then let go again.

"So you think someone put belladonna fruit into the strawberry jam? Why would anyone do that?"

"You do seem to be a favorite target. Maybe someone thinks you are too close to knowing the truth. Maybe you're just a distraction. Or maybe they wanted to make someone close to you look suspicious. I don't really know why."

"It wasn't anyone close to me who poisoned me. You know that, right?"

Terry gave a little grimace. "I don't want to think that either," he agreed. "But we still need to investigate. Sheriff Wilmot needs to investigate, since I'm still off this particular case. I just have… a vested interest in finding out the details."

Erin's face warmed. She'd never been called anyone's vested interest before.

"It wasn't Adele and it wasn't Vic. It doesn't matter if they both had access to the jam, neither one of them poisoned me. You can tell the sheriff that too. This wasn't my friends. My friends wouldn't try to kill me."

"I don't like to think about it either," Terry said, but Erin couldn't help noticing that he didn't agree that it was impossible either one of them had had anything to do with it. He was trying to keep her calm and happy, but he hadn't agreed with her.

"Why would either of them poison me?" Erin persisted. "Neither one has any reason. No reason at all."

"Unless one of them was the one who poisoned Joelle. Then it would make sense to poison you to keep you from finding out the truth. Being so close to both of them, you might know some little clue that would point to them, and they couldn't be sure that you wouldn't find it."

"I don't know who poisoned Joelle, though. I told the sheriff that. I tried to find out who… might have known something about poultices and folk medicine, but…"

"Why would you do that?"

"I wanted to know who might have helped Joelle with her poultice… to help to…"

"You're not supposed to be investigating. You're not supposed to be trying to solve this or to point the sheriff in the direction of the person who might have done it. You're supposed to be staying out of it."

"Well… I was," Erin stumbled, knowing it wasn't exactly true. She wasn't trying to solve the case. Not really.

"You were not staying out of it. Not if you were asking people questions about who might have poisoned Joelle."

"That's not exactly what I did."

"No. I'm sure. Erin... I don't know how you can keep walking into these situations blindfolded. You know that asking questions leads to... people getting defensive and trying to get you out of the way. So why do you insist on doing it?"

Erin squirmed under his gaze. "I don't know... I'm just curious. I like to solve puzzles. And I can't just sit back and not do anything when I'm a suspect, or when my friends are."

"If you're going to keep it up, you'd better get some training and become a police officer or private detective. Just bumbling around as an amateur, with no idea of how to properly conduct an investigation..."

"I don't bumble," Erin said with irritation.

"Well, you're not exactly unnoticeable."

Erin frowned. "Is that a word?"

"It is now. If you're going to keep getting yourself involved in crime investigations, then you should get some training. I hoped that with a burglar alarm, you'd be better protected, but so far, you've had someone disable the alarm and come after you with a gun, and someone else get right inside to poison you. We still don't know how that was done. You *do* turn on the alarm during the day when you're at the bakery, right?"

"Uh... no."

The dimple in Terry's cheek was long gone. His brows drew down in a fierce scowl. "What is the point in having an alarm system if you don't use it?"

"I do use it... at night, when we go to bed."

"I think that this shows you it needs to be on all the time. You can't have people sneaking into your house while you're gone and tampering with the food. You're gone for twelve hours or more every day. There should be some kind of security in place during that time."

Erin nodded, a little embarrassed. She should have thought of that. She should have known that her home needed to be protected just as much during the day as at night when she was sleeping. "Okay. Yeah."

The scowl smoothed away. Terry touched Erin's hand. "Okay," he repeated. "All right, then."

*E*rin was happy to see Willie and Vic together again, apparently just as happy and natural as they had been before, as if there had been no breach between them at all. Erin and Willie sat in the living room, watching Vic play with Orange Blossom with the laser pointer.

But the cat didn't seem quite as interested in the little red dot as he had the other day. He kept losing track of it and turning to look at Erin, meowing at her or jumping up on her to get pats and ear-scratches.

"He wants to make sure you're okay," Vic commented.

"I'm fine, you silly cat," Erin told Blossom, patting him, giving him a little cuddle, and putting him back on the carpet. "You go play."

Orange Blossom looked for the dot. Vic made it creep toward him, and then take a few dashes away. Blossom chased after it, swatting with both front paws, then pouncing to try to pin it down. No matter what he did, he couldn't seem to catch it or stop it from jumping around.

"Have you seen Charley lately?" Vic asked.

Erin had only been away from the house and bakery for a couple of days, so she wasn't sure why Vic was asking.

"Uh… she did come see me at the hospital once," Erin said. "Other than that… our paths don't cross a lot, even though it is a small town. Why?"

"I just wondered… I guess I'm hoping that she'll give up this idea of opening The Bake Shoppe. I don't know why she and Davis can't just give instructions for the estate to sell the shop and divide the money between them."

"For one thing, because they both want the whole kitty," Erin said.

Orange Blossom, on his back with his head stretched out looking for the elusive red dot, lifted his head and looked at her.

"Not that kind of kitty!" Erin laughed. "Neither one wants just their half of the estate. They both think they should have the right to get the whole thing."

"But the law says it's half and half."

"Davis thinks that he should get it all, because he's the only legitimate child. Charley never even knew her father, so why should she get anything just for being born? Especially since she wasn't born until after he was dead. Charley thinks that Davis shouldn't be able to get any of it because of his involvement in Trenton's death. He shouldn't be able to benefit from the commission of a crime."

"Well, they're both good points," Vic admitted. "So maybe neither of them should inherit. Who would it go to then?"

"I think we run out of heirs at that point. Maybe some cousin somewhere. Maybe you, you're a cousin. Is there anyone more closely related to Trenton who is still alive?"

Vic shook her head. "Me? I'm sure there must be someone closer. And if it goes to a cousin... it's going to have to be divided about a hundred different ways!"

"I suppose that eliminates any motive for gain."

"Oh..." Vic sat up straighter suddenly, startling Orange Blossom and making him leap to his feet. Vic laughed. "I was supposed to tell you Adele was looking for you. She said when you were feeling better and were back on your feet..."

"I should go over there." Erin picked up her phone and looked at the time. "She'll be up and around."

"You shouldn't be traipsing through the woods. Not when you're just recovering from being poisoned."

"The doctor said I'm fine. He said I can do anything I feel up to."

"You don't feel up to walking all the way over to Adele's."

"It's only ten minutes. I'm not that frail." Erin got to her feet.

"You could trip, or…" Vic trailed off, looking for some other terrible thing that could happen to Erin on the way to Adele's cottage.

"Nothing is going to happen to me. I've been over to Adele's plenty of times before and I've never lost a limb doing it."

"Think about what happened to Joelle. She just tripped and fell…"

Erin gave Vic a stern look. "Do you want to come with me?"

"Well…" Vic looked at Willie. "I suppose I should."

"You don't have to. I'll be just fine. You can stay and visit with Willie."

Willie gave a very slight shake of his head, and that made Vic's decision for her.

"I'll come along. Maybe I can feed Skye some peanuts today."

Willie and Vic got to their feet and said goodbye. Erin waited for them, shaking her head.

"You don't have to go. I can just walk over there myself."

"No, I want some fresh air," Vic said.

"You guys are plotting against me. Just because I was accidentally poisoned once doesn't mean it's going to happen again."

"Not if you don't eat or drink anything Adele makes," Vic added in a low tone.

"Don't say that. Adele didn't poison me. They tested the tea, and it was perfectly fine. The belladonna was in the jam. And… I don't know how it got there, but Adele did not put it in. The belladonna berries were jellied just like the strawberries. Adele didn't do that in the thirty seconds I was out of the kitchen."

"No," Vic agreed. "But—"

"No. She didn't do that. She didn't poison me. I'm going to visit her, and I will have a cup of tea with her if I feel like it!"

Vic didn't argue. Willie went on his way and Erin and Vic set out on the trail through the woods toward Adele's house. A pathway was getting worn between the two houses from the number of times they walked to and from each other's houses. It wasn't like the first time that Erin had ventured into the woods and to Adele's house, when it had been so wild and unfamiliar. Erin now knew each rock and tree along the way, and what had seemed like a long distance in the dark that first night seemed much closer.

Vic and Erin didn't have much to say on the way there. Neither one was looking for an argument or wanting to discuss Adele's possible involvement in Erin's poisoning.

They arrived at the clearing around the cottage and both stopped for a moment. Erin looked for any sign that Adele was outside, ears pricked for the sounds of movement or Skye's voice. Neither of them saw her, so they headed to the door. Erin knocked on the door. They could hear movements inside and waited patiently.

The door opened, but instead of the tall, slender Adele, they saw Tom Baker, part-time police officer. He looked at Erin and Vic and shook his head. "What are you two doing here?"

"Looking for Adele." Erin tried to see around Tom into the rest of the cabin. "Is she here? Nothing happened to her, did it?"

"Why are you looking for Adele? You know you're not supposed to be investigating this case, don't you?"

"Investigating what case? We just came to see Adele. She's our friend."

"Did she call you to come?"

"No... she told me she wanted to see Erin when she got out of the hospital," Vic said. She too was looking around for Adele. "Did something happen to her? Is she okay?"

Erin's stomach clenched, and her heart started to race. "She's not hurt, is she? Tell me she didn't get poisoned too."

She should have anticipated it. First Joelle, then Erin; Adele was bound to be on the list somewhere too. They were all connected. Somehow.

"Adele is fine," Tom finally assured them. "She's not here."

"Then, where is she? And why are you here? Did something happen?"

"Sheriff Wilmot has taken her into custody. He said she's the only one who could have poisoned Joelle Biggs and you, Miss Price. She's the only one who had the access and the knowledge necessary to poison both of you. And..." Tom's eyes darted back and forth, and he leaned forward slightly, his voice lowered, "because of her past."

"Her past?" Vic echoed.

Erin couldn't bring herself to ask for the details. Everybody had a past, and she didn't need to know Adele's. She knew what kind of a person Adele was. Erin had gotten cross-threaded with the law a few times herself, through no fault of her own, and it was more than possible that Adele could have too. Erin didn't want to hear about it. She didn't want to be prejudiced against Adele. She tugged on Vic's arm.

"Where is she?" Erin asked Tom. "Is she being held here?" She had no idea where Adele would have been sent once she was arrested.

"She's at the police department right now," Tom said slowly. "There's nowhere she can be held for any length of time in town, so they'll be getting a transport to have her taken to the county jail. Don't know how long it will take. Hopefully, by the end of the day. Always a problem if we have to hold someone overnight."

"We have to go see her," Erin told Vic. "Or I have to anyway. She's not the one who poisoned me, I'm sure of that. She doesn't have any motive to kill Joelle or to kill me. Does Sheriff Wilmot think it was just random? That doesn't make any sense."

"I don't know if they'll let us see her…"

Erin didn't ask Tom whether they would or not. She just tugged again on Vic's arm. "Come on. Please. Let's go. If they're transferring her out of town, I don't want to have to go chasing after her. I want to see her now."

"Okay," Vic finally agreed. "All right, let's go."

Tom Baker didn't try to stop them. As they turned away, he closed the door again. Erin wondered if he was in the midst of searching the cabin, or if he was there to see who came to visit Adele, or if there were another reason he was there. They started back toward the house. Erin heard a caw and looked around.

"Skye?"

She couldn't see where he was, somewhere close by, hidden by the branches of the trees. He cawed again. Or maybe it was another crow; it wasn't like Erin could tell them apart.

"Did you bring the peanuts?"

Vic held out a few nuts in the palm of her hand. Neither of them made any sound or movement. There was another caw closer to them and a curious little croak. Vic stood there, frozen, only her eyes moving, looking around for him and then glancing over at Erin. Neither moved. Erin didn't know how long they should stand there waiting. While it would be nice to make contact with Skye and make sure he was okay, he was a wild animal and would be just fine whether Adele was around or not. They needed to go see Adele before she was transferred to the county jail. Erin had no idea where it was, but she imagined that, like the prison where she had visited Davis, it was probably at least a couple of hours away, and there would be specific hours and procedures that had to be followed.

With a swoosh, the black bird swooped down and perched on Vic's arm. They both jumped, and Erin saw Vic's mouth tighten when Skye dug his claws into her arm. He didn't take a peanut right away, but cocked his head first at Vic, and then at Erin.

"Hey, Skye," Erin greeted. "How are you doing? You know us, right? You remember us?"

He didn't shy away, but kept looking at her, examining her with his glittering black eyes.

"Birds are very smart," Vic said, barely moving her mouth. "They're supposed to be one of the smartest animals. Way smarter than dogs."

"I know," Erin said, watching Skye. She really could see the intelligence in his eyes. It was like he knew exactly what was going on. "We're going to go see her, Skye. We'll find out what happened. She'll be back here soon, I promise."

He regarded her for a few more moments, then snatched up one of the peanuts in Vic's hand, and flew off.

"We'd better go," Erin said. "We can come back and feed him another time."

CHAPTER 26

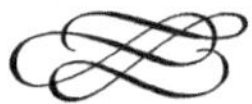

Clara Jones didn't look surprised to see Erin and Vic at the police department. She typed a few sentences into her computer, hitting the keys fiercely, then looked up at Erin and Vic again.

"What are you doing here?" she demanded. "You can't see her, you know."

Erin wasn't about to waste her time arguing with Clara about it. Clara might consider herself a cop, but she was just a secretary. "I want to talk to the sheriff."

"Sheriff Wilmot is busy at the moment. He can't see you."

"When will he be free?"

"How do I know? He is working on a very important case, as you well know."

"Considering I'm part of that case, I imagine he'll want to talk to me," Erin said reasonably.

"He's busy right now."

"Clara, just let him know we're here," Vic said irritably.

Clara fixed her with a glare. "I don't take orders from you, Miss Victoria Webster. Or whatever your real name is. I know my job, and the sheriff is not going to be interrupted when he's in the middle of an interrogation."

Erin turned her back and walked a few feet away, pulling out her phone and selecting Terry from her favorites list. After a few rings, Terry picked it up.

"Erin. Is everything okay?"

"Yes, we're fine," Erin said. "I just wanted to talk to Adele."

"She isn't—"

"She's at the police department. That's where I am, but your gatekeeper isn't letting us in to talk to her or the sheriff."

"That's probably not a good idea right now. He needs to take the time with her…"

"Adele was not the one who poisoned me. I don't know why she's been arrested for something she didn't do. I need to talk to her!"

"Erin," Piper's voice had that restrained quality that meant he wanted to censure Erin, but was struggling to be polite about it. "You need to let us conduct this investigation. I know you don't think Adele did anything, you've made that quite clear. But the evidence points toward her. We would be neglecting our duty if we didn't take action on it."

"When can I talk to her?"

Terry paused, not answering her right away. He sighed. "We need to interview her, and she needs to be transported to the county jail, so that doesn't leave a lot of time for you to be talking to her."

"So, when?"

"At least another hour… I'll try to get you ten or fifteen minutes before she's transported, but if we miss the transport, then one of us has to stay with her tonight, and we're not properly equipped to deal with prisoners here. Okay?"

"Please make sure I can talk to her before she's moved. I need to get back to work tomorrow, and I don't want to have to wait until the weekend to go talk to her at the county jail."

"You don't need to go to the bakery tomorrow. You can take another day to recover."

"No, I need to go. I don't want Vic to have to do everything. Even if Bella can get in for part of the day, it's too much work for just one person. She's already covered for me for two days."

Vic was trying to talk to Erin, to tell her that she could manage for another day, but Erin shook her head. She knew that Vic could do it if she had to, but Erin was trying to force Terry's hand.

"Okay," Terry said. "I'll do my best to make sure that you get a few minutes with Adele before she's transported."

"Even if you have to hold up the transport for a few minutes?"

"Yes. But I can't hold them for long."

"Okay. We'll be waiting."

Terry hung up. Erin looked back at Clara. "We'll be in the waiting area when Adele is free."

Clara shook her head as if she couldn't believe their nerve and continued to attack her keyboard with ferocity of a dozen pigeons fighting over a spilled bag of popcorn. Erin took a deep breath, and she and Vic went to sit and wait. It was going to be at least an hour, and quite possibly more. No one had said how long it would be before the jail transport arrived, but Erin imagined the police department would take as much time as they could get to question Adele before the transport arrived.

Erin pulled a spiral notepad out of her back pocket and began writing lists.

Eventually, Sheriff Wilmot approached the chairs where Erin and Vic were waiting, sore and numb backsides on the hard plastic seats.

"You really didn't need to come here," he said irritably. "If there was something pressing you needed to talk to Adele about, you could have gone to the jail to discuss it tomorrow."

"You know what our schedules are like," Erin said. "By the time we finished at the bakery, I'm sure their visiting hours would be over. Not to mention how tired we are at the end of the day, and how long would it take for us to get out there?"

Wilmot gave a shrug of acknowledgment. "A couple of hours."

"A couple of hours each way, at the end of a twelve or fourteen-hour work day? Do you really think that's feasible?"

Even though he had started the conversation, Erin sensed that he didn't want to argue about it. The sheriff just made a motion as if to wipe it all aside.

"You can come see her, but there's not much time. The transport will be pulling up any minute now."

"And you can tell them you're processing her out and she'll be ready in a minute," Vic said. "You do have to prepare some paperwork, don't you?"

"In fact, that's what I'm going to do now." He grimaced. "I did not choose the police force as a profession thinking that I would have all of this lovely paperwork to complete."

He led the way to the inner offices and opened the door to one that Erin had not been in before. Unlike Terry's and the sheriff's offices, it was not crammed full of file cabinets, desk, and visitor seating, but was quite empty, with just a table and a scattering of chairs inside. Erin was relieved to see Adele still looking like herself; calm, relaxed, and at peace with the world.

Erin and Vic hurried in. Erin had been planning to greet Adele with a hug of comfort, but it didn't seem appropriate with Adele looking so collected and unworried about the questioning she had just been through. She did, however, seem a little perturbed by Erin and Vic being escorted into the interview room.

"What's going on?"

"We wanted to make sure you're okay," Vic said. "And you said that you wanted to see Erin when she got out of hospital.

"Yes… well, I wasn't expecting it to be under circumstances like this."

"We went to see you at the cottage," Erin told her, "and Tom told us that you'd been arrested. I don't understand how they could do that! You didn't poison me!"

Adele shook her head. "No, I didn't. I'm glad you have the sense to realize that, even if the police don't. Why would I want to hurt you? As soon as something happens to you, I'm out a home. I can't support myself with my craft. I have to find a new home, a new job, not to mention, I'd be run out of town on a rail. The fact that I'm your groundskeeper is the only thing that makes me respectable enough to the town that they put up with me being here."

"Well…" Erin shrugged, embarrassed. Adele made her sound noble, when really, it was just a convenient arrangement for both of them.

"It's not an exaggeration," Adele said. "I've been through other towns like this. I know how people react." She motioned to the chairs and they all sat down.

"Are you okay?" Erin asked. "I don't understand why they've arrested you."

"As far as they are concerned, I am the only one who could have poisoned you. And with Joelle…"

"There could have been someone else in town who was helping her out. I'm sure you're not the only one who knows how to prepare a poultice."

"There is," Adele agreed, "since I'm not the one who put the poultice on her leg."

Erin was relieved to hear that. Adele could be lying, but at least there was still the chance that it could have been someone else.

"Do you know who? Did she tell you?"

"No. She didn't have it the last time I saw her. Someone else must have been there to help her. I guess you and I weren't the only ones who decided to be neighborly and drop in on her."

"I didn't give her the poultice either."

"No," Adele agreed.

"The church ladies are always dropping in on townspeople who are sick or hurt. They're very well-organized. She could have had a lot of visitors."

"Except I don't think any of them were too inclined to help Joelle. She wasn't part of the church group and she wasn't a very nice person."

"I don't know if that matters to anyone. They're supposed to help anyone, whether they like them or not, aren't they?"

"Sure they are," Vic agreed. "Love thy neighbor. But Christians are fallible just like anyone else. We don't always do what we're supposed to. It's easy to find excuses or not be available."

"I suppose. Somebody did go see her."

"We just have to find out who," Erin said.

Vic and Adele both turned toward her, frowning.

"Haven't you had enough?" Adele asked. "Leave it to the police."

"They've already arrested you; they're not going to find out who really did it."

"Well…" Adele's shoulders dipped slightly. "I would hope that they don't stop investigating just because they've arrested me. They still need to be able to prove that I was the one who poisoned you and Joelle, and that's not going to be easy, since I didn't."

"You don't have a motive. So that's one point in your favor."

Vic nodded her agreement. Adele wasn't so quick to agree. Erin waited for her to defend herself, but Adele didn't.

"You had a motive?" Vic asked.

Long seconds of silence ticked by. "I knew Joelle before I came here," Adele said finally.

"You knew her," Erin echoed.

Did that mean they had been friends? Was there significance to Adele's move to Bald Eagle Falls? It seemed like a stretch that Adele and Joelle had just happened to know each other and had both chosen to go to Bald Eagle Falls by pure coincidence.

"We grew up together," Adele explained. "Not friends, but in a community much like this one… the type of place where everyone knows everyone else's business."

Erin and Vic nodded, waiting for more.

"Joelle was the type of person who always wanted attention and was always trying to be part of the hip, popular crowd. But it didn't matter how hard she tried, she was never able to pull it off. Everybody could always tell she was poor and that she was trying too hard. Not that the girls in the popular clique were exactly happy or secure in their positions either."

"They never are," Vic agreed. "Everyone is insecure as a teenager and those girls just pick at each other, looking for any sign of weakness."

Erin didn't imagine that things had been easy for Vic, growing up with a transgender identity. She didn't know at what age Vic had started to transition; she had presented as female when Erin had met her at seventeen. She must have felt like an outcast in her small community.

Erin also felt empathy for Joelle, poor and awkward, trying to look like she fit in. Growing up in a series of foster homes, Erin had worn mostly odd hand-me-downs, faded, shapeless, and out-of-date. She had not been neglected, exactly, but new clothes had not been in the picture.

Joelle did the best she could with what Melissa had called 'thrift store chic.' Good enough to fool Erin into thinking she had plenty of money, but she hadn't fooled everyone and, as a teen, Joelle had obviously been aware of her failure to impress.

"But that's not a motive," Vic said. "You don't kill someone because you grew up together, whether you ran in the same circles or not."

"No," Adele agreed flatly. "You don't."

A couple of moments passed.

Adele shifted, looking uncomfortable. Not quite her usual poise. "Like I said. We weren't friends."

"Did you have something against her?" Vic asked. "Or… she had something against you?"

"She had a chip on her shoulder. She had something against anyone who she thought was getting ahead of her. When I first saw her in Bald Eagle Falls, I thought maybe she had grown up. She seemed pleasant, more comfortable in her own skin. But…" Adele trailed off.

"But maybe she wasn't actually so nice," Erin said. "Maybe she'd just learned a few new tricks."

As a teenager, maybe Joelle hadn't yet learned how to present herself. As an adult, she had played her part very cleverly, becoming Trenton's girlfriend and then giving him the cupcakes that would end his life. In the beginning, no one had suspected that she had done it all intentionally.

Adele was clearly reluctant to discuss the details. She nodded slowly, focused somewhere past Erin and Vic, avoiding their gazes. "She wanted me to give her money. Money to keep quiet."

"She tried to blackmail you?" Vic gaped.

"Yes."

"I thought that with Alton out of the way, everybody could relax and rest easy again," Erin said. "I never thought that Joelle…!"

She remembered Alton confronting Joelle at the Founders' Day Fair. Too far away for Erin to hear their words, but Erin had been sure that Alton had been trying to blackmail Joelle just as he had tried to blackmail Erin. But Joelle had shoved him away. She was having nothing of it. Had his attempt at blackmail inspired her? Or had she already been involved in such activities before?

"She's no innocent little lamb," Adele said dryly.

"No, I know that. Believe me, I know that! I just didn't see it coming. I can't believe that she would try to blackmail you! What did you ever do to her?"

"I don't think it would have mattered whether I'd done anything to her or not. She wanted money and she figured I was her meal ticket."

"I'm sorry she treated you that way."

But something wasn't right. Something was niggling at Erin's brain. It wasn't that she was worried about what Joelle might have been blackmailing Adele about. The fact that Adele was a practicing witch was enough. If word about that had gotten out, she would have been run out of town. But there was something more.

She heard a voice in her head. It took a while to identify whose voice it was and where it had come from.

Why would you take soup to a person who had tried to burn your house down?

Sheriff Wilmot had asked her that during her interview with him. Erin had been surprised at how suspicious he had been of her motives. She had just taken soup to someone who was hurt. There was nothing sinister about that. But faced with Adele's confession, it was suddenly easy to see why he'd been so persistent about it.

Why would Adele take boneknit tea to someone who had, just days before, been trying to blackmail her?

Adele could see the suspicion in Erin's eyes. She sat back in her chair, looking tired. "And… there it is. Now you see why they've arrested me. I was doing something nice for someone I knew could use my services. And obviously, Joelle wasn't suspicious of my motives, or she wouldn't have drunk the tea. But to an outsider… I had motive to see her on her way."

"Yeah," Erin agreed, nodding. "It was the same with me. Sheriff Wilmot kept asking why I would be nice to Joelle when she had tried to hurt or kill me. And I guess… I can see his point."

"Only you don't have the expertise to make the tea or the poultice. And I do. If the poison had been in the soup…"

"That can't be grounds to arrest you. There have to be other people in town who know about poultices."

"And who had the opportunity? And who had a motive?"

"There must be."

Adele sighed. "Your loyalty as a friend is admirable. But even you have to see that it looks suspicious. I didn't poison Joelle, but I can't prove I didn't."

"There must be something we can do," Erin told her. She could hear footsteps coming down the hallway and knew they didn't have any more time. "We'll try, Adele, okay? We'll do whatever we can." Seeing Vic's skeptical look, Erin amended. "Well, I will, anyway."

The door opened, and the sheriff was there with a uniformed man that Erin didn't recognize. The officer in charge of the transportation, Erin assumed.

"Sorry, we're going to have to break this up," Sheriff Wilmot said. "Mrs. Windsor, you just stay where you are. The rest of you need to go." He made a flapping motion to hurry them on their way. Erin and Vic got up, giving Adele waves and sad little smiles, walked out of the room and left her to the men.

When they got outside, Erin took a deep breath and blinked quickly, trying to banish the tears stinging her eyes. Vic gave a sigh as well. Then she looked at Erin.

"Mrs. Windsor? Did you know that Adele was married?"

They were getting into the car, but Erin wasn't ready to leave. She knew she needed to talk to Melissa before she could go home.

"I… think I dropped something," she told Vic, patting her pockets. "I'll be right back…"

Vic frowned, but didn't object or insist on going back with her. Erin moved slowly, making sure that the sheriff was back in his office and Terry hadn't shown up. Melissa was sorting through some reports. Erin went through the motions of checking the conference room for whatever it was she had dropped, and walked slowly by Melissa's desk. Melissa gave a frown and shook her head, acknowledging Erin's sadness over the arrest.

"Melissa," Erin approached the topic uncertainly. "I know you don't want to talk about what happened when you and Davis were young, or really anything about Davis…"

"That's right," Melissa gave Erin a stern look. "It's none of your business."

"I know… but I'm trying to help Adele out. You don't think she's really the one who poisoned Joelle, do you? She just isn't that type of person."

"I don't know what kind of person Adele is. I know she keeps herself to herself. I know she isn't from these parts and she doesn't go to church."

Erin opened her mouth to object, but Melissa shook her head. "She doesn't go to any church. Don't think I don't know that. I don't expect everyone to be Baptist, of course, but it does help me to know what kind of person someone is if I at least know what kind of church they go to. If they do. I just don't know what to think of you atheists."

"I know you'd rather we were your faith. But you've known me for almost a year, now. And you don't think I'm a bad person, do you?"

Melissa gave a little laugh and ran fingers through her wild, curly locks. "Of course I don't think you're bad, Erin… but I really don't know what to think of you. If you are a good person, then what do you have against being a Christian?"

Erin tried to steer the conversation back away from her faith—or lack of it. "Melissa… Adele didn't do anything to hurt Joelle."

"Maybe not." At Erin's look of reproof, Melissa amended. "No, of course not. Though in his report, the sheriff said…"

Erin waited for Melissa to finish, but Melissa gave her a teasing smile. "Oh, you're a tricky one! You thought you could get me to tell you what was in a police report. You know I can't do that."

"It's pretty obvious what the sheriff thinks."

"Yes, I suppose it is. I don't have to tell you."

"So if you could help me out, just a little… I don't want you to do anything that's against the law or unethical. I just want to know… What Davis has had to say about Joelle, I guess. Not if she committed a crime or helped him with anything, but just… the kind of person she was. We didn't really get to know her very well here in Bald Eagle Falls. She didn't really have anything to do with anyone else."

"Davis hasn't said anything about her," Melissa said immediately.

"Not even when he heard that she was dead? He wasn't shocked? He didn't say what kind of person she was? That he'd miss her—or that he *wouldn't* miss her?"

"I'm glad she's gone," Melissa confided. "I don't know how he feels about it, but I really didn't like her… slinking around here. She was a shady person. Not the kind of person you want hanging around Bald Eagle Falls. I know it was your sister, Charley, who invited her to come back here, but I can't understand why she would. You just don't want someone like that… always lurking around."

Slinking and lurking. Shady. Erin played a hunch.

"Does that mean she was trying to blackmail you too?"

Melissa's mouth dropped open and her eyes got wide. "Why would you say that? I never said anything like that. Exactly what would she blackmail me for? I don't have anything… nothing she could blackmail me about."

"Maybe it wasn't blackmail. Maybe she just asked you for money. Maybe she said she'd leave town if you gave her money, so she wouldn't be *lurking* around here anymore."

"You don't know what she was like. You only ever saw her at the bakery, and what would she do there? She couldn't exactly make trouble in front of all of the other customers. So you think she's just little miss perfect. You don't see that the whole thing is just a facade. She's about as genuine as a three-dollar bill."

"I believe it." Erin nodded encouragingly. "What did she do? What did she say to you?"

"She was all… lording it over me that she'd been with Davis. Like I wasn't good enough for him. Like I wasn't worth anything but her cast-offs. I'd never have talked to anyone that way! She was acting like she was 'all that' and I was nothing." Melissa leaned forward. "I told her that we'd been an item back when we were just kids, so if you wanted to get right down to it, she'd had my cast-offs, not the other way around. Hoo-boy!" Melissa puffed out her cheeks and rolled her eyes. "You should have seen her face at that! She was red as a rooster and mad as a wet hen! Then she started threatening."

Erin held her breath, not wanting to make any movement that would distract Melissa from telling her story. But once Melissa got going, it was like trying to stop a freight train. Nothing was going to deter her.

"She was threatening to tell everyone all kinds of lies! That I got pregnant by Davis and had to have an abortion! That I'd helped him to get drugs, because I was older than him. That I called him to tell him that Angela was dead, and that Trenton was here, and if he wanted to get anything out of the estate, he'd better come right now." Melissa shook her head in disbelief. "I never! Why would I do such a thing?" Melissa drew herself up as tall as possible. "I work for the police department!"

"Wow." Erin shook her head as well. "The nerve! And she thought she could squeeze money out of you by making these false allegations?"

"Can you believe it! I was never so angry in my life! I could have put my hands around her neck and strangled that woman!" Melissa mimed the gesture.

Erin swallowed. Melissa seemed to suddenly realize what she had done and dropped her hands to her side.

"Not really, of course. I've never harmed a soul in my life."

"And you didn't pay her anything."

Melissa's lips pressed together. She shook her head tightly. "Of course not."

Erin had her doubts. While Melissa might be a shameless carrier of gossip herself, she would have been horrified to have her reputation tarnished in front of all of Bald Eagle Falls. To have her virtue and uprightness challenged would be unendurable.

"Did you tell Davis what she was saying?"

Melissa nodded, still pressing her lips closed.

"What did he say about it?"

Melissa gave a tight shake of her head. Barely a twitch. But her eyes were blazing. "He laughed! Said she was just up to her old tricks. He said what does it matter what people think? Like my reputation didn't matter!"

"I guess that made you mad."

"You'd better believe it! I couldn't believe that he would tell Joelle anything about me. I wondered what I was even visiting him for, if he didn't care a lick for me and my good name. I was risking criticism every time I went to see him. What if word got around that I was visiting him in prison? I would be blacklisted. A pariah."

"For visiting someone in prison?"

"Yes! Oh, I'm not talking about you going to see Charley, of course. She was your sister and she needed your help. But with Davis and I… well, people might misconstrue it. You know what I mean?"

"I really don't know that it would be that bad, would it? People must know that the two of you used to be…" Erin hesitated. She had been about to use the word *sweethearts*, and suddenly knew it wasn't right and would just send Melissa off the deep end. "…Uh, friends. People must have known that you were friends when you were in school. So they wouldn't think anything of you checking in on him now…"

"You don't know what it's like," Melissa said. "You don't know how people would be. I would be ostracized."

And if they would ostracize her for visiting an old friend in prison, what would they do if they were told she'd gotten pregnant outside of wedlock and then had terminated the pregnancy? Erin didn't have to talk to Vic or any other advisor to know how the Bible-thumpers would feel about that. They didn't have any compunction about telling Erin she was a sinner for being an atheist, or Vic that she was going to burn for being transgender. They would definitely not have been gentle with Melissa, someone who had grown up in their midst, if they thought she had strayed and had kept it a secret all the years since.

"Davis said Joelle was up to her old tricks?"

Melissa nodded. "Something like that."

"So he wasn't surprised. She'd done this kind of thing before? Trying to blackmail someone?"

"Yes, that's what I thought. That's just the kind of person Joelle was. Someone who would say anything to get a few dollars."

Erin strongly suspected that asking how much 'a few dollars' was would not go over well. She was curious about what kind of numbers they were talking. How much had she asked Adele for? How much had she asked Melissa for? Were they talking a hundred dollars? A thousand? Ten thousand? Did a person like that start low, and then increase the demands as the payments were made? Or did she start high, and negotiate down according to what the victim could pay?

"Did he say who else Joelle had blackmailed?"

Melissa thought about it. "No... I don't think so. I was so mad, he might have, and I would have just kept shouting. What right did she have to ruin my reputation? I hadn't done anything to her."

"Of course not," Erin agreed. "What would you have done to her?"

Other than to supplant Joelle as Davis's friend. Once Davis was in prison, had Joelle cared what happened to him? She held Davis's Power of Attorney, so did that mean they were still a couple?

Or did Joelle believe that Melissa was taking Davis's affections from her?

As they worked through another routine day at the bakery, Erin let her thoughts wander. Who knew how many people Joelle had tried to blackmail. Erin was sure the list didn't end with Adele and Melissa. She would get as much dirt as she could on everyone she could. The more people she tried, the better the chances that she would get a good payoff.

"Vic, what does foxglove look like?"

Vic looked over at Erin. "What does it look like? People usually recognize it by its blossoms. They're sort of trumpet-shaped."

"And what does the plant look like? What do the leaves look like? It must grow wild here, does it? How would I know it if I walked by it in the woods?"

Vic did her best to describe the rosette shape of the leaves and pulled a picture of it up on her phone to show to Erin.

"Whoever put the poultice on Joelle's leg, they would have had to get it from somewhere. Would they have it in their own garden? Do people put it in gardens around here?"

"Sure. I can't say I've noticed anyone growing it in town, but they look very lovely in a garden."

Erin suspected that anyone who was planning on poisoning would not want to use a plant growing in their own garden. They wouldn't want something that pointed right back at them.

"Joelle didn't have any in her garden, did she?"

Vic thought about it. "No, I don't think so."

"What about Adele?"

"I don't remember seeing any in her yard. But she doesn't cultivate a lot. She mostly tries to find her plants and herbs in the wild, I think. Wildcrafting, they call it."

This fit with Erin's knowledge of Adele's activities. Often when Erin dropped by to see her, Adele was out gathering plants or sorting them and hanging them to dry. She didn't grow neat rows of herbs in the little cottage garden, but went out looking for what she needed.

"So there must be foxglove growing around here somewhere. No one has said where it was growing. If I could find that, maybe it would point to someone."

"Maybe," Vic said doubtfully. "It could grow in more than one place. And if it's in the woods around here, we could be looking for days. We could search for years and never find it."

Maybe it was the wrong way to go about solving the case, but it was the only course Erin could think of. Find the source of the foxglove. Find out who knew about its existence and could have gathered it. Who could have made the poultice and applied it to Joelle's leg?

Vic had covered the shop while Erin had been in hospital, so even though it was Erin's scheduled day off on Saturday, with Vic and Bella minding the shop, she had suggested Vic should get the Saturday off. But Vic had firmly instructed that they needed to stick to their written schedule, and Erin let herself be talked into it.

So Saturday morning found Erin traipsing through the woods, looking for foxglove plants. She had saved a picture of foxglove to her phone, so she had something to compare it to whenever she found anything that resembled the green rosette foxglove grew in. While she had stopped a lot of times to examine plants, she had concluded that none of them was foxglove and was still on the hunt.

Erin reached the river that bordered one side of her wooded property and, mindful of the series of accidents that had eventually led to Joelle's injured leg and ultimately her death, Erin was careful not to get too close to the edge of the embankment and kept an eye out for any roots that might trip her up or any other hazards. She didn't want to end up getting hurt out in the bush and having to call for help.

As Erin rounded a bend in the river, she was startled to find that she was not alone. A man stood nearby, staring out at the river, lost in thought. Erin took in his tall, thin frame, and studied his face.

"Roger…?"

Roger turned his head and looked at her. "Who are you? What are you doing here?" he asked in an accusing tone.

"My name is Erin Price. We haven't really met, but I know your wife."

"Mary Lou."

"Everybody knows Mary Lou, right?" Erin asked. "When you—when she needed help, I couldn't believe how many people turned out. Bald Eagle Falls really is a nice community."

"And Mary Lou knows you, Erin…?"

"Erin Price. Yes. I own the bakery in town. We really like your Jam Lady jam. We buy cases and cases of it."

"The Bake Shoppe?"

"No. Auntie Clem's Bakery. The Bake Shoppe had to close when Angela died. They haven't reopened it. But I run a gluten-free bakery that caters to all sorts of special diets." Roger didn't have much to say, and Erin found herself trying to fill the silence with words. "I really like helping to provide people with good food that's safe with their restrictions."

"Angela." Roger said her name with a sneer, clearly remembering her. "She's dead and gone now. Dead and buried!"

"Yes, I know. I feel bad for what happened to her, but I know she caused you and Mary Lou a lot of trouble and heartache."

"She was an evil woman. It's a good thing she's dead."

Erin was uncomfortable with this. "I don't know…"

"I went by there the other day." Roger frowned. "There was a man in The Bake Shoppe."

"A man?" Erin tried to think of who it would have been. A lawyer or trustee? Maybe a real estate agent giving an estimate? Or was he thinking of longer ago, and had seen Trenton or Davis there? "I don't know who it would have been. That's not my bakery. My bakery is across the street. Auntie Clem's. My Aunt Clementine used to have a tea room there. Do you remember that?"

She was afraid she was being patronizing. She had no idea how much he remembered. She didn't want to treat him like a dementia patient, but her past experience as a caregiver was kicking in, and she was testing him, exploring the limits.

"No, not there," Roger said. "I saw a man at The Bake Shoppe."

"Okay. You very well might have. People come and go… I don't keep track of who goes in there."

"I was afraid at first, at the woman screaming. I was afraid someone would find me there. When I went back again… he wasn't there anymore."

Erin chewed on her lip. A woman screaming? A man coming and going? She couldn't tie it together, but it didn't sound like it was anything to do with her current investigation. He was off in another time and place. Erin wanted to focus on the present, and on finding the plant that would help to prove Adele's innocence.

"Roger, you know your way around these woods, right?"

Roger's eyes went to her. They were blue. He seemed to be calmed by the water, not agitated like he had been when Terry had found him and brought him back to the church.

"I love the woods," he said simply, like a child.

"Do you know what foxglove looks like?"

"Of course I do. My grandmother taught me the names of all of the flowers."

"But do you know what the plant itself looks like when it isn't in bloom?"

"Sure."

"Is there any growing in these woods?"

There was no immediate response from Roger.

"If I wanted to pick some, where would I find it?" Erin persisted.

"Why would you want to pick it?"

"I don't know. If I wanted to make something with the leaves."

"You shouldn't touch it. The leaves are poisonous."

"You're right." Erin changed tack. "I actually wanted to pull it, if there was any around here, so no one would get poisoned by accident. I wouldn't want someone's child or pet to eat it."

Roger looked at her and Erin knew that he was not fooled. Roger Cox might have some issues with his brain, but he wasn't stupid. He wasn't buying into her changing story.

"Mary Lou talks about you," he said. "*Our little detective*, she calls you. Always trying to figure everything out. She says you're very smart."

Erin swallowed. She looked around for Mary Lou. Was it possible *she* was the poisoner? While she had previously told Erin that she didn't have any secrets, Erin highly doubted that was true. Everybody had secrets. And the people who were most reticent to reveal them were the ones who had the most to lose. Maybe Mary Lou wasn't the perfect mother and wife. She blamed her family's downturn in luck on her husband, but was that really true? What if she were the one who had made the bad investment with Angela? What if she had tried to kill Roger to cover it up, rather than it being a suicide attempt? If Joelle had something on Mary Lou, would Mary Lou have silenced her permanently?

Erin didn't like to think it could have been someone she knew, but Mary Lou had always been an enigma. She'd always been a little aloof, someone Erin couldn't quite connect with, even though she seemed like a very nice woman. Most of the time.

And while she hadn't been in Erin's house, she'd had access to the jam. She was the one who had given it to Erin. She'd had the opportunity to tamper with it before giving it to Erin.

"How is Mary Lou?" Erin asked, forcing a smile. "Does she know you're here?"

"She's having a nap. She hasn't been sleeping very well lately."

Was the reason Mary Lou was so tired and testy lately not because of her husband, but because she was being pressured by Joelle? Or because she had poisoned Joelle and was worried she might be caught? Maybe the reason she had been reluctant to call the police department when she couldn't find Roger was because she was afraid they would find out what she had done. Or maybe she was afraid Roger knew what had happened and would tell someone.

"I'm glad Mary Lou is getting some sleep," she told Roger. She felt her phone in her pocket. She should call Terry. See if he thought Mary Lou or one of the others Joelle was blackmailing might be the poisoner. Let him know that Roger was wandering again, unsupervised. "I guess I should be getting on my way."

Roger nodded vaguely. Erin didn't go back the way she had arrived, which had been a long, meandering path. It would be faster to get home by cutting across the woods. When she was sure she was out of Roger's hearing, she slid her phone out and dialed Terry.

"Hi, Erin," he greeted cheerfully. "Enjoying your day off?"

"I always do."

"What are you doing today? Catching up on your errands?"

Erin thought of the long lists of things she needed to do around the house or in the city and felt guilty for being out wandering in the woods looking for foxglove instead of focusing on the rest of the items on her list.

"Uh, actually, no. Just taking some time to walk in the woods. Smell the roses."

"That's good. I'm glad you're taking some time to relax. I was afraid you were doing too much so soon after being poisoned."

"I suppose. I feel like I'm back to normal, but the doctors did say it could be a while before I am fully recovered."

"Exactly. You need to take care of yourself."

"So, the reason I was calling you…" Erin wasn't sure how to approach the subject. "I wondered whether you had looked into Mary Lou. As the person who poisoned Joelle, I mean. And who poisoned me."

"Mary Lou. What makes you ask about her?" Terry asked, giving nothing away.

"I don't know. I just wondered… if Joelle was blackmailing her, then Mary Lou might have tried to—"

"What?"

"If Joelle was blackmailing her—"

"Who said Joelle was blackmailing her?"

"I don't know if she was. But she was putting pressure on others, so I'm just assuming she would get whatever she could on everyone. Mary Lou is one of those people who keeps her own counsel, and—"

"Erin. Stop."

Erin stopped. She didn't just stop speaking, but she stopped walking too, startled by his sharp tone.

"Where did you get the idea that Joelle was blackmailing anyone?"

"Oh… well…" Erin realized she had let her enthusiasm get ahead of her. "I mean, she could have been… that would have been a good motive for murder."

"You didn't just come up with blackmail out of thin air."

"Um… no."

"Was Joelle trying to blackmail you? Picking up where Alton left off?"

"No. Not *me*."

"Then who?"

"Well, a couple of the women in the community… and I thought if she was blackmailing a couple, there were probably more."

Terry let out an exasperated breath. "You didn't think this might be something that was important to tell the police?"

"I assumed you knew."

"Don't assume anything. If you find something out about an active investigation, you need to let someone know, not just go off and investigate it on your own."

"I didn't. It just occurred to me that maybe Joelle was blackmailing Mary Lou, and then I called you. So I did tell you. I'm telling you now."

"And I'm not the one investigating the case. You need to see the sheriff about this. Right away. Do you understand?"

"Yeah. Okay. Absolutely."

"Where are you now?"

"In the woods, like I told you."

"Not on your way to Mary Lou's house?"

"No! Of course not."

"What are you close to? I'll come pick you up, and you can get in to see Sheriff Wilmot right away."

"I'm just about home." Erin scanned the trees around her, feeling suddenly disoriented. "You can pick me up there, if you think it's that urgent."

"Whoever the poisoner is, she's already tried to kill you once. If you're making inquiries and she thinks you're closing in on her…"

"Okay. I'll see you in a few minutes then."

Erin hung up the call, a little irritated that he'd been so brusque with her. But she knew he cared about her. That was where he was coming from. She hurried along a less-worn path, looking for the connection to the main route she and Vic usually used. But as houses came into view, she realized she'd gotten herself turned around. She must have gone the wrong way when she had left Roger. Instead of heading back toward her house, she'd been heading for the opposite side of town.

Erin walked toward the houses so she could see what street she was on and get herself turned back around. She'd need to hurry to get to the house before Terry arrived. Or maybe she'd just call him back and have him pick her up wherever she had come out of the woods.

Erin studied the houses up and down the street, looking for any recognizable landmarks. She was at the complete opposite side of the woods from the house.

She stared at Joelle's house, reminded again about how close it was to her own, even though to drive there, she would have had to go all the way around to the opposite side of town. She turned and went back into the woods, cutting straight across to get to her house. There weren't any well-established paths through the middle, for some reason. Most of the paths that had been worn into the dirt tended to wander around the edges of the wood, shortcuts from one person's property to another, to Adele's cottage, to the river. Erin was moving quickly, pushing herself through the bushes and undergrowth, knowing she was going to end up with her legs all scratched up.

And then her way was blocked. She nearly ran right into Roger.

Erin moved to the side to let him pass, but he didn't go by her, standing right where she wanted to go.

"Hi, Roger," Erin greeted, as pleasantly as she could. "If I could just squeeze by you…"

He still didn't move.

Erin remembered Terry saying that he had found Roger near the river. She hadn't realized how close the river ran to Joelle's house. She hadn't pictured Joelle's odd accidents being in Erin's wood or Roger Cox wandering around her property.

Her stomach tightened. She looked back the way she had come, and then left and right, looking for established trails that she could use to get around Roger and back to the house. She shouldn't have gone back into the woods. She should have just had Terry pick her up on the other side. Instead, she had dashed right back into it, acting like there was no danger, when he had warned her there was. The poisoner had already tried to take her out once.

"Did you find the foxglove?" Roger asked.

"Uh, no. I got turned around; I was just going to go home. I think… I need a nap."

"You shouldn't do so much after you are poisoned."

Erin nodded, swallowing hard. "I know. Officer Piper was just telling me that." Erin looked back over her shoulder as if Terry might be right behind her. "I really do have to get on my way…"

She decided to make a dash to the side and continue to press forward toward her house. Terry would be waiting for her there. But when she tried to move to the side, Roger's hand snaked out and he had her by the wrist.

"You know!" he accused.

"Know what? I don't know anything. I just thought it was time to go home…"

"That woman. That snake in the grass. Coming to me and demanding money." Roger's face was pale, his eyes wild. "I told her I didn't have any money. We can barely scrape by on what we're bringing in, even with the boys working after school. She didn't believe it. She said she knew I had money, and if I didn't pay her, she would tell!"

Erin didn't move. If she tried to pull away from him, he would just tighten his grip, but if she didn't struggle and just let him talk, he might let her go on his own. That was the way it worked with a lot of the patients she had dealt with. Get them agitated, and they would just get more violent. Let them talk themselves down. Deescalate. Give them time to just calm down.

"She would tell what?" she prompted.

"*My secret.*" Roger said it in a strained whisper, as if the trees had ears. He looked around, eyes wide and unblinking. "She said she would tell Mary Lou."

Erin's curiosity prompted her to ask him what his secret was, but if she knew his secret then he might deem her a danger to him as well. Had Joelle gone one step too far by trying to blackmail Roger? It had never occurred to her that the poisoner might be a man. Poison was always seen as a woman's weapon, and the fact that it had been given in a poultice by someone who knew something about folk medicine had made her sure it was a woman. What man knew anything about herbal remedies and applications?

"Your grandmother," Erin said softly.

Roger's eyes riveted on her. "What?"

"You said your grandmother taught you all of the names of the flowers."

His expression softened. "Yes," he agreed. "I used to go out with her when she was gathering herbs. She told me all the names of the flowers, all of the different uses of medicinal plants."

"And which ones were poisonous."

"What is medicinal in one dose becomes poison in a higher dose. If you don't know how much to use, it's better you don't use it at all."

"So she was the one who told you about digitalis. And belladonna."

"After that woman fell and hurt herself, I helped her back to her house. She was in a lot of pain. I dressed her leg for her. Told her I would be back with something to help it to heal faster." Roger's eyes blazed. "She said it didn't matter if I helped her; she still expected me to pay up, or she was going to tell Mary Lou…"

Erin marveled at Joelle's nerve. Roger rescued her, gave her first aid, and offered his services as an herbal practitioner and, instead of being grateful, she had threatened him. Erin, Adele, and Roger had each put aside their grievances to help Joelle when she was hurt, but the woman had selfishly continued her campaign of blackmail.

"She shouldn't have done that," Erin told Roger, trying to pitch her voice to be low and soothing. "She should have been grateful to you. She should have shown you some respect."

"Yes," Roger nodded his agreement. "She should have acted like a decent human being. People like her and Angela, they can't be allowed to go on destroying good, innocent people. They have to be stopped."

Erin was startled by his mention of Angela. She probably shouldn't have been. She hadn't known Angela herself; they had only met a couple of times. But from what the others had said, Angela had been a sort of emotional blackmailer, holding power over those whose secrets and weaknesses she was able to ferret out. But Angela's secrets didn't keep her safe. Eventually, Gema had bent under the pressure, poisoning her and directing suspicion at Erin.

"Just like Gema," Erin said. "Angela just didn't know when to stop."

Roger's wide eyes got bigger still. "What do you know about Gema?" he demanded.

"Oh, not a lot." Erin gave her arm an experimental tug, just a little one, to see if he would let her go. He held on firmly. "I met her when I moved to town, but I didn't really get to know her. She killed Angela because she had found out about Gema's baby, the one she had out of wedlock, and was holding it over her."

Roger's grip tightened. "You know about the baby?"

Erin winced at the increased pressure. She pried at his fingers with her free hand. "Ow, Roger. You're hurting. Please let me go."

"How do you know about the baby?"

"From Gema. I saw her and her daughter at the store. I didn't realize it, but Gema thought I did and that I was trying to blackmail her. I didn't know until after everything was over that she'd been afraid of people finding out about her daughter."

"You can't know about that," he protested, his voice hoarse. "No one can know about that."

"It all came out after Gema was arrested. Everyone knows."

"Not Mary Lou. No."

Erin stared at him. "Mary Lou knows."

Roger shoved Erin into a tree. Her head slammed back into it and she saw stars. The bark of the tree was rough against her back, even through her shirt. Her head whirling. She tried to sort everything out. Clearly, she was not having success in keeping Roger calm, and there was something about Gema's secret baby that disturbed him greatly.

"No," Erin said, reversing her position, "Mary Lou doesn't know." Roger's grip relaxed just the tiniest bit. "Mary Lou doesn't know anything about Gema's baby."

"No," Roger agreed, his thin shoulders lowering a little.

"Nobody knows," Erin soothed.

"*You* know."

"I only knew that Gema had a baby. I don't know anything about it. I just moved to Bald Eagle Falls. I barely knew Gema."

"But you lived here then."

"No. I just moved here last year."

Roger pressed Erin more tightly against the tree. He put his forearm under her chin and pressed it against her throat.

"I remember you. You know what happened."

"I don't know. I'm sorry I said something to upset you. I was just joking around. Really. I didn't mean to upset you. Everybody has secrets. You are entitled to yours."

For a moment he relaxed the pressure on Erin's throat. Then his expression hardened. "Yes. My secrets. No one else can know."

He pressed his arm into her, cutting off her air. It was too late to decide that she should have screamed for help when all he was doing was holding onto her arm. Instead she had just stood there, trying to talk him down, not taking any direct action. She should have screamed, kicked him, wrestled away from him. He didn't look that strong. If she hadn't been in such a vulnerable position, maybe she could have fought him off. But she'd waited until his arm was cutting off her air before considering herself in any real danger.

"No one," Roger repeated.

CHAPTER 30

$\mathcal{E}$rin heard a shout, but it was far away and too indistinct to make out what he was saying. Roger didn't withdraw his arm, staring into Erin's eyes and waiting for her to lose consciousness.

"Go! Get him!"

There was a crashing as someone charged through the bush toward them, and then Roger let out a howl and released Erin. She clung to the tree behind her, trying to keep her feet. Roger was screaming and fighting with someone. As Erin drew in oxygen and her brain started to work again, she heard Terry shouting at Roger to get down and lie still and, when he finally did, Erin heard the ratcheting of handcuffs as Roger was secured. She blinked, trying to bring the world around her back into focus. Terry was leaning over Roger, who lay on the ground whimpering. Terry left him there, taking Erin into his arms.

"Are you okay? You need medical attention. Sit down. Can you breathe?" He fired questions and commands at her too fast for her to be able to sort out an answer and respond.

While Erin wanted to stay on her feet, he helped her sit down, his hands gentle. "Just relax, Erin, take deep breaths. Tell me if you think you're going to faint. I'm going to call for help."

Erin nodded.

"What happened?" Terry questioned, while he waited for the dispatcher to answer his call. "I've seen Roger get agitated, but never violent."

Before Erin could answer, he was talking to the dispatcher, relaying the best he could what had happened and asking them to send back up and get an ambulance if one were available. He terminated the call, checked on Roger, and returned to Erin, taking her pulse.

"I'm okay," Erin told him.

"Are you sure?"

She nodded. "Thank goodness you got there when you did." She swallowed, which hurt, and took a deep breath, which also hurt. "He's the poisoner."

Terry was looking back at Roger. "What?"

"Roger. He's the poisoner. He's the one who killed Joelle and tried to poison me."

"Roger? Why would Roger do that?"

"He had a secret. She was trying to blackmail him, and he couldn't pay her off. She said she was going to tell Mary Lou about… the secret."

Terry looked like he was about to ask another question, then stopped. "Oh."

"Oh?" Erin looked at him. "Oh? You make it sound like you already knew that. Like maybe this wasn't such a big surprise for you."

"I may… know his secret. And how Joelle found out about it."

"How?" Erin already figured she knew Roger's secret, but she didn't know how Joelle knew about it. How would Joelle, who hadn't ever lived in Bald Eagle Falls, know what had happened twenty years before? "Was it Davis? Did he tell her?"

"I don't think so. It's possible, but I don't think that's how." Terry hesitated. "I'm not on the case, though, so I should probably let the sheriff fill you in on the details. I only know the broad strokes. He'll be able to provide more details. Whatever he feels is prudent to share."

"Terry!"

"Sorry. You'll have to wait."

K9 nosed at Erin, whining and looking concerned over her strange behavior. She didn't normally sit around in the middle of the woods, and he wanted to know what was going on. Erin scratched his ears, something she also would not normally have done while he was on duty.

"Who's a good dog? That was you, wasn't it? You're the one who took Roger down."

"That's right," Terry answered for K9, who sat back on his haunches and panted proudly. "It was remarkably effective. He doesn't usually get to do that!"

"Is Roger okay?"

Terry shook his head. "You're too kind for your own good. The man tried to kill you and you want to know if he's okay? Just like you try to take Joelle soup and nurse her back to health when you know she pretty near killed you."

"I know. I shouldn't feel bad for him, but I do. I don't think… I don't think this is the kind of person he was, before his accident. I don't think he would have attacked anyone, the way he used to be."

She had only heard a few words here and there about Roger Cox and how he had been before his failed suicide attempt, but she gathered he had been quite gentle and unassuming. Not the best provider, but he had worked hard and done his best, and been a good husband and father. Except for one major failing.

"Is he the father of Gema's baby?" Erin asked.

"Did he tell you that?" Terry asked.

"Not exactly. But from what he said, I think he was."

"It was a long time ago. I gather Gema was separated from her husband, but Roger and Mary Lou were together. I don't think anyone ever guessed who the father was."

"No. That's why he killed Joelle. He didn't want it getting back to Mary Lou. Nothing was more important than keeping that a secret from her."

"And now it will all come out. As if the woman hasn't already had enough to deal with."

"What's going to happen to Roger? If he couldn't help it, because of his brain injury…"

"They'll still lock him up. You can't let someone who is a danger like that wander around where he could hurt someone. I don't know why he's out wandering now. Mary Lou promised they would keep better track of him. Not because we were worried about the public, but we wanted to make sure that Roger himself was safe. We didn't want him getting lost…"

"You don't think anything has happened to Mary Lou, do you?"

Terry considered. "I hope not. One of us will have to go make sure, after we get this dealt with. You are the equivalent of a five-alarm fire for our little department."

As if on cue, Erin could hear sirens approaching. The police cars probably didn't actually need their sirens on to get through Bald Eagle Falls rush hour, but they so rarely got to use them, they were taking advantage of the opportunity.

Tom Baker and Sheriff Wilmot arrived. Tom was instructed to take Roger in, but Terry held up his hand.

"He might be hurt. K9 took him down. Check him out before you take him anywhere, and then he should probably go to the hospital. Even if he's unhurt, he's going to have to go through some kind of evaluation—" Terry looked at Erin, "—to see how culpable he is in the commission of a crime."

Tom's mouth hung open. "What did he do?"

"Well, you know he attacked Miss Price. But it would appear he's also our poisoner. He's the one who killed Joelle Biggs and attempted to poison Erin."

"How do you know that?" the sheriff asked sharply.

Terry motioned to Erin, indicating she should explain.

"He told me that he's the one who treated Joelle's leg," Erin said, "he had to get rid of her to keep his secret."

"Is that a fact?" Sheriff Wilmot thought about this. He looked at Terry. "I guess that answers our question."

Erin frowned, trying to interpret the look that passed between them. "What question is that? Do you mean the identity of the killer? Or something else?"

The sheriff raised one eyebrow at Terry. "You didn't tell her?"

"I figure that's your job."

"Well." Sheriff Wilmot seemed pleased to be given the opportunity. "We found some interesting things when we searched Joelle's cottage. One of them was a diary written by your Aunt Clementine."

Erin blinked at him. She tried to get up to talk to him face-to-face. Terry wouldn't let her rise. "Stay there. Just relax."

Sheriff Wilmot bent lower to converse with Erin.

"Clementine's missing diary?" Erin demanded. "Joelle had it?"

"She did. I guess she or Davis must have stolen it sometime around the house fire."

"Clementine's diary! But why did they take it? It didn't have anything in it about Davis and Trenton, did it? Clementine never actually figured out what had happened to Adam Plaint."

"No. But it seems like it was a very tumultuous time in Bald Eagle Falls. Adam Plaint's disappearance, your parents and their accident. Your aunt seemed to be a confidante to a lot of people. The old woman with the tea shop… she must have been a good listener. Sympathetic, like you. So people told her things. And while she kept their secrets, some little bits and pieces did make it into the journal."

"Like Gema Reed having someone else's baby?"

"She went away on an extended vacation. Seeing all of the sights she'd always wanted to go to. When she came back to Bald Eagle Falls, she went back to her husband, and no one in town knew that she had gone away to have a baby. Or almost nobody. She did confide in somebody."

"Clementine."

Sheriff Wilmot nodded. "I assume Joelle and Davis took the diary because Davis was afraid it would implicate him in your father's death. But one of them decided to put it to use and see if they could extort money out of the townspeople to keep their secrets from coming to light."

Erin leaned back against the tree, closing her eyes. "Who would ever have guessed?" She looked from Sheriff Wilmot to Terry. "Did either of you ever guess that Roger was the one who had made the poultice for Joelle's leg? It never even occurred to me that it might be a man. That goes to show you how prejudiced I am!"

"Maybe we should have guessed," Terry said. "Given what we knew about how else he was spending his time."

Erin frowned, trying to figure out what else Roger might have been doing. "Maybe's it's just the lack of oxygen, but… what do you mean?"

"I mean his occupation. You did know, didn't you?"

Roger's occupation as the maker of the Jam Lady jams.

"Oh, that. Yes. I guess he was a little more… domestic than most men in Bald Eagle Falls. And why couldn't he be a healer? Lots of men are doctors. Why not herbalists? He said his grandmother taught him."

"I don't know anything about his grandmother," Sheriff Wilmot said. "I'll have to ask around. She was probably well known; but as you say, it's easy to assume that a poisoner and practitioner of herbal medicine would be a woman rather than a man. He did surprise us on that note."

They watched as Tom, having finished his examination of Roger, helped him to his feet and then escorted him to one of the waiting vehicles. Erin watched him drive away.

"Poor Mary Lou."

EPILOGUE

It was starting to get dark out, but Erin wasn't ready to go back into the house and turn in for the night. She was enjoying the company of Vic and Adele on the back porch and she didn't want the evening to end. It felt good to just relax with them and not worry about a murderer. The next day, she needed to be at the bakery bright and early. She had a new recipe for strawberry muffins to try out.

Adele heard the footsteps first. She went still, then got up and looked around the side of the house to see who was approaching.

"Who is it?" Erin asked. She took another sip of her mint tea, too lazy to get up and see for herself.

But in another minute, Mary Lou was there, gliding smoothly over the sidewalk as if she were on wheels. She looked at the three of them, her smile strained.

"Hello, ladies. Nice to see everyone this beautiful evening."

"How are you?" Erin got up to squeeze Mary Lou's hand and pat her shoulder comfortingly. "How are you and your boys holding out?"

"Oh, we're managing. As horrible as the whole thing is… at least I'm not up half the night trying to settle Roger and get him to stay in bed."

"That must have been so hard. I was worried about you."

"I wasn't myself, and I must apologize for that. I was very impatient and irritable…"

"Lack of sleep will do that to you," Vic said.

"It certainly will."

"I guess now we know what was bothering him," Adele said.

Mary Lou nodded. "I wish he had just told me. There was no need… for any of this."

Erin frowned, studying Mary Lou's face. "You already knew?"

"Not about the blackmail, no. But I did know… that he'd been unfaithful. I never confronted him. I never knew about the baby; Gema went away, and everything went back to normal. I was content to leave it at that and go on with our lives."

Erin tried to fathom how difficult it must have been to put her spouse's unfaithfulness behind her, never confronting him or making any reference to it.

"It's easier to bury something like that than you think," Mary Lou said, apparently reading Erin's face. "We went on to have two lovely boys and lived a happy domestic life… until the investment with Angela tanked. Since then…" She sighed. "We've had our share of challenges."

"I think that's the understatement of the century," Vic declared. "Y'all have been through H-E-double-toothpicks, if you ask me. I'm amazed you can keep a smile on your face."

"Well, thank you, Vic. It hasn't been easy. But I firmly believe the Lord doesn't give us anything we can't handle."

Erin couldn't help shaking her head. Roger had clearly been given more than he could handle, even if his wife could. He had attempted suicide, had killed Joelle, and had twice tried to kill Erin. If that wasn't a man pushed past his capacity, she didn't know who was.

"The Lord gives us strength," Mary Lou said firmly.

"What's going to happen to Roger?" Vic asked tentatively. "Do you have any idea?"

"They're doing all kinds of tests. All of those tests that they said weren't necessary and were just too expensive after his accident. They're saying all of the things I have been telling the doctors all along. He can't control his impulses. He gets agitated and overwhelmed. To talk to him in a normal conversation, you wouldn't think there was anything wrong. Maybe some hesitation in his speech. Some language issues. But dealing with him when he's tired or upset… he's a completely different person." Mary Lou sighed. "Now they agree with me. Now they say there's reason for concern."

Erin bit off a laugh. "I'm sorry. It's not funny. It's… tragic. They wait until after he's killed someone to admit there's a problem?"

"I want you to know that I didn't foresee this," Mary Lou said. "Especially you, Erin… if I had thought he was a danger to anyone but himself… I don't know what I would have done. But something. I would have gotten him admitted… warned people. When Joelle died, I had no idea he'd had anything to do with it. He never said he'd seen her or talked to her. I had no idea."

Erin believed her. She nodded. "It's okay. I understand that. I never even thought the killer might be a man."

"He's always been very… domestic," Mary Lou said, her eyes sad. "He's a good cook. Was always good with the boys and with taking care of their bumps and bruises and illnesses. It was providing for the family he struggled with."

Mary Lou looked at Vic, as if she would say something else, and then closed her mouth. Maybe some crack about men's and women's roles she'd thought better of. She stood there awkwardly for a moment.

"Anyway, I just wanted to let you know how sorry I am for everything. I really am."

"It's okay," Erin assured her. "Is there anything we can do for you and the boys?"

"No," Mary Lou sighed. "Just be there for us. There are a lot of people who aren't going to be."

Erin and Terry sat together in the family-style restaurant, having coffee after their meals.

Terry slid the black hardcover journal across the table to Erin. She didn't open it to examine Clementine's familiar handwriting. She didn't want to read it in front of Terry, but to have it to herself, the one precious account of what had happened when Erin had left Bald Eagle Falls the last time, on her way to becoming an orphan and leading a solitary life, never feeling like she belonged anywhere until she had returned to Bald Eagle Falls and the roots she could barely remember.

"Think you'll find anything interesting?" Terry asked. K9 panted at his side.

Erin carefully tucked the journal into her shoulder bag.

"Maybe," she said. "Though I don't think I'm up to any more excitement! My detective days are done."

COUP DE GLACE

AUNTIE CLEM'S BAKERY #6

To an unflinching look at the past.

CHAPTER 1

It was hard for Erin to believe that Bella and Vic were only a year apart in age, if that. Vic was her own woman, independent, knowledgeable, opinionated. Sometimes Erin felt like Vic was older than she herself. But Bella was definitely still a kid. Having graduated from high school, she was available to help out at the bakery more often, but Erin had a hard time thinking of her as a grown up.

Vic had taken the day off to go into the city with Willie. Erin was glad to see them back together again, working through their differences. There was still tension between them, not over Vic's transgender identity, but over the recent revelations of Willie's past and that he had kept back from Vic the fact that they were from opposing sides of a generations-long clan war. He'd known about it from the start, but had kept his involvement with the Dyson organized crime family from her.

Despite Vic's feelings about the deception, they had made up and were trying to get back on track again. A day away from Bald Eagle Falls would be good for them. It was easy to get caught up in the personalities of the small Tennessee town and to forget that things were not the same everywhere. Going somewhere else provided a little perspective. Vic had never been outside of Tennessee, and Erin hoped that someday she'd travel a little and broaden her horizons. As long as she still came back to Auntie Clem's

Bakery when she was done. Erin wanted Vic to grow, but didn't know what she'd do without her.

"Erin, can we make more of the gumdrop cookies and put chocolate chips in them?"

Erin was pulled from her ponderings. She looked at Bella, blinking to refocus herself.

"They're not gumdrop cookies if you use chocolate chips," she pointed out.

"Unless you put gumdrops and chocolate chips in them…"

Erin considered the suggestion. Chocolate and gumdrops. Erin's gumdrop cookies were pretty popular, but she'd never considered including both chocolate chips and gumdrops.

"That's an interesting idea. Do you think people would go for them?"

Bella's blue eyes twinkled. "You can't wreck something by adding chocolate to it!" Her curly blond hair was pulled back from her round face, making her look younger than her seventeen years.

Erin laughed. "Okay, we can give it a try. Substitute part of the gumdrops with chocolate chips, and we'll call them 'Bella's Dream' cookies."

"Can't we just add chocolate chips?"

"You have to have enough cookie dough for them to hold together, especially with gluten-free cookies. If you increase the add-ins too much, they'll just fall apart into a crumbly mess when you try to pick them up."

"Oh." Bella nodded. "That makes sense."

She got out the gumdrops and the chocolate chips and measured them into her cookie batter before turning the mixer on. "It's too bad we can't use peanuts," she said. "My mom makes these awesome Reese's Pieces and chocolate chip cookies. They are *so* good!"

"I'll bet they are," Erin agreed. "I like anything with chocolate and peanut butter. But no peanuts or nuts in Auntie Clem's Bakery. They are too common an allergen and I don't want even the possibility of cross-contamination."

"I know." Bella let out a sigh. "Your baking is really good, but sometimes I wish we could just do normal cooking and not have to worry about allergies and Celiac disease and all that."

"Imagine how you would feel if you had a life-threatening condition that meant you couldn't ever eat those things," Erin said. "It isn't easy going through life not being able to eat what you want. You and I can just go home and make Reese's Pieces cookies if we feel like it. Someone with an allergy can't. They just have to forgo it forever." Erin made a motion to encompass the baking they were each working on. "That's why we do this. So that people with allergies or intolerances can have some variety. If people without dietary restrictions want something that's not gluten- or allergen-free, they can just go into the city or make their own. It isn't so easy for someone with a life-threatening condition."

Bella nodded. She took a deep sniff of the cookie dough. "I'm sure glad that I can eat whatever I want. Although…" she patted her stomach, "I probably shouldn't eat it all!"

Erin just shrugged. She was careful not to eat too much of her own baking, but she didn't struggle with it like Bella. Bella had been overweight before working at Auntie Clem's and, while not obese, she had put on a few more pounds since starting.

"I might just have to go out and buy some Reese's Pieces after work," Bella said. "Now I'm going to be craving them all day."

"Have you ever seen *E.T.*?" Erin asked, trying to distract Bella from thoughts about the candy. "That is such a good show."

Bella shuddered. "No. One of my friends tried to put it on once, but it was so spooky, and I was really freaked out. I don't like movies about creepy aliens."

"But he's not creepy. He's just different. He's really lovable and funny."

"I couldn't get past the first five minutes." Bella shook her head. "No way, you can keep your supernatural stuff."

Erin shook her head and folded raisins into the muffin batter she was working on.

"I know," Bella said. "I'm a scaredy-cat about everything. I should grow up and act like an adult instead of a baby."

"I never said that. There are plenty of adults who are afraid of… supernatural things. It doesn't make you a baby."

"Most adults aren't afraid of everything that goes bump in the night. I wish I wasn't."

"Maybe you could see a psychologist or something. Someone who could help you to get over it. They have programs to help people overcome phobias and anxieties."

"No. I've been to them before. They never really help. They always want you to confront your fears. Desensitize yourself. I just… can't."

"So how are you supposed to do that? Watch scary movies?"

Erin expected Bella to laugh, but she didn't. She shook her head, face pale. "No…"

There was silence for a few minutes, Erin not sure what to say.

"They want me to go into the barn," Bella said.

"Into the barn? What barn?"

"At home. There's an old barn. It's… haunted."

Erin laughed. But Bella wasn't kidding. Her lips tightened. She was over-mixing the cookie dough, not paying attention to what she was doing.

"It is! I know you don't believe in ghosts, but that doesn't mean you're right. You wouldn't say that if you'd seen some of the weird stuff I have. That old barn really is haunted."

"Okay." Erin held up her hands. "I'm sorry. I shouldn't have laughed. You just caught me by surprise. You've never mentioned your haunted barn before."

Bella eyed her as if suspicious that Erin was making fun of her. She turned off her mixer and pulled out a couple of cookie sheets.

"It's never come up before."

"Do you know… who it's haunted by?" Erin asked tentatively. She wasn't sure whether that was the appropriate thing to do. Was it polite to ask people about their haunted outbuildings? Or was that a taboo topic?

Bella nodded. "My grandma." She started to scoop the cookie dough out onto the tray, carefully spacing the cookies apart so they wouldn't spread into each other.

"Oh."

Erin started pouring out the muffins. When she looked up, Bella was watching her intently, and Erin wondered if she'd missed part of the conversation while focused on the job at hand.

"You could help me! You're really good at solving mysteries. If you solved Grandma's murder, then maybe she'd stop haunting the barn, and I wouldn't have to be scared of going near there anymore."

Erin smiled and shook her head. "I'm a baker, not a detective."

"You haven't always been a baker, though. You've done all kinds of other things."

"I've done other things. But I'm not a private investigator or policeman and I never have been."

"But you've solved other mysteries. Lots of them."

"Just… lucky. Terry doesn't want me to get involved in any more police stuff. Not that I want to. It's always just fallen into my lap before."

"Officer Handsome can't control what you do. And if you were looking into a really old case, then it's not like you'd be in any danger, right?"

Erin grinned at Bella calling Terry Piper 'Officer Handsome.' He was that! Especially when he smiled at her and that little dimple appeared in his cheek. A lot of the Bald Eagles Falls women sighed over Officer Piper in uniform, patrolling and investigating with his canine partner at his side. He and Erin had known each other for almost a year and, while it hadn't been a whirlwind romance, things had progressed, and she did catch herself thinking of him as belonging to her, even though they weren't engaged and hadn't ever talked about an exclusive relationship.

"It's not just Terry. I don't really want to get involved in another mystery. The ones I've been involved with before now… Things have not always had a happy ending."

Bella nodded her understanding, but she wasn't ready to let the matter drop. "But like I said, this is a really old case. My grandpa isn't around anymore. No one would be trying to stop you from finding out the truth. There wouldn't be any danger, to you or anyone else."

"Just because it's an old case, that doesn't mean no one cares about it anymore." Erin was thinking about Bertie Braceling. "Sometimes, people get so caught up in trying to protect the past… people's reputations… histories that they've rewritten… what happened years ago still has an effect on today. Trust me."

"Okay." Bella sighed. "I guess I understand why you're scared to look into it."

The word *scared* irritated Erin. She wasn't scared. She was just cautious. She just didn't see the point in getting involved in something that wasn't any of her business. In the past, she'd had to get involved in cases because she or her friends had been the prime suspects. She didn't have any vested interest in what had happened to Bella's grandmother.

Bella picked up the cookie trays to put them into the ovens.

"Put them in the fridge for a few minutes first," Erin advised. "I think the dough might have warmed up too much. They'll spread too much and burn."

Bella considered the cookies for a moment, looking like she was going to argue, then nodded. "Okay." She took them to the fridge as instructed.

"It would just be really nice to be able to go to my own barn," she said with a shrug.

Erin wasn't so sure that solving her grandmother's murder would help Bella to go into the barn. She still couldn't go to the commode in the basement of Auntie Clem's bakery, even though Angela Plaint's murder had been solved and the loo was not haunted. Bella was still convinced that it was and refused to use the facilities. It was irritating to Erin that Bella couldn't retrieve any supplies from the storeroom and had to go down the street if she needed to use the toilet during her shift.

CHAPTER 2

From her attic reading room, Erin looked out the window to the loft over the garage, but there were no lights on. Vic and Willie had not yet returned. Vic had Sunday off as well; she and Willie could spend the night in the city or somewhere other than the loft apartment. While Willie had spent the night with Vic in the past, it had been when she had needed protection, and Vic had made it clear that they were not intimate. Erin didn't quite understand Vic's moral standards or why she cared if anyone thought she and Willie were sleeping together, but she just shrugged it off as part of what made Vic unique.

"Looks like it's just you and me tonight," Erin told Orange Blossom, the ginger cat who sat waiting for her to settle somewhere. "And Marshmallow, of course." She hadn't brought the rabbit up to run around and play with Blossom, nervous that he would fall down the stairs.

She picked up Clementine's previously missing journal, found in the deceased Joelle Biggs's possessions, and decided on the window seat. She sat down and patted the cushion beside her for Orange Blossom to jump up. He did so immediately, purr-meowing at her and chattering on about his day. It took a few minutes for him to find a comfortable position, kneading her thighs with his needle-sharp claws.

"Come on, Blossom…"

He finally settled and was still, purring his loud happy rumble. Erin opened up the journal. It was the one that Clementine had been writing when Erin's parents had been killed, and Erin was curious about what Clementine had known of the car accident that had left Erin an orphan and the intrigue that surrounded it.

To begin with, the mentions of her parents were general, "I have called Luke and Kathryn repeatedly, to no avail," and "Still no word from Luke." She obviously hadn't known about the accident right away. As far as she knew, her brother and his family had just gone away and refused to have anything to do with her. It sounded from Clementine's outpourings that she had perhaps had words with Erin's father about their parenting and the instability in Erin's life, and Clementine thought he was upset with her because of their argument.

There were also mentions of the Plaint boys. She hadn't known they'd had anything to do with her brother's disappearance, but she was clearly concerned about Davis. His descent into depression and drug use had not gone unnoticed. She had caught him squatting in the summer house that was now Adele's home, and had to send him on his way.

I couldn't let Davis hang around on the property, especially to crash at the summer house. I don't need teenagers or drifters setting up house there, running it down. I told him he needed to leave and not trespass on my property. If he needs something, he's welcome to come to the house. I'm more than happy to give him work, food, or just a listening ear.

Erin rubbed her eyes, telling herself they were burning because she was tired. What Davis had gone through because of his father's bad choices... even Trenton had suffered. He might have been a bully and a jock, but he hadn't been untouched by his father's unfaithfulness and his death. Adam Plaint might have thought that no one was being hurt by his affairs, but they had all been affected for decades to come.

Clementine had tried to reach out in kindness to Davis, even though she hadn't known the full extent of what he had been through. She had seen that he was hurting and had tried to offer him some kind of support.

"You missed your dad too, didn't you, Davis?" Erin murmured.

Orange Blossom raised his head to look at Erin, then decided she wasn't talking to him and put it back down to nap. Erin read on, trying not to get mired down in her own history. Yes, she missed her dad, and her mom too. But it had been twenty years and she wasn't a kid anymore. Sure, her childhood had sucked, passed from one foster home to another, yet life went on. She had worked hard and made something of herself.

The inheritance of Clementine's house and shop had made it possible for her to become her own boss, something she hadn't ever known if she would be able to do. So far, she was doing well, making a living at Auntie Clem's Bakery. Without the bakery, Erin would still have been trapped in dead-end jobs and Vic might have been out on the street.

But Clementine had more to report on than just her absent brother and the troubles of the Plaint boys. Erin's brow furrowed as she read on.

Strange happenings over at the Prost farm. I know that Ezekiel and Martha have always been strange ducks, but this is stranger than usual. Rumor has it that Martha has passed away, but Ezekiel will not let anyone into the house to see. He insists that she's just fine and will call them back later. But no one has gotten a call back from her and people are quite sure she's dead. The sheriff is seeing what he can do about getting in there, but apparently there is not much he can do if he doesn't have any evidence there has been a crime committed or that anyone is in immediate danger. Martha isn't in danger if she is dead, and Ezekiel wouldn't be guilty of anything other than misleading people and maybe improper disposal of a body if he's done something with her.

That was certainly an eye-opener. Another mysterious death or disappearance in Bald Eagle Falls? Even stranger, Erin had read through all of the newspapers around the time of her parents' deaths, and there had been nothing in the local weekly about a Martha Prost dying or disappearing under mysterious circumstances. That would certainly have caught Erin's attention.

But maybe it had just been a rumor. Probably, Martha had shown up again, perfectly healthy and happy, just like her husband said she would, and the rumor of her death was just that, a rumor, with nothing to back it.

Erin looked out the window toward Vic's loft again. She should have noticed if the light had been turned on, but she had been deeply interested in what she was reading. The apartment was still dark.

"I don't think she's going to make it back tonight," Erin told Orange Blossom. "They must be having too good a time."

Blossom sat up and yowled at her, a long, mournful sound that he made when she left him alone or took him in the car to the vet. Erin laughed and scratched his ears.

"We'll be fine if she stays away overnight. She doesn't sleep in the house anymore anyway."

Erin yawned, scrubbed at her eyes again, and decided it must be more than the dust from the journal that was making her eyes feel gritty. She needed to be up early in the morning for the bakery. Not as early as usual, because it would be Sunday, which was just the ladies' tea, and she didn't have to have everything baked that she would on a regular day. Just a few cookies and treats and an assortment of teas at the ready for when the women got out of their church services.

"It's my one night to sleep in," she told the cat, "I'd better take advantage of it."

CHAPTER 3

Things went well at the ladies' tea. It was pretty routine after a year, with no unexpected bumps in the road. Erin and Bella were cleaning up when Erin heard the jingling of the bells at the front door. She had a pretty good idea who it would be. Everyone knew that the tea would be over, and she would be closed. Erin looked out the kitchen doorway to the front of the shop.

"Come on in," she invited Officer Terry Piper.

He locked the front door for her and walked around the counter and through the kitchen door to join them. K9 panted at Terry's side.

"Do you want some water?" Erin suggested. "As Vic would say, it's almighty hot out there."

"Vic would not," Terry countered, "since this is still pretty mild for late spring."

"Fine, then *I'll* say it's almighty hot. Does K9 want a drink?"

Terry looked down at his partner.

"I'm sure he does," he agreed. "And a cookie. But you go ahead," he motioned toward the sink, "you finish cleaning up. I know where everything is."

Erin would protest that he didn't have to serve himself, but if she let him do it, she would be out of there all that much earlier. She shrugged. "Okay. Let me know if you need a hand with anything."

Erin went back to work and Terry got himself and K9 water and a cookie each. K9 seemed just as happy with his doggie biscuit as Terry was with his Bella's Dream cookie. Terry walked into the kitchen munching on it.

"Great idea, Bella," he told the girl, toasting her with the cookie. "I love them."

Bella turned pink and fanned herself with her hand. "Thank you, Officer Piper!"

"I'll be happy to test new combinations for you anytime."

Erin looked over at him. "Charley suggested that we try crickets in the protein bars."

A little wrinkle appeared between Terry's eyebrows. "Crickets? Is that some nickname for some kind of dried fruit or seed?"

"Nope. Crickets. Like she feeds to Iggy."

Terry made a face. "Don't even talk to me about crickets while eating. And remind me not to try anything labeled high protein if she ever reopens The Bake Shoppe. I'm not going to be *her* guinea pig."

"They are supposed to be very good for you. Low in fat."

"Well, so are a lot of things I don't intend to eat."

"K9 would eat them, wouldn't you, boy?"

K9 looked up at Erin with a little whine. They all laughed. They finished the clean-up together and Erin was free for the afternoon.

"Do you need a ride?" Terry asked Bella, as Erin locked the back door.

Bella shook her head. "No, it's okay. My mom is picking me up. She'll be here any minute."

"You're sure? Call Erin if you get stranded and we'll come back for you."

Bella waved him off. "I'm fine. Mom's coming."

Erin and Terry left her waiting in the back parking lot. They got into Erin's car; Erin knew his would be at the police department and they could pick it up later.

"Everything quiet this morning?" Erin asked.

"Like a Sunday morning in a small town."

Erin looked in her rear-view mirror at Bella. "Are you worried about her? Did you want to wait?"

"No, she'll be fine. I'm surprised she doesn't have a car of her own. Doesn't she have a license?"

"I don't think so. Her mom strikes me as a little… overprotective. She probably doesn't want Bella to be driving around on her own."

"Most kids out in the country are driving as soon as they are fourteen and have their licenses and their own cars as soon as they can. No parent wants to be driving around all over the county with them."

"I've noticed. I see kids who look like they're barely out of kindergarten with their own cars. I had my license when I was eighteen, but I didn't have enough money to get my own vehicle yet. And when I did have money to get my own…" Erin patted the steering wheel of the Challenger, "it was always a beater."

"With Bella living out of town, I would have thought she would have her own little beater by now. Maybe she's saving up for one."

Erin nodded, but secretly she wondered about Bella's mother. Erin hadn't seen Cindy very often, usually just a wave from behind the wheel when she dropped Bella off or picked her up. She didn't strike Erin as a very happy person.

Erin had been out on her own when she was eighteen. So had Vic. There was no reason Bella had to leave home when she was eighteen. Her part-time salary certainly wasn't enough to support her. Erin couldn't afford to give her more hours and pay her more, so she was glad that Bella wasn't too independent. She didn't want to lose Bella, but she wondered if Bella would be happier if she took a bit more initiative and stood up for herself.

"Family style for dinner?" Terry asked.

"Yeah, that sounds good."

Terry turned his head to look over at her. "You sound very far away."

Erin forced herself to look at Terry and smile, bringing her attention back to him. "Sorry. Just tired at the end of the week, I guess."

"Maybe Bella needs to take a few more hours on so you can cut back a little."

"Mmm. Maybe. Vic would agree with you."

"Where is Vic today? Did she and Willie have a good time?"

"I don't know. Haven't heard from them yet."

He looked at her, raising his eyebrows. "Oho? Is that so?"

"They didn't come back last night. Unless they went to Willie's. They didn't end up at Vic's."

"Well. That's a step forward in their relationship."

Erin nodded. "Hopefully, that means everything went well. He's stayed over before when bad things have happened… when she was being harassed. I just hope it wasn't anything like that."

"Not likely. Away from home, no one would know anything was different about her. She looks just like any other girl."

They pulled into the family restaurant and seated themselves on arrival. After ordering, Erin tried to relax and decompress from her day.

"What do you know about Bella's family?" she asked Terry. "She's never mentioned her dad and I've never asked."

"There's never been a man in the picture. It's just been Bella and her mom. Her mom had been away, but she moved back here before Bella was born. I don't know if her father was someone here in town or from somewhere else. I've never heard any explanation."

"Poor kid. It's tough being raised without a dad."

Terry shrugged. "These days, lots of kids are."

"If it's just the two of them all alone on the farm, I guess that's why her mom is so protective."

Terry nodded his agreement and had a sip of water.

"And probably why Bella is scared of her own shadow," Erin added. "I mean, not literally of her own shadow, but she's certainly got a thing about ghosts."

"Haints," Terry said with a teasing smile.

"Haints?"

"That's the local word for ghosts. Learn the lingo."

"I haven't heard that before. Well, maybe a couple of times, but I didn't know what it meant."

"Haints. Haunts. What haunts a haunted house."

"Oh, I see." Erin smiled and shook her head. "I don't remember Clementine ever using that one. But then, I haven't exactly been around for a long time."

"Bella is afraid of haints?"

"Mortally. Scared as a… I don't know. What's really scared?"

"A long-tailed cat in a room full of rockers?"

"I think that's jumpy, but it will have to do. She is really terrified of gho-haints. I don't think I can say that without cracking up! She's afraid to go downstairs to use the loo. She has to run down the street, where she doesn't have to go down to the basement. She's sure that my basement is haunted because that's where Angela died."

"But since we solved her murder and sent the culprit to prison, doesn't that mean she would be at rest now? Why would she be haunting you now?"

"Don't ask me. I don't know how it works."

Terry chuckled.

"She asked me to look into her grandmother's death years ago," Erin told him.

"Why would you do that? You told her no, right?"

Uh-huh," Erin nodded. "I told her I'm no detective."

"Her grandmother's death?" Terry stared off into space as if trying to remember what had happened.

The waitress brought them their plates, and Terry and Erin ate in silence for a few minutes.

"I only have a vague recollection," Terry said. "I wasn't with the police department back then. I was just a kid, but I remember there being talk about something happening to her grandmother." He shook his head. "I'll have to look it up. Why does Bella want you to look into it?"

"Because I gather her grandmother haunts the barn. So Bella can't go in there. She'd like to be able to go in there without being scared."

"Oh." Terry shoveled mashed potatoes into his mouth. "Okay, then."

"Like I said. She's scared of… haints. Really scared."

When Erin got back, she saw Willie's truck in front of the house and breathed a sigh of relief. Not because she'd been worried anything had happened to Vic. Not really. But she couldn't help being a little concerned when Vic didn't return when she was expected to. Erin was like a mother with grown children who still worried about them, just a little, and wondered where they were and what they were doing.

Erin parked her own car and went into the house, not sure whether Vic would be there or in her own apartment in back. She smiled when she heard Vic's voice addressing Orange Blossom.

"There she is, Blossom. There's your mommy, home again."

Marshmallow, the toasted-brown and white rabbit, hopped up to Erin before Orange Blossom got there, so he got the first scratches and pats.

"Hello, you soft, fluffy, beautiful bun!" She scratched behind his ears and let the rabbit snuffle her toes, investigating all the smells she brought home with her.

The cat sat on his haunches a few feet away, looking tall and regal and completely unconcerned with the attention his fellow was getting. Erin knew it was all an act. They had a strong rivalry going. Erin kept an eye on the cat while patting Marshmallow and giving him attention, until the rabbit decided he'd had enough for the moment and hopped away. Erin looked at Orange Blossom.

"I know. You aren't looking for any attention, are you? You just live here. You're a cat, not a lap dog."

Blossom gave her a long, slow blink. Erin stepped over to him and picked him up, pulling him to her chest and cuddling him. Orange Blossom immediately began to purr, loud and satisfied.

"Now are you going to talk to me?" Erin asked, not used to his being so quiet. He was always so chatty. The silent treatment was something new. Maybe it was a sign he was growing up and wasn't a needy kitten or adolescent anymore.

Orange Blossom chirruped in response. Erin talked nonsense with him for a few minutes, scratching his ears and chin. Vic stood in the doorway and watched them, her eyes sparkling.

"You ended up being longer than you expected?" Erin asked.

"Yes. A little," Vic agreed. She smiled.

"Are you going to tell me all about it?"

Vic considered, then shook her head. "Not all about it, no. Just… that we had a really nice time. It was a great break, I feel like I had a week-long vacation. I'm so relaxed. How did everything go here? Any trouble at the bakery?"

"No, everything went smoothly. Bella was there, and we didn't have any unexpected problems. Had dinner with Terry." Erin shrugged. "And now you're home safe and sound, so I'm happy."

"Good. Cuppa tea before bed?"

"That sounds good."

Erin followed Vic into the kitchen, the animals trailing them to get their treats. Erin put out some bread and jam while Vic put the kettle on and looked through the supply of teas to pick something out.

"I don't know if we're ever going to get through all of Clementine's teas," Vic said. "She must have put up a ten-year supply!"

"All the leftover inventory from when she shut down the tea shop. I don't think it will take ten years, but maybe a couple more, anyway."

While they waited for the kettle to boil, Vic got a stick of celery out for Marshmallow and Erin flicked a couple of kitty treats across the floor for Orange Blossom to chase. Vic giggled when the cat nearly skidded straight into the cupboards after galloping after one. Marshmallow kept one eye on Orange Blossom as he nibbled sedately on his celery.

They sat down at the table and Erin breathed in the lemon balm scent carried by the steam. Vic looked over the jars of Jam Lady jam and picked out the blackberry. Erin snagged the strawberry.

Vic shook her head. "I can't believe you can still eat strawberry jam after getting poisoned."

Erin looked down at it. "It's really good."

"You're not afraid that Mr. Jam Lady put poison in another one?"

"No." Erin didn't point out that if Roger had poisoned another jar of jam, it didn't have to be the strawberry. It could just as easily have been the blackberry that Vic had chosen.

"I guess this will be the last of the Jam Lady jam," Vic sighed.

Erin spread jam on her bread. "Unless Mary Lou or the boys take over. Or if Roger gets out."

Vic looked at Erin over the rim of her teacup. "They wouldn't let him go, would they?"

"I don't think so. Even if they decide he wasn't responsible because of his brain damage… they still can't just let him go free, because of the danger he could hurt someone else."

Vic nodded her agreement. "I feel bad for Mary Lou."

"Yeah. Things are going to be tough for them."

Erin smothered a yawn. "Sorry. I slept in, I shouldn't be tired."

"You work hard. Of course you're tired. You can head to bed as soon as we're done. Sooner, if you want."

"I'll want to read for a few minutes. Write a few things down."

"Read…? Oh, Clementine's journal? Come across anything interesting?" Vic was always careful not to ask anything too intrusive. She didn't ask specifics, like whether Clementine knew what had happened to Erin's parents or had said anything about the possibility of taking care of eight-year-old Erin.

Erin nodded. "She mentioned a missing woman. Strange, because I never saw anything in the local papers about it. And it's not like I would have missed it. I was looking for information about a missing man, I would definitely have noticed a missing woman."

"Maybe she was found again before the weekly was published. Or maybe it wasn't widely known. Just because Clementine knew about it, that doesn't mean the local media would have gotten ahold of it. We don't know."

"True," Erin agreed tentatively.

"Or they might have decided it was unsubstantiated gossip and they couldn't print it. Who was it?"

"I'd have to check the names again. Proust? I don't remember their first names."

Vic raised her eyebrows. "Proust? Or Prost?"

It wasn't until then that Erin made the connection. "Prost? You mean Bella?"

Vic nodded. "That is Bella's last name, isn't it?"

The pieces started to click together. "Oh, no…"

"What?"

"Bella asked me if I would look into her grandmother's death, a cold case. I told her no, I'm not a private investigator… and then Clementine's journal… I never made the connection. This missing woman must have been her grandmother."

CHAPTER 4

*E*rin didn't normally have Bella in on a Monday, unless it was to take the afternoon shift when she or Vic had a doctor's appointment or another errand that couldn't be put off. She didn't quite know what to say to Bella. She dithered around until it was late enough in the morning to make calls without waking people up, and then tried Bella's number. The number Erin had was, luckily, Bella's cell phone, so she wouldn't be waking the whole family by ringing the landline. Though 'the whole family' only meant Bella's mother. It wasn't like there would be sleeping children.

"Hello? Erin? Is everything okay? Didn't Vic get back? You should have called me last night."

"No, everything is fine. Vic did get back, and she's working today; we don't need you to cover an emergency shift."

"Oh. Okay… so what did you need me for, then? I put in my timesheet. I left it in your basket."

"Yes, I saw. It looks fine. I'm just… I'm having a staff meeting at the end of the day today, and I wondered if you would like to join in. Help us to make some decisions."

"Really?" Bella's voice perked up. "That would be awesome! I'd love to hear what you guys talk about, even if I didn't have any say in what the decision would be."

Erin felt a little bit guilty about that. There weren't a lot of decisions to be made at the staff meeting, but she'd have to be sure to ask Bella's opinion on a few things, just to get her involved. She probably should have been having staff meetings with both Vic and Bella for some months already, but it had never occurred to her to make it official and to invite Bella along.

"Great!" Erin said. "I'll see you here at about five, if that's okay?"

"I'll be there!"

Normally they were still open at five, but Erin could turn the sign over early. With Bella to help with the clean-up, Erin would be able to have the staff meeting and still not be home too late.

Bella's mother dropped her off just before five.

"Uh… mom wants to know how long this is going to be," Bella said, flushing pink. "What should I tell her? So she knows when to pick me up."

"It shouldn't be too long… maybe an hour? I guess that's kind of inconvenient, if she went home, she'd just have to turn around to get you again."

"It's okay," Bella assured her. "She can run some errands while she's waiting. That's not bad."

"Maybe we should drive you home after. Would that be better?"

"No, really. It's okay. Mom will pick me up. I just have to tell her when." Bella ducked back out and leaned down to talk to her mother in the car.

"Maybe this was a bad idea," Erin said to Vic.

"It's fine. Don't be so worried. It's about time we had a formal staff meeting."

In a few minutes, they had finished cleaning up. There wasn't a boardroom or any place suited for a business meeting, but they made do, using their stools at the kitchen counters.

"We've got a few things going on," Erin said. "I'm expecting the delivery of the new freezer sometime in the next week. Not sure what day it will actually show up here."

The residents of Bald Eagle Falls were used to how unreliable delivery service could be. No one wanted to make a special trip to Bald Eagle Falls, and it took too long for several deliveries to collect to make it worthwhile.

"Why do we need a new freezer?" Bella asked, throwing a glance toward the stairs to the basement, where the storage freezers were located. "I thought the old ones were working just fine."

"Not like those ones," Erin explained. "It's a display freezer with a glass front, so we can sell frozen goods and have them on display. Cakes, popsicles, frozen lemonade, whatever we want."

"Oh, great idea, with summer coming," Bella enthused. "Homemade ice cream would be amazing."

Erin nodded. She hadn't grown up in Bald Eagle Falls, and found the heat oppressive, but she thought that even the born-and-bred Tennesseans would appreciate the option of frozen treats in the summer. And it would allow her to freeze day-old goods and not have to waste as much. She was looking forward to the arrival of the freezer with more excitement than was natural.

They went on to other items on the agenda and were done in half an hour. Erin pretended to be studying her list of prioritized items.

"Bella, you were talking about your grandma and grandpa the other day. But I forget what you said their names were."

Bella frowned and tilted her head, not understanding why Erin would bring it up. "Uh… give me a minute… usually, it's just 'grandma and grandpa,' you know? Uh… Ezekiel and Martha, I think. I really should know their names better, they're the only grandparents I'll ever have. Why?"

"Well…" Erin considered lying about it. But she couldn't think of anything that would explain why she was looking for the names of her employee's grandparents. "You were asking me about looking into your grandma's death the other day, so I was curious about what exactly happened…"

Bella's eyes squinted slightly at Erin, frowning. "I don't really know much. My mom doesn't like to talk about it. I guess… nobody really knows what happened to her. People say maybe my grandpa had something to do with it, but why would he do that? They were old! They'd been married to each other forever. Men don't just suddenly kill their wives for no reason when they're that old."

Erin and Vic exchanged glances. "Well, we can't know anyone's motives without looking into it," Erin said. "Just because he was old, that doesn't mean he wasn't capable of doing something to hurt her. People still get jealous… greedy… or they have something wrong with their brains…"

"You think he was crazy? I don't think my grandpa was crazy."

"No, I don't know anything about it," Erin said. "I'm just saying… we never can be sure of what motives a person might have, without knowing everything about their past. Even knowing, sometimes we would never guess…" Erin thought about the murders that she had had an intimate peek at during her short stay in Bald Eagle Falls. Fear, jealousy, greed, an instant of anger… so many senseless deaths.

Bella pulled a lock of hair into her mouth and chewed on it. "Does that mean you changed your mind about looking into it? Will you see if you can solve what happened to her?"

"I don't know," Erin was honest. "I still don't want to be a detective. I'm just a baker. A full-time baker. But I admit I am curious…" she trailed off. "My Aunt Clementine wrote about it in her journal and I was just reading what she wrote. I don't know whether there is any real insight in Clementine's observations, but at least it is a first-hand account. Someone who was actually around when it happened, instead of it being a fuzzy memory from a long time ago.

"It's in your Auntie Clem's journal?"

Erin nodded. "I haven't read it all… but she's mentioned it once or twice so far."

"That's so cool! It's almost like we're related!"

"Mary Lou says everyone on the mountain is related. Everyone who's been here for any length of time, anyway. She says we're all kin."

"Will you at least let me know what it says? I'd really like to hear from someone who knew them."

Erin nodded in agreement. "Sure. I'll let you know what I find out."

Mrs. Sturm finally got poor old Ezekiel to let her in, and there is no sign of Martha anywhere. At least there is no moldering body in the living room or the bed, but that doesn't explain what has happened to her. Ezekiel said she's just off visiting, but Martha doesn't drive, and no one has driven her anywhere. At least not that anyone I have talked to knows about. Someone would have seen her if she'd taken the bus. Could Ezekiel have dropped her off somewhere? He can't explain where she has gone, other than general statements that she is off visiting, and it is no one's business where and the rest of the details. He is entitled to his own privacy, and yet…

Ezekiel still denies the sheriff access to his property. I asked the sheriff why he can't just go and take a look around, see if there are any new graves or disturbed areas, but apparently even for that, he needs permission. Mrs.

Sturm only looked around the house, she didn't get a chance to look around the rest of the property.

It remains a mystery.

Erin handed the journal silently to Vic, who took it from her without a word. Vic looked at Erin's face, then dropped her eyes to the paper. Erin watched her eyes go back and forth as she read the passage. Then she shook her head and handed it back.

"So they really do think that it was her grandfather? Not a stranger from out of town? An old man?"

"Being old doesn't stop anyone from making mistakes."

"But there's no evidence. None in there, anyway. If we are going to take the case, we'll have to talk to the people who knew them."

"But they'll just remember that they thought he was guilty, don't you think? Besides, we are not taking on the case. I'm just… looking."

Vic raised her eyebrows. "Sure. Just looking."

CHAPTER 5

*E*rin had no premonition when she got up in the morning that anything was going to happen. It was a bright, clear spring day, no 'dark and stormy night.' No spooky music. Everything about her day suggested that it was just going to be a normal, routine day like any other. Even her reading of Clementine's journal the night before didn't keep her from getting a good night's sleep and starting off bright-eyed and bushy-tailed the next morning.

She and Vic went to the bakery as usual, and everything proceeded normally.

Until the afternoon lull, when the bells jingling announced a new customer, and Erin looked up to see a tall, mysterious stranger.

It wasn't a strange man, it was a woman, her red hair in cornrows draped over her cheeks and shoulders, not gathered under the colorful scarf wound around her head. Her makeup was dramatic, eyelids smoky and lips red, and she had large gold hoop earrings. Her peasant dress was a shimmery blue. Her nails were red, and her hands adorned with numerous heavy, old-looking rings.

And she wasn't a stranger. because once Erin took a good look at her, she could see that it was the face of someone familiar.

"Well, there she is," Reg Rawlins said. "How's my favorite sister?"

"How can she be your sister?" Vic demanded. "I thought your only sister was Charley, and she's just a half-sister. Who is this Regina person?"

It was understandable that Vic was protective. Erin had taken care of Vic when she was in need. Vic had shot a man who had been trying to kill Erin. Erin was always ready to step in whenever Vic was being harassed. They took care of each other, lived and worked together, and were closer than sisters. Closer than Erin and Charley, anyway.

Erin glanced toward the door that led back out to the front customer area, trying to ensure that Reg couldn't see or hear them.

"She *was* my sister," she said. "A foster sister. But it's been a long time since we were anything to each other. Everyone goes their own way, and foster kids don't get the option of staying in touch."

"How did she know where to find you? And why? What's she doing here?"

"I don't know, since she only just got here, and I excused myself to talk to you."

"It can't be good."

"Well, it could be," Erin suggested. "Maybe she just came to let me know… how she's doing in life. That she's okay. Maybe she's getting in contact with everyone from her old life…"

"What are the odds of that?"

"Well… rare enough that I've never heard of it happening before."

"Yeah, that's what I thought."

Erin didn't tell Vic that Reg had been in contact with her before, after they were both out of the foster care system. And Reg hadn't just been looking for old friends to reconnect with. Erin wasn't happy to see her again.

Vic took a deep breath in, then breathed it out slowly. "She's here. So I guess you need to at least say hi to her. Give her a chance to say what it is that she wants." Vic wasn't going to be fooled into thinking that Reg just wanted to see her old family members again.

Erin nodded and took Vic out to the front of the shop.

"Hey, Reg, I wanted you to meet my friend, and my assistant in the bakery, Vic Webster. Vic… this is Reg Rawlins." Erin paused. "Are you going by Rawlins?"

"It's as good a name as any for now. What's in a name?"

Erin looked away from Reg, not wanting to be hypnotized by her new look. "It's good to see you again," she said automatically. "It's been a long time."

"Yeah. Well, it wasn't easy to find you, sis. Surprise, surprise, you're using your real name again. I didn't expect to find you under Erin Price."

Erin could feel Vic's eyes on her, interested and hoping for an explanation. But Vic wasn't exactly using her birth name either. She knew there were plenty of reasons for starting fresh, where no one knew you or your past.

Erin gave a shrug. "What's in a name?" she echoed.

Reg laughed. She looked at Vic. "Has she told you all about the mischief we caused in foster care?"

Vic smiled. "No, I haven't heard about this."

"It's nothing, Vic," Erin said quickly. "Kids do stuff. I tried hard to be good, so that foster families wouldn't send me away. I wanted to just stay in one place, with one family."

"Sure," there was a hint of a sneer in Reg's tone. "You wanted to stay with a family, runaway Erin? You had a funny way of showing it."

Erin shrugged again. "Kids do stuff."

Reg nodded, looking over the treats in the display case. "They sure do. And you were a runner. Caused foster moms no end of trouble. What's good here?"

"Everything is good," Erin said briskly. "It's all made from scratch. All gluten-free and nut-free. There are options if you are vegan or are allergic to one of the other major allergens; I try to make sure everyone can eat something."

Erin thought of Bertie Braceling and experienced a pang. She had thought she'd have years to try to develop a line of treats that were good for him. But like Carolyn, he was gone. It was too late to help him now.

"I don't have any allergies," Reg said. "How about... chocolate zucchini muffin?"

"Good choice," Vic approved, helping to take some of the weight of the conversation away from Erin. "They are always so moist and flavorful." She used the tongs to put one into a package for Reg.

Erin didn't bother to ring it up. "First one is free."

Reg slid the muffin partway out of the wrapper and took a large bite. "Oh, yeah. That's good stuff! This is gluten free? It tastes pretty good!"

"That's the idea," Erin agreed coolly.

Reg munched on the muffin, analyzing Erin. "No need to order fireworks and a big brass band. But you could show a little more excitement over seeing your long-lost sister."

"I found out recently that I actually do have a biological sister I never knew about," Erin said. "I was really nervous about meeting her. But it has been a while since I saw you last. Are you… just passing through?"

"Not exactly. I was hoping you could put me up for a few days and we could talk old times."

"Reg…" Erin glanced over at Vic, wishing that she'd leave them to have a private conversation. "I really don't have the time for old times. I have a new life now. I don't want to screw it up."

"I'm not doing anything to get you into trouble. What's wrong with reconnecting with an old friend? You and I *were* friends. We used to do things together. Even after we were both out of foster care."

"I know… I'm not trying to be stuck up… I just… stuff from the past… things didn't work out so well in the past and I don't want to repeat the same mistakes. You like to… stir things up."

Vic gave a little snicker. "I think I've heard the same said about someone else around here a time or two."

Erin glared at her. "Not helping, Vic."

"Sorry." Vic held her hands up. "Ignore me. I'm not even here. In fact, I'll go in back and wash some dishes. Just give me a shout if you need a hand with customers."

Vic retreated into the kitchen. Erin turned back to Reg.

"So how about it?" Reg asked. "Can we do supper?"

⌇

Erin was reluctant to close the bakery at the end of the day, knowing that once she was finished, she was going to be meeting Reg at the Chinese restaurant for supper. Her stomach was tied in knots and her head whirled with memories of her and Reg in foster care and later as young women out on their own, and the crazy stuff they'd been involved in. Reg was always the leader, and it seemed like Erin was always game to join in whatever nutty scheme Reg had devised. Some of them had been innocent games where no one was harmed. Others…

"She seems nice," Vic said.

Erin was jarred from her memories. "What?"

"Your foster sister, Reg. She seems like she's nice. The two of you must have had a lot of fun together."

"Uh… yeah. Of course. It was nice having her in the picture, back then. I needed someone who… liked me and wanted to do things with me."

Vic nodded as she scrubbed the cooling racks. "Her makeup and everything was very dramatic. Does she always look like that? Like a fortune teller looking for a place to happen?"

Erin hesitated. "She's had… a lot of different looks over the years. I don't know what this one is about yet. I guess she'll tell me at dinner."

"You'll have a nice time," Vic said firmly. Erin was obviously radiating her anxiety about the meal. Vic could read it in her face and body language just as clearly as if she'd been announcing it out loud.

"I'll try. I'm sure it will be nice… it's just… it's been a long time, and things have changed a lot since we saw each other last."

"Sure. You've grown up. A lot of things change between when you're a kid and when you're an independent adult," Vic agreed with authority.

Erin looked at her. Vic was *barely* a legal adult. Erin had been older than she was when she'd seen Reg last.

Vic grinned and got a little pink. "Just because I'm young, that doesn't mean it's not true."

"I suppose not. I'm just… I've got a bad feeling about this. Reg Rawlins is trouble."

"You can always tell her no. She can't just roll into town and expect you to take her in. Southern hospitality only goes so far."

Erin put mixing bowls away in the cupboard. "I can't even figure out what she's doing in Tennessee. She's never been this far south in her life. She can't have come this far just to see me."

"All the way from…?"

"Uh…" Erin thought back, trying to place the memories of Reg in a concrete time and place. "Massachusetts, I think. Yeah… pretty sure…"

"It is a long way," Vic admitted. "Who knows, maybe she is on her way to see someone else. Just a few days in Tennessee… we could handle that. You do have a guest room."

"Once she gets in…"

"You make her sound like a disease. Is she really that bad?"

"No. She was a good friend… we helped each other out… I just don't know what to think."

"Wait and see what she has to say. Then you can decide."

CHAPTER 6

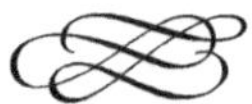

Maddie Burns, one of the hostesses at the Chinese restaurant, greeted Erin and gave her a look of puzzlement as she looked for Terry or Vic, and found Erin to be alone.

"I'm supposed to be meeting an out-of-town friend here," Erin explained. "Anyone unfamiliar here?"

"Oh, the gypsy." Maddie turned and pointed Reg out. "Right over there. Do you want a menu?"

"No, I don't need one. Thanks."

Erin went to Reg's table. 'Gypsy' was a good description of Reg. She didn't have the bone structure of a Roma gypsy, but she looked like a gypsy straight out of a children's fairy tale with her colorful headscarf, dramatic makeup, and loose skirt. Erin sat down across from her. She looked her old friend over one more time.

"Okay… tell me what this is about."

"What? I came to see you. To connect with you again. Why are you acting like there's something wrong with that?"

"You're all dressed up for some scam. So tell me. What's it all about?"

Reg tilted her head to the side, considering her answer. She ran her fingers through her narrow braids and rubbed the back of her head. "Just looking to make a little green."

"This is just a little town. You can't make anything here."

"I can't make anything here?" Reg snorted. "The looks I'm getting… people are falling all over themselves to get a good look at the stranger in town. Once they hear that I'm a medium, they won't stop knocking at my door."

"A medium?" Erin rubbed her face, tired after the long day and not wanting to hear about Reg's newest scheme.

"You know I've always had a talent for figuring people out," Reg said evenly. "I've always had a special intuition about things…"

"And that makes you a medium? Like a psychic?"

"So much more than just a psychic," Reg protested. "That doesn't even begin to describe my range of talents. Psychic readings are just one of the many spiritual gifts that I have. Healing, communing with the dead, palm and card reading, tea leaves…"

"You think people will fall for that?"

"What do you mean 'fall for' it? It's the truth. It doesn't matter whether people believe it or not. That's up to them."

"You want people to pay you for looking at their hands and making up some nonsense about what is going to happen to them in the future."

"Nonsense? No. I want to help people to realize their full potential. I am more like a life coach. Not some… charlatan who is just trying to bilk people out of their hard-earned money."

"You're not a psychic."

"I didn't say I was. I said that I am sensitive to impressions about people. I can help them to become who they are really destined to be. To find their true path to happiness."

"And how are you going to do this?"

"Talking with them. Picking up clues in their speech and manner. Reading them. You can tell a lot about a person just by looking at them. Add in some visiting to find out who they are and where they are going in life, and I can give you an accurate reading of just about anyone in the world. You don't think I can?"

"That, I can believe," Erin agreed. "But why do you have to surround that with this…" Erin flipped her hand to indicate Reg's costume, "this mysticism?"

"Because people like it. They're impressed by it. It signals to them that I'm serious about what I do, and they can trust me. If you meet people's expectations, they will take you for a professional. This is just me... meeting people's expectations."

"And you're going to tell them that what you're doing is just a cold reading?"

"I'll tell them what they want to hear. If they want me to couch it in spiritual terms instead of straightforward like you do, then that's how I'll explain it. Why would you have a problem with that?"

Maddie Burns brought over the dishes that Reg had ordered while she'd been waiting for Erin to arrive. Both women helped themselves to a sampling from the platters.

"My problem is that it's nonsense," Erin said. "There's nothing spiritual about it. There's nothing mystical. You're just someone trying to make a buck off of being observant."

Reg *tsked*, shaking her head. "Okay. You don't believe in God, right?"

Erin nodded. "That's right. I am an atheist. I don't believe in any of these secret powers you claim to have. Or that anyone else claims to have. I don't believe in prophecy or revelation or any of the things that happened in the ancient texts. Stories are stories. They change over time. Their purpose changes over time. But they are still just that—stories."

"And you go around telling that to everyone you meet."

Erin pressed her lips together. "No. I don't tell that to anyone."

"You just keep it to yourself and let them believe and practice what they like."

Erin nodded. "Yes. Exactly."

"Then why would you expect me to do anything different? I just frame the experience in the terms they are familiar with. I'm not lying to them. I'm just meeting them at their own level."

Erin shook her head. She ate a few bites of her dinner. "Whatever it is you're doing, don't expect me to help you with it."

Reg didn't say anything.

For a few minutes, they just ate, making routine comments about the food and what they liked. Just as if they were two friends who had met for dinner because they enjoyed each other's company.

"I need somewhere to stay until I can get myself established," Reg said finally, as they were both getting full and slowing down. "Not for long. I'm sure I can find a little rental somewhere that I can afford."

Erin had already told her no. She clenched her teeth in irritation but did her best to keep her expression calm and pleasant. "You can't just drop in on people and expect them to put you up."

"Not just anyone," Reg agreed. "But when it's your sister? Your best friend?"

"We haven't been sisters for a long time."

"Come on, Erin. The number of times I pulled your butt out of the fire? Erin and Reg Rawlins against the world. You don't remember?"

The trouble was, Erin did remember. Every time Reg had rescued her, it was Reg who had gotten her in trouble in the first place. It had been the two of them against the world, when maybe they should have been trying to get along in the world instead of fighting it every step of the way. Reg had encouraged Erin to fight her foster parents, social workers, school teachers, and anyone else in authority over her. She had encouraged Erin's natural propensity to rebel if someone told her she had to do something. She'd thought it funny when Erin ran.

Mrs. Bloom, her social worker, had seen the dynamic between them and had tried more than once to convince Erin that Reg was bad for her, which only served to push Erin closer to her. When she had eventually found other homes for the two of them, splitting them up, the decision had caused an irreparable rift between Erin and her social worker. Erin would never again trust Mrs. Bloom or anyone else at social services with any information about her life.

"What are you thinking about?" Reg prodded, her voice soft.

"Mrs. Bloom."

"The dragon! Man, she was terrible, wasn't she? She had it out for me right from the start."

"Yeah, she did," Erin agreed. "She saw right through you."

That gave Reg pause. She considered Erin's words. "Are you saying she was right about me?"

Erin raised her brows. "She *was.*"

Reg laughed it off. "I suppose you're right. But you needed someone on your side, Erin. You had to learn how to stand up for yourself."

"I stood up for myself."

"I mean using words, not just being stubborn or running away. Actually telling people what you thought."

Erin chewed on the last piece of noodle on her plate, considering. "Well, now I'm telling you. I'm not putting you up."

"But you are," Reg insisted, mischievous eyes sparkling.

"No, I'm not. Why would I?"

"Because I'm your sister, and that's stronger than your personal preference. Maybe you don't want to put me up, but because I'm your sister, you will anyway."

"It's a long time since we were sisters."

"Sisters forever. That's what you promised. That's what we promised each other. Not just sisters until we went to different families. Sisters forever."

Promises of devotion. Fierce hugs. Lots of tears. Erin could see the two of them together in her mind's eye. *Sisters forever. No matter what.*

The world could end, and they would still be sisters. No matter what any parent or social worker did, they would always be sisters.

Maddie Burns brought their bill, together with two factory-produced fortune cookies on a little plate. Erin unwrapped one of the fortune cookies and broke it open.

Be prepared for the unexpected.

Erin rolled her eyes and dropped the slip of paper onto the table. How could anyone prepare for what wasn't expected?

"I thought you didn't believe in fortune telling," Reg said.

"I don't."

"Then why did you open your cookie?"

Erin's face warmed. "I just wanted to see what it said. That doesn't mean I believe it. Just that it's interesting to see what they come up with."

"Sure. And because deep down inside, part of you wants to believe that it's true. Part of you wants to believe that you can catch just a glimpse of your future by reading a fortune cookie. The little girl part of you still wants to believe that the fortune inside is true, and that it will bring you something good."

When Erin had been little, she had not been a non-believer. She had hoped that there really was something to religion, mysticism, and magic. She wished on stars and birthday candles. She crossed her fingers, jumped over sidewalk cracks, and knelt by her bed to pray in the homes where she was told to. But there hadn't been any breaks. None of her prayers or wishes came true. By the time she turned eighteen, she was a firm non-believer against anything supernatural or unworldly. By then, she knew that it was all nonsense, no matter how many people believed. They were just holding on to something for comfort. Like a child dragging her teddy bear from one home to the next, thinking it would keep her safe in the night. But it never did.

"A few days," Erin finally said. "No more than a week. You start looking for a place of your own now, this minute. You can't stay with me forever."

"Never intended to," Reg agreed. "I just need to crash on your couch for a day or two while I get on my feet."

"Not the couch. I have a guest room. And you're there as a guest, so act like one. Not like you own the place or have some right to be there. You're there because I'm a nice person, not because I owe you anything."

Reg nodded. "Sure. Of course. And I'm sorry to be crashing on you like this. I didn't plan it that way."

Erin wasn't sure she wanted to know exactly what Reg had been planning.

CHAPTER 7

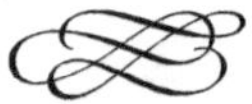

$\mathcal{R}$eg got her meager belongings settled and decided on a hot bath, so she was out of the way for a while. Erin breathed a sigh of relief. When Vic came into the house, her head turned toward the sound of the water running in the bathroom immediately. "I thought you weren't going to…?"

"She talked me into it," Erin sighed. "Just pretend she's not here. That's what I'm doing."

"How long?"

"Just a few days."

Vic shook her head. "Always taking in strays, aren't you?"

"I didn't want to. She's not a house cat, she's a tiger kitten. Sooner or later, it's going to turn out badly."

"I hope not."

Erin shrugged. "That's just the way it is with Reg. It always ends with disaster."

Vic stooped to pick up Orange Blossom, another member of the family who was not happy about a newcomer in the house. He bumped his head against Vic's chin, demanding attention. Vic's eyes were troubled.

"It will be okay," Erin reassured her. "It won't work out how Reg has planned, but… mostly that will be bad for her, not us. She'll get over it."

"Oh, it's not that. I get it. Some people just bring drama with them everywhere they go. I gather your sister is one of those people."

"Lots of drama," Erin agreed.

"Yeah. I wasn't thinking about her. I was thinking about Willie."

Erin was startled by the change in subject. She sat down on the couch and drew up her feet under her. "Willie? What about him? Everything is... okay, isn't it?"

Vic hadn't had much to say about her overnight stay with Willie. Erin hoped that the two of them had gotten along all right and hadn't run into any irreconcilable differences.

"Everything is great. We're working through things. Taking our time. Sharing what we feel comfortable with. Really good."

Erin nodded. She sensed a 'but' in there somewhere.

"He's looking for a new job."

"Oh," Erin nodded. "That's great."

In all the time she had known Willie, and from what she understood about his past, for a long time all Willie had done were odd jobs. He had his mines, and Erin didn't know what sort of metals he got out of them or how he refined them. That didn't take all of his time or provide the living he needed to take care of his own needs or Vic's. So he always had other things going on. Courier deliveries, flyer distribution, helping the seniors with their yard work. He was one of the busiest people Erin knew.

"I don't think it's great," Vic objected. "Why does he need to change his path now, just because we're together? He should still be able to do what he wants."

"Well, no one is stopping him from finding things he likes."

"I feel like I am." Vic sat down on one of the recliners, still holding Orange Blossom.

"What do you mean? You haven't told him where he can or can't work, have you?"

"No. But he's gotten into his head that he has to have a steady, stable job. Nine to five, five days a week. Like a 'normal' person."

Erin was horrified. It didn't sound like a bad idea on the surface but, knowing Willie as she did, she knew he would be miserable in a job like that. He liked the ability to be flexible, to decide how much work he wanted and when he would complete it. While these odd jobs often took him out of town for a day or two, he found ways to be with Vic the rest of the week, and the varied jobs kept him happy and productive. She had no idea how he would manage the stresses of a routine office job. He'd be bored. He'd be overwhelmed. He wouldn't know what to do with himself. Maybe it would still allow him enough time to do his mining; his weekends would be free, at least.

"Why is he doing that?"

"I don't know." Vic's voice was anguished. "I've told him he doesn't need to do it. That I don't think he'll be happy with a job like that, but he's sure it's the only way to go. He says if he's going to be a family man, he needs to have something stable."

Erin raised her brows. "A family man?"

"We were talking, when we went into the city. About what we wanted, where we wanted to go with our lives. I said that I wanted a family, and he thought he did too. We were both happy with that. I was glad to hear that he was interested in the same things as I was. But then when we got back here, and he decided he was going to get a full-time office job…" Vic shook her head, eyes shiny with tears.

"An office job? He's not even going to find something that is outside…?"

"That's the plan. White collar worker. That's what he thinks I want or expect from him, what a family man should do."

"There are plenty of family men who don't have white collar office jobs. That's just silly. Didn't you tell him…?"

"Don't you think I tried to tell him that I wasn't expecting him to change what he was and didn't want him to give up his… his way of life? Of course I did. I've told him every which way to Sunday. But he thinks it's just words, that I'm just being nice. He's sure that I really want him to be… normal."

"Do you want me to try to explain it to him?"

"I don't know. I don't know if that will make it better or worse. I can't tell him that he can do whatever he wants, and then say that he can't switch to banker's hours if he wants to. If it's what he really wants… I can't tell him not to."

Erin frowned. "I suppose. But you and I both know he's going to hate it!"

"Of course he is."

Vic stroked Orange Blossom briskly, in a way that made him yip and yowl, squirming to get comfortable.

"You both want a family?" Erin asked, changing the direction of the conversation slightly. "So… you would adopt?"

Vic nodded. "Seeing as I don't have the equipment. Or use a surrogate. Maybe we'll foster."

Erin's feelings warred. The product of the foster care system herself, she wasn't inclined to recommend it to anyone. But until someone came up with a system that worked better, there would always be foster kids in need of good parents. Vic and Willie would be good parents, given some time and experience, but the children they parented wouldn't be their own, and Erin didn't want them having to suffer the heartbreak of separation when children inevitably had to move on to new situations.

"Just… make sure it's what you really want. A lot of people think they do, but… it's not an easy job."

"Yeah." Vic's smile seemed forced. The water in the bathroom stopped running, bringing them both back to the present. "Speaking of foster care, tell me about Reg. You guys seem like you were close."

"Yes. Maybe the closest I ever was to a foster sibling. But she also… got us in a lot of trouble. She's a… not a troublemaker, exactly. But someone who agitates others…"

"And you were her favorite target."

"I guess so," Erin agreed, surprised at how quickly Vic grasped the situation. "Even after we were both adults, out of the system, she still tracks me down, shows up in my life at the most unlikely times, and gets me involved in some grand new scheme."

"What is it this time?"

Erin shook her head, not sure how to put it into words. Calling Reg a fortune-teller or medium didn't begin to describe the grandness of what she had in mind. "I don't know. That's her own business."

The bathroom door opened, and Erin felt the moist air expanding outward, dissipating into the house. The fresh smells of soap and shampoo wafted over Erin. When Reg stepped out of the bathroom, she was wearing one of the nightgowns that had been hanging in the closet in Clementine's room, which Erin had assigned to Reg. She was already making herself at home, digging herself in, making it harder to extricate her when it was time.

"Oh, you have company. Hi, there. You're… Vic, from the bakery."

Vic nodded.

"She lives over the garage," Erin advised. "Her apartment is just across the yard," she gestured.

"I didn't know you were such good friends. That's awesome."

If Reg's intuition had been as powerful as she said it was, she should have been able to discern the strong friendship between them, especially with her knowing Erin so well.

"Yeah. We're just going to visit for a few minutes, and then I'll be heading to bed. We need to start work pretty early in the morning…"

Reg didn't take the hint. Instead, she settled in, making herself comfortable in the other recliner. "So, what's been going on with you lately?" she asked Erin. "We kind of talked about what I'm up to, but you didn't say what's up with you."

Erin blinked at her. "Well… running the bakery. That takes up most of my time. I'm up really early, work until evening, and then have a short break before bed and starting all over again."

"I don't get how you ended up with the bakery. Did you buy it? Is it like… your own start-up? I know you liked to cook, but I never thought you'd have a place of your own. Pretty hard for a foster to get up capital like that."

"It was my aunt. Clementine. She left it to me in her will. It was a tea shop when she was running it, but I didn't want to run a tea shop, I wanted a gluten-free bakery. So that's what I did."

"The muffins are good." Reg patted her stomach, as if she'd just eaten one, instead of having consumed it early in the day. "If everything else measures up, I can see why it's popular. Normally, I see gluten-free, and I think 'cardboard.' But your baking is really nice."

"Thanks. I hope I can keep growing it. I notice we've started to get some out-of-town traffic lately." Erin glanced over at Vic for her input.

"You're right," Vic agreed. "Seeing more and more people from towns nearby where people have heard there are good gluten-free treats to be had in Bald Eagle Falls. If we can get more and more of those people, we don't have to rely just on the Bald Eagle Falls residents, which would be really good."

"Especially with Charley trying to reopen The Bake Shoppe," Erin agreed.

"Who is Charley?" Reg asked.

"My half-sister. I just found her recently. She was my mom's daughter, but not my dad's, and I never knew about her. She inherited a bakery from her dad's side, or half of it, and she wants to open it up again as soon as she can. And I guess they're doing the transmittal before too long, which means she'll be able to open it if she wants to. As long as Davis, her brother and the owner of the other half of the bakery, doesn't object." Erin glanced over at Vic. "She wants to get full ownership, but I guess she'll be fine just to have control of it. She'll get it open as soon as she can, and then we'll have competition."

"What does she need to do to get full ownership?" Reg asked, her eyes shrewd. "Buy out her brother?"

"That would do it," Erin admitted. "But what she really wants to do is to take it away from him without paying for it. She wants to prove that he had something to do with killing his brother, and he can't profit from his crime."

"Ah," Reg nodded sagely. "Makes sense."

Erin was a little surprised at Reg's interest in business matters. The Reg of the past had always been in it for fun and fast money, and things like building a business would not have interested her. But maybe she was maturing, and she was getting interested in more than just quick, easy money.

"I still think she'll do it," Vic said. "Prove that Davis was involved in Trenton's murder, I mean. She's driven."

"And what do you do besides the bakery?" Reg asked. "You can't work all the time. What do you do for your own entertainment?"

Erin had a hard time answering that one. She spent almost every second of the day at the bakery or wrapped up in running it somehow. If she wasn't baking and selling her wares, she was working on paying the bills, writing ad copy, working through marketing plans, or thinking ahead to the next party or holiday.

"Well... not a lot," she admitted. "It takes up most of my time."

"Solving murders," Vic suggested.

Erin shot her a look. "I don't solve murders," she said quickly.

"Well, not all of them, but you've got a pretty good track record so far."

"Solving murders?" Reg repeated with wide-eyed interest. "How many have you solved?"

"Uh... well, Angela Plaint; her son Trevor; her husband, Adam; and my father. Charley's boyfriend. Joelle Biggs. That's it."

"Six," Reg counted. "And how long have you lived here?"

"About a year."

"That's one every two months. That's amazing. I know full-time PI's who don't have a record like that."

"It's just been… luck. I haven't been looking to solve murder cases and haven't been paid for it. I just sort of… fall into things…"

"You get any money for it?"

"No. I was trying to stay out of prison for most of them!"

Reg laughed. "Right in the midst of things, our Erin. Man, I miss you, sister! You always did get into the most interesting scrapes."

"Not without your help."

"Come on, you would have gotten into trouble whether I was there or not, am I right? You just couldn't help yourself."

"No," Erin protested. "I was quiet and kept to myself. I wouldn't have gotten into any trouble without your help."

"Ha!" Reg looked at Vic for help. "Tell me you don't believe her. You've seen how it happens, haven't you? She just attracts trouble, like bees to honey."

"Well…" Vic screwed up her nose and tried to think of what to say. "It's not that she's trying to, though. So I don't know if it counts."

"It counts. It goes to show that she can find trouble all by herself without me at her side."

"I suppose," Vic admitted.

"You're supposed to be on my side, traitor!" Erin said with mock hurt.

There was a knock at the door and they all looked up. Erin wasn't expecting anyone else. She went to the door and peeked through the peephole, expecting to see Terry, or maybe Mary Lou. Other people just didn't stop by for a visit. Not usually. She twisted the deadbolt and opened the door to Bella, standing there looking embarrassed and much smaller than usual.

"Bella? What are you doing here?" Erin couldn't think of what would have brought Bella to the house, especially when she didn't drive.

"Sorry," Bella apologized. "I probably should have called instead of just showing up on your doorstep. It's just, my mom is visiting a friend, and I was with her, but I was getting bored and thinking about things, and I thought I'd stop by here and see…"

Erin waited for her to finish her sentence. "Yes…? See what?"

"See if you'd figured anything out yet about my grandma."

"Uh…" Erin looked at Vic and Reg. "I haven't looked into anything. I told you, I'm not a detective. I don't think I'm going to get very far looking into an old case."

"You did before. You figured out what happened with Adam Plaint."

"Well… but I had Clementine's journal to help me out there. I wouldn't have known where the boys hid the body without the journal. And I wouldn't have known about the men being switched, if it wasn't for Bertie Braceling being involved. It was just luck…"

"But you said Clementine talked about my grandma and grandpa in her journal. So you do have a starting point. Couldn't you at least… think about it? Read it over and try to imagine what had happened?"

Reg had a big grin on her face and was obviously enjoying the fix Erin was in.

"I'm not a detective," Erin repeated, giving Reg a glare. "I'm just a baker."

"Why won't anyone talk about what happened to my grandma? Doesn't anybody care? I know it happened twenty years ago, but she must have had friends. People who cared about what happened to her."

"The journal didn't say what happened to her," Erin said. "Just that she disappeared, and Clementine was concerned about your grandpa and what had happened."

"I want to know. If you can find out what happened to her, then I can stop worrying about the barn."

"The barn?" Reg asked, leaning forward. "What about the barn?"

"It's haunted," Bella said. "Maybe if we can figure out what happened to my grandma, then she'll be able to rest, and I won't have to be scared of the barn anymore."

Reg's eyes turned to Erin, eyes inquiring whether Bella was really serious. Erin gave a slight nod.

"Maybe *I* could help you," Reg offered.

"How? Erin is the one who is good at figuring this kind of stuff out."

"I'm sure she is. Did you know I'm her sister? And I'm trained to find things like this out. To see what other people can't see. I have a special talent."

"Really?" Bella's eyes were big. "How can you find things out?"

"I have a talent." Reg was wearing a nightgown rather than the headscarf she had been wearing earlier in the day, and had washed all of her makeup off, so there was no way for Bella to guess about her newfound psychic abilities. "What if I could talk to your grandmother?"

"You can't," Bella said, frustrated with having to explain it all over again. "She's dead. Or disappeared. She must be dead, or she wouldn't be haunting the barn. But I don't know what happened to her or how to fix it so that she can be at peace."

"If she's there, I can talk to her," Reg promised. "You just take me to your barn and I'll talk to her. We'll figure out what happened to her and what to do next."

Bella's big eyes got bigger and rounder. "You can talk to haints?"

Erin glanced over at Vic, amused. Score one for local dialect. But Reg was still in the dark about what a haint was. She frowned and blinked.

"Ghosts," Erin told her. "She's asking if you can talk to ghosts."

Reg nodded solemnly. "Yes! Exactly. If you take me there, I will talk to her, and we'll sort this all out."

Bella looked suddenly cautious. "I can't bring anyone to the farm unless my mom says."

Reg's brows drew down. "You're not allowed to invite anyone to your house?"

"Uh…" Bella shifted nervously. "No. Not really. I can check with Mom, she might say it's okay. But you can't tell her that you're coming to talk to my Grandma, or she'll say no."

"Doesn't your mother want to find out what happened to her mother? Why would she block it?"

"Talking to ghosts is…" Bella looked around dramatically, "that's *spiritualism*," she whispered. "Mom would never agree to that. And she's never wanted to talk to me about what happened to Grandma. She clams right up. Nobody knows what happened, but I think Mom's afraid that… people would think badly of us, if word got out."

"But people know your grandma disappeared," Erin said. "My aunt knew. What do people think happened? That she just fell off the face of the earth?"

"She's always kept it real quiet. No one ever proved that she died or that there was any foul play. She just… wasn't around anymore."

"Maybe I can come out there one day when your mom isn't around," Reg suggested. "We wouldn't have to get permission and she would never know about it. That way we wouldn't be stirring things up. I could talk to your grandma and send her on her way. Then you wouldn't have to worry about being afraid of the barn."

Bella nodded her understanding. "I guess… it's just that… she's almost always home. She doesn't go out very much, and when she does, it isn't for long. I don't know when the next time is going to be."

"The opportunity will present itself," Reg promised. "You'll just have to be patient while we wait for it. It will happen. And when it does, you give me a call." Reg felt for her pockets, but then realized she was wearing Clementine's night gown. "I'll get you my number, wait here for just a minute."

She disappeared into the guest room, and returned a minute later with a business card, which she insisted Bella take. "How else are you going to call me? Keep that. Let me know when she's gone, and I'll come straight out."

Bella handled the business card as though it were hot, holding it gingerly by the edges. "I don't want my mom to see this…"

"Then memorize it and get rid of it. Just make sure you know it when the time comes."

Bella stared down at the card, nodding dubiously.

CHAPTER 8

After Bella was headed back on her way, Erin said her goodbyes to Vic. Neither of them could say much in front of Reg, but they were familiar enough with each other's facial expressions and body language to communicate the basics. Erin didn't like Reg having anything to do with Bella. Vic wasn't sure what she felt about Reg herself, but she was willing to give Reg a chance and see how things turned out. They would talk about it at the bakery in the morning, where they could do it without being overheard.

"Nice to meet you," Vic told Reg, giving her a social hug where they barely touched each other. "I guess I'll see you around."

"Maybe we'll come see you at your house next time," Reg offered. "Save you the long trip."

Vic gave a little laugh, but her eyes when she looked at Erin were worried. She didn't want her sanctuary disturbed by the likes of Reg Rawlins, medium.

Erin gave a wide yawn, motioning Vic toward the door and herding Reg into the guest room. "You found everything you needed? I'll see you in the morning… you can call or come by the bakery once you're up and around, I assume you won't be when we get up. And don't worry if you think you hear a baby crying or someone being murdered. Erin looked down at Orange Blossom. "I'll try to keep Blossom quiet, but he can be very loud and bothersome. We haven't had a guest before, so I'm not sure how he's going to react. Hopefully, he'll just come and sleep with me like usual and won't bother you."

"He won't bother me," Reg said, though her nostrils flared a little and Erin suspected Reg didn't want anything to do with a cat. "I like cats. He could come and keep me company."

"I'll try to keep him quiet," Erin repeated. She called Orange Blossom to follow her to the bedroom and shut the door most of the way behind him. He could still get out if he wanted to, but she hoped he would just settle in and sleep when she did.

Wednesday, morning Erin was surprised by the delivery of her new freezer. She had the deliveryman put it into position and plugged it in to start it cooling. It was a beautiful, modern-looking steel and glass affair, and Erin could just imagine what it was going to look like filled with frozen treats. While finding gluten-free ice cream and popsicles was not difficult, she would be able to offer the vegans and dairy-allergic and intolerant some lovely dairy-free options.

"That's going to be popular when the heat hits," Vic commented.

Erin, quite warm enough with the late spring weather and the bakery ovens, wiped her forehead with the back of her arm.

"We'll start stocking it tomorrow," she promised.

Vic grinned. Taller than Erin, she didn't have to watch what she ate quite as carefully, and she had a sweet tooth. She would enjoy sampling Erin's new creations.

Terry stopped by in the afternoon for a cookie and a water bottle refill. He leaned on the counter and watched K9 lap water from his bowl.

"So, you got yourself a cold case," he commented.

Erin breathed in sharply. She had told Terry she wasn't going to look into Grandma Prost's disappearance. How had he found out so quickly that she had agreed to look a little further? Erin hadn't exactly said she would take the case, but she was curious to see what she could find out, just asking around a little and studying Clementine's journal.

"Uh… how did you hear that?"

"Word gets around town pretty quickly," Terry pointed out. Gossip did spread through Bald Eagle Falls like wildfire. All Erin had to do was sneeze, and everyone would be asking her how her cold was for the next three days. "Especially where it involves desserts," Terry added.

Erin stared at him, bewildered.

"Your cold case," he repeated, nodding to the freezer and raising an eyebrow.

"Oh, that!" Erin said with sudden understanding. "Yes, of course. We're going to fill it up with all kinds of tasty desserts."

Terry studied her. "What did you think I was talking about?"

"Nothing. I just didn't connect that you were talking about the freezer."

"What else would I be talking about?" His eyes narrowed as he thought about it. "Don't tell me you've gotten yourself mixed up in another investigation!"

"Well… no… not really. I mean, I don't know that it was a murder. No one is sure what happened. It's probably nothing at all. It's not like I can go back and interview people from twenty years ago."

"Bella's grandmother? I thought you told her no."

"I did, at first, but then… I came across it in Clementine's journal. I was curious when Bella had just been talking about her…"

"Your Aunt Clementine must have been just as big a busybody as you are! What did she write in her journal?"

"I haven't read all of it yet. I might have to pull out the next volume or two, depending on how long things went on before everyone forgot about it."

"You really should just mind your own business."

"I wasn't reading the journal because of Bella's grandma, I was reading it to see what Clementine had to say about my parents and about me. Family history."

"You should just leave it alone."

"Bella wants me to look into it. It isn't like I'm digging around in something that's going to upset people." Erin remembered Bella's concern about her mother not knowing anything about Reg going to the barn to talk to Grandma's ghost and felt a twinge of guilt. Bella wanted Erin to investigate, but Erin had a feeling Bella's mom wouldn't want her to have anything to do with it.

"Erin, no good can come of poking around in old murders. I thought you would have figured that out by now."

"We don't even know it's murder; she just disappeared. She might have left town. Maybe she had a fight with her husband. Maybe she's living the good life in California. It could give the family closure."

His brows drew down. "You know she's not living in California. She would have had some kind of communication with her family by now."

Erin hesitated. "Clementine's journal did kind of assume that she was dead. Either she had passed naturally, or her husband had had something to do with it. But there wasn't enough evidence for the sheriff to get in and have a look around."

"And you think there will be now, twenty years later?"

"No. We're not looking for the police to go in there and tear everything apart. I don't know. I'll talk to Bella. Maybe talk to some people who were around at the time and might know something about what was going on between Grandma and Grandpa. Talk to Bella's mom, if she'll see me. And probably… I won't find anything. Maybe there's nothing to find. But Bella did ask me for help. She's old enough to make her own decision."

"Is she paying you?"

"No, this is just a favor. Doing something for a friend. I don't want anything for it. I'm not a private investigator. I'm just going to have a look. That's all."

K9 had finished his water and his biscuit and sat on his haunches, watching them. Terry signaled K9 to go with him. "I really wish you wouldn't, Erin. I don't think you should be poking your nose into this."

"Don't look now," Vic said, watching a couple of figures approaching the door. "This looks like trouble."

Erin looked to see who it was. Melissa stepped in the door, her dark curls bouncing around her face, smile bright and cheerful. She was followed close behind by Charley.

Charley had the same petite build and pleasant, small facial features as Erin. She had the same dark brown hair and her eyes were the same shape and slant. Beyond that, they could have been strangers. Charley didn't carry herself the same way as Erin, she didn't talk the same way or have the same mannerisms. They weren't cookie cutter copies of each other. Just enough features to be familiar to each other.

Erin had longed for a blood sister when she was a little girl. Maybe she had known that her mother was expecting when she'd had her accident, or maybe it was just a natural fantasy for a lonely child shuttled from one family to another. It was normal for her to want someone like her, someone she had a bond with. Something to anchor her.

But Charley was trouble. She walked in with Melissa, looking like normal and natural friends, maybe a mother-daughter pair, considering the difference in their ages. There was nothing to suggest that Charley had been in an organized crime syndicate. Where Erin had stayed soft, raw from her experiences, Charley had been hardened. She had, as far as Erin could tell, been raised by loving, doting, law-abiding parents, but had rebelled and gone badly off the rails.

Having been kicked out by the Dyson clan after the murder of their heir apparent and their discovery that Charley was blood related to the Jackson clan, Charley had lost her place and position in the Tennessee underworld and was suddenly on her own with no real prospects, except for her half share in The Bake Shoppe, inherited from Trenton Plaint, her brother. She was determined to turn that into a successful venture. Preferably by taking over Davis Plaint's half share as well.

The friendship with Melissa was something new, but it was obvious that they were together and hadn't just shown up at Auntie Clem's at the same time. Erin agreed with Vic that it likely meant trouble.

Pushing all negative thoughts aside, Erin gave the two of them a welcoming smile. "Melissa, Charley! Good to see you again. What can we help you with today?"

"Melissa has been telling me all about her job with the police department," Charley commented. "She's been telling me all about the interesting cases that they've been handling over the last year or so. So many interesting twists and turns!"

Melissa liked to make it sound like she was a police officer herself. In fact, she just helped part time with some of the administrative tasks Clara Jones couldn't keep up with or didn't want to do. Filing, transcription, photocopying. A police department ran on paper. Unfortunately, Erin had been involved in several of those interesting cases over the past year. She didn't exactly want Charley to know all of the details or to think that Erin was some kind of criminal herself.

"Yes, it's been an interesting time in Bald Eagle Falls," Erin agreed, keeping the smile pasted to her face. "I already told you about most of that…"

"I think you might have left a few things out," Charley returned. She had the look of a mean cheerleader saying something nasty while pretending to be the all-American girl.

Erin looked at the display case. "We've got fresh brownies," she told Melissa. "I know you're always partial to the ones with white chocolate chips."

"Oh, the dominos," Melissa said, zooming in to look at them. "Have you seen these, Charley? They're so good, and they look so classy! Like brownies, that got all dressed up."

Erin nodded, smiling.

Charley looked at Erin for a moment longer, and then joined Melissa in looking over the day's baking and deciding what they wanted. They didn't seem to be there for any take-home baking, just a treat to eat while they visited. Erin rang up their purchases, exchanging a dubious look with Vic. *Just what was Charley up to now?* She wasn't the type to hang out with a more mature woman just for kicks. She might go out for margaritas with her pals back in Moose River, but hanging out with Melissa was something different.

After making their purchases, Melissa and Charley sat down at one of the little tables at the front of the shop to eat and gossip. They weren't loud enough for Erin to make out much of the conversation, but they seemed very chummy and comfortable with each other.

CHAPTER 9

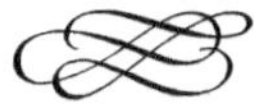

hen Bella was next covering an afternoon shift, Erin made use of the quieter time between customers to get Bella talking about her family.

"I don't know your mom at all, just to wave and say 'hi' to. What's she like?"

"I don't know. She's pretty strict, I guess. But we get along okay. I know teenage girls and their moms usually have a lot of tensions and arguments, but that's never been us."

"I don't get the feeling that you're particularly rebellious."

Bella grinned. "No. I'm home with her most nights, not out with friends drinking or tipping cows. I have to push sometimes to get her to trust me to handle myself, but I can usually get through to her."

"And no dad in the picture?"

"No. She's never said much about my biological father. She said it was a mistake, that they were never really together. I don't know if that means he was a one night stand, but I kind of get that feeling."

"There are so many kids being raised by single parents, it's not really such a big deal anymore, is it?"

"No. I think if you've got one good parent, you're in pretty good shape. It's the people who don't have anyone they can rely on that I feel sorry for."

"Yeah." Erin nodded, thinking back to the long list of foster parents she had lived with. Some better, some worse, but no one permanent. No one who would be there for her once she turned eighteen.

"Sorry," Bella said. "I didn't mean you. I just meant… people."

Erin gave her a reassuring smile. "It's okay. Things could have been worse."

"So… yeah. Mom's okay. She can be hard-nosed about things, but she's just trying to protect me."

Erin nodded. "And you don't remember your grandparents at all?"

"No. Grandma was gone before I was born. I guess Grandpa died when I was still a baby. Maybe a year old? I have a picture of him holding me, but I don't actually remember him."

"What did he die of?"

"Just old age, I guess." Bella gave a shrug.

Erin frowned, thinking about it. "Old age? How old is your mom?"

"Uh… not quite fifty."

"Then your grandparents, if they were thirty-something when your mom was born, would be eighty now. But they died when you were a baby; they would have been in their sixties. People don't die of old age in their sixties. Not in this century."

"Oh." Bella thought about that while she moved baked goods around in the display case to fill the empty spaces. "Well, I always thought of them as old. The picture of my grandpa holding me, he looks ancient."

"Your mom never said what he died from?"

"I don't think so. It's not exactly something that comes up in conversation."

"Maybe you could ask her about it. Say your doctor wants to know your family history."

"Yeah, maybe. But Doc has been around here longer than I have. He's probably the one who declared Grandpa dead, if they actually do that in real life."

"Maybe develop an interest in family history? I could show you some of the books my Aunt Clementine pulled together. Naomi at The Book Nook has some genealogy starter sets. You start putting in the names, dates of birth and death, start prompting your mom to tell you what she remembers about them, so you can record it for posterity…"

"I could do that," Bella agreed, brightening. "That would actually be pretty cool. I'd like to have some kind of record. With it just being me and

Mom at the farm, I feel sometimes like I don't have any other family. But I know our family has been in Bald Eagle Falls for a long time. I think the farm has been in the family since before the Civil War."

"That's quite a history. Looking through all of the records that Clementine kept has made me view myself and my family differently. I never had any family before I came here, and now… I can look through those books and see generations and generations."

"Maybe you even have some Prosts in your line!"

Erin grinned. "I wouldn't doubt it. You and I could be fifth cousins."

"That would be so cool. I'd love to be related to you."

The bells over the door jangled, and Erin looked over to see Mary Lou coming in.

Mary Lou had always been prim and pressed and presentable. Everything she wore looked like it had been tailored just for her. When Roger's behavior had grown more erratic, Erin had seen Mary Lou looking tired and worn for the first time. Her clothes had not been as neat and carefully presented and Mary Lou had been flustered and irritable.

Now that Roger was under state care so she could get a good night's sleep again and didn't have to be worrying about what he was doing all the time, Mary Lou once more looked calm and collected; but Erin felt that something about her had changed. It wasn't obvious. Maybe a little more gray in her roots or deeper wrinkles around her mouth. Or maybe it was just the way she held herself, a little more tentative, eyes a little lost or sad.

"Hi, Mary Lou," Erin greeted, putting as much genuine warmth into her voice as she could. She wanted Mary Lou to know that she harbored no bad feelings toward her or Roger. What had happened hadn't been Mary Lou's fault; it hadn't really even been Roger's. It was Joelle's meddling and threats that had triggered Roger's reaction. He would have done just fine living a peaceful life and making the Jam Lady jams and would not have been a threat to any of them if she hadn't gone messing around and making threats. "How are you today? How are your boys?"

"We're all doing better than could be expected," Mary Lou assured her. Her return smile wavered only slightly. "Everything is just fine."

"I'm glad. What can I help you with today? Something for supper, or a treat for your menfolk?"

Mary Lou gazed at the display case. "I should do both. Some of that harvest loaf for lunchboxes. A couple of pizza shells. Maybe some dinner rolls? Just plain white?"

Bella went to work packaging it all for Mary Lou.

"And something sweet?" Erin suggested.

Mary Lou let out a breath, her eyes glistening. She stared into the display as if she were facing the most important decision of her life and wasn't quite ready for it. "Erin…"

Erin hurried around the end of the counter to join Mary Lou on the other side. She grasped Mary Lou's arm and gave it a squeeze. "There… it's okay. Everything is going to be fine." She hugged Mary Lou around the shoulders, pulling her close.

"Oh, this is silly." A couple of tears raced down Mary Lou's cheeks, and she rummaged in her handbag for a tissue. "Why can't I make a simple decision?" She found a tissue and dabbed delicately at her eyes, trying not to smear her makeup. "I just feel like… I can't possibly be expected to make one more decision."

"No. No, you shouldn't have to. It can't be easy for you, having to take responsibility for everybody else. How can I help you? Do you want me to just put together a variety box? You know those boys will eat anything, they're not picky about it."

Mary Lou sniffled. She nodded and wiped her nose. "Yes, of course. That would be just fine. Only make sure you put two of each thing—" Mary Lou cut herself off. She frowned and shook her head. "No, don't. The boys are old enough that they can work it out between them who gets what. I don't have to make sure they both have exactly the same thing, do I? That's just silly. What a mother hen I am."

"You're just trying to take care of them and raise them right. You want to be fair to them. They know that."

"Life isn't fair. Maybe that's why I felt like it was so important. Maybe I was trying to make up for life not being fair, us losing everything like we did. But you know what? They're stronger than that. They can certainly navigate through the treacherous waters of choosing their own desserts."

Erin nodded and gave Mary Lou's shoulders another squeeze. She wasn't sure how long she should stay there and comfort Mary Lou, or if she should go back around the counter and package up the treats for the boys. Mary Lou patted Erin's hand.

"You're so sweet, Erin. It must be all the sugar you use. I'm okay now. I don't want to hold you up."

Erin nodded and let go of Mary Lou. She went back around the counter to put together a box of cookies and desserts for Mary Lou's teenagers. "They sure are getting big," she told Mary Lou. "Every time I see them, I marvel at how grown up they look."

Mary Lou nodded. "Oh, yes. They're a big help to me. A comfort to have them around. There are some days when I just can't do anything. I get home from work, and I just want to crawl into bed and pull the blanket up over my head. I freeze up and I just can't function. But they're always there, to help take over and look after their poor mother."

Erin counted out the items in the box.

"Go ahead and make it a baker's dozen," Mary Lou said. "Let them figure out what to do with the last one." Then she hesitated, reconsidering. "Oh, maybe not, maybe just twelve." Then her resolution hardened. "Thirteen. They can figure out whether to share the last one, or negotiate, or just toss it in the garbage. They're almost grown men."

Erin smiled and put the last cookie into the box. "Thirteen, there you go," she announced, before Mary Lou could change her mind again.

Bella looked shyly at Mary Lou. "I've always liked Josh and Campbell," she offered. "They're nice boys, always smiling and friendly. Lots of boys…" Bella looked down at her generous figure, "lots of them can be real jerks. But Campbell and Josh have never been that way. You'd be proud of them."

Mary Lou gave Bella a grateful smile. "Thank you! It's always good to know that they're behaving properly when they're not under mother's watchful eye. You never know what kids are going to behave like when they're not being supervised. You hope they'll do you proud, but you can never be sure!"

Bella blushed slightly. "My mom probably thinks the same thing. But I try to behave like she would want me to." She looked over at Erin, maybe thinking about trying to find out what had happened to her grandmother when her mother so clearly did not want her to. "Mostly, anyway. I try. I wouldn't want her to be ashamed of me."

"I've never seen you do anything that should embarrass your mother," Mary Lou assured her. "I've always thought you were a responsible, mature girl."

Erin went to the register to ring everything up and handed Mary Lou her bags. "There you go. Take care, okay?"

Mary Lou nodded, her eyes glistening again. "I will, Erin. Thank you so much for your help."

The bells jingled as Mary Lou left.

Bella sighed. "That just makes me want to go hug my mom. I've never felt like I am less fortunate because I don't have a dad, but I never thought much about how hard it must have been for my mom to take all that responsibility herself. It couldn't have been easy. Now, I'm all grown up, and she really doesn't have to do anything for me, even if she insists she wants to. But when I was little… for her to work and take care of the farm and raise me all on her own… I never thought about how hard that must have been."

"Well, like you said, she did a good job. And I don't think it's bad that you want to find out more about your grandma and your ancestors. Wanting to know the details about where you came from and what those people were like, that's natural. That's showing that they're important to you. It's not like you're disrespecting your mother." Erin tidied up, even though everything was already neat and laid out properly. "I can tell you… when I was a teenager, I told more than one foster mom 'you're not my real mother.' Like they could help it. Like they weren't just trying to raise someone else's thankless child."

"You couldn't have been that bad," Bella said. "You're so sweet, I can't imagine you ever saying a mean word to anyone."

"Not true, I'm afraid. I've said lots of mean and nasty things in my life. And foster moms definitely took the brunt of it. Foster moms, social workers, teachers, foster sisters…" Erin thought about Reg. How many times had Erin told Reg that she hated her in a fit of teenage pique? How many times had she tried to push Reg away? And why? Because she was annoying? Because she had yet another idea for the two of them to make boatloads of cash? Or was it just teen hormones? Any two hormonal girls living in close quarters with each other would have behaved the same way, blood related or not. "Growing up is hard. I felt so lost and alone and I took it out on whoever was closest."

Bella nodded sagely.

"See what you can find out from your mom," Erin said. "Maybe this whole thing is a way for the two of you to get closer."

CHAPTER 10

$\mathcal{E}$rin traced the lines in the diary. Clementine's long, looping hand was a little difficult to make out at times, written so closely together that the ascenders and descenders got tangled up with each other.

Cindy Prost is in town to see what she can do with Ezekiel. I think it was probably Lottie Sturm who got in touch with her, the two of them were always pretty close. Cindy came into the tea room the other day, but seems to be at a complete loss as to what to do with her father. He won't tell her what happened to Martha, insisting that she is still alive and just out of town. Cindy knows very well it isn't true. Martha never left the farm without Ezekiel in her whole life, why would she start now? But she's just at sixes and sevens as to what to do. Ezekiel won't leave the farm and she has no proof that he's done anything wrong or that he's become unbalanced.

Lottie figures Martha is probably buried in the barn or the garden, but there is no way to know for sure. Cindy hasn't come across anything suspicious at the farm other than her mother's absence. Ezekiel seems happy to have Cindy in town and is putting back on some of the weight he has lost since Martha's disappearance. He obviously wasn't eating very much without someone to prepare meals for him. How a grown man can be so helpless, I have no idea. At least my mother always taught her boys how to take care of themselves. Even if you get married, there's no guarantee you'll be with that person for the rest of your life or that they'll be able to take care of you.

464

I suggested to Cindy that if she needed any physical labor done at the farm that her father wasn't doing or wasn't up to, that she give Davis Plaint a call. I think he could use the attention and a little bit of cash to help him out. Trenton always seems to have new clothes, but Davis looks grubby and worn, like he's been sleeping in the rough rather than living at home with his mother and siblings. I've asked the sheriff to check in on the summer house at regular intervals to make sure no one is using it illicitly.

Erin read over the spare account of Bella's mother, Cindy, returning home to take care of Ezekiel.

What was it that made Clementine and apparently Lottie Sturm and Cindy Prost so sure that Martha Prost was dead? If she had died, wouldn't Ezekiel have told someone? Even if he had done something to hurt her, would he really keep insisting that she was alive and well and would be home soon? Was he in denial? Was it the beginning of dementia? Perhaps, like Roger, his behavior had been erratic for some time, and Martha Prost had been doing the best she could to take care of him and to hide his condition from everyone else. Maybe in a moment of anger or confusion he had turned on her but, having hurt her, he couldn't admit to himself what had happened and made up a story to go with it.

Erin wrote down a few notes in her own notebook. Even with Vic's teasing, she couldn't bring herself to keep her notes and lists on her phone rather than hard copy. She was sure that if she put them on her phone, they would end up being erased. Having her thoughts on paper, all neatly marshaled before her, gave Erin a kind of comfort and reassurance. If it was all down in black and white, she wouldn't lose or forget it. She could rest her anxious brain, taking peace in the fact that everything was in proper order.

Lottie Sturm was Cindy's generation, older than Erin. Erin was not close to Lottie, but Lottie did come into the bakery every now and then to pick something up, when she wanted fresh baking and didn't feel like making the trip into the city. Erin had never been favorably impressed with Lottie. She was a mean woman, always out to humiliate Vic or call her down to repentance, to spread some gossip, or otherwise disturb the peace in Bald Eagle Falls. If she had some recollection of what had happened on the Prost farm, some tidbit that Cindy had shared with her or something she had observed herself at the farm, Erin might have to find a way to connect with her.

She wasn't sure she could do that, given the way that Lottie had treated Vic in the past. It felt like a betrayal. Even if she told Vic and Vic understood why she was doing it, Erin wasn't sure she could forgive Lottie's past behavior.

She'd do well to learn a lesson from Melissa and Charley, putting any past differences behind them and apparently enjoying some time together.

～

There were footsteps behind her, and Erin turned to see Reg coming up the stairs into the attic. For a few minutes, she had actually forgotten that Reg was there.

"Oh, hi Reg."

"Hi yourself. There's a woman here to see you."

Erin looked at the time on her phone. It obviously wasn't Vic, who would have just let herself in and whom Reg had met before. There weren't a lot of other people who would call on Erin in the evening when it was getting so close to her bedtime.

"It must be Adele."

Erin shut the journal and put it neatly away. She followed Reg back down the stairs. After pushing the stairs back up into the ceiling, she went out to the living room. It was indeed Adele. She looked uncomfortable to be waiting for Erin in the living room. She often made a cup of tea for Erin before bed, and the formality of waiting like a guest didn't suit her.

"Erin, I didn't know you had company. I'm sorry to interrupt you."

"No, not at all. Adele, this is Reg. She's just staying here for a few days while she looks for a place of her own. She's... thinking of moving to Bald Eagle Falls. Reg, this is Adele." Erin wasn't sure how to introduce Adele. As her groundskeeper? Her tenant? "A friend of mine."

"I think I've heard your name in town," Reg said slowly, looking Adele up and down with a suspicious, cat-like gaze.

Adele was obviously also taking Reg's measure. Reg didn't like to go to bed as early as Erin and hadn't yet changed for bed, which meant she was still in her fortune-teller costume, looking ready to run a carnival booth at a moment's notice.

"What is it you do?" Adele asked baldly. "Are you... a practicer of the arts?"

Erin looked from one friend to the other, the tension drawing out between them.

Reg gave a dramatic, mysterious smile. "Are you a kindred spirit, maybe?"

Adele wasn't in costume. She didn't wear costumes. But she did tend to wear long, flowing dresses and a hooded cloak. Her skin had a pale, ageless cast to it. To Erin, Adele looked just like she would have expected a modern witch to look. But as most of Bald Eagle Falls hadn't immediately identified her as one, Erin figured she was biased by her prior knowledge.

Adele raised her eyebrows at Reg's flamboyant outfit. "Perhaps *not.*"

"I'm a medium. I foretell the future, read palms, communicate with the dead, whatever my clients need."

"Your clients? So you do this for recompense?"

"If you've got it, you might as well use it. You don't use your... talents to support yourself?"

"I sell some crafts and herbs," Adele said slowly. "My... faith... is not for sale."

Reg snorted. "Oh, you're very good," she said admiringly. "I'd almost believe it. A girl can't expect things to just fall into her lap these days. We have to take care of ourselves, don't we? You sound like a real soul sister." Reg looked over at Erin. "I might have known you wouldn't drift that far from your roots. You give me a big lecture about how you don't scam people, but your close friend is doing just the same thing we always did. Not quite as high and mighty as you were pretending, are you?"

Erin looked over at Adele, worried she was going to be offended. An attack by Erin's guest might as well be an attack by Erin herself. She was worried Adele would think that Erin had been talking about her, but Erin always avoided any mention of Adele and what she was or wasn't.

"Are you aware of the power you are playing with?" Adele asked Reg. "Do you really know what forces a medium employs?"

Erin didn't believe in magic or sorcery or any other unseen powers, whether they were those discussed by Adele or by one of Erin's Christian friends. She believed what she could see and hear and touch. And Reg didn't believe it either. She might pretend to for her scam, but she knew there wasn't actually anything to it.

Reg laughed. "You're even better than I thought. I know my 'powers,' don't you worry about that. I know exactly what I'm doing. People will see and believe what they want to."

Adele shook her head. She made a slight movement toward the door. "If you play with fire, you are going to get burned. Don't say I didn't warn you."

Adele gave Erin a nod and left the house. Erin wanted to hurry after Adele and reassure her that she was not mixed up in Reg's hocus-pocus. Just because Reg was staying in Erin's house, that didn't mean Erin agreed with her about anything. They were just sisters, and Reg had called in a sister's privilege. Erin shook her head at Reg.

"You were not very nice to my friend," she snapped. All at once, she was fifteen and furious over Reg getting her in trouble yet again. "I would expect better from a house guest. But I guess you don't understand southern hospitality. You don't know how to treat a sister; how would you know how to treat my friend?" Erin's eyes burned with angry tears and her throat constricted. "I expected better from you, Regina Rawlins!"

Reg withdrew into herself, shrinking before Erin's eyes. She ducked her head and looked ashamed. "I wasn't trying to insult your friend." Under Erin's stern gaze, she turned pink. "Okay, maybe I was. I just thought… she shouldn't have… okay, I shouldn't have behaved that way. I was rude to your friend. I'll apologize the next time I see her, okay? I'm sorry."

"You're the guest here. You should know how to behave. I did you a favor putting you up. I didn't have to do that. I could have sent you back to the city to find a motel."

"But you wouldn't—Yes, okay, you could have. I didn't think you would be able to turn out your own sister, but you could have just said no, and you probably wanted to. I'll try to be a more gracious guest."

"You'd better," Erin agreed. "Or you'll find yourself out in the street, middle of the night or not."

"Well…" Reg looked at the wall clock ticking away. "It's actually not exactly the middle of the night."

Erin froze her with another stare.

"Okay. It's the middle of the night for you. So I'd better let you get to bed."

Erin glanced to the back of the house. She hadn't had tea with Adele. What about bread and jam with Vic? It was getting late, and Erin should be getting to sleep instead of looking for other things to do. "Yes, I'd better do that. You're in for the night, right?"

Reg shrugged. "There isn't exactly a night life in Bald Eagle Falls, is there? You chose a pretty sleepy town to live in. I wouldn't have pegged you for the quiet life."

If only it were. In the past year, Erin had learned not to take the quiet persona of Bald Eagle Falls at face value. There was always something more sinister bubbling beneath the surface.

"Goodnight," she told Reg. "Keep out of trouble."

"Who, me?" A smile of mischief spread over Reg's face. "What kind of trouble would I get into?"

CHAPTER 11

Bella's tentative invitation to go out to the Prost farm came that Friday, much sooner than Erin had expected. She had figured it would take at least a week or two for Bella to dither around and find a time Reg could put on a show of visiting with Grandma.

Covering up the phone mic, Reg explained to Erin that Bella wanted both of them to go to the farm together. She knew Erin and trusted her judgment and her ability to figure out what had happened twenty years earlier. Erin hesitated, then agreed. While she didn't want to go out at the same time as Reg and appear to be sanctioning her talking to spirits, she didn't know when Bella would be able to arrange for her to go out again. And if she went along with Reg, she could keep an eye on her sister and make sure she didn't go overboard.

"Do you need directions?" Reg asked and, when Erin nodded, Reg got driving instructions for the Prost farm. They would head over in the early evening, when Cindy was going into the city for a doctor's appointment and to run some errands.

"Now you remember she's already scared of ghosts," Erin told Reg sternly once she was off the phone. "I don't want you making her worse. You want to convince her that Grandma's spirit is at peace and no longer haunting the barn, got it?"

470

Reg sighed. "Fine. You know there'd be more repeat business if we drew it out, though."

"We don't want repeat business. We want to help a friend. And you are not going to charge her."

"What? How am I supposed to make the money to get out on my own if you won't let me charge her?"

"This is a favor," Erin repeated.

"Fine. Hopefully, she'll spread the word to all of her friends, and we'll get business out of her that way." Reg scowled. "It's not very hospitable of you to say I can't even earn a living."

"Nice try," Erin told her, unconcerned. Hospitality only stretched so far.

The Prost farm was farther out of town than Erin had expected. She had thought that it would be one of the houses clinging to the outskirts of Bald Eagle Falls, but it was another half hour of driving before they got to the access road. There were three mailboxes at the turnoff from the highway, suggesting to Erin that there were several farms down the road. The Prost farm was, luckily, the first, so they didn't have to rattle their teeth going over the washboard road any farther.

Erin pulled into the graveled clearing in front of the house, where there were vehicles of varying vintages parked or abandoned. Several of them looked like they had been there for decades.

Bella came out of the yellow and white farmhouse that had to be at least a hundred years old. If the Prost family had been on the mountain since before the Civil War, who knew how old it was or how many different farmhouses had stood on the same patch of ground over the past two hundred years.

Bella gave a jerky wave. Erin parked the Challenger and got out. It was obvious on approaching Bella that she was nervous. Maybe she was having second thoughts about having them over. Most likely, about having Reg over.

"Uh, hi Erin. Reg. This is… so weird. I can't believe I'm doing this. Do you really think I should? Maybe I should just leave it alone. Wait until Mom is ready to tell me about her parents. Maybe what happened to

Grandma isn't really the point. Maybe it's just learning about them and the rest of my ancestors."

"If that's what you want," Erin agreed.

Reg gave Erin an irritated look. "I thought you wanted some peace," she told Bella. "Are you going to get peace from a restless ghost just talking about what she used to be like? You could just wait to see if it goes away, but usually restless spirits don't get quieter over time. They just get more insistent. They want the living to pay attention to them when they have something to say."

"Yeah." Bella nodded. Erin could tell she was clenching her jaw, steeling herself for what was to come.

"Maybe we can just visit in the parlor for a few minutes first. Did you find any books or old albums with family pictures?"

"Actually, yes." Bella motioned for Erin and Reg to enter the house with her. Reg glared at Erin.

"Quit trying to sabotage me," she hissed.

"I'm not! I'm just trying to help Bella. I'm not here to put on a show. I'm here to help a friend work through a loss."

"A loss? Her grandma died before she was born. She's not suffering from a loss, believe me."

"It's still a loss. Whether you remember or not, it hurts to lose a loved one."

Reg shook her head stubbornly. They followed Bella into the house.

The interior had been updated, but it was obvious that it was an old building that had been through several renovations and refittings. The big panel TV on the wall was at odds with the rustic interior. There was modern furniture mixed with old hand-turned wooden pieces. There was a startling contrast between the scarred coffee table that had been worn down with hundreds of hands and boots over the years, and the tablet computer laying on top of it.

"Home, sweet home," Bella said, making a wide motion to indicate the house.

"It's very homey," Erin said.

"Have a seat. I'll show you the albums."

Erin and Reg made themselves comfortable at opposite ends of the couch, and Bella sat between them. She flipped through the thick pages of the book, browsing through the faded pictures showing her grandparents, her mother as a little girl, and then eventually a picture of Grandpa holding baby Bella in his lap. He looked much older than he had in the other pictures, thin, his hair sparse, eyes distant behind his glasses. He had just a hint of a smile on his face, looking down at his granddaughter.

"Weren't you just the cutest baby," Erin said. "That's a sweet picture."

Bella ducked her head. "Thank you."

"Did you ask your mom anything about your grandparents since we talked?"

"No, not really. She saw me looking through the albums, and I asked her if she missed them, but…"

"I'm sure she misses them, even after so many years."

Bella nodded. "She said she did. She said she wasn't that much older than me when she lost them," Bella's brows drew down. "But she must have been… in her thirties. Almost twice my age."

Reg laughed. "It's all relative. She means she was too young to lose them, that she wasn't ready to be independent and all on her own so soon."

Bella looked impressed. "Yeah, I guess. I wouldn't want to be all on my own now, either. I've still got so much to learn… and I want to go to college…"

"What do you want to study?" Erin asked.

"Business management. I'd like to get an MBA, but I probably won't be able to do that right away. Need to make some money before I can afford to get a masters."

"Wow. That's quite an undertaking. Not a lot of women go into business administration."

"I think it would be really cool," Bella enthused. "I've always been interested in how businesses work and all of the financial formulas and benchmarks." She shrugged awkwardly. "And baking. I like that too."

"Sounds like you're set to cook the books," Reg offered.

Bella giggled. "No way, I'm not getting involved in anything shady. I'll only use my powers for good."

The conversation gradually petered out, and Erin was trying to figure out how to tactfully ask Bella for more information about her grandmother, and maybe a tour around the property and the barn. There wasn't much she could get from sitting on the couch looking at old photos.

"Do you have anything that belonged to your grandma?" Reg asked. "I think it's time…"

Bella turned a shade paler. She'd been relaxing and having a good time and was maybe trying to convince herself that she wasn't actually going to have to deal with her grandmother's ghost.

"Something that belonged to her? I don't know…"

"Maybe an article of clothing? Jewelry? Hairbrush? Your mom must have kept some of her things."

Bella thought about it for a minute, then nodded. "Uh… yeah. My mom has this locket that used to be Grandma's. It even has a lock of her hair in it, from when she was a baby."

"Perfect. That makes it even better."

Bella didn't move.

"Go get it," Reg encouraged.

"It's in my mom's room."

"Okay."

"I'm… not supposed to get into her stuff."

Reg scowled. "What are you, two? You're not messing anything up. You're just borrowing it for a few minutes to enhance our chances of speaking to your Grandma. Your mom would want that for you. You're not keeping it, and neither am I. It's going to go right back into the jewelry box when we're done, and she'll never know the difference."

"I don't think she would want me to."

"Of course she would. She wouldn't want to take away an opportunity for you to know your grandma. Never."

"Well…"

"Come on. Tell her, Erin. It's not going to hurt anything for her to borrow her grandma's necklace for a few minutes."

Before Erin could open her mouth to answer, Reg was already talking over her. Maybe she had anticipated that Erin wouldn't be quite so quick to tell Bella to disobey what she knew her mother would want her to do.

"Why don't I go up with you? You can show me where it is, and you won't even have to touch it. Maybe I'll be able to feel something more when I go into her bedroom. Is she in the master bedroom where your grand-mother used to sleep?"

Bella was looking a little dazed as Reg got to her feet and encouraged Bella to stand and take Reg to the bedroom.

"Yes, the master bedroom. It's really not any bigger than the other bedrooms, but that's where grandma and grandpa slept, and probably their parents too, for generations."

With more encouragement from Reg, Bella walked with her to the bedroom to get the necklace. Erin stood up as well and walked around the room looking out the windows and studying the various pictures and knick-knacks. It was only a couple of minutes before Reg was returning with Bella, waving the old locket at Erin.

"Got it. We're going to head out to the barn."

Bella caught Reg's arm. "Do we have to go out to the barn? Can't we just do it here? It's more comfortable, and you've got the locket, so you can call her, right?"

"This is a complex process, Bella. You can't oversimplify things. It's not just like dialing someone up on the phone. If the place that your grandma has been haunting is the barn, then that's where we need to go. Where her energy will be the strongest."

"But I don't really even know if she is. I mean… she might be… but maybe it's somebody else, who's been haunting it for years. Maybe there's something else going on. I don't know for sure that Grandma…"

"Quit being such a scaredy cat," Reg snapped. "Just pull yourself together and come. This is what we're here for."

Cowed, Bella followed along behind Reg. Erin caught up to them and put her arm around Bella.

"It's okay. I don't think there's anything to be scared of. And you can always change your mind. If you don't want to do this, then just tell Reg. Stand up to her and don't let her run over you."

"No…" Bella's voice was small. "She's right. I keep trying to find excuses not to do this, when I know it's what I want. What I need. It's just so frustrating… to want something and to be scared of it at the same time."

"I know."

They followed Reg toward the barn in silence. It was a big red affair, just like on TV and all the picture postcards. But as they got closer to it, Erin saw that it had fallen into disrepair. The wood sagged and buckled. It hadn't been painted in a long time. There were no sounds of animals coming from it.

"What do you farm?" she asked.

"Goats," Bella advised, giving Erin a smile. "Milk, meat, hair, hide. Everything but the bleat, my mom says."

"Where are they?"

Bella moved forward to help Reg to open the barn doors.

"Not in here. They're in the pasture right now. When we bring them in, it's to a more modern barn back there. This one—" She grunted as she pulled the doors open, "—isn't being used anymore."

CHAPTER 12

Stepping into the shadow of the old building, Erin felt a chill. Just the results of being out of the blazing sun. Nothing to be scared of. They were all quiet as Reg led the way into the barn. Bella seemed paralyzed at first. Erin could see the panic in her eyes. She wasn't going in there. The whole point of Reg and Erin being there was to rid the barn of the ghost so that Bella could go in there. She had no intention of going in until the ghost was gone.

Reg spun in a slow circle as if trying to pick up the ghost's psychic vibrations. Erin rolled her eyes. She knew it was all for show. She hoped Bella wasn't actually falling for it. She was a smart girl with a good head on her shoulders, if she'd just stop being scared of spooks.

"Grandma…" Reg called in a low, faint voice. "Grandma Prost, are you here…?"

There was a sudden flapping of wings and Erin jumped. She looked up into the barn's rafters, fully expecting to see them lined with bats, but they were not. Instead, there were birds. They were disturbed by the visitors, but they didn't all rush out in a cloud of mad flapping and shrieking. A few flew out. Others fluttered around, alighting here and there, not settling back in. Others simply eyed the visitors with cold, black eyes and then ignored them.

"Creepy," Bella muttered. "It's all too creepy."

"It's nothing," Erin said lightly, though her heart was still thrumming too fast in her chest, "it's just a few birds. Nothing to be scared of."

Reg walked around, eyes closed, the locket clasped between two hands and held over her head. Whether or not her little haint Geiger counter was supposed to be working or not, Erin didn't know. Reg didn't say whether she could feel the ghost there.

"Grandma Prost," Reg intoned again, "Bella is here to talk to you. She wants to commune with you and to know why you haunt this place. Can you give us a sign that you hear us?"

More flapping of wings distracted Erin from other potential signs. She forced herself to ignore the birds and the overwhelming ammonia smell of their guano, and to look around the barn. There were pieces of equipment that she didn't recognize, that had been sitting there rusting for a long time. Other hand and garden tools that she recognized. A thick layer of dust and frosting of bird excrement over everything made it look as if it had been standing empty for generations, not just since Cindy had returned to her childhood home.

"How long since it has been used?" Erin asked Bella.

"What? Oh, the barn? I don't really know. Not since I can remember. I don't think it was ever used for the goats." Bella poked her head in the door and looked around with more interest and a little less fear. "No, this isn't outfitted for goats. Mostly this is equipment for clearing and gardening."

Erin took a couple of steps so that she was inside the barn. She didn't walk in very far, not wanting to risk a bird taking aim at her head. There was an ancient fridge or freezer on one wall. More garden implements. Some dangerous-looking knives that Erin assumed were for clearing brush or hand-cutting crops. They hadn't been used for a long time, but Erin figured they were probably still sharp enough to do damage. She hoped that Grandma hadn't been killed with something like that. It was hard enough to deal with a death in the family, without it being by gory violence.

Reg saw the direction of Erin's eyes and started walking toward the knives, arms outstretched as if groping in the dark.

"I feel something. It's... drawing me this way..."

"No, it's not," Erin snapped. "It's definitely coming from the other way."

Bella's eyes got wider. "Do you feel it too?" she asked eagerly.

Erin shook her head, but her eyes were on Reg. She didn't want Reg putting any thoughts in Bella's brain. Not thoughts of violent or bloody death.

Reg stopped, then backed up a little, acknowledging Erin's dictates on the matter. She could have told a good story with the knives, but she would find something else instead.

"Grandma Prost… come join me, Bella, it will be stronger if we can magnify the pull by both of us being close together."

"No, I'm just going to stay out here."

"Come inside, Bella. You need to be in here. You have Prost blood and I don't. She wants to know that a member of her family is here, and it isn't just someone trying to fool her."

Erin wanted to ask who would be trying to fool a ghost, but bit her lip and kept her comments to herself.

Bella wavered, her toes just over the line formed by the doors. "I'll just look in. I can see from here."

"Come in. Nothing is going to hurt you. Why would your grandmother do anything to hurt you?"

"I've seen *Poltergeist*. Ghosts are fed by feelings. They take all of the negative feelings from the air around them, and they use their power to make things happen. To hurt people."

"What bad feelings, Bella?" Erin asked softly. "Are there a lot of bad feelings around the farm? In the barn?"

Reg's eyes flickered over to Erin. She liked the role Erin was playing, acting as Bella's confidante. Providing balance to Reg's role.

"No," Bella said, forcing a laugh. "What bad feelings would there be in the barn? No one has used it in years. And the farm has been my home, where I've been loved and cherished. It's not a bad place."

"Then you don't think there are any bad feelings for a ghost to feed on?"

Bella frowned. She looked quickly around the barn. "No, nothing bad happened here. It was just shut up after Grandma died."

"Why?"

"Because…" Bella made a helpless gesture. "Because they did, I don't know why."

Erin walked around the edge of the wall, exploring a little further. "Did your grandma garden? Were these things hers?"

"I don't know. Maybe."

On a workbench, Erin could make out a bundle of cloth with a flower print. A gardening smock? An old men's shirt that Grandma could pull on over her dress when she didn't want to chance getting it dirty? Erin didn't touch it. Just made note of it and went on. "There's nothing to be worried about here," she told Bella. "You can come in."

Bella tentatively took one step into the barn. She looked around, eyes wild, expecting something bad to happen the instant she set foot inside.

"See?" Erin prompted. "Nothing to worry about."

Like Erin, Bella didn't seem to want to walk under the rafters full of birds.

"Your grandmother's spirit is strong here," Reg announced. She stood absolutely still, then her eyes rolled back in her head so that only the sightless whites showed. Her face was a mask. Bella gave a little shriek and grabbed Erin's arm for stability.

"It's okay." Erin wanted to tell Bella that it was all just an act. She and Reg had spent many hot summer afternoons trying to come up with the worst, scariest faces possible. Inside-out eyelids, cheeks puffed out, tongue dangling lifelessly… they had come up with some pretty gruesome ones. Reg's eyeball rolling was just the beginning.

"What do you want to say to your grandmother?" Reg asked in her spookiest rasp.

"I don't know. Nothing. I don't want anything."

"Why would you disturb my rest without a reason? You must have had a reason!" Reg's voice was not her own. It was a good approximation of a Tennessee accent. The low, gravelly quality covered up any imperfections or slip-ups. It was the shaky voice of an old woman. But one who had just awakened from the grave? For some reason, Erin didn't think so.

Bella was rooted to the spot. "I'm sorry… I just wanted to… I just wanted to make sure you knew that you were loved. That people cared when you disappeared. Grandpa too. Mom said he was really broken up about it. He just went downhill the years after you were gone. He wasn't ever the same. Whatever happened… he mourned you. He did."

"Where is he? Where is Ezekiel?"

"He's… in the cemetery. There's a plot there… for you too. But we never had a body to bury…"

"Why didn't you bury me?"

"We didn't know what happened to you. It was before I was born. I don't know. Nobody wants to tell me about it."

"It's so cold here," Reg drew the words out, "why is it so cold?"

"I don't know. Cold in here? Is that what you mean?"

"It's so cold." Reg wrapped her arms around her body. She swayed back and forth. "It's so cold and cramped in here. Please let me out."

"In here?" Bella spoke urgently. "Where? Where are you? I'll make them take you out and put you in the grave beside Grandpa's, if you'll show me where you are. I'll take care of it. Then you won't need to haunt the barn any more, and we'll all be happy."

"I've been so cold for so long…"

Bella covered her mouth. She stumbled backward, out the barn doors again. She took a deep breath and continued to retreat, until she was in the sun. She lifted her face up toward it, eyes closed, letting it beat down on her face and warm her. Erin followed her out, worried she was going to faint if she tried to go back to the house on her own.

"It's okay, Bella. Bella, it's just Reg. There isn't any—"

"There isn't any reason to be scared," Reg covered easily, reaching them. "She's restless and confused, but she isn't malevolent. You can understand how confused she is, can't you?"

Bella nodded. She lowered her face and opened her eyes to look at Reg. "I'm confused, so I can only imagine how hard it would be for someone who didn't even have a brain to sort it out. Can you imagine being alive one minute, and the next thing you know, you're dead? You can't do any of the normal things anymore. You can't talk to the people you love. You just watch everything going on without you."

Reg looked impressed. This mark had a good imagination, even if she did lean more toward finances than storytelling.

"I think that with another session or two, we'll be able to figure out what's bothering your grandma and to sort it all out—"

"No." Bella's hand closed around the locket that Reg held in her hand, and she took it away. "No more. I didn't know if this was a good idea from the start, and now I know it's not. My mom would be horrified if she saw what you were doing in there. We're good Christian people, we don't go around communing with the dead."

Reg blinked in surprise at this. "Plenty of Christians commune with the dead," she protested. "Seances and Ouija boards and other methods of communication, they're just as big with Christians as with pagans and mystics."

"No," Bella shook her head emphatically. "No more. I don't feel right about this."

There was a loud snap in the trees beside the barn, a brittle branch someone or something had stepped on that sounded like a gunshot in their ears, their nerves stretched taut by Reg's performance.

Bella grabbed Erin's arm. They all looked as one in the direction it had come from.

"Who's there?" Bella demanded. "Who's back there?"

CHAPTER 13

They all waited, straining for another sound. Erin thought she could hear the soft rustling of footsteps. The wind was rushing through the leaves and there were birds calling back and forth to one another, all of the little wilderness noises competed with each other so she wasn't sure what she could hear.

"Is someone there?" Bella demanded again, her voice loud in the stillness.

Erin and Reg looked at each other. The three of them started moving, slowly and as quietly as possible, into the trees that grew right up to the walls of the barn. Erin scanned back and forth, searching for the shape of a person or maybe a deer in the thick growth. The smell of the grasses and weeds they crushed under their feet as they walked was fresh and pungent. Everything seemed peaceful, but Erin's guts churned, her heart thudded hard and fast, and her muscles were bunched, ready to run.

They didn't see anyone else. The property was isolated, and Erin couldn't imagine that anyone was out walking in the woods. It had to be an animal. A random noise. That was all. They stood there, looking around, for a few minutes. Bella was scanning the ground, but apparently didn't see anything that was worth pointing out to Erin and Reg.

"That was weird," she said breathlessly.

"You haven't had that happen before?" Reg asked.

483

Bella shifted uneasily. "I try to stay away from the barn," she said. "It always freaks me out. Mom said—" She cut herself off abruptly, frowning.

"Your mom said what?" Erin prompted.

"She's always told me to stay away from the barn," Bella said.

Erin was sure that wasn't what she'd been about to say. "Why?" Had Cindy said that it was dangerous in there with all of the equipment? It wasn't necessarily a great place for a young child to be hanging around. Or was she the one who had planted the seed in Bella's mind that it was haunted?

Bella shook her head. "I don't know," she said abruptly. "She just told me to stay away from here." She looked around once more. "This is creeping me out. Let's go back to the house."

They made their way back the way they had come through the trees. There was a blur of motion from a tree right beside her, and Bella shrieked and threw her hands up in front of her face to protect herself. It was Erin who recovered first.

"It was just a cat," she said, looking at the sleek, silver gray form that had stopped at the edge of the clearing and was looking back at them, clearly as spooked by them as they were by it.

"Oh!" Bella let out a whoosh of breath. "Thank goodness! I though the ghost was going to get me for sure!"

"Here, puss!" Erin called softly. She made kissing noises, trying to call it over like she did with Orange Blossom. "Come here. Come see us."

"We have a lot of feral cats around here. They aren't tame," Bella explained. "There are one or two of the mommas that will come up to you, but not that one. I've seen it around once or twice. It's pretty wild."

Erin made a few more noises. The cat watched her, then eventually slunk away, disappearing into the trees.

Cindy was expecting Davis to be by today to help with the farm and called me to find out if I had seen or heard from him. If the boy wants to hold down a job, he needs to be more reliable! There are too many days that he sleeps in or "isn't feeling well enough to work." I hate to unjustly accuse him of doing drugs, but I'm afraid that may be the case.

But today it was not his fault. This time it was Trenton. He had a serious allergic reaction and Davis drove him at breakneck speeds—without a license, I might add—to the city hospital to get him emergency treatment. The doctors said that Trenton was lucky to make it in time; he might easily have died on the way. Apparently, he is allergic to soybeans. He's lucky he had his brother to look out for him.

Curled up in the living room with the two animals for company, Erin read and re-read the journal entry. There was the proof in black and white that Davis knew about his brother's allergy to soy. It might not be proof that he and Joelle had conspired to murder Trenton, but it was close. It would shore up the case being developed against Davis. Throughout the journal, there were a number of underlines and annotations that Erin had come to believe Joelle had made while the journal had been in her possession. She had marked little bits of knowledge and gossip that she planned to use in her blackmail campaign. There was a margin bracket marking the passage about Trenton's allergy attack, with a little smiley face beside it. Erin felt a rush of anger at Joelle over her callousness. A smile for the fact that Trenton had had a life-threatening allergy that she had used to kill him? Even if it could be argued that Joelle hadn't intentionally killed Trenton, the smile removed any doubt that she had been happy about the result. The woman really was cold-blooded.

"I have to say I'm not unhappy that you are gone," she told Joelle aloud.

Orange Blossom and Marshmallow both looked up at the sound of her voice.

"Not one bit," Erin reiterated, shaking a scolding finger at the absent party to emphasize her point. The animals looked at her for a moment longer, then went back to napping.

There was the sound of a door slamming behind the house, and Erin looked up, frowning. In a few moments, there was a soft knock at the back door.

"Come on in," Erin called.

She was a little surprised when Willie poked his head in the back door. She'd been expecting Vic, though Vic would not have knocked.

"It's me. Are you decent?"

"As decent as I'm going to get. Come in."

Willie slunk into the kitchen, closing the door behind him. He looked at the burglar alarm panel. "You should have this armed. What's the point of having a burglar alarm if you don't use it?"

"I'll arm it before I go to bed and when I go to the bakery in the morning. Just like always. It didn't exactly stop my last burglar."

"No… I suppose that's true."

Willie stomped into the living room and slumped into one of the easy chairs. Erin didn't say anything about Willie's apparently grimy face and hands and whether he was going to get her furniture dirty. She knew from experience that his skin was stained dark from the mining and refining work that he did. It wasn't going to wash out, it was like a permanent tattoo.

"What is it about women?" Willie demanded.

"I don't know. What happened?"

"Why can't a woman just accept it when her partner tries to do something nice? Why do they have to suspect your motives and argue about it and act like you're just doing something to irritate them? It doesn't make any sense!"

Erin closed the journal and put it to the side. Orange Blossom yawned, stretched, and curled up the opposite direction. "What did Vic say?"

"I'm doing this for her! I want her to have a good, stable life. I want her to be happy. I want her to know she can rely on me. Why can't she just accept that? Why is she fighting me?"

"About what?"

Willie snorted and lapsed into silence, folding his arms across his chest. Erin waited.

"I don't know what you two are actually arguing about, unless you tell me."

"I'm sure she's talked to you about it already."

Erin thought back over what Willie had said and anything Vic might have said that was related the last couple of weeks.

"Oh. About you getting a regular job."

Willie nodded. "It's not like I'm not bringing in good money right now, but it ebbs and flows, and I can never predict how much I'm going to have in any particular month. Women want stability. A predictable flow so that they can save and plan household expenses. No one wants to be left not knowing whether there's going to be five dollars or five thousand dollars coming in during a given month. A salaried job gives you that. A regular, predictable income."

"Until it doesn't," Erin pointed out. "You get downsized or get fired or quit. Or a huge expense comes up that you weren't planning on and you have to figure out how to pay for it."

"Obviously that stuff can still happen." Willie flapped his hand to wave it all away. "But at least with a regular, salaried position, you have some expectations."

Erin let a few breaths pass in silence. "But that's not what Vic wants."

"It's so maddening!" Willie huffed. "I go to all of this work to try to change my lifestyle to something more suited to a long-term relationship and shared household, and she doesn't appreciate it at all! In fact, you'd think I had offended her by suggesting she deserves a partner who can provide a steady income!"

"Maybe she didn't want anything to change. Maybe she doesn't actually mind the way you work at several different projects at once."

Willie stared at Erin. "I should have known you'd automatically be on her side. Vic deserves to have someone who can take care of her properly."

"Maybe she doesn't want to be taken care of. She does already have her own job and her own place. She's not looking for someone to come rescue her. She's looking for someone to spend time with her and cherish her."

"That's what having a proper job would do. I wouldn't have to go away to deal with out-of-town projects. I wouldn't be off at the mines by myself, with her wondering if I was safe. I'd be there for her."

Erin raised her brows and shifted her position, bothering Orange Blossom. "You wouldn't even continue your mining on the side? You'd close the mines? Sell your claims?"

He spread his hands apart in a dramatic shrug, like that should have been obvious. "She wouldn't have to worry anymore. I'd be working a safe office job, home with her during the evenings and weekends. Isn't that what she wants?"

"I don't know. What did she say to you?"

"She said she liked me just the way I am."

Erin laughed at how exasperated he sounded. "Well, maybe she does!"

"But that's stupid! There are already enough differences between us without her having to worry about where I am, if I'm safe, and how much money I'll bring home. She should be happy that I'm willing to change for her."

"Would you want her to change the kind of person she is? Maybe you'd like her to be the kind of person who shrieks at spiders and needs a big strong man to protect her from all of life's disappointments and inequalities. Maybe you'd like her to be home all day instead of working, just waiting for you to finish your new office job and make her feel fulfilled."

Willie opened his mouth to snap back at her. He closed his mouth and scowled.

"Don't you want her to be a fragile little homemaker?" Erin persisted. "That's what all men want isn't it? Someone to protect?"

"I'd never want Vic to turn into something like that. I'd never want her to think that she has to pretend to be something else just to make me happy."

"Maybe that's not what she wants from you either."

"But I'm not talking about… I mean, she shouldn't have to…" Willie blew out his breath. He sat there for a few moments, stewing and occasionally sputtering out a few words of protest.

"Is that what I'm doing?" he demanded finally.

Erin shrugged. "I don't know. Is it?"

"Well… I didn't *know* I was."

She laughed.

Willie swore and pushed himself up out of his chair. "Don't ask me why I should apologize for trying to be nice and be a good provider," he growled.

He marched back out of the house. Erin saw his silhouette cross the yard to the garage and climb the stairs. She couldn't hear his knock, but saw the sliver of light as the door opened and stayed open just an inch or two while Willie talked to Vic, before she finally opened it the rest of the way and let him in.

Vic was in a better mood the next morning than she had been for several days. Erin eyed her as they mixed and poured batters, getting ready for the day ahead.

"I gather you and Willie came to an understanding?"

Vic laughed. "I thought he was gone for good last night. I mean, not forever, but for the night. I never expected him to come back telling me that he'd been wrong and maybe he should have asked me what I wanted before he decided to go and make a big life change like that." Vic shook her head. "Nothing like an abject apology to improve a relationship!"

"You guys have certainly had your ups and downs. I'm glad Willie decided he could see your point of view. That's the first step!"

"I could see *his* point of view all along. It's just that it was wrong."

Erin laughed and started spooning out dollops of filling into tart shells from the freezer. "In your humble opinion."

"It's my opinion, all right. Humble it is not."

"I gather."

"Thanks for talking to him. It was good for him to have someone else to talk to about it. He doesn't really have a lot of friends around here, and I don't know what any of his guy friends would have told him. He needed to hear a woman's perspective."

"Glad to help. Do you want to return the favor and do something for me?"

"Sure," Vic agreed, without waiting to hear what it was.

"You could really get yourself into trouble, agreeing without knowing what it is first!"

Vic shrugged. She wiped a smear of flour off her chin with the back of her wrist. "It's not like you're going to ask me to murder my grandmother. It's probably not even anything very big. I know you."

"I need someone to go with me when I go out to the Prost farm again to interview Cindy. I don't want to do it alone."

"Why don't you take Terry with you? He wouldn't let anything happen to you."

"Terry and I… don't exactly see eye to eye on this. I haven't told him I'm going out there, and I don't think he'd be too happy if he knew."

Vic *tsked,* shaking her head. "Here you are, fixing my relationship, and running yours into the crapper. I think sooner or later Officer Terry Piper is going to have to realize that you've got a mind of your own and he isn't going to be able to stop you from looking into every crime that happens in your area code."

"It's not that bad. And I'm not going to keep looking into other crimes, this is just… once. For a friend."

"Mm-hmm." Vic did not sound convinced.

"So will you?"

Vic gave her batter a stir. "Come out with you? Sure. I'll tag along."

"Good! I appreciate it. And if Terry knew, he'd be happy you were coming with me too."

"Do I need to bring my gun? Keep an eye out for any dangerous varmints?"

"I don't think so! There were a lot of birds in the barn and a cat scared the heck out of Bella, but we're mostly going to be indoors talking to Cindy, if she'll let us in. I'd like to look around the property, but I don't know if she'll permit that."

"Just tell me the time and place, and I'll be there."

Erin stopped by the police department after work, not knowing when the next time was that she'd be able to see Terry. It was late enough that Clara Jones was gone for the day, but Melissa was there filing.

"Hi, Melissa. Is Terry in?"

"He's not, but he shouldn't be too far. Were you guys going to meet for supper?"

"No, I wanted to show him something. Police business."

"Oh." Melissa raised her brows curiously. "Really. Well, let me page him for you."

"I could just call his cell," Erin suggested.

"If it's police business, then I should page him. I don't get to do it very often! It always makes me feel… official!" Melissa gave Erin a wide smile and tossed her wildly curly hair.

"Oh, well… okay…"

Erin waited while Melissa sent the page from one of the computers. Melissa pressed the last key with a flourish.

"Like I said, he isn't far, so it shouldn't be very long."

Erin waited a little awkwardly. She hadn't thought about the possibility of Melissa being there; if she'd known, she would have picked a different day or time. But there wasn't much she could do about it. She was there, she couldn't exactly duck out and say she'd come back another time.

"So… you and Charley seem to have become fast friends," Erin commented, looking for a safe topic. "That's kind of cool."

Melissa's smile faltered. "I thought so at first," she said tentatively.

"Oh… things didn't turn out so well…?" Erin immediately felt guilty. She didn't have any control or influence over Charley, but she still felt responsible for Charley being in Bald Eagle Falls to begin with. If Charley had done something to hurt Melissa…

"She seemed like a lot of fun. I don't have a lot of close friends, even though I've always lived here. I thought… it was kind of like being in the popular clique at school all of a sudden. I should have known it would turn out to be a joke."

"She didn't… a joke? I'm really sorry, Melissa…"

"I don't mean… it wasn't like she was laughing and making fun of me. Not overtly. But I started to feel like… she was laughing behind my back. That it wasn't really me she was interested in, she just wanted to pump me for information about Davis."

Erin sighed. She had been afraid of that from the start. Charley was far too mercenary to be making friends with an older woman for no reason.

"I'm sorry she did that. I never said anything to her…"

"Of course not. I know you wouldn't be like that, Erin. But not everyone is like you, and I was… fooled at first."

It was about five minutes before Terry got there, K9 panting at his side. He smiled at Erin. "An official visit? What's up?"

Erin cleared her throat. "Could we go into your office?

Terry led the way and Melissa clucked in amusement, as if she thought it was just a ploy on Erin's part to get Terry alone. Terry motioned Erin ahead of him into the office, and stood with his hand on the door handle, his body language clearly asking whether he needed to shut it. Erin nodded. Terry shut it and went around his desk to sit behind it, treating it as an official interview.

"So…? This is all rather mysterious."

"I wasn't expecting Melissa to be here. It's just that it's about Davis, and you know…"

The rest went unsaid. That Melissa and Davis had recommenced their decades-old relationship and visited him at the prison. Terry needed to keep anything to do with Davis confidential from Melissa.

"Ah. Got it. So what do you have?" His expression was puzzled, not sure what else she could have come across about Davis.

"I've been reading Clementine's journal, you know."

"Sure."

"There is evidence that Davis knew about his brother's allergy."

"Well, we always suspected as much. What evidence?"

"He had a serious reaction. Davis took him to hospital. They told him it could have been fatal." Erin slid the book out of her shoulder bag and opened it to the marked page. Terry took his time reading through the passage a couple of times before looking up at Erin.

"You're right. They might be able to use this."

"Do you see… the margin marking and the smiley face?"

Terry nodded. "I wondered what that was about."

"That was Joelle. She marked a number of things in the journal."

"Really." Terry flipped back a few pages, noting other annotations. "Well, well, well. That made her smile, did it?" He pondered for a few minutes. "This could certainly be helpful to the case against Davis. Thanks for bringing it by. I'll make a copy and get it back to you."

CHAPTER 14

$\mathcal{E}$rin's familiarity with the route to the Prost farm made it seem like it wasn't quite so far away as it was the first time. They were definitely out in the bush, but maybe it wasn't quite as remote as it had felt the first time. They pulled into the parking area, and Erin and Vic climbed out of the Challenger. A large black and white shaggy dog came streaking toward them, barking and growling so fiercely Erin was sure he was going to take a chunk out of her. She backed up into the side of the car, and fumbled behind her for the handle to get back in.

"Rasher, shut up!" a gruff voice shouted. "Go on, get out of here."

The dog lowered his head and looked back at the door of the farmhouse, where Cindy Prost stood with her hands on her hips. She pointed to the dog house.

"Go on. Back to your house. Leave the company alone."

He slunk obediently away and lay down in the dog house, head and front paws out the door.

Erin breathed heavily, holding one hand over her pounding heart. "Thank you. I guess we should have stayed in the car until after you came out. I didn't realize."

"It's a good practice if you're going to be visiting homes out in the bush. Most of us keep dogs to guard the house. Nobody is going to break into my house with Rasher in the yard."

"No," Erin agreed weakly. "I don't think so."

Cindy stood there for a moment gazing at them, hands on hips, then jerked her head.

"Come on in, then."

Erin walked up to the door. She was glad that Vic was there with her rather than Reg. Reg would enjoy getting this woman wound up, and that wasn't what Erin wanted. She would catch more flies with honey. Vic was far more sociable and wasn't likely to get them kicked off the property without what they had come for.

Bella was inside the house, hovering nearby, as if afraid she might get into trouble for acknowledging their presence. Cindy didn't say anything to Bella, neither telling her to leave nor encouraging her to stay.

"Come and set," Cindy invited, motioning to the living room. Vic and Erin found themselves seats. A good southern hostess, Cindy brought them tall glasses of iced tea and fiddled with the fans, trying to make sure they were pointed in Erin's and Vic's general direction. "I don't rightly understand why Bella wanted me to talk to you. This whole thing seems a little silly. If Bell wanted to know about my mother and father, she only needed to ask me."

"I have, Mom," Bella protested. "I've asked you about them lots of times, and you never want to tell me anything."

Cindy gave no sign that she heard a word her daughter was saying.

"I guess it's a bit of a local mystery," Erin said. "Family history can be so fascinating."

Cindy sat down in a carved rocking chair. She rocked back and forth a little, her movements slow. She took a sip of her tea and put it on the side table.

"It shorely is," she agreed. "I could tell you many stories about the history of the area. My family has lived here for hundreds of years. One of the first families to settle the area."

"That's what Bella was saying. What a long tradition. That's really amazing. I guess my family has been here for quite a while too, but I don't know all of the history and how our lines might intersect."

Cindy considered. "I don't rightly know. Been a long time since I pulled out those dusty old books. And..." Her eyes narrowed as she studied Erin and Vic in turn. "...I get the feeling that's not why you're here."

Erin shifted uncomfortably. She took a drink of her tea. "Uh... no. It's not really about my family. Or about ancient history. It was your parents I was curious about."

"And why?"

Erin tried to keep her eyes steady on Cindy and not let them drift over to Bella. "Like I said. A bit of local color. It sounded like an interesting story, and I was hoping you could fill me in on the details."

"You want to capitalize on our loss? Write a book about it or sell the story to the newspapers?"

"No. Nothing like that. I'm a baker. I'm not writing a book or articles for the paper. I just want to know what happened. Whatever you know, even if some of it is still a mystery today."

"This is Bella's doing. She put you up to it. I didn't like it when she took the job at the bakery. Told her she didn't need to be working while she was still going to school. She has everything she needs. Didn't need to be associating with…" her eyes shifted from Erin to Vic, "…odd people."

Vic gave a little snort at Cindy's pained expression. People like Lottie Sturm had already done their best to take Vic down a notch, to make her life miserable and drive her away. Cindy's distaste wasn't going to drive Vic to hysterical tears.

"Mom!" Bella said, red with embarrassment. "These are my bosses! You can't talk to them like that!"

"Because you might get fired? That's a risk that you faced by inviting them here. If they want to know what went on here, they're going to get the full Cindy Prost, undiluted."

"Just don't… call them names. Honestly!"

"I didn't call her *queer*," Cindy protested. "I said odd."

"That doesn't make a difference. Don't call them anything."

Cindy rolled her eyes and spread her hands in a 'what can you do about kids these days?' shrug at Erin and Vic. "Fine. So you came here to find out what happened to my mother. You think you're the only one who has ever asked?"

"No," Erin knew from Clementine's journal that more than one person had attempted to reason with Ezekiel Prost and to get him to allow them to search the grounds for any sign of Martha. But Ezekiel had denied them. If Cindy had been asked after she moved back to the farm, she suspected the inquirers didn't get much further with her. "I'm just hoping you'll share what you do know with us."

Cindy rocked. She had physical similarities to her daughter. Heavy. Blond hair—though Cindy's had a lot of gray in it. Her facial features were similar, though, of course, her skin was more wrinkled.

"Don't know what you think you're going to figure out that no one else has up until now. It's all pretty simple. My father told me that my mother was out every time I called to have a conversation. I started to wonder what was going on, whether she was ill and didn't want me to know about it, or maybe she'd even left him after some big blow-up. Some couples do that, you know, break up after all of the kids have moved out and they are on their own again."

Erin nodded. "Yes. It always bothers me when I hear about a couple that has been together for twenty-five or thirty years has broken up. It seems like such a waste."

Cindy made no response. Erin had the feeling that she was irritated by Erin's interruption to her carefully-considered narrative.

"So I was already wondering what was going on with my parents. Then I got a call from a friend."

From Lottie Sturm, as Clementine had suspected? Erin supposed it didn't make any difference who had called Cindy to tell her.

"She told me about how everyone was worried about Dad, and that Mom seemed to have disappeared. And just like that… my life changed forever."

Erin nodded. "So… you decided you'd better come home and see what was going on."

"You bet your sweet behind I did! Dropped everything, my whole life, and just came back out here."

"Did you find anything? Any sign of what had happened here?"

"Not a thing." Cindy shook her head. "You might think it's an exaggeration, but it's the truth. There was nothing to find. My mother wasn't here, but there was no indication she had planned to go on a long trip. I couldn't see any missing suitcase or clothes. All of her favorite things still seemed to be here. And no, there wasn't any sign that something violent had happened here, either. No bloody fingerprints. No rotting corpses. Just an old man…"

When Erin opened her mouth to ask about Ezekiel's age, Cindy talked over her.

"No, he wasn't that old in years. But it was like he was forty years older than he had been when I'd seen him the last Christmas. He had turned into an old man overnight. He wasn't eating, and his clothes just hung on him. He didn't say he was worried about my mom or that he was missing her, but he was obviously pining after her. Whyever she was gone… he was missing her something terrible. I think if I had taken another week to get here, he would have been dead."

Erin breathed out. "Wow. But you nursed him back to health. You took care of him, and he lived for a few more years."

Cindy ran her fingers through her hair. It wasn't curly, like Bella's. Bella had either inherited that from her father, or Cindy had outgrown her curls.

"My mother has been gone twenty-one years. Dad lived long enough to see his only grandchild, and she's seventeen now."

"Another four years." Not bad, for someone who had apparently been at death's door. But it was probably more than Cindy's cooking that had brought him back from the brink. It was Cindy herself. Family. Something to live for. Someone else to fill the empty spaces that his wife had left behind.

"That's really all there is to it. Nobody has ever found any trace of my mother, living or dead. I imagine sometimes that she's off enjoying life somewhere, that she started over and found the life that she couldn't have while she was living here and raising her children. But do I think she's off in Florida or Spain, enjoying the local color? Not really. I don't have proof of what happened, but I think she died."

Bella moved into the room to better hear or provide comfort. "Mom… is that what you really think? Why didn't you ever tell me?"

"I don't know how it happened. I hope he just woke up one morning and found that she had passed in the night. Or maybe she keeled over in the vegetable garden in the heat of the day. Just a natural occurrence. I don't like to think he might have done something to her."

"He wouldn't have," Bella said, as if she were the one who had known Grandpa and her mother the one who hadn't. "He wouldn't have done anything to hurt her, would he? He wasn't ever a violent person, right?"

Cindy didn't immediately jump in and say, 'Of course he wasn't. He'd never harmed a fly in his life. He'd never have laid a hand on his wife.' Instead, she pressed her lips together tightly, not answering for a few minutes.

"I don't know. When I was a kid, I was scared to death of him. He was bigger than life. If he told me to do anything and I questioned it, I'd get a whipping. There was never any doubt of that. But in the time I'd been away from home, he'd mellowed. He didn't have to be the authoritarian figure anymore. When I was little… I don't know if he ever struck my mother. I kind of assumed he did, but I never saw him do it. Maybe I just figured that if he whipped me, he must have hurt her too. My mother never said he did, but what woman would ever admit that to her child?"

"So it might have been violence. He might have killed her accidentally, or in a fit of anger," Vic suggested.

Cindy glared at her, clearly communicating that she was talking to Erin and didn't expect to hear any comments from Vic. She looked back at Erin and answered as if Erin had been the one to ask.

"I told you, there were no signs of violence. Nothing out of place. No blood. If he did hurt her… he cleaned everything up. He never said what he'd done. He never said my mother was dead."

"The townspeople assumed that he had done something to her. Or at the very least, that he'd disposed of the body."

"The townspeople have never had any idea about anything. Gossip and rumors. I've never had any reason to talk to anyone in the town about it."

"The Sheriff at the time? He never came out here?"

"He called me. Talked to me in town. I told him what I told you. There was no sign of anything on the farm. Nothing my father said ever convinced me that he had done anything to hurt her. She was just gone, and he was grieving for her."

"So the sheriff never came out?"

"He'd tried a couple of times before I came back. I made it clear to him that I would not be allowing anyone on the property either." Cindy picked up her glass and took a long drink, as if parched from her speech. "I never let anyone in here to talk about it, until now. The only reason I allowed you in was because you're Bella's boss."

"I really appreciate it," Erin said. "I know we don't have any right to just barge in here and demand details. You've been very gracious about it."

Cindy nodded her agreement. Erin didn't think she was only doing it for Bella. She had avoided Bella's questions in the past. Maybe she had just decided it was time to talk about it. Twenty years was a long time to stay quiet about something so life-changing. It had turned Cindy's life completely upside-down, putting her in the role of caregiver before she was prepared for it. Had Cindy ever considered abandoning her family property once her father was gone? Selling the farm that had been in her family for generations and going back to the city to work? It couldn't have been easy for her to eke out a living and to be isolated there for so much of the time. Just she and Bella.

"Would it be possible for us to look around the property a little?" Erin suggested, sure Cindy would say no.

But Cindy pursed her lips and considered. She rocked back and forth, and her eyes went over to Bella.

Bella leaned forward a little. "I could show them around, if you want. Then you wouldn't have to, but I'd make sure they didn't leave open any gates."

Cindy took another sip of tea. "All right," she agreed finally. "You can take them around. But stay away from the old barn. It isn't safe in there."

Bella nodded her understanding.

"We really appreciate it," Erin repeated. She swallowed and looked at Bella. "Do you want to show us around the house first?"

Again, she was sure that Cindy would jump in and snap at them, telling them they couldn't intrude on her family life. Looking outside at the goats was one thing. Poking through bedrooms was quite another. But Cindy just looked back at them, her eyes dark.

Bella managed to nod. "Sure, of course. We'll start upstairs."

There was a pause as everyone waited for an explosion, but one wasn't forthcoming. Had Cindy decided that she wanted them to look around? She wanted them to figure out the truth and expose it to the light of day twenty years later? It had been a burden that she had carried by herself for too long.

Erin and Vic stood up and followed Bella to the stairs. They all traipsed as quietly as possible up the squeaky risers. Bella hesitated for a moment, then indicated the first bedroom at the top of the stairs.

"I don't really know what you want to see. I mean… it's been years since Grandma and Grandpa lived here."

The first room appeared to be Cindy's room, the master bedroom. It was a small, cramped room, large enough for the bed and dresser, with patterned wallpaper that made Erin feel claustrophobic. She had lived in old houses, but none as old as the Prost farmhouse. What progenitor had originally erected those walls? Had it been one man? A family working together? A community project like a barn-raising? It was hot inside, which told Erin that it was not well-insulated and was probably freezing in the winter. Tennessee winters were nothing compared to the northeastern United States where Erin had spent most of her years, but they were still cold for someone with blood thinned by Tennessee summers. The closet was small by modern standards, but it had been built to hold all of a couple's clothes. Two pairs of pants, two shirts, and a good suit for the man. Two house dresses and a good dress for the woman. It wouldn't have accommodated much more.

"This is Mom's," Bella said unnecessarily. She looked around, as if seeing it with fresh eyes. "I guess when she moved back here, it must have been Grandma and Grandpa's."

Erin could see nothing that would give them any clues about Grandma's disappearance. What did they think, that the room would have been preserved as a shrine, still awaiting her return after twenty years? Cindy had moved on. She'd gone on to live her life.

Erin retreated to the hall and Bella took them on to the next room.

"Mine," Bella offered.

It was a typical teen girl's room. Vestiges of her childhood: dolls and middle grade books, posters of the current teen idols; an adult study desk, carefully arranged. Bella gave a shrug. "Mom's room when she was a girl. I guess she wanted me to have the same one as she had. Or to be in the room closest to her. I could pick one of the other ones if I wanted, but this is fine, and it's a pain to have to move everything."

Erin nodded. She didn't go in or spend long studying it. It wasn't like Grandma would have left a secret note for them to find, or Grandpa might have hidden a confession of guilt. It had been their daughter's room. Nobody was playing games.

There were two more bedrooms, one set up as a guest room and one holding excess furniture and other items they wanted to store. There was no upstairs bathroom.

"Was either of these used by your grandparents as a sewing room or study?" Erin asked.

Bella's shoulders lifted and fell. "Just bedrooms. I think they were both pretty outdoorsy, that's where they spent their time."

Erin nodded. "Okay. I don't think… I can't think of anything we need to see. We should look at the kitchen downstairs, but… I don't think we're going to find anything significant."

Bella took them back down the stairs. They nodded awkwardly at Cindy, who was still sitting in the rocker in the living room.

The kitchen was bright, with modern appliances that looked oddly out of place fit between old cupboards and counters. It was big enough for a small family to eat in. There wasn't a lot of space to store dishes or pantry items, but there was ample counter space for food preparation. No twenty-year-old blood spatters.

"And there's a cold room downstairs," Bella offered, but didn't indicate any desire to go down there herself.

"We should probably check that out," Erin said.

"No… there's nothing down there. Just shelves and canned goods."

Erin raised her eyebrows. "Then it will only take a minute to look. Where are the stairs?"

Bella reluctantly led them to the narrow door and opened it. She clicked on an electric light and stood to the side to allow Erin and Vic to go down.

"You're not coming?" Erin didn't really need to ask; the answer was obvious. Bella had no intention of venturing down to the basement. Maybe it wasn't haunted like she thought Auntie Clem's basement and the barn were, but it was still spooky enough that she wasn't going to go with them.

Erin led the way down the stairs. She tried not to let Bella's anxiety infect her. It was just a dug-out basement beneath an old house. There was nothing to worry about. No haints. No animals. Nothing that was any threat to them.

The lighting was dim, barely enough to see by. The stairs were bare wood, as was the handrail mounted on the wall beside them. It was much cooler than the rest of the house, enough to make Erin shiver. There had been some attempt made to put up wallboard and a subfloor, but it was clumsy and haphazard and didn't do much to enhance the space. Erin walked out into the middle of the cold room and gazed around at the jars of home-canned fruit together with commercial cans of vegetables and other products. There were some large sacks of grains and other dry goods, and the distinctive smell of rotting potatoes. Vic and Erin looked around at their surroundings and then each other.

"Could have buried her under the floor," Vic said, tapping the wood floor with her toe. It was still yellow rather than the gray that older wood turned. Of fairly recent vintage.

Erin nodded. "I don't smell anything dead."

"You wouldn't after twenty years."

"No, I guess not."

Erin looked at the floor, seeing whether there was a way to lift some of the floorboards up to have a peek underneath, but everything seemed to be nailed down securely. The floor had been laid before the walls, so it disappeared under the wallboard rather than ending before it.

"Nothing else to see," Vic said.

"Okay. Back up."

They both tried to look as if they were not hurrying for the stairs, and there wasn't exactly a scuffle at the bottom to see who would go first, but there was definitely a moment of awkwardness as they shifted and tried to decide who would go first. Erin had led the way down, so she figured it was her right to be the first one up and, in the end, she got the first position, walking back up into the oppressive heat of the day.

"I told you there wasn't anything," Bella said.

"And now we checked, so we know," Vic agreed.

"So you want to see the rest of the farm?" Bella led them out of the house.

Stepping out into the sun, Erin immediately regretted the choice to search the Prost property in the heat of the afternoon. They should have been there in the early morning as soon as the sun came up, or the evening as it went down, not right in the middle of it. She couldn't imagine how they were going to traipse all over the farm without fainting of heat and dehydration. Erin put her sunglasses on, but she needed a hat. And an air-conditioned car.

Bella led them to the parking area and pointed to a small vehicle that seemed to be a cross between an ATV and a jeep. "Climb on."

Vic didn't hesitate; in fact, she seemed eager to climb aboard. Erin was the only one who seemed to have reservations about the idea. She stood looking at the dirty, chipped, open-air vehicle.

"Uh… you drive?" she asked Bella.

"Sure, I've been driving this thing around for years. Trust me, you don't want to have to walk."

Erin reluctantly climbed into the vehicle. "Is this safe? There are no seatbelts."

"If it rolled over, you'd be pinned underneath," Bella said blithely, "so no seatbelts."

Erin looked at Vic. "If it rolled over?"

"Don't think about it. Bella knows what she's doing. Enjoy it!"

Erin hung on to whatever she could reach, thinking more about how to remain in the vehicle than of enjoying the ride. Bella keyed the ignition and the engine roared to life. Clouds of exhaust billowed out behind them. Before Erin had the chance to prepare herself, Bella put the car into gear and they started moving.

They bounced over the uneven ground. Erin felt every bump and clung tightly to her handholds. Vic give a whoop and leaned forward, looking like she was having the time of her life. She and Bella shouted to each other over the roar of the engine, but Erin couldn't hear most of what they were saying. She was supposed to be paying attention to the landscape, looking for any clues as to what might have happened to Bella's grandma. It wasn't like she would find disturbed earth or new growth where a fresh grave had been dug; Mother Nature would have reclaimed the area over the ensuing decades. She tried to force herself to pay attention to the passing landscape anyway and strained to hear Bella's comments as she gestured to various areas.

The road, if it could be called that, was rough and rutted, just a trail worn through the ground cover. They broke free of the thick growth of trees into a clearing, and Erin shaded her eyes from the sun in spite of her sunglasses. Bella pulled the car over to the side and parked it. The engine quieted a little.

"This is the lower pasture," Bella explained, motioning to the goats grazing or resting in the field. It wasn't flat like a farmer's field. It was hilly and rough and the pasture itself was on a fairly steep slope. But Erin knew that goats could climb just about anything. They looked tranquil and happy in the pasture and paid no attention at all to the roar of the engine intruding on their peaceful munching.

Erin evaluated it and found nothing unusual or out of place. "This is the same pasture as your grandma would have used?"

"Sure. Same one as has been here forever."

"And goats aren't like pigs, they won't eat just anything, right?"

Vic looked at Erin questioningly. Bella shook her head. "Goats will eat all kinds of things, food or not. You have to make sure there's no poisonous plants or anything else that might harm them in the field."

"But they're herbivorous. Not omnivorous, like pigs."

"Yeah." Bella gave a little shrug, her mind not following the same tracks as Erin's.

But Vic's face showed that she knew exactly what Erin was thinking. Pigs had been used by more than one serial killer to dispose of human bodies. She wrinkled her nose and shook her head at Erin. Erin gazed at the goats in the field.

"And you've always had goats? Not any other animal?"

"Goats are the best," Bella said. "In these parts, there isn't lots of flat land and it takes time and effort to clear the trees. You can't grow wheat here. Cows don't do well here. But goats do. That's what we've been raising for generations."

Erin nodded. "Is there anything else to see?"

Bella put the car back into gear, and they bounced around some more, winding around through the trees. They stopped at a large, curve-roofed metal structure. "This is the barn. The goat barn. This is where they come to shelter at night."

"How long has this been here?"

"I dunno. Thirty, forty years."

"So it was here when your grandma disappeared."

"Yeah, I guess so. Not much has changed since then. Everything is done pretty much the same."

"And the red barn was never used for goats? The one that—"

Bella waved away the rest of the question. "No. Back when they had horses, that's probably where they were kept. Maybe a milk cow. Garden stuff. Farming equipment."

"And it hasn't been used since your grandma… disappeared?"

"No. Mom had a horse when she was a little girl, but it died… maybe when she was a teenager, I'm not sure when. I think that was the last horse they had. And I don't know when they had a cow last. Mom doesn't talk about having to milk cows, so I don't think they had one when she lived here."

"Should we go in?"

Bella raised her eyebrows. "Do you want to? Not much to see."

"I'd like to, if we're allowed."

"Mom said to stay out of the old barn, she didn't say we couldn't come to this one." Bella shut off the car engine, and Erin and Vic followed her to the barn.

Even before they stepped inside, Erin was regretting the request. The pungent smell of goat filled her nostrils, making her nauseated. She breathed as shallowly as she could, through her mouth, but she could still smell and almost taste the rank, muddy smell of the goats. They weren't as bad as pigs. Erin remembered going to a farm on a field trip when she was younger. The pig pens had been so revolting, she had thrown up her lunch, causing chaos among her classmates. She was glad she hadn't stayed too long in that family. She had endured all kinds of teasing at school, and introductions always included 'the one who threw up on the farm trip.'

"Are you okay?" Vic asked.

Erin swallowed and nodded. "It's just… the smell."

"Takes some getting used to," Bella admitted. "I've been around them all my life, and it still bothers me when the wind is blowing from the west."

But she didn't seem to have any problem marching up to the building and throwing a door open. She groped for a switch in the darkness inside the door and turned on some lights. Erin held her breath and stood in the doorway for a quick look around, then backed out again to breathe. Vic went into the barn and took a few minutes before coming out. She made no comment on Erin's swift departure and spoke in a low voice before Bella finished up and joined them.

"The floors are slatted so that waste flows down into pits under the building. I don't know what the procedure is for getting them flushed or mucked out, but I assume they've been cleaned at least annually since Grandma disappeared. If there were any remains down there, I doubt if anyone could find them now."

Erin nodded. Bella exited the barn, shutting the lights back off and pulling the door shut. She didn't, Erin noted, lock the door. Why would they need to? It was out in the middle of nowhere, and why would anyone want to break into a goat barn? If they did, what harm could they do?

They all walked back to the vehicle. Bella seemed happy to be outdoors, unaware of the grisly conversation Erin and Vic were having. They all climbed into the car and proceeded on to another field, this one without any goats, that Bella said was the upper pasture. Erin could see that the growth there was longer, with leggy weeds and hardy grasses. Presumably, when the lower pasture got too short, the goats would be moved to the upper pasture.

Erin couldn't think of anything to ask. She nodded and looked around. Off to the right, she could see white posts and dark shapes. "What's that?"

"Family graveyard," Bella said. "You want to see?"

"Yes."

Bella put the car in gear and took them in a curving route to a little cemetery in a glade. The posts Erin had been able to see had been crosses, and the dark shapes various statues and monuments. Erin was first out of the car, and the others followed her. Erin explored the cemetery, fascinated. She'd rarely been to a regular cemetery before, and never to a family cemetery. She walked from one grave to the other, looking at the family names, the husbands and wives buried side by side. The tragic little gravestones with cherubs for babies who had died in infancy. Most of the marker stones were modest, but there were a few big ones with statues that towered over the others. Erin heard approaching footsteps, and Bella came up beside her. They browsed over the stones, Bella pointing out a few relatives or telling what she knew about this person or that. They made their way down an aisle, and Bella pointed.

"Over there, that's Grandpa's grave."

Erin approached it and looked down at the stone. Black with gray engraving. Just Ezekiel's name and the dates of his birth and death. No scripture, no 'loving father and husband,' no angel motif. Erin studied it.

"You said your mom is Christian?"

Bella nodded. "Yeah. We don't go to church every week, but she's still Christian."

Erin nodded thoughtfully. Maybe Cindy hadn't told them everything she knew about Ezekiel and what had happened to Martha.

"It's been a long time since I've been here," Bella mused, gazing around. "It looks different. I guess it's just because of growing up. Everything from your childhood seems smaller than you remember."

Erin withdrew her focus from the one gravestone to again take in the neat rows and columns of the plots. Somebody kept it maintained. Not the golf-short grass of a city cemetery, but it wasn't overgrown either. Some of the plots, like one of the ones next to Ezekiel, didn't have markers. Maybe they'd had wooden markers that had rotted away, or maybe there had never been markers, but slight depressions in the ground showed where the ground had settled in the graves.

"It's a beautiful little place," Erin said. "Maybe it's a weird thing to say, but I love it. I've never been in a cemetery like this before."

Bella beamed. "I like it too. Even though there are lots of bodies buried here, I've never felt like it was haunted. It's not spooky." She shrugged. "I guess that's because it's consecrated ground."

Erin nodded. She wasn't sure exactly what that meant, but it probably wasn't the time to ask.

With Bella beside her and Vic somewhere behind looking at other gravestones, Erin was startled by a movement in the trees ahead of them.

"Who's over there?" a man's voice demanded.

ella didn't seem perturbed to be addressed in such a way out in the middle of the bush. She peered through the trees.

"It's me, Mr. Ware. Bella Prost."

"Bella?" the man's voice repeated.

Erin watched him emerge slowly from the cover of the trees. An old man, solidly built and slow moving, each step deliberate. Erin tried to estimate his age. Sixty? Seventy? His hair was gray, his face deeply wrinkled by many years in the sun. It took a few minutes for him to make his way over to them.

"Erin, this is Mr. Ware," Bella introduced. "He lives the next property over. The boundary line is just over there. You see the fence posts…?"

Erin squinted at the trees Mr. Ware had come through. She could just barely see the fence posts. The wire in between them was invisible from where they stood. Apparently, there was a break or a gate somewhere that Mr. Ware had come through. It wasn't an old, weathered fence like Erin expected to see, but something newer that had been erected in the last five or ten years. The posts were too white to be wood, but were maybe some kind of plastic or other synthetic.

"It's nice to meet you, Mr. Ware."

"Erin is my boss," Bella told him. "She's the owner and head baker over at Auntie Clem's Bakery."

"At the bakery? I thought the bakery closed."

"The Bake Shoppe closed, this is a new one. Erin opened it where the tea room used to be."

"You run the tea room?" Mr. Ware asked Erin, apparently either hard of hearing or deliberately misunderstanding.

"I have a bakery where the tea room used to be," Erin said in a loud, firm voice. "You should come by sometime and have a look."

Mr. Ware barely glanced at Erin, looking instead at Bella for clarification. "Is that the new-fangled place?" he asked. "I hear they have all kinds of inedible, weird stuff there."

Bella's face was flushing red. "Mr. Ware! I've told you about the bakery before. Erin bakes great bread, and all kinds of treats too!"

There was a twinkle in Mr. Ware's eye that gave him away. Erin shook her head. "You're a tease, Mr. Ware. Don't think I don't see you for what you are."

Just a hint of a smile peeked through Mr. Ware's craggy face. "Who, me?"

Bella gave him a playful punch in the arm, just skimming his sleeve. "You're so bad! I never know when you're being serious."

"I've dealt with people like this before," Erin said gravely. "There's a trick to it."

Both Bella and Mr. Ware looked at her expectantly. Erin could hear Vic somewhere close behind her as well. She leaned toward Bella slightly, and said in a low voice. "You don't believe a word that comes out of his mouth."

Bella laughed, and Mr. Ware chuckled appreciatively. He put a hand over his heart.

"You've wounded me, young lady! Wounded me deeply."

Erin cocked her head, looking at him. "How long have you lived here?" she asked. "I assume this is your family farm?"

Mr. Ware made a little wave to the land behind him. "This has been Ware land for a long time," he agreed. "I was born here, lived here my whole lifetime."

"Then you must have known Ezekiel and Martha."

He stilled. The twinkle had disappeared from his eye. Together, the three of them looked down at Ezekiel's marker.

"Yes, I knew Ezekiel and Martha," he admitted. "Tragic how we lost them both. But you live out here long enough, and you learn that sooner or later, everyone departs this earth at some point. Some earlier, some later, but eventually, everyone."

"That's true," Erin agreed. "My mom and dad were both gone years ago. But what do you mean about the way we lost Ezekiel and Martha? I thought nobody knew what happened to Martha, and didn't Ezekiel just die of natural causes?"

Mr. Ware scratched his chin, considering his answer. "Everyone in these parts figured that Ezekiel knew what happened to Martha, even though he would never say. A woman just doesn't up and leave after thirty years of marriage without any warning. She didn't drive. No one picked her up. So where did she go? No, I'm afeared that something happened between her and Ezekiel." Mr. Ware stared down at the headstone. "I'm not saying what. The only one who knows for sure is Ezekiel and the good Lord, and Ezekiel's been gone these sixteen, seventeen years. He took that secret with him. We won't know until the hereafter."

"But you think Ezekiel had something to do with it? He had a fight with her…?"

"Everybody knew the two of them had their problems. But somehow, she disappeared. A lady who doesn't drive just doesn't up and disappear without someone helping her along."

"No," Erin agreed. She hoped to hear something more concrete from Mr. Ware, one of the only remaining witnesses as to what might have happened. But it sounded like it was just the same rumors as she'd heard elsewhere. "Martha never said anything to you? That she was planning on leaving her husband? That he had hurt or threatened her? That things weren't good between them?"

"I wouldn't want to speak ill of the dead. I can't say she ever said anything like that to me. But he wasn't an easy man to get along with."

Erin was going to repeat what Cindy had said about Ezekiel being abusive, but Bella might not want this repeated to someone else. She glanced over at Bella and decided against it.

"But you don't know. What happened to Martha, I mean."

Mr. Ware shook his head slowly. "I can't be certain he did something to her. But I don't see what other explanation there is."

"She might have died naturally, or accidentally, and he just… didn't report it."

"But why wouldn't he? Only if he had something to do with it and didn't want anyone else to know."

Erin sighed. "Maybe."

He stared at her closely for a moment, then looked over at Bella. "Why are you asking these questions? You're not part of this family. You're not even from these parts. Why do you care?"

"Erin is helping me," Bella said. "I always wanted to know the real story, and she's helping me out. And she is from here. Clementine Price was her aunt. She lived here."

Erin was going to correct her, as they hadn't actually lived in Bald Eagle Falls, but had only stayed there temporarily. But Bella wasn't intentionally misleading him, and it was probably better if he thought she was a native.

"You shouldn't go digging up the past," Mr. Ware said. "Just let things be."

"We just want to know the truth," Erin said. She didn't tell him that Bella wanted to know so that Martha would stop haunting the barn. That might be a bit too much honesty.

"You should just leave it alone," Mr. Ware repeated. "What's going to change even if you did find out what really happened? It isn't going to make any difference to anyone, it will just smear Ezekiel's good name."

"Since everybody thinks Ezekiel killed her, I'm not exactly smearing anyone's name. Maybe we could even clear him. Maybe he had nothing to do with her disappearance."

Erin wasn't sure how she could prove this. So far, she wasn't having much luck with finding anything out.

Erin had spent the evening in the bakery kitchen with Vic, blending up a number of sweet concoctions and pouring them into molds. Thursday morning, she would have the cold case at the bakery filled with frozen treats. She was excited to see how the kids—and the adults—enjoyed eating dairy-free ice creams and gourmet popsicles to beat the heat. The days were getting warmer and warmer, and during the days while she had sweated by the sweltering ovens, she had dreamed up the most delicious frozen concoctions she could think of to cool off with in the coming months. Not just frozen lemonade and watermelon, but dairy-free chocolate caramel ice cream sandwiched between two gluten-free vanilla cookies, sunflower butter pies in chocolate shells, popsicles with colorful layers of blended berries and fruits, and traditional dipped banana pops.

It was extra work to be preparing frozen treats on top of the usual baking, but she figured that once they took off, she could cut down on some of the hot baking in the morning as people chose frozen treats in place of their usual cookies and cakes.

"You know, I think the orange creamsicles are going to be my favorite," Vic offered, as she took another batch of molds to the freezer. "I know they're not anything fancy or new, but sometimes the traditional foods have stayed around for a reason."

"I'm not going to diss the orange creamsicles," Erin agreed. "They're lovely."

"You really know your stuff, Erin. These things are going to sell like hotcakes—or coldcakes!"

"I hope so."

There was a knock at the back door, and after a moment the door opened, and Erin turned to see Terry looking in.

"Let yourself in," she called. "We just have our hands full right now."

He entered with K9 and shut the door behind him. In the kitchen, he looked around at the counters full of fruits and various concoctions.

"Working on your cold case, I see."

Erin looked sideways at him. "Yup."

"And how is the other cold case going?"

"Not really going much of anywhere, as far as I can tell. Everywhere I go, they pretty much just confirm what I heard in the beginning. Grandma Prost disappeared, everybody assumed Grandpa killed her or found her dead and took care of the body, but no one could find anything out for sure. I think interest died out when Cindy got home and didn't have news about finding her mother's decomposing body in the bed."

"Your partner in crime seems to think there's been progress in the case."

Erin looked over at Vic, puzzled.

"Not Vic, your sister."

"Oh." Erin's stomach turned queasily. "Reg."

"She's spreading talk around town about the ghost of Grandma Prost demanding justice, wanting to know why her killer was never pursued and prosecuted."

Although Reg was still staying with Erin, things had been quiet the last couple of days and she had hoped that Reg was losing interest in Bald Eagle Falls and Bella's grandma.

"I didn't know that. She hasn't said anything to me about it."

"That's a little difficult to believe."

Vic looked at Terry. "Erin hasn't been encouraging Reg. Right from the start, she's been trying to get Reg to just move on."

"By inviting her to stay here and taking her to the Prost farm."

"I didn't invite her here," Erin protested. "She invited herself. I couldn't leave her out on the street with nowhere to live. She's supposed to be finding a place of her own to rent. And I didn't take her to Bella's. She could have gone in her own car; Bella invited her over. I went to keep an eye on things and make sure it didn't go too far."

"It's gone too far."

"Okay. I'll talk to her. Or at least, I'll try to talk to her. I don't know how much good it will do."

"Is she here?"

Erin shook her head. "No. I think she's gone into the city, but she didn't tell me where she was going or what her plans were. She doesn't keep a baker's schedule, so our paths don't cross much, unless she has something she wants to talk to me about."

Terry considered for a moment, then nodded and pulled out one of the kitchen chairs and sat down. Erin recognized this as a signal that he was done interrogating her and was ready to step out of his law enforcement role and relax.

"It's hard to believe that the two of you came from the same family. Reg is so different from you."

"I hope so. And we're not from the same family. We both came from other families, and then had several foster families. Just because we shared one foster home, that doesn't mean we were raised together. We only lived together for a few months. Not even a year."

"She calls herself your sister."

"Reg says a lot of things. You need to take anything that comes out of her mouth with a grain of salt."

"She's quite the con artist, isn't she?"

Erin nodded slowly. "Yes… if you want to call it that."

"What would you call it?"

Erin considered. "She's… creative. She always has a new scheme for making some money. Not necessarily anything illegal, but sometimes it crosses the line."

Terry raised one eyebrow. "And how often were you involved in these… schemes?"

"She was older than I was. She would involve me with things… use me as a scapegoat if we got caught. She figured I wouldn't get in as much trouble as she would."

"Sounds like a sibling."

Erin took a deep breath, determined to make a clean breast of it. "When we had both aged out, she kept in touch, and she pulled me into a few other schemes, before I thought better of it and told her I wouldn't do anything else with her."

"When you were old enough to know better."

"Does an eighteen-year-old have that much more sense than a fifteen-year-old? I don't know. Figuring everything out at that age is hard. I had to support myself and Reg had ideas of how to do that. I wanted it to be easy."

"But making a living isn't easy. There are no easy answers."

"That's what I eventually figured out. I'm not sure if Reg ever will."

"What is her background? Why hasn't she learned that?"

Erin grimaced, trying to figure out what to tell Terry. "Her history is her own business. We learned in foster care that people's pasts and families are their own. Reg has a right to her privacy."

"The citizens of Bald Eagle Falls have their rights too. Don't you think they have the right to know her history?"

"Not really," Erin said honestly. "They should be able to see what she is and judge for themselves. *You* could see what she was up to."

"And I have access to databases where I can see what kind of record she has. Regular citizens don't have that."

Erin scraped out the contents of one of the blenders, and half-filled a cup, which she set in front of Terry.

"If people are looking for a medium, they want to be deceived. If they want to pay to be deceived, then they get what they pay for."

"I can see how you would adopt that position, because you're an atheist and you don't believe in spirits and mediums. But people around here do. So that's what they are paying for. They think they really are getting someone who can talk to spirits."

"Like I say, they want to be deceived."

Terry scowled, looking for a way to better express his position.

"I don't think you're going to talk Erin out of it," Vic said. "You have to believe in spirits to think that people are paying for something other than a show."

"I suppose," Terry grumbled. He took a sip of the smoothie Erin had given him. "Mm. This is good. What is it?"

"Watermelon raspberry."

"Very nice."

"Thanks. And I am sorry about Reg. I didn't ask her here or plan on her following me here. It's one of the hazards of using my real name."

Terry looked as if this aspect had never occurred to him before. "Is that why you assumed other names?"

Erin hesitated. "Well, it's one of them," she admitted.

Terry studied her as he had another sip of his watermelon raspberry smoothie.

When Erin got home from the bakery, Reg was just getting home as well. Her cheeks were pink and her dark eyes sparkling, signs that she was pleased with herself. When she saw Erin, she lowered her eyes, trying to suppress her mood.

"Oh, hey, Erin. How was your day?"

Erin nodded. "Okay. Busy, as usual. You're looking happy. You find an apartment?"

That threw cold water over Reg's mood. She attempted to school her expression, but couldn't keep her smile from faltering.

"Uh, no. Still looking."

"So what's up?" Erin let herself into the house and Reg followed.

"Just making contacts… networking…" Reg said vaguely.

"Officer Piper was around today. He said you're causing problems."

"Problems?" Reg raised her brows, affecting an innocent expression. "I don't know what he could mean."

"He said you're spreading rumors around and stirring things up."

"Do you expect me to not talk about my business? I made contact with Martha Prost; that's news. That's something that people want to hear about. Maybe they have relatives they want to get in touch with."

"You shouldn't be capitalizing on someone else's loss." Erin lowered her voice to a confidential tone, even though there was no one there to overhear them. "You really upset Bella, you know. You were supposed to be reassuring her, not getting her more upset. She's been quite troubled about the idea of her grandma being cold somewhere and not being laid to rest with her husband."

Reg shrugged. She slipped off a heavy shoulder bag and sat it on one of the kitchen chairs. "It isn't my fault that her grandma isn't buried there. I can't help it if she finds that upsetting."

"You're the one who suggested it was a problem."

"She wanted to know why her grandma's spirit wasn't at rest." Reg lifted her hands, palms up in offering. "Well, there you are. The reason she isn't able to rest."

"But it isn't something that Bella or Cindy can do anything about."

"That's not my problem."

Erin blew out her breath in frustration. "You were just trying to leave things open so that she'd ask you back again."

Reg put a hand dramatically over her heart as if wounded. "Erin! You think I'm trying to take advantage of your friend?"

"Yes! Exactly!"

Reg laughed and had the grace not to deny it.

"I don't think you realize how what you're doing can affect people's lives," Erin said. "You have the opportunity to make people feel better, but instead, you're making them worse. You don't know if someone might be really depressed. You might be pushing someone over the edge."

"You sound like your friend Adele." Reg rolled her eyes dramatically. "'You don't know the powers you're dealing with.' Please. I don't have any special power or influence. People are going to believe what they want to believe. Bella wants to believe her grandma's spirit is restless, because she feels disconnected. She wants to pretend to be doing something." Reg gave a shrug. "I'm just a mirror, reflecting back what she wants to see."

"If you keep spreading around town what happened at the farm the other day, it's going to get back to Cindy. You'll get Bella in trouble with her."

"It was Bella's choice to invite us and Bella's choice to do it behind her mother's back. She's the one who set it up that way, not me."

"You need to stop talking about it."

"I didn't sign a nondisclosure agreement. This is my business. Word of mouth is the best advertising."

Erin shook her head, clenching her teeth together to keep herself from saying anything that might cross the line. She wasn't responsible for Reg Rawlins. She couldn't control what Reg did. If people judged her as being part of what Reg was doing, that was their problem. They should know Erin better.

"Did you ever apologize to Adele?"

"Apologize for what?"

"You said you would apologize for being rude to her."

Reg waved the issue away. She probably didn't even remember what she had promised. She wasn't one to get all in a knot over keeping promises or what someone else thought was right. She never intended to do what she had said, she had just wanted Erin off her back. "I haven't seen her around. She must not spend very much time in town. I'll tell her next time I see her."

"You were rude to her. You said you'd apologize."

"I just said I would. What do you want me to do? Go to her house?"

Adele's house was her sanctuary. Erin didn't know if Adele would ever forgive her if she sent Reg over there. And if Erin pushed it too much, Reg might start spreading rumors about Adele. Adele had a tenuous reputation as it was. If the townspeople decided she was more witch than wise woman, she could get run out of town, just as she had been run out of other communities.

"Just… tone it down a little," Erin suggested. "If you don't want to get into trouble, you should be trying to keep a low profile."

She should have known that telling Reg not to do something would not go over well. Erin herself had the same failing. Telling her what to do always stirred up feelings of rebellion. No longer a teenager, Erin tried to control those inclinations, but Reg was different. Erin needed to appeal to Reg's self-interests rather than urging the 'right' course.

"Terry's suspicions are already up," Erin persisted. "I'd hate to see him arrest you on some trumped-up charge because you're disturbing the usual balance of things here."

Reg considered this. "Yeah, okay." She nodded. "I appreciate the heads-up."

CHAPTER 17

The heat of the afternoon brought even more customers than usual, as word of Erin's frozen creations spread through town. Mothers brought their young children in, towing them back out into the fresh air with flushed faces and popsicle smiles.

Then the older children started to arrive as they were let out of school. Erin did a brisk trade, accepting pocket change and distributing the ice cream, frozen lemonade, and other cold desserts.

Erin recognized one of the childish voices and looked over the customers to pick out young Peter Foster, one of her favorite customers. He introduced his friends to the bakery, telling them about Erin's delicious baked goods. Some of the other children had eaten her food before, their mothers picking up bakery items or at the Halloween party Vic and Erin had thrown in Erin's back yard. They did everything they could to introduce new customers to the delicious gluten-free baking, proving that it really could be just as good as its gluten-filled counterparts. It didn't have to taste like cardboard or have the texture of sand.

"Hello, Peter," Erin called over to him. "How was school today?"

Peter gave her a brilliant smile. "Hi, Miss Erin! We came for popsicles."

"You're not the only ones. What would you like?"

"I don't know. Everything sounds so good! What's your favorite?"

"Hmm…" Erin considered the available selection. "I really like the cherries jubilee frozen lemonade. If you like sweet and tart. If you like something richer… the chocolate cheesecake frozen cones."

Peter considered, and discussed those and other options with his friends. Just like when Peter came in with his mother and sisters, he encouraged his friends to all pick something different, so everyone could share a bite of each different treat. He finally went with the chocolate cheesecake cone, his little friends made their selections, and all of the money was pooled together.

"Okay, you're all paid up," Erin told them. "Enjoy!"

They had all grabbed their selections from the cold case, so they headed outside to sit in the benches outside the bakery's front door, shaded by the colorful awnings that stretched away from the buildings, to visit with each other and enjoy their purchases.

~

Erin looked at her watch again, frowning. She understood that sometimes employees were going to be late or absent. They were held up at a traffic accident. They got up in the morning with a sore throat. Something unexpected happened.

But Bella or any other good employee should know to pick up the phone and give Erin a call to let her know what was going on. It was common sense.

But it was opening time and Bella wasn't there. She hadn't shown up for the prep. She hadn't called to say that she'd slept in but would be there for the start of business. Erin flipped the sign on the door to open and went back behind the counter to serve customers. The first few customers trickled in, some of them yawning, some of them bright-eyed. It was amazing how differently people's bodies handled the early morning.

She was too busy to think of much else as she tried to greet people, help them with their choices, and then ring them up at the till.

Erin was surprised when Terry walked into the bakery during the busy time. He knew the general ebb and flow of customers at Auntie Clem's and usually timed his visits for when it was quiet, and Erin would be able to chat. The second surprise was that he walked around the lineup of customers waiting for their turns, barging in front of the queue.

"Terry? Is something wrong?"

"Is Bella here?"

"No, she didn't show up for work today."

"She was scheduled, though?"

"Yes."

"Did she call you? Explain why she wouldn't be here?"

Erin put her hands on the counter, bracing herself. "No. What's going on, Terry? You're scaring me."

"She's missing."

"Missing?"

"Her mother called the police department this morning."

"But… what happened? Did Cindy wake up in the morning and Bella was gone? Did she go out and not come back? What?"

"She was apparently supposed to go out and put the goats to pasture. When she hadn't returned, Cindy went looking for her. The vehicle Bella should have been using was in the driveway, but she was nowhere to be found."

"Had Bella left and returned, or not gone out?"

"The goats were in the pasture."

"So she had done it and come back."

"Except there was no sign she'd come back, other than the vehicle. I'm going out there to help search for her. But we're pretty confused as to what might have happened."

"I didn't hear anything from her this morning. I thought… she'd slept in… I was pretty angry she hadn't even called." Erin felt sick to her stomach with guilt and worry.

"You couldn't have known there was anything wrong."

"Where are you going to search for her?"

"We'll start with the farm. That's the last place she was seen and where she should be. All of the Prost vehicles are there."

"What can I do?"

Terry turned his head to look at the customers waiting in line. "I think you've got your hands full at the moment. We'll get started and I'll let you know what we find."

Erin breathed out. "Okay. Thanks. Did you let Vic know?"

"I'm going to see if she can pin down Willie for me. He would be helpful out at the farm."

"Yeah. For sure. He's always willing to help; it's just a matter of finding out where he is and if he can get over there. He likes Bella, I'm sure he'll want to be part of the search team."

Erin didn't want to tell Terry goodbye; once he was gone it would really sink in that something was wrong, and Bella wasn't just going to show up late with an apology. Erin felt like if she could keep Terry from leaving, it wouldn't really be happening. That was silly, and she should let him get out of there as soon as possible so that he could find out what had happened to Bella.

"Did Cindy check the barn? I know Bella's not supposed to go in there, but maybe she did…?"

"I'll check when I get there. When you were out there, there wasn't anywhere else that made you uneasy? Maybe something Bella said she would check later?"

"No." Erin closed her eyes, trying to marshal her thoughts and put all of the memories in order so she could pull out anything important or unusual. "We toured around the farm… everything in the house seemed perfectly normal. The barn was rundown and gross, but I don't think there was really anything dangerous there. Certainly not Grandma Prost's ghost. There was…"

"What?" Terry prompted impatiently, when Erin couldn't quite catch the fleeting thought.

"When we looked at the goat barn—well, Vic went in, I couldn't get past the door—but we were looking for places that a body might had been disposed of and never found—and Vic was talking about the waste pit under the barn. She was talking about how deep it was…"

Terry gave a small shudder. "Well, that won't be a fun job. I hope we don't have to dredge it out."

"No one would have put Bella down there. Tell me no one would be sick enough to do something like that. Bella's our friend. She's only seventeen."

"Assuming that Bella's disappearance is not a coincidence… what's the difference between murdering an old woman and a teenage girl? If you can kill with cold disregard for human life… age really doesn't have anything to do with it. Whoever did this—if they are related—has already proven to be cold and cunning."

Realization washed over Erin. She hadn't actually equated the disappearance of Bella with the disappearance of her grandmother.

"If someone took Bella because of our investigation into her grandma…"

"It's not your fault, Erin. It's the fault of whoever did it. If anyone. There might be a perfectly innocent reason she didn't go back to the house, and she's still somewhere on the farm, unharmed…"

"But if someone took her…"

"What?"

"That means it wasn't Grandpa Prost. Right from the start, everyone assumed he knew where Martha was, and he had done something to her. But if Bella's disappearance is related, that means Grandpa Prost didn't do it. We've been looking at the wrong person for twenty years."

Erin felt like she was in a daze for the rest of the work day, trying to stay focused on her customers and their needs, but continually trying to take in the fact that Bella was missing and that she might hold a key to what had happened. Vic showed up an hour or so after Terry's visit, advising that she and Willie had cut their day off short and Vic figured Erin could use the help while Willie went to the farm to help Terry.

"I can't believe any of this," Vic said. "We were just there. Everything seemed so… innocuous. Whatever happened to Martha Prost, it was twenty years ago. Why would anyone care about it now?"

Erin counted out the cookies she was packing three times before she was sure she had it right.

"There's no statute of limitations on murder. If they thought that they were going to be discovered, they might have panicked."

"And kidnapped Bella? How is that going to make things any better?"

"If Bella knew something."

"But you and I know she didn't."

"Somebody thought she did."

Vic pressed her fingertips to her temples, massaging them briefly. "I just don't get it. What could she have said to tip anyone off?"

"I think pretty much everyone in town knew we were looking at the death again. Even if you and I and Bella kept it quiet, Reg has been spouting off about it all over the place."

"Reg! Where is she? Has anyone talked to her about this?"

Erin looked over at Vic. "Why would anyone talk to her?"

"To find out who she talked to. If she accused anyone. If she said she was close to finding out the secret of what happened to Martha. All of that."

"I don't know. Terry didn't say he had talked to her. I think they've been focused more on searching and seeing if they could find her on the farm."

"I'm sure he's already thought about it, but he's got so much on his mind right now, it could be overlooked. Are we going to go over to the farm after we close today?"

"I don't know. Terry is supposed to update me on what they find. Right now we would probably just be in the way."

Vic's nostrils flared. "This isn't just a job for the men. We can help too."

"I don't think anyone meant that. It's what they do professionally. Our job is the bakery. Their jobs are law enforcement and search and rescue. We'll find out after work what we can do to help them out."

hen Erin and Vic did get to the farm, things were eerily quiet. Erin had expected to find the place crawling with people, law enforcement professionals from other agencies and volunteers from town in addition to the little police department, Willie, and Cindy and the friends who had shown up to support her. But there was no one there to stop them and tell them where they could park the car, no volunteer search team being given instructions on how to do a grid search, no crowds of people milling around looking for something to do and waiting for word.

Erin parked the Challenger and walked with Vic to the farmhouse. She waited, watching for the dog, but then saw that he was tied up to the doghouse. As they got out, she saw the fleeting form of the silver-gray cat headed toward the barn. They knocked on the door but then let themselves in.

"Anyone home?" Vic asked.

Cindy was sitting in the living room, along with Lottie Sturm and a couple of other women from town that Erin recognized, but didn't really know. Erin felt awkward about showing up without something in hand. No casserole, no fresh bread or treats from the bakery; she hadn't even thought about what she should do to support Cindy.

Cindy looked at them but didn't demand to know what they were doing there. She didn't chase them back out again, either, which was what Erin had been worried about.

"Uh, hi. We're just wondering… how things are going, and where we can help."

There was no immediate answer. Erin and Vic went into the living room and found places to sit. Erin thought she should give Cindy a comforting squeeze, but she was too far away to do anything.

"Have they… found any sign of Bella?" Erin asked tentatively.

Cindy looked at her for a long time, as if she were far away and had to return to see and hear Erin. "No. They haven't found her. They don't know what happened."

"What do you think happened?" Vic asked. "Do you think she wandered off or got hurt somehow? Do you think someone would take her?"

"Why would anyone take her?"

Vic looked at Erin, silently inquiring about whether she was going to explain.

Erin swallowed. "Because… it could be related to your mother disappearing."

"That's ridiculous, and I told the policeman so," Cindy said strongly. "How could this have anything to do with my mother? She was gone years before Bella was even born."

"If the person who hurt your mother thought that Bella was getting too close to discovering the truth, then they might have… done something."

"This isn't anything to do with my mother."

"So you think she just… had an accident?"

"My mother?"

"Bella. You think that after she put the goats to pasture, she brought the car back to the house, and then disappeared between the parking pad and the house?"

Cindy stared at Vic, unflinching. "You don't know anything about it."

"No. I'm asking."

"She shouldn't have ever had anything to do with you people. You were putting ideas into her head. Filling her up with your perversions."

"Whoa!" Erin held her hands up to stop Cindy. "Neither of us ever said anything to her about anything but bakery business."

Cindy looked at Erin and Vic, her lip curled in a stubborn sneer.

"Are you saying that Bella was getting ideas from somewhere?" Vic suggested. "Ideas you thought she was getting from work?"

There was another delay in answering. Cindy turned and looked at Lottie Sturm, clearly indicating where the bizarre suggestion about Vic and Erin warping Bella's mind had come from. Erin already knew that Lottie Sturm disapproved of Vic and thought they shouldn't have anything to do with a young girl like Bella.

"She never said anything to me," Cindy admitted.

"Then what?" Vic persisted. "She came home smelling like perfume? Partied late? Brought questionable items into the house?"

"No," Cindy shook her head more definitely. "Nothing like that."

"So you just don't like the fact that she was working with a transgender person. Somebody told you they thought it was a bad idea," Vic looked over at Lottie, raising one eyebrow in question.

"Yes," Cindy agreed. "I just thought it wasn't a good idea."

"You don't think it has anything to do with her disappearing," Erin repeated.

"No."

"What do you think happened, then? Do you think she got confused or hurt? That someone picked her up? What?"

"I don't know." Cindy shook her head. "It's just so unbelievable. She's never done anything like this. She never ran away. She never threatened to run away. She wasn't ever one of those girls who argued and said she hated her mother or that she couldn't stand it anymore and was going to leave. She was never that kind of girl. We always got along together."

"Except she wanted to know what happened to her grandma and grandpa, and you didn't tell her the whole truth."

Cindy looked at Erin with a completely blank expression.

"You didn't fight over it. But she wanted to know things about her grandma and grandpa and you didn't want to talk to her about it."

"I don't know anything about it," Cindy insisted.

"How would your father have reacted if the same thing happened to him? Martha was supposed to be in the garden or the barn, and when he went out to see her, she was gone. And she never, ever came back again." Erin paused. "How do you think that would have made him feel?"

Cindy's gaze sharpened. This wasn't something she'd considered before. Erin was not blaming Ezekiel for Martha's disappearance, but empathizing with how he might have felt if his mate had simply disappeared from the yard one day, never to return again.

"He never said that was what happened," Cindy said.

"Maybe not. But how do you think he would have felt if that was what had happened? How would he have reacted to such a shocking, illogical thing? Would he have called the police about it?"

"Or would he have filled in the blanks," Cindy finished softly. "Would he have just explained it away by saying she had gone to visit someone or to run an errand, and she'd be back soon?"

"It could have happened that way," Erin said. "This might be exactly the same thing that happened to your mother."

Cindy shook her head. "People don't just disappear into thin air."

"No, they don't," Vic agreed. "So let's start making lists of how she could have disappeared. If this farm swallowed up two people, where did they go?"

Cindy turned her head to look out the window, across the lawn of weeds and drying, hardy grasses, toward the driveway.

"All she had to do is walk across the yard. She couldn't have just fallen into a hole."

"A hole," Vic repeated. "Is there… an old well on the property? A bore hole? A sink hole? A crevasse?"

"There have been several wells," Cindy said, her brow knitting. "One will stop producing, so another is dug…"

"Where are the old wells?" Vic asked. "Are they covered? Filled in?"

"Yes. Of course. It would be too dangerous to leave them open."

"What if the dirt that filled them in has settled or washed away again? What if the hole opened back up?"

"That couldn't happen," Cindy scoffed. "We would have known. We would have seen it."

"But what if you didn't see it. What if someone stepped into it without seeing?"

Cindy shook her head. "They would be hollering for help when we went out looking for them. If a well needed to be filled in twenty years ago… someone would have noticed it."

"You get around here on the roads, mostly. What if it wasn't near a road?"

Cindy continued to shake her head, but Erin thought that Vic had a good point. She pulled out a notebook and wrote down the idea. *Well hole.*

"What about other kinds of holes?" Vic asked. "Anyone digging for oil or mineral deposits? Even just a couple of core samples?" Vic held up her hands, forming a six-inch circle for reference. "Over the years, the rain and erosion could widen it into something much bigger."

"Not on our land."

Erin heard the emphasis on *our.* Maybe Vic was onto something.

"Someone else's land? The Wares or some other neighbor?"

"Robert Ware… his daddy was sure there was riches in the land. Not in growing on it or raising animals on it. But in mineral deposits… underground mines."

"Are there any mines near here?" Vic asked excitedly. "Near the house?"

"No, no. Robert Ware. His daddy wanted to drill holes. What did he call them? Sample holes?"

"Test holes."

Cindy nodded. "Yes. Test holes. On his property."

"Did they find anything?"

Cindy wrinkled her nose. "The Wares are as poor as dirt. Do you think they'd still be living like that if they had found minerals? There's nothing out here but limestone and shale."

"Were there any natural caves?" Erin tried. "Where people go exploring or mining?"

"Spelunking," Vic corrected.

"There's all kinds of caves and tunnels through the mountain," Cindy said. "It's like Swiss cheese. But we fill in any entrances that appear."

At Erin's baffled look, she explained further.

"We fill them in to keep the goats out. Goats are very curious creatures. You don't want a goat falling down into some cave and getting killed or climbing down and getting stuck. Especially not if he calls all of the other goats and they go to see what's happened to him too. When you make a living off of your livestock, you can't take chances. If there are caves or wells or bore holes, we fill them in." Vic and Erin followed Cindy's gaze back out the window. "There are no holes between the driveway and the house."

"But what if something attracted Bella's attention," Vic suggested. "What if she saw a cat, or a wounded animal, or some predator, and she chased after it into the woods?" Vic gestured to the thick trees on the other side of the parking pad. "If she ran into the woods and didn't look down in time to see a hole that had opened up…"

"The men have been searching the perimeter of the house all day. What do you think they've been doing?"

A fair question, Erin supposed. She wrote these other options down in her notebook. What if two decades before, the ground had opened up and swallowed Martha Prost? Traumatized, her husband had made up a story to explain her disappearance. No one had ever looked for the hole she had fallen down. Then twenty years later, Bella had walked into the same hole, chasing after the silver-gray cat or something else. It had a certain sense to it.

"A hole like that doesn't need to be very big," Erin said. "You read about young children falling down wells, and they're not talking about big holes two feet across. They're talking about four or six-inch pipes. For an adult Bella's size, that might translate to…?" She looked at Vic for help.

"I have no idea," Vic said apologetically. "But it wouldn't have to look that big. With grass and weeds growing over it, you might not see anything more than a depression in the ground, and not realize that there was a hole."

"We need to do a grid search like on TV," Erin determined, "where they poke sticks into the ground. Like when they're looking for an avalanche victim."

"You think my mother fell into a hole and no one ever found her?" Cindy demanded.

"It's possible. No one combed the woods when she went missing. And in the twenty years since, have you ever done a thorough search of the whole property? There are other options too. A hole is just one possibility. She might have chased after an animal and had a heart attack, and nobody found her body in the thick undergrowth. Scavengers might have—" Vic cut herself off. There was no benefit to filling Cindy's mind with gruesome images. There were large predators in the woods. There were smaller scavengers. Animals that would make short work of a body if allowed to work undisturbed. In a few days, there would be little left but bones, which would quickly be overgrown with foliage.

"Bella didn't have a heart attack," Cindy said. "Bella is as healthy as a horse. She's only seventeen, and she's strong and capable. She wouldn't have gone off chasing something in the woods when it was almost time to go into work. She's always very concerned about getting to the bakery in time."

Erin nodded and gave Cindy a warm smile. "She's a very responsible girl. Very hard worker. You should be proud of that."

Cindy didn't respond with a smile of her own. Erin shouldn't have expected her to. The woman had just lost her daughter. Expecting her to act like a proud, doting parent in the midst of her loss was ridiculous.

"Does anyone trap in these woods?" Vic asked. "Have there been any animal sightings that anyone has been concerned about? She could have gotten caught in a trap someone had put out for a bear or cougar."

"No." Cindy shook her head as if this were just too much. "No one would put traps on our property."

"And Bella wouldn't have gone onto someone else's property?"

Cindy shrugged. "We're not like that with our neighbors. When I was little, Robert Ware would yell at me and threaten me if he thought I'd been on his land. Believe me, I was always careful not to trespass. But he's mellowed out and he's kind to Bella, and nowadays there isn't anyone around here who would give us a lick of trouble for going on a stroll and crossing a property line."

"They're all pretty clearly marked anyway, aren't they?" Erin said, remembering the white fence out past the cemetery. "There are fences."

"My father was always very particular about fences," Cindy agreed, nodding. "He always made sure that they were in good repair, every year, making sure that nothing was broken or cut. If he thought a fence had been moved, even a couple of inches, he would be on the phone and making threats." Cindy gave a little shudder. Not being melodramatic, Erin didn't think. The memory actually did make her cringe.

"Ezekiel had a temper, didn't he?" she asked.

"I thought you believed he didn't know what happened to my mother."

"I do believe it. Or I'm willing to consider it, since there's no real way to know one way or the other. I was just… observing." Erin hesitated to share anything more personal, especially in front of the other women, but decided to chance it. "I was a foster kid," she said. "I've been in more than one home where… the dad was real mean. Sometimes physically abusive, sometimes not. But even the ones who didn't hit still scared the heck out of me."

"We breed them tougher than that out here," Lottie sneered. "It's not like the city where everyone is so sensitive. You can't raise your voice at a child these days without being accused of being abusive."

Erin had been watching Cindy for her reaction. Cindy looked toward her friend, but didn't agree with her comments. Her face remained a mask. She looked at Erin.

"He had a temper," she agreed, ignoring the rest of the conversation. "That doesn't mean he would have done anything to my mother, I could never picture him killing in a fit of rage. He'd never struck her in front of me. But he was very… opinionated, and very protective of the family's property and rights. He wasn't about to let anything interfere with the running of the farm and our ability to make a living. He and the neighbors were often getting into fights over boundary lines, water rights, timber, deadfall… In the time that it's been just me and Bella here, it's been much quieter. We have a much better relationship with the neighbors now, more cooperative instead of competitive." She shrugged. "With men, it's all about who's the bigger dog. Women do things differently. Daddy might not have approved of how I've handled negotiations, but I think he'd be happy with the farm and the way that it's running."

Erin tried to picture Ezekiel and how he had related to his family, neighbors, and the townspeople. The tall, spare man she had seen in the pictures had not been a self-effacing, soft-spoken farmer. He'd been an alpha male, standing guard over his territory, making sure his family and property were protected. How would he have reacted if Martha had said she was leaving him? The children were gone, and it was just the two of them; maybe she had decided the situation had become intractable. She had no more reason to stay with him.

But that didn't fit the facts. Not if Bella's disappearance was related to the disappearance of her grandmother. It was an accident or mishap. A fall, an unexpected injury. Or maybe something darker—was it possible there had been something more malevolent at work? Blackmail, jealousy, an affair. Some secret that was still important to keep even twenty years later. She'd seen it play out several times in Bald Eagle Falls. What made them think that Martha Prost's disappearance was any different?

"When you went through your parents' things after your dad died, was there any hint that either of them had had an affair? Or had been hiding some other secret?"

Cindy rolled her eyes. "Now the smear campaign starts. I thought you were going to be different because you said he might not have done it, but you're just going right back to it all being his fault."

"No, I'm not," Erin protested. "I'm just looking at the facts, trying to figure out what might have happened."

"Bella's disappearance has nothing to do with my father. He died almost twenty years ago. I don't know why Bell was so obsessed with the two of them lately. It's a dark part of my life I would like to just forget. I don't understand why she needed to bring it all up and make a big deal of it. Some things are better just forgotten"

It was a long day, especially since Vic and Erin had started so early and had been working extra hours lately getting the freezer stocked. They met with Terry and Willie and the others who were in the police department or had been asked to help with the search, coming in from the forests surrounding the farm house as night fell and they couldn't continue their search. Their faces were grim, voices low. They obviously had not found Bella nor any clear sign of what had happened to her. K9 nosed at Erin and whined when he saw her, not something he usually did. He was obviously just as tired and footsore as the men. Erin rubbed his head and fetched a water bottle out of the car for him to drink. Terry looked down at K9 as Erin fussed over him, obviously too exhausted to do anything.

"You didn't find anything?" Erin asked, even though it was clear in their faces. "No sign of what happened?"

Terry slid the backpack he wore off his shoulder and dug out a bag. "Was this Bella's?"

Erin looked down at the locket in the evidence bag. "That was her grandma's."

Terry's shoulders sagged. "Her grandma's? It hasn't been out in the elements for twenty years. It's not weathered."

"No. It was in Cindy's bedroom before. Bella got it out for Reg, when she wanted something to… help her connect with Grandma Prost's ghost." Erin gave an uncomfortable shrug, an attempt to apologize for Reg's actions.

"When was this?"

"The day that Reg and I came out here. Last Friday."

"Did she drop it that day? Lose it somewhere?"

"No, not that she mentioned. I remember her taking it back from Reg in the barn, but after that… she must have put it in her pocket."

"Did you see her with it any time after that? Did she wear it?"

Erin closed her eyes, trying to envision it. Ask her about smells and tastes, and she could recollect perfectly. Visual input was harder for her. Bella hadn't talked about the locket again after that, Erin was pretty sure of that. But had she worn it?

"I don't know," she said. "We don't wear jewelry while we're baking. Anything we wear has to be taken off, so Vic and I don't generally bother to wear anything in. Bella comes here after school, so sometimes she has jewelry that needs to be removed. She's pretty good about remembering to do it before she starts to work." Erin tried to picture Bella taking the locket off and putting it into the pencil box she used to corral such odds and ends. She could see rings and bracelets in her mind's eye, but not the locket. "No… I don't remember her wearing it."

"How about when you were out here with Vic. You guys toured all the main points of interest?"

"Yes. We started at the house, and then she gave us a tour around the property. The pastures, the goat barn, all that. Where did you find the locket?"

"Was she wearing it that day?"

"I don't think so. She didn't want her mom to know that she had taken it the day that Reg was here, so I would have expected her just to put it back in the jewelry box. I don't remember ever seeing her wearing it."

"But she could have had it under her shirt instead of over."

"Yes, sure. No one would know it was anything other than a chain."

"Or Cindy could have been wearing it," Vic suggested. "It was hers."

Terry nodded slowly. "It's a possibility," he agreed. "How much did she tell you about her mother's disappearance?"

"The basics," Erin told him. "I didn't feel like she was telling us every-thing. Maybe that's not fair, but I thought there was more to it than she would say… especially about her dad. Not necessarily that he knew what had happened to her mother or had been involved, just that… there was a lot of family history that she didn't want to talk about. Things about her dad. Maybe about both of them."

"History of domestic violence?"

"She said he had never hit Martha in front of Cindy. But she's ambivalent on whether she thought he was violent with her in private. He was a disciplinarian when Cindy was a child. Physically punished her."

"Are you going to organize a bigger search in the morning?" Vic asked. "Get volunteers from town and do a grid search? I wondered if she could have had an accident, fallen down an old well or a crevasse…"

"Maybe." Terry wiped his forehead with the back of his hand, looking utterly exhausted. "We'll have to decide that in the next few hours."

"Where did you find the necklace?" Erin asked. "Was it near the house?"

"No."

"I'm amazed you found it. With all of the thick underbrush, it could have disappeared forever. Cindy will be very glad you found it."

Terry said nothing.

"It was…" Erin tried to pin down further details. "Was it dropped along a pathway? Or did it get caught on something? Is it broken?" Erin hadn't even thought to look when Terry had shown it to her.

"It isn't broken," Terry advised. "It wasn't caught or torn off."

Erin felt her body loosen a little, relieved that there was no indication of violence.

"So it just fell out of her pocket while she was working. Do you think she lost it today? Or sometime in the last few days?"

Terry hesitated, seriously considering his answer. Erin looked over at Vic to see if she thought this was odd behavior.

"It wasn't dropped," Terry said finally. "It appeared to be deliberately placed."

"Deliberately…?"

"It was looped around the corner of Ezekiel's gravestone."

Erin blinked, surprised by this. Eventually, she shrugged. "I guess that's a logical place to put it. Sort of a memorial for Martha, reuniting her and Ezekiel. Reg told Bella they should be together, but no one knows what happened to Martha, so she couldn't be interred there…"

Something tickled at the back of Erin's brain, but she couldn't quite grasp it. She shook her head.

"She didn't do that the day we were up there," Vic said.

"No, not that I saw," Erin agreed. "She must have gone back and done it after that."

"Today?" Terry asked.

"She wouldn't have had time today. Not if she had to take the goats out to pasture and then come in to the bakery. There wouldn't have been time to go all the way up to the cemetery."

"She was already there. It wouldn't have taken more than a minute."

Erin frowned. "Why was she there?"

"To take the goats to pasture."

"To… the upper pasture?"

"Yes. That's where she took the goats this morning."

"I thought she took them to the lower pasture. That's where they were the day when we were here."

"The grass was long in the upper pasture," Vic said. "They hadn't been up there for quite a while. They must have been finished in the lower pasture, so Bella took them up instead."

Erin nodded. "Right. No reason why they wouldn't. I was just picturing that she'd gone to the lower pasture."

Vic looked at Erin, and Erin looked at her. Terry sensed the tension and waited for Erin and Vic to work it out and tell him what was going on. Erin couldn't shake the vague sense of unease she felt, knowing that Bella had gone to the upper pasture instead of the lower.

"What is it?"

"Nothing. When we were up there, we saw one of their neighbors, Mr. Ware. The fence between their two properties is up there."

Terry nodded. "We'll talk to neighbors. Today we just checked whether anyone had seen Bella. We'll have to interview them more deeply later."

"He seemed nice," Vic said.

"Yes. And Cindy said she hasn't had any trouble with them since Ezekiel died," Erin contributed.

Terry scratched his chin. "But Ezekiel and he had issues?"

"Just some competitiveness. Territoriality…"

"Had there been any dispute over property rights lately?"

"Cindy said not. She said everything has been quiet, there haven't been any issues."

Terry nodded. "I'll talk to Cindy about the necklace, maybe she knows whether Bella was wearing it today or whether she left it in the cemetery sometime last week. We can't assume it means anything at all if she wasn't wearing it today."

~

Erin had crawled into bed much later than her usual bedtime. Vic planned to take a sleeping pill so that she'd be able to get in a few hours before morning. Terry wasn't headed to bed, but he didn't need to be up as early as they did, either. The townspeople would not be ready to start a search until a decent hour. They all separated, going their different directions. Erin lay in bed, patting Orange Blossom and making notes in her notepad as she waited for her brain to start winding down so that she'd be able to sleep.

She didn't like to take sleeping pills, which always left her feeling groggy and hung over in the morning. She had an herbal tea Adele had left with her earlier, along with some valerian, hoping she'd be able to settle in for sleep, which seemed a long way off.

Orange Blossom purred and snored. Erin tried to match her breaths to his, resting her eyes.

She started to doze with the bedside lamp still on, unwilling to turn it off until she knew for sure she'd be able to fall asleep. She didn't want to toss and turn in the darkness, getting increasingly frustrated.

Her restless, waking dreams took her back to the meeting in the barn. She saw all of them as if from up above. Reg, Bella, and herself. Reg twirled and hummed and called for Grandma Prost to come, holding the locket up over her head like a beacon or a lightning rod. She heard the rustling of wings and the low murmur of the birds as they called to each other and watched the bizarre show going on down below.

"Grandma Prost," Reg chanted, "come and commune with us. Bella wants to talk to you."

"Leave me alone," Erin said from her viewpoint up above them. "Why don't you leave me in peace?"

"You can't stay in the barn," Bella told her. "Mom said. It's not allowed. It's too dangerous in here."

Erin tried to explain that she didn't know where she was, and Reg shook her head, sending her skinny braids dancing around her head. "Ghosts belong in the graveyard. Not the house. Not the barn. The graveyard."

Erin felt herself being pulled away from the barn. She tried to hold on, but there was nothing for her to grasp. The tug that started behind her belly button increased until she felt sick, and she had to let herself be pulled by it. She stared up at the stars and tried to count them. She looked for the familiar constellations but couldn't find them.

"You're on the other side," Reg told her, "so they're backwards."

Erin tried looking for their mirror images, but still couldn't find them.

"Count goats," Bella told her, "they're much healthier than sheep."

Erin tried to gather the stars to her but couldn't gather them together. Looking more closely, she saw that they were goats, and they followed behind Bella, bleating and complaining about the way they had been treated.

"You didn't put the goats away," she told Bella.

"I couldn't. He took me away before I could."

"Who did?"

"Pan. The goatherd."

Erin blinked. Her eyes were sticky, and she couldn't quite wake up.

"Where did Pan take the goats?"

"Over here." Bella led her to the cemetery, which was much larger than it had seemed when Erin had been there in real life. It went on forever, with rows and rows of crosses and tombstones, and many statues of sheep and goats and angels. A lot of the angels seemed to have pig snouts.

"I told you not to bring the pigs," Erin told them. There was no answer. She started to wander up and down the aisles, looking for the others. "Where did you guys go? Are you going to leave me here forever?"

"It is forever," Reg told her gently. "A ghost can't come back. You can talk to us, but you have to stay there forever."

Erin shivered as a cold wind blew through her. "But it's cold here. I don't want to stay here. Can't I go in the house, where it's warmer?" She remembered the barn that she had come from. "I'll go back to the barn. I'll stay there, and I promise I won't bother anyone."

"The grave is always cold," Bella said. "Wherever it is. You take the cold with you."

Erin didn't think that was true. She tried to push her way out of the cold, to look outside of the graveyard and see back through the stars to the barn again.

"It's getting smaller," Bella said. "We're getting bigger, so it's getting smaller."

And it was. She could see the white boundary fences around the cemetery. She could count the rows and columns that before had seemed endless. Erin tried to touch one of the grave markers. She could see Bella's name on it. On the one beside that, she could see Clementine's name, and then her parents. Erin hadn't realized that her family was buried in that cemetery. She'd never seen the gravestones before.

The tombstones were just beyond her reach. Every time she tried to touch them, the distance changed, and then she was standing at the edge of the cemetery where there were no new markers. While she watched, a hole opened up in the ground. First it was round, like an animal burrow, but it got bigger and bigger until she was afraid she could fall into it. As it expanded, it took on a rectangular shape, until she knew she was looking at a grave.

"You'll be fine here," Bella said tenderly. "Goodbye, Erin."

"I don't want this one," Erin objected, looking around. "I want to be buried with my family."

"They're here. Don't you worry. This is the right place."

"No. I don't want this. I still have to make the mud pies."

"The mud pies will always be there. They'll make themselves. This is your place."

As Erin watched, the rectangular hole started to fill in, and she knew it was her grave and she was already in it. They were going to bury her, whether she was ready or not.

"Wait," she insisted. "This isn't right. Wait until I'm ready."

"Death waits for no man," a man's voice insisted. "This is where you will be, until the angel blows the trump."

Erin looked at the gravestones around her, at all of the cherubs with pig noses waiting to blow the trump.

"I don't want to."

"You belong here."

The grave had filled with dirt. Grass grew over top of it, but Erin could still see the outline in the grass, the slight depression where the dirt had settled over time.

CHAPTER 20

The morning alarm went off, making Erin's whole body convulse with surprise and panic. What had happened? What had she done? Where was she, and why couldn't she just run away again?

The bedroom at Clementine's house resolved around her. She was home. It had just been one of those restless dreams like she had when she was camping or wasn't able to get to sleep at the right time. How much had she managed to get in? A couple of hours? Not nearly enough, but she needed to get up and get moving anyway. She would catch up on her sleep the coming nights. The searchers would need to be fed. Something sturdy and portable, like the energy bars she made for hikers. People who were upset about Bella's disappearance would want comfort food. And she needed to replace at least some of the many popsicles and frozen treats that had been consumed the day before.

Erin forced herself to swing her feet off the edge of the bed to start her on her way to the bathroom where she would shower to wake herself up. Orange Blossom stretched all of his legs out and opened his mouth in an incredibly wide yawn that ended with a tiny squeak. She smiled and shook her head at him.

"You're just trying to be cute, aren't you?"

He curled himself into a ball and looked at her upside-down. He would go back to sleep while Erin was in the shower, but once she was dressed, he would trip her all the way to the kitchen, yowling and complaining like he hadn't been fed in days.

By the time the animals were fed, and the tea kettle was whistling, Vic had made it into the kitchen. She yawned almost as widely as Orange Blossom and covered her mouth after it was done.

"Some mornings come way too soon," she commented. "Whose idea was it to become a baker, anyway?"

"I feel like I was up all night," Erin said. "The dreams that I was having… you couldn't have made up anything more bizarre."

"I slept like the dead."

Erin had to laugh at the turn of phrase, after the subject of her dreams. "I guess I did too, but not the kind of dead who just go to sleep and stay there!"

Vic gave her a quizzical smile. "But you don't believe in any other kind of dead, do you? You think that once a person dies, that's it and they're gone from this earth for good, don't you?"

"Yes. Other than the legacies they leave behind. I don't believe in an eternal spirit… but I did dream that I was one last night."

"You dreamed something you don't believe in? Doesn't that tell you something?"

"I've dreamed about being able to fly or breathe underwater, but I didn't wake up being able to do those things!"

Vic considered. "Well, yeah, I suppose."

Erin took a sip of her tea that had not yet had enough time to steep. She made a face and put it to the side. "I think I was Bella's grandmother, at least for part of the dreams. I could see myself from outside, because I was a ghost."

"Uh-huh."

Erin did her best to remember and describe the progression of the dream to Vic. It was already slipping away from her, in the way that dreams did, and in a few days, she probably wouldn't be able to remember any of it. She described the filling and settling of the earth inside the grave.

Vic nodded. "That's pretty macabre. I guess your brain was disturbed from everything that we talked about yesterday. Worry about Bella."

Erin frowned. She took another sip of her tea, trying to get her fuzzy brain to complete her mental processes.

"Whose grave was next to Ezekiel's?"

"I don't know… I guess his parents on one side. And then a plot beside him for Martha. But like Bella said, they didn't have any remains to bury there, so it was still empty."

"Then why would they dig it up?"

Vic shook her head. "They didn't. They didn't even put up a memorial headstone. If it was me, I would have at least put up a headstone, even if no one ever found my wife. It's just the right thing to do."

"The empty plot was to the right."

"Uh-huh."

"The ground had settled. There was a rectangle of ground that was lower by an inch."

Vic opened her mouth to answer, and then she understood. "Like it had been dug out and refilled, and then the ground had settled. But there would be no need to do that if there was no body to bury."

Erin nodded.

"You don't think someone…?"

Erin nodded again.

"We'd better call Terry!"

"Let him sleep. He won't be able to get anything done this early in the morning. He'll have to wait until everyone else is up anyway."

Terry came by the bakery later in the morning to let Erin know what was going on and what their plans were for the day. As Erin had anticipated, portable snacks and meals would be wanted, and she already had rows of granola and energy bars molded and ready to be wrapped. She tentatively explained to Terry about the empty plot next to Ezekiel's, which she suspected wasn't quite as empty as they had thought. He frowned, thinking back to his investigation of the day before.

"I was so focused on the necklace on Ezekiel's headstone, I never even looked at the empty plot," he said. "It never even registered."

"I didn't really think about it either, but I guess I noticed it subconsciously. Who would have done it, though?" Erin asked. "Cindy? I don't think Bella knew. I don't think it could have been Ezekiel, because if it was him, wouldn't he have put his wife in the next plot in line, not leaving a space for himself and then burying her in the next one?"

"First of all, you're jumping to conclusions by assuming it is Martha in that grave, if it even is a grave. And if it is, it could be an old one, from generations ago."

"Why would somebody have skipped over the plots for Ezekiel and his parents and whoever else generations ago? They wouldn't just put people in random places in the graveyard. They would have followed some kind of order or pattern."

"There may be a logical layout we don't know about. More questions than can be answered right now. I'll talk to Cindy and see what she knows. She may be able to explain it. We don't want to waste time on something that might be totally unrelated to the disappearances of Bella and her grandmother."

"Yeah. You're right, I guess. What did you find out from Cindy about the locket?"

"She wasn't even aware that Bella had it. She doesn't know when Bella might have put it on the gravestone."

"So maybe yesterday, maybe not."

Terry nodded. "And does it make any difference? What if she did put it on the grave yesterday? We already know that she was up there, she's the one who took the goats to graze. The necklace doesn't prove anything."

"What if Bella was seen putting it on the grave? What if someone took her because of that?"

"Why?"

"Because… they thought it meant she knew about Martha being buried there. Or maybe she said something to someone about the grave next to it."

"Maybe," Terry said, giving a hesitant shrug.

"When we were up there with her, she said it didn't look right."

"What didn't look right?"

"She didn't know. She said maybe it was because she hadn't been there for a while. But maybe she figured it out yesterday, like I did in my dream."

"Who was there when she said it didn't look right?"

"Just me and Vic. Mr. Ware was there for a little while too. I don't remember what parts of the conversation he was there for."

~

The first order of business was to take Cindy to the cemetery to see if she noticed anything out of place. She kept asking what was wrong and what she was supposed to see, but Terry shook his head and asked her to just look around. He looked at the depression in the ground in the plot next to Ezekiel's and looked at Erin. She hadn't imagined it. That part hadn't just been a dream. It had been a memory that her brain had been working away at, trying to tell her that something was wrong.

But Cindy barely even glanced in the direction of the plot. She looked at her father's headstone. She looked around at a few others, which apparently all looked just the same as they always had. She looked around, staring off into the distance, where Erin could see the white fence between the Prost farm and the Ware property.

"It seems so much smaller," she said, gazing around the cemetery again.

"That's what Bella said," Erin agreed. "She said it must be because she hadn't been there for a long time. Like when you go back somewhere you knew when you were a little kid, and it's so much smaller than it was, because you're bigger." Erin had felt much the same way when she had seen Clementine's shop again. *It was only that big? Hadn't it once been much bigger and grander?*

"Yes," Cindy agreed. "That must be it."

They all stood there quietly.

"That fence is new," Cindy said finally.

"Mr. Ware must have replaced it in just the last few years."

"Maybe. I don't think I've been up here since Ezekiel was buried."

"Seventeen years ago?"

"More or less."

"Cindy…" Erin ventured.

"What?"

"You said that Ezekiel used to fight over the property lines. When he thought fences had been moved, even just a few inches."

"Yes."

"Was it Mr. Ware he got angry with?"

"Any of the neighbors… but yes, he and Mr. Ware had a number of arguments over boundaries and land rights."

"And that new fence… is it in the same place as the old fence?"

Cindy studied it, considering, before slowly shaking her head.

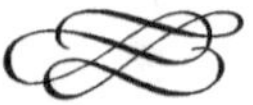

"No, that's not where the old fence was," Cindy said slowly. "It's much closer."

"And you don't know when he put it up?"

"No. He keeps the grounds," she motioned to the cemetery, "so that I don't have to. I always thought it was very kind of him. Not like he was when I was a little girl and he was always angry and yelling at us."

Eliminating the need for Cindy to go to the cemetery herself. She obviously didn't visit her father's grave.

"But why would he move the fence line?" Cindy asked. "Who cares where the fence is?"

"Your father did."

"I know, but he was fussy about things like that. I never could understand why it mattered. So what if it's not exactly on the property line? That doesn't change anything. Just because he moves the fence, that doesn't mean he moves the boundary."

Erin frowned and looked at Terry. He pursed his lips. "Actually, Miss Prost, it can."

"Whatever do you mean?"

"It's something called adverse possession. Squatter's rights."

"He wasn't living on our land. He can't claim that."

"No. But if you don't object to the placement of his fence line, and it remains there for twenty years, he can claim adverse possession and get the legal property line moved."

Cindy stared at him blankly at first, then as she gradually processed what Terry had said, her face turned into a mask of fury. She cussed Mr. Ware out. "He's trying to steal my property? That's the reason he's been so nice and offered to do the cemetery for me? So he could steal my property?" She shook her head. "Why would he? What makes an acre of my property so valuable to him? It's not even cleared to pasture."

Terry gazed toward the fence line. "Why don't we take a look?"

They all moved toward the new fence. Erin thought about how Mr. Ware had previously approached them when they were at the cemetery, demanding to know who was there as if it were his own land. Had he been worried that Bella had noticed something out of place? That one of them would wonder about the grave next to Ezekiel's? Or had Bella gone back there after taking the goats to the upper pasture, placing the necklace on her grandfather's tombstone and he had struck her down while she knelt over the grave?

She was nervous and wanted to take Terry's hand for comfort, but he didn't even seem to be aware of her as he marched through the trees, eyes ahead on the fence line. Cindy was still muttering angrily, bristling like an angry dog. They both moved faster than Erin, more used to tramping through the wilds, more confident of themselves than Erin. They climbed over the fence. K9 slipped under it. They moved in opposite directions, looking for something to indicate why Mr. Ware would want to add that land to his property. Surely it couldn't be just more forest.

Erin stopped at the fence, loath to go over and trespass on Mr. Ware's land. But it wasn't Mr. Ware's land, it was Cindy's. She had gone over the fence without a second thought. "Do you see anything?"

Terry glanced in her direction briefly but didn't answer. He watched K9 sniff around and studied the ground. Erin climbed over the fence, still feeling like she was invading Mr. Ware's space, though she logically knew that she wasn't, and he wasn't going to come and run her off his land like a child who'd stepped on the neighbor's lawn.

Terry was looking down and appeared to be following something along the ground. Erin followed a distance behind. She wondered where the actual boundary line was and looked for the old fence posts or holes where they had been. But if it had been ten years or more since the new fence was erected, any sign of the old fence would be long gone.

K9 barked and Terry hurried after him. It wasn't an alarming sound; Erin didn't think it meant that he had found anything worrisome, but something had caught his interest. Cindy had ranged off to the right, and when she heard K9 bark and saw Terry follow him, she hurried after him.

"What is it? What did you find?"

They disappeared behind a hillock and a stand of trees and brambles. Erin picked up her pace, not wanting to be left behind. She got close enough to see Terry kneeling down and Cindy leaning over.

"Some kind of cave," Terry was saying.

There was the snap of a twig behind Erin, making her jump.

Erin turned her head quickly.

It was Mr. Ware. Not the smiling, chuckling tease this time. His face was red, and he held a big heavy handgun that looked like it might have been used during the civil war. It was pointed at Erin.

"You're trespassing on private property," he growled.

Erin swallowed and cleared her throat, having difficulty getting the words out. "It's Prost property. Cindy's right there…" Erin gestured, before thinking better of it and thinking that maybe she shouldn't have pointed to where Cindy and Terry were crouched. But it was too late to take it back, Mr. Ware was already looking at the additional intruders, his brows squeezing down in a heavy scowl.

"Get your hands up, all of you," Mr. Ware shouted, loudly enough that Cindy and Terry heard and looked up to see what was going on.

Erin raised her hands tentatively. She didn't know if that was the correct response, but she wasn't armed and didn't want him to think she was. Her heart was pounding so hard she was sure everyone must be able to hear it.

She had turned to look back at Cindy and Terry to see what they were going to do and make sure that they had heard Mr. Ware. In a couple of seconds, Mr. Ware had closed the distance between them and wrapped one long arm around her, pulling her against him.

"Don't do anything stupid," Terry warned in a calm, reasonable voice. "Stop and think things through. You don't want to be in more trouble than you are already in. Threatening people isn't going to help anything. Let's just all back off and take a breath while we think this over."

"You back off. Right off of my property."

"Your property?" Cindy screeched. "This is my property! Just because you put a fence on it, that doesn't make it your property. My daddy was always on the lookout for people like you, trying to take what wasn't theirs. I should have remembered that. I should have been watching out for you too!"

"Your daddy was a pain in the neck," Mr. Ware said. "He was paranoid about those stupid fences. What did he think he was protecting? More pasture land for the goats? There isn't anything out here that's worth fighting over."

Was there really not anything of value on the other side of the fence? Had he just misjudged the property line?

Terry made a calming motion with his hands. "Let's just talk about this. Let go of Erin, and we can all have a civilized conversation. If there's any confusion over where the boundary line is, we can get a surveyor out here to establish it. There's no need to go to such lengths…"

"Nothing out here worth fighting for?" Cindy spat. "What's this, then?" She gestured at the ground. "If there isn't anything on my property that you want, then why did you move the fence?"

"What? There isn't anything over there. You people think every fox hole is a buried treasure. It's worthless land. Just more trees and weeds."

Mr. Ware was clearly bluffing.

Terry was watching Erin and Mr. Ware, assessing the situation, but he couldn't help dropping his eyes to the ground too, studying whatever he and Cindy could see there.

"I think there might be more to this," he said. "It's more a cave than a fox hole, and there's a path worn in the ground. That means someone has been traveling over this path repeatedly. There's only one thing I can think of that makes someone keep going back to a hole in the ground."

"I don't know who you think you are, cop, but you can go back to the city and forget you were ever here. This is my property."

"It's my property!" Cindy argued back. "And this mine—if that's what it is—is on my property. And I want to know what happened to my daughter! What did you do to her?"

"You mean did she come snooping around here just like her mother?" Mr. Ware tightened his grip on Erin, his arm so tight around her that it hurt. She breathed shallowly. "You all think you can just come around here and poke your noses into my business? My legitimate and rightful business?"

Terry started moving toward Erin and Mr. Ware. Erin stayed as still as possible, worried about the big gun.

"You can just stay back there, young fella," Ware growled.

"I thought you told me to get off of the property. I need to go back the way I came if I'm going to do that."

Ware considered it for a moment. "Cindy first," he said. "Get out of here and stay out. And you, just stay where you are, or I'm going to use this thing." He waggled the gun in his hand to show it off. "Let me tell you, the mess that it leaves behind isn't going to be pretty."

"No need to make any threats," Terry assured him. "I'll stay still. Miss Prost, I want you to do what he says. Go back to your car. We don't want any violence."

"You think there hasn't already been violence here?" Cindy's voice was a howl. "Where is my daughter? What have you done with her?"

"Just get out of here, woman! I never could abide the Prost women and their never-ending nosiness! Why can't you just stay at the farmhouse and mind your own business?"

Did he mean Grandma Prost? Bella? Cindy herself?

Cindy had, Erin was relieved to note, begun to walk back toward the cemetery and her car, though not at all happy about it. Ware pulled Erin off the barely discernible path, causing her to stumble, so that Cindy could walk by. After Cindy walked past him, Ware looked back at Terry.

"Take off your gun and drop it on the ground."

Terry didn't protest, but immediately did what he was told, unsnapping his service weapon, removing it from the holster, and dropping it on the ground. K9 whined and sniffed at the gun, concerned about his master's strange behavior. Terry stood with his hands at his sides, looking calm and relaxed. "You're in charge," he said. "Should I go with Cindy now?"

Ware nodded. "Walk slowly, and if that dog makes even a twitch toward me, I'm going to blow him away."

As worried as Erin was for her own safety, she didn't want anything to happen to K9. The dog was Terry's loyal partner and she couldn't bear to see anything happen to him.

Terry looked at Erin, his eyes unreadable dark holes. She knew he would do whatever he could for her, but she didn't know what he could do. Would

Ware let her go once the others were off of 'his' property? Erin had a pretty good idea that he wasn't going to be satisfied there. He knew as well as they did that kicking them off the property wasn't going to make it his. It wasn't going to keep anyone from returning.

"Can I go now?" Erin asked, her voice quavering even though she tried to keep it strong.

Ware looked toward the cave, uncertain. "Did they go inside?"

"No. No, they just came over and saw the hole. No one went in."

One strong arm around her and the gun jabbing painfully into her side, Ware dragged her over to the hollow that Terry and Cindy had been in. Erin averted her eyes, not wanting to see the cave. If she didn't see it, he couldn't kill her for being a witness. He could let her go, knowing that she wouldn't be able to tell anyone anything.

"Doesn't look like much of anything, does it?" Ware asked his hot breath in her ear. He bodily turned her toward it. Erin stopped trying to look away and obeyed him, looking down.

It didn't look like a cave or a mine. Erin had been spelunking with Vic and Willie and Terry, and she had been in the entrance of one of Willie's mines. But neither experience would have led her to believe that the crevice in the ground was anything of importance.

"Get down and take a look," Ware told her.

"I… I don't want to."

"Get down." He pushed her away from him, throwing her down with surprising force. He might be an old man, but he wasn't weak and frail. "You're the one who started all of this, asking questions about what was none of your business. So you take a look."

Erin was on her hands and knees. She reached out and swept her hand through the long grasses and wild plants to find the entrance. What had looked like just a small hole and a twisting crack in the soil was actually much bigger, it had simply been camouflaged by all of the overgrown weeds. Erin parted them, crawling forward on her knees, to reveal a hole large enough for a man or woman to crawl in through. She nodded and backed up.

"Yes… I see it now. I'm sorry to have bothered you. I don't want to stay here anymore. I'll leave you alone. You can…" she waved her hands at the cave, "do whatever."

"Go inside. Have a look around."

Erin felt like she was choking just at the thought. "I don't like caves," she confessed. "I don't want to go inside."

He smiled at her words. "Crawl in. It's bigger inside."

"I can't. I was hurt in a cave once. I can't do it."

He put his booted foot on her backside and shoved her. Erin fell on her face. A red and yellow lightning of pain shot from her face into her brain and, for a moment, she could see nothing else. She pushed herself back up, grit in her mouth, afraid that she'd broken her teeth or her nose. She tried not to inhale through her nose, afraid of sucking in blood. She crawled forward, finding her way more by feel than by sight.

"Please," she begged.

He didn't capitulate. Erin crawled farther in, feeling rocks under her knees, blinking and hoping that her eyes would get used to the dimness inside and that she wouldn't be left in total darkness. Not again. Erin tried to breathe slowly, finding herself gasping, already worried that she was running out of air. When she had been lost in the caves before, Willie had brought oxygen. Where was Willie now? Why hadn't they found the cave when they had searched for Bella the previous day?

Because they had not known to search beyond the marked boundaries of the property. They hadn't realized that the fence was in the wrong place. How were they to know? How would anyone other than the Prosts know?

"That's far enough," Erin said. "Please. It's dark. I can't see. I can't breathe."

He threw something at her that hit her in the elbow and made the nerve tingle all the way up to her fingertips. At first, she was disconcerted, thinking he had thrown the gun at her. Then she realized it was a flashlight. He had no intention of letting her come out, he wanted her to go farther. He wanted her to see what she was being consigned to.

Erin fumbled with the flashlight. She found the switch and used both hands to get it turned on. She shone it around her and was surprised to see that she wasn't in a narrow tunnel, but a large room. A natural cave. Tall enough for a person to stand up in. She looked back at Ware, who was in the narrower cave entrance behind her, holding the gun on her.

"It's… big."

"Yeah, and this is just the front lobby." He crawled in and then got to his feet. He pointed to a tunnel that branched off to the right. "Over there. Take that one."

Erin shuffled forward. She didn't want to trip and fall. Her face was already throbbing. So were her knees and palms. Her elbow was numb. She didn't want to go any farther. What if he only wanted her to go in so that he could kill her and leave her dead body there, perhaps never to be discovered, like Grandma Prost? Had he walked Bella into the same cave the day before? How many women did he think he could kidnap? Surely, he understood that the police were onto him and there was no longer any escape. Cindy and Terry knew what he had done. They had seen him take Erin. Only a lunatic would think he could get away with further violence.

"I'm tired," Erin protested. She touched her face. "I'm hurt. It's bleeding. Can't I go home now?"

"No. Take that passage."

"I don't like caves. I can't breathe in here." Her breaths were coming in short, sharp gasps. With the two of them in there, the air couldn't last for long. "Please just let me go."

He shoved her. Erin didn't fall, but she was afraid that she was going to stumble over her feet and take another face-plant. She shuffled forward, aiming for the passage Ware pointed to. She probed the darkness with the flashlight, trying to see what she was walking into as far ahead of time as she could. What was she going to find down there? Bones? A decayed body? Rats? Bats? She felt suddenly woozy, and before she knew what was happening, Ware had caught her and lowered her to the cave floor, pulling the flashlight away from her.

Erin covered her mouth, trying not to vomit. Her breathing was so fast she could no longer control it at all. She hunched over, her arm over her stomach and her hand over her mouth.

"You really *don't* like caves, do you?" Ware asked, chuckling.

"No."

CHAPTER 22

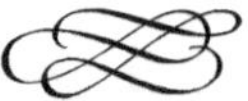

$\mathcal{H}$e let her kneel there for a few minutes, then grasped her arm and pulled her to her feet.

"Please let me go home," Erin urged.

"Just shut your whining. Come with me."

Her body moved automatically as he pulled her along, putting out one foot and then the other to keep her from falling, but all the while she just wanted to curl up and cry.

The tunnel was narrower than the big room Ware had called the front lobby. Erin could feel it closing in around her. She still felt dizzy and sick, but Ware ignored her moans and drunken swaying, taking her down the passage.

They kept going. Erin saw tools along the way. She saw areas where there had been chunks taken out of the walls, though whether with a pickaxe or explosives, she didn't know. She could see darker striations running through the rocks, but she didn't know what she was seeing. Willie would have known. He was the miner. He would have been in heaven in the little underground cave system. It was just the type of place he was always looking for.

"What is it?" Erin asked. "What kind of mine?"

"Most of what you find in Tennessee ain't worth spit," Ware told her, and he spat on the rock floor in front of them to emphasize his point.

"Semi-precious quartz, copper, bitumen. You can cart it out of here your whole life and not make enough to keep body and soul together. But every now and then, you find something else. You won't find diamonds or sapphires in here, like in South Carolina. But you can find gold."

"Gold?" Erin stared at one of the darker striations. "Is that what that is?"

"Nah. The gold is deeper down. There's a whole little world down here. You could walk through these passages your whole life and not find your way out. This system probably runs under half of Tennessee."

Erin felt the walls closing around her again. She could picture the labyrinthine tunnels he described. She'd seen them before. She could have died down there, and maybe she still would.

"I've seen your cave," Erin moaned. "Please let me go now."

Ware shook his head at her. "Don't you have any spirit of adventure? Even that stupid girl at least took some interest in seeing what was down here."

"Bella?" Erin croaked. "Did you bring her down here? What did you do with her? Where is she?"

"Do you want me to take you to see her?"

Erin held both hands over her stomach. "No! Yes. I don't want to see her if she's dead. Did you kill her?"

"I've never killed a thing intentionally in my life." He paused for her reaction. "Can you believe that? Living out here in the wilderness, and I never once shot a deer. Not even a rabbit or a thieving raccoon. I'll tell you, my pappy wasn't too impressed with me. What's wrong with a boy who doesn't want to go out hunting or fishing? Back then, it was a matter of life and death. There wasn't no grocery store where you could just go pick up whatever you needed. You ate what you got for yourself, and sometimes one deer was all that stood between you and starvation."

"That must have been very hard."

"Pappy whipped the hide offa me, trying to get me to give up my sissy ideas and help provide for the family. But that just convinced me all the more that I didn't want anything to do with causing another creature pain. He never did break me, but he did his darnedest." Ware's voice softened. "He did at that."

"I'm sorry. That sounds awful." Erin ventured a glance at him. "I've had a lot of different parents, and some of them... they think if they hurt you bad enough... I don't know if they really think you'll change, or if it just makes them feel better." She shook her head. She tried to see the boy this old man had once been. The little boy who had not wanted to hurt any living thing and was beaten mercilessly by a father who felt that he had to if they were going to survive. "I'm sorry he was like that."

Ware gazed back at her, his eyes far away. "I found these caves way back then. Looking for somewhere to shelter. Somewhere I could sleep and be safe. My pirate grotto to run away to, when things got too rough at home."

Minutes of silence ticked by.

"Can you show me where Bella is?" Erin asked.

"You're going to have to go farther."

"Okay. I'll do my best."

"Don't know how long it will be before your friends get reinforcements. They're not going to stay above ground forever."

"I can talk to Terry. We can explain…"

"Nothing to explain. He already knows the lay of the land. He's got a job to do."

Erin didn't know what was going to happen. It wasn't going to be good. She didn't want another case to end with more bodies than there were when she started investigating it. Too many lives had been lost already.

"Where's Bella?"

Ware escorted her through the tunnels. She tried to trust that he knew where it was safe and where the dangerous places were. She had to trust that he wasn't just going to push her off of a ledge or let her walk out into nothingness. The flashlight wasn't strong enough for her to be confident of her footing.

Everything he had told her could have been a lie. Some people lied compulsively. Without even knowing why, they told story after story just plucked from the air.

For all she knew, he could be a mass murderer. And still she felt sorry for him.

The cave system had been getting cooler and cooler the farther they went into it. Erin was past goosebumps into full-blown shivering. Ware was dressed for the cave, with a long-sleeved flannel shirt and long pants, thick and sturdy.

Then they stepped into a cave that radiated warmth. Erin's mind jumped illogically to volcanoes and lava and the center of the earth. Had they gone so far that they had reached a source of natural heat?

But as she looked around, she saw that wasn't the case. There was a fire. Built where there had obviously been a lot of fires before it. There was lots of white ash on the rock floor and the cave walls were coated with black soot. Up above, there was a natural chimney that drew the smoke out, so cave didn't just fill with smoke to smother them all.

Erin saw a shape beside the fire. A full figure and mop of curly blond hair that she recognized. Erin moved forward of her own accord for the first time.

"Bella! Bella, are you okay?"

Bella stirred and looked at Erin. Her eyes were distant, and it took her a few minutes to focus in on Erin. She pushed herself up. She was tied up, but still had some freedom of movement and didn't seem particularly aware of her situation.

"Erin?" Her voice was vague and uncertain. "What are you doing here?"

"Are you okay? Did he do anything to hurt you?"

"I'm fine."

But there was clearly something wrong with her. Had she gotten too cold? Not been able to get the oxygen she needed? Erin took in a deep breath, but the air in the cave smelled fresh, not stale.

"They're going to come for us," Erin told Bella, squeezing one of her hands. "They know where we are, and they're going to come and get us."

"Okay," Bella agreed.

"You're not hurt?"

"No. But you are. What happened?"

"I… fell…"

Erin looked at Ware. The angry man was gone. The man who had teased and joked with Bella was gone. Even the little boy who had been beaten for refusing to hunt for the family was gone. He just seemed like an empty shell. Like a meringue egg, which, broken open, turned out to be empty.

"Why did you bring us here?"

"This is where I used to come," Ware said, turning in a slow circle to look around the chamber. "Before I was worried about finding any gold or minerals in here. Before… when the only thing I wanted was somewhere warm and sheltered, where I was safe."

"So this was your pirate grotto."

"Yes," Ware agreed tiredly. "This is where it all began."

They were all quiet for a while. Erin strained her ears for some sign of Terry or the others. As Ware had said, sooner or later they would descend into the caves to find her and Bella. They would bring their guns. They would arrest Ware, assuming they could talk him into putting down his little cannon. If not, his pirate's grotto would be the site of his last stand.

Erin felt like she needed to keep Ware talking, if only to cover up the sounds of their rescuers' approach for as long as possible. To give them a way to find the shelter among all of the labyrinthine passageways. Erin would never forgive herself if something happened to one of the rescuers because they got lost in the tunnels.

"Mr. Ware…"

"Maybe you could call me Grandpa," Ware said. "That's what the little girl has been calling me."

It was funny for him to call Bella little, but Erin supposed that Ware's years gave him the right to think of her as just a tot if he wanted to. And if it meant he wouldn't hurt them, she didn't care what he wanted them to call him.

"Okay… Grandpa…"

"That's nice. I don't have any granddaughters of my own, and I always felt like I missed out because of it."

"What happened to Grandma Prost? You buried her beside Ezekiel, didn't you?"

He stared into the fire. "It was a long time ago, now. Sometimes it's just best to let things be."

"Some things need closure. The townspeople thought that it was Ezekiel. That he had gone crazy and killed her. Or that he had found her dead and buried her himself. For twenty years, people have blamed him for it."

"He didn't go crazy. Not until after she died."

"So do you know what happened? Can you tell me?"

"It was that darn fence… why did he have to be so stubborn about it? Why did he have to say no? I told him I'd swap with him. Hills and trees he couldn't do anything with for flat pasture he could use. Why would he say no to that? It was a good deal for him. He wasn't losing anything. He would get good pasture land out of it."

"Why did he say no?"

"Because of the cemetery… the title for this land includes the cemetery, and it includes caveats that the land can't be developed or subdivided, so that the cemetery will always be protected. I told him I'd take care of it. I wouldn't develop it. I wouldn't try to move it or develop it. I just… wanted the caves."

"Did he know that was what you wanted? And why?"

"Of course not. I would never tell him that. I learned from my Pappy to keep my mouth shut and not act like a sissy."

"And when he said no to the land swap, you tried moving the fence line."

"Not to where it is now. Just… a little at a time. So that he'd never know what I was doing…"

"Except he did."

"He had eyes like an eagle. Even though I only moved it a foot, a few inches, he knew it as soon as he saw it. He knew it, and he made such a big fuss about it that everybody else knew it too." He was silent for a time. "Martha was up here tending to the graves. She was always such a great gardener."

She didn't die tending the graves. Something had happened.

"When she saw me working on the fence, she guessed I wasn't just repairing it. She came after me, screaming about the property line, that I'd better leave the fence alone and keep to my own property. She said that when Ezekiel was upset, he'd take it out on her, even though it wasn't her he was angry with." He swallowed. "If she'd been my wife, I would never have done anything to hurt her!"

Erin looked at Bella to see if she was taking in all that Mr. Ware said. But Bella didn't seem to understand what was going on or being said. She dozed by the fire, giving no indication of being interested in the conversation. This was the revelation she was looking for, what she had asked Erin to find out for her, but she was too dopey to understand it.

"What happened?"

"She tried to wrestle my tools away from me. What did it matter? I could come back later. I could buy new tools. There wasn't any point in fighting over them."

"But you did. You didn't know what was going to happen."

"No. I was just reacting to her trying to take something that was mine.

They wouldn't let me have the caves. She tried to take away my tools. Threatened to call in the sheriff and have me arrested. I just wanted what was rightfully mine!"

But discovering the caves and making them his boyhood refuge didn't make them his. He was trying to steal them, just as surely as Martha had tried to take away his tools.

"I pushed her away and she fell." Ware shook his head bleakly.

Erin tried to picture it. What had happened? Had she hit her head? Had a heart attack?

The cave was full of paraphernalia that had built up there over the years. Things that he had brought as a boy to make it more comfortable. Precious possessions he had perhaps wanted to hide from an abusive father. Tools that he had used for mining those first years, hand tools that must have taken weeks to get results that would have been instantaneous with power tools or explosives. Ware was staring at a basket of tools. At first, they didn't look any different from the rest of the tools littering the room. But then Erin realized it was a basket of gardening tools.

Grandma Prost had been tending to the graves. Digging and edging and using the long shears to clip the grass around the headstones. Long, sharp blades. If she fell while holding the shears or the basket of tools, she could have been badly injured. Out in the wilds, away from any help, far from hospitals and medical care, there might have been nothing Ware could do for her.

"You never meant to hurt any living thing," Erin said softly.

"My pappy thought I was a coward. Maybe he was right. Maybe there is something wrong with my head. He said it's only natural, taking a life to preserve your own." He shook his head, eyes glistening. "You couldn't expect me to tell anyone. Ezekiel would kill me. They would put me in prison. I'd never survive there. Not a… a *pacifist* like me."

"It was an accident. Maybe you wouldn't have had to go to prison."

"Things were different those days. You don't know what it was like. They would have killed me."

Erin couldn't think of what else to say.

<h1 style="text-align:center">CHAPTER 23</h1>

It seemed like they were stuck in the cave for an eternity. It wasn't like it had been the last time. Erin was hurt, but only superficially. She wasn't lying alone in the dark wondering if she was going to be able to survive. She knew that Terry would come. It would take time to get reinforcements and to devise a plan, but he would come back for her. It was important not to agitate Ware. She couldn't know what he was capable of if he got worked up. He said that Martha Prost's death had been an accident, but that might just be how he chose to color it twenty years later.

He might be a pacifist, incapable of harming another living soul by choice, or he might be dangerous, lying to cover up a cold-blooded killing for profit. He couldn't deny that he had a gun and that he had held it on her, threatening her. He'd grabbed her and pushed her around. He'd already made her hurt herself once, no matter how innocent he claimed to be.

The fire made Erin drowsy once the adrenaline started to seep away. She shivered at first, all of her muscles quivering, and then the shakiness was replaced by the overwhelming desire to just curl up and go to sleep. Ware withdrew into himself, not talking to her, holding the gun in his lap and staring at it. He moaned and he whispered to himself, a man who had been alone with his own company for many years.

Erin cuddled up to Bella, trying to protect her and to reassure herself

561

that everything was okay. She closed her eyes, drifting in the suffocating warmth of the fire.

∼

She awoke with a start, hearing them coming. In the quiet of the caves, sound carried. As stealthy as they tried to be, the men couldn't completely mask the sounds of their footsteps and their words with each other as they coordinated the search through the caves. Erin sat up, trying to force alertness. She had to protect herself and Bella in whatever was to come. Bella was even dopier than Erin was, and she thought it more than just the warmth of the room. Maybe Ware had given her something to keep her quiet. Bella hadn't answered the calls of the searchers, who had been at least as close as the cemetery. Maybe their voices hadn't penetrated that far, or maybe she had heard them but been unable to answer.

"Mr. Ware!"

Erin recognized Terry's voice. She couldn't see him, but his sudden call made Erin jump, startled.

"I want you to put down the gun and come out with your hands behind your head."

Ware looked up from the gun in his lap, eyes unfocused. He made no move to obey.

"Please, Grandpa," Erin said to him. "Listen to what they say. Do what they say, and you'll be okay."

He looked in her direction. "Grandpa. I like that."

"You would have made a good grandpa. It's too bad you didn't have any grandchildren."

"I never even had a sweetheart," he said sadly. "Last in my line, and not even fit to marry."

"Couldn't you have found a girl like you, who respected your values?"

"A man had to be able to provide for his family. How could I have done that? I was worthless. Worse than worthless, needing to be fed by the efforts of others. Consuming but never giving anything back."

Erin turned her head slowly, trying to catch a glimpse of Terry. Wherever he was, she couldn't see him.

"Since you aren't going to shoot anyone," she said in a little louder voice, "why don't you just put the gun down?"

"This gun has been in the family for generations. Generations of Wares who have protected their homes and killed for their families. This country was built by guns like this." His voice was loud, as if he were trying to make it sound like he meant what he said, but it was flat and unconvincing.

"But you've never fired it, have you? Does it even work?"

He fiddled with the gun. Erin swallowed. Even if he hadn't ever fired it, that didn't mean they were safe. People got killed all the time by someone who didn't know how to handle a gun. Weapons that weren't supposed to be loaded and were just being handled casually. She was pretty sure that the police weren't going to take Erin's word for it that Ware wouldn't shoot them, or his hostages, or himself. Erin herself couldn't be sure that what he said was true.

"Mr. Ware," Terry's voice came again, loud and firm and in control of the situation. "Put the gun down on the floor in front of you."

Ware didn't move.

"Please, Grandpa," Erin coaxed. "Put it down or give it to me. I'll look after it for you. I don't want you to get hurt."

He looked across the dimly-lit cave at her. "I never meant for that woman to die."

"No. It was an accident. You couldn't have predicted what was going to happen. You hadn't planned to hurt her."

"She was trying to take away my home."

Erin ran her eyes around the walls of the cave. Mr. Ware had lived in the family home since he was born, as far as she knew. He'd probably been completely alone there for twenty to forty years, depending on when his parents had died. But the place he was attached to and considered his home was not the house, but the sanctuary he had discovered as a child. Adverse possession said that a squatter had to occupy the land he claimed for twenty years, but Erin doubted that the law would extend to an underground cave, even if Mr. Ware had used it since childhood.

"I know, Grandpa."

"The little girl… she was there, in the graveyard. She saw the extra grave. She knew what it meant."

Erin nodded. She pictured Bella putting the necklace over the headstone, marking the place where she now knew her grandmother was buried as well. "And she knew something was different. That the fence had been moved from where it was when she was little."

Too close to his secrets.

"I couldn't let her take it away. I told her… I'd show her…"

"And you brought her in here." Erin looked at Bella sleeping by the fire. Had he tied her up before or after bringing her inside? Had she been able to put up a fight? Or had he taken her off guard?

"And the car? How did it get back to the house?"

"I drove it." He shrugged, as if that were obvious. It was a bold move; Cindy could have seen him driving it back or getting out of it at the house. It was in sight of the front door. The dog might have gone after him, or at least sounded the alarm. But he'd gotten cleanly away, so they wouldn't know where Bella had disappeared from. He was a neighbor, so maybe the dog knew him and didn't consider him a threat.

"It's time for us to go," Erin told him. She pushed herself to her feet and stood there for a moment, waiting for her head rush to settle. Her mouth and face still throbbed, but she felt curiously removed from herself. She didn't look in the direction of the cave entrance, where she knew Terry was watching for his opportunity. She walked up to Mr. Ware. "Give that to me now," she told him firmly.

At first, he didn't respond to her any more than he had obeyed Terry's commands, but then he raised his eyes to her, frowning.

"Come on," Erin insisted. "You're not going to shoot me, so just give it to me before someone gets hurt. We don't want any accidents."

Mr. Ware turned the gun around and held it out to her, grip first. Erin hated to touch the weapon, but she swallowed her aversion and took it from him.

"Thank you."

She turned toward the entrance to show Terry that she had it. He emerged from the shelter of the tunnel where he was hidden by the darkness, giving low instructions to someone behind him. He held his gun in front of him, outstretched, pointing directly at Mr. Ware.

"Step back, Erin. As far away from him as you can."

Erin shuffled back away from Mr. Ware, her heart pounding again. The big gun was heavy in her hand, and she held it down at her side, worried about the possibility of triggering it accidentally. Vic and Willie had both suggested that she get firearms training and at least keep a gun in the house, but she was too afraid of accidents. She wished she'd humored them and at least held one before. Then maybe it wouldn't feel so awkward and menacing in her hand.

Terry gave Mr. Ware instructions, pointing the gun at him in a two-handed stance. His voice was sharp, but he wasn't yelling. Not like some of the cops on TV, always screaming and rushing suspects, trying to be as intimidating as possible. When he had Mr. Ware face-down on the rocky floor, he first patted his pockets and body for a hidden weapon before finally holstering his own gun and doing a thorough pat-down. He arrested Ware with a long litany of charges and the usual spiel about his rights. Others came into the cave, which quickly became crowded with bodies. The sheriff and Tom. K9 was already with Terry, whining and watching the suspect closely in case he became a threat. Willie was there. He was the one who took the gun from Erin's hand and passed it to the sheriff.

"Are you okay, Erin? You're bleeding."

Erin touched her face and drew it back slippery with blood, almost black in the firelight. "It's fine. I'm okay. Check Bella, he might have given her something."

Willie gave her arm a comforting squeeze and moved on to check out Bella.

After securing Mr. Ware, Terry passed him on to Tom with instructions, then turned to Erin. He enveloped her in a big hug, holding her close against his warm body. "Erin, I was so scared. I'm sorry. I'm so sorry I let him hurt you and bring you down here. I wanted so badly to help you, but I didn't want to escalate him. I needed to get Cindy out of there and to give him a chance to calm down…"

"I know, I know," Erin assured him while the words flowed out in a torrent. "I know. And we needed to find Bella. All of these tunnels… we might not have found her in time if he hadn't brought me here to her."

She remembered her own ordeal, lying hurt and alone in the pitch black, afraid that no one would ever find her. A shudder went through her. Terry felt it and squeezed her more tightly.

"It's okay, Erin. It's all over. You're safe. And Bella is going to be okay. Nobody else got hurt."

"I know." Tears were running down Erin's cheeks. She didn't know why. She hadn't cried while Ware had been holding her. She didn't cry until she was rescued, and then there she was, bawling like a baby.

Terry just kept holding her, rocking back and forth, waiting for her to calm down. "You're probably in shock. We need to get you out of here."

"I can walk." She didn't want to be taken out of there on a stretcher. Not again. She wanted to be able to get out under her own steam, her hands and feet free.

"Let's go, then. Come on."

With a supportive arm around her, he led her to the tunnel she and Ware had entered through. Erin hung onto him, glad to have something to hold on to.

"What if we can't find our way out? What if we get lost?"

"Do you think Willie would let us get lost? Do you think he let me just run in here following your voice and get all turned around? He's too much of a professional for that. I call him in as a consultant, and then he takes charge and I have to listen to what he tells me!"

Erin couldn't help but laugh at his aggrieved tone. "You did the right thing," she assured him. "I'm glad you didn't get lost."

She saw that there were small glow sticks dropped at regular intervals, guiding their way all the way back to the entrance.

Cindy was waiting with other townspeople outside. She pulled away from Lottie, almost tackling Erin in her anxiety. "Where is Bella? Was she in there? Is she okay? They won't let me go in!"

Erin tried to pat Cindy's arm comfortingly. "She's there. She's alive. They'll bring her out in just a minute."

Cindy collapsed. Erin could do nothing to catch her, but Lottie was there and another of the ladies from the town, and they kept her from landing on the ground.

"It's okay, Cind. She's okay," Lottie repeated. "Just hang on. She'll be right out."

"My baby. My baby girl..."

Her earlier fortitude and her anger at Mr. Ware were gone. Just like Erin breaking down once she knew she was safe, Cindy finally gave herself permission to express her anguish over Bella's disappearance. She cried and wailed, her friends doing the best they could to comfort her.

Terry led Erin away from them. He took her to a quiet patch of grass where they sat down and took a breath.

"Did he tell you anything?" he asked. "Why he took Bella and what happened to her grandma?"

Erin nodded and told him about Mr. Ware's emotional claim on the caves and the confrontation with Martha Prost that had led to her accidental death. She told him about the gardening tools in the cave, and he said he'd look after them later.

"We'll need to have a look at everything in that cave. There may be more to the story than he is telling us."

Erin nodded. The feeling she'd had that Ware might not be telling her the full story was validated by Terry's words. "I don't know exactly what happened, but at least we know one thing—it wasn't Ezekiel Prost who killed his wife. He's been blamed for it all these years, but it wasn't him."

They turned toward the cave entrance as a hush fell over the group gathered in the glade. Willie came out first, turned around backward. He was holding on to Bella's arms and helped to pull her up. She leaned on him for support and looked around in a daze. Cindy fell on her, crying and cuddling her daughter to her. Willie hovered close by, hands out to catch Bella, but Cindy held on tightly and didn't let her go.

"She's dehydrated," Willie said. "I don't think she's had anything to drink since she disappeared, and she's been lying by the fire. Give her some water, and we should probably get her to the hospital where they can put her on an IV for a few hours."

Erin watched the ministrations over Bella, grateful that she wasn't the one who had been languishing underground this time. She'd only been there for a few hours and didn't need to go to the hospital. Terry got back to his feet to talk to Cindy about interviewing Bella as soon as she was settled at the hospital.

"I don't want you talking to her about it," he warned. "Don't ask questions and taint her memories. Just be supportive. Leave the questioning to me."

Cindy nodded. She and her friends walked Bella back toward the car so they could take her to the hospital. Bella walked slowly but seemed to be unharmed.

"How about you?" Willie asked Erin. "Are you okay?"

Erin dabbed at her sore mouth. "I'll be fine. Thanks for coming to our rescue—again."

"Any time you get stuck underground, you can expect me to come looking for you." Willie looked around and motioned to someone in the crowd. It wasn't until then that Erin saw Vic.

"Oh, Vicky! Come on over. It's okay," Erin told her.

Vic separated from the crowd and hurried over to Erin. She sat down beside Erin and gave her a hug around the shoulders. "You gotta stop doing this," she said. "It just kills me to stand around waiting for someone to find you and bring you up."

"It wasn't planned," Erin assured her. "I didn't come here to go caving."

"Spelunking," Vic corrected, smiling because she knew Erin had said it just to tease her.

"Spelunking. I just came to look at the graveyard again. I had no plans to go into any cave."

"But it doesn't seem to stop you." Vic shook her head. "Now y'all been down in that cave and I haven't! Is it at least a good one?"

Erin rolled her eyes. She turned her head to get Willie's opinion. "It's big, lots bigger than you'd ever guess by the entrance. I don't know how many tunnels there are; Mr. Ware said they run all over Tennessee."

"That's an exaggeration," Willie said with a wry smile. "But there are definitely a few miles of passages."

"And Mr. Ware said there was gold," Erin said, keeping her voice very low so that the other spectators nearby wouldn't overhear her. "He said that was pretty rare in these parts."

"Almost unheard of," Willie agreed. "In fact, I'd be surprised if it was true." He cracked open a water bottle and took a sip, then offered it to Erin. "Just don't get blood in it."

"You don't think there's any gold?" Erin asked.

"Probably not. I don't see any sign of a vein or that he's been moving any ore out of there. If he was doing any actual mining, there would be rock to be taken out. But you'd have trouble even getting a small wheelbarrow through that opening, let alone anything that could move large amounts of rock."

"There could be another entrance, something where it's easier to get out."

"Could be. But I didn't see any indication of any real work going on. Or any mineral deposits that would lead me to think there was gold in there. Or anything else valuable."

"Just his memories," Erin decided. "He said he found it when he was a little boy. It's where he used to go to escape his father."

Willie nodded. "That, I can believe. Most miners don't actually have any desire to live underground, but he had a lot of personal stuff down there. Mementos. Things to make him more comfortable. It makes sense that it was sort of his private clubhouse."

"A refuge."

"Well… his daddy died a long time ago. Time for him to face life."

"I hope he *isn't* facing life," Erin said, twisting the meaning of his words. "If Martha Prost died by accident… then what sentence is he looking at? For kidnapping and whatever else…?"

"I'm not the expert. Terry might have an idea, but neither of us is a lawyer."

Willie motioned for Terry to join them to talk. Terry looked at his watch, then walked back over. "I have to head over to the hospital before too long. Sheriff and Tom can take care of the scene. What's up?"

"Just wondering what kind of time Ware is looking at. What is he being charged with?"

"Two kidnappings, weapons charges, resisting, maybe Mrs. Prost's murder. He'll probably spend the rest of his life behind bars. Don't know if he'll actually make it to trial or not. He's not a young man and jail conditions are not exactly conducive to good health."

"He's afraid of how he'll be treated by the other prisoners," Erin told him.

"He's not a child molester or murderer, so he won't be segregated. I doubt if anyone will really care about an old man who's not associated with any cartels or gangs. They have more important things to worry about."

"So you think he'll be left alone?"

Terry looked at her and couldn't come up with an answer. Eventually, he just shook his head. He looked at his watch again and said he needed to get to the hospital.

"I'll catch up with you tonight, okay? You'll be okay? I can get your statement tonight or tomorrow, you don't need to hang around here."

"Okay," Erin said with a nod of relief. "I think I'd just like to go home and relax for the rest of the day."

"Go ahead. You deserve it. Especially after the way you handled Mr. Ware and got him to give you his gun. I was really worried about gunfire and hostages in an enclosed chamber. It could have turned out very differently."

"Was it loaded? He said he'd never used it."

"It was loaded," Willie said. "But I believe the part about him never having used it before."

"Why? Was it… loaded the wrong way?" Erin asked uncertainly.

Willie smiled. "No firing pin. He couldn't have shot anything if he'd wanted to."

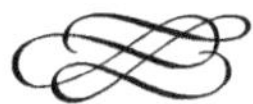

CHAPTER 24

*R*eg was home when Erin got there. She seemed surprised to see Erin and Vic.

"I thought you'd be at the bakery. What are you doing home already?"

"Things have been a little crazy today," Erin said, shaking her head. "Didn't your powers of divination tell you that?"

"My...?" She actually looked at Erin. "Holy heck. What happened to you? You didn't have a fight with that boyfriend of yours, did you? Cops always think they can get away with it, especially in small towns like this. Don't you put up with it!"

"It wasn't Terry! That's two strikes," Vic said in delight. "Once more, and you're out. I thought you were so good at reading people."

"It's different with Erin," Reg excused herself. "She's known me for so long, she can block me. And I wasn't ready to do a cold reading. I just got up from a nap, and I haven't had a chance to get my motor running yet..."

"Erin has been busy catching Martha Prost's murderer. You know, the ghost you talked to?"

"Really?" Reg's eyes got big. "You solved the ghost case? I'll bet she was somewhere cold, wasn't she? I've been getting chills all afternoon, I knew something was happening on the case... You should have taken me with you. I could have helped you to figure it out faster."

Erin rolled her eyes. She remembered when Reg had been the big sister, someone Erin looked up to, so much more sophisticated and knowledgeable than Erin. Reg had known everything, and Erin had idolized her. Wanted to do everything like her. How many stupid schemes had she participated in and how many times had she gotten in trouble, because she'd been stupid enough to buy into Reg's nonsense?

Reg was still stuck in the same place, still trying to scheme and talk her way into wealth or a reputation, but Erin had grown up.

Erin gave her a little smile, though it made her cut lip crack again, causing a flash of pain.

"It's all done, now, Reg. You missed out on it."

"You should have called me," Reg complained. "You should have let me come with you. If it was me, I would have included you."

"Have you found somewhere else to stay yet?" Erin changed the subject. "You said you'd have somewhere inside a week."

Reg looked uncomfortable. "I didn't count on how small this town is. No one has anything."

"Maybe you'd better find another town, then," Erin said unsympathetically. "You've about worn out my hospitality."

Reg looked at her sullenly, then shrugged. "Fine. I'll get out of your way. Tomorrow."

"Thanks. Sorry things didn't work out for you here."

Reg stared at Erin for a few long moments. "You've changed," she said finally. "I thought you were still the same old Erin underneath all of this professional baker stuff. But you're different."

"It's called growing up. Finding your place in the world. What is it you actually want to do with your life, Reg? You want to keep acting like a carnival fortune teller? Or is there something else you'd actually like to do with your life?"

"I don't know, but I can tell you I don't want to be tied down to a place like this. If I had inherited the bakery and this house, you can bet I would have liquidated it. I wouldn't be tied to all of this."

Erin nodded and didn't argue. They were two different people, and while she hadn't thought she'd ever have the opportunity to settle down with her own home and her own business, she'd been quick to do it when the chance came along. Reg wouldn't have taken the opportunity. She would have just tried to get whatever money she could have out of it and blown it all on some new scam.

"Well, good luck with whatever is next. Me… I'm going to take a nap."

Erin said her goodbyes to Vic and Reg and retired to her room.

Orange Blossom had obviously been sleeping in Reg's room, but when he heard Erin going to her bed, he jumped down from Reg's bed and hurried after Erin, yowling inquiringly after her, confused by her strange behavior. Erin rarely had time for a midday nap and, even when she did, she rarely took it. There was too much to do. Too much planning. Too many lists. Too many frozen treats to be made.

"Come on, then," Erin told the cat. "Come and get some cuddles."

Soon, he was curled up under her chin, his whole body vibrating with purrs. Erin closed her eyes and went to sleep.

Monday everything was back to normal, with Erin and Vic at the bakery early, baking the day's bread and then opening to the usual morning crowd.

What wasn't usual was that Bella was there even though it wasn't her shift. Erin had watched her drive up to the bakery in her mother's car, but with Cindy nowhere in sight. Bella was driving herself.

She came in and ordered a cookie and tea just like any other regular customer. Erin sensed something different in her. A new determination and independence. Far from withdrawing into herself after the horror of the kidnapping, she had instead remade herself. She was the new and improved Bella, confident and unafraid.

"You look really good," Erin told her. "No one would guess that just two days ago…"

"I'm not even going to talk about it," Bella said, holding her hands up. "Yesterday is over and today is a new day with new opportunities. I'm not going to waste another day fussing and worrying about things that are outside my control."

"Good for you. I don't know if I could ever stop myself from worrying. But I agree about taking on every new day… like a gift. Who knows what tomorrow will bring. Just deal with one day at a time."

"What good did worrying ever do for anyone? I spent my whole life worrying about what my mother would think, what the people in the town would think, what the right thing to do was… but I'm done that now."

Erin considered this. "Your mom loves you."

"I know that. But I'm not a little kid anymore. I can't just stay there my whole life, sheltered by her. She shouldn't have stayed there all this time. She should have gone to the city or somewhere she could be her own person. Like she was before Grandma disappeared."

"You think she should have sold the farm and done something else?"

"She's never been happy here. I don't know about selling the farm. Maybe someone else could stay here and look after it until she was ready to retire. But she hates it here. She should have gone on to do what she wanted."

Erin nodded. She didn't know Cindy Prost well, but the woman had never seemed particularly happy. If she'd left a happy, independent life to look after her father and then her daughter, her resentment was understandable.

The bells over the door jingled, and she and Bella looked up to see who it was. Reg stood in the doorway for a moment, looking first behind the counter where Vic was, then at the table where Erin stood talking to Bella.

"Oh, there you are. I just came to tell you… I'm heading out. I guess this is it."

"You can call me," Erin said. "Keep in touch. I'd like to know how you're getting on."

"As long as I'm not living here."

"I don't think it was a good fit," Erin said, keeping the comment as neutral as possible.

Reg swept back her hair. "No, I thought a little backwater town would be a good place to set up shop. Lots of superstitious people, don't get out much, they could use some entertainment." She shrugged. "But it wasn't like I thought it would be."

"Is that all this was to you?" Bella demanded. "Entertainment?"

Reg looked at her. "I tried to help you," she said. "That wasn't fake. I never said I'd be able to solve your Grandma's murder… but in the end, it did get solved."

"By Erin, not by you."

"I didn't say I did. But I did communicate with her. Maybe that helped Erin to figure out what was going on." Reg gave a shrug. "You never know how these things are meant to unfold. What we call coincidence and intuition…"

Bella gave her a scornful look. "You said that she was cold where she was and that she wanted to be buried next to my grandpa."

"Yes. That's what she communicated to me."

"But she *was* buried next to my grandpa."

"Err…" Reg looked for an answer. Then she looked at her phone, feigning surprise. "Is it that late? I'd better be getting on my way."

She stepped closer to Erin, gave her a hug and an air kiss, resting her cheek against Erin's for an instant, then pulled away.

"I'll write," she promised. "Or something."

EPILOGUE

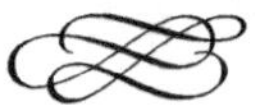

$\mathcal{E}$rin was cleaning up when her phone rang. She had a good idea who it would be and pulled it out of her apron pocket.

"Hi, Terry."

"Are you okay to get together for a while this evening, or are you too tired?"

"Either way, I need to eat." Erin wouldn't really be sure how she felt until she'd had a chance to sit down and relax. Then it might all catch up with her.

"Do you mind eating at home today? Would that be too much work? We can just have sandwiches."

"That's fine. Why don't you pick up a packaged salad at the grocery store? I'm not sure what's in the fridge."

"Okay. I'll see you in half an hour or so."

Erin ended the call and slid the phone back into her pocket. "Terry's coming over. You want to join us?"

Vic shook her head. "Willie and I already have plans. You guys can have the house to yourselves." She winked. "Don't do anything I wouldn't do."

Erin felt herself blushing for no reason. Rather than protesting, she tried to raise her eyebrow in an enigmatic quirk, but wasn't sure whether she succeeded or just ended up making one of the crazy faces she and Reg used to practice on each other.

It was obvious when she let Terry in at the house an hour later that he had something on his mind. He took the salad into the kitchen to put it in a bowl and mix it, but said barely a word to her. Erin started to get the sandwich fixings out.

"What's up?"

"What makes you think something is up?"

"I may not be a detective, but I think I can tell when something is wrong." She studied him. "Is it work? Something go off the rails with Mr. Ware?" She remembered how he had said he wouldn't last in prison and hoped something hadn't already happened to him. Surely, they would be careful when introducing a new prisoner into the general population.

Terry's dimple was nowhere to be seen. His lips were pressed tightly together and there was a frown line between his brows. K9 watched him, panting.

"It's not Mr. Ware."

"But it is work? I guess it's not something you can talk to me about?"

He seemed to be torn. Erin lifted her hands in a questioning gesture.

"It's about Reg."

"Reg is gone. You don't need to worry about her anymore. I told her she'd been imposing on my hospitality long enough and sent her on her way."

"Did she say where she was going?"

"No. I asked her to keep in touch… but it could be another ten years before she decides to talk to me again. She's like that."

"No idea where she might go? Any mutual friend who might be able to put you into contact with her?"

"Uh… I don't know." Erin thought through their various acquaintances. Was there anyone Reg might keep in closer contact with? "What's wrong?"

"Your sister made off with several family heirlooms when she left town."

Erin's stomach clenched. She turned away from the table, where she had been laying down plates. "No! Oh, tell me she didn't!"

Terry didn't recant. Erin had known he wouldn't. He wouldn't have joked about something like that. And it wasn't something Erin would have put past Reg. Erin reached for the nearest chair and sat down with a thump, her knees weak.

"Oh, Terry, I'm so sorry. Who? What did she take?"

"I can't give you a list, those reports are confidential. But I did get reports from several women that are remarkably consistent with each other."

"What did she do? Did she steal from their houses? I said she was trouble. I knew this wasn't going to turn out well!"

"She apparently would ask for an item that the dearly departed would have valued, for her to hold on to and get a clearer picture of the person they wanted to talk to. She asked to hold on to them for a day or two, so she could really get to know them, and then set up appointments to return the valuables and give a reading. But when word spread that she'd left town… we started to get anxious calls."

"Oh, Regina," Erin groaned.

"Do you mind if I check her room, just to make sure she didn't leave anything here?"

"You don't think she'd leave heirloom jewelry here."

"No. I'm hoping maybe a note scribbled on the bedside table, a reservation number, something that might indicate what direction she was going."

"Of course. You know which room she was in. The one that used to be Vic's."

"I thought you were going to take back the master bedroom after Vic left."

Erin shrugged. "Mine is too cozy. I can't bring myself to take Clementine's room."

Piper clicked his tongue at K9 and went to search Clementine's bedroom. Erin hadn't yet had a chance to see what needed to be tidied away and to change the sheets; everything was just as Reg had left it. Terry was back a couple of minutes later shaking his head.

"Nothing there. In fact, you might want to check and make sure she didn't abscond with any of your valuables."

She shook her head. "No… if she had the nerve to steal from me… I don't want to know about it. I really don't."

They turned their attention to their supper, both quiet and pondering over the developments individually. Orange Blossom was under foot, while K9 stayed politely by Terry's chair and Marshmallow kept to the side of the room, watching them all with one eye.

They avoided any further discussion of Reg during dinner, instead talking about the weather, their friends, and the bakery, occasionally returning to the subject of Mr. Ware and Martha Prost.

"Bella even went downstairs to the storeroom today," Erin told him after they had adjourned to the living room couch. "She hasn't gone down the hall to the commode yet, but she went downstairs, and that's a huge improvement. I wouldn't be surprised if she actually made it to the loo one of these days."

"She's a brave girl," Terry said. "I don't think she knew that about herself before."

Erin nodded. "She's spent too much time worrying about ghosts and being safe from things that were never really a threat. I think this experience… forced her to see that there are a lot worse things in life. There's no point spending your time worrying about things that don't really matter."

"A good lesson," Terry agreed pointedly.

"I don't spend a lot of time worrying. And I'm not afraid of ghosts."

"I still think you worry more than you need to. And like Bella… you worry about what other people are saying about you."

"I'm going to try not to."

The doorbell rang. Erin looked at the clock on the wall. K9 lifted his head and looked in the direction of the door, his ears pricked curiously, but he didn't give any sign that there was danger lurking outside.

Erin went to the door. She flicked on the outside light and looked out the peephole. She didn't have the burglar alarm armed like Terry thought she should in the evening, but she couldn't be much safer, at home with the town cop. She opened the door.

"Charley, hi! Come on in."

Charley entered. She saw Terry on the couch and gave a sly smile. "Well, I'll be sure not to interrupt you for too long."

"Come visit with us for a few minutes."

Charley sat down in an easy chair, and Erin slid back into the warm spot next to Terry. He put his arm around her.

"I just got word from the estate lawyers," Charley said, leaning forward excitedly. "They've finally agreed to let me open The Bake Shoppe!"

Erin's stomach tightened into a knot. "They did? That's great news for you. Does that mean…" She frowned, trying to sort it out. "They've decided to give you Davis's portion as well?"

"Not yet. They're going to hold half of the estate in trust, but for now, they're letting me control the decisions about what to do with the bakery. They said that since Davis hasn't been proven guilty of causing Trenton's death, they can't take his portion away from him yet. If he's found guilty, they will. Until then, they're just going to hold it."

Erin nodded. "Well… I'm glad it's working out for you. I guess that means we'll both be in the baking business." Erin's job was going to be that much more difficult with a direct competitor.

"I'm still not getting up that early in the morning. I'll have other people to do that for me."

Erin laughed. "You're not exactly a morning person."

"No. But…" She made a gesture like she didn't know what to do with her hands. "I wanted to thank you for what you did."

Erin glanced over at Terry. "I just did what anyone would have. There was written evidence that Davis knew about Trenton's allergy and that it could be fatal. There's enough circumstantial evidence piling up to show that he and Joelle knew exactly what they were doing and were happy with the results."

Terry nodded.

"So… thanks for that," Charley said again. "I don't know that it was the smartest business decision for you, but I appreciate it. I'm sure people in town will be happy to have The Bake Shoppe open again. No offense to your baking—you make some amazing stuff—but some people just want traditional wheat breads."

"I'm sure there's enough business for two bakeries." Erin had said it many times before, but had never doubted her own words so much. She gave Charley a reassuring smile she did not feel. "I'm looking forward to it."

Did you enjoy this book? Reviews and recommendations are vital to making a book successful.

Please leave a review at your favorite book store or review site and share it with your friends.

Don't miss the following bonus material:
Sign up for mailing list to get a free ebook
Read a sneak preview chapter
Other books by P.D. Workman
Learn more about the author

PREVIEW OF SOUR CHERRY TURNOVER

AUNTIE CLEM'S BAKERY #7

CHAPTER 1

$\mathcal{E}$rin arranged the cupcakes carefully in the display case, carefully adjusting the space between them and making sure the icing shapes would all be oriented right-side-up for her customers.

"Well, if it isn't your favorite person in the world," Vic drawled.

Erin didn't need to look at her assistant to know who was approaching. She raised her eyes to look through the glass of the display case to the young woman about to walk through the front doors of Auntie Clem's Bakery, the muscles of her stomach clenching into a hard knot. She tried to school her expression to keep a pleasant smile on her face, and smushed the cupcake in her hand against the bottom of the shelf above it.

She groaned and pulled it out. It was a good thing there were no customers in the shop at that moment.

"Sorry." Vic gave a little grimace and a shrug.

Erin grabbed a damp cloth to wipe the smear of icing from the shelf, then straightened to greet her half-sister.

"Hi, Charley."

"Oops," Charley looked at the cupcake in Erin's hand. "Looks like that one didn't make it."

"No." Erin chucked it into the garbage can. She put her hands on her hips, unconsciously retreating into a defensive stance. "What can I help you with today?"

Charley smiled. Having only recently met Charley, Erin still found it disconcerting to see the dark hair and delicate features she was used to seeing in the mirror on someone else's face. And she knew that particular smile was just as fake as her own.

"I came to see if I could borrow a muffin pan," Charley said. "Every time I turn around, there's some other piece of equipment I am missing. The Bake Shoppe should have been fully-stocked. I'd really like to know who has been taking stuff home with them. If I could afford it, I'd hire help from the city instead of Bald Eagle Falls, just so I could be sure I wasn't hiring back whoever has been helping themselves to everything!"

Erin wavered between sympathy and irritation. She knew that she would have been pretty angry if she'd found someone had been stealing from her, especially when the bakery was her livelihood, but she was also increasingly annoyed with Charley and dearly wished that she wouldn't reopen The Bake Shoppe. And not just because she would be in direct competition with Erin's bakery.

"You must be madder than a wet hen," Vic said, without a trace of sympathy in her voice.

Erin avoided looking at Vic.

Charley nodded. "You bet I am. Half of Angela's recipes use weights for flours instead of measuring cups, so you'd think there would be an electronic scale in the place, but do you think there's any sign of one?" She sighed. "Anyway, I need to whip up some muffins before opening and I really don't have time to go into the city to get a jumbo muffin pan, so I wondered if I could borrow one of yours just for a couple of days and then I'll bring it back to you."

Erin had already explained enough times that she shouldn't have had to tell Charley again. "I can't, Charley. They would be contaminated with gluten and I wouldn't be able to use them again."

"I'd clean them really well. And it would be cooked, so it shouldn't cause a problem for your *special* clientele. Please, Erin, this will be the last thing that I ask for."

"It doesn't matter how well you clean it, there could still be microscopic traces of gluten or other proteins on the pan, enough to trigger a reaction in someone. None of the equipment I use has ever been used for gluten-containing batters. Nothing is cross-contaminated, so people who are celiac or allergic don't have to worry about reacting to my baked goods, no matter how sensitive they are."

"But like I said, it will all have been cooked anyway. So they shouldn't be allergic."

"Baking doesn't denature gluten proteins enough for someone to stop reacting to them."

"I had a friend who was allergic to eggs. She couldn't eat them scrambled or boiled or fried up for breakfast, but she could eat cake and cookies that had egg in them, because baking changes them."

"Some people can tolerate eggs that have been baked," Erin agreed, "but it's not the same with gluten. Or they'd be able to eat regular bread and there wouldn't be any need for specialty baked goods! I can't use pans that have been used for regular muffins. Even though you scrub the pans and they look perfectly clean, there could still be microscopic amounts of gluten that would get into my baking. I'm not willing to risk it."

Charley folded her arms across her chest and pressed her lips together, clearly irritated. "Can't you help me out just this once?"

"I'll help you any way I can," Erin promised, "just not in any way that will endanger the health of my customers."

She suspected that, like a large portion of the population, Charley figured that anyone who claimed to be gluten intolerant was just trying to get attention, and that they didn't really have any health concerns at all. While some people did avoid gluten some of the time just because it was a trendy thing to do or they thought it would help them to lose weight, Erin had customers who could end up in hospital if she glutened them. She wasn't about to take chances with their health.

Erin looked over at Vic. As usual, Victoria Webster had her long blond hair put up and corralled inside a baker's cap. Her makeup was perfect in spite of the Tennessee heat and she could have just as easily walked off a runway as out of the hot kitchen. Vic arched one eyebrow at Erin. She knew how much Charley had been driving Erin crazy as the reopening of The Bake Shoppe approached. Her advice had been to stop helping Charley. Family or not, Erin wasn't under any obligation.

"So you're going to make me drive all the way into the city to pick up new muffin tins, when you could just loan me a tray for a few days," Charley accused.

"Sorry, I can't."

"Thanks loads."

"Sorry."

"You're lucky you don't have employees who steal from you." Charley looked at Vic for a moment, then back at Erin. "If I knew who was stealing from me…"

Erin imagined the former organized-crime soldier could have made some pretty good threats, but Charley didn't put them into words. "Do you think someone is stealing from you now, or is this stuff that disappeared before you got The Bake Shoppe?"

"It's still theft, whether they knew they were taking it from me, or decided to take things home after Angela Plaint died and the bakery closed. It wasn't theirs to take."

"No," Erin agreed. "You're right. I just wondered whether you were still having stuff disappear."

Charley shrugged. "I don't know. All I know is that for what should have been a turnkey business, there are an awful lot of things missing!"

Erin nodded sympathetically. "Maybe you should do an inventory before you go into the city, make sure you get everything you need in one run."

"The trouble is, I don't really know what's missing until I go to make something and it's not there."

Erin nodded. That was exactly her point.

"You should make a list," Vic suggested. Her face was smooth, no sign of the laughter bubbling under the surface. She was always teasing Erin for her endless lists. But Erin couldn't imagine trying to run a business—or her life—without them.

Charley rolled her eyes at Vic and didn't bother to comment. While she didn't bully Vic for her transgender identity like some of the Bald Eagle Falls townsfolk—knowing how Erin would react if she did—Charley clearly didn't intend to take any advice from Erin's eighteen-year-old employee, no matter how on-point it was.

"So that's it?" Charley asked Erin. "That's your final answer, you won't help me out?"

"I can't help you with your muffin tin problem."

"Fine. You have yourself a nice day." Charley shook her head and stormed out of the store, making the front door bells tinkle wildly.

Erin didn't say anything immediately. She just stared after Charley. Eventually, she spoke. "Is it just me, or…"

"Is your sister on the verge of a mental breakdown?" Vic suggested, cocking her head.

"I don't know if I'd go that far, but she does seem to be a little… stressed."

"And you weren't before you opened Auntie Clem's?"

"Well, yeah." Erin thought back to the days before she had reopened her late aunt's tea shop as a specialty bakery for those with celiac disease or allergies. "I was pretty nervous… but I had my lists."

Vic giggled. "She didn't seem to appreciate the suggestion. Really, when I think about the two of you being sisters… I don't know if I could find two people less alike."

"Charley is a little… rough around the edges. She just has some… maturing to do."

"She's older than I am."

"*Everybody* is older than you are," Erin teased. "But you're remarkably mature for your age. Charley is still in a sort of rebellious stage…"

Vic polished a few smudges off of the display case of baked goods. "I think my family would tell you I'm right in the midst of my rebellious stage too. Running away from home, coming out as a girl…"

"You being you is not a stage," Erin said firmly, looking Vic in the eye. "Don't let them get to you."

Vic hadn't said anything about having had contact with her family recently, but she normally didn't mention them in conversation unless she'd heard from them. They weren't exactly supportive of her transition.

"Thanks," Vic said softly. She looked down at the glass and polished away another invisible smudge. "And my advice to you is to make sure all of your pans and equipment have your name on them."

Erin smiled. "I'm not exactly worried about *my* employees walking off with them."

"I was thinking more about Charley," Vic said, with a nod in the direction of the door. "It would be a lot less work for her to raid your kitchen than it would be to drive into the city."

"She doesn't have a key."

"Maybe not, but having worked for the Dyson family, I suspect she probably wouldn't need a key."

Erin thought about that. "Well… you might have a point there. Do you think Willie has engraving tools?"

"Sure. I'll tell him you need him to mark everything he can?"

"Yes. It's probably a really good idea even without Charley in the equation. If we had a break-in, or even did a catering job and left something behind, it's a lot easier to recover if everything is marked!"

Vic nodded. She tapped her temple. "I'm putting it on my list."

CHAPTER 2

*E*rin was more tired than usual at the end of the day and wondered whether she was coming down with something. Or maybe it was just the additional stress of having to deal with Charley and worrying about a competing bakery opening in Bald Eagle Falls.

She had said from the start that there was enough business in Bald Eagle Falls for two bakeries, but it had been a lot easier to stay in the black when she was the only one. People who wanted to get freshly-baked treats had to either go to her bakery and get gluten-free, or to go into the city. Now anyone who didn't have special diets to deal with would have the option of a regular bakery, and Erin was a lot more worried than she let anyone know.

She didn't have much appetite for supper, opting for just a day-old roll from Auntie Clem's and a cup of ginger tea. Vic was out with Willie, so Erin didn't have anyone to nag her that she needed to eat a well-rounded meal. Or at least as well-rounded as anything that came from a box in the freezer could be. She took her tea into the living room. Orange Blossom followed her to the couch and made a place for himself on her lap, meowing and yipping chattily about how he had passed his day in her absence. Erin encouraged his story with *mm-hmms* and ear scratches until he got settled. Marshmallow, the toasted-brown and white rabbit she had rescued nibbled at the pant leg of her pajamas and snuffled her bare toes, and then eventually flopped down on top of her feet.

Erin wiggled her toes. "Do you really think I need foot warmers in this heat?"

Of course, she had air conditioning, so it wasn't like she had to put up with the outdoor temperatures. Marshmallow just stared at her out of one eye, his nose wiggling busily.

Erin tried to focus on the job at hand, which was brainstorming what areas she could specialize in; what reasons people had to choose Auntie Clem's Bakery over The Bake Shoppe. The top ones were, of course, people who required special diets. Sufferers of celiac disease, allergies, and intolerances. Vegans. And… nothing else was coming to her. There were other untapped possibilities, such as those who followed special diets with acronyms like SCD or FODMAPS, who had PKU or other digestive enzyme disorders, were trying to lose weight or gain muscle, were sugar-free, fat-free, or low carb. But she couldn't cater to them all.

She could possibly develop a low carb line; paleo recipes were popular, but they tended to revolve around almond or coconut flour and eggs, which were bad for her allergic clientele. She had been nut-free from the beginning and didn't want to leave those who had potentially fatal nut allergies in the lurch. That meant she was choosing a smaller customer base over the larger one, which was not a particularly good business decision.

There was a knock at the door. Erin glanced out the front window and saw the squad car parked at the curb. Removing the animals from their comfortable spots, she got up to open the door for Officer Terry Piper— Officer Handsome, as Vic had been known to refer to him—and his partner, K9.

"Personal safety check, ma'am," Terry said, affecting more drawl than usual, "just wanted to make sure you're safe and secure."

Erin laughed. Terry wasn't usually so playful. She liked seeing that side of him. "I could use some personal protection," she breathed, putting her arms around him and giving him a kiss. They stayed like that for a moment, just looking into each other's eyes. K9 interrupted the tableau with a high-pitched whine followed by a low grumble, as if to say, "Oh, please!"

They both laughed. Erin drew back, allowing her personal protection to enter the house. He closed and locked the door behind him.

"On that note," he said in a more serious tone, "I didn't see you check the peephole before opening the door."

"I didn't," Erin agreed. She motioned to the window. "I could see your car from the couch."

"How did you know it wasn't some *other* police officer?"

"Because my date with the sheriff isn't until Friday."

Terry chuckled. He took his place on the couch, making a motion to K9 that indicated he was allowed to lie down and no longer be on guard. K9 did so, sprawling like a teenager. He nosed Marshmallow, snuffling curiously. Marshmallow wasn't in the mood to play, and kicked K9 in the nose with a back foot. K9 sat up, affronted, and sneezed. He looked at Terry and gave a snort.

"If you're going to poke your nose where it doesn't belong, you risk getting kicked," Terry said unsympathetically. "You go doing that to a porcupine or skunk, and you'll really regret it."

"Or even Orange Blossom," Erin contributed. "He'd probably take your nose off."

K9 approached Erin. He bumped up against her leg and nosed at her hands. Erin scratched his ears and was rewarded with a lick, but that wasn't what he was after.

"Oh," Erin scratched his neck and chin. "You're looking for a treat."

Both Orange Blossom and Marshmallow perked up at this suggestion, looking at Erin to see if she were going to give them something.

"He doesn't need a treat every single time he comes over here," Terry pointed out. "You spoil him."

"It's my house, I'll spoil him if I like." Erin patted K9's head and walked toward the kitchen. "Come on, boy. You can have a cookie."

He went with her eagerly, tail waving back and forth in wide arcs. The cat and the rabbit followed close behind. Erin picked a gluten-free doggie biscuit out of the cookie jar for K9, some soft treats from a snack can for Orange Blossom, and a stick of celery for Marshmallow. She handed K9 and Marshmallow their treats directly, but for Orange Blossom, skimmed the treats along the kitchen floor, making him go careening after them in wild pursuit.

"Doggie treats," she murmured as she went back to the living room and sat down next to Terry. "That's another thing."

Terry raised his eyebrows. "What's that?"

"I was trying to think of all of the reasons people come to Auntie Clem's

Bakery, and that's another one. Grain-free doggie treats. A lot of dogs are sensitive to grains and the grocery store doesn't stock grain-free biscuits."

Terry nodded. "Right. We'd have to go all the way to the city to get them."

"And that's not something Charley is going to want to stock, is it? She just wants a regular bakery, and most bakeries don't do treats for dogs, gluten-free or otherwise." She picked up her list and wrote the thought down.

"What else have you got on there?" Terry looked down at the short list. "What about the ladies' tea?"

Erin had revived Clementine's tradition of an after-services tea Sunday mornings for the churchgoing ladies.

"There's nothing to stop Charley from doing a ladies' tea," she countered.

"Well, I suppose not, but people will go to yours because that's where Clementine's Tea Room was. Having it somewhere else wouldn't be the same."

"But you don't think they'd choose Charley over me if she did offer one? Because I'm an atheist and she's... not?"

"Charley isn't exactly religious herself. Does she even attend services?"

"I wouldn't know, since I don't go," Erin teased. "But seriously, no, I don't think she ever has. And I don't think she goes into the city or back to Moose River for services. But she's Christian in name, and that matters to people around here. Better a Christian who beats his wife and goes fishing every Sunday than an atheist."

"I don't think they're quite that bad."

Erin considered. "Maybe not quite," she admitted. She held up her fingers, pinched close together. "But it's close."

"Has someone been getting on your case?"

"No more than usual. I think they've adjusted to the idea that they're not going to convert me, but they're not happy about it and people still... make comments."

"You're never going to get people to stop talking."

"No."

They sighed in unison, then laughed.

"Does it ever bother *you* that I'm not a Christian?" Erin asked.

He raised his brows. "Me? Not a bit. Never even crossed my mind."

"It doesn't bother you that I'm not going to your heaven?"

"You might be surprised where you end up! No, it really makes no difference to me what you believe. I'm not entirely sure what it is that I believe. I'm born and bred Christian and have never considered myself anything else, but do I believe the whole thing?" He shrugged. "That the Bible and everything in it is meant to be taken literally? I don't know about that. I'll take it on faith for now… and see what happens."

"Hedging your bets? Making sure you're covered just in case it is all true?"

"Our society is built on the Ten Commandments and the Bible. That's where our most basic laws stem from. So… yes. I'll do my best to keep the top ten and uphold the law. Whether that will get me anything in the afterlife or just keep me on the right path in this life, I don't know."

Erin shook her head. "Okay…"

"What does that mean?"

"I thought one of those top ten was going to church on Sunday, and you don't do that. You go to work like usual."

Terry looked away, grimacing. "Well, it doesn't exactly say that…"

"Oh."

"It says to keep the Sabbath day holy, and I…" he trailed off.

Erin waited for him to finish. He didn't come up with anything.

"You'll take that one under advisement?" she suggested.

"Well, maybe I'll do better at that one when I'm retired."

"Sounds good to me."

They sat in silence for a few minutes while the animals gathered back around them and found comfy places to nestle. Erin added the ladies' tea to her list and read over it again. There still wasn't enough there to keep a business running. If everybody who didn't have to eat a special diet decided to go to The Bake Shoppe, Erin's business was going to be in trouble.

~

Sour Cherry Turnover, Book #7 of the *Auntie Clem's Bakery* by P.D. Workman will be available at pdworkman.com

ABOUT THE AUTHOR

Award-winning and USA Today bestselling author P.D. (Pamela) Workman writes riveting mystery/suspense and young adult books dealing with mental illness, addiction, abuse, and other real-life issues. For as long as she can remember, the blank page has held an incredible allure and from a very young age she was trying to write her own books.

Workman wrote her first complete novel at the age of twelve and continued to write as a hobby for many years. She started publishing in 2013. She has won several literary awards from Library Services for Youth in Custody for her young adult fiction. She currently has over 60 published titles and can be found at pdworkman.com.

Born and raised in Alberta, Workman has been married for over 25 years and has one son.

∼

Please visit P.D. Workman at pdworkman.com to see what else she is working on, to join her mailing list, and to link to her social networks.

∼

If you enjoyed this book, please take the time to recommend it to other purchasers with a review or star rating and share it with your friends!

facebook.com/pdworkmanauthor

twitter.com/pdworkmanauthor

instagram.com/pdworkmanauthor

amazon.com/author/pdworkman

bookbub.com/authors/p-d-workman

goodreads.com/pdworkman

linkedin.com/in/pdworkman

pinterest.com/pdworkmanauthor

youtube.com/pdworkman